CLAIMED BY LUCIFER

THE COMPLETE SERIES

ELIZABETH BRIGGS

DEMON KING

CLAIMED BY LUCIFER BOOK ONE

1

HANNAH

Only a desperate woman made a deal with the devil—and I was on my way to ask him for a favor.

I couldn't help but wring my hands while we went up, up, up in the elevator. Generic club music played softly in the background as I stared at the sleek mirrored walls and dark silver buttons, trying to avoid looking at the two imposing men either side of me. There was no escaping them. They filled the entirety of the space with their broad shoulders, thick necks, and well-pressed black suits, barely leaving me room to suck in a breath. They were hot as hell, just like everyone I'd seen in The Celestial Resort & Casino, but scary enough to make me wonder if coming here was a huge mistake.

Who was I kidding? Of course it was a mistake. But it might be the only way to find my best friend.

The elevator dinged, signaling we'd reached the penthouse, and when the door opened, I let out the breath I'd been holding. More models-turned-security guards stood outside a big, black, shiny door. As I stepped out of the elevator, that black door was thrown open and a man in a disheveled gray suit rushed out. His wide eyes were full of something like panic or fear, and he jostled hard against my shoulder as he tried to escape.

"If you're smart, you'll turn around and run," the guy yelled before one of the muscular guards grabbed him by the arm and dragged him toward the elevator. He didn't even struggle, and soon the elevator door shut him in, barely drowning out his last word. "Run!"

I swallowed hard but steeled myself as I headed for the open door. Each footfall felt like one step closer to my doom. I glanced between the guards perched on either side of the door, but they barely acknowledged me as I walked through. I'd already gotten approval to speak with Mr. Ifer from a man in a suit downstairs, so I supposed they were expecting me.

Just inside the door was a small foyer with a huge painting of stylized black wings spread wide on a pure white canvas. I knew little about art, but found myself staring up at it, drawn to the way the brush strokes looked like angry slashes.

I shook myself and continued down the hall, along black marble floors with a touch of silver veining in them, and entered a large living room. The sight of expensive, black leather couches and a grand piano made me freeze. I'd expected to meet Lucas Ifer, CEO of Abaddon Inc and the rumored mob boss of Las Vegas, in his office, not his own home. Momentarily stunned by the sight of it all, I took in the backlit mirrored bar along one wall, the large, sleek fire-place across from it, and the floor-to-ceiling windows on the end with an impressive view of the Las Vegas Strip, not to mention the infinity pool on the balcony.

The man I'd come to see leaned with his hand on one of those large windows, staring out at his domain like a brooding king. Or a kingpin, maybe. I could only see his profile, but it was striking enough to make my heart miss a beat. I cataloged him while I waited for his attention to land on me, as I didn't dare disturb such dark, dangerous perfection. An impeccable black suit framed broad shoulders and tapered down to narrow hips, before hugging a perfectly rounded ass. Sunlight kissed short, thick hair that looked almost black except for highlights of rich, chocolate brown. Below that, perfectly trimmed dark stubble accentuated a chiseled jaw, leading up to the cheekbones of a god.

Whatever I'd expected from the man they called "the devil" in hushed whispers, it had not been this.

"Come to ask for a favor?" His voice washed over me with a delicious British accent that somehow made his words sound both smart and sensual. "As you saw, it didn't go so well for the last fellow. Then again, he tried to renege on our bargain. I trust you won't do the same."

His words rolled off his tongue like sex and sin, but also reminded me why I was here. I shook my head a little to clear my thoughts and to snap out of the daze he'd put me in. "Yes, I am. Here for a favor, that is."

He turned from the window to face me, and the light and dark played over his face in the most beguiling way I'd ever seen. The full force of his presence hit me in the gut like a fire bursting into life from the strike of a match. Forget the men outside—they were nothing compared to him. I actually forgot how to breathe under the weight of those eyes, an emerald color I hadn't realized was humanly possible until today. And that mouth...dear lord, was that a mouth made for sinning. I could already imagine it whispering naughty things in my ears before his lips left a trail of lust down my skin.

Something about him was familiar too. I searched my limited memory for a time I could have met him, but surely I would've remembered someone this remarkably gorgeous. No. There was no way we'd met.

Yet... I knew him somehow. Instinctively, primally, deep in the core of my being, he felt like something I... It was right on the tip of my tongue. The thought I couldn't grasp before it slid away. I refocused, but it was no use. I couldn't put my finger on it. Maybe I knew him from before the accident? Seemed unlikely, and surely if he knew me, he'd say something.

I realized I was staring and jerked my gaze away, out over the view. Las Vegas in the daytime wasn't nearly as impressive as at night, when the city was lit up as if some preschoolers had sprinkled giant tubs of glitter over an expanse of desert. Even so, the bustling city against the backdrop of the mountains in the distance momentarily took all of my focus, giving me a second to gain my bearings again.

"Tell me your name," Lucas said.

His voice, that accent, *my god.*

"Hannah." I finally met his eyes again. "Hannah Thorn."

"Hannah." My name rolled off his tongue like a sip of expensive Scotch. I shook my head and blinked away the thought. I didn't drink. Why would I think about the smooth burn of a drink I'd never had?

He tore his eyes from me like it was difficult for him to do so. Almost as if he was drawn to me as much as I was to him. A fanciful notion, and one I immediately dismissed as he walked behind the bar.

"Drink?" Lucas held up a decanter and a crystal tumbler that sent a rainbow of light shards bouncing around the room.

"No thanks. I don't drink."

He hummed low in his throat, a sound of dissent. "Pity. We could have a lot of fun if we got drunk together."

He reached for different glasses and shoveled ice into them. Three perfect cubes hit the sides of the glasses with a chinking sound. Then he grabbed a jug of clear liquid from under his counter, and I held up my hand in the universal gesture for *stop.*

"I meant it. I don't drink."

"And I don't give alcohol to anyone who isn't a willing recipient." He picked up his glass and took a big swallow of the contents. "Sadly, just water."

He held the second glass out to me. As I wrapped my fingers around it, our hands brushed against each other, and the fire in my gut erupted again, sending heat all over my body and down to my core. The feeling that I knew Lucas redoubled, like a memory just outside my grasp, or a word on the tip of my tongue. And with it came a rush of desire so strong it took my breath away.

His gaze intensified. Did he feel it too?

"Sit." Lucas gestured toward the black leather couches.

I perched on the edge of one and held my glass in both hands, my grip tightening as my nerves stretched thin. Anxiety wound in my chest and mixed with the desire pooling between my thighs, making me feel light-headed. I glanced at the nearby piano, trying to bring my emotions back under control. This was all too big. Much too big. What the hell was I even doing here?

Lucas sat on the couch across from me and spread one arm along the back. He rested an ankle on his knee in the perfect picture of poise and calm control. "Now, how can I be of assistance?"

I took a deep breath, trying to channel some of that calm control for myself, even if I only pretended. I was perfectly happy to fake it, even if I would never make it. Not around someone so disarming.

"My best friend is missing," I blurted out. *Way to fake poise.* "Her name is Brandy Higgins. She was staying here, in this hotel, for a conference, but she never came home. I tried to find her myself, but I haven't had any success, and when I went to the police they were dismissive. Especially when I told them she'd been staying here."

"You must be a very loyal friend. Very few are brave enough to ask me for a favor." He looked at his drink and shook the ice around in the glass, the sound it made almost musical. "The rest are extremely desperate. I wonder, which one are you?"

I glanced down at my hands, but then forced myself to meet his eyes, trying to channel bravery along with my desperation. "Both. Brandy is more than a friend. She's like a sister to me, and she has a little kid and a sick mom at home counting on me to find her. I've been living with them ever since her divorce to help out, but if she doesn't return..." The thought was too terrible for me to consider. I straightened my spine and stiffened my shoulders, shoving my anxiety into a tight ball in my chest as I faced Lucas with determination. "I heard you're called the King of Las Vegas, and that nothing happens here without you knowing about it. I figure if anyone can find Brandy, it's you."

I didn't mention the other rumors I'd heard about him, like the fact that he was basically a mob boss who ran the city, and how people referred to him as the devil in nervous whispers and behind locked doors. Even the police seemed afraid of him.

"You both sound like a proper pair of saints," Lucas noted, his lips quirking at the corners. "You said she went missing here, in The Celestial?"

"Yes, a few days ago."

He nodded slowly, like a man in no kind of a hurry, a man with nothing to lose and with the luxury of time on his side. Time I sure as hell didn't have. "You understand there is always a price for my help?"

Panic wrapped an iron band around my chest, and I sucked in a shaky breath. I'd known this was coming, and I had no idea what he'd want in return for his help. "I don't have any money."

"Oh, I don't trade in money." He laughed, but his face flashed with something villainous. "My currency is dark deeds and dirty secrets."

I swallowed hard and glanced at the hallway, wondering if it was too late to escape. I had no secrets, none that I remembered anyway, which meant he would want a dark deed of some kind. Would he ask for something illegal? Something dangerous? Something I would regret for the rest of my life? I nearly ran out the door, but then I pictured Brandy's son looking up at me with barely contained tears as he asked when his mom was coming home, and my resolve hardened. I looked Lucas in the eye and nodded.

He leaned forward, no longer casual. "Are you willing to do whatever it takes?"

"Yes," I said breathlessly. "What do you want?"

"You."

My jaw dropped, and my stomach dropped lower. Possibly through the floor. All the floors. "Me?"

He chuckled, the sound a dark melody full of wicked promises. "Six nights with you. Here in my penthouse. Mine to do with as I please."

I gasped at the sensual pause between each of his last three words. Then I shook my head, certain I'd misheard. Misunderstood perhaps. Yes, that last one. "Excuse me? You expect me to give you carte blanche to do anything to me? For six nights?"

"Would you prefer seven?" A sinful grin crossed his lips as he leaned back against the soft leather of the couch. "I will warn you, I don't rest on the seventh day."

"*Seven?*" My thoughts scrambled, and all I could do was stare at him. Was he serious?

He nodded. "Yes, let's make it seven nights. One for each deadly sin. Even better."

Shit. I really shouldn't have questioned that six nights thing. I ran the scenarios through my head, my face warming as I saw many of them in glorious detail. Yes, the man was insanely attractive, but he was proposing something six degrees of indecent. Not to mention, he was a total stranger. A very gorgeous, very *dangerous* stranger. What he was asking of me...it was too much. Maybe there was some other way I could find Brandy. Someone else I could go to for help.

Lucas watched me, waiting for my decision. "Tick-tock. Time is slipping away. The longer you wait, the less likely we'll find your friend alive."

Fear pulsed through me at the thought, but he was right. She'd already been missing for days. I needed to make a decision quickly, but I had to be sure about what I was getting myself into. I cleared my throat. "Let me get this straight. You want me to stay here with you for seven nights while you...do whatever you want to me. Sexually."

His gaze darkened to a glower, and I nearly trembled at the intensity of it. "I have never forced myself on a woman, and I never will, if that's what you're worried about."

A breath of relief left my lips. "I had to be sure. I've never done anything like this before."

"I promise no harm will come to you by my hand. But as for sex..." He rose to his feet and walked the few steps toward me, making me look up at him. Then he bent forward and rested his hands on the back of the couch on either side of my head, caging me in. "Don't you know who I am? They call me the devil for a reason. Temptation, lust, sin, all wrapped up in a neat little package. Oh, who am I kidding? A *huge* package. Trust me, before the week ends you'll be begging for every single thing I do to you."

He was entirely too close, his face inches from my own, his green eyes burning like a fire had been lit from within. Desire rushed through me like I'd never felt before, but it was mixed with a heavy dash of fear. My gaze dropped down to his mouth, only a breath apart from mine, and I ached for him to close the space between us, even as I wanted to run from him.

I forced my eyes back up to meet his intense gaze. I couldn't think of another way to find Brandy. I'd tried everything I could, but nothing had worked. If I didn't do this, I'd fail completely.

This was my last chance.

"I agree," I said, with as much courage as I could muster.

"Excellent." He straightened up and walked to the other side of the room casually while my heart raced in my chest. He picked up a pad of paper and a pen, then handed them to me. "Write down everything you know about your friend's disappearance. Names, dates, and so forth."

As I scribbled down all the details, apprehension making my handwriting look like someone else's, he watched me closely. I kept glancing up as the pen scratched along the paper, unable to keep my eyes off him. Why did I feel like I was signing away my soul with our deal?

When I'd written down everything I could think of, I gave him back his notepad and pen. He closed his hands around mine to take them, and heat shot down to pool between my thighs again. Unexpected longing rose in my chest, and I swallowed as I tried to bring order and coherence back to my thoughts.

"Where are you staying?" he asked.

"This cheap place off The Strip." I looked away, embarrassed to say the name of it. I'd scrambled up every penny I had to come here, but it was nothing compared to this penthouse. "Double Down Motel."

His face twisted with disgust. "Give me your room key. I'll have all your things brought here."

"What about my car?" I asked.

"My people will handle that as well."

I raised an eyebrow at that, but pulled out my keys and handed them to him. He had *people?* I thought people who had people were just a myth. Who actually had *people* to do shit for them?

"Good." He pocketed them and held out a hand. "Now follow me."

Every time I touched him I felt...things. I kept my hands to myself. "Where?"

"To your new room." His voice dripped with promise. "Though I suspect you'll soon prefer mine."

We walked down a corridor and he threw open a door at the end. Unlike the rest of the penthouse I'd seen so far, which was all decorated in black and silver, this room was done in neutral tones. The queen-sized bed had one of those padded headboards behind it and was covered in lush blankets, a thick duvet, and soft-looking pillows. On the other side of the room was a cute sitting area and a desk in front of windows looking out at The Strip. A door led to a walk-in closet as large as my old apartment, and another opened to a massive bathroom all done in Carrera marble.

"This is your guest room?" I asked, as I took it all in, spinning in a slow circle. If this was for guests, what did his bedroom look like?

His lips quirked up in amusement. "It's yours now. Make yourself comfortable. Order anything you like from room service. My people will bring your things along shortly, while I begin my investigation into your friend's whereabouts."

I shook my head, part in denial, part in wonder. This situation made no sense, and I was starting to wonder what the catch was. Maybe this was a case of mistaken identity of some sort. After all, why would he want me—*me*, of all people—for seven nights? I was just a basic bookworm with a nice set of boobs and a cute smile, who worked in a flower shop and wore flip-flops and jeans. Nothing special. Not compared to the women he probably surrounded himself with all the time.

Nerves churned in my gut as I considered the full force of what I'd just agreed to. Me. Here. In this penthouse. For seven nights.

And *him*. Doing whatever he wanted to me.

For the next week, he owned me. Completely. But it would all be worth it if he kept his side of the bargain.

I turned toward him. "Do you promise to find Brandy?"

"I will. Dead or alive, I will find her."

He looked me in the eye, and I didn't doubt his conviction. Lucas Ifer was a man who got things done, and if anyone could find my friend in the dark underground of Las Vegas, it was him.

He offered me his hand, and I took it to shake. The moment his skin touched mine, an electric tingle rushed through me, with that same fleeting sensation of familiarity and long-lost desire.

His fingers tightened around mine almost possessively. "It's a deal."

2

LUCIFER

T he door to the guest quarters closed behind me with a barely perceptible click as I stepped into the wide hallway. There I paused to draw in a deep breath as the enormity of what had just transpired hit me fully.

She was *back*.

My heart raced with anticipation. I could hardly believe it when she walked into my penthouse without warning, but the second we touched all doubts had vanished. She'd returned to me. Finally.

Hannah Thorn. A new name. A new look. But still undeniably *mine*.

I pictured her on the other side of the door, probably examining her new bedroom. Long golden hair framed a heart-shaped face with blushing cheeks and bright blue eyes, not to mention her very kissable lips. Lips I would soon be claiming, along with the rest of her small, curvy body. I only had to convince her over the next seven nights that she belonged to me.

While I found her friend, of course. Couldn't forget that part. She'd led Hannah to me, after all. Yes, I needed to find this Brandy woman, if only to thank her.

Besides, I didn't take lightly the disappearance of a human

female in my hotel. Though demons fed on the energy of humans, I had strict rules about not harming them, especially within my domain. Of course, now that we'd made Earth our permanent home, the entire world was technically my domain. Still, even the youngest demons knew not to break the rules in the king's own castle.

The Celestial Resort & Casino was my flagship hotel, a shining gem on the Las Vegas Strip, designed to entice humans to sin in any number of ways, all so my demons could feed safely while still remaining hidden from the world. In fact, I'd covertly built the entire city over the last forty years to be the perfect haven for demons. Sin City, they called it, and I was its King.

I stepped outside my penthouse and adjusted my suit as I eyed my guards. "No one goes in or out, except by my command."

They bowed their heads as I entered the elevator. If Hannah really wanted to leave, I wouldn't stop her, but I couldn't have her running around the city alone either. Now that she'd been returned to me, she needed to be protected at all times.

For years my heart had been cold and black, a hard piece of coal waiting for her to return and ignite it. I'd searched for her for so long to no avail, only to have her walk into my life out of the blue. Looking for *me* this time. Oh, the irony.

I took the elevator down one floor to my war room. As I stepped inside the large space, I could almost inhale the power of my rule—a heady scent indeed. I paused as I took in the room, dark lord of all I surveyed. Live feeds and surveillance footage filled huge TV screens, and my industrious staff operated computers on too many desks to count as they followed every thread and whisper of sin this city had to offer. Greed, envy, lust...all mine, mine, mine. A huge switchboard took up an entire wall as they made connection after connection, following people, emotions, and things. Flashing lights moved around on a large world map on the wall, showing various demon, angel, and fae activities.

Samael was in his office, as I expected him to be, from where he oversaw everything in the command center. He acted as my right-hand man in most matters, and he'd been by my side ever since I left Heaven to rule Hell. Gadreel was in there too, looking at an open file atop the black desk. He was one of the younger Fallen, only about two centuries old, but he'd proved his loyalty many times and had risen in the ranks to become Samael's assistant.

I poked my head into the office. "Meeting. Now. Get Azazel too."

They both snapped their heads up, one dark and one light. Samael furrowed his brow. "What's this about?"

"She's returned." I didn't need to elaborate. They knew who I meant.

Gadreel's blond eyebrows darted up. "Are you sure?"

I thought of the sparks I'd felt when I touched Hannah's hand. "Yes, I'm certain of it. Funny enough, she found me this time."

Without waiting for a response, I turned and headed for our meeting room. The windows facing out to the rest of the command center turned opaque as soon as I flipped a switch, giving us complete privacy. The room was soundproof too, even from supernaturals with enhanced hearing. I took my seat at the end of the conference table, sinking into the plush leather executive chair. Seconds later, Samael walked inside, followed by Gadreel and Azazel. They shut the door behind them, and took seats around the table.

"I hear she's back," Azazel said, as she kicked her legs up on the table, showing off studded black leather boots. She was my top security official and my fiercest blade, able to wield any weapon with ease. Tight black leather was her armor of choice and anger her fuel to fight.

"Yes, and I need you to guard our new guest," I said. "She's in my penthouse, and I can't allow her to leave it unless you're by her side. I want you protecting her at all times."

Her face twisted with annoyance, but she nodded. She would never disobey a direct order from me, even if she didn't want to follow it.

I leaned forward and caught her eye. "I realize being a bodyguard may seem beneath you, but in truth I've given you the most important task of them all. Hannah's life will soon be in danger, and you're the only one I trust to keep her safe."

Her annoyance faded and she bowed her head. "I won't fail you, my lord."

"What is her name now?" Samael asked, his hands folded calmly on the table.

"Hannah Thorn."

"Ah. The woman asking about her friend."

I should have known Samael would already have some information on her. Little happened within these walls that he didn't know about. "Yes, and we need to find this friend with all haste. She went missing in The Celestial a few days ago." I pulled out the pad of paper and handed it to him. He scanned it quickly, while I continued. "I also want everything you can dig up on Hannah's life. Family, boyfriends, work, what she eats for breakfast—I want every single detail."

"It will be done," Samael said, with his usual smooth confidence.

I pulled out Hannah's car keys and room key next, then tossed them to Gadreel. The blond man caught them with quick reflexes. "Gadreel, I need you to go to the Double Down Motel" —I shuddered simply saying the name— "And retrieve her things, along with her car. I trust you can figure out which one it is."

"Won't be a problem, my lord," Gadreel said, as he examined the room key with distaste. Hannah had referred to the Double Down Motel as *this cheap place off The Strip*. That description oversold it.

"You have your orders. For the time being, let's keep Hannah's presence here between the four of us." I rose to my feet and glanced between my loyal Fallen, while determination burned in my chest. "I lost her before, but I'm not letting her go this time. Not again."

3

HANNAH

As soon as Lucas closed the door behind him, I glanced around the guest room in wonder, still struggling to believe this was all real. Two days ago I'd been packing my bags to head to Vegas to find my friend, and now I would be living here for the next seven nights, at the whim of a man they called the devil. Sure, I'd agreed to the deal, but that didn't make it any less terrifying. Especially now that Lucas was gone and I was alone with my thoughts.

He'd better find Brandy. And alive, too.

Please let her be alive.

I moved to the large window overlooking The Strip and wondered for the hundredth time where she was and what had happened to her. Sunlight glinted off the various hotels and casinos, and I remembered how excited Brandy had been to come here. She'd been invited to a librarian conference over a three-day weekend, winning some award that paid for the entire trip. She'd asked me to come too, to have a girls' weekend with her in Vegas, but I'd turned her down. My florist shop was small, but it demanded almost all of my attention just to keep it afloat. Plus, I enjoyed working there in the place once owned by my parents, finding exactly the right flowers to brighten people's homes or convey the things they couldn't always bring themselves to say. No matter how much I'd wanted to go to Vegas with Brandy, I'd said no. Now it was one of my biggest regrets.

She'd gone to Vegas alone, and then she never came home.

The last time I heard from Brandy was after she checked in to this very hotel, when she'd called to say goodnight to her son. That was six days ago.

When she didn't answer her phone or come home at the end of the weekend, I knew something was wrong. I felt it right in my gut, and I never ignored my instincts. With a sick mom and a little kid, no way would Brandy run off. Someone must have taken her.

Over the next day I made dozens of phone calls, trying to find her, but it was useless. It soon became obvious I'd have to go to Vegas myself and figure out what happened on my own. I begged my part-time helper Maggie to watch the flower shop for a few days, and then I scraped together every penny I had and hit the road in my beat-up car, driving the five hours through the desert until I reached Sin City.

Before I left, Brandy's mom Donna had taken me aside and begged me to find her daughter, while she'd sobbed into a tissue streaked with blood. Donna had terminal lung cancer and could barely find the energy to make herself a sandwich these days, but she promised she'd manage looking after Brandy's son Jack while I was gone. Then, on my way out of the house, Jack grabbed me around the waist and asked me to bring his mom home soon. Both times I'd blinked back tears, and swore to them that I would find Brandy.

What else could I have done? Brandy had treated me like family from the moment we'd met in the library where she worked, and she'd given me a place to live when I needed it most. I should have gone with her to Vegas, and guilt was eating me alive for that decision. I'd chosen my responsibilities over my friend, and I wished more than anything that I could go back in time and redo everything. If I could get Maggie to step in and help at the shop now, why couldn't I have done that before? Brandy would have done it for me in a heartbeat. Why, why, why did I let her go alone?

I had to find her, and it was all on me. Brandy had nobody else in the world to go looking for her, and I couldn't let her drop off the face of the Earth. Vegas would eat her alive and forget her, allowing her to become another statistic. The police here were proof of that. When I went to report her disappearance they blew me off, especially once they found out Brandy went missing in Lucas's hotel. They'd closed ranks immediately, speaking in low voices to one another with pointed glances, suddenly all deferential about Mr. Ifer. He probably had each and every one of them on his payroll. They eventually took my report, but I had a bad feeling it was in a pile somewhere never to be seen again.

My only option had been to start doing some detective work myself, but I kept hitting dead ends. First, the staff at The Celestial Resort & Casino couldn't find any information about a librarian conference. When I looked it up myself online I only found one sparse website for it, and no other mentions anywhere. It was almost like it never existed at all. Or like someone had set up the whole thing just to lure Brandy to Las Vegas. But why? Had she gotten herself involved in something bad? Some sort of business with the mob? I found that hard to believe.

I started poking around the hotel, asking questions and playing detective, but I was no Nancy Drew. I had no idea what I was doing, yet I asked people as many questions as I could think of, and slowly but surely my intuition tugged at me, telling me something wasn't right. I wore my cheap flip-flops up and down The Strip, visiting all the places Brandy might have visited. No one gave me any information, almost like Brandy hadn't existed at all. I hit brick wall after brick wall. I needed access to video cameras, phone records, and credit cards, but I didn't have a badge or any connections. And I was running out of time and money.

Then I heard about Lucas Ifer, the owner of The Celestial, along with a lot of other places in Vegas too, according to rumor. They called him the devil in hushed tones and made him sound like a dangerous mob boss, but it soon became apparent that not much happened in Vegas he didn't know about. Plus he was known for making deals, and he was able to get you anything you wanted. For a price, of course.

By all accounts, Lucas Ifer was the King of Las Vegas. If the police couldn't help me, and the people on the street couldn't help me, I had to come to the castle. I just hadn't expected the castle to be in the sky. Now I was trapped in this tower like Rapunzel, except my hair was definitely not long enough to get me down.

I sat on the edge of the bed, my heart pounding. I was basically being held captive as a sex slave for a mob boss, and there was no telling if he was going to find Brandy. Or if she was even alive.

No, I had to stop thinking that way. I believed Lucas would honor our deal as long as I did. I felt it in my gut, and my gut was never wrong. Even if my gut also told me that he was the most dangerous man I'd ever met.

I leaned back and ran my hands along the smooth, soft duvet cover and blankets. This guest room was huge and luxurious, but it was sparse too, and I got the feeling it wasn't used very often. I debated ordering room service, but my stomach was too twisted up in knots to eat anything. Still, if I had to stay somewhere for seven nights, I would be hard-pressed to find a hotel room nicer than this one.

Damn it. Seven nights away from home and from my shop. I sincerely hoped Maggie was able to keep an eye on the place that long. She was in her late sixties, and I worried running the whole thing might be a hardship for her. I'd had to agree that she could say cash or check only, which was going to suck. Most people preferred credit, but Maggie was hopeless with the card machine. I grimaced at the thought of returning to a business that had collapsed under the weight of going old-school. The place wasn't doing all that well before I'd left, and I owed it to my parents to keep it afloat.

Taking out my phone, I dialed her quickly. No answer. It was almost five, and she was probably closing up the shop. I sent a text instead. At least she was pretty good with texting.

I'm delayed in Vegas. Please do your best at the shop. Will be gone 7 more days.

I'd deal with the fallout when she replied. As I waited, I considered texting my sister too, but Jo was an enormous worrywart. She tended to be overbearing, and I didn't need that on top of everything else. If it had been up to Jo, I never would've left Vista. If I told her about what I'd agreed to now, she'd completely fly off the handle.

Maggie's reply reassured me. **I'm fine. Take your time. Win lots of money.**

She ended it with a bunch of money bag emojis. I shook my head, wondering if she was unclear on why I was here, or just perpetually optimistic. I took a few moments to call Donna, but she didn't answer either. Probably making Jack something to eat. I sighed and left her a message telling her I was doing everything I could to find Brandy, but I would be here for another week. I apologized profusely for being away so long, and my throat tightened with emotion as I hung up.

With all my bases covered, there was nothing else to do but wait, which I wasn't very good at. If nothing else, I could explore my new surroundings. Surely that was allowed.

I got up and opened all the drawers in the room but they were empty. I stepped inside the giant walk-in closet and twirled around, but it was bare except for a few hangers. I moved into the massive bathroom next, my eyes going wide at the sight of all that marble and the huge shower and even bigger soaker tub. I'd never been in a bathroom this fancy before. Or this big. I was tempted to take a bath and try to wash away my worries, but I was curious about the rest of this place. If this was to be my home for the next week, I should get familiar with it, shouldn't I?

I opened the bedroom door wide enough to peer out into the hallway, but didn't hear a thing. Lucas was gone, off to investigate Brandy's disappearance, or so I hoped. I walked back out across the marble floors into the living room, gazing across the black and silver space that exuded power, danger, and luxury. The place could really use a few flowers or ferns to give it some life and color. Maybe some succulents even. Something to make the space feel less cold and dead.

Then I realized I wasn't alone after all.

A gorgeous Black woman stood in front of the entrance to the penthouse. Leather crisscrossed her body like some sort of armor, and her dark hair was scraped back so tight it drew her skin taut over the most wicked cheekbones I'd ever seen. The hilt of a blade peeked above her left shoulder. Something about her tickled my instincts, but not like the familiarity I felt around Lucas.

"I'm Zel," she said, like she didn't care if I remembered or not.

"Is that short for something?" I asked.

"Azazel."

I could see why she went with Zel. "I'm Hannah."

"I know. Lucas ordered me to protect you."

"Protect me or prevent me from leaving?" I asked, raising an eyebrow. I had no doubt she could snap me in half with a lazy bend of her pinky finger, and she didn't sound pleased about her new job as my bodyguard.

Her dark eyes surveyed me with something like disdain. "If you leave the penthouse you need an escort at all times."

"Why?" I tilted my head with a frown. "Is Lucas worried I'll run away?"

"Lucas protects what is his."

And that included me now, I realized with a shiver. "What if I leave the city?"

She pinned me with a threatening gaze. "You won't."

I truly was a captive. I had the illusion of freedom, but Lucas had made sure if I went anywhere, his bodyguard-slash-spy would keep tabs on me at all times and make sure I didn't run away.

Zel didn't seem inclined to chat, so I continued through the living room and around a corner, discovering a small, well-appointed kitchen on the other side of the bar, along with a dark dining table that seated six. I couldn't imagine Lucas doing much cooking, although this kitchen seemed like a chef's dream come true. I didn't recognize the brand names of any of the appliances, which made me think they were ridiculously high-end. I opened up the stainless steel fridge out of curiosity, and was surprised to find some food inside, including an impressive selection of fancy-looking cheese. I spotted foods with labels in foreign languages, and I examined tins and jars containing things I'd never even heard of. To my relief, I spotted a container of Heinz ketchup in the door. Something I recognized. Something that proved Lucas wasn't all pomp and circumstance.

I shut the fridge door and headed down another hallway, with the distinct sense I was going down the rabbit hole and through the mirror. Nothing in this penthouse felt at all real. Everything was spotless, like dust didn't even dare to exist within these walls, and I'd never witnessed such luxury or wealth so prominently and unashamedly on display. I was hesitant to touch anything, for fear of breaking something. I didn't need to add to my tab with Lucas.

At the end of this hall, I found a big set of double doors like the ones that led out of the penthouse to the elevator. I tried the handle, but each one was locked. Certainty flowed through me that these doors led to Lucas's private chambers. I rested my hand on the smooth wood and felt an intense craving to know what was on the other side, along with a whisper of something that felt a lot like desire. I shook off the feeling and turned around.

I wondered what Lucas would think of me looking around his space, and then I realized he almost certainly had cameras everywhere. He likely already knew that I'd been poking around like a mouse when the cat was gone. Well, what did he expect? I couldn't sit around the guest room all day staring at my nails, waiting for him to return. I snorted at the thought.

I walked out onto the huge balcony that wrapped around the entire penthouse, and marveled over the pool that seemed to flow right over the edge and into the sky. The sun was starting to set, and Las Vegas was waking up with all its noise and lights. Soon my first sinful night with Lucas would begin. With a tremor of fear running down my spine, plus a heavy dose of curiosity, I wondered what he had planned for me.

Back inside, I found another set of double doors and assumed they would be locked too, but to my surprise, they clicked open— and then I walked into a librarian's own personal heaven. A vast room filled with hundreds of books stretched before me like something out of a movie. The bookshelves around me seemed impossibly high, and Belle would've been at home tucked into a corner here, waiting on her Beast. Old leather editions were housed with glossy modern volumes, and I longed to flip the pages just to inhale all the scents the paper released. Brandy would've chained herself to the ladder that provided access to the upper shelves.

In one corner of the room was a seating area with plush, dark chairs and large paintings on the wall behind them. On the other corner stood a massive desk with nothing on top of it, and a silver sword hanging on the wall behind it that seemed to glow with an inner light. The legs on the desk were exquisite carved wood, wrapped in tiny wraith-like figures that turned out to be horned demons and gothic angels on closer inspection. Every time I blinked, the carvings seemed to move, and I stepped back and shook my head. I'd never been a good sleeper, and it had only gotten worse since arriving in Vegas. The long nights must finally be catching up to me.

I turned in a circle, taking in the library with awe. I wasn't sure what the next seven days and nights would hold, but this library might make it all worth it. Like Brandy, I was a total book nerd, which was how we'd met, after all. I'd strolled into the Vista Library looking for something to read during the boring shifts at work, and we'd been best friends ever since.

Dark wooden pedestals stood around the room, displaying ancient-looking vases and other pieces of art under spotlights, like in a museum. I had no doubt each one was priceless. An old Greek vase caught my eye, and I moved closer to inspect it. Intricate black figures depicted a scene on an orange background of a large man in a crown sitting on a throne, offering a plate of berries or seeds to a woman standing before him. A small placard on the pedestal read, *Hades Tempts Persephone, c. 350 B.C.* My mouth fell open as I studied it with reverence. I was a huge history and mythology buff, and this vase hit both of those notes.

I'd expected a lot of things from Lucas Ifer, but I hadn't imagined him as a connoisseur of ancient art and old books somehow. I stared at the vase for far too long, and then turned to the bookshelves to get lost in them. Row after row, both fiction and nonfiction, covering so many genres and topics it made my heart sing. I soon got overwhelmed and grabbed a notepad and pen to make notes on which books I had to read during my time here. There was no way Lucas would be around twenty-four-seven, even within the bounds of our deal, not if he had a city to run. This was the perfect way to distract myself from worrying about Brandy all day.

"I see you found my library." Lucas's smooth voice interrupted me, and I turned toward him. He stood in the doorway in his impeccable suit, all brooding darkness and beguiling shadows.

"It's incredible. I could stay here forever getting lost in these shelves." I was halfway through the room and my list had already gotten longer than I could manage.

A wicked smile danced across his lips. "I can arrange that, you know."

I stiffened, remembering why I was here and how he controlled everything in my life for the next few days. "On second thought, seven nights is plenty."

He let out a low, dark chuckle, the sound so sexy it made my toes curl. "What do you like to read?"

"History and mythology mostly, but I also love romance. Historical, paranormal, fantasy romance... It's my guilty pleasure, I guess you could say." I clamped my mouth shut the second the words came out. I wasn't sure why I'd confessed that to him, especially when men were often so derisive about romance novels.

"No reason to feel guilty when it comes to pleasure...or romance." He sounded amused, but at least he wasn't mocking me or putting down the genre. "Those are my favorite genres as well."

I gestured at the Greek vase. "I guessed that from the art. Very impressive."

He followed my gaze with a mysterious smile. "I find history so... fascinating, don't you? Especially how it can be depicted so differently from what truly happened."

"But how would you know what truly happened?"

His smile grew wider and became downright devilish. "That is the question, isn't it?"

"Excuse me." A voice interrupted us just as I was about to lose myself in Lucas's dark gaze. I shook myself and turned toward the door, where another far-too-attractive man stood. He wore a suit like Lucas, but didn't pull it off quite as well, even with his broad shoulders. The tips of his sandy blond hair touched eyelashes of the same color, and big blue eyes looked out at me from a face that could have belonged to any boy next door. Only this place didn't have a next door, so where was this guy from? Where were any of these people from?

"Yes, Gadreel?" Lucas asked.

"I've brought her things from the motel, as you asked." Gadreel's eyes landed on me and lingered, like he was intrigued by my presence. I wondered if Lucas made these sorts of deals with women regularly, or if I was the first one to become the devil's plaything for seven nights.

Lucas idly waved a hand. "Put them in the guest room."

"Of course, my lord." Gadreel gave a quick bow before exiting the room. Did Lucas really demand such old-fashioned obedience from his people?

Lucas's intense gaze turned back to me. "If you're wondering about our deal, I assure you my best people are looking into your friend's disappearance and should have some leads soon. I expect we'll know a lot more tomorrow."

I swallowed, feeling a tiny trickle of hope and relief. "Thank you."

"I always fulfill my end of the bargain." His emerald eyes drew me in, and I was powerless to look away. "Now, it's time for you to fulfill yours."

4

HANNAH

A long black limo drew up at the curb outside the front of The Celestial. I was pretty sure we got in at the back while the front was arriving at our destination. The spectacle was even more eye-opening than my low-cut black silk dress, which Lucas had delivered after he'd discovered I'd brought nothing formal to wear to Las Vegas. Or more accurately, that I didn't own anything formal. Nothing that would live up to his standards anyway.

I'd never been in a limo, as far as I could remember. It was leather-everything with windows tinted so dark they seemed to be part of the interior walls rather than actual windows. My gaze kept drifting to the sunroof and the Vegas lights that played through the glass like some kind of neon kaleidoscope. I pictured myself hanging out of it and waving at passing cars like in a movie, but I refrained. This wasn't a joyride, or a date even—this was part of a deal with a dangerous man to find my missing friend. I couldn't forget that, no matter how glamorous it all was.

Or how gorgeous my captor was.

Lucas was the epitome of cool, calm, and collected as he sat back in his seat and straightened his tuxedo cuffs. Yes, he wore an actual tuxedo. Even in my new dress, which probably cost more than my monthly salary, I felt completely out of place at his side.

"I've decided each of our seven nights will represent one of the Deadly Sins," he said, with a roguish smile that made my knees weak.

My breath caught as I imagined what those sins were. Wrath, envy, *lust*. "And tonight is...?"

His mischievous green eyes danced with amusement, as though he knew exactly which sin I was thinking about. "Tonight is gluttony. I hope you're hungry."

A silent sigh of relief left me. Gluttony I could handle. "Starving, actually. I haven't eaten since this morning."

Lucas tutted. "I did tell you to order room service."

My hands twisted in my lap. "I've been too worried about my friend to eat much. Do you have any leads on what happened to her?"

"Not yet, but my people are combing the hotel's security footage now." He looked me right in the eye with complete confidence and seriousness. "I promised you I would find her, and I will. Do not doubt that."

I nodded slowly and looked away before I lost myself in his dark, burning gaze. Worry for Brandy still stifled me, but I tried to push it aside. There was nothing more I could do at this point, except have faith that Lucas could find her.

The limo stopped outside the Bellagio, a massive hotel that looked like some kind of fairytale castle framing the huge lake of water and gorgeous fountains. The window slid smoothly down in front of me and music floated on the night air, while the fountains moved in time to it and lights splashed across the water.

"Look at the fountains," I said with a gasp. When I turned to Lucas, he watched me with an unreadable expression on his all-too-handsome face, and I turned quickly back to the fountains.

The car drew to a smooth stop right in front of the hotel. Other cars raced by, but I lost myself for a few moments in the spectacle and the music. I'd never seen water sway like that before. Like it was alive.

Lucas stepped out of the limo when the driver opened the door, then he turned and held his hand out for me. I scooted over as best I could in the snug dress, trying not to snag it on my gorgeous heels. They'd arrived with my dress, and I'd nearly died when I saw the red bottom of the heels—the signature style of Christian Louboutin. I didn't know much about fashion, but Brandy did, and she'd always coveted his shoes. Maybe I could sneak these back to Vista when this was all over and give them to her.

I took Lucas's hand as I stepped out of the limo, and his eyes raked over me with something like hunger in them. Then he slowly lifted my hand to his lips, pressing a lingering kiss inside my wrist. I released a breath and met his gaze in surprise. The heat from his lips traveled right through me, straight to my core, and probably scorching my panties right off. How did he know that was my spot, the one that drove me wild and stoked my desire like nowhere else?

"You look exquisite," he said in a low voice.

"Thank you." I smoothed the dress, my cheeks flushing. "Anyone would look nice in such an amazing dress."

"I wasn't talking about the dress."

He took my arm like a true gentleman, even if the look he gave me was anything but gentlemanly. Being this close to him made my heart race, and it wasn't only with fear. He was far too good-looking, and the power and danger he radiated both intrigued me and made me want to run away all at once.

We entered the hotel and I tried not to have wide tourist eyes as we walked down the gorgeous entryway. Everyone scrambled to make sure our path was clear, parting like waves in front of us, and more than one person gave Lucas a deferential nod. He strolled by as if he owned the place, even though this wasn't his hotel. That swagger was something billionaires always had, I guessed. People whispered as we walked by, my ears picking up the hiss of the sound but none of the words. Their eyes followed us, and more than one woman lost interest in her date as Lucas passed in front of her. Others shot me curious or even dirty looks. I was on the arm of Vegas's most handsome, richest bachelor, and people definitely noticed.

At Lucas's side, I felt like the queen to his dark king. Most surprising of all—I found myself secretly enjoying the thrill of it.

We stopped in front of a restaurant called Picasso. I knew nothing about the place, except that it was one of those restaurants that listed the chef's name under the sign, so you knew it was going to be expensive and have dishes you couldn't pronounce. Lucas led me across the shiny floors to the hostess, who waited at the entrance like she was expecting us.

"Mr. Ifer?" She was polite, but her deferential body language said she knew exactly who he was. "It's a pleasure to welcome you to Picasso. We have the terrace all ready for you. Right this way."

We followed her inside the restaurant, which was completely empty other than the three of us. A bit creepy, but it allowed me to marvel at how beautiful everything was. We walked along colorful carpet under mosaic ceilings and between tables covered in white cloths, past walls decorated with unusual geometric art.

As the name of the restaurant clicked in my head, my jaw dropped open. "These paintings. Are they *real* Picassos?"

"They are," Lucas said casually, as though we weren't basically walking through an art museum.

I didn't think anything could top seeing real Picasso paintings up close, but then we walked outside and I gasped at the view. We were directly behind the gorgeous fountains, which towered over us against the backdrop of the Vegas lights, and close enough that I could feel the spray of water in the air.

He tightened his arm around me as I watched the fountains, mesmerized by how they danced and twined to the music with the kind of grace I'd never master. The droplets were like sprites or fairies and a lump formed in my throat as I imagined what Brandy's reaction would have been to this magical sight.

"Your box for the fountains is on your table." The hostess indicated the white-covered table with two red chairs on either side of it. The rest of the large terrace, which likely seated many guests on a normal night, had been completely cleared out, giving us a lot of space and privacy—plus this amazing view.

Lucas held out my chair for me, and I sat as gracefully as I could, praying I could keep it together in such an exquisite place. It would be just my luck to drop my dinner or spill my drink all over this dress. The whole thing was completely overwhelming, and it was hard not to gawk as the server came over and launched into a spiel about how the restaurant featured both authentic Picasso master-pieces along with decadent food inspired by the regional cuisine of Spain and France. Oh and over 1,500 selections from the finest European vineyards—not that I drank wine, but it still sounded impressive.

The server then handed me a tiny menu, just one sheet of embossed paper with six different things on it. I scanned it and picked the item that looked the least strange, because most of it was gibberish to me. "I'll have the lobster salad please."

The server gave me a pitying smile and spoke with a French accent. "Oh no, you don't need to choose anything. These are the six courses you'll be receiving throughout the evening, personally selected by our master chef. I guarantee it's the finest food you'll eat in Las Vegas."

My eyes dropped to the menu again. Six courses? Yes, I was hungry, but could anyone eat that much? And what were half of the things on this menu anyway? Suddenly I just wanted a hamburger and fries. And to be back in Brandy's house sitting on the couch in my yoga pants, with her by my side while we watched Netflix.

The server handed Lucas the wine list, and he perused it while I stared at the table, feeling completely out of place and over my head. When I told the server I would only be drinking water, he gave me a look that made me shrink down into my chair. Luckily Lucas ordered a bottle of wine for himself, and the server seemed pleased with his selection and disappeared.

A second later, another man in a uniform brought out some toasted bread with fancy little tomatoes drizzled in sauce—our first course. I grabbed a piece of bread and nibbled it, ultra-aware of where to put my hands. Anywhere but on the dress. Don't want to ruin this thing before giving it back to Lucas.

I glanced up and noticed him watching me again with those inscrutable eyes, looking impossibly handsome in his tuxedo against the backdrop of the fountains. Like something from a dream or a fairy tale.

"You seem nervous," he said, in his sexy, lilting voice.

I let out a sharp laugh. "Is it that obvious? Expensive dresses, Picasso paintings, and fancy meals are really not the norm for me. Not to mention..."

"Not to mention, what?" he asked.

I swallowed hard. I'd been about to say that I'd never been the woman on a billionaire's arm before, but that didn't seem polite. "I just don't understand. Why? Why are we doing this?"

"It will all make sense in time, I promise." He studied me for a moment longer and then picked up the small box in the middle of the table. "I love this restaurant, and not only for the food and the art, but because of this feature reserved for its most...exclusive guests."

"What is it?"

He opened the box and showed me the list of songs inside, which had buttons next to them. "You pick a song, then push the button beside it and it'll start the fountains to that song. It's spectacular."

Straight away, my gaze focused on *Con Te Partiro*. It made me cry every time I heard it, but I pointed at it anyway. "This one," I whispered.

Lucas's gaze dropped to my finger and his jaw tensed, just the smallest shift in his muscles. "Time to Say Goodbye," he said, with a degree of emotion I didn't expect in his voice. "A fitting choice."

I pressed the button next to the song title and the music started slowly, the illuminated fountains arching and winding together sinuously like lovers about to be parted. A rush of emotion suffused me straight away, like I knew it would, and I lifted my napkin as stealthily as I could to dab at the corner of my eye, careful not to smudge my mascara. I should have chosen a different song, but this one had called to me.

We sat in silence as the fountains danced in time to the music, while the opera singers' voices surrounded us. We were so close to the fountains it felt like we were inside them, and the mist made goosebumps on my skin in the cool night air. Lucas watched with a stony expression, but his jaw clenched when the song got to the big climax and the fountains shot high into the sky.

When the fountains' dance ended and the water stilled, Lucas returned his attention to me again. It was at that moment our second course, the lobster salad, was brought out to us. I'd already eaten most of the bread with tomatoes—it had been delicious—and I was ready to dig into this too. I just wasn't sure how I'd eat four more courses after that.

"Tell me about your life," Lucas said, as he picked up his fork.

I shifted in my seat, uncomfortable with this line of conversation. "There's not much to tell. I live in Vista, a small city near San Diego. I run a florist shop there."

"A florist shop?" He let out an amused chuckle. "How appropriate."

I wasn't sure what he meant by that. Was it an insult or a compliment? I decided to ignore it and instead took a bite of salad. Flavor exploded across my tongue. Wow.

He barely touched his food, but instead continued his interrogation of me. "And you said you live with this friend, Brandy?"

"Yes, after she got divorced she needed some help with her son, and I was struggling to pay the rent on my apartment. It worked out for both of us. But now her mom's sick too..." My chest ached as I thought of my second family and how they were all counting on me to find Brandy—before it was too late. "I'm just really worried about her."

He tilted his head as he studied me. "I can tell you truly care for these people."

"They're all I have. Well, them and my sister, but she lives in San Francisco and I don't see her very often. She runs a company and she's pretty busy with that."

Our plates were swept away by quick-fingered servers, and another course laid in front of us. This one was some fancy scallops dish with potatoes, and it was also delicious.

"So you're not in a relationship then," Lucas continued.

I let out a nervous laugh. "What's with all these questions?"

He pinned me with an intense gaze. "Answer me."

His directness and abrupt focus on my relationship status startled me, and I considered lying to protect myself, but I couldn't do it. Honesty was important to me and I prided myself on never lying. Not even to someone who probably had no trouble bending the truth...or worse. "No, I'm not in a relationship right now."

He leaned forward. "But you've been in relationships in the past. How many? Were any of them serious?"

His tone sounded so possessive it made my spine stiffen. I shook my head, setting down my fork. "That is really none of your business."

He sat back, languid and casual again. "I'm simply trying to understand you. Are you the type of woman who has long-term relationships, or are you more into casual flings?"

I snorted. "More like the type who sits at home and reads books instead of going out on dates."

That got a laugh from him, low and husky and sexy as sin. "Lucky for me then that I have such an extensive library. Still, I find it hard to believe you've been single all this time. You're a gorgeous woman, Hannah. Surely some men or women have taken an interest in you in the past. Did none of them strike your fancy?"

"I've dated a few guys before, but it never got serious," I admitted, my cheeks flushing at his compliment. "It never felt right with any of them, and besides, all my time is spent managing the shop."

Satisfaction gleamed in his eyes at my answer. I expected him to continue this line of questioning, but instead he sipped his red wine and asked, "You're the manager? Or the owner?"

"Both." I paused, debating how much to reveal. What could it hurt? This would only last seven days and then I'd never see him again. "It was my parents' shop, but they died five years ago. My sister and I inherited it in their will. Jo is too busy with her own business, so I run the place myself."

"I'm sorry to hear about your parents," he said.

My throat grew tight with that familiar sadness and the loss I felt every time I thought of the accident five years ago. Not because I missed my parents, but because I didn't remember them at all. Not only were they taken from me, but I'd lost all my memories of them too, in an especially cruel twist. Was it any wonder I would fight tooth and nail to hold onto my loved ones now?

Before he could fire off any more questions about my parents, I asked, "What about you? Why does the King of Las Vegas need to bribe a woman into spending a week with him? I thought you were a billionaire playboy. That's what the internet says about you, anyway."

"Don't believe everything you read on the internet." His expression became distant as he looked out at the water as the fountains splashed a playful rhythm. "I had a great love once. The kind they write books about."

"What happened?" I asked in a hushed voice.

He turned his hypnotic eyes back on me. "I lost her."

"I'm sorry," I found myself saying, echoing his words to me a minute ago. The tone of his voice made me think that his great love had passed away, and my heart squeezed in sympathy. I couldn't imagine having something like that and then losing it.

He gazed at me with unblinking intensity. "Perhaps it will be different this time."

I wasn't sure what he meant by that, so I took a long sip of water just as our next course was brought out, some tiny pieces of steak with figs and honey. I'd already forgotten what course number we were on. All I knew was that the food kept coming, and it was all amazing.

I pushed another button in the little box and the fountains started up again, this time dancing to that Celine Dion song from Titanic. Soon another course came, some lamb with kale and asparagus, but I was already so full I could only take a few bites.

"Tell me about your life," I finally said, once I gave up on trying to eat anymore. "It's probably a lot more interesting than mine."

A perfect eyebrow arched up. "What would you like to know?"

"How did you do all this?" I asked, gesturing around us. "This restaurant is obviously very expensive, and we've got the place all to ourselves, plus control of the fountains at Bellagio. How?"

"Easy—I own it all."

My brow furrowed. "I thought you owned The Celestial."

"That's what I want most people to believe, but for you, the truth." He gestured toward The Strip, where I could see the glowing signs of the other casinos through the mist of the fountains. "I own nearly every luxury hotel and casino in Las Vegas. Some through shell companies, so it doesn't seem as though I dominate The Strip quite as much as I do, but for all intents and purposes, Las Vegas is my city."

I sat back in my chair, stunned. I knew he was a powerful billionaire and that he controlled Las Vegas, but to own all of that—damn. "Is that why they call you the King of Las Vegas?"

"One of the reasons." He paused before sipping his wine. "But that's not what you really want to know, is it? You want to know why they call me the devil."

My face grew warm, embarrassed that my thoughts were so obvious, or that he could read me so easily. Of course that was what I wanted to know. I'd heard those whispers—the ones people muttered when they thought I'd turned away and was no longer listening. There were also the rumors about what happened to people who crossed him. "Why do they?"

His eyes flashed with dark humor for a second before he answered. "Because I *am* the devil. My true name is Lucifer."

I couldn't help but laugh. "Seriously? That's your birth name? No wonder you go by Lucas. Your parents must have hated you."

"My father certainly does, but that's beside the point. I am *the* Lucifer, formerly known as the Lightbringer, also called Satan, the Prince of Darkness, Father of Lies, King of Hell, and a number of other titles that people have bestowed upon me over the years."

My laughter faded as I realized he was completely serious. "I'm sorry...what?"

Our server brought our final course, a fruit tart for dessert, while I stared at Lucas. As soon as we were alone again, Lucas picked up his fork, as though we were having a normal conversation. "I realize it's difficult to believe, but I only speak the truth to you."

While he took a bite, I could only watch him, my stomach twisting. "You're trying to tell me you're *actually* the devil. Fallen angel. Evil incarnate."

"You absolutely must try this tart, it's truly divine. I should know." He met my eyes again, and this time the look in them made me tremble. "Evil? Probably. Fallen? Definitely."

Shit, what had I gotten myself into? My thoughts swirled chaotically, and I poked at my tart with my fork as I tried to gain control over them. I was being held captive by a crazy billionaire who believed he was the devil. I should run away right this instant and never look back. But I couldn't. He was probably the only man in Vegas who could find Brandy, and I'd sacrifice myself any number of times for the safe return of my friend.

"Is that why you make deals?" A nervous laugh bubbled out of me. "Are you going to steal my soul? Should I be afraid?"

"Oh, Hannah. Your soul already belongs to me." His eyes smoldered and a villainous smile spread across his lips. "And you should be *very* afraid."

5

LUCIFER

My spoon guided my coffee into a slow swirl in my mug—an exercise in controlled chaos—as I skimmed the newspaper front page. A relic of an older time, but one I refused to give up, even if I managed most of my business online these days. Hell, I still remembered when newspapers were invented. To see new technologies change the world and then become obsolete years later—such was the curse of an immortal.

Besides, the headlines about Earth's latest problems were a good distraction from thoughts of Hannah. Just knowing she was in my penthouse brought me a sense of calm that had been missing for years, but I was certain she didn't feel the same. Ever since I'd told her the truth about who I was she'd become closed off and nervous, and had retreated to the guest room as soon as we'd returned from dinner. She didn't believe me. Not yet. But she would.

As I sipped my coffee I gazed out at the midday sun. Normally I spent my nights awake and slept during the day, as fit my role as Lord of Darkness, though I didn't need much sleep after all this time. However, with Hannah here, I'd adjusted my schedule to accommodate her mortal needs. Besides, I had plans for us today.

The elevator opened outside the penthouse door with a familiar ping, capturing my attention. Samael walked inside a moment later, his dark brow furrowed as he approached. Like many former angels, he had an ethnically ambiguous look with dark bronze skin and rich brown eyes. Many humans guessed he was Middle Eastern, or perhaps Latino, but the truth was often too much for their fragile mortal brains. Like me, Samael had been born in Heaven, though we'd lived in Hell for much longer. Not that either Heaven or Hell was home anymore.

"Good morning," he said, in his usual serious tone. "I have an update for you on the missing woman, along with a complete report on Ms. Hannah Thorn."

I nodded and sipped my coffee as he slid a thick beige folder toward me with Hannah's name on it. "What have you found?"

"Our surveillance footage of Styx Bar showed Ms. Brandy Higgins sitting with Asmodeus on the night she disappeared."

My attention piqued, I stopped in the act of opening the folder. Asmodeus was an incubus who ran most of my strip clubs in the city —and Samael's son, with the Archdemon Lilith. "Is that so?"

"They spoke for a short time, and then they left the bar together."

"Have you questioned Asmodeus about this?"

"I tried." A muscle in his jaw ticked. "My son is missing as well."

My hand tightened around the folder. Asmodeus was old and powerful, not to mention extremely loyal to me. If he was missing too, that pointed to a much larger problem than a lost human woman. Who could kidnap him? And why would they do such a thing? Was Asmodeus the target, and Hannah's friend simply in the wrong place at the wrong time? It felt too much like a coincidence, and I'd learned those were rare among immortals.

I opened my mouth to issue Samael further instructions, but before I could speak, Hannah's bedroom door opened with a quiet click. She shuffled sleepily into the kitchen and her eyes widened when she saw we were already in there. Her startled gaze flowed over Samael, curiosity obvious in her body language, then landed squarely on my naked chest. Interest flickered in her eyes, but she quickly dragged her gaze away from my body as her cheeks flushed.

Her obvious desire for me stirred heat at the base of my cock, but I needed to take this slow, to bring her to me willingly. Still, it seemed she wasn't above a bit of temptation, judging by the way she'd eyed me. And I did love to tempt.

I stood quickly and pulled out a chair, gesturing for her to take a seat beside me. "Hannah, this is one of my closest advisors, Sam."

"Nice to meet you." She clutched her robe—which looked as ancient as I was—tight at her throat, a hopeful look lighting her eyes. "Are you helping to find my friend?"

"Yes, I am." Samael held himself stiffly, though his words were polite. His dark eyes scanned her, no doubt taking in every detail and filing it away in his vast mind.

"Find Asmodeus and find the girl," I told him.

His gaze snapped to me and irritation crossed his face. "Of course I will."

He sounded almost offended, and I wasn't sure if he thought I was questioning his capabilities, or his devotion to his son. In truth, I simply wanted both of them found immediately. "I have no doubt you will."

He bowed his head, somewhat mollified, and then left the kitchen. I took a long sip of coffee as I tapped my fingers on the report about Hannah. Once I was alone, I would pore through it and memorize every detail.

"What was that about?" Hannah asked, still clutching her robe. The thing was pale pink cotton and so thread-bare I could almost see through it—not that I minded that part. However, it was definitely a sign she wasn't living to the standard she should be, and no doubt required a full wardrobe intervention. Exactly what I had planned for today.

I reached for another mug and walked toward the coffee machine. "Do you take your coffee with two sugars and no cream?"

"I do." She said, and then her still-sleepy brain caught up. She stared at me with a healthy dose of suspicion in her eyes. "How did you know that?"

I handed her a mug and winked. "Lucky guess."

She considered a moment, her distrust clear in her guarded

expression. Then she appeared to arrive at a decision. "I'm not buying that, but I'm willing to move on to get information about Brandy. As part of our deal." Her words were curt. Business-like, almost, and I appreciated her cool efficiency as I longed to make her mouth move in more sensual ways. "Did you learn something new?"

"I did." I drew my chair alongside hers, sitting possibly a touch closer than she felt comfortable with. I couldn't help myself. The desire to be near her was too strong for me to resist. "Our security cameras show Brandy left the Styx Bar downstairs with Asmodeus. He's an incubus who runs my strip clubs." I added that helpful detail and side-eyed her, awaiting a reaction.

She coughed on the sip of coffee she'd just taken. "Incubus? In your...strip clubs?"

I should have suspected she had no memory of any type of demon or supernatural entity, but perhaps I could help jog her memory. "Yes, strip clubs. I own many of them throughout the city catering to all sorts of different themes and kinks. They allow the Lilim to safely feed on humans without hurting them, and thanks to their gifts, the humans are immensely satisfied. After all—" I leaned closer to Hannah and dropped my voice. "I like all of my customers to leave my establishments satisfied. Including you."

She watched me from under her dark lashes, the suspicion in her gaze increasing as she flicked a glance between the direction of her bedroom and the main doors like she was calculating an escape. She could look around the penthouse all she liked. There certainly wasn't any escape for her. The men outside the door would see to that if she tried, and Azazel was certainly *very* good at her job.

"Lilim?" she asked after a few moments, obviously choosing to ignore my question.

Damn. Nothing I said seemed to be sparking any memories. "The collective term for succubi and incubi. They're a type of demon that feeds on lust."

"Uh-huh." She sipped her coffee, disbelief heavy in her tone like she was merely humoring the crazy billionaire. "There's only one problem with what you're saying. Brandy isn't the type of person to go to bed with a man she just met in a bar."

"She's human." I shrugged. "She wouldn't be able to resist an incubus no matter how hard she tried. Especially one as old and powerful as Asmodeus—he can enchant a human female without the slightest effort. But the problem is that he's missing too."

"Do you think he took her?" she asked, obviously ignoring the parts about the demons and focusing on Asmodeus's disappearance. There was a fierceness in her crystal blue eyes, and I had no doubt she'd try to take down anyone she thought might be a threat to her friend, even though she had no chance of actually injuring a demon like Asmodeus.

"No, I can't imagine he would do such a thing."

"Then we need to find them. We should go looking around, or question some people, or—"

She'd let go of her robe in her excitement, revealing why she'd been clutching it closed so tightly. The fabric was so frayed that the knot at her waist kept loosening, and her cleavage pressed against the edges of the collar enticingly, baring the sweet curve of her breasts. I'd barely heard what she said as my fingers itched to touch that soft, smooth skin.

"Hannah." I rested my hand on her knee, making her freeze. "There's nothing more we can do. My best people are looking for them now. I have every confidence they'll find your friend soon."

Her shoulders fell. "We can't help?"

Samael's people would find Brandy, I was sure of it. Nothing on Earth or in any of the other realms was as important to me as the woman sitting beside me, clutching her robe. We had a deal, and I'd hold up my end. I always did.

I shook my head. "If we get involved, we'll only slow them down. Let them do what they're trained to do. This isn't Samael's first time heading up a search and rescue, and the best thing we can do is go on about our lives. In fact, I have something planned for today that I think will keep your mind off of things."

"Day? I thought we were only doing nights." She blew out a long breath. "What's today's sin?"

"Greed." I gestured toward her room. "There's a fresh outfit hanging in your closet in a black garment bag. Please wear that today." I tried to keep my smile subdued, but the idea of her wearing clothes I'd selected for her sent a possessive streak of lust through me. *My* woman. *Mine*. I hadn't felt like that since... Well, since the last time.

"What are we doing?" There it was again, that suspicion threading through her tone. It was one of the reasons I liked her. She never did let me get away with anything.

"Shopping." I deliberately kept my voice casual, and she lifted her chin in question. "We'll be purchasing some new clothes for you."

She groaned. "What's wrong with my clothes?"

I stared pointedly at her threadbare robe. "Everything."

She crossed her arms. "Excuse me for not realizing I'd be playing the role of billionaire's mistress this week."

"Exactly. You need a wardrobe suiting your new position at my side." I looked back down at my newspaper, effectively dismissing her. My feigned disinterest wasn't because I was finished looking at her, but because if I continued to watch her, I'd want to touch her, to kiss her, to possess her, and she wasn't ready for that...yet.

She huffed and then turned on her heel to head back to her room, hopefully to get ready. I glanced up and caught sight of her perfect ass and the swish of her long golden hair. She looked different from before, but there was no doubt of who she was. The tug inside me, the rapidity of my heartbeat, and the twitch in my cock... Every part of me knew exactly who she was.

She must have felt it too—the pull, the longing, the need. The unbreakable connection between us that stretched back for all eternity. But it must be buried deep this time.

It was an exquisite torture to know the truth about us, and to be the only one who remembered. I wanted to tell her, but I'd wait until she was ready to hear it. This was certainly a game for a patient man, and I'd bargained on a week.

Over the next few nights I would remind her who she really was —and why she belonged by my side as my queen.

6

HANNAH

Another car whisked us out of The Celestial and down The Strip, but at least it wasn't a limo this time. Not that the sleek, silver Aston Martin sports car was any less glamorous. Lucas drove with a casual hand on the wheel, and with his eyes focused on the road, it allowed me to study him without his intense gaze staring back at me. He was too handsome to be real, like something out of a dream, and every time I looked at him I wanted to touch him to prove to myself I wasn't imagining it. He exuded a heady mix of sensual charm and dark, dangerous power that was impossible to resist. This time he wasn't in a tux, thank goodness, but his black suit was perfectly tailored and no doubt cost a fortune.

My outfit probably did too, for that matter. In my closet I'd found white shorts with a label I didn't recognize, but no doubt couldn't afford, and a sleeveless button-up shirt in lavender. I looked like I was ready to head to the country club and eat stupidly small sandwiches or drink tea with my pinky outstretched while laughing at poor people like me.

And then there were the shoes, sparkly black flats with Miu Miu on them. I'd heard of that brand and had to stop myself from getting on my phone and searching for the price. I couldn't stand the thought of walking the sidewalks of Las Vegas in shoes that cost more than my car. I chose to believe they weren't *that* expensive. I couldn't think about them any other way or I'd need to carry them and walk about barefoot. I was in so far over my head it wasn't even funny, and my gut twisted at the idea of what he'd want in return for all of this...kindness.

And how I'd probably give it to him.

At least Lucas was fulfilling his bargain to find Brandy. As we drove along The Strip, I stared out at the tourists walking past the brightly lit stores, casinos, and restaurants, while thinking back on what I'd heard this afternoon. I found it hard to believe Brandy would leave a bar with a stranger, no matter how sexy he was, and Lucas's explanation of the man being an incubus didn't make me feel any better. They had a lead though, which was more than I'd been able to get. I just had to stick through this bizarre experience for another few days until she was found and we could go back to our normal lives.

And that whole thing about Lucas being the devil? Yeah, I'd been trying hard to forget that ever since he'd brought it up last night. The only explanation I had was that he was using it as a metaphor to try and intimidate me.

Or he really believed it, which was even more disturbing.

We entered a parking garage, going down several levels until we reached an area filled with a selection of the flashiest looking cars I'd ever seen. I'd only heard of some of them—the names almost always Italian and spoken in reverent tones.

"Where are we?" I asked, as a man in a suit stepped up to open the passenger door, while a valet moved forward to park the car for Lucas. Rich people never parked, I'd quickly learned.

Lucas got out of the car and walked to my side, stepping in front of the valet to take my hand and help me out, almost like he wouldn't dare let the other man get near me. "This is a special entrance to the Shops at Crystals for their premier customers. It's a shopping center that houses only luxury brands. I own it through Abaddon Inc, which also owns thousands of malls across the world."

"You own this place? And thousands of malls?" My jaw fell

open. During my short stay in Vegas while searching for Brandy I'd walked past the Shops at Crystals and marveled at them from outside, but knew there was no way I could afford anything inside.

He buttoned his jacket as he replied, "Just another of my holdings. Shall we?"

He led me down a red carpet—an actual red carpet—into a mall that was unlike any I'd ever been in before. We walked along shiny floors that had thick veins of gold running along the edges, meeting champagne-colored walls with intricate sconces every few feet to light the way. At the end of it were steps that actually looked like they were plated in gold, with lush greenery on either side. I picked out black mondo grass with pink and white periwinkles and some lilac hibiscus. I breathed in deeply as we passed them, feeling a touch of homesickness for my florist shop.

"This is a mall?" I asked in a hushed voice.

Lucas's lips quirked with amusement as he walked by my side. "This is a secret part of the mall, a special tunnel for VIP guests. Vegas brings lots of celebrities and high rollers, and they like to shop without being observed. Each of the shops has a separate entrance so we can retain our privacy."

Personally, I would have preferred to people-watch everyone else in the mall, but I supposed a man like him wanted that kind of privacy, with his darkness and obvious underworld connections—because how else would he gain that degree of power? Nothing about Lucas Ifer was like anything I'd ever known before. I'd heard about how the other half lived, but I'd never expected the difference to be so vast. It was obvious he just expected the world to bow down before him. And the world did bow.

The tunnel we were in was empty except for the two of us, but I read all sorts of signs like Gucci, Dior, Louis Vuitton, and others I'd never even heard of. Was he expecting me to buy clothes here?

I cleared my throat. "You do know I can't afford much, right? I barely had enough money to pay for gas to get to Vegas."

His hand curled around my elbow, and even that light touch made my breath hitch and my thighs clench together. "Hannah, I would never expect you to pay for any of this. It's my gift to you."

I bit my lip. "And what do you want in exchange?"

"Only the pleasure of your company."

He led me inside the first shop, where a sign over the door read Versace. It was all white, with white leather couches, white floors, white tables. The only thing that wasn't white in the whole room was the clothes we had on and the name of the shop printed repeatedly on the floor in gold.

As soon as we walked in, a saleswoman ran from the other side of the room, her pert bob bouncing in her haste. "Mr. Ifer," the saleswoman exclaimed. For a second, I thought she was going to curtsy. "It's such a pleasure to see you. How can we assist you today?"

"Please measure my companion and bring us an assortment of clothing for her to browse."

With wide eyes the saleswoman turned to rush from the room, giving me the impression of a startled deer. She was terrified of him, I realized. Was everyone in this city?

He sat on the edge of one of the couches, then patted the spot beside him for me. I shook my head, too intimidated to sit down.

Within moments, more salespeople ran in and out of the room with clothes on racks, hanging them in front of me. I could only gawk at the expensive clothes, soft fabrics, and shimmering materials. Someone handed me a bottle of ice-cold water with a fancy-looking label I didn't recognize, and I took a sip, my throat dry. I hated to admit that the water tasted better than any water I normally purchased for myself. Shit, I usually drank tap water, even when it tasted like dirt or was so sun-heated it rivaled the temperature of my coffee.

"Try on anything you like." Lucas waved in the general direction of the clothes. "It's all yours, should you desire it."

Suddenly, I felt very small and very alone, surrounded by all of these nice things I couldn't afford, under the complete control of a man who could either shower me with riches and gifts or end my life altogether, if he so chose.

"Lucas," I said, trying to speak to him around the rush of people. "I can't accept all these expensive clothes."

He stood up and crossed the room to me, then took my chin in his hand as he gazed into my eyes. "You can and you will. After all, if you're going to be seen in public with me over the next few days, you need to look the part."

I swallowed, my throat dry again, and this time from the mix of lust and fear pulsing inside me. "Is this some kind of Pretty Woman thing?"

"Not at all. I'm not paying for your body. I only bargained for your time." His thumb trailed across my lower lip, tracing sensual patterns that made me breathless. "And as part of spending time together, I demand you dress properly for the occasion. I assure you, I will not miss the money, and the gifts come with no strings attached."

I nodded slowly, hypnotized by his eyes and the low, melodious sound of his voice, not to mention the way he touched me—like he owned me already. He looked at me as if nothing else existed in the entire city, and it was hard not to want to be his completely.

I tried on some of the clothes and set aside the ones I liked, but then I found myself wanting to put some back. It just seemed like way too much, especially when I glimpsed a price tag. My monthly rent to Brandy could pay for one of the shirt sleeves and that was about it.

"She'll take it all," Lucas said in a commanding voice. "Pack it up and send it to my penthouse."

The treatment was the same at the next several stores, with the result of my head spinning and me feeling like some sort of kept woman. Or a mob boss's wife. That was probably more accurate.

We sped through Louis Vuitton, where he insisted on the rarest bag they had. Apparently, only three had been made, and I got one of them. I carried it on my arm—empty— to the next store, stiff as a corpse as Lucas wound an arm around my waist. I tried not to lean into him, but it was pretty much impossible, especially when he was so much bigger than I was and my body seemed determined to melt against him, even when my brain said it was a bad idea.

Fendi, Prada, Chanel. We got more clothes, plus matching shoes and accessories, creating a wardrobe fit for a princess, but one I could never wear in my normal life. Why would I need so many clothes for a week's worth of time? I kept trying to tell Lucas it was enough, but he ignored me. At one point I saw an outfit I loved, and he must've read my mind or something because I was *very careful* not to show any reaction. I didn't want him to think I was taking advantage of his generosity when really the weight of it left me cold, but he told the salespeople to pack it up like everything else.

The next stop was Tiffany's. I hesitated at the door, below the sign in the iconic blue. "Lucas, really. This is too much."

"I insist."

He took my hand and I didn't react quickly enough to stop him. With a short tug, he had me walking through the door and into another private showroom, just as fancy as the last five or six, or however many we'd been to at this point. As soon as we were spotted, sales people practically fell all over themselves to help us. I tried to refuse everything, even as I marveled at the jewels, but Lucas picked out several pieces, including diamond necklaces and stud earrings.

"For everyday wear," he said.

I snorted. "My everyday wear does not consist of diamonds."

"No?" He gave me a charming smile that wreaked havoc on my brain. "I thought diamonds were a girl's best friend."

"Not this girl," I muttered. "Give me books over diamonds any day, thanks."

"I can do that too, you know. But perhaps we can find something that's a bit more you." He stopped in front of a case that had a matching set including an emerald necklace, earrings, and a bracelet. The gems were exactly the color of Lucas's eyes.

I held up a hand. "They're gorgeous, but—"

"Yes, these are perfect," Lucas said with an air of finality. He looked from the jewels into my eyes. "Emerald is your favorite, isn't it?

My breath caught. First the coffee, now this. Was he stalking me? "How did you know?"

He gave me a devilish grin. "Consider it a lucky guess."

"But where would I even wear them?"

The hunger in his gaze made my heart race. "You can wear them for me in my bed, with nothing else on."

"That's not going to happen," I said with a very unconvincing laugh.

He gestured for the salespeople to wrap the set up for him, but then he caught sight of something behind me that made his eyes narrow. "Excuse me for a moment."

He rushed past me and out the door like he was going to battle, and the swift change in his demeanor made my head spin. I watched the Tiffany employees pack up my things in cute little blue boxes and bags, wondering how this was my life.

"Should we put this on Mr. Ifer's account?" a salesman asked.

"I assume so." I glanced behind me. No sign of Lucas anywhere.

I poked my head out of the shop door, searching around for Lucas, and spotted him down the hall. He was talking in a low voice with another man with red hair, and their body language told me it was not a friendly conversation. Then suddenly Lucas grabbed the man around the neck and lifted him up into the air and slammed him against the wall.

No. *Into* the wall.

Plaster went flying and the man left a body-sized dent in it. Meanwhile, Lucas's hand was still around his neck, holding him there with impossible strength. I could only see his back, but it was enough to send a cold wave of fear through me.

Lucas dropped the man in the rubble at his feet. "Do not cross me again, or I won't be so lenient next time."

"Yes, my lord." The man kneeled on the floor and nodded, keeping his head low. He didn't appear injured, even though he'd just been sent through a wall.

Lucas brushed plaster dust off his hands and turned toward me, leaving the man kneeling there. He spotted me watching with my mouth hanging open, and gave me a dazzling smile, like everything I'd just seen was totally normal.

He joined me in front of Tiffany's and rebuttoned his suit jacket. "Sorry, darling, demon business. Now where were we?"

"How?" I gestured at the man, who got up and ran out of there as fast as he could.

"Don't worry, he's a shifter. Fox, if you must know. I barely scratched him." He took my elbow again, his fingers strong and possessive as they dug into my skin. "Shall we continue? I have one more shop I'd like us to visit."

I dimly nodded, my throat tight, as Lucas led me down the hall, leaving the plaster rubble behind, to another shop—Alexander McQueen. I had to practically pick my jaw up off the floor as we walked inside past all the beautiful clothes, shoes, and purses. There were actual runway gowns here on display in this secret back room, with capes and feathers and jewels. Real jewels, not tacky sequins. It was almost enough to make me forget what I just saw.

Lucas had picked that man up by his neck and thrown him into a wall. How did he have that kind of strength? And how had that man walked away without a scratch?

Could all this stuff about demons actually be true?

No. Impossible.

I had no explanation for it, but what I saw did confirm one thing —Lucas was more dangerous than I'd thought.

"I need a gown fit for a queen," Lucas said to the salesman. "One of a kind. In her size."

"I have the perfect thing," the smartly dressed man replied in a respectful tone. "I'll bring it out immediately."

Lucas nodded and the man disappeared. I stared at Lucas with fear trailing down my spine, wondering how he could look so casual after such an act of violence. And so disturbingly gorgeous. Fuck, maybe he was the devil. Or at least the closest thing to it.

The salesman returned carrying an ethereal ball gown that was all black except for tiny crystal stars trailing down to the different phases of the moon along the bottom hem. At the shoulders, silver moon clasps held on a long, sheer black cape with more crystal stars running down it. Everything about it was soft and billowy except for the bodice, which was low-cut and form-fitting. It was the most beautiful gown I'd ever seen in my life.

Lucas nodded. "Have it fitted for her."

I instantly reached out to touch the crystals on the gown, but then pulled my hand back. "It's lovely, but I can't imagine I'll ever have anywhere to wear it."

He pinned me with his dark gaze. "On your final night, you'll be attending the Devil's Night Ball as my guest."

I counted the nights in my head. That was the night before Halloween. "What's the Devil's Night Ball?"

"It's when the demons honor me as their King."

I had no time to process his absurd words before I was whisked away into a dressing room, where a woman helped me put on the gown. Then I stared at myself in the mirror, my face pale, my eyes scared, while I stood in the loveliest dress I'd ever worn. Was this what Persephone felt like when she was kidnapped by Hades? Did Lucas think all the glitz and glamour would hide the dark, seedy depths of his underworld?

He moved behind me and met my eyes in the mirror, then rested his hands on my shoulders possessively. "Yes, this is the gown. And when you wear it by my side, everyone will know you're mine."

"Only for seven nights," I said, my voice defiant, even though I was secretly wondering if escape was still an option.

His lips curled into a dark smile. "We'll see about that."

7

HANNAH

When we returned from our shopping trip, a whole spread of food awaited us in the apartment, with gourmet sandwiches, fancy meats and cheeses, and a salad with feta cheese. I needed some time to myself after the day's events, and grabbed some food and retreated to the guest room. But when I opened the door, my breath caught and I nearly dropped my entire plate.

Flowers and plants now packed my previously sparse guest room, and I inhaled the fresh, floral scents I loved so much. Each corner had a weeping fig tree, and flowers grew in pots along the windowsill, on the desk and side tables, and inside the bathroom. I spotted white lilies, purple violets, blue irises, and white-and-yellow daffodils. No roses, which I found curious, but I didn't mind. I'd always thought roses were overdone and overrated, especially when there were so many other beautiful plants out there.

Then it hit me. These were all my favorite flowers.

How did he know?

How did he *always* know?

Lucas's voice at my back made me jump. "I thought they might help you feel more at home."

"They're lovely," I said, trying to keep my voice steady. Between this and his earlier comments I was starting to think he intended to keep me here longer than seven nights. That was never going to happen though. As soon as Brandy was found and my time was up, I was out of here. No matter how rich, powerful, or sinfully sexy he was. Or how thoughtful and generous he was being. "Thank you."

"Try to relax and enjoy the rest of your day," his voice purred. "Take a bath, perhaps. Eat anything you like. We'll meet at nine for our evening's festivities."

I swallowed and nodded, and he retreated on silent footsteps. Once he was gone I closed the door, let out a long breath, and sat at the desk to eat my sandwich and salad. A small pot of daffodils rested on the table beside my plate, and I admired the star-like white petals circling a yellow center. Even though they were pretty common, daffodils were my favorite flower because they always lifted my spirits. Like harbingers of spring, they popped out of the ground when nothing else in the garden had yet dared to declare victory over winter. Plus, once they were cut, they secreted sap that was poisonous to other flowers, which meant you had to keep them in their own vase. They were like the plant version of introverts, except they poisoned anyone who got up in their space. My kind of plant, indeed.

The daffodil was also called the narcissus, when you wanted to sound sophisticated anyway. The narcissus was known for being the flower Persephone picked just before the earth opened up and Hades kidnapped her and took her to the underworld. At the thought, I remembered the ancient Greek vase in Lucas's library and wondered if the daffodil here was connected somehow.

I shook myself out of my dark thoughts and finished my food, while scanning my phone for any messages or updates, then resorting to glimpsing through old photos of Brandy while praying she was still alive. Then I took Lucas's suggestion and took a bath in the huge tub, luxuriating in the shampoos and soaps, losing myself in the floral scents with a richness beyond the usual cloying smells I purchased at the local dollar store.

When I got out, I discovered an entire collection of makeup lined up for my perusal, arranged like the most expensive department store counters. I stared at the pots and tubes and brushes for several minutes. It was hard to break the perfect seals and mar the powders pressed in their little dishes. Once they were used, they were used, and I couldn't shake the feeling they were all wasted on me. I was an eyeliner and lip gloss kind of gal, and I didn't even know what to do with most of these things. Did they come with a tutorial?

Fuck it. If I was being held captive by a dangerous billionaire who called himself Lucifer then I deserved all the perks that came with the situation. Like the luxurious toiletries and makeup, along with the clothes and jewelry. Even the fancy shoes. Worst case, I gave them back at the end of my seven day sentence.

I cracked open the makeup, found a YouTube video explaining how to use it, and went at it. Sometime later, I walked out of the bathroom and found all the clothes from our shopping expedition hanging in the massive walk-in closet. While I'd been playing with eyeliner and foundation, someone had been in my room without me even knowing it. I never expected having staff would actually make me feel *more* vulnerable. From now on, I'd make sure to lock the doors.

Then, once I'd ascertained I was safe, I returned my attention to the clothes and tried to decide what to wear tonight. Lucas had mentioned in the car ride back to The Celestial that we were going to an exclusive nightclub, which was so not my normal scene. I wasn't kidding when I told Lucas I usually spent my nights at home curled up with a book.

Eventually I picked something that was bolder and sexier than I'd ever normally wear, but I had an idea for how to make the evening less intimidating. If I felt like I was in costume, I could pretend to be someone else for the night, and leave all of my worries here to come back to later.

After tugging at the tight red dress and sucking in a deep breath, I opened the door and stepped out into the penthouse's living area.

Lucas whirled, the night view of the city framing him with a neon glow, contrasting with his stylish, tailored suit and dark hair. He looked me over and a muscle flexed in his jaw, while his gaze turned hungry. "You look like—" He paused as if searching for the word, and then his lips took on a wicked curve when he found it. "Sin."

I found myself unable to tear my gaze from his mouth, as the word sin settled over me like a seductive caress on my exposed skin. If there was ever a man who embodied sin, it was him.

"Shall we?" he asked, offering his hand.

I lightly rested my fingers in his, and let out a sigh at the little shock that always ran through me when we touched. "Where are we going?"

"My rooftop nightclub, Pandemonium. There's a band playing tonight that I think you'll like."

We exited the penthouse, ignoring the guards, and entered the elevator. I didn't know if I'd ever get used to having handsome, burly men standing outside the door, but at least I only had a few more nights to deal with it. Soon all of this would be like one of those dark fairytales, a cautionary story I'd tell about how I once was a billionaire's side piece for a few nights.

"Thank you for the flowers," I said, as soon as we were inside the elevator. "But how did you know they were my favorite? And then there was the coffee this morning, and the emeralds... Are you stalking me?"

"I do my research." He raised one of those perfect dark brows at me. "I like to know who I'll be making deals with and allowing into my home. Need I remind you that you're the one who came to me to ask for a favor?"

My cheeks flushed, but I wasn't satisfied with that answer. Nor with the ever-present feeling that he was familiar somehow. "Did we know each other before the accident?"

He tilted his head. "Accident?"

The elevator opened onto the roof before I could answer. Music and lights blasted me in the face as soon as we stepped out, and all previous thoughts died away when I saw who was playing on the small stage.

"Is that The Hellions?" I asked, raising my voice to project over the music.

Without waiting for his reply, I hurried forward to get a better look. The rooftop club had a pool on one side of the stage and a bar on the other, and was open to the night sky above us and the flashing lights of Vegas all around. It was also so exclusive that I didn't even have to push through a crowd to get to the stage. People stood around, dancing to the sound of The Hellions' newest songs, but I was able to go straight to the front.

How was this possible? The Hellions were huge, like selling out giant concert venues huge, but here they were in a tiny, intimate venue. I could almost reach up and touch the singer's black combat boot while he crooned about lost love.

As I moved in time to the beat, I noticed Lucas standing beside me, watching me with unblinking intensity. I turned toward him. "Was this in your report too? My favorite band?"

He leaned close with one hand on the small of my back, in the spot where the dress had an intricate cut-out. When his fingers touched my bare skin, I stilled, unable to focus on the music as heat rushed between my thighs. His sensual voice came through loud and clear in my ear, as if we were in a room alone. "I'm very thorough. As you'll soon learn for yourself."

"You got them to play here, in your nightclub, on such short notice?" I drew in a shaky breath. "For me?"

He let that hand trail a tiny bit lower, hovering just above the curve of my butt. "I did, yes."

I couldn't help but be impressed. I hated to admit it, but he was winning me over a tiny bit, no matter how hard I tried to resist his charms. Clothes, jewels, shoes—those felt like buying me off. But my favorite flowers? My favorite band? That was something else.

"They couldn't say no to me," Lucas continued talking as if my thoughts hadn't carried on racing forward at a million miles per hour. "They're demons, you know. Imps, actually. Their kind tends to become musicians, actors, that sort of thing. Imps always crave the spotlight. Don't worry, I paid them handsomely too."

And now we were back to the demon talk. It had to be some sort of quirky billionaire eccentricity—a way to amuse himself when he could already afford every other sort of amusement in existence, no doubt—but it was really getting old. Of course, it would explain what I saw earlier today... But no. There had to be a more reasonable explanation for that.

Lucas caught my hand and pulled me close, still laughing. "Dance with the devil?"

Maybe he was crazy, but as he drew my body flush against his, I found myself melting in his arms. No matter how hard I tried, I couldn't bring myself to want to pull away from him. I soon lost myself in the song and the feel of Lucas's hard chest pushing against mine. Though he was much taller than me, his masculine body molded against mine perfectly, and the sense of rightness I felt in his arms was unlike anything I'd ever felt before.

His hand on my bare back led me across the floor, and for a few minutes all I knew was the pounding of the bass drum and the tingle where Lucas touched me. I couldn't deny how much I wanted him at this moment, even if getting involved with someone like Lucas was a terrible idea. Even without his obvious eccentricities, he was powerful, and it was the kind of power tainted by danger. He bargained for the things he wanted but couldn't buy, and fear as much as lust slid cold fingers down my spine as I considered my position at his side.

When the song ended and another one began, Lucas left his hand lingering on my back and turned me toward the bar. "Come, let's get a drink."

We walked toward the bar, and many people stopped to notice us, especially the way his hand claimed me. There would be no doubt in any of their minds that I was Lucas's woman, at least for tonight. For all I knew, he had a new woman on his arm every week.

As the thought of that made my stomach clench, someone in the crowd shouted. We both turned and watched as something on the stage exploded with a burst of light and a deafening boom, setting off multiple screams in the audience. One of the screams might have been from me.

The members of The Hellions ran off stage as blue flames shot into the air, quickly engulfing everything and spreading unnaturally fast along cords and into the audience somehow. People began to run toward the exit in a panic, while Lucas wrapped an arm across my shoulders and turned us away from the conflagration.

"Ignore it," he said, as he signaled to someone on the sidelines to deal with the fire. "It's all an illusion."

"What?" I glanced behind my shoulders as the flames danced across the pool's water, my head spinning and my heart pounding.

"An illusion. Imps can create them. Someone is causing a distraction, though I'm not sure why."

As he rushed me away from the burning stage, I spotted Zel running forward with Gadreel and some others, presumably to put out the fire...or whatever you did with illusions. Then the panicked crowd swallowed us up and I was bumped into by several people. In the chaos, I was separated from Lucas and surrounded by strangers, while blue flames suddenly sprouted up near us, so close that many people jumped and screamed. I took a few steps back, until I was pressed up against the wall surrounding the edge of the roof, but the flames kept coming while people around me tried to escape.

Then something hard and fast plowed into me with such force it sent me flying.

No, not flying. Falling.

The sudden force of the collision knocked all air from my lungs as I somehow went over the wall of the roof and plummeted toward my death. I couldn't even scream, because I couldn't suck in any air. Time slowed as I suffocated on my own panic, my limbs flailing, trying to grab onto something, anything, while my body dropped toward The Strip below me.

Then it hit me—I was going to die.

My life didn't pass through my eyes. There were no moments of clarity. Instead, I felt only regret for all the things I hadn't done and for not finding Brandy, along with an unexpected pang of loss for not getting to finish my seven nights with Lucas.

There was something else too. A sense of inevitability. As if I'd always known my death was coming swiftly and violently, sooner than later.

Like in my dreams.

The rush of air ripped tears from my eyes, but through the haze

I saw something dark falling above me. For a second I thought a man had jumped off the edge of the roof, but that was absurd. Until the man came closer, and I made out Lucas in his black suit. I watched his eyes glint red as his determined face drew near, and I laughed, because surely this was some kind of near-death delirium. Or maybe I was already dead?

Just as he wrapped his strong arms around me, enormous, black-feathered wings erupted from his back. My stomach lurched as we stopped falling, and I sucked in a huge rasping breath of air, my heart nearly leaping out of my chest from the impact.

"I've got you," he said, as he tucked me close against his chest.

I could only stare in shock and wonder as his wings moved like shadows against the bright city lights. Darkness trailed away from each feather like smoke as we flew through the air, rising until we reached the balcony of his penthouse. He landed easily beside the pool, but didn't let me go, his arms wrapped protectively around me as I leaned against his chest. Probably a good thing, since I wasn't sure I could stand.

I looked up at Lucas's impossibly handsome face. His eyes had lost the red glow, or perhaps I'd imagined that, but the black wings were still there. They looked like they were made of night itself, and I watched the way the darkness curled around him, the shadows clinging to his body and maybe even forming the hint of horns above his head.

"Am I dead?" I managed to ask. "Are you an angel?"

"You're not dead." He gazed down at me with such fierce protectiveness it took my breath away. "And I'm definitely no angel. Not anymore, anyway."

My heart was still beating out of my chest, but I had to see if this was real. I reached up with a trembling hand to touch one of Lucas's wings, running a hesitant finger along one of the night-colored feathers. He sucked in a breath and closed his eyes for the briefest moment, and it surprised me to see how much such a light touch could affect him. How *I* affected him.

Our conversation from last night came back to me like a voice on the wind, as everything he'd told me connected with everything I'd seen in a rush of clarity.

"*I am the devil. My true name is Lucifer.*"

"*You're trying to tell me you're actually the devil. Fallen angel. Evil incarnate.*"

"*Evil? Probably. Fallen? Definitely.*"

I could no longer deny it.

Lucas Ifer really was the devil.

And I'd made a deal with him.

8

LUCIFER

W ith one last look at the star-filled sky I'd plucked Hannah from, and the bright lights below where everything could have ended, I cradled her closer to my chest and strode inside the penthouse to settle her on the sofa. Her blonde hair spread over the black leather cushions like spun gold, and her blue-eyed gaze watched me with a mixture of shock and something else. Fear? Curiosity?

Fire raced through my veins as I turned in a circle and raked a hand through my hair as I tried to figure out what to do. Water. That was what she needed. I headed to the bar and poured some for her, and a whiskey for me. This certainly called for a drink.

That was too close. I'd nearly lost her. How had she fallen? By the time I spotted her in the panicked crowd, it was already too late. If she hadn't screamed, I wouldn't have seen her in time. Someone must have shoved her, and hard too. Only supernatural strength could have gotten her over that wall.

Was *he* after her already? Or was it someone else? Fuck. I couldn't even keep her safe on the roof of my own building. Would it be better to send her away? Would she be safer?

No. *No.* She was safest by my side. This time would be different. It had to be.

When I returned with her water, Hannah sat on the sofa in the exact position I'd left her in. She hadn't moved or said a word, she just stared off into space with her perfect lips slightly open. This was definitely shock. Falling from a roof would do that to anyone, not to mention being saved by the most infamous villain in the world.

As soon as I realized she was shivering, I waved a hand at the fireplace and it ignited, instantly. Then I snatched a velvet throw from the chair by the fire and covered her with it. As I tucked it around her shoulders, she finally moved her eyes upward, focusing on something behind me. I whirled, expecting to find someone there, but we were alone.

As I returned my attention to Hannah, I realized her wide-eyed gaze was glued to my wings. I tucked them away quickly, making them vanish.

"I was planning to show you my wings, and prove to you all I'd been saying," I said in my softest voice—the one I reserved only for Hannah—as I squashed all the fury still roiling inside me. "But not like this."

She jerked her gaze to my face, and her perfect little mouth formed an *o*. "It's true. It's all true."

"Yes, it is." I reached up to stroke her cheek, but she flinched back from me and I stopped myself. "Do you know what happened back there? How you fell?"

She shook her head silently, her eyes still wide.

"Whoever attacked you will pay." This time, I wasn't able to keep the menace from my voice, and she recoiled again. I drew in a sharp breath and regained control of myself. "Hannah. You have nothing to fear from me."

Hannah's chest began to heave under the blankets as she took rapid breaths. "But you're the *devil!*"

Without waiting for a response, she threw her blanket to the side and kicked her heels off. Her red dress rode up her legs with the movement, revealing inch after inch of pale, soft skin. My cock twitched as I remained ever aware of how perfect she was, inside and out, even in the midst of an existential crisis. I averted my eyes.

"God," she whispered. Ah, she'd discovered the larger implications of me being...well, me. "Does God exist? What about the Bible?"

"I've known many gods in my time, and I've been a god or two as well, but I don't know if *the* God, an all-powerful and all-knowing deity, actually exists. No one does."

She jumped to her feet and scurried across the room, but she didn't leave, which was promising. I had a sliver of hope I hadn't completely scared her away. "And the other demons you keep talking about. Imps, succubi, incubi.... Those are real too? What about angels?"

"Yes, all real. Everything I've told you is true." I wanted to reach for her, to help her through this difficult realization, but I stayed back. She was still here. She knew where the door was, and she hadn't left. That was the important thing.

Hannah stopped pacing and stared at me with her jaw hanging open. "But...how?"

"Demons come from a..." How to describe it? "Parallel universe of sorts, known as Hell. Angels came from another realm known as Heaven, and fae come from Faerie."

Her eyebrows rose with every sentence I spoke. If I carried on, she'd lose them somewhere in her hair. "Fae?"

"Let's focus on angels and demons for now and worry about the fae some other time." I walked over to the bar and poured myself another whiskey. Sometime in the last few minutes I'd downed mine without realizing it. "Drink? If there was ever a time for alcohol, it's when you realize your entire view of life has been upended."

"No, thanks." She walked over to the armchair by the window and collapsed into it, completely unaware of how the dress had shifted on her frame, exposing those thighs again, not to mention most of her midsection. Another inch and I'd see the lower curve of her breasts. Not that I was complaining. "The last thing I need is for this revelation to be muddled by alcohol."

"Many humans find life preferable when muddled by alcohol.

Alas, it has no effect on me." I took a sip of whiskey anyway, mainly because I liked the taste. The burn reminded me of Hell.

Hannah finally realized she was holding a glass of water and took a sip. A tiny bit of clarity returned to her eyes, and I could almost see her thoughts working inside that smart brain of hers. Her true nature would allow her to accept these revelations easier than a normal human would—some of them never recovered from learning about supernaturals. I had no doubt Hannah would be fine by the end of the night. She always was.

She turned those big blue eyes on me, peering at me from under her soft lashes. "You were an angel once."

"Archangel," I corrected. "But I rebelled against Heaven, much as the lore says I did."

"Why?"

The answer to that was too much for her to handle tonight. "Let's just say I disagreed with a few of their policies regarding Earth."

"And then you became the devil?" she asked.

"Then I left Heaven for Hell." I ran a hand down my suit, smoothing the rumpled fabric. "There I united the warring, chaotic demon tribes and crowned myself King. I've ruled the demons ever since."

I debated telling her how she played into it all, but she seemed shell-shocked enough as it was. She'd had enough for tonight. Soon she would know everything, with no more secrets between us, and I longed for that day. But she needed time to process everything first.

I stepped forward and offered her my hand. "I can tell you have more questions, but I think it's time you got some rest. You've had an...eventful night."

"But I have more questions," she said, as she slid her hand into mine.

"And I promise to answer them. Tomorrow." She wobbled a little as she stood, and I bent down and picked her up again. The second she was in my arms, everything in the world felt right again.

"What are you doing?" she squealed, kicking her legs as I carried her across the living room.

"Taking you to your room."

"I can walk!"

"That's debatable." I kicked open her door and set her down on the bed. "You just had the shock of a lifetime, and nearly died as well. Allow me to help you get undressed."

She stood up without wavering this time. "I can manage just fine, thanks." But then she paused. "Although if you could unzip the back of this dress, that would be great. I could barely get it on by myself earlier."

A low chuckle escaped me as she turned around, and I dragged the zipper down her back, exposing her pale, perfect skin. Oh, how I longed to trail my lips down it, and to continue sliding this dress to the floor. I had to have her. Soon.

She turned around and shot me a look that reminded me of a kitten trying to be ferocious, and muttered thanks. Then she grabbed something from the closet and escaped into the bathroom, shutting the door behind her.

I lounged on the bed while I waited for her, admiring the flowers around the room. Gadreel had done a good job following my orders, as I knew he would. I breathed them in, remembering a time long ago when we'd also been surrounded by narcissus.

When Hannah stepped out she did a double-take when she saw me on her bed. Her face was hesitant, but she licked her lips, and I knew she felt desire too. She could never resist me, no matter how hard she tried.

Her hair was loose around her shoulders, her makeup gone, and she wore a thin black nightgown with spaghetti straps. Restraining myself from slipping those straps off her shoulders was sheer torture, but I prevailed and rose to my feet.

"I'm leaving," I told her, as I unbuttoned my suit jacket. "I simply wanted to make sure you were all right before I left you alone."

She let out a long breath. "I feel like my head's been taken off, shaken about, and put back on again."

I chuckled softly. "That sounds about right. Come. Lie down."

I eased forward and took her hand, drawing her toward me. She allowed it, to my surprise, which only showed how tired she was. A near-death experience really took it out of humans, even one as extraordinary as Hannah. I drew her blankets back and when she slipped into the bed, I covered her up. When she looked up at me with her golden hair spread out on the pillow it took everything I had not to climb in bed with her. Her eyes were wide though, and I sensed her tired brain was resisting sleep, coming up with even more questions to ask me.

"Sleep. We have another big day tomorrow." With the faintest push, I added a bit of power to my words, just enough to make her yawn and her eyelids begin to flutter closed. The command wasn't very strong, but it would allow her body's own instincts to take over and help her sleep off most of the shock.

She yawned and pulled the covers up to her chin, before whispering, "Why me?"

"Because you're mine. You've always been mine." I pressed a kiss to her forehead as her eyes fluttered shut. "And you will *always* be mine."

9

HANNAH

When I woke, the sheets had twisted around me like I was being pinned to the bed by coiled snakes. A cool sheen of sweat lingered on my body, and damp strands of hair stuck to my forehead. I groaned and sucked in a long shallow breath. It wasn't enough. My body craved oxygen as though I'd spent most of the night running.

I'd always been a terrible sleeper, plagued by horrible dreams and then waking to find my body clenched tight around a pillow, my muscles aching from the tension in my limbs. But last night was especially bad.

Fractured remnants of my dreams floated through my mind. Fire and ashes, shadows and smoke, darkness curling into feathers and horns. So much fear, so much pain, so much death. And Lucas... always Lucas. His face drifted in and out of focus before being replaced by another's, though this one was blurred.

The only dream I remembered clearly was one with Lucas—no, *Lucifer*—sitting on a black throne, and the closer I tried to look at him, the more he seemed to become aware of my presence. Too late, I pulled back, but his red eyes gaze snapped to mine and he crooked his finger, beckoning me closer. That was right before I woke up, and my heart still thundered from the memory of it.

I sat up and shook my head, trying to clear it, but the fear from my dreams still lingered. I hesitated to leave the room because Lucas would be out there, with day three already planned for me. Which sin would it be today?

I swallowed the horror drying my throat. How could I possibly spend any further time with that man now that he'd revealed his secret? When I'd thought him a mob boss, I'd questioned my choices. Now I condemned them.

I moved from my bed like an old lady, slowly and carefully in case I broke. I'd nearly died last night, and my body felt tender, like it hadn't gotten the memo I was still alive. I walked to the closet on autopilot, and the hangers clacked together as I moved them from left to right. Like everything else I touched in this room, they were good quality. Expensive. And they belonged to the devil.

Did I belong to him too now?

I drew out the first outfit my hands touched—a linen, sleeveless pantsuit. I briefly wondered if it would suit today's activities but shrugged it off. I didn't care about the activities. I was only doing this for Brandy.

Once dressed, I couldn't delay any longer. I had to face Lucas.

No, not Lucas.

Lucifer.

Lu-ci-fer.

The syllables rolled around and around in my head, their sound enough to drive me crazy. Even after everything I'd seen last night, it was hard to accept it was all real.

When I finally walked into the kitchen, he was there and already dressed in another of his impeccable black suits, sipping coffee and reading a newspaper.

"Good morning." His warm voice washed over me, as if nothing at all untoward had happened last night. Except I'd all but plummeted to my death, and he'd grown a pair of wings as black as darkness itself. But then, the devil might not have a care in the world. Why should he?

"Morning," I murmured, although it was nearly noon at this point.

He looked me over, his eyes dark and unreadable. "You look lovely."

"Thank you." I couldn't look at Lucifer without memories of my dreams flickering through my head, or of the stomach-lurching jolt when he'd caught me mid-air and saved my life. Clearing my throat, I focused on the food instead.

An entire brunch buffet was laid out on the table with everything from eggs to pancakes to fruits. I picked at a couple of things, then glanced at the apples. Ruby red, juicy-looking, and tempting me like they probably once tempted Eve. Was that story real too? I shook my head, rejecting them.

Lucifer watched my progress back toward the table, and he eyed me as I began to pick at the small scoop of eggs on my plate, but I avoided looking at him. Every time I glanced his way, my breath caught at the memory of his protective eyes looking down on me, his arms clutching me tight, his wings unfurled behind him. The enormous, shadowy, impossibly beautiful wings that had saved my life. If he had wings and red eyes—because surely I didn't imagine those either—what else did he have? Horns? A forked tail? Goat legs? My brain conjured up all sorts of horrifying images from movies and tv shows, and I shoved my food away, my hunger gone.

Yesterday, I'd been trying to humor a sexy billionaire with a devil fetish. Today, I was dining one-on-one with Lucifer himself. It was a lot to take in. I just had to get through the next few days, and then I'd have Brandy back, and I could spend the rest of my life trying to forget I'd ever met the devil.

Yeah, right. As if that was possible.

———

That afternoon, we took another of Lucifer's fancy sports cars out onto The Strip. I didn't ask where we were going, and Lucifer left me to my silence, as if he knew I wasn't ready for conversation. We left downtown Las Vegas and drove just past the edge of civilization, to the start of where the desert could swallow us up. He turned the car down a road that led to a sign for the Devil's Playground Raceway, and we soon came upon a rectangular building set against the backdrop of a large racetrack with the arid, dry mountains behind it.

"What are we doing here?" I asked, as I gazed out at the race track.

"Letting off a little steam." Lucifer gave me a wicked grin. "I thought you could use a good distraction."

He parked in front of the building and donned a pair of black sunglasses, while I stepped out of the car and under the scorching desert sun. I was used to heat after living in Southern California, but this was brutal. Another sports car pulled up behind us and stopped on a dime, and then Zel and Gadreel jumped out. Zel was wearing her battle leather and had weapons strapped to her, and she glared at everything like even the sun offended her. Gadreel grinned and ran a hand through his sandy blond hair as he checked out the place, like he was a tourist on vacation.

"We have company today," I noted.

A muscle flexed in Lucifer's jaw. "You were attacked last night. I want you protected at all times from now on."

My breath caught. "Attacked? I thought it was an accident."

"We're looking into it now." He gestured at his two cronies as they approached. "I believe you've met Azazel and Gadreel, two of my most loyal Fallen."

"Are they demons too?" I asked, lowering my voice.

"Not exactly." Lucifer wrapped an arm around my shoulder and I stiffened, while he led me into a shady area. "Fallen were origi-nally angels, as I was, but they followed me into Hell and became... something else. Not exactly demons, but not angels anymore either."

I swallowed, absorbing this new information so casually spoken as if we were discussing the weather. "Do they have wings too?"

"They do, but mine are bigger." He lowered his shades to give me a naughty wink. "And in case you're wondering, yes, wing size does correspond directly with other body parts."

A startled laugh escaped me at that, and my guard relaxed a

little. I couldn't help it. The man was just too damn charming. Not to mention that when I was around him, I felt like I knew him on some deep level. But...how?

A thin, attractive man walked out of the building carrying two helmets, and bowed his head to Lucifer. "My lord, everything is ready."

"Brilliant." He waved a hand at me. "Just the helmet for the lady today."

The man before us raised his eyebrows and glanced at me with thinly veiled curiosity. "She knows?"

"She's under my protection," Lucifer said with a hint of a growl in his voice.

"Of course, my lord." He offered me the helmet and then backed away in a half-bow. "I'll get the keys."

After the man had left, Lucifer leaned closer to me. "Another of my demons. A cheetah shifter."

"A what now?"

"Shifters are another type of demon. They can transform into animals." He gestured for me to follow, and we walked around the side of the building, where a row of sports cars awaited us. Gleaming, beautiful, aerodynamic cars in bright colors from lime green to hot pink. Some of them looked like they were right off a NASCAR racing track, with huge spoilers and stickers all over them, while others would be right at home in Lucifer's garage next to his silver Aston Martin.

"Are we going to drive them?" I asked, as Lucifer pulled the helmet over my head. I'd have helmet hair for the rest of the day, but my excitement overcame any apprehension at the realization of what we were about to do.

"We are," he said, as he led me to the first car, the lime green Lamborghini. He wouldn't let anyone else but him buckle me into the passenger seat, but he knew exactly what he was doing. Before I knew it, we were off, while Gadreel and Zel watched from the sidelines under a canopy.

Lucifer raced to breakneck speeds like a pro in seconds, zipping us around the track. The force of the acceleration threw me back in my seat and took my breath away, but I hated to admit how much it thrilled me too.

"You've done this before," I said through the helmet's speaker, but I'd forgotten he hadn't put one on. It didn't matter, though. Lucifer heard me over the engine and shot me a wicked grin. Then he went even faster.

I screamed, except it wasn't out of fear this time but exhilaration, like when you're on a roller-coaster and go down a steep drop. Even though I held on for dear life, I couldn't remember a time I'd had so much fun. Excessive speed had always made me nervous since the car accident, but Lucifer had a way of making me feel safe. Like he was in complete control, and nothing could hurt me when he was by my side.

As we finished the circuit and slowed to a halt, Lucifer looked over at me and let out a throaty laugh. It was so sexy it made me melt a little into my seat.

"You liked that, did you?" he asked.

"More than I expected."

He helped me out of the elaborate safety system and took my hand, lifting me out of the car. His touch sent an unexpected thrill through me as he pulled me close against him. He lingered there, nearly holding me, drawing me in even though his eyes were hidden behind his shades. "I knew you would."

"How?"

"I'm the devil, darling. Give me a little credit." He lifted my hand and pressed a kiss to my wrist, like he did the other night, and everything inside me turned to hot, molten lava.

He's the devil, a voice whispered in my head.

Yeah, but he's really freaking hot too, a louder voice said back.

Okay, so I was probably losing my mind, but wouldn't anyone in this situation?

We drove around the track in three other cars, testing each one out, and it was easy to lose myself in the speed and the adrenaline. Every time I glanced over at Lucifer he flashed me a smile, like he knew just how much I was enjoying myself. Like this, he was just Lucas Ifer again, a man with too much money and too many toys.

When we got out of the fourth car, Lucifer asked, "Would you like to drive one?"

"Really?" My pulse raced as I looked up at him. "You have no idea how much I'd like to drive one. Or maybe you do."

He chuckled softly. "Then choose your car."

I went with the hot pink Ferrari, not because it was pink, but because it was a freaking Ferrari. I'd probably never get another chance to drive one of those, and I wasn't missing out on that. Once again, Lucifer strapped me inside, and gave me a brief rundown of everything I needed to know. Nervous energy raced through me, and I almost talked myself out of doing it, but then Lucifer got in the passenger side of the car and nodded at me. I couldn't back out now.

I gripped the wheel, shifted gears, and put my foot to the pedal. The car shot forward, too slowly at first, but soon I grew more confident and kicked it up a notch. Pure adrenaline raced through my veins and exhilaration ripped a laugh from my lips as the car zoomed around the track, hugging the road like nothing I'd ever experienced before. My poor beat-up Honda could never compare to this.

Lucifer let me take lap after lap until a man's voice told me to come in over the intercom. I was low on fuel. When I stopped, I let out a long breath as the excitement faded away. Then I practically tumbled out of the car, halfway pulled out by Lucifer, while my body still felt like it was moving at hundreds of miles an hour.

As Lucifer helped steady me in his arms, I looked up at him with a smile. "I felt like I was flying."

Something dark crossed Lucifer's face at those words and he glanced away. Maybe it was rude to reference flying to the guy who could grow his own pair of wings at will. Or was it something else?

While I chugged water in the shade, Gadreel and Zel took a turn on the track, opting to go at the same time so they could race. Standing back, I watched in delight as Zel kicked Gadreel's ass, but then let out a startled cry as something—no, *someone*—dropped from the sky at breakneck speed. I jumped back as charcoal gray wings filled my vision as another of Lucifer's henchmen landed hard in front of us. Sam, I remembered. The one who was investigating Brandy's disappearance.

He'd obviously flown here in a hurry. Sweat gleamed on his shaved head as his dark wings tucked behind him and then disappeared completely. Whoa. I wasn't sure I'd ever get used to that.

"What is it, Samael?" Lucifer stepped forward, while Zel and Gadreel leaped out of their cars and rushed over.

"I found them," Sam said.

Now that the shock of seeing another winged man was over, I rushed forward, my heart pounding, scared to ask the question that sprang to my lips. "Is Brandy alive?"

Sam drew himself up and nodded. "Yes. And Asmodeus too."

A huge wave of relief washed over me, so strong my knees nearly gave out. Alive. *Alive!* Thank god she was alive. Although maybe I should be thanking Lucifer, since he'd done this, at least indirectly. I closed my eyes as the dread of worrying she was dead lifted from me.

"Where?" Lucifer asked.

"They're being held captive at an abandoned motel out in the desert," Sam said. "By demons. Shifters, I believe."

And just like that, the worry was back. "Is she hurt? Why did they take her?"

Sam turned his dark gaze back to me. "We haven't determined that yet."

"Well done." Lucifer clasped Sam on the shoulder with something like affection. "I knew you'd find them. We'll mount the rescue tonight. Samael and Gadreel, you're with me. Azazel, stay with Hannah and make sure she's safe."

Zel and Gadreel glanced at each other with raised eyebrows. "You'll be leading the attack, my lord?" Zel asked, obviously surprised.

"Yes, I'll be handling this personally." Lucifer cast me a quick look. "I swore I'd bring Brandy back, and I always keep my promises."

I stepped toward him. "I want to come too."

Lucifer removed his sunglasses and pocketed them. "Though I applaud your bravery, I can't allow you to do that. It isn't safe. You're human, after all."

Gadreel nodded. "Let the demons do the devil's work."

I shot him a defiant look. "None of you would even know about this if I hadn't brought it to your attention."

"And we thank you for that, but there's nothing more you can do." Lucifer rested his hands on my shoulders and pinned me with his intense stare. "Trust me, Hannah. I will handle this with all haste, and soon you'll have your friend back. I will not fail you."

I swallowed and stamped down my stubborn determination. Though it pained me not to go with them, I knew they were right. What could I do against demons? A few hours ago I didn't even know they existed, and it's not like I was a fighter or anything. I ran a flower shop, for fuck's sake, and he was the *devil*. There was no comparison.

And for some reason, I did trust him. It made no sense, but every fiber of my being told me he was telling the truth, and that he would bring Brandy back safely.

I nodded mutely and stepped back. Lucifer reached up to cup my cheek, gazing into my eyes, as his large black wings extended behind him with a rush of wind. Samael's charcoal wings snapped out next, followed by Gadreel's pale gray ones. Without further word, the three of them launched into the sky, blocking out the sun with great flaps of their large wings.

Zel watched them go, her mouth tight. "Come with me. I'll take you back to The Celestial."

But I wouldn't budge. Not until their dark forms were just pinpricks against the bright blue sky, vanishing in the distance and leaving me with only a heavy dose of fear and worry. And not just for Brandy either...but for Lucifer too.

10

LUCIFER

The ground shook under my feet as I landed outside the motel and cracks formed in the cement, fanning out into the hard-packed earth of the surrounding area. Dust kicked up around me as the wind whirled, the elements in tune with my barely constrained anger.

Dozens of my Fallen soldiers landed behind me, many of them carrying Lilim—incubi and succubi—in their arms. The lust demons had volunteered as soon as they'd learned one of their own was being held captive. Asmodeus was well-loved among his kind for running the strip clubs many of them used to feed safely, and they were incensed by his kidnapping. Though many of them were strong fighters, their race didn't have wings, and thus they were relying on my Fallen for covert transport tonight.

We were in the middle of nowhere Nevada, far enough off the main highway that no one would see us. Dim lights were on inside the motel, but otherwise it looked truly abandoned, with broken windows, peeling paint, and a sign hanging on for dear life proclaiming it the Desert Paradise Motel. An empty, cracked swimming pool sat in the middle of the courtyard, half-filled with tumbleweeds. But I knew the place wasn't as empty as it seemed.

The October night air was lovely and cool, and I breathed in the darkness, my closest companion for centuries now. Though I'd once been a soldier of the light, I was truly the Lord of the Night now. I drank in the power of darkness, letting it fill me with strength.

With Gadreel on my left and Samael on my right, I stalked toward the run-down motel with fury burning inside my veins. One of my most loyal demons was being held there, along with Hannah's best friend. They had better be fucking alive, or there would be hell to pay.

Oh, who was I kidding? There was already hell to pay, and the devil was here to collect his due.

Before I reached the door to the motel lobby, it flew open and two men ran out and began shooting at us. Guns, really? How pedestrian. I raised a hand and enveloped the bullets in darkness, fading them into the night before they could hit me or the fighters behind me.

The two men then let out a roar as their bodies grew and changed, growing fur and claws. Bear shifters. Demons of passion and wrath, who should be loyal to me.

They charged forward, and other demonic bears, wolves, and even hellhounds emerged from the motel's various doors, crawling through windows, jumping through rotten walls, and leaping off the roof. My Fallen angels and Lilim immediately charged into the fray before any of the shifters could get near me, and I growled at the sight of demons fighting demons.

"Enough," I bellowed, my voice bouncing off the surrounding mountains with a crack like thunder and echoing back to us. "Bow to me, your King."

None of them backed down, and the fight continued all around me. I gestured for Samael to go inside and he charged forward with his sword raised, with a few angry, gorgeous Lilim at his heels. Gadreel fought a huge bear beside me, using his sword and shadow magic to subdue the beast. With a great slash, Gadreel rammed his sword through the bear's chest, then wrapped darkness around his throat until the shifter slumped in defeat. Gadreel may have looked like a cheerful angel, but in battle he was truly ruthless, a rival for any bloodthirsty demon.

Other shifters foolishly tried to attack me. Their sharp claws and gnashing teeth glanced off my skin without leaving a mark. All of the anger I'd been trying to keep hidden, to protect Hannah from, spilled out of me at the complete disrespect for my power. Perhaps it was time for a reminder of who I was.

I gathered the night around me, spreading my wings wide, before I unleashed it. Like shadowy tentacles, my magic reached out and wrapped around each shifter outside the motel and carved jagged clefts right through them, ripping them apart limb from limb.

Did I need a small army at my back? No. I could destroy everyone here with the slightest thought. I'd simply hoped to avoid bloodshed, thinking that a show of force would cause the shifters to back down and hand over the captives. But that didn't happen, and now I was really fucking pissed.

More shifters emerged from the motel, chased out by Samael and his Lilim warriors. A huge red fox decided to get brave, snapping at me. The same fucking fox shifter who'd been spying on me and Hannah while we'd been shopping.

As he leaped at me with sharp teeth, I clamped my fingers on the creature's neck and used darkness to reach inside him and crush his heart and his lungs. Then I tossed his body to the ground as the remainder of his flesh shifted back to human form. He should have heeded my warning earlier.

I looked around at the continued fighting, my chest heaving as I battled the desire to burn each of the remaining shifters to ashes. Perhaps they'd surrender now.

None of them did.

I pushed my darkness outward. As soon as the remaining shifters saw more of the twisting shadows swirling from me they ran, but they were too late. They'd forced my hand.

My darkness snaked around the throats of each of the rebellious little traitors, yanking them back. I sucked all the life out of them, drawing it back inside myself, their resistance only making me stronger.

Their lifeless bodies hit the ground and the battle was officially over. I turned toward the motel in time to see Samael emerge from the front doors with Asmodeus and a pretty Black woman. Her dark skin was dust-covered and there was evidence of blood congealing around small tears in her clothes, but her brown eyes still held a gleam of determination. This must be Brandy.

She was faring better than Asmodeus, by all appearances, and she held onto his arm, like she refused to be parted from his side. The incubus's olive skin was covered in more dried blood and dirt, as were his ripped and torn clothes. His normally vibrant green eyes were dull and exhausted, and he stumbled forward along the dirt, leaning against Brandy for support while Samael looked on with a frown.

I took a handkerchief from my suit pocket and slowly wiped off my hands. "Tell me what happened."

"They kidnapped us," Brandy said, and I was surprised she answered first. A brave one, for sure. "They tortured him, trying to get him to talk about you, but he wouldn't break."

"Did you feed on her?" I asked Asmodeus. It would be understandable given the circumstances, but humans could only handle so much of an incubus's attentions. I needed to know if he'd done any damage to Brandy before I returned her to Hannah.

"No, I didn't," Asmodeus said between clenched teeth. He obviously needed to feed, and was doing everything in his power to hold himself back.

"You heroic fool," Brandy muttered, her eyes softening as she looked at him. "I told you it was all right."

Heroic? Asmodeus? The incubus who ran my strip clubs and went through human women like candy? I nearly laughed, until I saw the way they looked at each other. With their gazes locked, something intense passed between them, like powerful longing. It must be a side effect of his powers. Asmodeus may have refrained from feeding on her, but the lust he inspired was impossible for humans to ignore.

"I would never hurt you," Asmodeus said to her.

Samael stepped forward and took Asmodeus's arm, yanking him

away from Brandy with a disapproving frown. "You need to feed, son. I'll take you now."

"Yes, go," I said, waving them off. "I'll handle things here."

Asmodeus reached out to Brandy like he was going to stroke her face, but then he dropped his hand and his expression turned grim. Samael's wings stretched out and he picked up his son, before they flew up into the sky. Unlike Samael, Asmodeus didn't have wings. He took after his mother, Lilith, instead.

Brandy watched them fly away and brushed her fingers across her eyes, wiping away tears she didn't wish me to see. Then her head snapped to me and she stared at me with something like curiosity.

"You know who I am?" I asked. As she certainly knew all about demons now, there was no sense in hiding my abilities or pretending to be other than I was.

She bit her lip and nodded, but I was impressed that she didn't drop her eyes or look away. "Asmodeus told me. I didn't believe it at first but..."

She was handling things very well, all things considered. I could see why Hannah would practically sell her soul for such a friend. "We're going to fly you back to my hotel, The Celestial, where you can recover in safety. Hannah is there already."

"Hannah?" Brandy looked around at all the bodies helplessly. "She can't be here. This place, this world..."

Perhaps this was a bit much for a mortal to endure. I waved my arm and the night devoured the bodies, causing them to vanish. That only made her jump though, and I wondered whether I'd over-done it. It had been a long time since I'd shown my true self to humans, and I forgot how skittish they became around blood and magic.

"Hannah is the reason we found you," I explained. "She'll be relieved to see you're all right."

"Am I?" she asked with a short laugh, as she rubbed her arms and gazed at the hotel with dark memories in her eyes. Yes, she defi-nitely needed to leave this place. After my people finished searching the motel for evidence, I'd burn it down in her honor.

I snapped my fingers. "Gadreel, please escort Ms. Brandy back to The Celestial and set her up in one of the luxury suites."

Gadreel stepped forward and nodded, his pale wings stretching out behind him. She stared at them with her mouth open, and then he said something quietly to her before picking her up. I could have carried Brandy myself, of course, but that felt like a betrayal of Hannah. Another woman in my arms? No. I only wanted the one who was meant for me.

I barked out a few orders to the remaining Fallen and Lilim at the scene, making sure they left no stone unturned in their search. I didn't know why those shifters had taken Asmodeus and Brandy, but their betrayal made my blood boil. I needed to know if this was an isolated rogue group, or if this was part of a larger act of mutiny. Hopefully when Asmodeus recovered he'd have some answers too.

I took one last look around before taking off into the sky, eager to tell Hannah that her friend had been rescued. My part of the deal was complete.

Now it was her turn.

11

HANNAH

I paced back and forth in the penthouse until my feet ached. Shouldn't they be back by now? I checked the clock for the fiftieth time but only two minutes had passed since I'd last looked at it. I groaned and turned away before I drove myself even more mad.

Azazel watched me from where she lounged on the black leather sofa in Lucifer's living room. With her rich, dark skin and black leather clothing, she looked like a panther—deadly but deceptively relaxed. While drinking a glass of red wine, she watched every single one of my movements like she had to report them all to Lucifer.

"You're making me tired, little mortal." She yawned and shifted her position, stretching like a feline.

I stopped and sighed. "I'm sorry my pacing exhausts you. Aren't you the least bit worried?"

Zel snorted. "Not at all. If your friend isn't dead already, Lucifer won't let her be hurt. And if she is, well, it's already done."

I threw my hands up at her infuriating response. "What about Lucifer? He's your boss, isn't he?"

She laughed in response to that. "You *really* don't need to worry about him."

Maybe not, but I was surprised at how much the thought of him being wounded made my chest tighten and my heart pound. Why did I even care? He was the *devil*, for crying out loud. Should I be rooting for him at all, or was that like siding with evil? But if he was rescuing innocent women from kidnappers, wouldn't that make him the good guy? Damn, this shit was confusing.

Still, I probably shouldn't be worried. I'd only known Lucifer for a few short days, during which he'd basically held me captive. Okay, he'd also bought me a lot of nice stuff and treated me like a queen, but I'd also seen some pretty terrifying things. Not to mention, I'd nearly died too.

To say I was conflicted was an understatement.

I sucked in a breath. All I wanted was for Brandy to be safe. I would focus on that and figure out everything else later.

With nothing to do but wait, I plopped into one of the armchairs and jiggled my leg. Zel moved again on the sofa, cat-like, adjusting so she could see me better.

"So you're a fallen angel?" I asked, trying to make conversation. Mainly to distract myself from glaring at the clock once more.

"If you *must* know, I was once an Erelim."

I gave her a blank look. "Am I supposed to know what that is?"

She sighed and began to speak like she was explaining something even a child would know. "Angels have four Choirs, each with different abilities. Malakim are healers, Ishim can go invisible, Ofanim detect truth, and Erelim are warriors of light."

I shrugged. I still didn't really know what she was talking about. "So what happened?"

She pinned me with a dark gaze. "I followed Lucifer into Hell and became a Fallen, like the rest of his loyal soldiers."

My mouth fell open. "Wouldn't that make you thousands of years old?"

She idly examined one of her perfect red nails. "Yes, I've been Lucifer's blade for many years of both war and peace."

"War?" At least Zel was a good distraction from my worries. "What war?"

"The Great War." She waited for my response, but I just

shrugged again, and she rolled her eyes. "The war between Heaven and Hell?"

"Oh, right." I probably should have guessed that. "Is the war still going on?"

"No, it ended a little over thirty years ago when Lucifer and Archangel Michael signed the Earth Accords, and we were all forced to leave Heaven and Hell to live in this dull realm." She sneered. "Supposedly angels and demons have been at peace since then."

"Why don't you sound happier about that?"

"I prefer war," Zel snapped.

Her words had a tone of finality, but clearly there was more to it than that. While I debated whether to let it go or ask more questions, because I still had a million of them when it came to angels and demons, the sound of windows shattering filled the room.

I screamed as shards of glass rained down on us. Zel was immediately on top of me, protecting my body with her own, pressing me to the marble floor. I managed to crane my neck up as people with demonic, bat-like wings and stony gray skin poured into the room, and I nearly screamed again.

"Gargoyles," Zel practically spat. "Stay down!"

Fine with me. No way was I getting near one of those things. If I'd had any doubts about demons existing, they flew right out the window the second I saw the winged monsters arrive.

Zel jumped up and sprang into action. I watched, mouth agape, as she whipped two daggers out of holsters at her thighs and began to mow the creatures down. She threw some incredible moves with the daggers, and they flew almost faster than I could see in her hands. One glowed with white light, while the other had a strange black glow that reminded me of Lucifer's wings. But the gargoyles seemed almost impenetrable, with skin like stone, and her kicks bounced off them. Only the glowing white dagger seemed to do much damage to them.

I scrambled back from an inhuman snarl behind me as hot, fetid breath wafted across the base of my neck. One of the gargoyles had gotten around Zel. With a panicked yelp, I crawled across the carpet on all fours, knees digging into the tiny beads of shattered glass. The gargoyle grabbed my leg, dragging me toward him with a vice-like grip, and sheer terror flooded me. I grunted and kicked at his face with my other leg, successfully connecting with his nose.

It was like kicking a boulder.

I was pretty sure I did more damage to my foot than to his face. These fuckers really were made of stone. His impossibly strong fingers dragged me toward him, no matter how much I fought back, but then Zel threw her light dagger at the beast's chest. The creature howled and released me, giving me enough time to scramble away.

The door to Lucifer's library was open and I bolted for it, running faster than I'd ever done in my life. I darted through and tried to close the door from the inside, but another gargoyle slipped his hand through and grabbed the door at the last second, stopping it from shutting all the way. He shoved the door open with inhuman strength, and I cursed and backed away.

I looked around the room frantically, searching for a weapon. Anything that would help keep this monster off me. My gaze landed on that ornamental sword mounted on the wall behind Lucifer's creepy desk. It seemed to call to me, and I was unable to tear my gaze away.

Before I could question my actions, I stood on tiptoes and jerked the sword from the wall, ripping it out of its jeweled sheath, then lurching forward when the weight of the blade surprised me. The tip nearly hit the ground before I corrected and swung it up, just in time for blinding white light to burst out of the blade as it slashed across the gargoyle's chest. The glowing sword cut through his stone skin like butter, and I gasped as he hit the ground, dead.

The impact of his stone body hitting the marble floor left cracks in it and sent rubble and dust flying. As soon as the life left him, his wings vanished and he changed, looking for all intents and purposes like a normal human. A normal, very dead human.

Holy shit, I'd just killed someone.

Before I could process what I'd done, another gargoyle charged into the library after me. By sheer instinct and some sort of survival mode I'd switched on, the sword kept moving, cutting down my attacker as I wielded it with the kind of skill I never dreamed I possessed.

I didn't have time to question it. More gargoyles poured through the door, and my hands kept moving, as did my whole body as I danced and sparred and killed. It was like I'd discovered a muscle memory I never knew I had, like I'd spent most of my life with a sword in my hand. And a good thing too, because here I was, swinging this damn sword and hitting my target every time like my life depended on it—which it totally did.

Gargoyle after gargoyle fell to the ground under the sharp, shining blade, and then Zel was fighting alongside me, her movements impossibly fast and shrouded in darkness. She'd throw a dagger, then use shadow tentacles to pull it back to her hand, and if I hadn't been fighting my own demons, I would have stopped to stare.

"You all right, little mortal?" Zel yelled, as she stabbed a gargoyle through the neck.

"I think so?" I called back, as I narrowly dodged a gargoyle's claws. With a mighty swoop, I chopped the head off of him, like some kind of bloodthirsty warlord riding a battle high. Okay, maybe I wasn't all right. But I couldn't stop either.

Zel cut down the last gargoyle, and then we were alone. Standing amid a circle of dead bodies. Panting heavily and covered in dust and blood.

I looked down at myself and the horror of it all finally hit me. The adrenaline left me in a rush, and the sword fell from my hand and clattered on the floor. I looked at my trembling hands, wondering if they were mine. How had I done all that? I'd never even held a sword before, as far as I could remember. Yet somehow I'd cut down my opponents like it was nothing. Like I'd been born for combat.

"How?" I looked up at Zel, my heart racing and bile rising in my throat. "How did I...?"

Zel leaned against one of the large bookcases, looking completely at rest as she wiped off her daggers with a small cloth. "That was some show. I have to admit, I'm impressed, little mortal."

"I killed them." My gaze flew over the lifeless bodies, knowing I'd been responsible for their deaths. "Oh god, I killed them."

She shrugged, like it wasn't a big deal. "It was you or them."

Pushing off the bookcase, she nudged the sword I'd used with her boot, then carefully picked it up with her cloth, like she worried it would burn her, even though the bright light had faded. I felt a pang of something like possessiveness when she touched it, like I wanted to snatch the blade from her and shout, "Mine!" I stepped back instead, shaking my head to clear it. What the hell was wrong with me?

"How did I do this?" I asked, my voice faltering.

"That's not my story to tell," she said. "You'll have to ask Lucifer."

She walked out of the library, leaving me standing amid a circle of death—one caused by my own hand.

12

LUCIFER

I landed hastily on the balcony of my penthouse, taking in the destruction. The windows of the living room had all been shattered, and tiny pieces of glass shimmered in the moonlight. Panic and dread fought for control inside me as I rushed inside.

"Hannah?" I yelled.

My furniture had been tossed about and broken, and a thin layer of dust and rubble coated the floor, along with blood. No bodies though, and no sign of Hannah or Azazel either.

I ran to Hannah's room, but it was empty and untouched except for the broken windows and the glass all over the floor. Where was she? I returned to the living room and turned in a circle. My rage and fear nearly overwhelmed me. Darkness slipped from my fingertips, eager to find someone to punish for this invasion. How dare they attack *my* penthouse? Where *my* woman was?

"She's fine."

Whirling, I nearly blasted Azazel with dark magic before I reined myself in. "Where is she?"

"In your room. She's asleep, and unharmed."

Relief settled over me and I let out a long breath, then rested a hand on Azazel's shoulder. "Thank you for protecting her. I knew you wouldn't fail me. Gargoyles, was it?"

She bowed her head slightly in acknowledgement. "They were trying to kidnap Hannah."

My fists clenched at my side and filled with hellfire, waiting to be unleashed. Someone was going to burn for trying to hurt her. First imps, then shifters, and now gargoyles. Were all my demons turning against me? And why attack now? They must have known we were going to be away rescuing Hannah's friend. Another betrayal against me.

"There's something you should see," Azazel said.

She led me into the library, where the gargoyles' bodies had dropped in a circle. The clean-up crew was still working here, and they all gave me a low bow before continuing their work. Even though much of the carnage was gone, I spotted some heads removed from their bodies, and there were many more attackers than even Azazel could face.

I arched an eyebrow at her. "You did all this?"

"No, I had help. From Hannah." Azazel crossed her arms and cocked her head at me. "She used Morningstar."

I glanced over at the spot on the wall where the sword usually hung, but it was missing. Then I saw it resting on my desk, beside its jewel-encrusted sheath. I picked it up and examined the sword I'd wielded back when I was an Archangel in Heaven, now covered in traces of gargoyle blood and stone but still glowing with the white light of the angels. I'd clean it later, after I checked on my mate.

"Impressive," I said, as I set the sword back down. "She must be remembering, finally."

I left Azazel in the library and stalked to my room. The door wasn't quite closed, and I opened it silently. Hannah was passed out on the bed, curled up in a ball, clutching my pillow tightly to her chest. She'd fallen asleep tense, based on the way her brows were furrowed together, and at some point she'd thrown the sheets off herself and pushed them into a heap on the empty side of the bed.

My rage quieted, turning into a strong relief to see her alive. When I'd arrived and found the evidence of an attack, I'd feared the worst. Though Hannah's eventual death would be inevitable, I wanted to spend more time with her first.

For a few seconds I simply stared at her, watching her breathe. She wore another of those slinky little nightgowns we'd bought yesterday, and it showed off every curve of her body. Her golden hair draped down her shoulders, and one of her hands was reaching out, like it was searching for me. Intense longing to claim her ran through me, but I pushed it down, back into its dark depths.

I sat gingerly beside her and rested my hand on her shoulder, needing to feel her soft skin, to confirm she was alive. I didn't intend on waking her, but the moment I touched her, her eyes popped open and she sat straight up, like she was ready to bolt.

Tension left her the second she saw me. "Lucifer?"

I kept my hand on her shoulder, hoping to keep her calm. "It's okay. I'm here. Brandy's safe."

Hannah surprised me by throwing her arms around me and letting out what sounded like a relieved sob. "She's okay? Really?"

I held her close against me, savoring the feel of her in my arms once more. Where she belonged. "Of course she is. I promised, didn't I?"

"Thank you." She slowly sat back and wiped tears from her eyes. "Where is she?"

"She's in a suite here at the hotel, with a human doctor tending to her, along with plenty of food and plenty of armed bodyguards. I'm having some clothes brought up for her too, and I sent someone to let her family know she's all right."

"You did all that?" Hannah asked, tilting her head as she studied me.

"It's the least I could do. She was kidnapped from my hotel, after all."

"Can I see her?"

I shook my head. "Your friend has been through a traumatic experience and is exhausted. Right now she needs sleep more than anything." Her shoulders slumped in disappointment and I quickly added, "However, I booked you both a spa day tomorrow. A slothful day, if you will."

"A spa day sounds good." Her eyes focused on my white shirt, and she reached out to touch a spot on it, her palms resting against my chest. "Are you bleeding?"

My muscles clenched under her touch. "I'm fine. It's not my blood."

"I guess tonight was wrath." Her words were barely above a whisper and she looked away, her face twisting to a grimace. "For both of us."

I sensed the turmoil inside her and guessed it had something to do with the attack. "Do you want to tell me what happened?"

She looked at me with wide, shocked eyes. "These...gargoyles flew in and attacked us. Zel fought them off, but there were so many of them. I ran to the library and got that sword off the wall, and it was like I'd been trained in how to use it. My body moved and worked on its own, without me controlling it. It was like..." She hesitated and frowned. "Muscle memory or something."

She looked at her hands, shocked and maybe a little excited. Of course, there was no mystery as to how this had happened, her being able to handle a sword. Not for me, anyway. But was it the right time to tell her?

"Perhaps you tapped into some deeply repressed memory?" I suggested, hoping my words might create some recognition.

"Maybe," she murmured, but nothing changed in her expression.

"That sword was mine when I was in the Angelic Army, created to cut through demons using heavenly light. Few others can wield it without it burning them." I reached up and stroked her cheek softly. "I'm glad it protected you tonight."

One bare shoulder lifted in a shrug. "Zel did most of the hard work."

"From what she said, it sounded like you held your own against them." I slid my fingers into her soft, golden hair. "Are you all right? You weren't injured?"

"I'm okay. Physically anyway. Emotionally... I'm pretty shaken up." She drew in a long breath, but then smiled weakly at me. "At least Brandy is okay. I'm so grateful to you for everything you've done for her. And for me."

"It's my pleasure and my duty." The way she looked at me made my chest tighten with longing. "I would do anything for you."

She raised her eyebrows at that. "Maybe the devil isn't the bad guy everyone thinks he is."

I laughed darkly. "I assure you, I'm every bit the villain they think I am."

"I don't believe that's true."

"Shall I prove my point?"

I took her chin in my hand and turned her head to the side, then leaned in close, breathing in her sweet scent. I wanted to fill my lungs with her, to drink her in until she suffused my empty, dark heart with her light. My soul ached to consume her, but it settled for me pressing my mouth to the spot just below her ear. The slight taste wasn't nearly enough to sate me, especially when I felt her pulse race faster and her breathing grow shallower. Was she growing wet for me? Did she crave me as much as I craved her?

I ran my thumb across her soft lips, imagining them wrapped around my cock or shouting my name as she came. Her eyes fluttered shut at my light touch, her breasts rising and falling in time with her heavy breathing, her nipples straining against the thin fabric of her nightgown. My mouth trailed down her neck ever so slowly and she arched her back toward me, unable to help herself.

"Lucifer," she gasped softly as my lips reached the curve of her neck. Her fingers grasped my shirt, digging into my arms, though not to stop me, but to pull me closer. Her desperate need matched my own, and a low groan of masculine satisfaction hummed deep in my throat. This woman would be my undoing and my absolution, as she always was.

I turned her face toward me and met her eyes, then captured her lips and claimed the kiss I'd long awaited. For years I'd dreamed of this moment, but the reality of it was even better than I'd imagined. As my mouth captured hers, time stood still. For the first time in an eternity, I felt *alive*. Whole. Complete. Blood pounded through my veins, and my senses sharpened, while darkness swirled around us. I deepened the kiss, wrapping my arms around her and probing her delicate mouth with the tip of my tongue. Her fingers slid around my neck, pulling me closer, kissing me back with as much passion as I felt. Even if she didn't remember the truth about us, her body did, her instincts telling her that she belonged to me.

When I pulled back, she licked her lips and stared hungrily at my mouth, eager for more, and fuck, how I wanted to give it to her. Everything inside me surged with the need to possess her body again, and I knew she'd let me do anything I wanted to her. Within minutes I'd have her begging for me, until she knew deep in her soul that she was mine, and mine alone.

But I couldn't do it.

Not yet.

Those crystal blue eyes were hazy with sleep and desire, but something held me back from making her mine. A slight hesitation in her gaze, a small tremble in her touch. She wasn't ready for this. Not after the night she'd just had. The act of restraining myself nearly undid me, but I told myself it would only make my claiming of her even sweeter when it did occur. I pressed one last hot kiss to the hollow of her throat, and then relaxed my hold on her.

She looked confused for an instant, but then footsteps sounded outside the door. Rage threatened to bubble up inside me again—who dared interrupt me with my woman in my bed?

Gadreel strode purposefully inside and then paused when he saw Hannah in my arms. She looked a little stunned as she touched her lips, like she was still dazed from the way I'd kissed her. I couldn't blame her.

"I'm sorry to interrupt," Gadreel said, averting his eyes. "I'll come back later."

"It's fine." I let go of Hannah, though it pained me to do so. "You have a report for me?"

"Yes, we managed to capture one of the shifters at the motel. We're holding him for questioning now."

"Very good. Did they find anything else at the motel? Any indication of who was leading them?"

He kept his head bowed. "No, my lord."

A low growl rumbled in my chest. Imps, shifters, and gargoyles had all acted against me or Hannah in the last few days. Ever since she came into my life, demons who were once loyal to me were turning against me. Was it a coincidence or part of a larger conspiracy? The Fallen and the Lilim still seemed loyal, but what of the dragons and vampires? I needed to question that shifter tonight and find out the depth of this mutinous plot. Either way, I would have to deal with this problem before more demons got any ideas about defiance.

I ran a hand through my hair, the anger and pent-up lust making my movements sharp. "Thank you, Gadreel. I'll meet you in the war room soon."

He bowed and then departed, and I turned back to Hannah, who'd watched the conversation with questions shining in her intelligent eyes. Damn it. I needed to tell her who she was, but first I needed to deal with this insubordination problem. Besides, she wasn't ready for any more surprises tonight.

"Sleep," I told her, easing her back into the bed, putting a touch of power in my words once more. "Stay here in my bed, where you belong. I'll make sure you're safe."

She nodded slowly as she settled down, her eyelids growing heavy. "Don't leave just yet."

My heart twisted at the soft plea. "I'll stay until you're asleep."

That seemed to satisfy her, and I stroked her head softly as she relaxed, no longer tense like before. I longed to crawl in beside her, to curl up behind her and wrap my arms tight around her small frame, but I had matters to attend to tonight.

Tomorrow. I'd tell her the truth tomorrow.

13

HANNAH

Sleeping in Lucifer's room was like an extra level of decadence. I'd escaped there because it was the only untouched room in the penthouse after the gargoyle attack, and sheer exhaustion and lingering shock had made me pass out in his bed, amid black silk sheets that smelled like him. When I awoke to his touch and his news that Brandy was alive, I'd never felt such overwhelming relief and gratitude. He said he was a villain, but last night he'd been my hero.

And then there was that kiss, and the way he touched me like he already knew every inch of my body. I grew wet again just thinking about it, imagining him here in bed with me now as I stretched out upon his soft sheets with morning sunlight filtered through sheer black curtains. I had no idea where he'd slept last night, or if he'd slept at all. The last thing I remembered was him stroking my hair as sleep overcame me.

Lucifer wasn't in the kitchen either, I discovered with a pang of longing. I was sure he was dealing with the aftermath of last night's events, and I wanted to go see Brandy anyway, but I still felt his absence in the big, empty penthouse. I quickly downed my coffee and ate a muffin, then threw on some yoga pants and a t-shirt from my own wardrobe.

Once I was ready, I hurried down to The Celestial's day spa to meet Brandy, with Azazel and a few other guards surrounding me. It was no surprise that The Celestial had its own luxury day spa. There seemed to be nothing that Lucifer's resort and casino lacked. I even saw a champagne vending machine on my way down the marble halls. I could probably live my entire life in this hotel without needing to ever step outside again—especially if Lucifer continued to bring the world to me. Memories of his kiss flooded back to me at that thought, practically setting my panties on fire. Maybe being the devil's captive wasn't so bad in the end.

I stepped inside the Diabolique Day Spa and marveled at the large, relaxing fountain in front of me. Everything was white marble, shining blue glass, and smooth, curved lines.

"Ms. Thorn," a beautiful woman said, stepping forward to meet me. I briefly wondered if she was a demon, and if so, what kind? "We've been expecting you."

"Is my friend here yet?" I asked.

"No, but we will bring her in as soon as she arrives." She gestured down the hall. "Follow me."

I was led down shimmering floors and through a frosted blue door into a room with two massage tables. Another woman approached with a glass of champagne, and I waved her away. "No, thank you."

They left me alone in the room. To change, I supposed. I'd never actually been to a spa, at least, not that I remembered, and wasn't exactly sure what all it entailed. Instead of getting undressed, I paced the room with butterflies in my gut. Brandy was supposed to be here any minute.

When the door opened again, I rushed toward my best friend. She looked too thin, and bags stained the skin under her dark brown eyes a purple-gray color, but she was alive and safe and that was all that mattered.

"Brandy!" I threw my arms around her. "I've been so worried!"

Brandy hugged me tightly. "Thank you for coming to Las Vegas to look for me."

"How could I not?" We didn't let go of one another for several moments, neither of us entirely steady. Tears filled my eyes, and I heard her sniffing too. "I'm so glad you're okay."

I pulled back and examined her again. I was right—her face was just this side of gaunt and her normally glowing dark skin looked ashy. She mustn't have eaten well in captivity, if at all. Thank goodness Lucifer had rescued her when he did. There was a darkness in her eyes too that hadn't been there before, like she'd seen and learned things that had shaken her to the core. I wondered if I had the same look in my eyes.

As we hugged and cried, the masseurs kept checking into the room to find us still clinging to one another, and it took us several attempts to separate and lie on the tables for our first appointment of the day. But full body massages waited for no one, and Brandy looked like she really needed the care and attention.

"We better let them do the massage before they combust," I said.

Brandy managed a ghost of a smile and nodded. "I could definitely use a good massage."

We stretched out and tried to keep the conversation vague while the women were in the room. I told her about her mom and son, how worried they'd been, and we discussed what we'd seen of Vegas, but the conversation made me prickle with an urgency to know more, and I could hardly wait until the massages were over so we could talk properly.

Once our massage was finished, the women led us to another room. It was dimly lit, with a long, expensive-looking counter and two reclining chairs, similar to those usually found in a salon. Various pots and machines sat on the counter. The tools of the trade, I assumed, although I couldn't begin to guess what some of the machines did. One of them offered us champagne, which Brandy gladly took.

"Your facialist will be here soon," the woman said. "Mr. Ifer instructed us to give you at least a half-hour break between each session. He said you'd be eager to catch up."

I thanked her with a smile, though I wondered if I should be thanking Lucifer. Again. How could he be the actual devil, with all the wickedness and darkness that brought, and still melt my heart with his small gestures of consideration? But my smile quickly disappeared as I looked at Brandy once we were alone, and I shuddered at the thought of the things she must have gone through.

I sank into one of the chairs. "Tell me what happened."

"This is some high-class shit," Brandy said, before she downed the champagne. I got it—it was easy to be distracted by the trappings of Lucifer's life, especially when the other subject might be more difficult to address. She stared into the empty glass. "I guess you deserve to know, more than anyone."

"If it's too painful to talk about, I understand."

She sat beside me and shook her head. "No, it will help to talk about it. It's so crazy I have to share with someone." She drew in a sharp breath. "Well, you know I came to Las Vegas for a librarian conference, right? But when I got here, there was no conference."

I nodded. I'd learned the same thing when I'd started poking about.

"I didn't know what to do. I mean, I was in Vegas, by myself, with nothing to do. In the end, I went to the bar to get a drink." Her face took on a far-off, dreamy look. "That's where I met Mo—Asmodeus, I mean. He was probably the hottest guy I've ever seen, and charming as all hell. Before I even got my drink, I wanted to take him back to my room and do naughty things to him."

My jaw dropped. Brandy had never been the hooking up in a bar sort of girl. Maybe that was his incubus powers at work? "What then?"

"He convinced me to go out to dinner with him. While we were leaving the hotel, we were attacked. By these...monsters." She shook her head like the disbelief was still real, and I gripped her hand as horror showed again in her eyes. "Giant wolves and bears. It's such a cliché, but it all seemed to happen so fast, and it was totally unbelievable at the time. Then I got knocked out."

"That had to be a big shock." From what I'd heard, it was shifters who had captured her. I'd never seen one in animal form myself, but I'd seen gargoyles and Fallen angels, and they were scary enough, thank you very much.

"I'll say." Brandy snorted before reaching over to grab the champagne bottle and pouring herself another glass. "When I woke, I was with Asmodeus in a small concrete room—some kind of basement I guessed, because there was a tiny thickened glass window at the top of the wall. It didn't open and there was no point banging against it." She laughed a little. "I mean, I tried. But it just hurt my fists and barely made a noise. We couldn't even see through it." Her eyes took on that distant look again. "Asmodeus was with me the entire time, and we talked a lot. There wasn't much else to do. He...filled some things in for me."

I looked at her, trying to figure out what she and Asmodeus had spoken about. I didn't want to dump a load of information on her that she didn't need. Being taken hostage was probably traumatic enough *without* learning all about Lucifer and associated paranormal beings. I could hardly believe it myself still—and that was after all the things I'd experienced. "What things?"

"Things I still find hard to believe," she muttered.

She knew. She had to know. I was just going to come right out with it. She was my oldest friend—we didn't have secrets. "He told you about demons, didn't he?"

Her shoulders dropped and a huge sigh of relief rolled from her. "So, you know? Please say you know."

I pulled Brandy into a hug and tried to reassure her, but what could I really say? She hadn't said what exactly Asmodeus had shared with me. I probably *did* know, but she didn't need to hear any kind of uncertainty from me. "Yes. I know. You can be totally open with me. Of all people, I'll understand."

"How?" Disbelief rang in her tone.

"You know the guy they call the devil of Las Vegas?" I asked. "Turns out he's the *actual* devil. Not just of Las Vegas."

"Asmodeus told me he worked for the devil. I didn't believe it at first, but..." She nodded slowly. "I met him last night. He was fine as hell, but...intense. You should have seen what he did to those demons who kidnapped me."

I sat up a little straighter, curious what he'd done. "Did he kill them all?"

"He sure did."

"Good." The word slipped out of my mouth, surprising us both. I'd never wished anyone dead before, but all I felt was a deep sense of satisfaction knowing the people who hurt Brandy had been punished.

"He saved us." Tears filled her eyes again. "And he said he found me because of you. Thank you."

I still hadn't let go of her hand, and I let her hold onto me as tightly as she needed. "Of course. You would have sent the devil himself to save me, too."

She flicked her tears quickly away, but her sadness hurt me, squeezing my chest. "I didn't think we'd get out. I thought we'd die in there."

"Do you have any idea why you were kidnapped? Did Asmodeus know?" Maybe she'd have some answers that could help Lucifer figure all this out.

"Not really. Asmodeus said he was investigating a conspiracy against Lucifer, but he also said he got a text from his dad, ordering him to seduce me, but he didn't know why. The library conference seems like a setup too, but why would demons want to kidnap me?"

"Seduce you?" I asked. There was something about the way Brandy said his name. "Did he succeed?"

She opened and closed her mouth several times. "Before I tell you everything, I should probably say that Asmodeus is an incubus, a demon of lust. He only needs to look at someone to seduce them, and he needs sex to survive. He requires a steady stream of lovers to feed on, and humans can't survive sex with an incubus more than once, which means the two of us... Well, it's not possible."

She spoke so matter-of-factly about the things I was only just starting to come to terms with. How much more did she know? And just how far had she and Asmodeus gone in their basement prison?

She looked at me like she could read my thoughts. "But to answer your question, no, he didn't seduce me. We kissed once, and frankly, it was better than any sex I'd ever had, but that was it.

Mostly we talked a lot and learned about each other. There was nothing else to do."

"So, you *didn't* have sex?" I asked. Given that Asmodeus was an incubus, that seemed almost impossible.

"No." She shook her head. "The shifters tortured him, trying to get info on Lucifer, but Mo wouldn't break. Even when they tried to get him to feed on me, he held back. At times, it was obvious how painful it was for him to be in the same room as a woman without feeding, especially when he was injured. But he was so strong." Her eyes took on that faraway look again, before a small frown forced the fledgling happiness away. She definitely had a thing for him. No doubt. But she also believed there was no way to work it out. I wished I had the answers for her, but there was still so much I didn't know about this world.

She shook her head and blinked rapidly. "How *did* you get the devil to rescue me? And this?" She gestured around the room. "This is so far above either of our pay grades."

As I explained how I came looking for her, and the deal I'd made with Lucifer, she grew somber. And then downright pissed off.

"You sold yourself to him for seven nights?" she practically yelled. "Like some kind of sex slave?"

I held up my hands, feeling the urge to quickly defend him. "He swore he wouldn't force himself on me, and so far he's been a perfect gentleman. I don't know why he's interested in me, but there's something there. Something I can't explain." I paused and tried to find the words. "I know I'm in a dangerous situation, but I made a deal, and he's delivered on his end. That just leaves my side of it." I sucked in a breath. "I have to see it through."

"Hannah, we can go. We can leave now. Nobody is here to stop us. We'll go straight back home and forget any of this ever happened."

I shook my head. "I can't do that."

Brandy looked at me, her gaze steady as it met mine. "I'm going home to my mom and son as soon as I can. I have to. You understand, right?"

I leaned forward and threw my arms around her. "Of course, I do. I wouldn't expect you to stay. I don't even really want you to—this whole trip has been about getting you home safe. That's all I want. We don't even have to do this spa day if you want to go now."

She shook her head. "No, Lucifer arranged a car to drive me back to Vista as soon as this is over. I can wait until then. Besides, I think I probably need the pampering. If I arrive at home looking like this, Mom will flip."

The facialist soon came in and gave us a treatment that was more massage than anything, but both of us moaned our way through it, so we didn't complain. When it was over, my skin felt like a baby's and practically glowed. Brandy looked about a thousand times better too.

Next, we were fed a ridiculously huge, fancy lunch, which Brandy devoured. Then we hit the salon and had mani-pedis while the experts did whatever they wanted to our hair. We gave them permission to do their thing, and they managed to give us both luscious waves that made us look like we were about to walk onto a movie set.

After we'd had lunch and another round of appointments, the day came to an end much faster than I wanted. Brandy had to get back to her family, and I couldn't go with her, and that was fine. But I'd just found my best friend, and I didn't want to say goodbye to her already. Plus she'd been my entire purpose for being in Vegas. With her gone, all I had was my deal with Lucifer. The thought made my pulse race.

Brandy and I stopped in front of a limo in the private parking garage and I pulled her into a fierce hug. Emotions flooded me—thankfulness that she was safe, pleasure that she was with me, and sorrow that she had to leave, even though it was what I wanted most in the world. "I'll see you soon. I promise."

She stared into my eyes. "I meant what I said. Just get in this car with me, and we can both leave."

"I can't. I promised Lucifer I'd be his for seven days and nights, and this is only day four. I owe him three more nights. I can hardly break a promise to the devil, can I?" My heart hammered with both lust and unease when an image of his face, all dark shadows and focused masculinity, flitted through my mind. Besides, there was obviously something strange happening with me, and I needed to know the truth.

"I don't know," Brandy said, eyeing me with brows furrowed. "You're hung up on him somehow. Has he seduced *you* yet?"

Heat filled my cheeks. "We kissed. That's it."

She let out a hoot. "I knew it!"

"It's nothing more than you and Asmodeus did!"

"That's all well and good, and maybe you'll get some good sex out of this, but be careful. Remember that these people are all about temptation. Guard your heart." She shot the driver, who waited with the limo door open, a look and lowered her voice. "I've seen what they're capable of, Hannah."

I remembered last night, and how I'd cut down the gargoyles who'd come for me, and I swallowed hard. "I've seen some things too, but I'm handling it. Trust me." I hugged her again. "Give my love to Jack and Donna."

"Will do. Come home when you can." She stepped back with a sad smile and then slipped into the limo. The driver shut the door, and the windows were tinted so dark the car seemed to swallow her up.

I waved as the limo pulled away, thinking about what she'd said.

She was right. I had to guard my heart. But with a man like Lucifer, was that even possible?

14

HANNAH

I headed back to the penthouse, completely deflated after saying goodbye to Brandy. When I arrived, with Azazel at my side, I looked around feeling at a loss. The mess from the gargoyle attack had been cleaned up while I'd spent the day at the spa, and even the windows had already been replaced. It was like it never happened. There was no sign of Lucifer though, and I wasn't sure what to do. I considered spending some time in the library, but in the end, exhaustion claimed me, and I headed to my room for an afternoon nap. Today was about sloth, after all.

Sleep came easily for a change, but it wasn't peaceful. I woke up curled in a ball and wrapped tightly around a pillow, as I often did. Tense, with my muscles sore and stiff, like I'd spent the day in the gym rather than at the spa. And the dreams... I never remembered specifics, just fear and darkness, pain and death. Only snippets, but always violent and tinged with terror and grief.

This nap was no exception. I was fairly sure my inability to sleep peacefully had gotten worse since I met Lucifer. It was probably being out of my element, in a strange place and a deeply unsettling situation, but I longed to just close my eyes and wake up hours later with no memories of anything at all.

Sometime during my fitful sleep the sun had set, and I sat up to look out my window at the night sky lit up by all the Vegas lights. The sound of piano music drifted through the crack under my door, luring me toward the living room like a siren's call. Where Lucifer was no doubt waiting for me.

I checked my spa-teased hair and makeup in the bathroom, glad to note they had survived my nap pretty well. I fluffed my hair and dabbed on a bit of lip gloss before stepping inside my walk-in closet and marveling at all the gorgeous clothes inside. It was still hard to believe they were mine, at least temporarily. I wasn't sure what Lucifer had planned for tonight, but I guessed my yoga pants and t-shirt weren't going to cut it. Instead, I selected a long black dress, the fabric soft and airy and with a gentle shimmer. Then I grabbed the first pair of black heels I put my hands on, and there were many, as if they were breeding in there. As I buckled the straps, the music escalated into a crescendo. Was Lucifer the one playing?

Curiosity drove me out of the room. Not just about the music, but about a dozen other things. Demons. Brandy's kidnapping. The attacks on my life. And most of all, how I'd swung that sword around like the world's mightiest warrior instead of a florist from Nowheresville.

Okay, and a big part of me wanted to continue what we'd started last night too.

Peeking into the living room, I watched Lucifer from behind as his fingers flew over the ivory keys of the grand piano. He seemed to be one with his music, and the effect was pure magic. I was completely entranced by the way he played, not to mention the slant of his shoulders in his black suit and the way his dark head bent over the piano. I'd never seen a man more gorgeous in my life, and I'd never wanted anyone more.

I didn't recognize the piece he played, but it was haunting, full of minor keys and slow melodies. The room was lit by dozens of red candles, and the ambient lighting turned low so the city's neon backlit the flickering flames. The shadows created by the effect were beautiful rather than scary, and I was drawn to them.

And to him. Always. Impossibly so.

The question was...why?

Lucifer must have sensed I was there because he cocked his head. "Please, come in."

"What's all this?" I rounded the piano and gestured at the candlelight.

"I thought we could stay in tonight. Nice and quiet. Safe." The music faded as Lucifer reached the conclusion of the song. He nodded toward the windows. "I've posted guards everywhere to ensure your protection."

I turned my gaze to the tall windows and focused on the darkness around the Vegas neon. It was almost like looking with my peripheral vision, but eventually I saw them. Dark-winged Fallen, circling the building, with shadows clinging to their feathers. I had no doubt Azazel was out there, and probably Gadreel too.

"All to protect me," I said slowly, still finding the situation unbelievable. "Why?"

"I won't let anyone harm you."

I nearly replied that he hadn't really answered my question, but then he rose from the piano bench and took my breath away. The flickering candlelight played across his face and only made him more alluring. A mixture of dark and light. A reminder that the devil was once an angel.

Lucifer stepped toward me and offered his hand. "I hope you're hungry."

I hesitated, not because I didn't want to take his hand, but because I so desperately did, and because I knew I'd feel that familiar rush of desire the second we touched. Eventually my resistance crumbled and I slid my hand into his. "Yes, I am."

"Excellent. I made your favorite meal." He led me around the bar to the kitchen and dining area, where a pristine white tablecloth had been laid out on the table, along with the finest silverware. All chairs had been removed except for two, and the red candles made the setting intimate. A single narcissus flower sat in the middle of the place settings.

Lucifer helped me into my seat like a gentleman, letting his hand linger on my back for a moment, before he stepped behind the kitchen island. There he began to serve something on two dishes, while steam rose into the air. The tantalizing scent of herbs and tomatoes drifted toward me, increasing my hunger.

"You cooked?" I asked, unable to hide the surprise in my voice.

"I'm a man of many talents. As you'll soon learn."

He set down a steaming bowl of spaghetti and meatballs in front of me, then laid out some garlic bread and a side salad. Finally, he poured some sparkling water into my wine glass, before sitting across from me at the table. I wondered how many other women had ever been served food by the devil. Or been cooked their favorite meal by him.

"How did you know this was my favorite?" I asked, as I breathed in the scent before picking up my fork.

He gave me one of his devilish grins. "I have a whole file on you, my dear Hannah. You'd be amazed at how much one can find online."

I flushed, thinking of him scouring my Facebook profile. That couldn't be all of it though. He knew too much, things that he couldn't have found from stalking me on the internet. Tonight I intended to get answers from him—after I bolstered my courage with some food.

My lips closed over my fork, and I moaned in delight. The sauce was perfectly spiced. Most people thought spaghetti was a little kid meal, but I didn't care. It was my favorite, and this was sheer perfection. "Wow, this is amazing. Did you make the sauce yourself?"

"I did." He arched a dark eyebrow. "Why are you surprised?"

I tore off a piece of garlic bread next. "I never thought you'd be the type to cook, let alone be a master chef."

His eyes danced with amusement. "Well, I have had thousands of years of practice..."

I nearly choked on my garlic bread at his words.

Thousands. Of. Years.

Sometimes I forgot he was so old, and then he just sprung it on me in casual conversation like that.

He took a sip of red wine. "I'll have you know I'm an expert chef of many cuisines, some of which you've never even heard of, since they've long faded from history."

Another reminder of how ancient and unfathomable he was. Why would he be interested in a normal human like me?

While I was contemplating his immortality and my mortal existence, he asked, "How was your day? Has your friend recovered from her ordeal?"

"She seems a bit shaken by what happened, but she's tough. She'll get past this." I twirled my spaghetti on my fork. "Although I think she has a thing for Asmodeus."

"Who wouldn't?" Lucifer smirked. "I'm lucky you haven't met the man yet. Let's just say he makes me look ugly."

"I don't think that's possible," I blurted out, then awkwardly changed the subject, answering his other question. "I think the spa day was exactly what she needed. Thank you again. For everything."

He inclined his head. "It was nothing."

"Did you learn anything about why she was kidnapped?"

"No. Not yet. It seems there may be a rogue group of demons conspiring against me, but I don't know who is leading them yet." He stirred his glass, swirling his wine around. "Have no fear. It will all be dealt with soon."

"Okay, it's just..." I chewed my lip, summoning the courage to voice my thoughts out loud. "It's going to sound crazy, but I'm starting to wonder if Brandy was brought to Las Vegas and kidnapped on purpose to bring me here. To you."

He pinned me with an intense stare. "Why would you think that?"

"It makes no sense otherwise. Why would someone set up a fake librarian conference to lure her here? And then there were those attacks on my life. I could have believed the roof attack was an accident, but there was nothing accidental about gargoyles coming after me. Or how I cut them down." My hands trembled as I laid out all the thoughts that had been whirling around in my head over the last few days. "There's something going on here, something you aren't telling me. I think it's connected to how I wielded your sword like some kind of ninja. And why I find you so familiar and...comfortable, even when I should find you terrifying. And why I always have horrible dreams full of death and violence, which have only gotten worse since I met you. I thought the dreams were related to the car accident when my parents died, but now? Now I don't know."

I fell silent, and my words seemed to echo between us as Lucifer gazed at me with an unreadable expression. The seconds ticked by, and neither of us moved, our food forgotten.

Finally, he sighed. "Oh, Hannah. Answering your questions is like opening Pandora's box all over again. Once you learn these truths, there is no turning back from them. Are you sure you want to go down this path?"

I'd never been more certain of anything in my life. "I need to know."

He nodded, his mouth twisting in a grimace. Then he rose to his feet, making me look up at his tall height. "Let's adjourn to the other room for this conversation."

I stood and he rested his hand on my lower back, the slight pressure sending heat between my thighs. Together we returned to the living room and I sank into one of the leather couches, while he perched beside me, his hand lingering on my knee.

"We've had this conversation hundreds of times, and yet it never gets any easier," Lucifer mused to himself. "You'd think I would have a script by now, wouldn't you?"

My brow furrowed. He wasn't making any sense. "What do you mean?"

Lucifer took both my hands in his and gazed into my eyes. "I told you I once had a great love, but I lost her. That love was you."

"Me?" I asked, even though his words rang with truth inside me. "Was it before the accident? Is that why I don't remember you?"

He shook his head. "No, it was before even that. Before this life."

I blinked at him. "I don't understand."

"Hannah, you have lived many lives, going back thousands of years."

"Like...reincarnation?"

"Exactly. And in each life, you're my mate. My destiny. My heart."

My pulse raced fast as he talked. I looked deep into his emerald green eyes, and I couldn't stop the feeling of falling. "Your mate?"

"Yes. Demons sometimes have fated mates, as do a few select angels, including Fallen. It's rare, but it happens."

"Like a soulmate..." I said slowly, feeling the rightness of it deep inside me, even as it sounded too impossible to be true.

He leaned closer, close enough that my gaze dropped to his lips, wondering if he would kiss me again. "We're meant, through all eternity, to be together. It is our fate. Our destiny. And our curse."

His words stirred something within me, something primal and true. The feeling of falling increased, and I gripped tighter to his hands, knowing he'd catch me. Everything he said was unbelievable, but then again, I'd thought the same thing about demons a few days ago. And with each word, it felt like a light was going off inside me, like something old and powerful finally waking up.

I closed my eyes and breathed in, searching deep in my soul. I always trusted my gut, and it told me that Lucifer wasn't lying. That everything he said, about reincarnation and destiny and mates, was all true, no matter how insane it sounded. Of course, that only brought up more questions.

"Is that why I was attacked?" I asked.

"Yes—because they know you're important to me. And why you could defend yourself so easily."

I stood up and began pacing as his words sank in, resonating inside me. "How many lives? How many times have I died and been reborn?"

"Hundreds. Sometimes we only get a few days before I lose you again. Sometimes we get many happy years together." He stood, but didn't come any closer, like he sensed I needed space. "I'm hoping this will be one of the better lives."

"And we're together in all of them?"

"Yes, Hannah. Every time you die, I wait for you to be reborn. Those years without you feel endless, and my heart withers and dies, only to return to life once I find you again. And I always do. I find you, I claim you, and I love you, in an endless cycle."

"Why?" I asked, the only word that came to my lips. "Why me?"

"Because you're mine." He stepped forward and took my face in his hands. "You've been mine since you took your first breath, and you'll be mine after you take your last. We are inevitable."

The truth settled over me like a warm blanket. I still didn't remember anything from before the accident, but everything he said felt...right, somehow. Like a truth I'd always known deep inside me. Some part of me had recognized him from the first time we'd met, and even though I should be terrified of Lucifer, I wasn't. Not anymore.

"You find me." It wasn't a question. My soul knew it was true. "Every time."

"Always." He looked at me with such longing, it cracked a piece of my soul. Something kept me from remembering him, a bitter torture that wouldn't clear from my mind. Maybe this would do it.

Pushing my mouth against his, I kissed the devil with everything I had in me. I was ready to give it all to him. He cupped a hand around the back of my neck and drew me in close, taking control of my mouth. His tongue slipped past my lips, and I knew the feeling. I'd felt it before. Not from another man, but from him. Always him. *Lucifer.*

My mind might not remember him, but my body sure did. And it craved more.

15

HANNAH

Need pulsed inside my veins and heat pooled in my core as Lucifer's kiss dominated me. His arms shifted around my waist, and he lifted me with an ease I still couldn't believe. My nipples ached as they pressed against his hard chest, and he carried me across the room while plundering my mouth with his tongue like he owned it.

He set me on the very edge of the large, black piano and finally broke the kiss to look at me with his infernal eyes. His hand found the thigh-high slit on my long dress, and he dipped a finger under it, stroking my skin. Teasing me. A master of temptation.

Then he grabbed the slit and tugged the fabric, grunting in pure male satisfaction as it ripped easily in his strong hands. The act was so surprising and carnal, I gasped. Then he removed his own jacket with quick, determined motions, like a man about to get down to business. The business of claiming me.

With strong hands he gripped my thighs and spread them apart, flashing him a peek of my dark red thong. I reached out and grabbed his expensive white shirt, the buttons digging into my palms as I pulled him close. The piano was the exact right height for him to fit between my legs and press his hard bulge against my core. I wrapped my legs around him, and his reaction was visceral as he let loose a low growl.

His lips brushed my ear. "I can't hold back if you do that."

I ground myself against him slowly, looking up at him with a challenge. "Don't hold back."

That glorious fire glinted in his eyes again, a turn-on even now that I knew what it was, and he pulled me closer, lifting me from the piano. I tightened my legs and twined my arms around his neck, running my tongue over the dark stubble along his jaw as he carried me toward his bedroom. Need pounded through my body. I couldn't remember ever being this desperate to be with someone.

When my mouth reached Lucifer's ear, I bit it— perhaps a little bit harder than I would've if I hadn't known he was the devil. His growl returned, and the next thing I knew, my back hit his plush mattress hard. Lucifer stood above me in the low light of his room, radiating power and control in his black suit, his face dark and his eyes hungry. For me.

With slow, measured movements, he yanked at the tie on his neck and removed it, while his eyes never left my face. My mouth watered, and I hoped he would continue removing his clothes, but he only stared down at me like the predator I instinctively knew he was.

And tonight, I was his prey.

He grabbed the hem of my already ruined dress before tearing it in half in one quick motion. The sound of the ripping fabric filled the room, and cool air rushed over my bared skin, heightening my desire. My pulse raced faster as I lay before him in nothing but my red lace bra and panties with my black heels. I waited for him to do his worst.

"So lovely," he said, with that sexy accent that drove me wild. "In every life, you manage to stun me with your beauty."

Heat rushed through as he finally lowered himself over me, then claimed my mouth again. His kiss was hot and desperate as his hands trailed down my naked skin, and then his lips followed, moving from my neck to my collar, then even lower. I tangled my fingers in his dark hair as his tongue glided along my skin over the top of my bra, my nipples so hard it was almost painful. Then he gripped the edges of the red lace and yanked the bra in half too with a loud rip, making my breasts spill out. I was losing a lot of clothing tonight to Lucifer's lust, but he'd paid for them, so I supposed he could do what he wanted to them.

Lucifer looked up at me with a devilish grin, then lowered his head again to my breast. His mouth enveloped one of my already-peaked nipples, sucking eagerly as lightning shot to my core. I arched my back and moaned, needing more.

"Lucifer." I gasped as his tongue swirled around my nipple. "Please."

He let out a low, sensual chuckle. "I did say you'd be begging for me."

Then he captured the other breast with his mouth, while his hands slid along my thighs, so close to where I needed him, but not close enough. His fingers brushed against my lace thong, but only for an instant before retreating again, just enough to make me wetter for him.

He really was the devil, and this was his way of torturing me.

"Please," I begged again. "Let me touch you."

"Tonight is all about you," he replied, his voice husky. "Always you."

I trembled as his words only increased the need inside me. My body built toward orgasm just from the tone of his voice and the touch of his tongue and mouth on my skin, but it wasn't quite enough. I felt like I'd been waiting for this moment my entire life, and only when he entered me would I be complete.

He lifted his mouth from my other breast, where he'd been teasing my nipple with his tongue, and then trailed hot kisses down my skin, which tingled with every brush of his lips. His mouth moved across my stomach, down my hips, and finally lower, his teeth nipping lightly at the lace between my legs. I gasped and lifted up slightly, and he used that movement to hook his fingers in the sides of my thong and tear it off me.

He gripped my knees and spread me wide for him. "Look at this beautiful pussy. Sheer perfection, and all mine. Forever mine."

He was so close to my core, his hot breath dancing across my slick, eager folds. I was writhing with delirium already and he hadn't even touched me where I needed him most. Then his tongue slid inside of me, and I nearly leaped out of my own skin.

He darted in and out, tasting me with a low hum of approval that vibrated through me. Then he licked upward, and the tip of his tongue touched my clit seconds before he sucked it into his mouth. I cried out at the sudden burst of pleasure, fingers digging into his silken sheets, while his lips and tongue consumed me.

His fingers joined in moments later, sliding inside of me, fucking me slowly in time with his other movements. With his other hand, he gripped my ass, using it to drag me closer to him, lifting me up like an offering to his greedy mouth.

And then I came apart. My hips bucked, pressing my wet pussy into his face as my inner muscles clenched over and over. Lucifer kept licking and sucking through my orgasm, pumping his fingers into me while I writhed on the bed and moaned, unable to control my own body anymore. It was his now, completely and utterly his.

"It's been far too long since I tasted you." Levering himself up on his elbows, he licked his lips as if savoring his favorite meal. "And far too long since I felt you come. But now I want you to come around my cock. Do you think you can do that?"

I nodded, unable to speak, unable to do anything but tremble with pleasure and anticipation. He rose up above me like a dark god, still fully dressed, and I could only stare as he slowly unbuttoned his shirt, reveling in each inch of skin he exposed. I'd seen him shirtless the other day and the sight had soaked my panties and fueled my dark fantasies when I was alone. Lucifer's chest was hard and muscular, a warrior's body hidden under a three-piece suit. I wanted to run my tongue along the valleys and ridges of his abs, then tease his dark nipples the way he'd tormented mine.

He removed his belt with a sharp snap, then unzipped his black slacks. I held my breath as he shoved them down, revealing his enormous cock. I'd thought he was bragging before when he joked about his size, but no. It really was that big, hard, and glorious.

He slowly slid up my body and then his mouth came down on

mine again, his strong hands gripped my aching thighs, settling himself between them. That hard length brushed against my sensitive skin as he grabbed my wrists and pressed them into the bed, holding me down.

"I've waited far too long for this," he said, as the head of his cock slid inside me, just enough to tease me. "Now I'm going to take what's mine."

My core clenched at his words, my body eager for him to fill me completely. I flexed my hips, pulling him deeper inside me. His name fell from my lips on a soft moan. "Lucifer."

That seemed to push him over the edge. His control slipped and his cock thrust into me, hard and fast. Completely filling me, stretching me around his size. I gasped at the sudden intrusion, and at the way it made me feel whole.

"You were made to take my cock." He punctuated each word with hard, deep strokes. "We always fit together just like this. Perfectly."

His words were like a drug to my libido, spiking my desire into a desperate, ravenous need. My hands were still pinned down by him, but I hooked my legs around his hips, drawing him closer. He set a relentless pace that gave me exactly what I needed, as he rocked into me with impressive force. Each thrust felt like he was laying claim to me, marking me as his own, erasing any doubt that I belonged to him.

He found a rhythm that made my body quiver. Fire danced in my veins with each delicious stroke of his cock. He yanked my arms up above my head, his hard, masculine body pressing me down into the bed, his fingers tight on my wrists. I surrendered to him completely, crying his name as another orgasm slammed into me. Pleasure broke me like a hammer against glass, and I so desperately wanted to be shattered.

"That's it," Lucifer groaned. "Come for me. Take me with you."

I lost all control of my body as it trembled and tightened around him, my hips rocking against him in a wild rhythm that he matched, stroke for stroke. Then he drove harder into me, throwing his head back, exposing his perfect, masculine throat as he erupted inside me.

Together we rode out the waves of pleasure, unable to stop ourselves, until we were both completely spent.

Lucifer released my wrists and pulled me into his arms, tucking me against his strong chest. My body was weak and languid, tingling with the after-effects of pleasure, and all I could do was curl against him.

It made no sense, but here in the devil's arms, I felt like I'd finally found home.

16

LUCIFER

Before I opened my eyes, I felt it. A lightness that hadn't been there the day before, the warmth in my chest that I only had when she was close to me. As the rest of my body caught up to my mind, the pure pleasure of waking with Hannah in my arms spread through me, and I lay still for a moment, just savoring it. Unlike the other times I'd seen her sleeping, she was relaxed and calm. I stroked her golden hair lightly, trailing my hands along her soft skin, marveling at the way she fit perfectly against me.

She stirred and pressed back toward me, waking my cock, while using my upper arm as her pillow. She had to know what she was doing. Had to feel my own arousal pressing against her from behind. Seeking out what was mine.

I skimmed my fingers along her side, along her naked skin, then dipped down, between her thighs. Finding her already soaking wet for me. She moaned a little, her voice still heavy with sleep, and that was enough for me.

I slid my cock into her tight pussy from behind, while my fingers teased her clit. She gasped at the sudden invasion, her back arching, which only pushed her ass harder against me and sank my cock in even deeper. Fuck, she was perfect, her body made to respond to me. She fit me like no one else ever could.

I slowly began to thrust in and out of her, taking my time, without the urgent need to claim her I'd felt last night. Early morning sex was meant to be leisurely, at least at first. She moaned and rocked back against me in time to my movements, while I teased her clit with my fingers. I bent my head over her neck and pressed hot kisses there, unable to get enough of the way she tasted.

In this position, all she could do was take what I gave her and follow my lead. I drew out the moment together as long as I could, until her hips pressed back harder, and I sensed she was growing close. Although I was tempted to delay her pleasure and torment her a bit, there would be time for that later. With a few hard strokes of my cock with my fingers on her clit, she began to tremble and moan, her pussy clenching around me, which sent me over the edge too. My hot seed filled her core as I crashed down with her into the abyss.

She turned in my arms and looked up at me with eyes heavy from sleep and the after-effects of pleasure. "That was a nice way to wake up."

"Good morning," I whispered into her ear before nuzzling the soft spot underneath. "I hope you slept well."

Hannah stretched, her lithe body pressing along the length of mine. I resisted the urge to repeat what we'd just done. As much as I wanted to spend the day in bed with my reunited mate, I had some answers to find.

After her long stretch, she nuzzled back into me and suppressed a yawn. "You know what? I slept better than I have in as long as I can remember."

She tucked her arms in between us and idly stroked my chest. She probably didn't realize it, but it was a position she'd preferred for countless millennia—with my arms enveloping her and her face in the hollow of my throat.

I sighed and hugged her close for another long moment, stretching out our time together and committing the very feel of her to memory, before rolling back. "I slept better than I have in a very long time as well." Since the last time I'd slept with her in my arms, at least.

"What's planned for the day?" she asked as I climbed out of bed. Her gaze followed me, roaming over my naked body in a way that made it exceedingly difficult not to climb right back into the bed with her. I might have preened a little, but I would have denied it if anyone asked.

I grabbed my phone to check it, and had a few messages from Samael. He wanted to meet immediately. "I have some devil business to attend to right now, but you're welcome to do anything you'd like today. Stay here and relax in the penthouse, or go out somewhere else with Azazel. Use my credit cards and take one of my cars. Everything that's mine is yours."

She sat up. "I can leave?"

"You're not a prisoner here, Hannah. You're my guest. Enjoy yourself."

I took a quick shower, leaving the door open in case she wanted to join me, but she didn't move from beneath the covers. Probably a good thing, because we both knew where that would lead.

After I'd wrapped a towel around my waist and walked back into the bedroom, I pulled a suit out of the closet and began to dress. She put her hands behind her head and continued watching me as I looped a tie around my neck. The comforter dipped to her waist, baring her naked breasts, and I averted my gaze before my cock thickened too much to ignore.

"Have you decided what you'll do today?" I asked. Knowing Hannah, she wouldn't spend much, but if she wanted to, she could.

"I don't know." She tapped her lips mischievously like she really did know. "Maybe I'll drag my favorite Fallen bodyguard out to do something touristy and fun. Like ride the roller coaster at New York-New York or something."

I laughed heartily as I sat on the bed and drew on my socks and shoes. Perhaps she had some of my predilection for torture after all. "That sounds perfect."

Then I leaned over and captured her mouth for a long kiss that I hated to end. Too many years had passed with a hole in my heart, but for the first time in ages I felt alive. I only ever felt this way when I was with her. The rest of the time, during the many long years alone, I was empty, a husk of a man simply waiting for the next time I would be with her. When she brought me back to life again.

But this happiness wouldn't last. It never did. I had to do whatever I could to defend what we'd just reclaimed. To stop her from being lost again.

I had to somehow delay the inevitable.

Damn this curse.

I touched her cheek lightly as I pulled away. "I'll see you after your adventures with Azazel."

She sat back against my pillows. "Have fun doing...whatever it is you do. Things I probably don't want to know about."

I gave her a wink. "Oh, I definitely will."

In the kitchen, I poured myself a cup of coffee, as strong and dark as my soul. Azazel was already there, and she gave me a salute as she drank her own black coffee.

On the way out, I found Gadreel perched outside the penthouse door, guarding it. He straightened to attention as soon as I approached.

"Good morning, my lord."

I paused a moment as I took a sip of my coffee, then addressed him. "Please stay with Hannah today. I want to make sure no harm comes to her."

He bowed his head in submission to me. "I will protect her with my life."

As I knew he would. I nodded in acknowledgement and headed straight for my war room to find Samael. Last night Gadreel had mentioned a captured shifter, and by now Samael should have questioned Asmodeus too. Someone had better have some fucking answers for me.

"Report," I barked as soon as I walked in the room.

As always, lights flickered over giant screens and cameras showed various views of the city, but I wasn't interested in any of that. Demons and Fallen scurried all over the place, some to get out of my way, and others simply to showcase how busy they were.

Samael walked toward me and gestured for us to enter the conference room, then shut the door. "Good morning."

"You have news?"

"We've captured an imp, a shifter, and a gargoyle, all of whom we believe were connected to the attacks."

I sat at the head of the conference table. "And?"

"Nothing. They won't talk." He drew up a chair, joining me as he spoke again. "Perhaps you can persuade them."

I steepled my fingers. I could be *very* persuasive. "And Asmodeus?"

Tension tightened around the corners of Samael's mouth, the only sign he was angry. "My son knows very little, unfortunately. He was investigating rumors spreading among the Lilim about some demons turning against you, and he thinks that's why he was kidnapped. The shifters tortured him for information on you while he was being held hostage, but he doesn't know who they're working for."

"How is he doing now?"

"He is...refusing to feed completely." Samael shook his head with a hint of disgust. "I think he has feelings for that mortal woman."

My eyebrows shot up as I leaned back in my chair. "That won't end well for either of them."

"Obviously." Samael grimaced, but then he returned to being all business. "He also claimed to receive a text from me ordering him to seduce this woman, but I never sent it. I suspect someone is trying to overthrow you again. Possibly one of the Archdemons."

"I suppose we're overdue for another attempted coup." This happened every century or so, but I'd been the King of Demons for thousands of years for a reason. It would take more than a few pathetic attacks to overthrow me. The only reason this was a problem now was because it put my mate in danger.

Perhaps that was the point.

"The timing of this coup is suspicious," Samael said, echoing my thoughts. "I believe Brandy was deliberately kidnapped to lure

Hannah here and distract you. They likely think Hannah will weaken you, or divide your focus."

"Nothing weakens me." I drummed my fingers on the table. "I've been thinking the same thing though. Something about this situation seems like a set-up, meant to bring Hannah to me and then take her away again."

"Do you think it could be her first husband?"

"I'm not sure yet." Red hot hatred filled my veins at the thought of that monster, but this didn't seem like his actions. "I want him found though. And we'll need to set up extra precautions around Hannah either way."

"I'll handle it." Samael paused, his dark eyes judging me silently. "Does she know yet who she really is?"

"I told her some of the truth last night. Not all of it. She isn't ready to know about the curse yet."

Samael's lips pressed into a tight line. "I don't like this. She is making you weak, even if you don't see it. The moment she came back into your life, your focus changed."

I slammed my hands on the table and stood, glaring down at him. "You're wrong. Hannah makes me strong. I need her by my side."

He bowed his head. "Where is she now?"

"Last I heard, she was taking Azazel to the roller coaster at New York-New York. I sent Gadreel with them too."

Samael chuckled low in his throat, the rich sound a welcome relief. "Azazel will hate every second of that."

"I'll speak with the prisoners now." I started to leave, but then paused at the door as my hands tightened into fists. "One last thing. Make sure all the Archdemons are at the masquerade ball on Devil's Night. I have something special planned for them."

"As you wish," Samael said.

I strode from the room to find the prisoners and make them talk. If torture wouldn't work, my special powers of coercion would.

The devil's work was never done.

17

HANNAH

I spent the day with Zel and Gadreel—who I'd started to call Gad —doing all sorts of touristy things on The Strip I'd never get a chance to do otherwise. Zel grumbled and complained the entire time, saying things like, "Roller coasters are for people who don't have wings," but she stuck by my side. I just knew there was a gooey center underneath that hard exterior, and I was determined to find it. Gad, on the other hand, gleefully joined me on every ride and for every silly photo shoot. We rode gondolas at the Venetian, stood at the top of the Eiffel Tower replica at Paris Las Vegas, saw the white lions and dolphins at the Mirage, and so much more. Anything that had a ride? We did it. At least once. Sometimes twice, just to annoy Zel.

I also lost a lot of Lucifer's money on ridiculously-themed slot machines, but somehow I didn't think he would miss any of it. Soon most of the day had gone by, and there was still so much more we could have seen and done in Las Vegas, but it was time to meet Lucifer. I'd have to take my two Fallen bodyguards out for another tourist excursion soon.

I met Lucifer at a helicopter pad on the roof of a building that was part of The Celestial's sprawling resort. When I saw him, standing in another black suit beside the Abaddon Inc helicopter he owned, his face was dark, his mouth set in a grim line, and I guessed his day hadn't been as fun as mine. Then his eyes landed on me and everything changed, the darkness parting like a curtain to allow the light to shine through, and a devastatingly gorgeous smile spread across his sensual lips.

I had that effect on him. Me.

It was a powerful feeling, knowing I could make the devil smile with my mere presence. I couldn't help but smile back as I approached. Then his smile shifted, becoming naughty, and he winked. Memories of last night and this morning flooded me, and my thighs clenched with desire, which was probably his intention. The man really was sin and temptation.

Lucifer swept me into his arms and gave me a kiss that ignited every one of my nerves and sent lust racing through my veins. According to him, we were destined to be together, and when he held me like this I began to believe it. The past lives thing? That was a lot harder to accept.

"How was your day?" he asked, as he led me to the helicopter.

"Fun." I glanced behind me at my two bodyguards, who trailed behind us. "Zel hated every second of it. Or at least, pretended she did."

That got a sexy, low chuckle from him. "Good. She could use some fun in her life."

"Where are we going?" I asked.

"I'm taking you on a helicopter tour of the Grand Canyon."

My eyes widened at that, and then he helped me inside the helicopter, which was another new experience for me. At least, I assumed it was. Then he got in the pilot's seat and we both put bulky headphones on so we could talk over the roar of the helicopter. Zel and Gad got in the seats behind us, but they didn't bother with headphones.

I was truly impressed when Lucifer guided the helicopter into the air. I supposed when you were as old and rich as he was, you could pick up some expensive hobbies. First we flew over the city, and I marveled at the view of The Strip from above. Then we set out over the seemingly endless desert, and excitement nearly spilled out of me at the sight of the world laid out before us.

I turned to watch Lucifer, who exuded masculinity and power as he flew the helicopter with practiced ease. "How was your day? You looked...troubled earlier."

He shook his head slightly, as if surprised by the question. "You always did catch everything. Yes, troubled is a good word for it."

"What happened?"

"We managed to capture some of the demons involved in the kidnapping and the attacks, but we couldn't get them to tell us anything. Not even when I questioned them personally..." His eyes burned with dark fire. "And I can be *very* convincing."

"Did you..." I drew in a breath and tried again. "Did you torture them?"

"Not physically." He glanced over at me as if considering something. "One of my powers is...coercion, you could say. I can convince people to tell me anything, or do what I wish."

A memory sparked in my mind of Lucifer telling me to sleep, and cold fear trickled through me. "You used it on me, didn't you?"

"Only to help you sleep. That was all."

I bit my lip. "But you use it on others?"

"Now and then, yes. It's a useful tool, but one I use sparingly."

I had a sudden realization and gasped. "The devil made me do it. That's really a thing, isn't it?"

He let out a low sound of discontent. "I can't *make* anyone do anything. That's more of a vampire power. What I do is tempt. Coerce. Sway. If someone is at a crossroads, I can nudge them down a path I choose."

"The darker path, no doubt," I muttered.

"Perhaps, but is darkness always evil? Or is it necessary for there to be light?"

I shook my head, unsure about his justification for what he did. Maybe to an ancient being like himself it seemed normal, but to me it sounded like mind control—and made me wonder what other powers he had that I didn't know about. And how many stories about the devil were true.

I sighed and turned back to the view, as we flew along a river that eventually led to a big bridge and a white dam behind it. Lucifer informed me it was the Hoover Dam, and I leaned over to get a better look at the impressive structure nestled between the arid mountains. At the entrance, two huge green statues with tall wings stood guard. When Lucifer caught me looking at them he explained, "I helped fund the Dam, long ago."

More conflicting feelings warred inside of me. Was he good or evil? Should I be worried about the feelings I was developing for him? And how right it felt to be by his side?

I stared out at the view to distract myself, which was easy when the sunset set the Grand Canyon ablaze with color. The immense size of it left me awestruck, as did the raised plateaus and steep canyons, with winding rivers cutting through them. My inner nature lover longed to be out there hiking the trails, checking out the plants that grew here and breathing in the wild scents.

Suddenly the helicopter swung low over the canyon, making my stomach drop, and impulsively I grabbed Lucifer's hand. He gave it a squeeze as he prepared to land the helicopter on top of one of the plateaus, and I spied a table with a white tablecloth with rocks holding it down so it didn't get completely blown away by the chopper wind.

When the blades quieted, Lucifer helped me step out onto the rocky terrain. Zel and Gad exited behind me and took flight, quickly disappearing from view somewhere among the crags of the steep walls.

The sun had just sunk behind the cliffs, leaving us in a glow of orange and red. Lucifer kept my hand as we walked across the hard, rough landscape over to the small table. He helped me into my seat, because if nothing else, the devil was always a gentleman. Then he opened a large black container, which he'd carried from the helicopter. A super fancy picnic basket. He quickly set the table with red candles, real plates, and silverware. No paper for this picnic. With a snap of his fingers, he lit the candles with pale blue fire—another of his powers, it seemed—and I tried to hold in my gasp.

Lucifer poured drinks for both of us, and when I was about to protest, he winked and showed me the label. It was a fancy sparkling cider. "Non-alcoholic, of course."

Warmth filled my chest knowing he'd remembered and respected my wishes, and that he'd set up all of this for me. I took the glass and gazed out at the incredible view, while the cool wind softly teased at my hair.

"What sin is tonight?" We'd done gluttony, greed, wrath, and sloth so far. That only left three more.

"I'm not sure." He raised his glass in a toast. "Let's see how the evening goes."

He opened a basket and set out fancy sandwiches, an impressive cheese plate with tapenade, and artisan chips. I had no doubt everything would taste amazing, because with Lucifer it was nothing but the best.

The light reflected in his eyes, bringing out that flash of flame even more as he bit into a piece of cheese. As I picked up a sandwich, I blurted out one of the many questions always rolling around inside my brain. "Do you really need to eat?"

His eyes danced with amusement. "Of course, all things need sustenance."

"But you said Lilim feed on lust. Do you need something else too?"

He raised his eyebrows like he was impressed. "A very attentive question. Yes, all supernatural beings must feed on energy of some kind. The fae, for example, feed on nature itself, while angels feed on light. Demons vary in what they feed on depending on their type, but generally speaking, they feed on the emotions of others. And Fallen are the inverse of angels. They need darkness to survive and fuel their powers."

"Including you?"

He leaned in close and lowered his voice. "I'll tell you a secret. I can feed on both light and darkness. It's one of the reasons I'm the most powerful being walking the Earth right now."

"Wow, cocky much?" I asked, with a sharp laugh.

He settled back and lifted a casual shoulder, giving me one of his devilish grins. "Is it cockiness if it's the truth?"

I grabbed a fancy chip from the bag. "So there's no one else as powerful as you?"

"Oh, there are a few. The High King of the fae, for example, but he's in Faerie and knows better than to set foot here. The Elder Gods certainly, but they're all banished or sealed away." His smile widened, showing teeth. "But on Earth? I'm the big bad, darling."

Well, shit.

I decided right then that when confronted with impossible, terrifying things that were hard to accept and understand, one could either run, or make a joke. I chose the latter.

I raised my glass and grinned. "Tonight must be pride, because you're certainly full of it."

He let out a deep laugh that was pure sex. "You're probably right. Pride is my sin, after all."

18

HANNAH

We continued eating as the sky darkened around us and the candles flickered in the soft breeze. Finally, I worked up the courage to breach the topic hovering in the back of my mind all day. "Tell me about my past lives."

"Which ones?" He poured us both more cider. "There's no way we could discuss all of them tonight. I have a better idea. Tell me about your life now."

"Don't you have everything about me stored in a little file somewhere?"

"I'd rather hear it from you." He passed me the cheese plate. "Last night you mentioned your parents died in a car accident. That was five years ago, wasn't it?"

I swallowed and stared down at my plate, wishing I didn't have to discuss this, but knowing it had to come up sometime. Better to get it over with. "It was a drunk driver."

"Ah. Hence the reason you don't drink."

I nodded and breathed deeply, trying to force myself to be calm as the emotions welled up inside me. "I was in the car with them, but I was the only one who survived. I lost my memory at the same time. I don't even remember them."

He reached across the table and took my hand. "How awful that must be for you."

My vision blurred, and I blinked back tears. "I wish so much I could remember them but there's just...nothing. My earliest memory is waking up and my sister telling me what happened."

His thumbs rubbed back and forth over my knuckles slowly. "Your sister... Jo, isn't it?"

I had a hard time believing he didn't already know everything about me, but I humored him. "Yes. She lives in San Francisco and runs a tech company there. She helped me get back on my feet after the accident, and then I started working in the florist shop we inherited from my parents. Not long after that I met Brandy where she works at the local library, and we became friends. She ended up getting a divorce, and I moved into her house after that."

He leaned back, releasing my hand, and began to swirl his cider as if it was wine. "Do you ever want more from life than working in a flower shop? Or is that your heart's desire?"

I bit my lip and looked away, his question touching something deep inside me, something I tried to ignore. I did want more. Desperately. But I also had a duty to run my parents' shop, and I couldn't run away from that. "I've taken a few online classes here and there, and sometimes I wish I could go to college and get a degree, but I don't really have time. I have to run the shop and keep my parents' legacy alive. That's enough. It has to be."

"Hmm..." He sounded as if he didn't believe me. "When you dreamed bigger, what did you want to do?"

"I don't know. Sometimes I dreamed of becoming a landscape architect and designing outdoor spaces for people." I shrugged and wiped my mouth on my napkin. "It doesn't matter, since it will never happen."

"A job involving nature and plants. Seems like that would suit you."

I glanced around at the amazing view with a small smile. "I love being around plants. Always have."

He nodded like he'd expected as much as he pulled a big, red pomegranate from the picnic basket. He held the fruit toward me. "Would you like some?"

I nodded as I inhaled the delicate, powdery fragrance. Just a touch of sweetness that hinted at the luxury within. He must have known it was one of my favorite fruits. I wondered if he knew my trick for cutting into one.

With a small knife, he sliced off the stem, revealing the center and the parts of the pomegranate that didn't have seeds. After turning it on its side, he scored down the fruit, following each section. With his hands, he broke the pomegranate into sections, the seeds both beautiful and bountiful on each one.

My eyebrows shot up. "Did you teach me that trick?"

"Actually, you taught me." He picked up one of the sections and held it close to my mouth. I bit into it and the tips of his fingers brushed my lips, sending tingles through me as juice exploded over my tongue.

His eyes stayed fixed on my mouth as my tongue darted out to gather the stray juice off my lips. "In one of our past lives, they called me Hades. You were named Persephone."

I nearly choked on the delicious fruit and stared at him in shock. "The goddess?"

"Angels, demons, and fae were often portrayed as gods in mythology. You were actually a fae of the Spring Court in that life." He winked, a naughty grin slanting across his mouth. "I snatched you away from Faerie to live with me in Hell, much to your parents' dismay."

I shook my head in wonder, trying to absorb his words. The vase in his library made a lot more sense, along with the narcissus flowers in my room. Was it my favorite flower because it subconsciously reminded me of my past life? What other things from my previous lives influenced me now? Favorite food, favorite color, even the way I drank my coffee—how much of that was from my current life and how much was from before? Having so much knowledge just out of my reach was maddening.

"It was a time of relative peace between the supernatural races, where we all moved freely between Earth and the other realms."

Lucifer kept feeding me the pomegranate seeds, holding them to my lips as he spoke. I let my tongue touch the tip of his finger, watching as his eyes flared, but he didn't miss a beat. "You ruled alongside me in Hell for many years, though your mother made you spend part of your time in Faerie too."

That did align with the myths about Hades and Persephone. I closed my eyes and searched my soul for some memory of this, but found nothing. "What happened to us?"

"All good things must come to an end." Something dark lurked in his expression, something that made me wonder if my memories were repressed for a reason. He stood and held out his hand, as his shadowy black wings erupted from his back. "Come. Let me show you the Canyon the way it's meant to be seen. At night, in my arms."

I couldn't refuse him, even though the thought of flying again made my hands tremble. All I could picture was my terrifying fall off the edge of The Celestial, and the way he'd caught me mid-air with a jolt. But he hadn't let me fall then, and I knew, deep down, he wouldn't let anything happen to me now either. The devil was dangerous and deadly, but he would never hurt me.

He lifted me up in his arms, carrying me like he did the other night, as though he was rescuing me from something. I squeezed my eyes shut and clung to his neck as his great wings flapped, sending a rush of cool air all around us, and we launched straight up. He held me close to his chest as we flew higher, and I tucked my face against his neck, afraid to let go.

"I've got you, Hannah. Open your eyes."

His wings kept us steady, and I dared a peek over his shoulder. The sun was very low on the horizon, just peeking above the mountains in the distance. Dusk had never been so beautiful before, as a rainbow of colors reached across the sky, painting a canvas over the entirety of the Grand Canyon. I relaxed my hold on him as I gazed around us, soaking in the wonder of nature.

"It's incredible."

He nodded, but his eyes were distant as he took in the moment when the sun vanished and the sky turned indigo. "This is what day looks like in Hell."

His voice held so much longing, and I wondered if he missed his other home. I wanted to ask him why he lived here and not there, but then we were flying and all thoughts rushed out of my mind. I tightened my hold on his neck as he flew along the cliff walls, through the winding valleys, and dropped down to skim just over the river. His grip on me never once faltered and he was always completely in control. Even when the gusts were strong, he used them to lift us up instead of being buffeted. I trusted him, in a way I'd never trusted any other man.

I shifted myself in his arms to see better as he flew up and spun around, before diving back down. Fear no longer seized my muscles and gripped my throat, and instead something new had taken over. Elation. Adrenaline. Joy. It was a lot like when we'd been in the race cars. It felt...natural.

As night fell, it got harder for me to see, though the myriad of stars above us made for a gorgeous backdrop. Somehow Lucifer's wings were even darker than our surroundings, like they were blacker than night itself. My focus shifted to the man holding me instead of my surroundings, since I could still make out the features of his face. I slid my hand along his neck, up to his stubbled jaw, then to his sensual mouth. "How can you see where you're going?"

"All demons and Fallen can see in the dark," he said, his voice easily carrying over the wind.

He flew around a curve in the canyon, but then something shot toward us from out of nowhere. Something huge. Lucifer suddenly dropped, plummeting down to avoid the thing hurling toward us, and my stomach lurched as I clung tightly to him again. There was a huge rush of wind as the thing flew past us, and then Lucifer turned to face it.

Then there was light—no, fire. Coming out of a huge mouth. With giant fangs.

Holy shit. Was that a fucking *dragon?*

The fire illuminated a winged, reptilian creature the size of an SUV, before flames hurled toward us. Lucifer stretched out a hand and darkness, even blacker than night, shot out and consumed the flames, until the light faded.

"Hold on tight to me!" Lucifer yelled, as he flapped his wings and hurled us toward the dragon.

With a shaky breath, I tightened my grip around his neck and tucked my legs in as close as I could. There was nothing else I could do, and I felt so damn powerless and terrified.

The dragon roared, sending shivers of terror through me, but it was hard for me to see him in the darkness until more fire emerged from his mouth. Before he could unleash it, tendrils of magic so dark they blended into the night erupted from Lucifer's hands and shot toward the dragon. The dark tentacles circled the dragon all around, coiling over it and tightening in place like a net.

But then Lucifer swore under his breath in a language I didn't recognize, his gaze on something to the right. I turned and spotted more fire emerging from two other dragons' mouths, as they loped toward us on reptilian wings.

Lucifer turned and flew faster, arms tight wrapped around me, toward the helicopter. As we shot through the air at breakneck speed, the other dragons chased after us, moving just as quickly. Lucifer moved instinctually, avoiding the bursts of fire that blazed hot trails toward us, and I tried not to scream when one came dangerously close.

Azazel and Gadreel descended on the dragons, and I watched in awe as they whipped, whirled, and surged around the enormous creatures, wielding glowing white swords. But then we turned a corner of the canyon, and in the darkness of night it was impossible for me to see what happened next.

Lucifer reached the helicopter and landed hard on the rough stone, the ground trembling under the impact. I glanced back, but didn't see any hint of the battle going on out there.

"Get in!" he yelled, as he helped me into the chopper. The very rock behind me shuddered with the rage in his voice, and I scrambled inside the cockpit.

He slammed the door shut and then vanished, literally just... disappeared into the night. A second later darkness surged into the cockpit with me and coalesced into his form, while my jaw dropped to the floor. Damn, how many powers did he have?

"What the hell was that thing?" I asked, as I hurried to buckle myself in to the seat.

"A dragon shifter. A demon of greed."

Shit, I really had seen a dragon. I'd started to doubt myself as soon as we were out of sight, like maybe it had been a trick of the light or something, but no. A fucking dragon! Breathing fire at us!

"How dare they attack us?" Lucifer growled, as he started up the helicopter. He was beyond furious, but also something else. Terrified, I realized. For me. "You're my mate. They know better than to hurt you. If they'd harmed a hair on your head, I'd wipe the rest of the fucking dragons off the face of this world."

The helicopter lurched into the air and my stomach plummeted as it rose higher and higher. I held my breath as we zoomed off, and in the distance I saw the flash of bright lights and burning flame, and prayed my two bodyguards would make it out alive too.

When we got back to The Celestial, Lucifer was still furious. He immediately summoned some Fallen guards to watch over me, and then he gave me a hasty kiss. "Now that you're safe, I have to go back."

I nodded, my hands trembling a little, my stomach twisted with worry for Zel and Gad. This time Lucifer took off on his wings, flying faster than he'd done with me, and then vanished into the night. With a sigh, I realized he would have stayed to fight the dragons if not for me. He probably could have defeated them easily, but he'd run because he was worried for my safety. My mortality was holding him back. He feared losing me again so soon.

I was the devil's weakness.

19

HANNAH

I fell asleep in Lucifer's bed alone, curled in his black silk sheets. He joined me late in the night, murmuring softly that both Zel and Gad were all right. The three of them had killed one dragon and captured another, but the last had escaped. Then he tucked himself around me and held me close as I fell asleep again, feeling safer in his arms than anywhere else in the world.

When I woke in the morning, he was already gone. A note told me he was investigating the attack and that he'd prefer it if I stayed in the penthouse today. Fine with me. I had a library to explore anyway.

After a front row seat at an epic dragon battle last night, plus all the mind-bending discoveries of the last few days, I was ready for some quiet time to myself. I took a long, hot shower in Lucifer's bathroom, which was even more luxurious than mine, and found it was already close to noon.

Lucifer had ordered an enormous spread of food from room service for me—from colorful tropical fruits I'd never even heard of, to smoked salmon and pre-massaged beef, artisan breads and tiny egg omelets with flakes of truffle. Then there were exotic chocolates dotted with gold and cheeses flown in from all over the world. It was probably the most expensive buffet I'd ever been to, and there was no way I could eat all of it.

I noticed Gadreel standing by the door, acting as my bodyguard today. He wore jeans and a faded t-shirt, showing off his impressive arms, and with that golden hair and those blue eyes, he looked like a college football player more than a Fallen angel.

"Where's Zel?" I asked, while I began making up a plate of food.

"She got hurt last night and Lucifer made her take the day off to heal." He smirked. "There was a lot of arguing. She takes her duty to protect you seriously."

My chest tightened at the thought of her getting injured. "Is she all right?"

"Yeah, just a little dragonfire on her legs. Nothing she can't heal herself in a day or so, but hurts like hell in the meantime."

I tilted my head as I popped a piece of cheese in my mouth. "Heal?"

"All supernaturals heal faster than humans. One of our many gifts. There's also a type of angel called Malakim that can heal others, but we prefer not to ask them for favors if we can avoid it. Old rivalries, and all that."

"Right," I said, nodding slowly. My plan today was to scour Lucifer's library for anything about angels, demons, or my past lives. I still had so much to learn.

I gestured at the huge buffet. "Please, eat anything you like. There's way too much for me."

He gave me a warm smile as he pushed off the wall and walked toward me. "Thanks."

With a plate of food in one hand, I headed into the library. My eyes immediately landed on the sword on the wall behind Lucifer's desk, and I swallowed back the memories of dead gargoyles it brought to the surface. Was I a fighter in one of my past lives? How many times had I wielded Lucifer's sword before?

I set the food down and found the area of the library with the books on history and mythology, and then spent the next few minutes pulling out everything that looked even remotely helpful. I spread them out on the floor and sat in the middle with my plate beside me, munching on food while perusing old tomes and newer books alike.

Hours passed, and I still felt like I knew nothing. I sighed and put the book on Hades and Persephone down in my lap. It was informative, but how was I to know how much was true and how much was legend? I'd been through a dozen books on angels and demons and the Greek gods, but I wasn't sure I'd really learned anything new. Now my neck was starting to crick from leaning forward over the pages, and my butt hurt from sitting on the hard marble for so long. I let out a long sigh and began massaging my neck, hoping it would loosen my tight muscles.

"Everything all right?" Gadreel asked, from where he sat in an armchair. He'd been alternating between eating and idly playing on his phone while I'd been in here. Not a fan of books, it seemed.

"Just a bit stiff." I stood and stretched some more, then crossed the room to sink into the armchair beside him. Sitting on the floor had been a terrible idea, but it was the only way to see all my books. "I've been trying to research angels and demons, but it's such a big topic. I'm not sure why I thought I'd be able to learn everything in a few hours."

Gad chuckled softly. "It's probably easier to just ask one of us. We'll tell you whatever you want to know."

"I appreciate that." I sat up straighter and tucked my feet under me. "How did you come to work for Lucifer?"

"I'm one of the younger Fallen, which means I'm only a few centuries old and was born in Hell as a Fallen, not an angel, unlike Azazel or Samael. I fought in Lucifer's army in the Great War back in the 19th century, and since then I've worked my way up through the ranks and proved my loyalty, until Samael made me his assistant."

It was something of a relief to hear he wasn't as ancient as the others, even though I would definitely not consider *a few centuries old* to be young. "The Great War—the war against Heaven, right?"

He nodded, with a sad smile. "I knew you then. In one of your previous lives. Do you remember?"

I shook my head, but the feeling that he spoke truth lodged in my chest. "Can you tell me about that life?"

"I'd be happy to. You were a beautiful Fallen angel named Lenore with raven-black hair and wings, born around the same time as I was in the 18th century. We fought together, side by side, and you were a fearsome warrior."

"A warrior?" My eyes slid to the sword on the wall again. Was that when I'd gotten my fighting skills?

He leaned his head against the high back of the chair and grinned. "Oh yes. You cut down so many angels in Lucifer's name. But you were also kind and funny, and like now, you loved books. You would often go to Earth and hang out in London, talking to the gothic writers there like Lord Byron, Mary Shelley, and Edgar Allen Poe. You inspired a lot of their stories, actually."

"Really?" My eyes widened at that. It was a relief to hear I'd done something in that life other than kill angels, and I'd always loved all those old gothic books—to hear I'd actually met the authors and inspired some of their stories was really incredible.

He chuckled at that. "Yes, and Lucifer encouraged it. He liked that they were writing about the creatures of the night."

I let out a long sigh. "I wish I could remember it."

"It might come back to you in time." But then his smile dropped and he looked away. "Although maybe it's better you don't remember."

"What do you mean?"

"You died on the battlefield of Hell. An angel in gold armor cut you down right in front of my eyes. You took your last breath in Lucifer's arms, whispering his name, and many of the Fallen wept for days over your loss." His face was a mask of regret, as he sucked in a deep breath. "For what it's worth, I killed the angel who did it. I just wish I'd been a little faster and could have saved you instead."

I'd scooted to the end of the chair as he talked, held captive by this glimpse into my own life and death. I wasn't sure how to feel about this new information—sadness? Regret? Confusion? All I had was loss and emptiness. "I had no idea about any of this."

Gadreel looked stricken as he leaned forward as if to comfort me. "I'm sorry. Did Lucifer not tell you about this?"

I shook my head. "No, he's been very sparse with details about my past lives so far."

He rested a hand on my shoulder and offered me a weak smile. "I'm sure he would have told you this eventually. He's been very busy lately with the attacks and all that."

"What's going on here?" Lucifer's dark voice made me jump.

Gadreel jerked his hand back as if he'd been burned. I took in our shifted positions as I'd moved closer to listen to his story. Our knees nearly touched, and we both sat on the edges of our seats. *Too close.*

"Gadreel was just telling me about how he knew me in a previous life," I said, as I scooted back in my seat again.

Lucifer stood in the doorway, and he took my breath away with how handsome he was, even doing absolutely nothing except filling out a black three-piece suit. "Is that so?"

I gestured toward my pile of books on the floor. "I've been reading up on angels and demons and mythology all day, but I still had so many questions. Gadreel was kind enough to share what he knew."

Lucifer crossed the room and bent down before me, sliding a hand behind my neck as he kissed me hard. Then his dark gaze shifted to Gadreel. "You're dismissed."

His kiss left me breathless, and he spoke in a low, threatening voice, but I couldn't figure out why. There was no reason for him to be jealous. I didn't have any feelings for Gadreel. That was even more obvious after such a hot kiss like that.

Gadreel brushed past us, back stiff, and strode from the room.

"That was rude," I said to Lucifer, crossing my arms. Days ago, I would never have spoken to him that way. Now? I'd lost all my fear of him. "Gadreel guarded me all day per your orders, and was just answering my questions."

Lucifer considered me with his fierce gaze, but then bowed his head slightly. "I suppose I overreacted. When I came in and saw you two like that..." His face darkened again, his hands clenching into fists at his side. "I always suspected Gadreel had feelings for you when you were Lenore, though you claimed you were only friends. But everyone loved Lenore. Entire poems were written about you."

"Why didn't you tell me about that life?"

He reached up to touch my face as he gazed at me with sadness in his eyes. "That was your most recent life before this one, and sometimes the pain of losing you is still strong. It's hard for me to speak of it, though I'd planned to tell you eventually. I'll tell you about all of your lives, if we have time. There's simply a lot of them to get through."

I nodded, leaning into his light touch. "I guess that makes sense. I'm just eager to learn."

"You always have been." He hit me with a devastating smile, then stepped back. "Come."

He led me across the room to one of the bookshelves, and his shadowy wings erupted from his back. With one powerful stroke, he lifted off his feet and hovered at a top shelf I hadn't reached yet. He grabbed a small black book and lowered to the ground, his wings disappearing behind him.

He offered me the book, bound in black. "This was yours."

I carefully took the tiny book, which was old but well preserved. *Collected Works of Edgar Allen Poe*. On the title page there was an inscription that read, "For my muse, my Lenore." Underneath it was Poe's signature.

I quickly looked up at Lucifer. "Is this real?"

"Oh yes. I've looked after that book for a long time for you."

"Holy shit. I'm *the* Lenore. In *The Raven*?" I turned the pages to find *The Raven* and read the poem to myself, then repeated one line out loud. "A rare and radiant maiden whom the angels name Lenore, quoth the Raven 'Nevermore.'"

Lucifer's lips quirked up. "He wrote another poem about you too, simply titled *Lenore*. Poe was quite obsessed with you."

"Wow." I flipped the pages, which cracked with age as I turned them, and found the other poem.

"Hannah, please trust me on this. I plan to tell you about Lenore and all your other lives, but I know from past experience it's better to introduce these things gradually, or otherwise it becomes quite overwhelming for you. Coping with past lives and being fated mates with the devil is a lot to ask of any woman." He leaned forward and cupped my cheek. "Even one as extraordinary as you."

It *was* overwhelming, but I had this urgent need to know too. I shook my head and closed the book. "I want to remember so badly. I often have these vivid dreams, and I always thought it was because I read so many books and had such a strong imagination, but now I'm wondering if it could be glimpses of my past lives."

"It's possible. I'm surprised you haven't remembered more by now, or at least remembered me, but more should come in time." He rubbed his hands together. "Now, we have two more nights of sin, and tonight's is lust. Oh, you should see what I have planned."

I held up a hand, as an idea hit me. "Hang on. You've picked the activities every night so far, but now it's my turn."

He blinked at me, cocking his head. "Your turn?"

"For days I've done everything you wanted, and yes, it's been pretty incredible, but tonight we're going to do what I want for a change."

"You don't even know what I have planned." His fingers trailed down my neck, brushing the top of my chest like a tease. "Trust me, you'll like it."

I sucked in a breath and tried to control my desire. "I'm sure I would, but I need a break from this lifestyle. A little sense of normality amid all the madness of the last few days. Please."

"Very well, I'll allow you to choose tonight's activities." He sounded skeptical, and I sensed it was because it was hard for him to give up control after many lifetimes of being king.

I lifted on my toes and gave him a quick kiss. "Don't worry. I'm sure we'll both be naked by the end of the night."

I was rewarded with a sensual grin. "Now that sounds more like it."

20

LUCIFER

"Here we are," Hannah said, as a bell jingled above our heads. I guessed she'd pushed a door open, but I couldn't see because she'd instructed me to keep my eyes closed, in a voice that said she meant it.

"You can open your eyes now."

She nudged my arm, but... Fuck, did I have to? I was deliberately keeping my eyes shut against the fear they might fall out once I opened them and saw wherever she'd brought me. If the stench of stale beer and too much cheap cooking grease—not to mention the undertones of puke and piss—were anything to go by, I definitely wanted to keep my eyes closed. Very firmly closed. Perhaps with a padlock.

I tried to grin, but it came out more like a grimace. "Are you sure we're in the right place?"

"Yep, this is it."

I took a deep breath, even though the alcohol in the air was so strong just inhaling it burned my throat, and opened my eyes. I looked around in apprehension. We were in some sort of seedy dive bar, the sort of place I would never visit on my own. The interior had neon lights that flickered and blinked, although due to short circuit rather than design. Far too many pool tables took up valuable seating space and an entire side wall was devoted to old slot machines, many with dark, cracked screens. Ripped vinyl seating seemed to be the order of the day along with dated plastic tables where the top coating was lifting and scorched.

An enormous man in dirty jeans and a leather vest—and nothing else—stumbled past us, and I glanced down at my Armani suit, feeling rather overdressed for the locale.

This was where she'd brought me? And they said I was a torturer.

"Is this truly what you chose for lust?" I couldn't hold the question in any longer as I tried not to look as horrified as I felt. Of all the places in Las Vegas we could have gone to, she'd picked this dingy old bar?

Hannah laughed, and seeing her eyes sparkle with mischief was almost enough to make up for this wretched place. "Come on, let's go order some food and drinks."

She led me to the bar, and I admired her in those tight black jeans and that draping top, both of which came from her new wardrobe, though she didn't stand out in this place like I did. I wouldn't have chosen to spend any moment of my immortal life with these other human specimens, but if this made Hannah happy, so be it.

She hopped onto one of the red barstools, and I took the one beside her. I nearly rested my elbow on the bar and barely contained my yelp as I yanked away from the surface. More than one layer of dirt and grease graced the dark wood. Enough that my jacket sleeve might have never recovered from such close contact.

"What are we doing in here when you don't even drink?" I asked Hannah.

"I found this place on one of those lists of 'best food in Vegas off The Strip.'" She shrugged as she flipped open a laminated menu with peeling edges. "I thought it'd be fun to do something different. Take you out of your element for a change and see what happened."

A crusty old bartender ambled over, acknowledging people left and right as he approached us. He made a pretense of wiping the bar with a stained rag. "What'll it be?"

"Four chili dogs with everything on them. Fries and onion rings." She paused and I stared at her in horror as she described six different ways to cause a heart attack. Not that I could have one, of course, but I worried about her own mortality. "And a root beer."

"What'll you have to drink?" The bartender tapped his fingers on the bar while I considered which wine would taste best with fried foods.

"Malbec?"

He stared at me, his face blank.

"You don't have wine, do you?" Instead of horror, I only felt resignation. I glanced behind him at the various bottles and waved a hand. "Just bring me some of the house beer, whatever that is."

At Hannah's giggle, I swung my attention back to her while the bartender walked away to get our drinks. I straightened my suit and asked, "Does this amuse you?"

"Very much so. It's a nice reversal, seeing you so out of place." She raised her eyebrows and gave my suit a once-over with a grin, although the hand she skimmed down my thigh spoke much more of appreciation than amusement. "This is how I always feel around you, with your fancy penthouse and gourmet foods and private helicopters. Tonight I wanted to see what Lucifer was like without all the money, luxury, and power."

I leaned close and brushed my lips across her ear. "You can take away the money and luxury, but power? Oh, I still have plenty of that, darling."

Her eyes flared with desire as I sat back, just as the bartender set two drinks in front of us. I picked up my plastic cup and took a sip. It tasted thin and watered down but wasn't completely undrinkable.

"Besides, I have a hard time believing you'd ever eat here if it wasn't to torment me," I added, once he'd left again.

"Probably not." She glanced around and wrinkled her nose. "But it's closer to the kinds of places I'd normally eat at than anywhere you'd take us."

"Then I shall endeavor to enjoy slumming it with you, as the mortals say."

She burst out laughing at that, and the sound of it made all of this worthwhile. I'd do anything she asked if it brought out that kind of reaction. Damn, how I'd missed being with her. She'd always loved to challenge me, and it was wonderful to see she felt comfortable enough already to do it now. Her fear of me had vanished, and though she may not remember me yet, she knew me on some deep, subconscious level.

Her laughter trailed off as the bartender plopped two grease-spattered plates of chili dogs and fries in front of us. Eating this meal without getting it all over ourselves was going to need a miracle.

Well, challenge accepted.

With my gaze meeting hers, I picked up the chili dog and took an enormous bite. Flavor and heat exploded in my mouth, but it was nothing I couldn't handle. Then I set the food down and grabbed a napkin from the smudged chrome holder and carefully wiped grease off my fingers. "Your turn."

She took a bite next, but her chili dog fell apart as she did, making a huge mess that tumbled down to her plate. She laughed as she tried to salvage it, and I handed her some fresh napkins. "Wow, that is good. Although I'm not sure it's worth the, um, ambiance."

"No food is worth this," I muttered, as two people in the corner started yelling at each other in high-pitched voices, then suddenly leaped up and started making out over the table.

We kept eating anyway, dipping fries in the chili as we watched a lady in a pink tutu who couldn't be a day less than ninety use one of the slot machines. At least we were never bored.

"What did you do today?" Hannah asked, as she grabbed an onion ring.

"I questioned the dragon we captured, but once again he proved resistant to my powers, which shouldn't be possible." I bit down hard on an onion ring, trying not to let my frustrations show. The fact that dragons were also turning against me and trying to kidnap —or worse—Hannah meant this truly was a larger conspiracy. One

I'd need to deal with soon. Tomorrow, in fact, at the Devil's Night ball.

"I nearly pissed my pants when I saw that thing," Hannah said. "I can't believe dragons are real."

"They are, but there are very few of them left. It's unheard of for so many to attack at once."

She lifted her eyebrows. "What does that mean then?"

"That someone powerful is trying to undermine me." I shrugged casually, even though my blood heated at the very idea. When she looked uncertain, I reached over and rested my hand on her knee. "You don't need to worry. I'll deal with it."

She nodded slowly as she drank some of her root beer. "How many kinds of demons are there?"

"Six, or seven if you include the Fallen, although there's some debate over whether they count as demons or not."

Her eyes lit up. "One for each deadly sin?"

"Exactly, although the deadly sins were so named by angels. Still, they mostly fit. Pride for Fallen, naturally. Shifters are wrath, though their emotion is more like passion. Imps are envy, although they mainly thrive on attention."

"You said last night that dragons were demons of greed."

"Yes, it's where the whole dragon hoarding stereotype comes from."

She tilted her head as she considered. "Lilim are lust, obviously. What about gluttony and sloth?"

"Gargoyles, like the ones who attacked you the other night, are sloth. They can turn to stone and they feed on sleep." I finished my food and used my napkin to wipe my hands. "As for gluttony, that would be vampires. They require blood to survive, just like in lore, and they're very charming."

"Glad I haven't met any of those yet." She gave my shoulder a playful shove. "I can't possibly handle any more charm."

We finished up our meal and I was surprised to find that in this dive bar with her I'd been having a great time. Even with the greasy chili dogs and weak beer. All I needed was Hannah by my side to feel complete, no matter the locale.

As we stepped outside I said, "Now that you've had your fun, let me take you to do one of the things I'd originally planned for tonight."

Her brow furrowed. "No more private helicopters and thousand-dollar dresses, please."

I held up my hands. "I promise I won't spend a penny on this particular endeavor."

She twisted her lips, like she was contemplating saying no, but then she nodded. "Okay. I suppose we can see the Mob Museum and the world's largest slot machine some other time."

"Wonderful." I held out my hand and my blood pumped harder when her fingers wrapped around mine. Then I cloaked us in shadow so any stray gazes wouldn't notice us before lifting Hannah in my arms and launching into the air. She tightened her grip around my neck, but not like she had with the dragons. She trusted me not to drop her.

My chest humming with pleasure, I took us higher and higher, holding Hannah so she could see the city beneath us. The hustle and bustle, the lights and the music, all of the chaos that was my home. We didn't talk, just held each other as we flew over the city, enjoying the feel of being close as the cool night air bent around us.

Eventually, I landed on the top of the Stratosphere Tower, the tallest structure in the city and the perfect spot to lord over it like a king and queen gazing across their domain.

"Welcome to The Strat. Best view of the whole city." I put my arm around Hannah's shoulders and she leaned against me.

"It's beautiful." She turned to look up at me with those bright eyes that missed nothing. "But why do you live here and not in Hell?"

My chest tightened with long-repressed pain. "After thousands of years of war against the angels, Hell became uninhabitable. Heaven too. Our numbers were dwindling, and it was clear both our races would die off if something didn't change. Archangel Michael and I met in private over many years, discussing how to negotiate peace between our kinds. In the end, we signed the Earth Accords and called a truce, then brought all the angels and demons to Earth, closing off Heaven and Hell permanently."

Her eyebrows darted up. "The angels and demons were okay with that?"

I let out a bitter laugh. "Hardly. Many were angry with us at the time. Hell, many are still angry. Archangel Michael even lost his life over it. But it was the only way to save our people, and I stand by the decision."

Her hand found mine and she squeezed it. "I'm sure you did what was best. But...why Vegas?"

"About forty years ago, when I realized we couldn't live in Hell anymore, I started building up Las Vegas to be a safe haven for demons, where they can feed on humans without harming them or exposing our kind to the world. Here, humans are allowed to indulge their sins, and demons can reap the benefits."

The wind whipped strands of her golden hair across her cheeks. "And the Fallen?"

"The Fallen act as the...keepers of the demons, you could say. I have strict rules about not harming humans, and one of the requirements of the Earth Accords is that we keep our presence hidden from the mortal world. My Fallen make sure the demons stay in line."

Her face softened as she gestured at the sparkling city below us. "You did all this, creating this entire empire, just to protect both humans and demons. To make sure we could live in peace."

"And angels," I said, deflecting her praise with a smile. "Can't forget them."

"And angels." She reached up and touched my face in wonder, and the look in her blue eyes captivated me like nothing else ever could. "Tell me again how you're the villain of this story?"

Before I could respond, she pressed her lips to mine and stole my breath. The kiss quickly grew heated, as my tongue explored her mouth and she tangled her fingers in my hair. I let my hands skim down her back to firmly cup her ass, so tight in those hot little jeans, and she let out a little sigh.

"Take me back to the penthouse," she whispered.

21

HANNAH

"Already?" Lucifer drew away with a small chuckle and a teasing glint in his eyes. "The night is yet young. We could still see the sights, grab a souvenir, eat a bite of dessert."

"I'm ready for the lust portion of our evening."

I gripped the front of his shirt, the small buttons pressing into my skin. I kissed him with renewed passion, trying to convince him of my need as he gathered me in his arms. The feel of his tongue gliding across mine distracted me from our surroundings so much that I didn't notice he'd taken off until we were already high in the air.

I pressed my lips to his neck as I watched the view over his shoulder as he flew toward The Celestial, his wings moving silently through the night. I wanted more of what he gave me the other night, and my body hummed with need as I pressed against him.

He landed on the balcony outside his room and the door pushed open ahead of us. It was hard to tell in the night, but it seemed as though a shadow had opened it. As soon as he entered the room, his wings disappeared and he set me down, but he didn't let me go.

"I need you." My voice came out husky and full of desire, and I began unbuttoning his shirt as he slid the jacket off his shoulders. I walked backward into the room as I slipped my finger under his belt, drawing him after me. His cock pressed against his pants, seeming to guide his way, and I smoothed my hand over the bulge, making him groan softly.

After one last stroke across the front of his pants, I returned my attention to his buttons before he grew impatient and yanked his shirt off and threw it to the floor.

"Mmm..." I pressed a series of open-mouthed kisses across his neck and collar bone as my hands explored the shifting muscles of his taut stomach. "Let me count the sins... Greed." I kissed his neck again. "Lust..." A deeper kiss to his mouth. "Gluttony." I stroked his tongue with mine before drawing it into my mouth. Then I pressed my hand to the bulge in his pants once more. "And pride."

He lifted an eyebrow as a corner of his mouth gave an amused quirk. "It is my sin, after all."

"Want to show me how proud you are, Lucifer?" I asked as I drew his zipper down. I caught my breath as his huge cock sprang free of his soft black slacks.

I sank to my knees, and his fingers immediately laced in my hair, his fingertips pressing to my scalp as all of my focus fell on the hard length in front of me. I closed my eyes as I traced my fingers lightly over the soft skin of his cock and a growl rumbled through him.

"Tease," he ground out, his voice rough as his fingers tightened in my hair.

"Not used to a little temptation, Lucifer?"

He rumbled another growl and I grasped him with a little more pressure as I stroked his full length. He inhaled sharply, and I took the sound as encouragement, pressing the flat of my tongue to his skin in a long lick. I swirled it around the head, listening as his breathing became ragged.

"Hannah." He murmured my name so quietly I didn't know if he was even aware he'd spoken.

In reply, I slipped the head of his cock between my lips. He groaned, driving his hips forward, and I opened my mouth wide as I accepted more of him. He was so big it was a challenge, but somehow I knew I could take it.

He pushed into me a couple of inches then pulled slowly back out, giving me a chance to even out my breathing. I chased him with my mouth to take more of him as I worked my hand at the base. I bobbed my head lower each time, and he moved his hips rhythmically with me, his breathing increasing in tempo with every thrust he made.

As I closed my eyes, all of my other senses took over. The texture, the taste, the smell, and the sound of Lucifer. It all rolled over me, and the moment took me home. I hummed my pleasure over his skin, while he thrust into my mouth.

"Hannah," he whispered hoarsely. "You always were the one to make me fall. Not pride. You."

With a groan, his fingers tightened around my head, forcing me to suck him deeper, just as his cock surged between my lips. Then his hot, salty seed shot into my mouth and down my throat. I took it all as I looked up at him, his face gazing down at me as he came.

He gripped my arms and yanked me to my feet, his eyes blazing with hunger. "Now it's my turn. Take off your clothes."

I stripped slowly, removing my shirt and jeans, then my bra and panties. He watched me the entire time, stroking that long cock, which was still hard, even after that. I should have expected that the devil could go for more than one round. My pussy pulsed with the knowledge of where he wanted to be, and where I craved him so badly.

He removed the rest of his clothes next, way too slowly for my liking, although I soaked up the sight of his sculpted, naked body. Both impatient and in the mood to tease him, I slipped my fingers between my thighs, gliding them over my wet slit. I groaned as I touched my clit, suddenly unsure who I was teasing more. "Envy."

"Don't let me get to wrath," he muttered as he reached for me, drawing me flush against him, his cock needy as it pressed into me. "That's my pussy, and I'm going to be the one to fill it."

I shivered at the darkness and sin in his low voice, but I glanced up at him with a smile. "Promise?"

He growled and walked me backward, faster than I could keep up with. My back hit the floor-to-ceiling window looking out over Las Vegas, and he grabbed my ass and yanked me up, wrapping my legs around him. His cock entered me hard and fast, without warning, filling me completely. He swallowed my gasp with his mouth, his kiss rough and demanding, while he plunged his tongue and his cock into me.

I reached across his back to where I knew his wings were hidden by some kind of magic, then wrapped my arms around his neck. I slid my fingers along into his lush, dark hair, holding on tight as he pounded into me relentlessly.

With my naked ass pressed against the window, I was on display for anyone who might look over. Maybe someone in one of the other hotels, or one of the Fallen flying outside on patrol. The thought that someone could be watching us made the whole encounter even more sinful.

Against my back, the glass was cool, but my skin felt like it was on fire. Lucifer's strong arms moved me up and down on his cock while his hips rocked into me. His entire body fucked me so thoroughly I wasn't sure I'd be able to walk afterward.

I was getting close, so close, thanks to his intoxicating rhythm, but then he suddenly pulled out of me, setting my feet back on the floor. My need for him skyrocketed and I started to protest, but then he spun me around, so my naked body faced the windows. He held me against him, snaking his hand down to my clit, pinching it hard as we gazed out at the bright city lights with our reflections imposed over it.

While his cock nudged me from behind, he played with me, teasing me, tormenting me. One hand on my clit, and the other on my breasts. My pussy throbbed, aching for him to fill me again, and I whimpered.

"Lucifer, please."

He buried his face in my hair, then nipped lightly at my ear as his fingers stroked my wet folds. "Tell me this pussy is mine."

"It's yours. Please. I need..."

He pinched my nipple hard. "Yes, what do you need?"

I gasped from the mix of pain and pleasure. "I need you inside me."

He pushed me forward, my hands splayed against the glass, then entered me roughly from behind. My nipples tightened painfully and I arched back against him, needing him to fill me completely. He felt so huge in this position, like he was tearing me apart, and I loved every second of it.

In the reflection of the mirror I watched him fuck me from behind, his hands on my hips, his eyes red and wild. His wings flared out behind him, his black feathers exuding darkness, and the sight of him in his true form made me want him more. Only I could make the devil lose control like this.

"This is what you want," he said, between hard thrusts. "You want me to fuck your tight little pussy so hard you feel me for days."

"Yes, yes, yes," I cried out, as he pounded into me, my breasts shaking from the impact.

He grasped my hair, yanking my head back. "Now you're going to come, and you're going to scream my name so loud everyone in The Celestial will know the devil's the one fucking you."

With that, he reached around with his other hand and stroked my clit, setting me off like a bomb. I convulsed around him, my knees growing weak, and only his hands holding me kept me upright. I screamed his name as a violent orgasm ripped through me, like nothing I'd ever felt before. My hips bucked back against him, wanting it to never end, while he kept rubbing my clit and filling me up. Only when I felt like I was bursting with pleasure to the point I'd surely die did he let himself go too. I felt it when he came, like a rush of power leaving his body, his wings flaring and his red eyes looking at me in the window's reflection. Like he was staring right into my soul.

Then he picked me up in his arms, our naked bodies cradled together, and he carried me to his bed. He set me down on it, while I tried to remember how to breathe, and he lowered himself beside me, his wings fading away into the darkness of the room.

I turned to his face and stroked his cheek, with a delirious grin on my face. "And now, sloth."

"I'm not done with lust just yet," Lucifer said, as he spread my thighs and ducked his head between them, wringing another orgasm out of me with his tongue and his fingers, making me scream his name again and again.

I had a feeling it was going to be a long night...and I was definitely not complaining.

22

HANNAH

M y hair tumbled over my left shoulder in shiny blonde ringlets. Damn, it looked good. I sat in a robe, feeling sexy and sultry before the gorgeous gown even went over my head. The matching bra and panty set under the robe did their part as well, the lace detail against my skin reminding me I was wearing bedroom underwear—the kind I wanted Lucifer to see.

I met Zel's dark eyes in the mirror. "For a badass killer, you do a great job on hair."

"What, a girl can't be multi-talented?" Zel tapped me on the nose before going back at it with the wand of black goop. "Hush, or I'll mess up your mascara."

This was it. My last night here with Lucifer, appropriately known as Devil's Night—the night before Halloween. But then what? I was free, I supposed. The devil's bargain hadn't extended past seven days. It would be time to head back to Vista and check on my shop. But the thought of leaving made my stomach clench.

"There." Zel stood back and squinted at me, casting a critical eye over her workmanship. "You'll do."

I gazed at myself in the mirror, amazed at how Zel had turned me into some kind of ethereal beauty. But sudden anxiety suffused me. "Will everyone know who I am tonight?"

"Without a doubt." Zel paused in the act of putting lids back on the makeup we'd used. "Lucifer doesn't look at other women the way he looks at you."

The words sent a shiver of pleasure-laced apprehension down my spine as they confirmed what I already knew. What Lucifer had told me. Still, it was nice to hear it from someone else, someone who was a... I paused, considering. Was Zel a friend?

I studied her closely, noting the slightly red skin on her legs, barely visible under her tight leather skirt. She'd mostly healed from the attack, but the traces of it were still there. A reminder that she'd protected my life over and over. "Zel, were we friends in any of my past lives?"

Her movements stopped as she stared off into space. When she finally looked up at me, it was through the mirror, her mouth set in a grim line. "Sometimes, yes."

"And the other times?" I touched her arm lightly.

Her face became hard as stone. "It's hard being friends with someone you know is going to die."

With those words, she walked out of the bathroom, preventing me from asking more. I sighed and stared at myself in the mirror, at the hair and makeup Zel had so carefully done. She must have been close to me in a previous life when I was also human. Compared to demons, our lives are short, our bodies fragile. I could understand why she'd be hesitant to get close to a mortal, only to lose them a few years later.

Did Lucifer worry about that too?

How could I be in a relationship with an immortal, knowing I would grow old and die, while he stayed exactly the same?

I left the bathroom and found Zel sitting on my bed, to my surprise. She was staring at nothing, and I wondered if she was distant with me because she wanted to protect herself against the pain of losing her friend again to the ravages of a mortal life.

She stood as I approached and went to the closet. "Let's get you dressed."

I nodded as she helped me step into the gorgeous, shimmering black gown with the crystal stars and moons on it. The fabric fell about me, lying softly over my skin with the lightest of pressure, skimming my curves and making me feel beautiful. When I turned, the cloak flared behind me, like something from a dream.

Zel pulled a matching mask out from behind her back. It was also black and covered in crystals, like a starlit night. As she tied the ribbon and wove it into my long ringlet with her dexterous fingers, I asked one last question.

"Can humans be made into demons? Or Fallen?"

She snorted. "No. Impossible."

Damn.

She handed me a tiny purse that seemed to be made entirely of sparkling crystals, and turned me toward the door. "Go. Lucifer is waiting and the ball is starting soon."

I hesitated, overwhelmed at the idea of attending a demon ball. "Will you be there too?"

"Yes. I'll be guarding you the entire time from the shadows."

I reached out and rested my hand on her upper arm, giving her a warm smile. "Thank you."

She shook off my hand, scowling without meeting my eyes. "Just doing my job."

I stepped out of my room and entered the living room, then paused to take in the man in front of me. Tonight was October 30, known as Devil's Night, and if any man looked like he deserved an entire night named after them it was him. In his shiny black tuxedo every inch of him radiated power, charm, and dark, dangerous masculinity. He looked like a sexy supervillain that people on the Internet wrote fanfic about. No mask, though. I supposed when the masquerade ball was in your honor, you were the only one who didn't need a mask.

"You're gorgeous," he whispered. "Absolutely stunning."

"Thank you." I did a little twirl, the fabric swishing around me. "You look pretty incredible yourself."

He held out his arm. "Shall we?"

I walked with him out of the penthouse and into the elevator. Was I ready to face a ballroom full of ancient demons?

No, I really wasn't. But what choice did I have?

The elevator kept going down, down, down, as if we were descending all the way to Hell. I hadn't seen which button Lucifer had pressed, but we traveled past the underground parking garage, and when the doors finally opened, an enormous ballroom was revealed in front of us. The room was dark, with only roaming spotlights and bright stars on the ceiling illuminating the room, making it feel like we were outside under the night sky. I glimpsed many people in masks and gorgeous clothes moving about the room, and a large silver throne at the other end, but otherwise much of the room was a mystery to me. Unlike the demons here, I couldn't see in the dark.

"The Devil's Night ball is always designed to look like Hell," Lucifer explained, as he watched me gaze across the room with an expression that probably looked a bit baffled.

"I thought Hell was supposed to be all fire and brimstone."

He gave a bitter laugh. "Only because of angel propaganda. Hell is the realm of night and darkness. It only burned when the angels set fire to our world."

As we stepped into the room, people started noticing he'd arrived and began to bow. Within seconds, the entire ballroom full of masked demons sank to their knees or bent at the waist, honoring the King of Hell in respectful silence. I tried not to widen my eyes too much behind my mask as we walked toward the throne, but every gaze was on us. On *me*.

Hundreds of demons, all watching me. They must know I was human, an imposter among them, only here because Lucifer demanded it. Every one of them could probably kill me with the slightest thought.

Lucifer gestured for everyone to rise, and then began pointing out people in the crowd, first nodding toward a woman in a slinky silver dress with shiny, jet black hair. "That's Belphegor, or Bella, the Archdemon of gargoyles," he told me in a low voice. "She lives in Paris and oversees much of the European demon affairs."

The mention of gargoyles made my skin tingle, and I studied her closely, but she kept her head bowed and never met my eyes. With her silver mask on, I couldn't see much of her face anyway.

Lucifer led me forward still, pointing out more people of note in the crowd. "The man in the red and gold mask is Mammon, Archdemon of the dragons. He lives in China and handles that part of the world for me."

Mammon was huge and built like a truck, with jet black hair and eyes that I swore were glowing orange. He glared at us as we passed by, and I really would not want to meet him alone in a dark alley. Or any of his other dragons, for that matter. I'd seen enough of those for one lifetime, thank you very much.

"The woman beside him wearing green is Nemesis, Archdemon of the imps," Lucifer continued.

My jaw dropped at that. Nemesis was a demon? Not some mythological goddess or abstract concept? She had bright red hair and sensual curves, but barely even glanced my way, too busy with a crowd of admirers flocking around her.

I couldn't help but feel a bit shell-shocked at seeing so many powerful people, and I didn't fail to notice that these were all the Archdemons who might be responsible for the attacks over the last few days. A whisper of fear trickled down my spine, but I had to trust in Lucifer. He wouldn't have brought me here if he thought I would be in any danger. Besides, Azazel would be protecting me from the shadows all night long. Only that knowledge made me feel a tiny bit better.

Closer to the throne, Lucifer stopped in front of a woman who was more beautiful and alluring than anyone I'd ever seen in my life, even with a red leather mask on her face. Her dark hair was in an elaborate coif that suited her bone structure, and she had green eyes that rivaled Lucifer's.

He gestured toward her. "Hannah, I'd like you to meet Lilith, Archdemon of the Lilim."

"It's good to see you again," Lilith said, and even her voice was sultry. "But you don't remember me, do you?"

"No, I don't. I'm sorry." Should I remember her? Was she another person who'd been close to me in one of my past lives?

"No matter." She leaned in close, as though sharing a confidence. "I'm incredibly grateful for your part in rescuing my son, Asmodeus. He should be around here too somewhere, and I'm sure he'd like to thank you himself."

I couldn't help but raise my eyebrows. "You don't look old enough to have an adult son."

"My dear, you flatter me." She made a dismissive gesture, her fingers fluttering. "It's but one of the benefits of being an immortal."

"How are your daughters, Lilith?" Lucifer asked. I sensed he was closer to this Archdemon than any of the others.

Lilith's face showed genuine affection as she spoke of her children. "Olivia is settling in nicely as mediator between angels and demons. Thank you again, Lucifer, for helping her get that position." She looked around and then smiled toward a couple talking to a tall man with long black hair. "Ah, Olivia and Kassiel are over there with Baal now."

The woman named Olivia looked a lot like Lilith, with the same seductive beauty that was hard to take your eyes off, but the dark-haired man beside her, Kassiel, sparked an odd reaction in my body. My heart beat faster, almost painfully, tugging inside my chest in a physical reaction I couldn't explain. I lifted my hand and rested it over the bodice of my dress as I waited for the response to the man to die away. Then it vanished as quickly as it came upon me. How odd.

"And your other daughter?" Lucifer asked, as if he was genuinely interested.

Lilith inclined her head slightly. "Lena is still recovering from her time with that awful cult, but she improves every day."

I had no idea who they were talking about. What cult? But I didn't ask. Lucifer had been a good sport when I took him to that seedy dive bar, so I figured I owed him this. I could smile and nod along with these people, even if their conversation did make me feel like a child at an adult party.

"Excuse me." Lucifer pressed a kiss to my cheek. "I must speak with Fenrir. I'll return in a moment."

He headed over to speak with a large, bearded man with wild gray hair who stood in the corner. The long-haired man named Baal joined them a moment later.

"I have no idea who any of these people are," I muttered.

"Fenrir is the Archdemon of shifters, and Baal is the Archdemon of vampires." Lilith cocked her head. "You know, I think this might be the first time all the Archdemons have been in one building in decades. Lucifer demanded our presence here tonight. I wonder if he has something planned for us."

Had he summoned them here because of me? But why?

Lilith slipped her hand in the crook of my elbow as she led me to the buffet. "Don't worry about the others. They're all jealous. Who wouldn't want to be on the arm of the Demon King?"

Maybe she was right. Tonight's sin was supposed to be envy, after all. I watched Lucifer as he prowled across the room with barely restrained power in every one of his movements, and noticed the way everyone responded to him. Treating him like a king.

And me?

I was Persephone being claimed by Hades, and I had no choice but to enter his underworld and become his dark queen.

23

HANNAH

Lilith and I grabbed a few fancy appetizers to eat at the buffet, and I was grateful to her for sticking by my side even though she didn't know me at all—at least, not in this life. As an introvert, parties were hard enough. Add in the fact that I was the lone human at a ball full of demons and it was hard not to run back to the penthouse as fast as I could.

"Ah, there's my son now," Lilith said, raising her hand to wave him over.

The man who approached could only be described as sex on a stick. With dark hair, bronze skin, and muscles galore, he looked like some kind of international model on a billboard somewhere. He wore a plain black mask and a black suit, oozing sex appeal with every step, although he didn't make my heart flutter the way Lucifer did. He looked like the kind of guy you had one crazy, unbelievable night with, and then never saw again. In that Fuck, Marry, Kill game he'd be Fuck every time.

Unless you're Brandy, maybe.

"Hannah, this is Asmodeus," Lilith said.

He reached out to take my hand, then bowed a little and brushed his lips against my knuckles, sending tingles through me. I hoped Lucifer wasn't looking, or Asmodeus might be flying against the wall soon. "An honor," he said, his husky voice sliding along my skin like silk.

I nearly fanned myself. Shit, I needed a cold shower after five seconds in his presence. How had Brandy withstood a *week* of this? No wonder Lucifer had said there was no way she could have resisted leaving the bar with him.

"I've heard a lot about you," I said, after extricating my hand.

"All bad things, I hope?" he said with a wink.

I laughed, unable to resist his charm. "Things I had a hard time believing until now."

Lilith pressed her hand to Asmodeus's face. "Have you been feeding? You still look a bit weak from your ordeal. I'm sure any number of demons here tonight would be happy to help."

He pulled away. "I'm fine, mother."

"All right, dear." She ruffled his hair with obvious love, then excused herself to speak to someone else, leaving me alone with the incubus.

"You're Brandy's friend." He said it as a statement, his voice becoming more serious. "I've heard a lot about you too, and it seems I owe you my thanks."

I shrugged, the action making my shimmering cloak flutter. "All I did was nudge Lucifer in the right direction."

"You're a good friend. Brandy is very fond of you." The way he said her name made me think he cared for Brandy too.

I remembered how she spoke of him at the spa. "I'm not the only one she's fond of..."

His shoulders stiffened and pain crossed his green eyes. "Brandy is special, but it's impossible for the two of us to be together. She knows that."

"Maybe, but I know Brandy better than anyone and she's never backed down from a challenge. She's also never spoken of any other guy the way she spoke about you."

He studied me. "May I tell you a secret?"

Err...me? I'd met the guy two minutes ago. But I nodded. "Of course."

He closed his eyes as if in pain and let out a shuddering breath. "I haven't slept with anyone since meeting Brandy. My parents want me to feed, and I know I need to, or I'll die. But I can't. I don't want anyone but her."

"But you can't have sex with her?"

"Only once, and then never again. Not without killing her."

"Is there no way around that?"

"No, there isn't. Unless..." He trailed off and looked across the room, his gaze landing on his mother. "There might be a way. But I'd have to give up everything. For a human I barely know."

I spread my hands. "I can't tell you what to do. All I know is that Brandy would love to see you again. Maybe all you'll have is one crazy, wild night together that you remember for the rest of your lives. Or maybe you both decide you want more and find a way to make it work. Either way, you should go to her."

"I think you're right," he said, his voice distant. Then he took my hands and bowed slightly. "Thank you, my queen. I always did appreciate your wise counsel. It's good you're back."

My mouth fell open. "You're welcome?"

He straightened the cuffs on his shirt. "I have a long drive ahead of me. I better get going."

"Give my love to Brandy."

With a nod, he vanished into the crowd, and I hoped I'd done the right thing. There was obviously something there between the two of them, and if nothing else they needed to get some sort of closure. Hopefully they'd be able to find a way to be together too.

And now I was alone again. I scanned the crowd for Lucifer, but didn't see him anywhere. Plastering a pleasant expression on my face, I worked my way to the edge of the room, nodding at people I didn't know and shaking more hands than I wanted to think about. The darkness along the walls was deeper, but there was also an area with tables. My feet throbbed in my heels, and I collapsed gratefully into the chair closest to the wall, then slipped off the expensive, sky-high heels.

Being a human among demons was intense to say the least, but it was far easier to handle from over here. The other guests barely paid any attention to the edges of the room, focusing all of their attention inward instead to observe each other, sometimes with suspicion gleaming in their eyes from behind those masks. It made for great people watching, though. *Demon* watching.

A small group sat at the table behind me, their faces shrouded in darkness. As I listened, relying on my mask to disguise exactly where I was looking, I learned that the demons were scandalized by some new woman who was half demon and half angel but was favored by Lucifer, and I was just leaning into the details of the story when a rough voice nearby caught my attention.

"It's true then. Lucifer's woman has returned."

"She's human though." The second person snickered. "We'll see how long she lasts."

My pulse kicked up a notch at their words. I glanced over, peering into the shadows and trying to make my movements so small that no one would notice my focus had shifted to the new conversation. I got a glimpse of a huge man with a red and gold mask. Mammon.

"Not long," he said. "Things are already in motion. Many of the Archdemons are involved. Soon Lucifer will be defeated, and it will be time to return to Hell."

His words were enough to strike fear in my heart. I had to tell Lucifer immediately. I bent to slip my shoes back on, then took a deep, fortifying breath and threw myself into the crowd. I darted between demons, trying to get to the center of the room so I could find Lucifer and warn him about Mammon.

When I was almost halfway there, one of the spotlights swung around and beamed down on Lucifer. I caught my breath at the sight of him, shadows playing across his face and his eyes burning with power. He stood in front of his throne and turned in a slow circle. A silver crown graced his head, throwing off fragments of the light as he moved, and it fit him as if he'd been born to wear it. The room quieted as everyone gave their attention to their king.

His commanding voice rang across the ballroom. "Someone in this very room has been plotting to overthrow me. Trying to take what is mine."

At first I assumed he meant his throne, but then his gaze found me in the crowd, like a caress only I could feel.

He meant me. I was the thing he considered *his*.

"All traitors will be punished." As he spoke, another spotlight illuminated the corner of the room, near where I'd been sitting, where Gadreel and Samael now led out four demons. I wasn't sure what kind they were, but I had a sneaking suspicion these were the demons involved in the attacks that had been captured.

The demons were pushed down so they knelt in front of Lucifer, facing the audience. Their faces were drawn with lines of tension and their hands were bound behind their backs, but otherwise they appeared uninjured. I could barely look into their eyes. Pure fear glimmered there as shadows began to snake round them. Like even the darkness was toying with them.

Lucifer began to pace slowly behind the traitors as he spoke. "These four—an imp, a dragon, a gargoyle, and a shifter—were all caught in plots against me. Tonight they will be punished."

I expected the audience to react in some way, but it seemed like everyone in the crowd was holding their breath, too terrified to move. Me included.

"I have been Demon King for thousands of years." Lucifer's voice boomed around the ballroom, echoing from the walls I couldn't see. "Though many have tried to overthrow me, all have failed. There's a reason I'm the King. Perhaps you all need a reminder?"

Then he bowed his head and took a deep, controlled breath. His shadowy black wings erupted behind his body, and I gaped at him along with everyone else in the ballroom. Tendrils of black, smoky energy crept around him coalescing and growing thicker, until they almost looked like inky black, swirling solids. I stepped forward, moving carefully through the crowd again as the lines of black shadow wrapped around each of the demon's necks. Nobody moved but me.

"I do not tolerate insubordination." Lucifer snapped his fingers, and suddenly bright blue flame erupted from the darkness wrapped around the demons. The traitors screamed as the unnatural blue fire consumed them, lighting the room with eerie, flickering light. Everyone gasped, their faces paling, their mouths falling agape, but nobody stepped forward. I heard a few people whispering in shocked voices about hellfire, as the four demons turned to ash before our eyes.

Then the entire room bowed as one, lowering to knees of submission on the floor, until I was the only one besides Lucifer standing. I stared at him in horror as he surveyed the people kneeling before him, his wings spread wide with darkness trailing off them like mist.

He'd just...killed them. Right there, in front of everyone. And his people *bowed*. My breathing came in shallow, fast pants, and my dress felt like it was tightening around me, constricting my chest until I had no space for air.

Lucifer's gaze met mine with a dark smile, and he was triumphant. Proud. His eyes glowed red as he looked at me like he was encouraging my pleasure as well.

Because I was his queen.

And the worst thing was...a part of me wanted to smile back. To applaud him for what he'd done. They'd kidnapped Brandy. They'd threatened my lover. They'd tried to kill me. They deserved retribution.

As soon as everyone was upright again, I used their cover to take off running, sliding between bodies and moving as fast as I could while staying upright in my heels. My chest heaved as nausea roiled through me and my heart practically leaped out of my body. I made it to the elevator without anyone stopping me, but when I pressed the button, it wouldn't light up. Turning to see if anyone was trying to follow me, I noticed a door off to the right. With a fluorescent glow behind a small window, I realized what it was. A stairwell. Even demons needed an emergency exit.

I burst through the door and slipped my heels off, holding the skirt of the gorgeous gown as I sprinted up the stairs, my legs pumping and my lungs threatening to burst. We were a few flights down from the parking garage, and I shoved through the doors, then raced across the lot in my bare feet until I found another door leading to another stairwell outside. I had to get the fuck out of here.

As I stepped out into a side alley, I gulped in the fresh night air as panic threatened to overtake me. I'd known he was the devil. He'd said he was a villain. What had I expected? That he'd be someone different with me? Had I willfully ignored his dark side, or had I craved it? He'd never been anything but honest with me about what he was, but I'd been drawn to him anyway. He should have inspired fear in me rather than lust. But that was his job, after all. Temptation. *Sin.*

It didn't matter. The deal was over anyway. Tonight was the seventh night—Devil's Night—and I was done. Maybe I was Lucifer's reincarnated love, and maybe I wasn't, but either way, it was time to return to my real life. I didn't belong here. Not in this fancy hotel, not in these expensive clothes, and definitely not with the demons.

I put the shoes back on, not about to walk barefoot in a Las Vegas alley full of broken bottles and old piss. Then I pretended my feet weren't on fire as I shoved my panic to one side and summoned enough confidence to walk a straight line. No way I was going back in that hotel. I had a tiny little purse with a wad of cash and my phone in it, and that was enough to get me home.

A flash of light exploded nearby, the force and shock nearly knocking me over. A pair of gleaming copper wings were highlighted against the dark night sky, swooping down toward me, and in my already-panicked state I screamed. Strong hands grabbed me, lifting me up...and then everything went black.

24

LUCIFER

As I surveyed the room, taking in my followers and their show of loyalty, I wore a dark smile, my eyes glowing red. I hated doing shit like this, but it was necessary. A show of force to ensure they all knew I was their king. Demons needed a firm hand. Whatever this newfound conspiracy was, someone would come forward rather than risk my wrath. Then it would be settled. This shit had happened before and would happen again, and I'd deal with it every time.

Before I became king, the demonic tribes fought each other. When I left Heaven for Hell, I united the tribes under my banner, bringing order to the chaos. If it weren't for me, the vampires and shifters would still be at war, the dragons would still be slaves to the fae, and let's not forget the angels, who would have wiped out the lot of them if they'd had a chance. No matter how heavy my crown became, I never forgot that someone needed to rule the demonic horde, and it sure as shit had better be me.

Besides, I'd do whatever it took to save Hannah's life. If a show of force was needed to prevent more attacks and show she was completely off-limits, so be it.

As everyone rose and the music began playing again, I sank

down on my throne, waiting for Hannah to join me. I should have made them bring a second throne out for her, but they'd planned this night before she'd come back into my life. If she was still alive for the next ball, I'd make sure she reigned at my side.

The demons and Fallen went back to their conversations and I gazed around the room, searching for a glimpse of Hannah. I'd seen her briefly, but then she'd been swallowed by the crowd. I noticed Gadreel flirting with Lilith, whose smile was tight and her eyes wandered, like she'd rather be anywhere else. He'd always had a thing for her, but who didn't at some point? And Gadreel had always been ambitious. It was one of the reasons I'd thought he was interested in Lenore too.

I rose to my feet and people hushed around me as I scanned the crowd. Where was Hannah? Earlier she'd been sitting at the side tables, but she wasn't there now. Nor was she with Gadreel and Lilith, or Samael in the corner, or at the buffet or the bar. I didn't see Azazel either, who was meant to stay on Hannah's tail all night.

My chest tightened in panic. Where could Hannah have gone? Had someone taken her? Was I about to lose her again?

Clenching my fists, I strode through the crowd. They parted in front of me, out of respect or fear, and a quick search confirmed Hannah wasn't in the ballroom anymore. I went to the elevator, wondering if she'd retreated to the penthouse, but it wasn't working for some reason. Someone was going to pay for that later.

My heart beat faster as I launched through the door to the stairwell and took the steps two at a time, up a few flights to the parking garage. I looked left and right as I reached the top, taking in the empty space, and spotted a tiny crystal on the ground in the distance. From Hannah's dress. She'd definitely come this way.

Maybe she hadn't been taken. Maybe she had run away.

Was she upset by what she'd seen in there? Killing enemies was par for the course among supernaturals, but she still thought like a human. Dammit. I'd forgotten she was mortal, and how sensitive humans were to death and violence. She remembered nothing of her previous lives, which meant all of this was new to her. I'd only known her for seven days, and that wasn't nearly enough for the truth about who she was to sink in. No wonder she'd panicked. She'd started the week meeting Lucas Ifer to beg for help in finding her lost friend, and she'd finished at a demon's ball where Lucifer himself had killed traitors in front of her.

Before I could tame my thoughts, Azazel ran around the corner, wearing a short leather dress with blades strapped to her thighs. "Hannah!" She stopped and sucked in a breath, her eyes wide. "She's been taken!"

"What happened?" I grabbed her shoulders and held her firmly at arm's length as I searched her wild gaze. Azazel never panicked, but there was definitely something that had her spooked.

"I kept my eyes on Hannah all night, staying close to her from the shadows. When you executed those traitors, she freaked out and split. She ran for the elevator, but it didn't come."

"Then what?" I tried to keep my own panic from increasing. There weren't many places I couldn't rescue Hannah from. Except death.

"She ran up the stairs and took off walking through the alley. I followed in the shadows from a safe distance. She clearly needed to be alone, and I tried to respect that."

My grip tightened on her shoulders. "And then?"

"An angel swooped down and picked her up before I could get close enough to stop them. I tried to go after them, but I was hit with a blast of light, stronger than I expected." She ripped herself out of my arms, her eyes furious—and upset too. "It knocked me back, and I lost them."

"Tell me exactly what you saw." Perhaps I could work out which of my Heavenly brethren would be so bold. Why would they take Hannah? Were the angels making a play against me?

"Copper wings. Female. I couldn't see any other details." She shook her head, her face tormented. "I'm sorry, my lord. It was my duty to protect Hannah and I failed. I accept whatever punishment you deem fitting."

I stepped back, seething. Copper wings... I knew an angel like that. What I didn't know was why she would want Hannah.

Azazel kept her head bowed, awaiting my command. She'd been

ordered to guard Hannah and she'd failed, and now my mate had been kidnapped. She should be punished for her failure, and she knew it. But Hannah wouldn't want that. I felt that in my gut.

I turned away from her. "You are dismissed, Azazel."

"My lord?"

"I think I know who took Hannah." My eyes narrowed as red hot anger pulsed through my veins. "And I will handle this myself."

25

HANNAH

My head swam as I tried to pry my eyes open, but they were so heavy. Eventually, I managed to get them to crack open. The room was blessedly dark, curtains pulled tight, though a sliver of light filtered through. It was daytime, but where was I?

Something didn't feel right. This didn't smell like my lightly perfumed room in the penthouse, where even the expensive fabrics had a scent all their own. And it definitely wasn't Lucifer's room with his decadent black silk sheets.

I sat up in bed and rubbed my eyes. I was in another luxurious bedroom, tastefully done in shades of cream and dusky pink. The enormous room was sparsely furnished, but it had more of a deliberate minimalist vibe than feeling half-finished, and I was struck by the sheer size of the space. If I yelled out, it would echo. As I let my brain wake up and recover from the night before, I took in the smooth wood dresser and intricate sconces on the walls, both painted the same shade of pink. It was like waking up on the inside of a strawberry cream dessert.

This certainly didn't look like Lucifer's style. Not when I remembered all the black and silver that filled his spaces or the very safe neutrals that his guest room boasted. Where was I?

The bedroom door opened, and sunlight filled the room from the hall on the other side, putting whoever had opened the door in shadow. The person flicked the overhead light on, and the room illuminated. It took me a second to realize who had walked in while my eyes adjusted to the unexpected brightness.

When I saw the person holding a breakfast tray, my jaw dropped. "Jo? What are you doing here?"

My older sister gave me a droll look. "I live here."

I watched her walk around the bed, barely believing what I was seeing. Jo looked like her normal, beautiful self, with hair almost the same shade as mine that ended just above her shoulders. She'd always had a grace and sophistication I could never match, with her billowy frame and radiant skin. Even her nails were shiny and perfect. Pink, naturally.

"You're safe." She set the tray in front of me and poured us both some coffee. The situation felt strangely familiar, and eerily close to when I'd woken up in my apartment after the car wreck. My mind tried to piece together what had happened last night, but everything was fuzzy after Lucifer's display. But as my brain cleared and the coffee worked, I remembered more.

Someone had grabbed me in the alley of The Celestial. Someone with wings. Someone who knocked me out.

Someone who looked a lot like Jo.

I scooted back in the bed, suddenly desperate to put distance between us, not caring that the tray wobbled as I moved. Was no one as they appeared anymore? And why the hell could everyone fly?

"How do you have wings?" My tone was accusing, but I couldn't help it. For fuck's sake, my own sister—the last family member I had left—had knocked me out and kidnapped me. I was allowed to be a little upset. "Are you a Fallen too?"

She drew back and huffed, visibly offended. "Of course not. I'm an angel."

"An angel?" That didn't make me feel any better somehow, and it made no sense. "How is my sister an angel when I'm human?"

She sighed and seemed to choose her words carefully. "We were sisters in one of your former lives, when you were an angel. I've tried to protect you ever since."

I stared at her, the weight of her revelation almost more than I could handle after all the other things I'd endured in the last week. Was *everything* about my life a lie? Was I nothing but a collection of past lives, with people and events I couldn't remember, while everyone else could? I wanted to bury my head in the pillow and scream.

Jo must have sensed my inner turmoil because she stood. "Take your time and rest. Eat some breakfast. The shower is through that door, and the closet is beside it. I've put a few things in there you can wear." She moved to the door, lingering there as she twisted her hands together. "Come see me whenever you're ready."

She left me alone, which was a relief because I needed time to get my head on straight. I was still in my ball gown, and it was wrinkled to high heavens. Hopefully not ruined.

I was starving too, since all I'd eaten last night were a few fancy appetizers, and I devoured the omelet Jo had brought me. Then I took a quick shower and quickly dressed in a cream blouse and navy blue slacks that were obviously Jo's. Now that I was fully awake, I wanted answers from my so-called 'sister.'

I found Jo in the living room, a massive space all done in white and gold, with huge windows offering spectacular views of the bay, from the Golden Gate Bridge to Alcatraz Island. I automatically moved toward them, pressing my fingertips on the glass as I looked out. We were up on a hill, and a view like this, in a house this enormous, had to have cost a fortune.

I turned toward my sister. "Shit, Jo. I knew you had money, but..."

"I do all right for myself." She sat on a soft-looking sofa and watched me like I was an injured deer about to bolt away. "You've never been here, have you?"

I didn't reply. She knew fully well I'd never been here. If I had, maybe I wouldn't have been as overwhelmed by Lucifer's shows of wealth. I'd offered to come visit her numerous times in San Francisco, but she'd always made some kind of excuse, and had come to see me instead. Had she been hiding this from me, maybe even purposefully keeping me away to protect her secrets? Was anything about her true?

"Well, you're here now." She gave me an encouraging smile. "And I'm glad to have you as my guest."

Was I her guest? Or was I a captive again? I moved through the vast living room, taking in all the displays of wealth. Her aesthetic was the exact opposite of Lucifer's, with white trimmed in gold, and just like his place, it was seriously lacking in plants and flowers. A display case held dozens of tiny little angel figurines, some looking quite old, others made of crystal. I studied them as I asked, "Why did you bring me here?"

Jo clasped her hands in her lap as she looked up at me. "I had to get you away from Lucifer. You're in danger around him. As long as you stay here, I can keep you safe."

"Jo, you don't understand. Lucifer is my mate. I've had all these past lives with him. He isn't a threat to me." Or was he? After what I'd seen last night, I wasn't so sure.

"I understand more than you do. I've lived an awfully long time, and I've seen many of those past lives of yours. What you don't understand is that Lucifer is the villain. He's been lying to you this entire time. Manipulating you. Controlling you. As he's done with all humans for thousands of years." She tilted her head, her eyes full of pity. "Did he even tell you about Adam and Eve?"

I hated to admit there was something Lucifer hadn't told me, but I had to know what she was talking about. "No, he didn't."

Her mouth took on a sad smile. "I thought not. Why am I not surprised somehow?"

Her superior tone grated at me. This particular tone was so familiar that it must've bugged me in one of my lives before, and my subconscious knew it. I tried not to glare at her. "What about Adam and Eve?"

"Your very first life was as Eve."

My heart skipped a beat, or maybe even stopped for a full minute. "*The* Eve?"

"Yes, the very one."

I blinked at her several times as I tried to process this new revelation. "How?"

"You were married to Adam and had three sons with him, but then Lucifer abducted you and claimed you as his mate. Adam wasn't happy about that, as you can imagine, and he sought revenge. He killed you."

I blew out a breath as I processed everything she'd said. Hearing about my past lives was always a combination of difficult and intriguing, but this one was especially hard for me to believe, if not for the sense of rightness in my gut when she spoke.

A week ago I'd been book-loving Hannah from the florist shop. Now I was Eve. Persephone. Lenore. All great women from literature and mythology. Talk about a heavy legacy to live up to.

I dropped onto the couch across from Jo. "That is pretty shocking, but I don't see why that puts me in danger from Lucifer."

The pitying look in her eyes increased ten-fold. "There's more. I'm just not sure you're ready to hear it yet."

"Just tell me already," I snapped. Damn, I was so tired of everyone knowing the truth about myself except for me.

"After your death, all three of you were cursed for all eternity. Your fate is to be reborn and die violently, usually in Lucifer's arms, in an endless cycle of death and agony. Lucifer's curse is knowing this will happen and being unable to stop it. And Adam's curse is to be reborn every time you are...and to kill you again and again, before dying at Lucifer's hand."

"No, that...that can't be true." I recoiled in horror, my pulse spiking through the roof. It was suddenly hard to breathe, but I managed to suck in a ragged breath somehow.

Jo came to sit beside me and rested a warm hand on my back. "I'm so sorry, Hannah. I wish it wasn't true. But deep down you know it is, don't you?"

I nodded, but then my head dropped and my vision blurred. I found myself in Jo's arms, leaning against her as she held me close, like she had in those early days after the car accident. Like she was still my sister.

Why hadn't Lucifer told me any of this? He'd been slowly

doling out information to try to stop me from getting overwhelmed, but this seemed important. Maybe he was right though—this was really fucking overwhelming.

Or maybe he worried I wouldn't live long enough for it to matter.

Was that what was happening here? Was it time for me to die now that I'd found Lucifer again?

And where was Adam in this life? Were all the attacks his doing?

"Who cursed us?" I asked, gripping Jo's shirt as I looked up at her with wide, desperate eyes. "Is there a way to end it?"

"I don't know," Jo said, as she drew me into a hug again. "I wish I did."

An endless cycle of death and agony. That was my fate. And there was no way to escape it.

26

HANNAH

Once again, I found myself in a vast library, although this one wasn't as impressive as Lucifer's. Jo had a large collection of books, but she lacked the ancient vases and dark artwork that made Lucifer's library so remarkable.

I'd retreated here after speaking with Jo, when everything she'd told me had just seemed too big and impossible. When life became too much, the best solution was to retreat into a good book, or turn to them in the hopes of finding answers.

With a book on demonology in my lap, I sat in a white suede chair near windows overlooking the bay. The sun had turned the sky the entire range of reds, golds, and yellows as it sank down to the horizon. Sunset on Halloween, and not at all where I'd expected to be.

I'd spent the last few hours reading up on angels, demons, and the devil. I'd perused everything from Dante's Inferno to some ancient scrolls Jo had that required me to use gloves. Every single thing I read depicted the devil as evil incarnate. A beast. A monster. In every story of good and evil throughout all time he was the villain.

How could I have been so wrong about Lucifer? Had he been

deceiving me, tricking me into caring for him? How could I reconcile the man I knew in private with the one I'd read about in these books, or the dark king I'd seen at the Devil's Night ball?

Was Lucifer the root of all evil, or the thoughtful, protective man who'd do anything for me? Was he the villain in this story, or the one keeping the demons in line and the humans safe from them?

Unfortunately, coming to the library had only saddled me with more questions this time.

The doorbell rang, and I decided that was a sign I should take a break anyway. I headed for the front door, just as Jo ran in with a sword in her hand and a fierce look in her eye.

"Don't open that!" she yelled. "It might be someone after you."

"I doubt they'd ring the doorbell if they were trying to kill me," I muttered.

Jo checked the security camera and lowered her sword, then grabbed a bowl shaped like a pumpkin sitting by the door. "Just some kids. I forgot it was Halloween."

With a chuckle, I opened the door to a trio of trick-or-treaters. One of them was dressed as a little red devil, to my great amusement, though Jo's tight smile told me she didn't feel the same. We dropped some candy in their bags and then they scampered off to the next house. I smiled after them, enjoying the brief moment of normalcy.

As I turned away and began to close the door, it suddenly slammed open, crashing against the wall. Something cold and dark passed through me, and when Jo and I whirled around, Lucifer stood behind us. His black wings were spread wide as darkness swirled around him and his eyes blazed red. Shadows played across his face and his hands were clenched in fists at his side. He looked pissed as hell, and my traitorous heart beat faster and filled me with longing.

His gaze raked over me, like he was checking I was unharmed, before they landed on Jo. The entire room got darker and colder, like his anger was sucking all light and warmth from the surroundings. Jo raised her sword, which now glowed white, while Lucifer conjured a shadowy blade of his own made of pure darkness. Then he surged forward toward her.

With my heart in my throat I dodged in front of him, blocking Jo with my body, certain that neither of them would hurt me. "Stop!" I yelled. "That's my sister!"

Lucifer drew back, his inky dark sword held high as he looked from me to Jo. "How is that possible?"

"It was in one of my past lives," I explained, though it hit me then that Lucifer should probably know that... Shouldn't he?

They stared at each other with hard expressions, until some sort of understanding passed between them, but that only made him angrier. His voice grew so loud it shook the walls. "Did you do what I think you did?"

"I had to," Jo said. "All I want is to protect her. From Adam. From you." She pointed her glowing sword at him. "It's always you!"

"I'm her mate!" he roared.

I watched them like I was a spectator at a tennis match, back and forth as they yelled and exchanged meaningful looks. There was clearly a lot more to this story than either of them had told me. I wanted to snatch away both their swords and give them each a time-out.

I held up my hands between them. "I wish someone would let me in on what the *fuck* you're both talking about! I'm sick of everyone hiding things from me. Can I have the whole truth, please? And put your damn weapons away already!"

Lucifer's darkness blade disappeared like vanishing smoke. He spread his hands and bowed his head, as if to say he'd play nice. I looked at Jo and narrowed my eyes a little. She sighed and put her sword on the entry table.

"May I have a moment alone with Hannah?" Lucifer asked. I was surprised by how polite his voice had become. "I promise I won't steal her away."

"Absolutely not," Jo declared. "Out of the question."

I turned to her. "I'll be fine. I spent a week with him and I'm unharmed, aren't I? And if I want answers, how else can I get them if I don't talk to him?"

"Fine." She huffed as she narrowed her eyes at Lucifer over my shoulder. "You can use the library, but I'll be in the living room. And leave the door open!"

I rolled my eyes. What was I, a teenager with her first boyfriend?

I led Lucifer into the library, where he eyed all the books I'd pulled out. He picked up the copy of Dante's Inferno and snorted, shaking his head as he tossed it back in the pile.

"I see you've been doing some research," he said, his voice dripping with disdain.

"Is it true?" I asked in a low voice. "Am I Eve?"

"Yes, it's true." He arched an eyebrow. "What else did Jophiel tell you?"

"Jophiel?" To me she'd always been Jo. I'd just assumed it was short for Joanna all this time. Now I was beginning to realize I didn't know a single thing about her.

"Indeed. Your 'sister' is an Archangel. Did she mention that?"

I pinched the bridge of my nose, trying to contain my frustration. "No, she left that part out."

"Of course she did." He reached for me, but I quickly stepped back, and he paused. "Are you afraid of me?"

"No, I just..." I turned away and drew in a breath. "I have a lot of questions."

He sank down in the chair I was sitting in earlier and leaned back, then gestured lazily at me. "Ask away, darling."

"Is it true that I was married to Adam before you? That you abducted me and made me your mate?"

He let out a sharp laugh. "Abducted is a strong word. Trust me, you weren't happy being married to Adam. He was still in love with his first wife, Lilith, and he had a horrible temper. He's the kind of man who charms you with flowers, poems, and promises, and only once he has you in his grasp does he reveal his dark side."

"And you're not the same?"

"No, I'm completely up front about my villainous nature." He smirked at me as he leaned forward. "You ran away with me to escape Adam."

I swallowed hard. "But he followed us. And then...he killed me."

Lucifer's eyes darkened. "He did."

"And this curse? Is that real too?" I clenched my throat, suddenly finding it hard to breathe. "Is my fate to die over and over at Adam's hand?"

He rose to his feet and stepped toward me, with pain and sadness written across his face. "I wish I could tell you that wasn't true, but I never lie to you, Hannah." He reached up to touch my cheek, and this time I didn't flinch away. "I've watched you die hundreds of times, and each time my heart shatters into a million pieces. My only solace is that I know one day you'll return to me, but it's little comfort as you take your last breath in my arms." Darkness swirled around him like angry tentacles. "And then I usually rip that fucker's heart out."

An endless cycle of love and death, for all eternity. I blinked back the emotions threatening to drown me. "Why didn't you tell me?"

He brushed his thumb under my eye, catching a tear before it fell. "It wasn't the right time. You were just beginning to accept the supernatural world and your place in it as my mate. How could I add this burden on top of everything else? I planned to tell you about the curse eventually, but only when you were ready."

"I'm not sure it's possible to ever be ready for a revelation like this." I drew in a ragged breath. "Do you know where Adam is now? Do you think he's behind the attacks?"

"I don't know." Tension tightened the corners of Lucifer's mouth. "My people have been looking for him, but haven't found anything yet. All we know is that he must be human, since he's reborn in a pair with you. It seems unlikely he could be behind the attacks unless he's sided with some of the Archdemons somehow. Though he has gotten very crafty over the years..." His voice trailed off as he considered, but then he met my eyes again. "It's more likely the Archdemons are trying to overthrow me again. It happens now and then, but my display at the ball should make them reconsider."

I shuddered a little at the memory. The darkness holding the traitors in place, the blue hellfire that turned them to ash, the way everyone bowed... And the worst part of all, how it had secretly thrilled me, deep down, to see them punished.

"It bothered you, I see," he said, cocking his head. "When I couldn't find you at the ball, I feared the worst, but then I suspected you might have run away. I was almost relieved when I'd learned Jophiel had taken you."

"I *did* run away." I stepped back from him, my eyes wide. "I'm not sure what to make of you, Lucifer. History doesn't exactly paint you in the best light. And in every one of these—" I indicated my large pile of books. "They tell the same story, over and over—that the devil is the personification of evil."

"They also say I have horns and a pitchfork, and that's obviously not true." He cast a dismissive glance at my pile of books. "History was written by the angels, who have long sought control over Earth. They've hated me ever since I rebuffed their control and fought for humans to have free will. They paint me as the villain, making me their scapegoat, blaming all evil on me. As if any one person could have such power."

He sounded bitter, but there was something else in his voice too. Vulnerability. Pain. Despite all my hesitations and fears, my heart ached for him. If he was telling the truth and they'd made him out to be this horrible monster that he wasn't, that was incredibly sad. It would be a hard life to live, and lonely too. Especially in the long years while he waited for me to be reborn.

But was Lucifer telling the truth? Or was he deceiving me? I couldn't tell. I'd learned so much about myself and the world over the past eight days, but I wasn't sure of anything anymore.

"Lucifer I... I need some time to think."

He moved close and touched my face again, with the lightest of caresses. "I know this is a lot for you to take in, but it will all make sense in time. Come back with me to the penthouse. You know in your soul we're meant to be together, even if you're uncertain about everything else. Your place is by my side, ruling as my dark queen."

I pulled back, out of his grip, and shook my head. "I'm not ready for that. It's too much. Please just...give me some space for now."

"You want me to leave."

"Yes. Go. Please. Before this gets any harder."

He searched my eyes, like he didn't want to believe what I was saying, but then he bowed his head and stepped back. Without another word, thick darkness swirled around him, the shadows dancing and claiming him as their king.

When it cleared, he was gone.

27

LUCIFER

S pace. Hannah wanted *space*.

Fine. I could give her that. For now.

But that didn't mean my business here was finished.

Using my power to become darkness, I slipped through Jophiel's extravagant house until I found her office. White walls, white distressed desk, white chair... What a bore Jophiel was. If she hadn't been an Archangel and the CEO of Aether Industries, she'd hardly be worth my notice. Except now it seemed she was apparently Hannah's sister, though that was impossible. To my knowledge, Hannah had never been an angel in any of her past lives, and she certainly wasn't one now. Her wings would have long emerged by now if she had been—plus I would have sensed it.

I pushed back Jophiel's white chair and sat in it, then kicked my feet up on her desk, knowing the sight of me invading her space would drive her mad. It only took a few minutes of playing on my phone before she arrived.

She jumped when she saw me at her desk, and then her eyes narrowed with a look of pure, unadulterated hatred. "What do you want?"

The sight of her made my blood boil too, but I flashed her a devilish smile. "I want the truth. Isn't that your area of expertise?"

Her mouth twitched at that. As an Ofanim, Jophiel was an angel of truth...and was one of the best at concealing it. All Archangels had a special, unique power—and Jophiel's allowed her to erase or hide memories. "The truth will only hurt Hannah."

"I'll be the one to decide that." I rose from her desk slowly, the shadows gathering behind me like menacing wings. "You stole some of my memories, didn't you? Of a past life where Hannah was an angel. And your sister, apparently. Now you're going to put them back."

She raised her haughty little nose. "Why should I?"

I turned to shadow for a split second to glide through the desk, then I grabbed her by the throat while my eyes turned red with rage. "Because I demand it."

We stared each other down, her body glowing with light and power as she faced me. The high and mighty Jophiel and I had never gotten along. For years, she'd blamed me for killing her former lover, Archangel Michael, even though I never would've done such a thing. He and I had once been enemies, that much was true, but we'd worked too hard to end the war and establish peace between angels and demons. Why would I kill him after all that effort? His death nearly undid the treaties as it was. Now we knew Archangel Azrael was behind Michael's death, and he was in Penumbra Prison —a place where the angels, demons, and fae kept the worst supernaturals locked up. Yet she still hated me.

"I don't take orders from you," she finally gritted out.

I tightened my fingers around her throat, my darkness filling the room like ink. "Not even you can resist an order from the devil."

"Villain," she muttered. "All you do is lie and kill."

I arched an eyebrow. "Enlighten me on the truth then. You know I didn't kill Michael."

"But you did kill my father!"

I rolled my eyes. Not that old excuse for her continued behavior. "Phanuel attacked me, as you well know. It was self-defense and we were at war then. We aren't any longer."

That only made her glare harder at me. "Not at war? Tell that to the angels and demons who died at Seraphim Academy last year."

"We both know that was Azrael's doing." I cocked my head. "Wasn't he your former lover as well? I heard the other Archangels have been suspicious about your loyalties lately."

"My loyalties are to other angels and to my family," she snapped. "Including Hannah. It's your fault she's doomed to die, over and over. I won't let you hurt her again."

I sensed she was talking about something specific, something from this past life of Hannah's that I couldn't remember. My anger exploded and wrapped inky darkness around her. "Show me," I demanded, and even the Archangel Jophiel couldn't deny a command from the King of Hell.

She finally relented with a sharp nod, and I let go of her. She drew in a ragged breath and then reached up to touch my forehead. Light burst in front of my eyes and warmth flooded my skull, radiating out from Jophiel's touch as memories rushed through my mind. My anger washed away, replaced with a potent mix of happiness, pain, and grief, and I nearly stumbled under the weight of it. Within seconds I was hit with everything from the relief of finding my mate alive again, to the joy of being with her every moment I could, to the heartbreak of losing her.

I stepped back and bent over, gripping my head, as the memories consumed me. Our first meeting, our first kiss, our first time making love. Long talks into the night where she made me question my beliefs. Flying together, her wings silvery white against the moonlight. And then losing her in a way too painful to even focus on.

When all of it faded to a bearable level, I was left with the true knowledge of Hannah's angelic life, and what the two of us had shared together.

And everything we'd lost.

My anger returned with greater fervor than before, making it hard for me to even think. An entire life with Hannah had been erased from my memories by Jophiel, who had no right to do such a thing. I held myself tense as I spoke through gritted teeth, then lifted my red eyes to Jophiel again. "How dare you? You've hidden this from me for years. Not to mention what you did to Hannah..."

"I only did it to protect her!" Jophiel said, as she stepped back from my rising darkness. There was nowhere for her to go. Her back hit the door and she glowed brighter, but she wasn't a fighter. Not really. We both knew she had no chance against me.

"I should make you pay for what you've done." My magic gathered around me as my wings unfurled, my darkness eager to do my bidding. I breathed through it, the desire to lash out and punish her for her actions almost overwhelming every other thought in my head. It would be so easy to let the darkness tear her apart limb by limb, a fitting punishment for her crimes, which I now knew went above and beyond erasing memories. But then I thought of Hannah in the other room, and the way she'd jumped in front of me to save this wretched angel. No matter what Jophiel had done, they were sisters, and I couldn't hurt her.

I reined in my dark desires with effort. When I folded my wings and snapped them away, the shadows receded. "I won't punish you." Then I smiled, and not in a nice way. "No, I'll let Hannah do that when she learns what you've done."

Jophiel shuddered a little, but then looked me in the eye. "We both know my actions have kept her alive this long. Leave Hannah here with me. I can protect her better than you can."

"Never," I growled. "Her place is by my side."

The second I said the words, doubt crept in. Perhaps the angels could do a better job of keeping Hannah safe. I'd done a shit job at it for thousands of years, after all. This newly remembered life of hers only proved that even more. Every time she was reborn, I swore to myself I'd protect her and that this time it would be different, and then I failed. Over and over.

My memories weighed heavily on me as though they were as fresh as the day they were created, and though I detested Jophiel, I knew she would protect Hannah with her life. Yet I couldn't give up my mate completely either.

I moved to the window beside Jophiel's desk. "I'll leave Hannah with you...for now. But when she wishes to return to me, you must allow her to do so."

She sniffed, back to being haughty. "Shall we make a deal for her time, like you did with Demeter over Persephone?"

I should have known she'd get in one last jab by reminding me of that mistake. "I'm done making deals."

I pinned her with a dark look, before turning to shadows once again and heading outside, into the night. I hovered there, invisible to any mortal who might look up at the sky, as I watched Hannah through the library windows.

Children walked along the street below me in their costumes, many of them dressed as the creatures of the night I ruled over, while Hannah leafed through book after book. Reading about me, no doubt.

Halloween had always been my favorite of Earth's holidays—a night when everyone embraced their inner wickedness and allowed themselves to love the darkness. Tonight though, it was me who was haunted.

My chest ached as I watched Hannah, wishing I could go to her, but doing my best to respect her wishes. I reached out as though I could touch her, imagining her soft skin under my fingertips, then clenched my hand into a fist. Damn this curse. It had killed her hundreds of times, putting her through so much agony, more than any one mind could possibly bear. No wonder she could only see glimpses of her past in her dreams. Anything more would shatter her mind. And me? The curse had destroyed me emotionally over and over, hundreds of times throughout the years, and would continue to destroy me still.

Could I go through this again? Could she? How many more times must we suffer?

Perhaps it was time to end this curse...but I didn't know if I could bring myself to do the only thing that would stop it.

The price was far too high. A sacrifice, and one I'm not sure I could make.

28

HANNAH

S unlight wanted me to wake up, but I clamped my pillow over my head and ignored the bright, shining ball of fire in the sky. After Lucifer had left, I'd sat at the table in the library, reading about angels and demons until well into the night. When my eyelids had started drooping, I'd come to lie down in the bedroom Jo had let me use, hoping that staying up so late would help me sleep better.

I should have known that wouldn't work. It never did.

Violence had crowded my dreams, and what I now knew were events from my past lives had echoed through my head, leaving me sweaty, rumpled, and still tired. Gadreel had been in one of them, wielding a sword, presumably from my life as Lenore. I didn't remember any of the other dreams except in snippets that disappeared like fog when I tried to chase them.

No matter how hard I tried, I couldn't get back to sleep. I rolled over and groaned. In all the time since the accident, only when I slept beside Lucifer had I slept well.

Lucifer... My heart ached at the thought of him. After only a few days of knowing him, I already missed his presence, even though I wasn't sure how I felt about him. Or what my place in the world was anymore.

When I walked into the huge, white, gleaming kitchen, Jo looked up in surprise. "I was just about to wake you. I made breakfast, if you're hungry. Eggs, bacon, and toast."

"Thanks," I mumbled, as I headed straight for the coffee pot. I still wasn't happy with my 'sister,' and I couldn't pretend otherwise. She'd hidden so much from me, and I suspected there were so many more things she hadn't told me yet. But she was an angel...one of the good guys? Right? Or was that a lie too?

"You made the right choice by staying here," Jo said with a self-righteous smile, as she made up a plate for me. "I can protect you from Lucifer."

I grabbed the plate from her hand, annoyed at her words, but also hungry. Did I need protection from Lucifer or from her? Jo —Jophiel—wasn't even my real sister, and she'd lied to me for years.

"Is anything about my life real?" I asked, as I sat at her round breakfast table.

Jo took a chair across from me. "Our relationship is real. That's never been fake."

"But you're an Archangel!" I sputtered, then glanced around the house, which was like something out of an HGTV show about mansions I could never afford. "I'm only realizing now how little I knew about your life. How separate you kept me from it. How you knew all this time I was Lucifer's mate and didn't tell me."

"Only to keep you safe." She spread her hands out on the table. "Hannah, I had to keep my life separate from yours to protect you. If you came to visit me, for example, you might attract the attention of others in the supernatural world, which I knew could lead Lucifer and Adam to you. But if you went about your life believing you were an ordinary human, you'd remain hidden."

I was getting tired of everyone knowing the truth except for me and using the excuse of trying to keep me safe like it absolved them of all their crimes. But at the same time, maybe I was alive now because of Jophiel's actions.

"What about the accident? My parents?"

Jophiel's face turned pained. "Your parents are dead. I didn't lie about that."

I sensed that was true, at least. I took a moment to eat some of my food, which was delicious. I wondered if Jophiel had really made it. I'd never seen her cook before.

"You can stay with me as long as you like," Jophiel continued, a smile lighting her face. "Now that you know about the supernatural world, I no longer have to hide things from you. I can tell you all about your life as an angel. Oh, you can even meet my sons!"

I nearly choked on my bacon. "Sons?"

She nodded, her eyes proud. "Yes, I have two of them. Callan and Ekariel. Callan is the son of Archangel Michael and Ekariel is the son of Archangel Azrael, though I hope you won't hold that against him..."

The more Jophiel talked, the more I felt like she was a stranger, and like my entire life was a lie. The only thing that felt real anymore was the time I'd spent with Lucifer. How did that make sense?

I pushed my plate away and buried my face in my hands. "All I want is to go back to my old life of a week ago, when I was just Hannah who worked at a flower shop and lived in Vista. Hannah, who didn't know about angels and demons and past lives, and had no one trying to kill her. But that's impossible now. There's no forgetting this."

Jophiel rested a light hand on my back, as if to comfort me. "Actually, it is possible. I can remove your memories and make you forget all of this ever happened. I could hide you from both Lucifer and Adam. You could go back to being an ordinary human again who knows nothing of the supernatural world."

I looked up at her. "How?"

"It's one of my angelic gifts."

The idea was tempting, but only for a second. I shook my head with a sigh. "No, I don't really want to forget. I don't think it's possible to run away or hide from this anymore. This is my life, my curse, and my fate. I have to accept it. Somehow." I drew in a ragged breath, but then sat up straighter. "And I will. Eventually."

"And then you'll die again and start all over," Jophiel said, her voice sorrowful. "I don't want to lose you, Hannah. I realize you feel like you don't know who I am anymore, but to me, you're still my sister and I love you."

I started to say the words back to her too, but I couldn't get them out. I didn't know how I felt about anything at the moment. Especially her.

From across the house came the faint sound of my phone ringing, saving me from having to answer Jophiel. I set the coffee mug down and hurried to the guest room just in time to see Brandy's name flash across the screen.

"Hey Brandy." I glanced at the hallway, out where Jophiel was, and decided to step onto the balcony. "Are you okay?"

"I'm fine. Good, actually. How are *you* though? I've been texting you, but you haven't answered. I got worried and had to resort to actually using my phone to make a call, ick."

I laughed, and it was so nice to have a moment of levity after the events of the last few days. Damn, I missed Brandy and her cheerful, stubborn exuberance. No matter how much life shit on her, she always found a reason to smile.

"Things are...complicated," I admitted. "I've learned a lot of things over the last few days that have made me question my entire life."

"What sort of things?"

I leaned against the balcony railing and stared across the bay covered with wispy fog, while the cool air tickled my hair. "Things like I'm supposedly Lucifer's soulmate. And I've lived hundreds of lives before this one."

"What? Like some reincarnation thing?"

"Exactly like that. Lucifer finds me in each life, but our happiness never lasts."

Brandy let out a low whistle. "That's some deep shit right there."

"No kidding. I'm at my sister's house now. Which is also complicated." I blew out a breath, suddenly really tired of my problems. "Tell me what's been going on with you. Did you get home safely? How's Jack? And Donna?"

"They're both good, and yes, I got home fine. Lucifer made sure of that. He also paid all our bills for this month and the next, to cover the time off we both had to take from work. I could hardly believe it."

"I had no idea." I pressed a hand to my chest as the longing for Lucifer became so strong it actually hurt. It was just like him to do something like that, without even telling me.

"I thought I was done with demons," Brandy continued. "I told myself it was for the best, too. But I couldn't stop thinking about Mo, I mean, Asmodeus. Then he showed up at my front door in the middle of the night. He said the two of you talked, and then he got in his car immediately to come see me. So whatever you said to him, thank you."

"I just told him he should talk to you. The rest was all him."

"And we did talk, and so much more..." She giggled, like she was sharing a naughty secret. "Let's just say the Lilim's reputation as sex demons is well-deserved. Then he went trick-or-treating with me and Jack. Can you believe that?"

It was hard to imagine Asmodeus going trick-or-treating with a little kid, but it definitely proved he cared a lot for her, and made me like him even more. "Asmodeus said there might be a way for you to be together?"

"He told me the same thing, but it sounds dangerous. He's gone back to Vegas to speak to his mother about it." She let out a dreamy sigh. "It's crazy but...I think he's the one. Maybe this soulmates stuff is actually real. I mean, I never in a million years would've guessed I'd fall for a demon, or that they even existed, but here we are."

I stared across the bay, though my heart was somewhere else entirely. "I know exactly how you feel."

"Do you?" Brandy asked. "Because if so, then what the fuck are you doing at your sister's house?"

I bit out a laugh at her bluntness. "Like I said, it's complicated." I closed my eyes as my voice lowered to almost a whisper. "He's the *devil*, Brandy. Red eyes. Black wings. Hellfire. The actual devil."

"Well, no man is perfect."

"I'm serious. I've... I've seen him kill people."

She was silent for a moment. "Did they deserve it?"

I chewed on my lip as I considered. "One was involved in your kidnapping. The others tried to kill me."

"Then you have your answer. He was protecting his family in the only way he knew how. Just like you did when you came to Vegas to find me."

"That's not really the same thing..."

Her voice softened. "Hannah, you have the best heart of anyone I know. Follow it, and I know it won't lead you astray."

My throat choked up a little at her kind words. Jophiel may call herself my sister, but Brandy was the one who'd always been there for me and never kept secrets. She was the true sister of my heart. If she thought I should give Lucifer another shot, even after knowing everything we did about demons, then maybe I wasn't crazy for wanting the same thing.

"I love you," I told her, my pulse racing faster as I made my decision. "And I'm going to follow my heart. Back to Vegas."

"I love you too, and you better call me and tell me everything that happens."

"I will, I promise. Say hi to Jack and Donna. I'm not sure when I'll be back."

"As long as Lucifer keeps paying your bills, it's not a problem," she said, with a joking tone. "But seriously. I won't ever forget what you did for me. I've got your back, no matter what happens."

"Thanks, Brandy."

We said our goodbyes and hung up, promising to keep each other updated. I wanted to hear what happened with Asmodeus too, and if they found a way to be together. But first I had to get back to Lucifer. I wasn't sure about much of anything anymore, except that I only felt like myself when I was by his side. Maybe he was a villain to the rest of the world, but to me, he'd always been a hero.

I went inside and put back on the sparkling black gown and uncomfortable heels from the ball, leaving Jo's clothes behind. Then I shoved my phone back in my tiny little purse and checked my cash. I had plenty to cover gas money and a pair of flip-flops, because no way was I driving for hours in these freaking heels.

I stepped out into the hallway and glanced around, but didn't see or hear Jophiel anywhere. I considered finding her and explaining that I had to go, but I honestly wasn't sure she'd let me leave. She'd try anything to make me stay. Anything to prevent me from returning to Vegas—to Lucifer.

But fuck that. This was my life, and I was taking control of it.

Yesterday Jophiel had given me a brief tour of her gigantic mansion, including her four-car garage, and that's where I was headed now. Once there, I found a panel by the door that had a row of key fobs, which no doubt unlocked one of the ridiculously expensive cars before me. I took a moment to eye up the cars—a burgundy Porsche SUV, a black classic Rolls Royce, a yellow Lamborghini, and a silver Audi—and then grabbed a pair of keys. I rushed over to the Lamborghini, because when you're stealing a car from your angelic 'sister', you might as well go big.

When I got on the street, I found the button to put the top down and cranked the radio. My hair blew out behind me, immediately getting tangled up, and I kicked off the heels and tossed them to the passenger seat.

Vegas, I was coming for you. Consequences be damned.

29

LUCIFER

After my encounter with Jophiel, I returned to Vegas, keeping my word to give Hannah some space even though it tore me apart to do so. Besides, my people still needed a king, and Samael said he wished to speak with me. I had some questions for him too.

The sun had barely risen by the time I arrived in his office. He was on his computer, completely absorbed in whatever he was looking at, but he glanced up sharply as I entered.

"Did you find Hannah?" he asked.

"Yes, she was taken by Jophiel." I slammed my hands down on his desk, making him jump. "The Archangel gave me back my memories. Turns out, my mate was once an angel, and we were together before the Earth Accords were signed, when our relationship was forbidden. No one knew about us, except Jophiel...and my most trusted advisor."

Samael's chair squeaked as he rolled back and looked at me in alarm. "Lucifer, I can explain—"

I clenched my teeth. "You kept this a secret for years. Why didn't you say anything?"

"I thought the pain would be too intense. I thought it might be better if you didn't know. Less agonizing. For both you and

Hannah." The look on his face, the twist to his mouth, said he was tortured by the decision, but that only made me angrier.

"Keeping those secrets was not your decision to make." I kept the desk between us, or I would've been too tempted to grab his throat like I'd done with Jophiel. "Did you set up Brandy's kidnapping to bring Hannah back to me? Are you behind the attacks on my mate's life?"

He held his hands up in supplication. "Of course not. I wanted to keep Hannah away from you, not bring you together. I assumed Jophiel had her hidden somewhere, but that suited my ends. It kept you both safe and alive."

"Not safe enough. Someone found her and brought her here." I fixed him with a glare as I asked questions I'd never wanted to voice. "Have you ever thought about taking my place? Or becoming the leader of the Fallen?"

He drew his shoulders back. "I'm offended you would even ask me such a thing. I've been your closest friend for thousands of years and have always served you well. You're questioning my loyalty when I've never given you any reason to do so."

"You're the only other person who knew about Hannah's life as an angel. What was I supposed to think?"

"There is someone else who knew. Adam." Samael returned to his desk and took a seat. "That's why I asked you to meet me, actually. At the ball, Gadreel told me he'd tracked down a human who might be Adam."

"Where?"

"He didn't say."

I took the chair across from Samael and stroked the rough stubble on my chin as I considered this news, my gut telling me something wasn't right. I scoured my memories, including the ones Jophiel had just returned to me.

When Eve had been reborn as an angel, I'd believed only Samael knew about our relationship, but maybe I was wrong. Maybe someone else knew too. I'd never found Adam in that life—normally I tracked him down and killed him as retribution for what he'd done to my mate, but Jophiel intervened first and took my memories. I never even knew what he looked like. Could he still be alive?

In every life, Adam was reincarnated as a pair with Eve. If she was born human, so was he. Except when she was Lenore. The one who'd killed her was an angel, according to Gadreel. When I'd found them, there'd been a dead angel beside her, his sword covered in her blood, and I'd simply assumed that the curse didn't differentiate between an angel and a Fallen.

But what if it did?

Now someone had lured Hannah to Las Vegas, for the sake of bringing her back to me. Why? Just to take her away again, knowing it would hurt me more now that we'd found each other. But how?

My mind followed the trail of clues. Asmodeus said he'd received a text from Samael ordering him to seduce her, but Samael claimed he'd never sent it. It had to be someone close to us, someone who knew too much, who had access to everything.

Someone like Samael's assistant.

Someone who spent too much time chasing both Lenore and Lilith.

Gadreel.

Could it be? Could Gadreel be Adam? Had he somehow defied the curse and stayed alive when Eve was reincarnated again and again?

I leaned forward, anger simmering under my skin. "Where is Gadreel now?"

Samael's mouth tightened. "I haven't seen him since the ball."

Darkness swirled around me. My fury couldn't be contained, and with it came fear for Hannah's life. She was in more danger than I'd realized. "Find him, and bring him to me. Now."

30

HANNAH

The drive from San Francisco to Las Vegas took way longer than I expected, and even with only a few quick stops, it took me the entire day to get there. By the time I rushed up to Lucifer's penthouse, night had fallen and The Celestial was waking up. Vegas truly was a perfect city for demons, where most of the action happened after dark.

I found Lucifer in his library sitting behind his desk, a glass of whiskey beside him and an ancient-looking tome in his hands. He rose to his feet as soon as he saw me, and my heart skipped a beat as our eyes met and I was hit with the full force of his magnetic presence. Then he quickly crossed the room in a few long strides and swept me into his strong arms. Before I knew what was happening, his mouth came down on mine and he kissed me hard, as if he hadn't seen me in years, while his fingers tangled in my hair like he was never going to let me go. My hands gripped his soft white shirt while his tongue swept against mine and I wondered how I ever thought I could live without this man.

My *mate*.

"You came back to me." He pulled back just enough to study my face. "You had us all worried."

I was still dazed from his kiss and it took a second for his words to register. "Worried?"

"Jophiel texted me when you drove off with her car. Nice choice, by the way." His lips quirked up in amusement as his thumb idly stroked my cheek. "Both of our people have been looking for you ever since. You shouldn't have driven all that way without anyone protecting you."

I shook my head. "Lucifer, I can't live in fear all the time. I may be cursed to die, but I'm ready to accept my life by your side. For however long we have."

"Even though I'm a villain? A monster? The root of all evil?" His eyes gleamed red as he spoke, as if he were challenging me to run away again.

I reached up to stroke his eyebrows and the dark stubble on his jaw while I gazed at him, accepting him completely, red eyes and all. "I don't care how the world sees you. You're not evil. Not to me."

He gripped my arms tightly. "Only because of you. Your light keeps me from turning completely to darkness. I would be lost without you."

I trailed my fingers down his neck. "I'm here. I'm yours."

He closed his eyes and inhaled sharply. "Say it again."

Sliding a hand behind his neck, I drew his face down to mine and brushed my lips across his. "I'm yours."

"Yes, you are." He yanked me against him and turned my soft kiss into something much more, something that made red hot desire race across my skin. "Across the vastness of time, you're the one thing that stays mine."

My heart beat faster with his words and his touch, my need for him becoming overwhelming. I quickly unbuttoned the top of his shirt, while his hands skimmed down my black, sparkling gown. The gown I'd worn to the ball as his guest. As his queen.

"You're still wearing this dress." He unclasped the attached sheer cloak, and it billowed to the floor. "I love seeing it on you."

I smoothed my hand down the front of it. "It's probably ruined now."

"It's perfect. Just like you."

He drew the gown above my head, and I raised my arms, delighting in the feel of the silky fabric drawing across my skin and leaving it exposed to the cooler air. When I lowered my arms, Lucifer's gaze raked down my body like a caress. Then he unclasped my bra, freeing my breasts, and I loved the way he looked at them with fire in his eyes. Like he'd never seen anything he wanted more.

He took a step toward me and the dark hunger in his gaze made me tremble. He took each of my breasts in his strong, masculine hands, feeling the weight of them, rubbing his thumbs along my taut nipples. Then he lowered his mouth to one of them, tasting me with a slow lick that made me moan. His mouth thoroughly explored my breasts, his rough stubble grazing my sensitive skin and leaving the slightest burn behind. I wanted that burn to continue all over me. I wanted Lucifer's fire to consume me.

After sliding his fingers across my midriff with agonizing slowness, he slid my panties down. His fingers tickled along my thigh, leaving a path of desire from my pussy to my toes. Ready to explode from the heat and desire coursing through me, I ground against him, desperate for a little relief from the ache inside. My fingers fumbled for his trousers, yanking them open, searching for his cock. It didn't disappoint as it sprung forward, and I wrapped a hand around it, savoring the feel of his size and length in my palm.

With one arm, Lucifer shoved everything off his desk, the ancient texts falling unheeded onto the floor, before he gripped my hips and set me on the edge of it. Then he dug his fingers into my thighs and pulled my legs far apart, exposing my wet folds to him.

He slowly kneeled in front of me. "It's been far too long since I tasted you."

"It's only been a few days," I said with a delirious laugh.

His tongue slid along my slit, one long, slow stroke before he looked back up at me. "Exactly. Far too long."

He lowered his head again and I moaned and grabbed his hair as he dipped his tongue inside my pussy, pushing until he filled my entrance with wet warmth. He fucked me like that with his tongue, driving me wild, and then suddenly moved to take my clit into his mouth. He hummed, the vibrations teasing while I writhed on the edge of his desk.

He kept a firm hand on my hips but adjusted so his arms wrapped completely around my thighs, holding me in place. He spread my pussy open and sucked my clit harder, causing me to cry out in earnest as I begged and moaned. My hips tried to thrust against his mouth as he took me higher and higher. With my hands planted on the desk behind me, all I could do was throw my head back and chase the pleasure as it built, my every nerve tingling in anticipation. But then he stopped.

"No." Lucifer pulled back and let go of my thighs. "Not yet."

"Lucifer," I begged. "Please."

He rose to his full height, then gripped his perfect cock and stroked it slowly, making my mouth water. When I was about to drop to my knees and start begging, he stepped forward and continued his torment by sliding his cock up and down my folds, getting the head slick with my desire. I whimpered a little, and a satisfied smile crossed his face at my desperation. When he looked at me like that, I knew exactly why they called him the devil.

When I couldn't stand a second longer of his teasing, his cock pushed inside me, and it was everything I needed. Thick, hard, and long, a perfect fit for me, like we'd been designed as a pair. He went slow this time, drawing out each thrust and retreat, and I felt every single inch as he moved inside me. He teased my breasts and stared into my eyes the entire time, watching my reaction when he stroked and pinched, when he plunged in deeper, when he claimed me again and again.

Then he pushed me back so I lay flat on the desk, and he grabbed my legs and lifted them up, hooking them over his shoulders. The position allowed him to sink even deeper into me, and put me completely in his control. All I could do was take what he was giving me.

His hips began to roll and lift in a slow, sensual rhythm, his cock hitting me in spots I never knew existed. With one hand he held me in place, and with the other he rubbed my clit, knowing the exact way to touch me to make me lose my mind. Of course he did. He'd been making love to me for centuries, whereas this was all new to me.

"Tell me you're mine and I'll let you come," he said, his voice rough with lust.

"I'm yours," I managed to gasp. "Always yours."

He moved harder and faster, hitting that spot over and over while he teased my clit, and the pressure built until I couldn't hold back any longer. Just as I began to tighten around him, he dropped my legs and reached down to slide one hand under my head to grip my hair. As the orgasm swept through me, he tugged my body up to press against his chest, then claimed my mouth with a rough kiss. He kept thrusting into me the entire time he came inside me, and all I could do was moan into his mouth against the delicious tug of his hand in my hair, while he drew out every last second of my orgasm.

He held me close against him, and I buried my face in his neck as our hearts raced together. Our breathing slowed to a normal rate, but he didn't let me go.

"Don't leave me again," he said, though it sounded more like a plea than a demand.

"I won't," I promised, as I took his face in my hands and stared into his shockingly green eyes. My favorite color, and only now did I realize why.

"You will," he said, with a sharp intake of breath. "You always do."

My chest tightened at the inevitability in his words. "And you always find me again."

"I'm not sure how much longer I can do that," he confessed. "Each time you die, I lose another part of my soul."

"We have no other choice." I stroked his face. "Not even death can keep us apart. Somehow we'll find a way to be together, no matter how much time or distance comes between us."

"Not even death," he muttered, his eyes turning distant.

"What is it?" I asked.

He finally pulled back from me and picked up the ancient books on the floor. "I need to do a little research. I'll join you in the bedroom shortly."

I stretched in a way that drew his eyes back to my naked body. "All right. I could really use a shower after my long drive."

He gave me a quick kiss, but I could tell his mind was elsewhere already. He sat behind his desk, cracking open one of the old books, and I watched him for a moment, wondering what research could be so important...and why his mood had shifted so suddenly.

31

LUCIFER

S he'd returned to me. I'd hoped for it, but I wasn't sure it would happen before the curse struck again and we began the cycle of love and death once more. A cycle I had grown weary of, but wasn't sure we could escape.

While my people had been searching for Hannah, I'd been going through Samael's old journals in Aramaic, the ones he'd written to document the ancient days. In those thin, cracked pages he described the curse as it happened, and once again I scoured the tome hoping for answers, but found nothing I didn't already know. There was only one way to break the curse, but it would destroy us both. And possibly the entire world with us.

Could I make the ultimate sacrifice?

For her, I would do just about anything... Except this, perhaps.

I quickly sent off a few texts anyway, calling in a few favors. Now I had to wait.

While I drummed my fingers on the cover of one of Samael's journals, Hannah returned to the library, her hair wet from her shower. Now she wore one of the slinky nightgowns I'd bought her, which just begged to be pushed up to her thighs or even ripped off completely.

She covered a yawn with her hand. "Quit reading those old books and come to bed already."

"Yes, dear," I said, as I rose to my feet. I'd worry about breaking the curse tomorrow. And find Gadreel, while I was at it. Where was that bastard now? I took Hannah's hand, realizing she didn't know about him yet. "There's something I need to tell you."

"I suspect there's still a lot you need to tell me." Then her eyes widened. "Actually, there's something I need to tell you too. Something I heard at the ball. I completely forgot about it until now, but—"

Her words were interrupted by a loud crash outside the library. I immediately shoved Hannah behind me, while shouting broke out from the entrance of the penthouse. Was it Gadreel?

I turned to Hannah and took her face in my hands. "Stay in the library. You'll be safer here."

She nodded, her eyes wide with fear, and I kissed her deeply, fearing it might be the last time. She hugged me tight and then I headed out of the library, closing the door behind me. Without any windows, the library was the safest place in the penthouse for Hannah at the moment, and I had to deal with whoever was invading my lair.

I rushed through the living room, and from the corner of my eye I spotted dark shapes outside my windows flying back and forth in ominous patterns. I had no time to worry about that though, because at the entrance of my penthouse stood a tall, hulking man with hands turned into reptilian claws, now dripping with blood.

The blood of my guards.

"Mammon," I growled, as I surveyed what he'd done. All of my hand-picked, loyal guards lay dead at his feet. "So you're the one behind all this."

The ancient Archdemon of the dragons let out a haughty laugh. "Hardly. I'm but the first of many who want your downfall."

I drew my darkness around me, preparing to fight. "Then you'll have the honor of being the first to die."

He let out a massive roar, making the floors and window shake, and dragonfire burst out of his mouth. I smothered it quickly with my darkness, almost offended. He should know better than to think that would work.

"Why?" I asked. "Has your greed overcome you? You think you can steal my throne and be the next Demon King?"

"It's time for someone else to lead the demons." He swiped at me with his claws, and I easily dodged and avoided them, my movements flowing like smoke around him. "You never should have forced us to abandon Hell. It was our *home*."

"A home that could no longer sustain us," I reminded him.

He ignored me as he kept attacking, knocking over all my furniture in the process. "And a truce? With *angels*? Come now Lucifer, surely you didn't think that would work."

"You'd rather we kept fighting forever, while our numbers dwindled to nothing?" I cringed as he threw a chair into my bar, destroying dozens of bottles of my finest alcohol. "I did everything to save our people. The future of our race was at stake."

"*Our* race? You're not even a real demon!" He blasted me with another mouthful of dragonfire, which I blocked with a wall of darkness. His face began to redden, his frustration becoming obvious. "Angels never belonged in Hell. Once we rid ourselves of all the Fallen, we'll reopen Hell and begin to rebuild it."

We'd neared the huge windows overlooking Vegas now, and I had a clear view of the battle going on outside. My dark-winged Fallen angels fought in the skies against both dragon and gargoyle attackers, with blasts of fire and shields of darkness fighting for dominance of the air. I spotted both Azazel and Samael out there, but no sign of Gadreel anywhere.

"You plan on destroying all the Fallen?" I asked, cocking my head. "But what of Gadreel? Isn't he working with you?"

Mammon snorted. "Gadreel is nothing but a tool the Archdemons have used to weaken you. He gave us the information we needed, but he's a pawn. An inside man, if you will. He serves us, like all your Fallen will soon. They'll be on their knees before the Archdemons, where they belong...or they'll be dead. Along with you."

His threats against my people made rage boil up inside me. "I am the true Demon King, and you will kneel!"

With a wave of darkness, I pushed Mammon through the windows into the night sky and launched after him, my dark wings spreading as I dove. Blood red scales slithered across his skin as his own wings erupted, his body shifting into his massive dragon form faster than I expected.

We wove and dodged through the sky amid the other fighters, though they gave us a wide berth. Mammon scraped at me with his enormous claws, but I pulled back, trying to avoid the pointed tips. He was too fast though, and one of the massive claws caught me, gouging a jagged split from my collar bone to my abdomen.

I went into a spin as I fell toward the city streets below. Pain washed through me, but the darkness forced my body to heal, and I fought for control over my flight. My wings beat strongly, lifting me back up, chasing the man who dared lead a revolt against me, who dared endanger Hannah.

He banked and whirled, flying high over the city lights, above the fighting around us. Pushing out my wings, I soared upward as fast as I could, and moved just in time as a blast of orange dragonfire erupted from Mammon's mouth, the heat intense even over the distance.

He'd left himself vulnerable by spewing the fire. It took him precious seconds to coordinate his massive body for movement, and while he swung his head to try to locate my position, I made my way around him. I dropped onto his back, almost grateful for the opportunity to rest a moment while my body burned with the effort of healing. His leathery wings beat against the night air as he fought against the sudden addition of my weight.

Dragon hides were nearly impossible to penetrate due to their scales, but I pushed my darkness into his ears, his eyes, his nostrils, choking him. I wished for a moment I had my sword, Morningstar, but it was in the library with Hannah. Probably for the best. Instead I unleashed my hellfire, bright blue and charged with the magic of both Heaven and Hell, fueled by both light and darkness. A gift I rarely used because it was so destructive, and one that only I possessed. Well, along with Belial, but I hadn't seen him in years.

In a desperate move, Mammon dropped from the sky, unseating me as his weight plummeted from underneath me. He spun frantically, trying to put out the hellfire, the only kind of fire that could harm him. It went out, but I'd managed to injure him at least.

I followed him down, but he banked again and maneuvered around me. Staying on his tail, I chased him high into the air, before I got close enough to sling out my darkness like a whip and wrap it around the base of his wings. I yanked hard, and the popping of his wing joints reverberated through the sky like thunder and skittered along the threads of my dark magic.

He plunged from the sky as he tried to escape, but I made sure my threads of darkness held his wings just enough so that he couldn't move. Pointing myself downward, I flung my feet onto his chest and held my darkness like a rope, pulling on his wings while letting another tendril of magic wrap around his throat. We kept falling, but I controlled it with my wings as Mammon struggled underneath me.

"You can't kill me," I said, glaring into Mammon's eyes. "Concede defeat and I'll let you live."

"Never," he growled, baring his fangs. "Even if you stop me, there will be others. This is just the beginning, Lucifer. You have no idea what's coming. For you and your little bitch."

Fury consumed me at his words. He could insult and threaten me all he wanted, but now he'd insulted Hannah, and I was done playing around.

Narrowing my eyes, I unleashed my hellfire again, the destructive magic rippling over his scales like lightning and tearing him apart. He let out a mighty roar as it consumed him, dragonfire spewing from his mouth in every direction, and I snapped my wings, sending me backwards and away from him. He lit up the night like a display of fireworks, until all that was left were his ashes as they blew away in the wind.

At his death, the other dragons below us let out a wailing roar, and then they loped away, giving up the fight. The remaining gargoyles hurried after them on their bat-like wings, the battle over. It surprised me to see it hadn't been just my Fallen fighting the gargoyles and dragons, but a few angels had joined the battle—the ones I'd texted earlier. I hadn't expected them to respond so soon, and I began flying toward them.

A scream and a crash from inside the penthouse struck me with sudden terror. Dread filled my chest as I rushed toward more battle sounds and noises of struggle echoing from the library—where I'd left Hannah.

32

HANNAH

Lucifer had been gone for only a few seconds before I grabbed the sword off the wall—the same one I'd used against the gargoyles, the one I seemed able to use without even thinking about it. Lucifer's sword, from back when he'd been an angel. Hopefully nobody would come into the library, but I had to defend myself if they did. Assuming I remembered how to fight again.

Long minutes passed by, and the noises outside the library filled me with fear and anxiety, including guttural roars that made the floor shake. Then I heard a huge crash as if the windows were shattering, like they'd done during the gargoyle attack, and I couldn't wait any longer. I had to know if Lucifer was okay.

I threw open the door and ran out, swallowing hard at the sight of the penthouse torn apart again and some of the walls scorched with fire. Outside, Fallen angels clashed against gargoyles and dragons, while fire lashed across the night sky. I wondered if any humans in the hotel or down on the ground could see this, and if they thought it was another Vegas attraction. The magic of Sin City. If only they knew what *really* happened in Vegas.

Then Lucifer flew into view, and my heart pounded harder as he fought a red dragon a good three times his size. Was that

Mammon? Dammit, I should have warned him earlier about what I'd heard at the ball, but it had slipped my mind after Jophiel kidnapped me. I gasped as Lucifer streaked upward, far out of my sight, chasing the dragon. I ran for the balcony, my slippers crunching on broken glass, hoping to see where they went.

My only warning of approaching danger was a faint whisper behind me. My instincts took over, and I whirled in time to yank up Lucifer's blade and slice through tendrils of shadow magic that had been about to grab me.

The sword glowed bright white as Gadreel stepped forward out of the darkness. His grim smile sent tremors of terror through my heart, especially when he squared off, pointing a sword at me that looked similar to mine, except it blazed with darkness instead of light.

As Gadreel and I shifted positions, like we were about to dance, I prayed my muscle memory would hold and that I was a good enough swordswoman to match Gadreel.

"Why are you doing this?" I asked. "I thought we were friends! Or at least we were, back when I was Lenore."

He slashed forward, on the offensive, and I blocked him with my glowing sword. We weren't fully fighting, not yet. He wanted to feel me out. Probably checking to see if I had enough fight in me in this body. Asshole, I had plenty.

"You know why," he said, his voice cold. All traces of fun-loving Gadreel were gone, leaving a stranger in his place. "Deep down, you've always known my true identity. Haven't you?"

I nearly dropped the sword as clarity swept through me. My hands trembled and I stepped back, but I managed to whisper his name. "Adam."

A cruel smile spread across his handsome face. "I've come for you, my wife. As I always do."

I leveled the glowing sword at him. "Stay away from me!"

His face darkened, and he attacked again. I had to dance and move quickly to block him. As we fought, we dodged upended furniture and broken glass, unintentionally moving back toward the library. The battle was balanced, and somehow I knew in my bones that this was a fight we'd fought a hundred times before. An exhausting thought that lent a feeling of inevitability to all of it. Was it even possible for me to win against him? Or would he strike me down just as Lucifer returned?

"Jophiel thought she could hide you, but I always find you," Gadreel snapped. "You belong to *me*, Eve, not Lucifer."

He found me... My jaw dropped, though I kept my sword raised. "Did you have Brandy kidnapped?"

He inclined his head slightly, with pride shining in his eyes. "I knew it would bring you to me."

"Why not just kill me in Vista? That seems a lot easier."

"Where's the fun in that?" He gave me a maniacal grin as he advanced, making me step back. "No, it's much more satisfying to bring you to Lucifer and give you some time to fall in love again, so it hurts him even more when I take you away. Like he stole you from me."

"Lucifer is my mate, not you," I shot back at him, as I stepped into the library. "I don't even know you!"

He looked oddly hurt at that. "How do you not remember me? *Me?* After everything I've done to you?"

The way he said it made me want to vomit, but I had an idea. "What if I left Lucifer for you? Would that make you stop?"

He let out a horrible, menacing laugh as he came toward me. "Oh, Eve, you're the same in every life. You think you haven't tried that before?"

Damn. I was out of moves. Except as he drew closer, I grabbed the vase of Hades and Persephone, silently saying an apology to the long-dead artist, and threw it at Gadreel's head. It hit him perfectly, using precise aim I didn't know I possessed, shattering into a hundred pieces. Giving me just enough time to stab him in the shoulder with the light blade. He screamed and stumbled back, like he was on fire. I already knew from the gargoyle attack that the blade seemed to do extra damage to demons—and Fallen too, apparently.

His dark blade glanced downward as he cradled the wound, and I used the second of vulnerability to my advantage. Darting forward,

I sank my blade into Gadreel's chest, driving it into his heart as his eyes widened with shock. The sword's white light increased, shining between us.

I gave him a triumphant smile. "Never expected me to kill you for once, did you?"

I yanked out the sword with a twist and stepped back. He rocked forward, clutching at his heart as he sank to his knees. He hit the floor hard, and I pressed a hand to my chest, sucking in a deep breath and trying to calm my racing heart.

Holy shit. I'd killed Gadreel.

Adam was dead. Was the curse broken?

Then a horrible laugh came from his body, even as his blood spread across the floor. Like some kind of zombie, he forced himself up off the floor with a groan. Ripping his shirt apart, Gadreel proudly displayed his chest, and I watched in confusion as the torn flesh and skin knitted back together.

I stumbled back, shaking my head, fear gripping my throat. "How?"

"Oh, Eve, don't you remember? Thanks to the curse, I can't be killed as long as you're alive. We're a pair in life and death." He stepped forward again, shadowy blade in hand. His eyes had changed. They were wild before, but now they were six steps past that. He'd gone totally dark. Pure evil.

"Together forever," he whispered, and terror rushed through me.

I tried to move, but I wasn't quick enough. I lifted my blade, but the dark swinging sword came at me so fast, with so much fury, all I could do was surrender to the inevitable. At least I would be reborn again.

The library door blasted open, breaking off its hinges, and a shield of darkness flew up around me, blocking Gadreel's attack. Lucifer strode through, his eyes blazing red, his shadowy wings fully extended. He crossed the room to me in a blur of darkness and threw me behind him, protecting me from any further attacks with his own body.

Gadreel took one look at Lucifer and paled, the color draining from his face. He turned and sprinted toward the broken library door, sweeping Lucifer's old book from the desk as he darted by—the one Lucifer had been reading when I'd found him earlier.

In the living room, glass shattered and fell toward The Strip below as Gadreel launched through the last remaining windows with a burst of energy and force I hadn't expected. His pale gray wings carried him into the night, and I almost expected Lucifer to go after him, but he turned to me instead.

His red eyes faded back to green as he held my shoulders and scanned me from head to toe. Probably searching for signs of blood or other injuries. "Are you hurt?"

"No, I'm fine." I threw myself into Lucifer's strong arms. "I'm so glad you're okay. When I saw you out there fighting a dragon, I feared the worst."

He held me close against him, running his hand up and down my back. "It was Mammon. He and some of the other Archdemons have been plotting against me, and they're working with Gadreel. He's Adam, you know."

"Yeah, I figured that part out," I said with a slight shudder.

"I was about to tell you when we were attacked." He looked in the direction of the library and his frown deepened. "And now he has Samael's journals. This is bad. Very bad."

With a ripple of magic, Lucifer's darkness snaked out and flipped over one of the leather couches. It had large gashes in it, like it had been shredded with huge claws, but he sat on it anyway. Then he sighed before rubbing his hands over his face—the most defeated I'd seen him.

I sank down beside him. "Why is that bad? What was in that book?"

"It's an account of what happened long ago, written by Samael. I was going through it to see if there was a way to break the curse. But there's more in that book. A lot more." Lucifer turned his gaze toward the window, looking in the direction Gadreel had flown off in. "And now Adam has it."

"I killed him." The fight played over in my head, and fear gripped my throat again. "But he didn't die. He said he can't die while I'm alive. Why didn't you tell me that part of the curse?"

Lucifer took my hand, turning it over as he looked at my skin, as if committing me to memory. "I assumed Jophiel told you about it."

"She must have left that part out." I had a feeling she'd left a lot of things out.

He wrapped an arm around me and held me close, and I leaned against him until the shock of the attack slowly receded. But when it did, I was left with a horrible dread for the next time it would happen. And the next, and the next...

"We have to end the curse," I said quietly. "I can't keep doing this. Living and dying, over and over. Finding you and losing you again and again. Living in fear of the day Adam would end my life once more." I turned toward him, but he was staring off into space, his brow furrowed. "Did you find a way to break the curse in Samael's notes?"

"Yes, there is a way." His dark gaze lifted and his eyes met mine, but now they were hard. Cold. A little terrifying. "But there's a price. There's always a price."

"Whatever it is, I'll pay it," I said, though a flicker of doubt lodged in my chest.

"Will you?" He let out a haunting laugh, as darkness began to gather around him. "Or am I the one who will suffer for all eternity for the crime?"

I stood up and backed away, my skin suddenly cold. "I don't know what you're talking about. How do we break the curse?"

He stood and stalked toward me like a predator, backing me against the wall. "Do you trust me, Hannah?"

Words failed me for a moment, as the darkness seemed to close in around us like a cage. Was he trying to scare me? If so, it was working. But I knew in my heart he would never hurt me. He was my mate, the other half of my soul, and he loved me.

"Yes, I trust you." I reached up and stroked his face softly as I looked into his eyes. "I love you."

Pain crossed his face just before the darkness turned the room pitch black around me. All I could see were his red eyes, glowing like brimstone, and then the shadows wrapped around my body like shackles, holding me tight.

"Lucifer... What are you doing?" I struggled against the bonds he'd twined around me, but there was no resisting the devil.

He wrapped his strong, masculine hands around my throat. "I'm sorry, Hannah. It's the only way."

I couldn't talk, couldn't protest, couldn't breathe. I could only watch Lucifer's red eyes burn like an inferno as his hands tightened, cutting off my air. I tried to fight, tried to scream, tried to beg, but I couldn't move at all.

Pain exploded in my neck and lungs. Tears fell from my eyes. It grew harder and harder to see his burning eyes clearly as the darkness creeped into my vision and I struggled for air.

Lucifer was *killing* me.

How could he do this? Had I been wrong about him this entire time? As my vision blurred and my body grew weaker, Jophiel's words came back to me. *Lucifer is the villain. He's been lying to you this entire time. Manipulating you. Controlling you. As he's done with all humans for thousands of years.*

You're in danger around him.

His voice came to me in the darkness. "I love you, Hannah."

How could that be true when he was ripping the life from my body? Was this how he ended the curse—by doing Adam's job for him?

I'd made the ultimate mistake, trusting the devil with my heart. And the price was my life.

The darkness closed in, enveloping me completely as my lungs burned for the last time. Everything turned black as death finally claimed me, as it had done so many times before.

Except this death would be my last.

33

HANNAH

With a bright flash of light, life surged back into me...and with it came power.

And memories. So many memories.

My mind flooded with events from my past lives. Every single one of them. Eve. Persephone. Lenore. Countless other humans who lived short, brutal existences.

All of their lives came rushing back to me, filling my head with their pain, joy, love, and death, stretching back thousands of years. Too many memories for one mind to hold, even an immortal one. I screamed and thrashed, clutching at my head, trying to make the torrent stop.

Then the flood died off and the memories faded away like smoke. Only a few impressions remained, fragments from some of my lives, though I knew others were within my grasp if I needed them. Only one life remained just out of reach, clouded by another's magic. My true self had been stolen from me, my powers stripped from my body, now returned in death. But I still couldn't access those memories.

I sucked in a breath that felt like my very first one. Power swirled inside me like adrenaline. My skin tingled with magic. How was this possible?

Lucifer had killed me, but somehow I was alive.

No, better than alive. I was *whole* again.

But that didn't mean I forgave him for what he'd done.

I opened my eyes and slowly sat up, glancing at the small crowd of people gathered around me, before my eyes landed on Lucifer. My mate. My killer. My savior.

"Hannah?" he whispered.

Hannah? Hannah was dead. But like a phoenix, I was reborn. I didn't remember my name, but I knew one thing.

It was time to raise some hell.

DEVILISH MATE

CLAIMED BY LUCIFER BOOK TWO

1

LUCIFER

I n all my thousands of years of existence, killing my mate was the hardest thing I'd ever done.

The light faded from Hannah's eyes, along with a look of betrayal I'd never be able to forget in all my days. As her life left her, anguish gathered in my chest, growing and pressing outward until I barely held myself together.

She slumped in my arms.

Dead.

"I'm sorry." I settled her back against the leather couch and swallowed against the emotion trying to claw its way from my heart. "It was the only way."

My regretful apology wasn't enough. It would never be enough. How could I apologize for this? For killing her? Even if I did it to break the curse, with every intention of bringing her back to life, I wasn't sure my actions could ever be forgiven. Even if she forgave me, could I forgive myself?

My Hannah lay on the couch, her chest still. So still. I grazed my knuckles across her soft, pale cheeks as I watched her face and waited. The more seconds passed, the more certain I became that I'd made the wrong decision. What was taking so long?

Samael rushed in, visible in my peripheral vision. He stopped short and stilled completely as he took in the scene. I couldn't tear my gaze away from my love, the other half of my soul. *Come back to me, Hannah.*

"What have you done?" Samael asked, the horror evident in his tone.

My voice came out tight. "I had to do it to break the curse. Don't worry, her death won't be permanent." But her skin grew colder under my fingertips as I stroked her jawline, trying to wake her up with the strength of my will. "I hope."

My attention shifted from Hannah's face when five winged people flew through the broken glass of the windows and landed in the penthouse, their feet touching the ground with barely a sound. As their wings folded shut with a snap, I breathed a sigh of relief.

Kassiel adjusted his tie and straightened his suit as he gazed at the destruction and death before him. At his side was his lover, Olivia, along with her three other mates, Bastien, Callan, and Marcus. As a half-succubus, she required four of them to keep her sated, just like her mother, Lilith. I'd called them earlier today in the hopes they could help me with this matter—and I'd only gone forward with breaking the curse once I'd seen them outside, fighting Mammon and his dragons beside my people.

I rose to my feet and faced them. "Thank you for coming with all haste."

Kassiel strode forward with the others at his heels. "It's fortunate we were already nearby when you called us."

"That was quite the skirmish." Olivia nodded toward the broken window and the skies outside where we'd all fought the dragons and gargoyles. All our enemies had fled after I'd taken out their leader, but unfortunately Gadreel—now revealed as Adam—had fled too, and taken Samael's ancient journals with him. Something I would worry about later. All that mattered now was bringing my mate back.

Kassiel's green eyes landed on Hannah's prone body. "Although perhaps we were too late..."

I focused on one of Olivia's other mates, Marcus. As an angel of the Malakim choir, he had the ability to heal, and as the son of Archangel Raphael, he also had a unique and miraculous ability. One I needed right now.

"Resurrect her," I demanded. It wasn't a request. It was a command, laced with power, and it resonated from the depths of my soul. Even if these angels hadn't owed me a favor, they'd find it difficult to refuse me.

"I'll try, but I can't guarantee it'll work." The dark-haired angel walked to Hannah and examined her quickly, before glancing at me with hesitation.

"Just do it," I barked. I had no patience for doubt today. The longer we waited, the harder it would be to bring her back. And we had to bring her back. I would accept no other possible outcome.

Marcus rested his hands on Hannah's chest, just under her collarbones, and a white glow surrounded her. I held my breath in anticipation. If she came back, I'd go to the ends of the Earth to keep her safe and make up for all the years of pain we'd been through. I'd do whatever it took to make her forgive me for what I'd done.

Olivia held out one hand and Marcus took it, enveloping it in his larger one. Her other mates crowded around and put their hands on her back. They all closed their eyes, sending Marcus their combined strength and energy to help him save my Hannah. My Persephone. My Eve.

My heart pounded in my ears, warring with the roaring of the wind outside the broken windows. Samael hovered nearby with a tense frown. No one moved as the white light suffused Hannah's body, and I held my breath as I waited for the longest minute of my eternal life. Would this truly work? Or had I made the biggest mistake of all time?

Finally, Marcus removed his hands and the light faded. At first, nothing happened, and I fully expected him to tell me it was impossible.

Then Hannah sucked in a desperate, ragged breath.

Relief overwhelmed me, and I rushed forward without hesitation. I dropped to my knees beside her, ignoring the crunch of glass as it cut through my trousers. Her blue eyes fluttered open, and all the tension in my body faded away.

"Hannah," I whispered, my hands already on her cheeks because I couldn't go another moment without touching her. I needed to feel the warmth in her cheeks and the breath escaping her lips to believe she was truly alive again.

As her eyes focused on me, her beautiful mouth twisted, and her gaze registered confusion and horror. Fine, yes, I deserved that. We'd work on that problem later. All that mattered was that she was alive—and that the curse was broken. A sense of triumph filled my chest knowing I'd once again beaten my father at his own game.

"Just breathe," I said in a low voice as Hannah struggled to sit up. I held out my hand, which she took with some hesitation.

But then Hannah shrunk back against the couch as if trying to get away from me. She stared at the other people in the room, her eyes wide, but her gaze kept returning to Kassiel. Understandable. I settled beside her, ready to say or do anything she needed as she came to grips with what had happened.

"Our debt is repaid now."

Without even turning, I knew who'd spoken. The gravelly, flat voice could only belong to one person. Callan, Jophiel's son, and Olivia's most hard-headed mate. I turned his way with a sharp, withering look. If only he knew who Hannah truly was...

"Thank you all for your assistance," I said, glancing between all of the people gathered around us.

"Who is she?" Kassiel asked.

Hannah jerked slightly when she heard his voice, and her hand moved to grip the arm of the couch, her knuckles whitening as she squeezed. She was freaking out and trying not to show it. Who could blame her? Being murdered by your mate and then brought back from the dead would be a lot for anyone to take in.

I rose to my feet and adjusted my poor suit, which was covered in dragon blood and devil knew what else. "We'll speak later. For now, I need to be alone with her. Samael, can you find rooms for our guests and arrange for cleanup to begin?"

Samael nodded curtly, obviously displeased about the situation. I'm sure I'd hear about it later in great detail. "Follow me please," he told the others, and his strides were sharp as he walked away. Kassiel gave Hannah one last curious glance before following Samael and the others out of the penthouse.

As soon as they were gone, I turned back to Hannah to offer her comfort and perhaps a glass of water. Her eyes locked onto me and she suddenly burst into movement, jumping to her feet, her face twisting with rage, her blond hair flowing behind her.

"You killed me." Her chest heaved as her eyes blazed. "You killed me!"

"Hannah..." I stepped forward to take her into my arms and reassure her, but she stumbled back and held up her hands to stop me.

"Stay away! Don't come any closer!" The color drained from her face, and she brought her hand to her throat. Clutching it gently, as if remembering.

I sighed, wishing I could take that memory away, the memory of my squeezing her neck until life left her. "Hannah, let me explain. Killing you was the only way to break the curse, but I had a plan all along. I called in a favor with the angels and had Marcus resurrect you. He's the son of Archangel Raphael and, like his father, he can bring people back from the dead."

Hannah reared backward, her eyes wide. "Were you certain it would work?"

"No, but I had faith."

"You had faith?" She grabbed a vase, one of the few breakable things in the room that had survived the battle unscathed, and hurled it across the room. "I might have died!" she screamed. "Fuck you. I did die!"

As the vase hit the ground and shattered, I stayed calm, trying not to do or say anything that would add to Hannah's distress. "Yes."

She stopped and stared at me, more shock blooming across her face, if that was possible. "And this time I wouldn't be reborn."

"Yes."

She picked up a wine glass and threw it toward me. "You could have told me that was your plan first!"

I lifted my hand and caught the glass just in time. "I couldn't warn you. Believe me, I wanted to tell you everything, but I couldn't. It had to be an act of passion, done with my own hands, and you had to look at me and know I was killing you. My father made that very clear when he cursed us. If you'd known my full plan, it might not have worked. I couldn't risk that. Even if we have to live with the memory for the rest of our days."

She held up a hand to her head, as if in pain. "Why now? If you knew how to break the curse all along, why wait til now?"

"Because until recently I had no way to bring you back." I set the wine glass down and braced for more flying objects. "About a year ago I helped some angels—the ones who just left—escape from prison, placing them in my debt. I couldn't have brought you back and cheated Death without their help."

Hannah sucked in a shuddering breath before she spoke. "Is the curse broken then?"

"I believe so, yes." I'd felt it when she died. Like a rubber band snapping in half deep inside me.

"So if I die, that's really the end of me?" She looked lost as she said the words.

"As it is for all living things." I spread my hands and cocked my head, unsure of how to respond. She'd wanted to break the curse as much as I had, if not even more. I'd done it for her, after all. For *us*. "We must all face our demise at some point. At least now we can face it together."

"No, no, no..." she muttered to herself, as she backed away from me, shaking her head. She grabbed her head with her hands as agony claimed her face. "It's too much... I can't..."

I rushed forward as she bent over and cried out, but then she held up one hand while her other arm clutched her waist.

"Stay away from me!" she screamed.

Golden light shot out of her skin, illuminating the room and knocking me back. As I stumbled and threw up a hand to shield my eyes from the light, Hannah ran toward the broken windows. She charged right through the jagged holes before leaping off the balcony into the night without a backward glance.

I hurried toward the railing and gripped it tightly, watching as Hannah flew away on silver wings.

2

HANNAH

I was flying. On my own wings. How was that possible?

I'd been overwhelmed by the knowledge of my own death at Lucifer's hands, the thousands of snippets of memories crowding my brain, and this rush of power inside me that I couldn't control. In my panic to escape it all, I'd run toward the penthouse balcony. Some instinct had made me jump off, but I didn't fall. No—I'd done the opposite of falling. *Flying*. And only when I was soaring through the night sky did I realize I was gliding on silver wings.

My wings.

The wind ruffled through my feathers as I swooped on air currents without any thought, and I marveled at the feeling of freedom and power. It was enough to calm me for a few seconds, and I allowed myself to exist in that brief moment. It felt...right. Familiar. Natural.

But then the memories flooded back and filled me with anguish and pain. I'd *died*. At Lucifer's hand. My own mate had killed me! Sure, he had a reason for it, but he should have told me about his plans first. Or given me some kind of warning. *Something*. Even if I could forgive him, which I wasn't sure was possible, I'd never be able to forget the feel of his own hands suffocating me to death.

Anger and agony filled me at the thought, and golden light shot out of my skin again, lighting up the night sky as if I'd turned into a star. Power pounded through me, and then a rush of memories that were not my own overloaded my brain. *Flying through the darkness of Hell on black wings. Running barefoot through a vibrant garden and laughing. Looking up at Gadreel as he yanked out the spear from my chest. Holding a small naked baby boy in my arms.*

I shook my head as I tried to bury the memories deep inside me and find my way back to the present. Lucifer's horrible act had unlocked something within me, and now I didn't know who I was anymore. If Hannah had died, then was I Eve? Lenore? Someone else with wings—an angel?

Flying was the only thing that made sense to me, that my body somehow knew how to do instinctively, so I kept moving, pumping my wings to rise higher and go farther. Every time a new question or memory popped into my head, I flew harder and faster, outrunning my panic, unable to stop and succumb to my thoughts.

A figure made of darkness itself suddenly flew in front of me and then coalesced into the form of my mate. Lucifer's shadowy black wings spread out behind him as he blocked my path, looking devilishly handsome with his dark hair blowing in the wind and his green eyes bright with worry. My heart panged at the sight of him, both with love and with pain.

"Hannah, stop!" He took my hand in his, but I yanked it away.

"I can't!" I cried out, as I swooped away from him. "What the hell is happening to me? Who am I?"

"I can explain everything if you come back to the penthouse with me." He sounded so calm and reasonable, and that only made me more angry. How could he be calm when everything inside me had imploded?

"I'm not going anywhere with you!" I said with an angry flap of my wings, sending silvery streaks of light through the night air. "If you have an explanation, tell it to me right here, right now."

Lucifer let out a long sigh before he spoke, his words slow and deliberate. "You're an angel named Haniel. Your powers and memories were taken from you by your sister, Jophiel, for your protection.

My memories of you were taken too, and I only got them back on Halloween."

Haniel. An angel. Yes, that made sense. But the rest... The pain in my chest flared. "Jophiel did this to me? How?"

Darkness trailed off his wings, making him blend into the night. "She had your best interests at heart, I believe, but that doesn't excuse what she did—to either of us. I'm still processing all of the returned memories myself. I hoped your resurrection would restore you to your full self, but it seems it only restored your powers."

My full self? An hour ago I'd been human—or so I'd thought. Now I'd died and been reborn, and discovered I was actually a freaking angel. Except I was also all of these other people from my past lives also. It was enough to make me want to scream.

"How do I get the memories back?" I asked, my voice shaking.

"You'll have to make Jophiel return them, as I did." A villainous smile teased his lips. "She didn't want to do it, but I can be quite persuasive."

I pressed my palms against my face, filled with so many emotions, powers, and memories I felt like I might explode. Now I'd learned my own sister had betrayed me too? And taken not only my memories but my powers? No. It was too much. I already had hundreds of past lives vying for attention inside of me, and I didn't know who I was anymore. Was Hannah even real? Who was Haniel?

I had to find the truth about who I was as Haniel. I knew that, deep in my core, even if I couldn't explain why.

I lowered my hands and took a deep breath. "I need to see my sister."

"Of course. But before you go, I will warn you that you may not want those memories back." Lucifer's mouth twisted and he looked away. "The truth of what happened might be too painful to bear. Even now I wonder if I was better off not knowing."

"I have to know. No matter how bad it is." I crossed my arms, using my wings to keep me alight. "And really, can it be any worse than being killed by my own mate?"

Lucifer gazed up at the heavens. "Will I pay for that crime for the next century?"

"At the very least!"

His voice lowered as his eyes landed on me again. "Don't forget I did it for you. For *us*."

I let out a long breath. "I understand why you killed me, but that doesn't mean I'm okay with it. I'm not sure how to forgive you, or how to move forward from this."

His face darkened and he shot toward me on his black wings, until he was only a breath away. "Forgive me or not, it matters little. You're my mate. You always have been, and you always will be." He took my arms as he stared into my eyes with intense focus. "Even if you can't see it now, you'll realize in time that this had to be done. The curse had to be broken. This was the only way."

I let out a burst of golden light and used my wings to jerk back from him. "That doesn't make it okay!"

He shook his head. "You need to rest. In the morning, we'll take the private jet to visit Jophiel."

"No. I need to confront my sister, but I'm doing it alone. Besides, the last time we were all together, you and Jophiel nearly killed each other."

He pressed his lips into a tight line. "I can't let you go alone."

"You can't stop me either."

"Then take Azazel at least."

"Fine." My wings flapped slower, and I felt the weight of the evening dragging me down. "After I get some rest."

Lucifer suddenly swooped me into his arms and flew me toward the penthouse, holding me close as his shadowy wings carried us forward. I tried to protest, but was too exhausted to do anything but glare up at him. My traitorous body wanted to curl up against him, and my heart beat faster at being pressed close against his hard chest. My brain might be screaming that it was all wrong, but the rest of me wanted to savor every second in his arms. Lucifer was right—he was my mate, and no matter how angry I was, I'd never be able to escape that fact.

As soon as he set me down in the penthouse, I turned from him and ran, my shoes crunching on broken glass from the earlier fight. I couldn't spend another second with Lucifer and all my conflicting emotions. I headed straight to the guest room where I'd been staying, and it was a relief to find it untouched from the battle that had raged earlier.

I closed the door and leaned back against it, feeling out of breath and shaken to my core. My knees were weak, and my mind almost demanded I give in to my panic, but my newfound powers were draining me fast. Or maybe it was dying and coming back to life—I imagined that would really take it out of a person. I collapsed on the bed, my limbs weak and useless, and the sweet relief of sleep took me quickly.

But I didn't sleep for long.

Four hours after I'd gone to bed, when everything was deathly quiet in the penthouse, I shoved some clothes into a duffle bag. Enough for a few nights. Maybe more. Maybe forever.

Then I slipped out of the penthouse. Alone.

3

HANNAH

No one stopped me on my way out of the penthouse, or down the long elevator ride to the lowest level of the garage in The Celestial Resort and Casino. Why would they? Everyone who worked in Lucifer's hotel knew I was his woman. They had no idea of the turmoil inside me at the thought of being his mate for the rest of my life. My only life now, thanks to Lucifer breaking the curse.

I headed through the private area of the parking garage, where Lucifer kept all his expensive sports cars, toward the yellow Lamborghini I'd borrowed (aka stolen) from my sister Jophiel yesterday. I wasn't looking forward to another long drive back to San Francisco, but I also needed to speak to her immediately—and without Lucifer present.

A sharp footstep behind me made me jump and spin around, my wings flaring out behind me and a bright glow emanating from my skin. Azazel stood before me, her long hair framing her muscular shoulders, her dark skin gleaming under the light I was radiating. She was dressed for combat in black leather with her daggers strapped on, and she stared at me with open hostility. "What fresh hell is this?"

"I'm leaving." I gripped my bag tighter. "You can't stop me."

"Not that. Your wings." Zel gestured at them with blood-red nails, and when she spoke her voice dripped with disgust. "You're an *angel* now?"

I looked over my shoulder at the silvery feathers, and then with some effort managed to make them vanish, along with the glowing light. Damn these powers. I still wasn't sure how to control them.

"It appears so," I muttered. "Trust me, I'm just as shocked as you are."

Her dark eyes narrowed. "How? Lucifer would've noticed if you were an angel. We all would have noticed."

I let out a long sigh. "I don't know. All this time I thought I was human too. That's why I'm leaving—to get answers. Lucifer says my sister Jophiel hid my powers and my memories from me, and I'm going to confront her now." I stared back at Zel. "Is this going to be a problem for you?"

"I have no love for angels." She sounded like she was speaking through gritted teeth. "But I swore to protect you, and that hasn't changed. I failed once, and that won't happen again—even if you are an angel." She curled her lip when she said the last word.

I fought off a pang of disappointment that a pair of silver wings could change so much between us. "I'll gladly accept your protection, but I could really use a friend," I confessed.

"I don't make friends with angels." Zel stalked toward the yellow convertible. "Is this our ride? Not bad. I'll drive. We all know angels are useless after dark, and you look like you're about to fall asleep standing up."

She wasn't wrong. I tossed her the keys with a yawn. "Thanks."

"Where to, little mortal?" She threw open the car door and then paused. "Hmm, I suppose I can't call you that anymore."

I opened the small trunk and threw my bag inside. "San Francisco."

"Long drive." She slid into the driver's seat. "We'll switch once the sun comes up."

I nodded as I sank into the leather seat on the passenger side. As she started up the car and drove us out of the parking structure, I wadded up my jacket as best I could to make a pillow, then leaned against the door of the car and closed my eyes. Four hours was definitely not enough sleep after what happened last night, but I had to find answers.

Yet as I closed my eyes and willed myself to get some rest, sleep proved elusive. My thoughts were too wild and chaotic, too full of questions that had no answers and memories that only brought pain. I could barely grasp my head around the fact that I was an angel now, that I'd died and been reborn again, and that everything I thought I'd known about my life so far was wrong.

I'd only been away from home for a little over a week, but already my flower shop seemed like a distant memory. In that short time, I'd learned about the supernatural world and that I was part of it. First I'd learned I was Lucifer's mate, cursed to die and be reborn in an endless cycle. I was Eve, and Persephone, and Lenore, and many others whose names had long been lost. But now I'd also learned I was an angel. Not Hannah. *Haniel.* My entire identity had been swept away and replaced in a matter of days.

And Lucifer had killed me.

Maybe for good reason, but not with enough surety that I'd be resurrected. Not nearly enough. He had assumed the angels could bring me back, but what if it had failed? I should have been given a choice in the matter at least, but he took that away from me. He made the decision to break the curse on his own, acting like the big arrogant king he was, and now we both had to live with his terrible crime for the rest of our lives. Our *immortal* lives.

As an angel, I wouldn't age. That was a huge shock right there. Of course, with the curse broken—if it really *was* broken—this was also my last life. I thought I'd feel relieved about that, and yet it sent a trickle of fear down my spine. If Gadreel—who we now knew was Adam reincarnated—killed me again, that would be it for me. A final death.

Of course, with the curse broken it also meant we could kill him too. For good this time.

I sure as hell hoped he could be killed anyway. I had memories flickering in my head of Adam in numerous incarnations, and all the times he'd murdered me. Even in lives Lucifer never knew about, where Adam found me as a child. I shuddered especially hard at those memories and all the wretched, disgusting things he'd done. That monster had to be stopped.

I had no idea where he was now though. He'd taken off after stealing Samael's ancient journals from Lucifer, which sounded like it was going to be a problem, though I wasn't sure how exactly. I shoved the missing journals out of my mind—I'd leave that one to Lucifer. I had more immediate problems to deal with. Like confronting my sister and figuring out who the fuck I was.

Adam would find me eventually though. He always did. But this time I would be ready for him.

While Zel cruised down the freeway at breakneck speed, I adjusted my makeshift pillow and tried to get comfortable. Lamborghinis were sexy little cars, but not exactly designed for one to sleep inside. Not that the car was the real problem. No, the problem was that I couldn't get my mind to turn off. Over and over the moment of my death played through my head on repeat, like a bad horror movie I couldn't turn off. Sometimes other images broke through from my past lives, just to fuel my anxiety. Some were memories of other times I'd fought with Lucifer in the past, like my brain couldn't help but drag up the worst things to torment me with.

Dammit. Focusing on the past wouldn't help me get answers now. I forced myself not to care about Lucifer, not to even think about him. I focused on slowing my breathing in an attempt to calm down. I wouldn't achieve anything by allowing my frustration to overtake me. And what I needed more than anything was rest.

Sleep sank its claws into me eventually, but just before it claimed me completely, another face flickered in my mind of one of the men who'd been there tonight when I'd been resurrected. Dark hair. Green eyes. Lucifer's smile. I'd seen him at the Devil's Night Ball too. My heart clenched at the thought, and something about him spoke to me on an almost cellular level. He was important to me somehow, but I had no idea why. The memories were too tangled, and they wouldn't obey my commands yet. They came and went as they pleased, even as I sought desperately for one involving this man.

Finally, a name came to me as I succumbed to sleep. *Kassiel.* Who was he?

———

After the sun rose, Zel woke me up by shoving my arm, hard. I yawned and took over in the driver's seat, while Zel immediately fell asleep beside me. I envied her for that. I'd always been a terrible sleeper, plagued by what I now knew were flashes from my past lives. The only time I'd ever slept well was when Lucifer was by my side. I shoved that thought away before the anxiety came back.

As I drove, the sun hit me through the windows and filled me with warmth and strength, and eventually we made it to San Francisco. I found my way easily to my sister's house, as if I'd always known the path, and someone buzzed us past the gate. I parked in front of her two-story mansion that looked like a French chateau, which sat on top of a hill with amazing views of the bay. Everything inside and out was white and beige, although at least the outside had a few touches of color from some pink roses.

Zel made a sound of disgust as we got out of the car. I ignored her as I made my way to the door, which opened before I reached it. Jophiel stood on the other side with a smile, her straight blond hair gleaming in the sunlight. She wore a white suit with a skirt and a pink shirt, and every inch of her was far too perfect to be human.

She came forward on her white heels and took both my hands in hers. "Hannah! I was worried when you took the car, but I'm so glad you've returned. Did you realize I was right about Lucifer all along?"

I jerked my hands away and bit my tongue. I wasn't sure how to answer that. Instead, I met her eyes and said, "I'm here for answers."

"Answers?" my sister asked, cocking her head as if she was the picture of innocence.

"About my life." I swallowed against the anxiety making my throat tight. "About Haniel."

I had the satisfaction of seeing Jophiel's face pale at that name.

Her fingers splayed at the base of her throat, and if she'd been wearing pearls, she probably would've clutched them. "Lucifer told you. I knew I should never have given him back those memories."

"Don't blame Lucifer for this one." With some effort I made my wings flare out behind me, making Jophiel's eyes widen. "He had to tell me when these things sprouted from my back."

"Shit," she said, dropping the innocent act entirely.

An angry bright glow surrounded me. "My powers have returned. I want my memories back too, along with an explanation. And it had better be a damn good one."

Jophiel nodded slowly and gestured toward her front door. "Come inside."

4

HANNAH

I hid my wings and stepped inside Jophiel's entryway, but she held up a hand when Azazel tried to follow me.

"The demon isn't welcome in my house," Jophiel said.

"Fallen," Zel snapped. "And I go where she goes."

"Azazel is my bodyguard," I explained.

"You don't need protection here," my sister replied curtly.

"I'm not so sure of that," I muttered. "But we can do this out on the porch if you'd prefer. I don't care either way."

Jophiel let out a sniff, but then stepped back to allow Zel to enter the house. If I'd thought Zel was sneering before, it was nothing compared to the look on her face as she walked inside and saw the white marble floors, gleaming chandelier, and sweeping staircase. I'll admit, it was a bit much, but it wasn't like Lucifer's penthouse was much better.

My sister led us into her living room, which was spotless and shining, as it had been every time I'd visited. We passed the display of angel figurines, which Zel eyed with distaste before plopping down on the white couch.

Jophiel's lips pressed in a tight line as she watched Zel, like she worried the Fallen might drop dirt on her pristine white furniture.

Then Jophiel turned her eyes back to me and gave me a thorough examination. "Are you all right? Has something happened with Lucifer?"

The concern in her voice broke through my anger and impatience, reminding me that she cared about me, at least enough to notice when something was wrong. But how could I respond to that question? If I told her everything that had gone down in the last twenty-four hours she'd give me an "I told you so" speech, and no one in the history of the world wanted that from their older sister. I also wasn't sure how much Zel knew about my death and rebirth. And frankly, I just didn't want to talk about it right now.

"I had a rough night," I managed to say. "Adam attacked me, but I fought him off and he escaped. But that's not why I'm here." My hands clenched at my side as I stared my sister down. "I need to know who I really am. You took my powers. You took my *memories*. Why? How?"

She barely reacted, except for the slight twitch of her mouth. "Please, sit down and I'll explain everything. Then you can decide if you still want your memories back. But first, allow me to get you something to drink at least. You look exhausted."

"Coffee," Zel said. "Black."

Jophiel shot her a glare before leaving the room, and I sank down into a white armchair with golden piping. I put my head in my hands and waited, trying not to let the anxiety overcome me again.

A few minutes later, my sister returned with a silver carafe of coffee and a tray of fancy-looking pastries. She poured me a coffee as she said, "Perhaps your guard can give us some privacy for this discussion. Some of it is of a sensitive nature."

At her words, another wisp of memory floated to the front of my mind. I was in a pub with wooden tables and beams across the ceiling. The smell of stale beer lingered in the air, and the raucous calls of the barmaids and customers echoed in my ears. Zel sat beside me, along with another woman with fiery red hair. They both wrapped their arms around me as we laughed and toasted to something, though the details eluded me. A warm sense of friendship and belonging surrounded me, and then the memory faded.

I shook my head to return to the present. I couldn't live like this, with half-memories making themselves known at random. This had better be a temporary side effect of my resurrection and nothing more.

I realized Jophiel and Zel were waiting for my response. I didn't know very much anymore—certainly not things I'd counted on as true only two days ago—but I knew I could trust Zel. I'd had few true friends over my many lifetimes, but she was one of them.

"Azazel stays." My voice was firm, leaving no room for argument.

Zel smirked and poured herself a coffee, then grabbed a tiny fruit tart with powdered sugar off the pastry tray and popped it in her mouth. Jophiel offered me a pastry as well, but I shook my head. My stomach was in knots, and I had a feeling it wouldn't get any better during this conversation.

"Tell me about Haniel," I said.

Jophiel sat in the other armchair and crossed her legs primly. "Very well. As you probably have realized now, you are not truly Hannah, but Haniel, an angel of the Ofanim Choir, and my half-sister. You were born in the early twentieth century in Heaven to two Archangels—Anael and Phanuel, our father."

My mouth fell open, but I was too stunned to respond. I was over a hundred years old, and born in another realm. To two Archangels. I searched my mind for any glimpses of the parents she spoke of, or of my childhood in Heaven, but those memories were gone. Not even a tiny flicker of familiarity remained. And yet, I sensed she was telling the truth. That only made it worse somehow. After spending the last few years desperately wishing I had memories of my parents, whom I'd believed were killed in the car accident that gave me amnesia, even the briefest flash of them would be a blessing.

"Go on," I said.

"The Great War was still ongoing at that time, and together we fought against the demons, until Lucifer killed our father and kidnapped you." She sighed and sipped her coffee before continuing. "Somehow you fell in love with him, much to my dismay. You always do."

I sat up a little at that. "Lucifer killed our father?"

"Oh, he left that part out of his story, did he?" She shook her head. "Why am I not surprised?"

"If Lucifer killed him, I'm sure he had a good reason," Zel growled.

"I'm sure the death of an Archangel seemed like a good enough reason at the time," Jophiel snapped back.

I held up a hand before they started going at it. "What happened after that?"

Jophiel set down her coffee mug and met my eyes. "Eventually you returned, claiming Lucifer had let you go. As an Ofanim, I could tell you were speaking the truth, but I knew there was more to it than that. When we were alone, you told me you'd started a secret romance with Lucifer. I was appalled, naturally, but you explained about your past lives and your mate bond with Lucifer. Since you're my sister I agreed to keep your secret, though I later regretted that since it only led to your doom when Adam killed you."

I swallowed hard, but had to ask, "How did it happen?"

"I don't know. I wasn't there at the time. You managed to escape and flew to my house, bleeding everywhere." Her face tightened and she stared into her coffee mug with pain evident in her eyes. "I called Raphael to heal you, but he didn't arrive in time to save you. However, he did manage to resurrect you."

Archangel Raphael was Marcus's father, I remembered. I'd now been resurrected by both father and son. How lucky for me. "That doesn't explain why my memories are missing."

Her voice grew urgent, her eyes pleading with me. "Everyone thought you were dead. Only Lucifer, Raphael, and I knew the truth. Knowing that your fate would only be to return to Lucifer and then be killed again by Adam, I saw an opportunity to protect you— and I took it. I wiped your memories, along with the others', and allowed everyone to believe you were another tragedy of war."

I raised my eyebrows. "And you didn't think to ask me if I wanted that?"

"I did, actually, and you agreed. The pain you felt at the time was too much to bear. You wanted to forget."

"Why? Why was it so bad?"

Jophiel looked away. "You lost more than just your life that day. I cannot say any more than that."

I glared at her, wishing she would give me answers, and annoyed at my past self for agreeing to that plan. "How long ago was this?"

"About forty years ago."

I nearly knocked over my coffee mug. "Forty years?" I practically yelled. I only remembered the last few years of my life as Hannah. Where was the rest of it?

Jophiel tried to offer me a small blueberry scone. "Dear, you should really eat something. You'll feel so much better."

I knocked the scone out of her hand. "I don't want a fucking scone! I want to know what happened during the last forty years! Where were my wings, my powers? Who was I all that time?"

"Yes, I'd like to know also," Zel said, and I felt grateful she was there to back me up. "Especially since even Lucifer thought she was human."

"For all intents and purposes she *was* human," Jophiel admitted, before turning back to me. "I took away your powers and turned you human. The only thing I left was your immortality. I couldn't bear the thought of you growing old and dying. I didn't want to lose you."

"How is that possible?" I asked.

"Because she's an Archdemon," Zel said with obvious disdain.

Jophiel nodded. "Archangels—and Archdemons, for that matter —have a unique ability to turn angels and demons into humans, stripping them of their powers and immortality. It's almost never done, and in fact few people know it's even possible. In the old days the power was abused, so now we try to never use it, unless someone asks us to do so."

I stared at my sister, my hands trembling. "Did I ask?"

"No. You simply wanted to forget. But that wasn't enough. I couldn't send you back out as an angel. Lucifer and Adam would find you again!" She reached for me, but I pulled back. "Don't you see, I did this to protect you."

"You did it against my will!" Fuck, she was just as bad as Lucifer. Both of them claiming to love me, and then making life-changing decisions without actually consulting me. I stood up and paced the room, running a jerky hand through my hair. Did anyone actually give a damn what *I* thought? Or what *I* wanted? Or did they all think they knew better than me?

"Haniel, please," my sister said. "I only wanted you to be safe."

"But you never asked what I wanted!" I roared, as golden light flared out of me like an explosion.

Jophiel shrank back and Zel threw up a hand to shield her eyes. I quickly got the light back under control and took a deep breath, trying to calm myself before I accidentally destroyed my sister's house. Not that she deserved anything less. Besides, there was still more she wasn't telling me.

"Why do I only remember the last five years of my life as Hannah?" I asked.

Jophiel smoothed her skirt. "Even though I did my best to give you a normal, human life, after a few years you figured out that something wasn't right. I wiped your memories and started again, giving you a new identity and a new life, but it never lasted. You'd miraculously heal a wound, or realize you weren't aging, and then grow suspicious. So we'd have to do it again."

My mouth fell open and all I could do was stare at her. "How many times?"

"Seven," Jophiel said in a low voice. "I've wiped your memories seven times."

"Seven times! And each time you gave me a new life," I said, still pacing, my hands clenched tight. "Was any of it real? What about the accident with the drunk driver? That was fake, wasn't it? Just a way to easily explain away my lack of memories?"

She dropped her head. "Yes."

"And our supposed parents who died in the crash? They weren't real, were they?"

"No. They never existed. Not the ones you're thinking of anyway, although all of our parents are gone. We really are orphans."

As if that made it any better. Fury pounded behind my eyes, nearly giving me a headache. Everything I'd believed for my entire life—or as it turned out, only five years of my life—was all a lie. A story. Something Jophiel simply made up to keep me under her control like I was a child she needed to coddle.

"All this time you lied to me," I said, seething with anger. "Aren't Ofanim supposed to be the angels of truth?"

"I'm sorry, Haniel," Jophiel said in a low voice. "I only did what I thought was best."

Shock and rage unfurled in my chest, and I picked up my coffee mug and threw it at her display of angels, knocking a few of them over and splashing liquid everywhere. "No! You can't use that excuse anymore. You took my choices away. You took my *life* away." I whirled around and stalked toward her, until I stood over her, trembling with barely-contained emotion. "And now you're going to give me my memories back."

Zel jumped to her feet and moved behind me, backing me up with a growl. "Do it."

"All right, yes." Jophiel rose to her feet and lifted her chin. "But don't forget that you asked me to remove them. You didn't want these memories. Sometimes it's easier to not remember."

Lucifer had said something similar, but what could be worse than existing in a world of fleeting half-truths? If I was going to move on with the rest of my immortal life, I needed to be whole again. "Do it. I don't care how bad the memories are."

Jophiel pressed her lips together in a thin line, a crease marring her forehead. "You may want to sit down for this."

I reluctantly took a seat in the white armchair, and Jophiel moved close. She rested her hand on my forehead and light filled my gaze as her palm heated. I closed my eyes and braced myself for whatever was to come.

The memories rushed in, all at once. They filled my mind with decades of life, but it was too much and too quickly. I wanted to scream, and if I was standing I surely would have fallen to my knees. As it was, I could only grip the arms of the chair tight as memories buffeted me. Things I should have known, things I never should've forgotten. Love. Pain. Loss.

Such incredible loss.

I clutched my stomach and cried out in anguish, as tears filled my eyes. The pain was too much, and way too raw. Pain I'd never had time to recover from, and loss I'd never had a chance to grieve. I didn't know how to handle it, or all the other feelings surging inside me.

Maybe Lucifer and Jophiel were right. Maybe it *was* better not to know.

5

LUCIFER

When I woke, Hannah was gone. As I knew she would be.

I could have stopped her. I could have gone after her. If I wanted her by my side, nothing on Earth would prevent me from getting my way. But Azazel was with her—I'd made sure of that—and I would allow Hannah to confront her sister on her own. She needed some time to think, and to recover. Then she'd return to me...or I'd drag her back here, kicking and screaming if I must.

While Hannah sought her past, I had other problems to deal with. My destroyed penthouse, for one thing. I immediately ordered it cleaned and repaired, and I knew my staff would have it looking like new within a few hours. It certainly wouldn't be the first time—even in the last week—that they'd had to restore order to the place. As they worked, I headed to my war room one floor below, searching for Samael.

As soon as I stepped into his office, Samael's face darkened, his eyebrows lowering into a glower. He stood from his seat, pacing in front of the large window that separated us from the main hub of the control room, where giant screens flashed with demon locations and global activity. My staff rushed about out there, taking phone calls and exchanging information, but Samael and I were trapped in a quiet bubble. I moved to the small bar in the corner and poured us both a whiskey, then took a seat in front of him.

We sat together for some time, the silence thick and heavy in the room. He shook his head and parted his lips like he was finally ready to speak. Then he closed his mouth and shook his head again before glancing out of the window and clearing his throat.

"I can't understand how I missed it." He slowly swirled his whiskey around in his glass. "For over a century Gadreel deceived us. How did I miss that he was truly Adam? I was with him the most. We worked together. I trusted him!"

"He spent years earning our trust, only to betray us all," I said, my rage quietly simmering under the surface, but threatening to boil over. The rage I always felt whenever I thought of Adam.

Samael stood and poured himself another drink. "Yes, but he was my assistant. I trusted him with *everything*. And all that time he was lying to us and plotting his attack. I should have seen it. I should have stopped it."

"We all should have seen it." I'd trusted Gadreel too. He'd been at the center of many of our operations. I'd let him get close to Hannah, even left him alone with her. I shut my eyes briefly, not wanting to consider the things he could have done while he'd had my trust.

Fuck—the things he *had* done while he'd had my trust.

"He killed Lenore. And Haniel." My chest clenched with pain at the old memory, newly recovered. And the other memory of him last night, standing over Hannah, about to finish the job. "He must pay."

Samael knocked back the whiskey in one gulp. "He will."

"Find him," I ground out, my voice low and angry.

"What do you think we've been doing?" He set his empty glass down on his desk with a heavy thump. "I have all my best people looking for him, but he's proving to be elusive so far."

I downed the rest of my whiskey as well, hoping the slight burn would calm my smoldering fury. "The Archdemons must be hiding him. Mammon said Adam was working with some of the other

Archdemons. They wish to overthrow me and return to Hell. Fools, all of them."

Samael poured another glass for both of us. "There will be fallout from you killing Mammon. There are so few dragons left, and you killed the oldest, most powerful one." He tipped his glass toward me in an almost salute. "Not that I blame you. He deserved it. But they might retaliate."

"If they're that stupid, let them come." I was in the mood to remind some more demons who was in charge of them.

He arched an eyebrow at me, a gentle rebuke. "Perhaps you should consider making peace with them, if you can. It would be a shame if you had to wipe out the few remaining dragons."

"That's up to them. They can swear loyalty to me—or they can die."

"That's not our only problem," Samael said. "Gadreel took my ancient journals, the ones that spoke of the curse, and other things from our distant past. It contains knowledge he and the Archdemons should never know—like where certain Elder Gods are sealed away." He looked at me, his gaze full of warning. "Including your father."

My chest tightened and fury whipped through me like fire as things started to make sense. "They must be trying to release them. The Elder Gods are the only ones who could defeat me." It was a foolish, dangerous plan that was likely to backfire on them, but would also result in many casualties along the way.

Samael furrowed his brow. "If Adam and the Archdemons release those four, destruction will rain down upon Earth."

My fingers tightened around my glass until it shattered. Those four Elder Gods could not be unleashed upon the world. Especially my father. "I won't let that happen."

"We'll do everything in our power to stop it," Samael said, before letting out a long, frustrated sigh. "But first I need to find a new assistant."

I rose to my feet and adjusted my suit. "Try to find someone who isn't plotting our destruction this time."

6

HANNAH

The last thing I remembered was darkness claiming me, taking me to a place where the memories couldn't hurt me anymore. Now the sound of metal slipping against metal wormed its way into my dream, waking me from a vision of Gadreel glaring at me with eyes full of rage. I rolled over and slowly realized I was in Jophiel's luxurious guest room. Azazel sat in a chair in the corner, sharpening one of her knives.

It was dark, with no light visible through the curtains, so I must have been out a while. I sucked in a deep breath and tried not to panic as everything hit me again, returning in a wave as big as when Jophiel had released the memories into my head.

I remembered it all.

Everything.

A gleaming white house built upon a hill with many places for an angel to land. A woman with golden hair and a radiant smile taking me into her arms. A man with serious blue eyes handing me a book. Jophiel, already hundreds of years old by the time I was born, taking my hand and leading me outside into bright sunlight. All memories from my childhood in Heaven. And my parents—my real parents. I remembered them strongly, along with the pain of losing them.

My mother, Archangel Anael, had simply disappeared soon after I gained my wings at twenty-one. No one knew what happened to her, though many suspected the demons had killed her. And my father, Archangel Phanuel—Jophiel was right, Lucifer *did* kill him. What she left out was that he'd done it in self-defense. It was during the middle of the Great War, and I was serving under my father, who commanded a group of spies. He led our team in an assassination attempt against Lucifer, but we failed. My father died in the attack, and Lucifer captured me.

At first, I hated Lucifer. I burned with the desire to strike him dead. I'd been raised my entire life to hate demons, and especially Lucifer, and then he'd killed my father. But I couldn't deny my bond with him either, and soon I came to know the real Lucifer. I also began to remember my past lives, just snippets and feelings more than anything, but it was enough. I couldn't deny the truth that he was my mate.

We began a secret, forbidden relationship, and in private we spent hours discussing the endless war between angels and demons. Slowly we each began to realize that the two sides had both lost sight of why they were even fighting by that point, and we agreed that the war was hurting both our races. Heaven and Hell had each become ravaged by the ancient battles, and the population of angels and demons were dwindling. Despite that, we couldn't see an end to the war. Neither side would concede. Pride was perhaps the greatest enemy of all.

Lucifer was the only one who could put an end to the war, and I'd tried to convince him to do just that—and for a while, I really thought he might do it, especially when we discovered I was pregnant. The first child ever created from the forbidden love between and an angel and a Fallen. A perfect blend of light and darkness. A daughter.

We were overjoyed—especially since children among immortals are so rare. But the joy didn't last long.

The memories played out in my mind like a film I couldn't stop.

When I was seven months pregnant, Gadreel found out about us, and he got me alone and attacked me. My thoughts faltered in a wave of pain. He hadn't only taken my life. He'd taken my unborn daughter's life too.

A sob lodged in my chest and I tried to choke it down, trying not to feel the pain that swept over me, but it was impossible. Agony wrapped around me like cold tentacles as the loss hit me all over again, binding me in unexpected raw sadness.

I couldn't stop the memories. Gadreel stabbed me, and the blood... So much blood. I managed to escape and fly again, even though the pain was unbearable. All I could think was that I had to get to my sister. She would be able to save me and my daughter. But it was too late. I died, and though Raphael resurrected me, he couldn't save my child.

Another sob escaped me at the memory. She was gone. My daughter was gone. I still remembered the first time I felt her move inside me, and the unbearable grief when I realized I would never feel her again. The pain was as fresh now as if it had just happened.

After my resurrection, the despair had been overwhelming. I couldn't shake the belief I should have died with my daughter. I was angry, so incredibly angry that Raphael had brought me back without her. How could I go on with my life, knowing what I'd lost?

I'd begged Jophiel to wipe my memories. Begged her to kill me again. Begged her to let me start over fresh as a new person, leaving Haniel behind forever.

And in a way, she'd done just that.

The tears flowed freely now as the memories swept through me, so hard and fast I could barely breathe through them. Gasping, I clutched my chest as true despair radiated through me, so strong I could barely stand it. My daughter was an innocent victim of the curse, and I would give anything to trade places with her, to give up my life so she could live.

I felt so helpless. So alone. I understood now why Lucifer told me I might not want to know.

Zel sank down beside me on the bed and wrapped her arms around me without a word, enveloping me in a tight hug. I was so surprised by the gesture, especially since Zel had no idea why I was upset, that at first I nearly jerked away from her touch. Then I leaned into her, pressed my face against her shoulder, and cried against her.

She held me the entire time, offering me silent, strong comfort. She didn't ask me to explain. She didn't tell me it would be okay. She simply allowed me to find my way through the grief while showing me I wasn't alone in it. Like a true friend.

Eventually, I tried to talk, a garbled stream of consciousness punctuated by sobs and uncoordinated inhales and gasps. "It hurts too bad. I—I wish I'd never remembered. Why did I have to know so badly? I should have listened. I should have let the past die..."

Zel pushed back enough to look me in the eyes. "No. It's better that you know, even if the memories are painful. I know you believe this. You're an Ofanim. Truth is everything to your kind. No matter how hard it is to bear it."

I hated her at that moment because she was right. I'd never be satisfied without the truth. But even accepting that, I didn't know how to stop the overwhelming tide of agony. All I could do was let it wash over me, burying my face as I let more tears fall. It was pointless trying to hold them back. I surrendered and let the grief take me away, because I didn't know how to bring it to an end any other way.

———

At some point, I fell asleep and didn't wake until sunlight brightened the day outside, shining through the windows. This time when I opened my eyes, it was my sister sitting beside me. She stroked my head like a mother looking after her child, and that only made my chest tighten up again.

"Do you understand now?" she asked. "Why I had to do it?"

Her questions and her tone instantly put me on edge. I sat up and stared at her, feeling hollow inside. "I asked you to do it."

"Yes," she said with a sigh of relief. "I'm so sorry. I wish you never had to remember any of it."

I shook my head as more memories returned, this time of my life after my resurrection—as a human. Living fake lives in different cities, oblivious to my true self, believing all the lies my sister told me about who I was. Jophiel always kept me close to her, in towns big enough that people wouldn't notice me much, but small enough that I wouldn't be easily found. But I inevitably uncovered something that made me question everything about myself, and then she would swoop in again. Over and over she gave me a new life and a new identity, wiping my brain so many times I'm surprised I didn't have permanent damage from it. And any new friends or connections I'd made in that time? Any interests or accomplishments I'd achieved? All the places I came to call home? Gone. Forever.

Yes, I'd asked to forget. Yes, I'd asked to die and be reborn again. But I hadn't asked for *that*.

My voice was hoarse and my throat scratchy as I said, "What you did was unforgivable."

"I only did what you asked me to do," she said, and the look she gave me was exasperated rather than apologetic. "I was *trying* to help you."

"You were trying to control me." I threw off the covers and got out of bed, needing space from her. "You took away my ability to have a real life. With friends. With family. With a home or a career or anything of my own."

"I know it seems extreme, but I also kept you alive and safe for forty years. If you'd gone back to living as Haniel, Adam would have killed you again." Her tone was so reasonable, and that only upset me even more.

"You took *everything* from me. My memories, my power, my identity..." My heart twisted. "And my mate."

"You asked me to take away the pain, and that's what I did. You must remember now how distraught you were. I only wanted to help you get through the grief." A flicker of pain marred Jophiel's perfect features for a moment. "I understand the loss of a child. I know how it breaks you. You might remember that I lost a daughter too once, before you were even born. More recently, my son, Ekariel, was taken from me when he was a child. For years I believed he was dead, but a few months ago he was rescued from a cult, yet that didn't erase the suffering I endured all that time. There's nothing as painful as losing a child. I didn't want you to have to go through that too."

"When I asked you to wipe my memories, I wasn't in my right mind," I said, as tears slipped my eyes again at the reminder of my loss. "For fuck's sake, I asked you to kill me too! You should have comforted me and given me time to grieve with Lucifer over our loss, instead of trying to fix the problem by taking everything away from me!"

She reached for me, but I sidestepped her touch. "You're my little sister. If you're in pain, I'll do whatever I can to fix that."

"But you turned my life into a lie! I don't even know who I am anymore!" Fury and despair pounded through me, throbbing in my head, filling me until I couldn't contain it anymore. My wings burst from my back, and golden light shot out of me, knocking over a lamp behind me and throwing the bedsheets back.

Jophiel stood, one hand outstretched like she was trying to stop me from doing something rash. "Haniel, please. I know this is a lot to take in. But you must stay calm."

I was about to tell her to shove calm up her ass, when Azazel ran into the room, her daggers out—one gleaming with white light, the other seething with darkness.

"What was that?" Zel asked, scanning the room for any apparent threat.

"Her powers are coming back too quickly," Jophiel said, before turning to me with urgency in her voice. "You need training to control them, or you'll hurt someone."

"I'll take care of it," Zel said, her eyes never leaving my face even as she addressed Jo.

"This is only something an *angel* can help with," Jophiel replied in a frosty tone.

"I *was* an angel," Zel snapped. "Once."

"That was thousands of years ago!"

"Enough," I yelled, holding up my glowing hands. I couldn't seem to make them stop.

"Stay with me," Jophiel said. "I will help you regain control of your powers and remind you about your angelic side. You're the daughter of two Archangels. You belong with us—not with the demons."

"No. I don't." I stared at my sister, who'd lied to me so many times and stolen so much from me. If Lucifer hadn't killed me, I'd still be a clueless human with my powers locked away. I wasn't sure where I belonged, but it wasn't with her. It wasn't with Lucifer either though. Not after what he'd done.

The two people who claimed to love me the most had hurt and betrayed me, all supposedly to protect me. They'd left me broken. Shattered. Alone.

Well, not entirely alone. Zel stood beside me, even knowing what I was. And Brandy, back in Vista—she'd always been a loyal friend. My heart clenched thinking about her. She was my real sister, and she was the one I needed now. Maybe with Zel she'd find a way to put me back together again.

I went into the bathroom and cleaned myself up, changing into fresh clothes, and then headed back out. Zel and Jophiel were still there in the guest room, glaring at each other. I grabbed the rest of my things.

"We're leaving," I said to Jophiel. "And we're taking your car. Don't try to follow us."

"No, you can't go," Jophiel started, but I brushed past her without listening and headed for the door. Would I ever be able to forgive my sister? I wasn't sure. But it definitely wasn't happening today.

As we headed outside, Zel grabbed the keys. "Where are we going?"

"To Vista." I drew in a deep, shuddering breath. "Back to Hannah's life."

7

HANNAH

The drive took nearly all day, and I spent a good bit of it telling everything to Azazel, detailing all of Lucifer and Jophiel's crimes. She listened to everything without complaint, and weathered all of my crying without making me feel any less for it. When I was done, she simply said, "That's some messed up shit," and the brutal truth of it actually made me laugh through the tears. Messed up shit indeed.

I was comforted by the thought of seeing Brandy again, and when we pulled up outside the sand-colored ranch house she owned, relief settled over me. It all looked the same as when I'd last seen it. So familiar. So simple. I was a different person now than when I'd left—many people, really, and holding far too many memories—but I craved this return to my normal, ordinary life.

"Hannah!" Brandy yelled, after throwing open the front door. She must've seen the Lamborghini pull up. It wasn't exactly subtle in a quiet suburban neighborhood like this one.

I jumped out of the car and met her halfway across the yard. She wrapped me in her arms and I breathed in, so happy to be home I nearly started crying again. At least Brandy was still my friend.

Something constant in a world that had turned completely upside down.

"I'm so happy to see you," she said, as she pulled back to look at me. I stared at her too, trying to suss out how she was doing ever since returning home from her ordeal. Her kidnapping in Las Vegas had started all of this, but surprisingly she looked better than ever. Her dark skin glowed, her brown eyes danced, and her curly hair gleamed. I could only imagine what a wreck I must look like in return.

She looked over my shoulder, her gaze resting on Zel. The Fallen had stepped out of the car, looking dark and dangerous, though luckily her knives were hidden.

I gestured back at my companion. "This is Zel, my...friend."

"Nice to meet you," Brandy said, then grabbed my hand. "Come inside so we can catch up. I want to hear everything that happened after you went back to Vegas."

That seemed like a lifetime ago, even though it had only been a few days. I tried not to think about that as we walked in and I glanced around the familiar living room with its cozy furniture. Brandy's son, Jack, was sitting on the gray couch, playing video games with Asmodeus, who I recognized instantly. Not only from the brief time I'd met him in Vegas, but from before that. All the times I'd known him during my past lives flickered through my head, threatening to overwhelm me. I rested my fingertips on my forehead as I sucked in a quick deep breath and shoved the memories back down.

"Hello, my queen," Asmodeus said with a dashing smile, and I tried not to cringe at the reminder of who I was. With dark hair, bronze skin, and the facial structure of a god, he was still incredibly hot but...something was missing. He seemed different. Dialed down somehow.

I was surprised to see him here, especially in such a casual position. Asmodeus was an ancient, powerful incubus, and though he'd obviously developed feelings for Brandy while they were both held captive together, it was impossible for them to be together. As demons of lust and sexual energy, Lilim could only sleep with a human once without killing them. Yet somehow he was here, playing video games with Brandy's son like it was a normal thing for an incubus to do.

His mouth opened like he might say something more, but instead he grunted as Jack squealed and leaped off the couch, throwing his game controller in Asmodeus's lap on the way.

"Hannah!" Jack ran the last few steps to me, his arms out before he caught me around my waist, barreling into me and nearly knocking me over with his exuberance. He was sticky, I could tell without even touching him, but I didn't care. My heart swelled as I held him close.

"Did I hear Hannah?" I turned at the familiar voice as Brandy's mom, Donna, walked in, her lips forming a gentle smile. "Oh, my sweet girl. Thank you for saving my daughter."

Donna had once been a bigger woman before cancer ravaged her, but she still gave big hugs. In her arms I inhaled her familiar strong perfume, and a fresh wave of emotion threatened to overwhelm me. These people were genuinely happy to see me, and I'd missed them too. I regretted that everything had changed so much since I was last here.

But then I remembered they were happy to see *Hannah*. Was I even Hannah anymore? Was I perpetuating a lie by coming here?

"Let me take Jack outside for a bit before dinner," Donna said, grabbing the boy's hand. "I'll let you kids talk."

"What happened to you?" Zel asked Asmodeus once they were gone, her words abrupt and to the point—and confirmation I wasn't the only one who'd noticed he seemed like a lesser version of his usual self.

He looked down at himself and shrugged like the next words were no big deal. "I asked my mother to make me mortal so I could be with Brandy. As Archdemon of the Lilim, she alone has that power over our kind."

Zel snorted and gave me a look, her eyebrow raised as high as I'd ever seen it. "Lots of that going around it seems."

Oh. My chest tightened. It was the same thing Jophiel had done to me. The difference was that he'd requested it, whereas it had been done to me unknowingly.

"That's a big sacrifice to make," I said, and now I understood why Brandy looked so radiant. What an amazing act of love. He gave up everything to be with her. Just like that.

"But you're going to grow old and die now," Zel said, sounding horrified.

"Yes." Asmodeus took Brandy's hand and seemed excited by the idea. "I've had plenty of immortality, and it was time for a change. I just hope she'll still want me when I'm old and gray."

Brandy looked at Asmodeus, her brown eyes full of warmth and love. "It's more likely he won't want me when I'm old, and will regret giving up his immortality and powers."

He reached up to cup her face, gazing into her eyes. "I'd never feel that way. I couldn't."

The truth of his words ricocheted within me. Even as a human I'd always had this gut instinct about truth and knew I was a good judge of character, but now I realized that was my Ofanim powers all along. Now they'd returned in full force, and Asmodeus's truth was strong and pure, like a shining light inside him.

"I'm so happy for you both," I said with a faint smile. And I was, even if I was concealing shock that Asmodeus was willing to give up so much after knowing Brandy for such a short time. But I supposed when you met your fated mate, there was little that could stop you from wanting to be with them. I felt that unbreakable bond with Lucifer even now, hundreds of miles away, no matter how upset I was with him.

Zel plopped on the couch beside Asmodeus. "Mad Green Zombie? I love that game. What level are you on?"

Brandy rolled her eyes at another gamer in the house and looked at me. "Hungry?"

"I could eat." We'd stopped for lunch briefly during our long drive, but with everything else going on in my head and the turmoil of my emotions, food had seemed like the smallest of worries.

We walked into the kitchen to find Donna had taken Jack outside into the yard, where he was riding his bike around in circles.

I watched him out of the window for a moment with a pang in my chest. I'd missed this. But I knew I didn't belong here either.

Brandy began getting some things out of the fridge as she talked. "I've got lasagna in the oven. Good thing I made a big one. Should be about fifteen minutes. Enough time for you to tell me what's been going on...and why you're here instead of with Lucifer."

I sighed and shook my head as I registered her implied question. How could I answer her? My entire life had been upheaved in the last few days. I didn't even know how to begin—and wasn't sure I wanted to drag Brandy back into this dark world with me. Not now that she had gotten out of it with Asmodeus and had a chance at a happy ending. But there were definitely things I needed to tell her. Truths I couldn't keep hidden.

"I had to get away for a while," I finally said. "I needed to get back to my normal life, and wanted to see you."

She threw some lettuce in a large bowl, then grabbed some croutons. "I'm really glad to see you, but I can tell something's up with you. Spill it."

"I found out something about myself, something that's changed everything." I sucked in a breath and positioned myself in the center of the kitchen so I didn't knock anything over, before spreading my wings. "I'm an angel."

"Oh shit!" She dropped the salad dressing she was about to open, and the plastic bottle bounced on the floor. "You have wings! Like actual wings!"

Crap. I probably should have given her some more warning before letting the wings out. "Yeah, I do. Turns out my name is really Haniel, and the reason I couldn't remember my past was because Jophiel kept it from me, along with my powers. But now that's over."

"I always hated your sister," Brandy muttered. "Can I touch them?"

I nodded, and she lightly ran her fingers over the silver feathers. It sent a weird tingle through me and felt way too intimate, but I kept myself from squirming at her touch.

"Holy shit. An angel." She gazed upon my wings with such

reverence, it made me feel self-conscious, and I quickly tucked them away again.

"I hope this doesn't change anything between us. I know my whole life as Hannah was a lie, but..."

"No way. You're still my best friend. Sure, you didn't remember who you were for a while, but so what? Our friendship was never fake. Everything we had was real."

Warmth filled my chest as relief settled over my shoulders. "Thank you, Brandy."

"Of course." She wrapped me in a tight hug. "Now what's going on with Lucifer?"

My back stiffened at his name and the rush of emotions that came with it. "It's...complicated. We've had a bit of a falling out. Hence why I needed to get away."

"Well, I'll help you however I can," Brandy said, as she went back to making the salad. "If you need to crash here for a while, that's fine. Technically you still live here anyway. Your friend Zel can take the couch."

"I'm not sure what we're going to do. I have a lot to think about. But thank you for the offer."

She nodded and waved me away. "Dinner will be ready soon. Why don't you go to your room and take a minute to clean yourself up? I love you girl, but you look like a hot mess."

Her brutal honesty made me laugh, and I looked down at myself and realized she was right. After two days on the road and a lot of crying along the way—and no showers either—I could really use some freshening up.

I headed up the stairs toward my room, except once I stepped inside, it hit me then that nothing about this life was truly mine anymore. Not like it had been.

This room was the smallest one in the house, big enough for a bed and not much else, but that had never bothered me. I'd just been grateful Brandy had let me stay with her. I didn't have much stuff either, and all of it seemed like something from a dream now anyway. I'd earned the money and purchased it all myself, but everything felt like trinkets from another life. A double bed with emerald green throw pillows. Piles of books. Cute little houseplants that desperately needed to be watered.

On my dresser was a framed photo of my parents. Or rather, the people Jophiel had said were my parents. I picked it up and studied it, but I had no memory of any of these people. With a huff, I slammed the frame facedown on the dresser. Probably a damn stock photo.

I pressed my palms to my eyes, willing back the tears I didn't want to cry. I'd done enough crying already and I was damn tired of it, but I didn't know how to move on from this either. I'd come back here in the hopes of returning to my ordinary life, even for just a short time, but that life was a lie. These things weren't mine. They belonged to Hannah. And Hannah wasn't real.

How could Jophiel have done this to me? Not just once, but again and again?

The more I tried to ignore my memories of those other fake lives, the more I saw and remembered. Other homes where I lived by myself, with few friends or other connections. Jobs that tied me to one spot and kept me too poor to do much of anything. Relationships that never went anywhere. I even had a dog once, a little mutt with big brown eyes and a shaggy coat. What happened to that dog? I had no idea.

Jophiel had kept me close-by and completely clueless so she could control me. Supposedly for my protection, but that didn't excuse her behavior or her actions. That didn't make it right. Nobody should be able to take over someone else's life like that.

And she'd kept me from my mate.

I was still upset with Lucifer, but she had no right to keep me apart from him for so many years. She'd taken his memories too, I remembered now. We should have had a chance to grieve our unborn daughter together, and instead we'd been torn apart and made to forget. Now we had the memories back, but we were both too broken to deal with them.

Brandy called out that dinner was almost ready, and I realized I was supposed to be pulling myself together. I stared at myself in the mirror, noting my stringy blond hair and the dark circles under my blue eyes. I really was a mess. I tried to clean up a bit, changing my clothes, brushing my hair, throwing on some deodorant. The best I could do without taking a shower.

As I headed down to dinner, plastering on a fake smile for my companions, I felt more lost than ever. What in the world was I supposed to do now? Where did I truly belong? And who was I, really?

8

HANNAH

I n the morning there was only one place for me to go—my flower
shop.

I'd crashed in my bedroom overnight, though I'd barely slept. I'd
been too plagued by nightmares and memories to get much rest.
Now I covered my mouth with a yawn as the Lamborghini
approached the familiar little shop with its dark green awning and
elegant white script spelling out the name Elegant Thorn.

Thorn. My last name. I'd always been amused by how perfect it
was for the owners of a flower shop, like perhaps the name had influenced my parents' profession somehow. Now I knew the last name
was completely fake. I wondered if it amused Jophiel to give me that
name, or if she was just that uncreative and went for the obvious.
Probably the latter, knowing my sister. I was lucky she didn't name
me Hannah Blossom or something.

I got out of the car, but held up a hand when Zel started to
follow me. "I need a moment in there alone. Please."

She huffed and looked like she might argue, but then said, "Fine.
I'll be right outside though."

With a deep breath, I approached the front door. The place was
closed and empty, the windows still displaying jack-o-lanterns and

other Halloween decor, even though it was days past the holiday. We should have moved on to Thanksgiving preparations already, but there was no sign of Maggie, who was supposed to have been running the place for me in my absence.

I pulled the keys out of my pocket and unlocked the door before walking inside. The shop smelled musty, like greenery that was giving up, like death was already taking some of my beloved plants. They all needed tending, and it broke my heart to see them in such a state. Petals were starting to curl, and leaves drooped and had lost their shine. I sighed, knowing this was my fault. I hadn't been the most attentive boss while in Las Vegas, especially with everything going on, and it's not like I paid Maggie much either. It had probably gotten to be too much for her, and I couldn't blame her for walking away.

It didn't matter now anyway. The shop was another lie. My parents had never owned this place. They weren't even real. For the last five years, I'd kept the business going out of loyalty to their memory and a desire to keep their legacy alive, but it was all another of Jophiel's fabrications.

The shop hadn't ever made a lot of money, but I'd worked so hard to keep it going. And for what? In the grand scheme of things, what had been the point? Oh, the work was enjoyable, sure. I loved dealing with plants, and seeing the joy and beauty that flowers could bring to the world. How could I not, when I was the reincarnation of Persephone? But I'd always wanted more. I'd always known, deep down, that my life was meant for bigger things than running a small flower shop.

I filled a can with water and began giving the plants a drink, talking to them as I went, reassuring them they'd be okay. They'd have some water and perk right back up in no time. I touched a leaf here and there as I passed, willing it to grow strong again. I breathed in the scent of the roses, and smiled faintly at the bright daffodils as I walked through the place I used to call mine.

I was deep in the back row of plants when the bell chimed to announce that someone had come in the front door. "Zel, I said wait outside."

Nobody answered, and I paused. Zel would have shot back a mouthful of attitude, and she would have stopped anyone who was a threat. Shit, what if it was a customer? I sucked in a deep breath and tried to put a pleasant expression on my face as I walked toward the front of the shop. But then I spotted him through the rows of greenery.

Lucifer.

He wore a crisp black suit and a white shirt with the collar unbuttoned, radiating sex, power, and dominance with every step he took toward me. My emotions warred inside me. Seeing him again was torture now, with the knowledge of what he'd done, along with all my recovered memories. But I'd missed him too. Of course I did. How could I not? He was my mate. We were bound together for all eternity...like it or not.

"What are you doing here?" I asked, keeping my voice as even as I could manage.

"I allowed you to leave Las Vegas," he said as he stalked toward me. "But you've been gone far too long. It's time you return home with me."

His arrogant, commanding tone immediately annoyed me. I put my hands on my hips as I stood my ground against him. "And if I won't go?"

A dark smile crossed his sensual lips. "Then I'll make you come. In both senses of the word. Should I get the handcuffs? That could be fun."

"You're impossible," I muttered, as I tried to ignore the erotic thoughts his words brought to mind. "I'm not going anywhere."

His smile dropped and his green eyes burned with dark power. "You belong by my side. You're my mate. My queen. My *wife*."

"We are not married!" I blurted out.

"Oh, yes we are. I know you went to see Jophiel, and she must have given you your memories back. Surely you remember our hasty wedding with Samael as our officiant, done at your request after we discovered you were pregnant. I thought the whole thing was silly—angels and demons tend not to bother with the marriage thing—but you insisted. I assumed it was an eccentricity from all the lives you spent as a human."

Shit. I remembered that now that he'd brought it up. We'd had the private ceremony at his palace in Hell, and he'd chuckled at me for wearing a white dress and insisting on a bouquet of flowers. I'd wanted the whole human ceremony because I was just so happy about the pregnancy and so head over heels in love with Lucifer. With our relationship forbidden and secret, I wanted some way to make it feel official before our daughter was born. Samael had married us outside in a private garden, under the endless stars, and for a short time everything had seemed perfect.

But I also remembered something else. Seeing Gadreel poke his head into the garden, looking for Samael, then apologizing profusely for interrupting us. That's when he found me. And only a few weeks later, he killed me...and our daughter.

I couldn't even reply to Lucifer, because the memory of our wedding only brought back pain now. What once had been a joyous day only reminded me of everything we'd lost. My face crumpled and I turned away, covering my eyes with my hands to try to stop the tears from escaping.

Lucifer's arms wrapped around me, pulling me against him and holding me tight. "So you do remember."

"Part of me wishes I didn't. Our daughter..." The pain returned, and it was too much. I couldn't breathe. I pressed my face into his shoulder, craving his familiar strength.

"I know," he said in a low voice. "I understand."

Yes—he was the only one who truly understood. Jophiel had taken his memories too, and he'd only just regained them a few days ago. The pain was fresh for him also, which was why he'd warned me I might not want the memories back.

I gripped the front of his suit. "I should have listened to you and stayed in the dark."

"No, it's better that you know. Harder, yes. But better." His hand moved slowly across my back as he held me close. "I knew you'd choose to get the memories back. You always did want the truth."

The truth...the truth brought pain. But it brought clarity too. I took a deep breath and looked up at Lucifer with determination burning inside me. "Adam. He took our daughter. He has to pay."

Lucifer growled in response, his chest rumbling with the force of his rage. "My people are searching for Adam as we speak. With the curse broken, we can defeat him once and for all."

I nodded, focusing on the anger to get through the pain. Vengeance wouldn't return what was lost, but it would help. And as long as Adam was out there, he would continue trying to torment us and everyone we loved. I was going to kill that fucker, once and for all, even if it was the last thing I did in this life.

"Adam has taken everything from me a thousand times, but that night I thought he might truly have broken me," Lucifer said, his voice distant as he recalled his own memories. "You vanished, leaving behind only a trail of blood, and I knew it was bad. I managed to track you to Jophiel, but by then it was too late. She told me you were both gone." His hands tightened around me, pressing me harder against him. "I'm very familiar with grief after watching you die so many times, but this...this was different. It was unbearable. I could barely think straight, and Jophiel was able to overpower me and remove my memories. Perhaps I didn't fight it too hard. Perhaps oblivion seemed preferable."

I sensed the great depths of grief inside Lucifer, akin to my own, even though he was good at hiding it from his face. "I wanted the same thing. It seemed easier at the time to forget."

"But now the pain is back, just as raw, and you want to tear the world apart," he finished for me.

Emotion made my throat tight. He knew me so well after hundreds of lifetimes together, no matter what body I was in. "Yes."

He cupped my cheek in his hand, his eyes intense as he gazed into mine. "Then return to Las Vegas with me as my dark queen, and together we'll burn the world down and rebuild it from the ashes."

I stepped back from him and glanced around the flower shop that had once meant so much to me. Now all I wanted was for Adam to pay. I wouldn't find justice if I stayed here in Hannah's life.

I wouldn't find peace either, if such a thing was possible. But leaving this place behind was harder than I expected. For the last five years, this had been my life. Real or not, it was everything I'd known...until I'd met Lucifer.

I turned back to him, my decision made. "I'll go with you, but just because I'm returning doesn't mean I forgive you for what you did. If you want me to be your queen, you have to start treating me as your equal. You can't keep making decisions that turn my whole world upside down without discussing them with me first."

His eyes narrowed. "I already explained why I had to kill you the way I did. You're welcome to be mad at me for the next few hundred years, but I stand by my actions."

"But you didn't give me a choice! Just like Jophiel, you took away my options and had all the power in the situation. I know you had your reasons, but I still can't accept that this was the only way, and I'm not sure how to move on from it. You *killed* me, Lucifer. With your own hands."

He scowled at that, his jaw clenching, but after a moment he managed to say, "I suppose I'm so used to making all the decisions on my own after ruling the demons for thousands of years, and most of that time without you by my side. I will do my best to consult with you in the future."

It wasn't an apology, but it was something. An acknowledgment that maybe he'd fucked up a little at least. I wasn't sure Lucifer could really change at this point, but he was my mate. The two of us were inevitable, and I couldn't escape him even if I wanted to. Which meant I had to find a way to live with him. More than that, I *wanted* to find a way. I couldn't imagine my life without him.

"What will you do about the shop?" he asked.

"Close it, I guess. It was never really mine anyway. Jophiel is the real owner."

He rested a hand on my shoulder possessively. "I'll send someone to deal with it. My people will handle everything."

I nodded and looked around the place for what was probably the last time, and all I felt was an aching hollowness deep inside me. "I'm ready."

9

LUCIFER

H annah was silent the entire drive back to her friend Brandy's house. I couldn't blame her. She'd been through a lot these past few days, but now she would return home to Vegas where she belonged, and together we would get through this. It was clear Hannah needed time, and I had plenty to give her—we had forever, after all.

But first, she wished to say goodbye to her friend and collect her things. We left the limo behind and approached the front door of the quaint little house, while Zel waited in the Lamborghini. I was probably going to have to send Jophiel a bill for that car, since my mate seemed to have claimed it as her own. Or, if Hannah preferred, I'd buy her a new one in every color if that would make her happy. I owed her that much.

"Oh," Brandy said, when she opened the door and caught sight of me. She didn't shrink back, but her eyes got huge when she realized the devil was standing on her front porch. We'd met once before, when I'd rescued her from an abandoned motel in the middle of the desert where she was being held captive by shifters. Needless to say, I'd made a strong impression.

"I believe you've met Lucifer," Hannah said, gesturing at me.

I took Brandy's hand and kissed it, which only made her look more shocked, much to my amusement. "A pleasure to see you again. You seem to have recovered nicely from your ordeal."

"Thank you again for saving us." Brandy stepped back and allowed us entry into her home. "Please come in."

I followed Hannah inside and surveyed the living room with furniture that had obviously seen better days. A rug that curled slightly at the end. A couch with arms worn thin from use. A pillow with frayed edges. But most shocking of all was Asmodeus standing in the center of the room in his black suit, somehow looking as though he belonged there.

"I'm going back to Las Vegas," Hannah told Brandy. "I'm just here to get my things."

Brandy shot me a quick glance and nodded. "I'll help you pack up."

The two of them went up the stairs, leaving me alone with Asmodeus. He cleared his throat.

"My lord," he said, bowing slightly.

I scanned him from head to toe, noting how much he had changed. No longer did he radiate his incubus sensuality, that innate power that drew people to him and made them want to rip their clothes off. To all of my senses, he was completely human.

"It's true then," I said. "You gave up your immortality."

The ancient demon bowed his head, his black hair catching the light. "Yes. I've made all the arrangements to pass control of my Lilim duties to my assistant Himeros. Everything shall continue to run smoothly, my lord."

I held out a hand to him. "I'll be sad to lose you. You've always been one of the few I could trust, and a good friend too. I wish you all the best."

He clasped my hand in a warm shake, and seemed relieved by my words. "Thank you, Lucifer. That means a lot."

"Was it worth it?" I asked in a low voice. "Giving up all your powers and your immortality?"

Asmodeus stared at the stairs Brandy had gone up. "It's worth it. I'd do it a million times over for my mate."

I understood perfectly. I would've done the same if that was what it took to be with my woman too. "Take good care of her. Hannah is very fond of her."

Asmodeus stood taller, his chest puffing out a bit. "I will. I plan to take Brandy and her son to Disney World soon, and then I'll get us a huge mansion on the beach and spoil the crap out of them." His gaze softened. "Brandy's been through a lot. So has her son. I'm going to treat her like a queen and give them both the life they deserve."

"Good," I said. "You certainly have the money for it, but please let me know if there's anything you need from me." For decades, Asmodeus ran strip clubs under my command in service of the Lilim, and though he was passing on that responsibility now, he'd been rewarded generously for his work over the years. Besides, Asmodeus was almost as old as I was, and no doubt had a large stash of money tucked away after all this time.

Asmodeus hesitated. "Actually there is something. I wondered if I could have one last favor from you for all my years of loyal service."

That sounded ominous, but I'd always been one to grant favors, usually in exchange for a favor in return at some point. "What is it?"

"Brandy's mother has terminal cancer. There is nothing the human doctors can do. Might you ask one of the angels to heal her? I know you have some allies among the Malakim now."

I clasped his shoulder and gave him a firm nod. "It will be done."

"Thank you, my lord," he said, his shoulders dropping in relief. "You are a fine king, and it was an honor to serve you."

Hannah came down the stairs then, carrying a bag on each arm. "I think I have everything I need."

Brandy also returned with her son and the older, frail woman who must be her mother. Hannah looked at them all with sadness in her eyes, and I took the bags from her arms, along with the one Brandy was holding.

Hannah gave me a nod in thanks and then turned to the others. "I guess this is it then. Thank you for letting me live here with you for the last few years. I'm sorry to leave in such a rush."

Brandy shook her head and grabbed Hannah's hands. "No,

thank you for helping around the house with Jack and everything else. It won't be the same without you here. Promise you'll come visit sometime."

"I will. And you all have to come to Las Vegas to visit us."

"Yes, my hotel would be happy to host your family whenever you'd like," I said. "My treat, of course."

Donna's face lit up. "That sounds lovely."

"Yes, it does." Brandy fixed a glare on me. "But listen. You better not hurt Hannah. I don't care if you are the devil, I will kick your ass."

I raised an eyebrow at the feisty human. We both knew how that would end, but I had to give Brandy credit for her courage and loyalty to Hannah. "Noted. And now we really should be on our way."

Hannah nodded, and then gave each person a long hug before saying her final goodbyes. I shook Asmodeus's hand one last time, and then gripped Hannah's bags and led her outside.

"Took you long enough," Zel said, from where she leaned against the Lamborghini.

Our limo driver rushed out and took Hannah's bags from me, then loaded them into the car. He was a young vampire and eager to serve, but I couldn't help but wonder if he was truly loyal or only spying on me for his Archdemon, Baal. When we returned, I'd have to deal with the Archdemons and find out who among them was loyal to me.

As I ushered Hannah toward the limo, the hair on the back of my neck prickled, just as Zel drew her knives. The sky was cloudy and full of the promise of rain, a rare and precious thing in Southern California, but it darkened even further as a large shape flew over the nearby houses.

"Something's coming." I pushed Hannah between me and the limo as I scanned the sky for the threat. "Get in the car."

The shape flew close enough that I could identify it. Large wings with dark red scales. Reptilian black eyes. Huge talons and fangs. A fucking dragon. Out here in suburbia in the middle of the damn day when anyone could see it. The outright insubordination made me furious, and I quickly spread darkness around the area, obscuring us from any neighbors who might peer out their windows.

"What's happening?" Hannah asked, and I realized she was the only one who couldn't see through the murky shadows. The rest of us all had eyes accustomed to living in the eternal darkness of Hell, but as an angel, Hannah was more suited for the land of light.

Zel jumped into action, spreading her black wings and launching into the air toward the dragon. I maintained a defensive pose in front of Hannah, who'd ignored me when I'd ordered her into the car, naturally.

The dragon immediately sliced at Zel with its talons, though he seemed to have enough sense not to shoot flames from his mouth. If he set fire to Brandy's neighborhood, he would quickly see the true depths of my rage, just before I ended his life.

Zel managed to catch the tip of the dragon's wing with her light-infused dagger, making the beast roar loud enough to shake the windows of the nearby houses. I hoped the residents would write that off as an earthquake or a loud truck passing by, but this had to end quickly or someone would get suspicious. The last thing I wanted to deal with was a bunch of nosy humans showing up and asking questions.

The dragon retaliated by knocking Zel back hard. She crashed against a nearby roof, then rolled off it and dropped onto the grass, sending shingles flying. Oh, for fuck's sake.

"Can't we help her?" Hannah asked, and I noticed she was glowing again, like a lighthouse in the middle of a storm. The dragon noticed too, and immediately honed in on us.

"She's fine," I said. "You just focus on keeping your powers under control. I'll handle this."

I had to get control of this situation, fast. As the dragon tucked its wings and dove toward us, I reached out with tentacles of darkness and wrapped them around the beast. He tried to shrug them off and managed to get a wing free, but then Zel slammed into his side, distracting him enough for me to encase him completely in my shadows. Shadows which Hannah's bright light was quickly burning through. She didn't even realize she was doing it either.

The dragon spun and twisted, but couldn't escape the dark coils wrapped around him, and his momentum carried him straight down into the middle of the road. He hit it so hard he sent out fractures and cracks in the asphalt where he landed. Zel set down beside him, brandishing her daggers, and the dragon hissed at her with hatred in his eyes.

I stood over the dragon, looking down at the captive beast. Fury pounded in my veins, and I allowed darkness to swirl around me menacingly while brilliant blue hellfire sparked in my palms. "You dare to attack me and my mate in the middle of a human area in broad daylight. Explain yourself."

"I seek vengeance!" The dragon roared the words in my face, his fangs dripping with venom. "You killed my father!"

Ah, of course. This must be Mammon's oldest son, Valefar. I'd met him a few times before, but never in his dragon form. With some effort I clenched my hands, extinguishing the hellfire, as I remembered Samael's words about making peace with the remaining dragons. I supposed he had a point. There was a reason I kept him as my advisor, after all.

"You're right. I did kill your father. Mammon conspired against me and attempted a coup. He attacked me in my own home. I couldn't let such insurrection go unpunished." I held up a hand before he could say anything in return. "Like it or not, I am your king, and you are now the Archdemon of the dragons. There are very few of your kind left, which means you have a choice. You can bow before me and swear loyalty, or you can go to war with me, as your father did. You know how well that went for him." I paused, letting my words sink in. "I don't want to wipe out the remaining dragons, but I will if I must."

The dragon growled, but then his reptilian eyes closed, and I sensed he had given up the fight. I nodded at Zel so she'd back away. She scowled, but sheathed her daggers and gave the dragon some space. Hannah had managed to get her glowing under control by now, and the street fell silent, the area still unnaturally dark.

Valefar got to his taloned feet and shook out his wings, his gaze still on me. "This isn't over."

With a heavy flap of his wings, he took to the skies and flew out of sight over the rows of houses. I waited until he was gone and then released the darkness, allowing the sun to shine down on the street once more through the clouds.

Hannah let out a long breath as the shadows receded, as if relieved to see the light again. "You're letting him go?"

I smoothed the front of my suit and shrugged. "He needs to step up and become a leader to his people now. If he doesn't, we'll deal with it."

I helped Hannah into the limo so we could resume our journey to the private jet that would take us home to Las Vegas. But as she slid across the black leather seats, her face was troubled.

"What is it?" I asked.

"My powers. I'm having a hard time controlling them. I think it's because I have so many memories clambering around inside my head, it's hard to keep them straight and sort through them all." She leaned her head back on the leather seat, as if exhausted. "Jophiel offered to help me remember how to use them, but I don't want anything from her."

"I know some angels who might be able to help. The ones who helped resurrect you." I rested a possessive hand on her knee, and though she stiffened, she didn't move away. A small sign of progress. "I'll take care of everything."

Anything she needed, I'd get her. If she wanted me to go to the depths of Hell or the heights of Heaven, so be it.

I'd do whatever it took to win Hannah's heart back.

10

HANNAH

W alking back into the penthouse was like returning to the dark depths of the underworld. Lucifer wanted me to be his queen again, the Persephone to his Hades, but how could I rule by his side when I couldn't forgive him? Or when he didn't treat me as an equal?

And would any demon accept me, an angel, as their queen?

I returned to the guest room, unable to share a bedroom with Lucifer for the time being. I was pleased to see someone had brought my bags up, and that my plants here were all still doing well. Oddly, this space felt more like home than any of the other places I'd visited over the last few days, especially once I began unpacking the belongings I'd brought from Brandy's house. The green throw pillows did a nice job of touching up the otherwise bland furnishings, and on the nightstand I added a photo of me with Brandy and Jack when we went to the San Diego Zoo, which made me smile every time I looked at it.

When I stepped back into the main room of the penthouse—which had all been restored to its former glory, even the destroyed bar—the five people who'd been there when I'd been resurrected were back, sitting around the room on leather couches and black barstools. I looked at Lucifer, waiting for him to properly introduce me to them, but then my eyes landed on the dark-haired man beside him and I inhaled sharply.

Kassiel.

My son.

The knowledge hit me in the chest so hard and with such surety I was shocked I hadn't realized it before. Rapid, brief glimpses of his childhood lit up my mind like the flash of a camera, all from my life as Lenore in the 19th century. He looked so much like his father, both as a child and now. He even wore a similar well-fitted black suit.

I stepped toward him, my heart nearly bursting out of me with the need to be with him again after all these long years. "Kassiel..."

"Hello, mother." He gave me a warm smile, but his voice seemed reserved, and his English accent only added to the effect. I moved close and he embraced me, and now I was crying again, but for once they were tears of joy. I didn't even care that all the other people in the room were surely staring at us. All I knew was that I had my son back after decades apart, and I wanted to savor every second with him.

I reached up to touch his face as I looked him over, marveling at how he hadn't physically changed after over a century, yet he somehow looked different. Older. Wiser. Damn, I'd missed so much of his life.

"I'm so happy to see you," I said, unable to contain my huge smile. "I want to know every single thing that's happened to you while I've been gone."

"We'll catch up later. I promise." Kassiel squeezed my hand and stepped back, then gestured to the curvy brunette sitting on the sofa. "Let me introduce you to my mate, Olivia."

She was distractingly beautiful, her eyes a clear green, her skin almost luminescent, and her curls a rich, dark brown. In the past I would have felt intimidated by her beauty, and I nearly took a step back, like I would have done as a human—but then I remembered I was an angel too. More than that, I was Eve and Persephone and so much more. Besides, I was Kassiel's mother. If anyone should be intimidated, it was her. I stood my ground and gave her a nod in acknowledgment.

"It's an honor to meet you," Olivia said, as she rose to her feet.

"Olivia is the only known half-succubus, half-angel hybrid," Lucifer said. "She currently acts as the official liaison between angels and demons, working for Archangel Gabriel and myself to keep the peace. I thought she might be able to help you balance living between both worlds."

"I would appreciate that," I said. So many of my memories were of war between angels and demons, a war I'd fought on both sides. Now we were at peace, but things between the two races still seemed strained, and I was definitely caught in the middle as an angel surrounded by demons.

"I asked Olivia's other mates to join us as well," Lucifer said. "As angels, they can answer your questions and work with you to control your powers." He nodded toward a serious man with cool, calculating eyes and glossy black hair. "Bastien, in particular, should be able to help with that. He's also an Ofanim."

Bastien bowed his head in response. "I shall assist you however I can."

"Thank you," I said.

Lucifer turned toward the handsome olive-skinned man sitting at the bar, who flashed me a charming smile, his eyes sparkling. "This is Marcus. He's the one who resurrected you. I plan to send him to heal Brandy's mother."

I stepped forward and took Marcus's hands, giving them a light squeeze. "Thank you for using your powers to bring me back, and for helping my friend. I owe you so much."

"It's what I do," he said, with a quick wink.

Lucifer nodded toward the last person in the room, a broad-shouldered, muscular man with golden hair and a square jaw. "Callan is Jophiel's son. Your nephew."

My eyes widened as I studied Callan closer. He did have some of Jophiel's look to him, though I suspected he had a lot of his father in there too. He stood near the window overlooking Las Vegas, as if trying to remain as far away from Lucifer as possible, and I wondered if there was some history there.

"I look forward to getting to know you. My relationship with my sister is..." I hesitated, searching for the diplomatic word. "Strained. But I hope that won't stop us from being a family."

Callan grunted. "My relationship with my mother is strained too. She's not exactly an easy person to love."

"No, she's not," I said with a faint smile. "Jophiel mentioned she had another son too."

"Yes. Ekariel." Callan's jaw clenched. "He was kidnapped as a child and held for years by a human cult bent on killing all supernaturals. He's currently taking some classes at Seraphim Academy so he can catch up on everything he missed over the years."

How terrible. Jophiel had mentioned the same thing, but it had happened after I was turned human. Maybe I should be taking classes with him also—I obviously had a lot to catch up on also. "I hope to meet him too someday."

"I should get going so I can heal your friend." Marcus set down his glass and stood. He leaned forward and kissed Olivia on the cheek. "I'll be back as soon as I can."

I watched their interactions closely. Was Olivia with all four of these men? And they were just...okay with it? Including my son? How interesting. I supposed if she was part succubus she'd need more than one person to satisfy her needs, but in my vague memories I'd never seen a Lilim with actual mates before. They tended to not form attachments, from what I recalled. Then again, Asmodeus had given up his incubus powers and immortality to be with Brandy, so I supposed anything was possible.

"We should probably head out too," Olivia said.

"We'll begin training tomorrow after you've had a chance to rest," Bastien told me.

"Thank you." I swallowed in an attempt to bring my emotions back under control, but it was hard. I looked again at the people in the room, including my nephew and my son, remembering all they'd done for me. I wouldn't be alive now if not for them. "I can't thank you all enough."

Once everyone had left, I spun around to face Lucifer. "Why didn't you tell me about Kassiel?"

He let out a frustrated sigh as he moved behind the bar. "As I've mentioned before, I've been slowly doling out information about your past lives to not overwhelm you. When you walked into my penthouse and asked me to find your friend, I couldn't exactly say, 'hey, I know we just met, but we have three sons together.'"

Three... Yes.

I remembered now. In the back corners of my mind, I'd known I had children, but now the feeling inside me sharpened, and with it came two other names: Belial and Damien.

"Where are they now?" I asked. Belial was the oldest, born during my original life as Eve. Damien came second, when I was Persephone, and Kassiel was the youngest. They each had centuries between them, but that was fairly normal since having a child as an immortal was difficult and rare.

Lucifer scowled and poured himself a drink. "I haven't seen either of them in years."

"Why not?" I sat on a barstool and watched the amber liquid pour into his glass. "I'll take one too."

Lucifer arched one of his perfect, dark eyebrows, looking every inch the handsome devil he was. "I thought you didn't drink."

"That was back when I thought my parents were killed by a drunk driver." As soon as he poured me a glass, I downed it and set the glass down, feeling the burn in my throat. Not that it would affect me now that I was an angel again. And if there was ever a time for a drink, it was now.

Lucifer looked amused as he poured me a second drink. "Damien lives in Faerie and acts as a spy in High King Oberon's court. We pretend to be estranged so Oberon will trust him, but he secretly reports back to me."

"Sounds dangerous." I bristled a little, wondering how he could put our son in such danger.

"It was his idea." He lifted a shoulder in a casual shrug. "Damien can handle himself. We made sure of that."

I stared into my glass, reminding myself that my sons were not boys anymore, but ancient, powerful men in their own right. How strange to realize your own children were older than you were—at least in this body.

"And Belial..." Lucifer finished his whiskey and slammed the glass down on the counter. "I don't know where Belial is. We haven't spoken in centuries."

Centuries? How was that possible? I vaguely recalled that our eldest son had always had a difficult relationship with Lucifer, though the details were still fuzzy. I hoped more of them would come back to me soon. "And Kassiel? What's he been doing all these years?"

"He's been working as a spy among the angels for me for some time," Lucifer said, practically swelling with pride for our son. "He recently helped take down a secret society of angels bent on sending all demons back to Hell permanently."

A smile lit up my face upon hearing of our son's accomplishments, but then it dropped when I remembered there should have been a fourth child. Our first and only daughter. I quickly looked away before the emotion could grab hold of me again.

Lucifer slowly walked around the bar, then put his arm around me, drawing me against him. "I know. I mourn her as well."

I let him comfort me, putting my head on his chest as I thought about the little girl that should've been. The pain haunted me as if it had happened yesterday. When I looked up at Lucifer I sensed he felt the same grief, though he was much better at hiding it.

Unable to help myself, I reached up and touched his jaw, slowly rubbing my fingertips across the dark stubble. That light touch seemed to ignite something inside him, because his eyes suddenly blazed just before he lowered his head and pressed his lips to mine. Fire coursed through me as his mouth claimed me, reminding me he was my mate and we were meant to be together. That I was his, always his, for all eternity.

My body begged me to surrender, to lose myself in him, but somehow I managed to pull back. Our eyes met, and I felt short of breath, my blood racing with desire. Lucifer's lips were parted slightly, practically demanding I kiss them again, and it took every ounce of willpower not to close the gap between us. The bond between us was strong, drawing us together at all times, and we'd been through so much together, it was natural for us to want to find comfort in each other again. But I wasn't ready to be with him. Not yet. He still had a lot to answer for, and I still had to figure out who I was, both with and without Lucifer.

"I'm going to bed," I said.

"Yes, you are," Lucifer growled. "With me."

I hated how sexy he was when he was arrogant and demanding, and I hated how much I desperately wanted to give in to him. But I wouldn't. I refused. "Not a chance."

The look he gave me was absolutely smoldering. "I'm tempted to haul you over my shoulder and carry you back to my bed, but I'll give you tonight to rest. But that's it. One night."

Heat pooled between my thighs at his words, despite my objections. "And then?"

Darkness gathered around him as he gave me a villainous smile. "And then I'll remind you that you're *mine*."

11

HANNAH

The next day, Bastien joined me just after breakfast to begin my training, and I suggested we head outside onto the balcony since it was such a nice day. You'd never know it was November in Las Vegas, with those perfect blue skies and the warm breeze. My angelic side wanted to let my wings out and preen in the sun like a bird, but I restrained myself.

We took seats at a table near the infinity pool, with a view of the famous Vegas Strip below us. Bastien's sharp eyes focused on me, and I had a feeling he never missed anything. "We're going to start by learning about auras," he said. "In your position you'll need to be able to discern truth."

I nodded, eager to learn—or remember, rather. "I can already tell if someone is lying. Even when I was a human I...felt things. Like a gut instinct. I just didn't know what it was then."

"That was your Ofanim powers coming through even though they were suppressed. Now you must do it with intention. Viewing auras allows you to see the truth about someone even if they don't speak. Do you remember how to see them?"

I filtered through my memories, but nothing came to mind. I took a deep breath and closed my eyes, but I shook my head as frustration prickled through each of my nerves. "No, I can't seem to bring the ability to mind."

"That's understandable after what you've been through. The memories you've lost and regained." His voice was calm and level, like a professor giving a lecture. "When I look at someone's aura, it's like instead of smelling or tasting, there's another sense. You simply need to turn that sense on."

"But how?"

"It's like examining the light around us in a different way, and bending it to our will."

I wasn't sure what that meant but I tried again. Nothing worked. It was like I was blocked somehow.

After a few minutes of failure, he sat back and stroked his chin while he considered me. "I suppose we could try a trick they use to teach the new Ofanim at Seraphim Academy, though it seems rather silly to me."

"I'm open to anything at this point," I said.

He let out a sigh, as if the idea was distasteful to him. "Very well. First, close your eyes. Then imagine you have a pair of sunglasses, perfectly shaped for your face."

"Sunglasses?" I asked with a laugh, but I did as he said, picturing a pair of black shades in a slightly retro style, the kind you'd wear while sitting at the pool and sipping a margarita.

"Yes. Now hold them in your hands and pretend to put them on your face, imagining that lens going in front of your eyes and how it changes the way you see the world." He spoke slowly, and I did what he said. "When you open your eyes, you will now view the world through the lens of truth."

The whole thing felt ridiculous, and I was about to laugh it all off, but when I opened my eyes, everything had changed. It was as if my eyes had relaxed behind the pretend lenses, allowing me to truly *see*.

Bastien's bright aura circulated around his body, the color predominantly ice blue, like a frosty winter morning, with a ring of white light shimmering around the edges. Other colors swirled throughout the aura too, but there wasn't a speck of darkness there.

"It's beautiful," I whispered.

"Yes, most of them are. Can you see the bright light around my aura? That tells you I'm an angel."

I nodded slowly as it began to come back to me. "Demons have a ring of darkness."

"Indeed. And do you remember what the other colors mean?"

"They give you a hint about personality. Yours is predominantly blue." I spoke faster as I remembered. "You're calm and thoughtful. Intellectual. But there's a thread of red throughout too—you're in love."

He cleared his throat and looked away. "Very good. Now I want you to tell me if I'm lying solely by looking at my aura. My favorite food is broccoli."

His aura didn't change, just continued to swirl with bright beautiful colors, and I had to laugh. "True. But seriously? Broccoli?"

"It's versatile," he said with a slight shrug. "My right hand is dominant."

"Also true."

"I grew up in Georgia."

His aura became murky and dim as he spoke the words, and I nearly jumped out of my chair. "False!"

"Correct," he said with the faintest hint of a smile.

The success emboldened me, and we continued on for a few minutes, before Bastien decided we could move on. Since I was having trouble controlling my powers of light, we worked on that next. My emotions seemed to trigger it, and Bastien helped me remember how to summon light when I wanted, and how to keep the power contained when I didn't.

We kept going until lunchtime, and by the time Bastien stood to leave, I was well along the way to being able to control my Ofanim powers and feeling a lot more confident in myself as an angel. He promised we'd meet again tomorrow, when he'd help me remember some other Ofanim powers, and I found myself looking forward to it.

A fter my session with Bastien ended, I got a text asking me to meet Olivia at the Ambrosia Cafe, one of the restaurants in the hotel, and I headed down to join her for lunch. I hadn't seen Lucifer all day, but that suited me just fine at the moment, although my pulse raced when I thought about what might happen tonight.

Olivia looked as gorgeous as she did when I saw her yesterday, even in casual jeans and a black t-shirt, and her innate succubus allure made numerous heads turn as she waited outside the restaurant for me. She greeted me warmly, and then the host seated us in a private booth in the corner, which I had a feeling was reserved for VIP guests. Like the owner's woman.

"Thanks for inviting me to lunch," I said, after we were seated and had ordered some food.

Olivia smiled at me across the table. "I thought you might like to talk about what it's like to straddle both the angel and demon worlds. Kassiel told me a bit about what you've gone through, and it sounds like you might need a friend who knows about being stuck in the middle."

"I would love that. This is my first life as an angel, and I'm not sure what the demons will think of me being Lucifer's mate. Especially since as Haniel I fought in the war on the other side." I played with my fork idly as I thought back on all my lives. "Although I also fought on the demons' side as a Fallen, and spent many lives as Lucifer's mate in Hell. But I'm not sure if the demons will see it that way."

"I understand. Both angels and demons had a hard time accepting me at first too. Even now, I'm constantly torn between both sides, never fully belonging on one or the other. My loyalties are always divided, because that's the essence of who I am. Half angel. Half demon. And in a way, you're the same. You may be in an angel's body now, but you remember being other people in the past."

"Yes, that's exactly it." I let out a long sigh, feeling a little lighter. "It's nice to talk to someone who gets it."

"You and I are probably the only two who could understand," she said with a laugh. "I'll admit, I'm selfishly glad we met just so I could have someone to vent to about it."

I chuckled at that. "Lucifer said you're working as a liaison between the angels and demons?"

She twisted her mouth a little before she spoke. "Yes, I'm trying to keep the peace between them, but it takes a lot of time and effort to overcome thousands of years of hatred. Both sides believe the other one is the villain, but we're hoping to change that."

"Yes, I remember that from this life. Before I knew who I was, I was convinced that demons were evil and that Lucifer was, well...the devil. In every sense of the word. Only once I met him and began remembering my other lives did I see how wrong I was, and I realized I'd thought the same thing about angels when I was a Fallen. I urged Lucifer to end the war, but I died before I could see it come to pass."

Olivia's eyes soften. "But it did come to pass. Lucifer and Michael signed the Earth Accords over thirty years ago. I'm sure you had something to do with changing Lucifer's mind about angels."

"Perhaps," I said, just as the server brought our fancy salads along with some breadsticks. "I also vaguely remember being Persephone and spending some of my time ruling with Lucifer in Hell, and the rest of my time in Faerie. That was a struggle too, but at least demons and fae weren't at war then."

"No, the fae have always managed to stay neutral, although in my opinion, they're really trying to manipulate both sides for their own gain. I wouldn't be surprised if the High King has plans to move on Earth someday." Olivia paused and her cheeks colored. "Sorry. I hope that's not offensive, since you were a fae once."

I waved a hand. "It was long ago, and you're not wrong about the fae. Even among their own courts, their intrigues are legendary. Let's just say I didn't struggle too hard when Hades captured me and took me to the underworld."

"I bet. I mean, who could resist Lucifer? Or his son, for that matter?" Then she slammed a hand over her mouth, her eyes wide with horror. "Oh shit, I am so sorry. I completely forgot that you're Kassiel's mother. You just don't look anything like him in this life, and um, wow I have really messed this up, haven't I?"

Her embarrassment and awkwardness made her so much more

relatable, and it only made me like her more. "It's okay. Really. In fact, maybe you can tell me about Kassiel. How did you two meet?"

She seemed relieved, and then launched into a story about how she'd pretended to be a full-blooded angel to attend Seraphim Academy, the school where angels went to train, in order to find her missing brother. There she met her brother's friends, Callan, Bastien, and Marcus, along with Kassiel, who was one of her professors at the time. She explained that Kassiel had been sent there undercover on a mission for Lucifer, and was also pretending to be an angel. Together they all found Olivia's brother in Faerie and uncovered a vast conspiracy of angels trying to send demons back to Hell, led by the former Archangel Azrael, who was now in Penumbra Prison. I listened raptly as she described how my son had helped take down Azrael's secret society, and how Lucifer had orchestrated their release when they were all sent to Penumbra Prison. My heart swelled even more with pride for my son...and for my mate. Despite once being the number one enemy of the angels, Lucifer had helped them on numerous occasions in the last few years, and now was working directly with Archangel Gabriel—Olivia's father—to make sure the two sides remained at peace.

"Thank you for telling me your story," I said, as we were finishing up our meal. "I had no idea about any of that."

"It's why we were happy to help Lucifer when he asked us to resurrect you and why we're eager to remind you about your angelic side now. We owe him a lot, and we also want to make sure the treaty stands between angels and demons." Her voice softened. "Until recently, I was forbidden to even exist, but now I can hold a privileged position in both societies, and have angel and Fallen lovers. I will fight to keep that peace however I can."

My eyebrows shot up. "Can I ask about that?"

"About having four mates?" Olivia laughed. "Of course. I'm surprised it didn't come up sooner, especially since Kassiel is one of them."

My cheeks heated. "Sorry, am I that obvious?"

"No, I'd want to know too, if the situation was reversed." She met my gaze and lowered her voice. "As part Lilim, I have to feed on the sexual energy of multiple people to survive. I tried once to do it with fewer people, and it only ended up draining them of life. Four seems to be the perfect number to keep all of us healthy and happy, and if none of the guys complain, I'm certainly not going to either."

I considered her words as we headed outside the restaurant. "Do you know Asmodeus? He recently fell in love with a human friend of mine and gave up immortality to be with her."

She smiled, but there was a touch of sadness in her eyes. "Yes, he's my half-brother actually. Mom—Lilith—told me she'd turned him mortal, and I couldn't believe it at first. I was planning to go visit him once we were done helping you." She sighed, her voice dreamy. "I hate that he's going to grow old and die, but it is rather romantic he gave everything up to be with her. And honestly, probably a lot less work than managing four mates. Sometimes it can be *a lot*."

I chuckled softly. "I can't even imagine. One Lucifer is already enough for me."

More than enough...and I had a feeling he was going to prove that to me tonight.

12

HANNAH

After my lunch with Olivia, I returned to the penthouse and found my nephew waiting at the door, looking like he'd stepped out of some comic book universe, from his broad frame to the muscular arms to the stony blue eyes.

"Hello, Callan," I said with a smile, eager to get to know more of my family. It was turning out to be much larger than I'd ever realized.

He put his muscular arms around me in an awkward hug, his breath seemingly trapped in his chest at his moment of hesitancy. "I'm not sure what to call you. Aunt Haniel?"

I'd debated going by my former name, once I realized my life as Hannah was a lie, but decided I wasn't totally Haniel anymore either. It didn't feel right, taking that name, when I hadn't been her in forty years. I wasn't sure who I was anymore, but Brandy and her family knew me as Hannah, so I decided to stick with that. Now I had to reclaim that name from the persona Jophiel had created and take control of this new, final life.

"Just Hannah is fine," I said. "At times, depending on which memory I'm riding, I don't really feel any older than you."

He nodded. "I'm here to train you in angelic combat."

"That would be great." I already knew how to fight, of course. I'd taken down gargoyles with Lucifer's sword, and defeated Gadreel too. But that was more like instinct or muscle memory, and I was nervous it might fail me when I needed it the most. I'd fought in many battles in my previous lives, and hopefully a bit of practice would awaken those memories. I'd need them if I was going to go after Adam again.

The thought of taking him down made my adrenaline race. "Where should we do this?"

"Lucifer's arranged a room for us to use on the fourth floor."

I rolled my shoulders. "Awesome. Let me change into some more forgiving clothes, and I'll meet you there."

I quickly shoved on leggings and yanked a workout top over my head, then took the elevator to the fourth floor. When I stepped out, Callan was already there, and he led me down a corridor to an empty room clearly designed for sparring. The floors were slightly padded, the ceilings were unusually high, and mirrors lined one of the walls. As Callan shut the door, I also realized the room was sound-proofed.

Callan turned to me with a satisfied nod. "Lots of room so we can fight with our wings out. We'll work our way up to that though, along with weapons and angelic powers. For now, let's see what you remember."

As soon as I turned my head, he was already there with his huge fist swinging toward my face. I ducked and moved before the gasp even escaped my mouth, my muscles reacting instinctively. When he next attacked, I was ready this time, and I used his momentum against him so that I could spin around and kick him from behind.

"Seems like you remember a lot," he said.

"More than I expected." I couldn't help but grin, my blood already pumping from the exertion...and from excitement. It felt like my body and my soul were both waking up, reminding me of who I was—a warrior. I'd shed blood on countless battlefields since the dawn of time. Sure, I was a bit rusty after a forty-year intermission, and I needed to retrain some of those muscles again, but it was all coming back to me.

Callan lunged for me again, and we began sparring in earnest. My back hit the mat more times than I could count, but I kept getting up again. The man was an incredible fighter, and I was so out of practice there was no way I could defeat him. Not yet, anyway.

We both paused when the door opened, and Zel walked through, her face twisted with rage. "What the fuck do you think you're doing?"

I stepped forward. "It's okay, Zel. He's training me."

After giving Callan a nasty look, she turned her snarl to me. "I should be the one training you. Not some *angel*." She practically spat the word. "I've known you in most of your previous lives. I've fought at your side for centuries. I know your strengths and weaknesses."

Her words rang with truth inside me, and I remembered us on a battlefield in Heaven, overlooking the carnage we'd brought to the angels. Azazel stood on my right, my dark avenger and fiercest protector. But on my left there was another woman with red hair, who was both gorgeous and deadly. The one I'd seen in another memory before. I searched for her name, but it eluded me. Who was she? What had happened to her?

Callan's gruff voice broke me out of the memory. "Hannah needs an *angel* to train her in *angelic* combat. Not a demon."

"Fallen," Zel corrected. "You forget I was an angel once too. For longer than you've been alive." She stepped forward and spoke through gritted teeth, frustration radiating from her in waves so thick I could almost see them. "I'm thousands of years old. I actually fought in the war, which ended before you were even born. There is nothing I cannot teach her."

Callan crossed his arms, and I had to give him credit for staring at Zel without backing down. He lifted his chin in a challenge. "Let's see what you've got then, Fallen."

I barely had a chance to move out of the way before the two of them went at it. They were pretty evenly matched, each of them blocking and attacking, ducking and weaving. Their wings quickly came out, hers black as night and his almost blindingly white, and their movements became so fast it was hard to watch.

Zel grunted as Callan sent her spinning through the air, but she recovered quickly, and zipped toward him with a speed he hadn't expected before using her weight to push him toward the floor. He twisted and launched them both back up before grabbing her in a headlock. She shoved him off and tackled him around the waist one last time before they sprang away from each other.

Zel stared at him, her dark wings beating slowly behind her to keep her aloft. "Not bad, son of Michael. I can see why they wanted you to lead the Angelic Army. Why did you turn the job down?"

"I fell in love with a half-demon," Callan said dryly as he wiped a bead of sweat from his brow. "My priorities changed."

I held up my hands before they started fighting again and called out, "Enough already!"

They both looked down at me as though they'd forgotten I was there, and then they quickly dropped to the floor and sheathed their wings.

"I can see I can learn a lot from both of you," I said, glancing between the two of them. "I'd like both of you to train me."

They shot each other wary looks before returning their attention to me. "Fine." They spoke in unison, but I wasn't sure how much unity we'd have. Still, we would try.

After all, it was my destiny to straddle the line between the angel and demon worlds, like Olivia. This would be my first test.

When I got back to the penthouse, all I wanted was a long shower and a bite to eat. What I got was Lucifer sitting at his piano, playing a haunting melody that had me lingering in the doorway so I could better take it in.

He looked up at me and paused, his fingers lightly resting on the piano keys. His suit jacket was missing, and his shirt collar looked like he'd yanked it open after a long, hard day of work. My eyes were drawn to that bit of revealed skin, yearning to press my lips there.

"Come here."

His sharp command echoed through the otherwise silent room. Heat pooled between my thighs, and I found myself walking toward him as if in a dream, unable to stop myself. I held my breath as I got closer and closer, the anticipation making my pulse race, especially with the way he looked at me—like he might devour me at any moment.

When I stood before him in front of the piano, I became all too aware of what I must look like in my tight workout clothes, my hair a mess from training, my cheeks pink from exertion...and now from desire.

"I'm all sweaty," I said softly. A feeble protest, and we both knew it. "I need a shower."

"Not yet."

His hand gripped my arm, then he drew me toward him and dragged me into his lap, with my back against his chest. My breath hitched at the sudden close contact, and how he pulled my hair to the side to press his mouth against my neck in a hot, feverish kiss. His hands slid all along my body, feeling every inch of me through the tight clothes, moving across my breasts, my hips, my thighs.

Then he gripped my leggings and yanked them down roughly, probably ripping them in a few places. His other hand held my breast, rubbing his thumb along the taut nipple, an effective way to hold me in place. I was caught in the devil's grasp, and he made sure I knew there was no escape. Not tonight.

My panties were torn off my next, making me gasp. Lucifer forced me to spread my legs, his hands rough and demanding until he found how wet he'd made me already. I could only lean back against him and moan as his fingers slid into my pussy easily. He had me completely under his control as he fingered me and kneaded my breasts, teasing out little gasps of pleasure from me when his thumb stroked my clit.

I closed my eyes and allowed myself to melt into the moment. I shoved away all the pain and the anxiety from the past few days and accepted his touch. Fuck, I needed this so bad. I needed *him*.

He quickly and silently brought me to orgasm, making my hips thrust against his fingers desperately as he wrung out every last second of pleasure. I felt his hard cock pressed against my ass through the fabric of his trousers, and wondered if he would free it now and take me like his, with me sitting on his lap. Or maybe he'd bend me over the piano. Or press me down against the hard marble floor. I didn't care how, really. I just wanted his cock inside me already.

"No matter how much you hate me, you're mine, Hannah," Lucifer said, his mouth right by my ear. "Every inch of you." His hand slid over my pussy, like he was claiming it. "Now and forever."

Then he let me go.

I rose to my feet, my knees a bit shaky, and turned to look at him in confusion. He stood and let his hungry eyes linger on my half-naked body, which was aching for him to continue. He knew it too. I could tell by the wicked grin he gave me.

"Go take your shower," he said, as he kissed me on the cheek. "I have business to attend to, but I'll see you tomorrow."

He adjusted the cuffs on his shirt and then walked away. Just like that.

Leaving me desperately wanting more.

13

LUCIFER

I took Hannah's hand as we stepped through a door that led us outside, to the grounds of The Celestial.

"Where are we going?" Hannah asked with a huff.

"You'll see soon enough."

I could tell she was annoyed at me for last night, but I loved seeing Hannah all fired up about something, and I'd rather her annoyed than sad.

Besides, she wasn't really annoyed. She was *hungry*. For me.

Exactly how I wanted her.

We walked past the paths to the resort's different pool and recreation areas, and I could hear the sounds of my guests enjoying themselves all around us, while the hot sun beat against my skin. Eventually, we reached an area that was fenced off, and I used a key to open the gate. Hannah shot me a confused look, before stepping through to the empty lot on the other side. Flat land stretched before us, most of it dirt with a few sad little weeds sticking out of it, along with some trash and tumbleweeds blowing in the breeze.

I spread my arms wide. "This is my gift to you."

She cocked her head. "Um, thanks?"

I laughed at her bewildered expression. "I bought this land a few months ago so I could add another pool area to The Celestial, but I've decided we have enough pools. What I think we really need is a garden."

"A garden?" Hannah asked, perking up immediately.

"Your garden."

She sucked in a breath. "Really?"

"I want you to design it. Something huge and impressive, the kind of garden that people can wander through for hours. A tranquil respite in the middle of the desert." I watched her face as she gazed across the empty lot, her blue eyes dancing with excitement. "I know you had to leave your flower shop behind, but here you can still work with plants, and this time you can create something that's completely your own."

She threw her arms around me, which was a better response than I'd hoped for. "Thank you. I think this is the best present anyone has ever given me."

"I don't know, I've given you some pretty impressive gifts over the years," I said with a grin, before capturing her mouth in a kiss. She slid her arms around my neck and pressed against me, a bit urgently. Still wanting more from last night, though she tried to contain it. My cock strained against my trousers too, begging me to take her right here in the dirt, like an animal. But I was nothing if not patient.

"How did you know?" she asked, looking up at me, still in my arms.

"Know what?"

"That I was already missing the flower shop and wondering how I would fill that void in my life."

I slowly brushed my thumb across her lower lip. "Because I know you better than I know even myself. You've always loved gardens, ever since I got you kicked out of one as Eve." I smirked at the memory. "As Persephone you had the power to make plants grow and to bend them to your will. You transformed our palace in Hell from a cold, barren manor to a home filled with life and color. I knew if you could do that, you'd be able to work magic on this plot of land too."

She turned in my arms, leaning back against me, as she considered the lot. "We can call it Persephone's Garden."

"Perfect." I'd never understood nor much cared about plants or flowers, but I'd always loved the way her face lit up around them. "You can already picture it, can't you?"

"Yes, although I want to sit down and brainstorm some ideas before I get started. I can't wait."

"I'll have someone get you the dimensions of the lot so you can get to work on it. The Celestial has a landscaping team, so all you need to do is tell them what you want, and they'll work with you to make it happen."

"Thank you." She rested her head against my chest, letting me hold her close. "I really love it."

"And I love you."

She didn't say it back, but that was all right. A part of her was still upset with me. Maybe it would always be upset with me. But most of her was coming around.

———

Hannah spent the rest of the day training with the angels, which was fine because I had business of my own to deal with. Samael's people were still on the hunt for Gadreel, while our other spies sought information about the Archdemons. In today's report, I learned that Valefar had returned to Hong Kong and declared himself Archdemon of the dragons. My spies said he had no further plans to move against me at this time, and I hoped he'd taken my advice. If not, we'd be ready to go to war with the dragons. A war we would undoubtedly win.

In the evening, Hannah joined me in the penthouse for supper. There were a dozen restaurants in The Celestial, and I owned even more across The Strip, but Hannah always loved it when I cooked for her. Besides, I wanted her alone for what I had planned.

"You won't win me back by cooking for me." She took another bite of the meal with a soft sigh. "Even if this is the best steak I've ever had."

Watching her savor the meal I'd prepared was its own kind of foreplay. "We both know I don't need to win you back. I'm your destiny. You're my fate." I lowered my voice, as I locked eyes with her. "In many of your lives you've tried to resist me, but it never works. You always succumb eventually. As you will now."

Hannah shook her head, but she didn't argue. How could she? She'd already given in.

With a smug little smile, I sliced off another piece of filet mignon, which I'd cooked in a peppercorn sauce. Beside it were rosemary roasted potatoes with a touch of onion, and broccolini sauteed in garlic. "How is your training going so far? I didn't have time to ask you last night. I had...other things on my mind."

Heat rose to her cheeks at the reminder of our encounter at the piano. "It's going well. I'm starting to remember more about myself, and I'm gaining control of my powers."

"Good." I took a sip of red wine. "I meant to ask, what would you like me to call you? Hannah? Haniel? Eve, perhaps?"

"I'm sticking with Hannah. I don't feel like I'm really Haniel anymore after all this time." She dropped her eyes to her food. "Of course, Hannah was created by Jophiel, so I'm not really her either. I'm honestly not sure who I am anymore."

"You do know who you are. You always have, deep down. No matter what name you go by, the true essence of who you are never changes." I reached across the table to take her hand. "I've found you hundreds of times, and your soul is always the same. Jophiel might have created a fake life for you, but your true self still crept into every single aspect of it. Your affinity with plants and flowers. Your love of books and history. Your commitment to honesty and truth. In every life, going all the way back to Eve, you had a light inside you that made the world better for everyone around you. Losing your memories could never take that away."

She blew out a breath and squeezed my hand. "I suppose you're right. I just wish I didn't feel so damn confused all the time, and so out of place. Am I an angel? A Fallen? Am I on the side of the angels or the demons?"

"You're on the side of peace, as you always have been." I paused as I considered my next words. "When Jophiel returned my memo-ries, it filled in a lot of gaps in my past. Do you remember when you came to me as Haniel, and how much you hated me? But then we had long talks about the war, and about how it was destroying both angels and demons. We each saw that it couldn't continue, or both species would be wiped out. You convinced me to swallow my pride and try to end the war for the good of my people, even if I didn't think it was possible. You urged me to work with Michael and try to come to a truce. And I did. Even after you were taken from me, after I had no memory of Haniel, I ended the war." I leaned forward, as she hung onto my every word. "Jophiel might've been able to erase my memories of you, but not how you affected me. You changed me, Hannah. Part of you was still with me, even if I couldn't remember."

That got a faint smile out of my lovely mate. "I'm still impressed you managed to end the war. I know how hard that must have been. And from what Olivia told me, you've been working to make sure the peace lasts too."

I sat back and picked up my wine glass, swirling the dark liquid inside. "I've done what I can to protect my people, and peace has been beneficial for both sides. Though it was painful to leave Hell behind, our population is increasing again now that we're living on Earth. For whatever reason, it's easier for immortals to have children in this realm. For that benefit alone we must maintain the peace."

Sadness touched Hannah's brow at the mention of children, but then her eyes took on a look of determination. "Then that's what I'll dedicate the rest of my life to—keeping that peace. After I deal with Adam, anyway. Do you know where he might have gone, or what his plans are?"

"I have my suspicions, though we haven't found him yet." I watched Hannah's expression, debating whether she was ready to hear this, before deciding there could be no more secrets between us. "The ancient journals he took were Samael's accounts of things that happened to us in the early days, when you were Eve and I had just left Heaven to rule Hell. It contained information about the curse, along with many other things... Including the locations of the Four Horsemen and how to release them."

"The Four Horsemen?" Hannah's jaw dropped, her fork dangling uselessly from her fingers. "They're real, too?"

She said *too* like she'd only just started believing in angels and demons, and I wondered if telling her this was a mistake. "Unfortunately, yes. How much do you remember about the Elder Gods?"

She stared off into space as she searched her memories. "Not very much. They're ancient, powerful beings who created all the races and the different realms. But I don't remember what happened to them."

"Their children—angels, demons, humans, and fae—rebelled against them, as all children do in the end. It was the first war I fought in, back when I was an angel. The Elder Gods eventually retreated to another realm called Void. All except four of them. Pestilence. War. Famine." My mouth twisted in distaste. "And Death."

"Death..." Hannah whispered. "He's the one who cursed us."

Though I hated discussing this, I was pleased she was finally remembering her life as Eve, even if in only tiny snippets. "Yes. My father."

Her eyes widened at that. "Death is your father?"

"Indeed." Bringing up my father demanded another glass of wine, I decided, before I poured one for both of us. "He's gone by Death, the Grim Reaper, Thanatos, and many other names throughout history. Adam was always his favored human, and I was always a disappointment. Too much like my mother, Aurora, he always said. He thought it amusing to curse you in order to torment me for all eternity."

"But now you've broken the curse."

"Yes." I raised my glass to that. "Once again, I've defeated him."

She arched an eyebrow. "Once again?"

"After the other Elder Gods left, the Four Horsemen began destroying the realms of Earth, Heaven, Hell, and Faerie as punishment for our rebellion. A group of us, gathered from all the different races, fought and defeated them. Since it's impossible to truly kill an Elder God, we buried the Four Horsemen in secret locations across the realms of Earth, Heaven, Hell, and Faerie, and four of us—you, me, Archangel Michael, and High King Oberon—used our blood to seal their tombs." I scowled and finished off my wine. "I believe Adam and the Archdemons plan to release them now."

"Why?" she asked. "Why would they even consider doing that?"

"They know it's the only way they can defeat me." I shot her a wry smile. "None of the Archdemons are strong enough. They need the power of the Four Horsemen to take me down."

She took a bite of her potatoes chewing slowly, and then asked, "If the Four Horsemen are released, is that the beginning of the apocalypse? Like in the Bible?"

"Possibly. They nearly destroyed all four realms before we managed to stop them. I can't imagine what destruction they would unleash now after thousands of years in a tomb." My jaw clenched. "And even if the other Horsemen are released, we absolutely cannot allow my father to walk the worlds again."

"What can we do to stop it?" Hannah asked, her face pale.

"The Horsemen must be released in the order we sealed them, just as it says in the Bible. That means Pestilence is first. I've already sent people to that location to watch for any sign of Adam or the Archdemons. When they make their move, we'll be ready to stop them."

She nodded, though I could see our discussion was weighing heavily on her mind. It was a lot to lay at her feet, but I wanted her to know everything now. No secrets. No lies. No reason for us to be apart.

At some point during our discussion we'd finished our meal, and I rose to my feet and crossed over to her, offering my hand. "Come with me."

Her delicate fingers reluctantly slid into mine. "Where to?"

"We're going flying."

14

HANNAH

I dragged my feet as Lucifer led me outside to the edge of the balcony overlooking The Strip below. The thought of flying again made me nervous for some reason. Maybe because as I stared off the side of the building, I remembered the time I'd nearly plummeted to my death. My wings would have really come in handy then, I thought bitterly.

Or maybe it was because allowing my wings out and using them to fly meant accepting the truth about who I was. Not a human, but an angel. Something I hadn't even believed existed until a few weeks ago.

Or maybe it was because the thought of flying reminded me too much of that terrifying, confusing night when I'd been resurrected, when nothing had made sense and all I'd wanted was to escape.

"Have you flown since the night you regained your wings?" Lucifer asked, as if he knew exactly what was going through my mind.

"No." I shook my head, backing away slowly. "I can't."

He gently pulled me back to the edge of the balcony. "The longer you wait, the harder it will become."

I swallowed hard, knowing he was right. Every time I backed

down from flying, it would become a much more daunting task. I had to rip the bandage off and just do it already, but that was easier said than done.

"Trust me," Lucifer said. "I won't let anything bad happen to you."

"Other than kill me?" I asked, before I could stop myself.

"It worked out in the end, didn't it?" His cocky smirk made me want to smack him over the head. "If I hadn't done that, you wouldn't have your powers or your wings now."

"Did you know that would happen?" I asked, staring hard at him. "You had your memories back then. You knew I was really an angel."

"I suspected rebirth would return you to your angelic state, yes, but there was no way to know for sure. I considered it an added bonus to breaking the curse."

"Still not okay," I muttered, shaking my head.

Lucifer's wings suddenly unfurled behind him, so dark they made the night sky look bright. The area around us darkened slightly, as if the shadows were drawn to his power. In his three-piece suit, with his wings spread, he radiated danger and masculinity like no other man in this world, or any other. There was no doubt when looking upon him that he was the monster spoken of in every dark tale throughout history. The devil himself.

"I believe it's time to show me yours," he said, and I realized I'd been staring.

After a moment's hesitation, I let my wings out, my silver feathers expanding at my back, eager to be freed. It felt good to let them out—like taking off a bra at the end of the day.

"Beautiful," Lucifer said, as he reached out to lightly brush one of my feathers. "Look how you light up the night sky. My bright star."

His touch sent a shiver through me. Among angels, touching another's wings was an intimate act only done among family or lovers. That much I remembered, and yet I didn't pull away. Not when he looked at me like I was his entire world.

I tore my gaze away from him and stared down at the bright lights of The Strip. I could do this. I could. I'd already flown once, without even realizing I could do it. How much harder could it be now?

Lucifer took my hand and drew my eyes back to him. His quiet confidence lent me some strength, and I nodded to signal I was ready. Together we leaped off the balcony, spreading our wings wide, and though my heart leaped into my throat, Lucifer's firm grip on my hand kept me from panicking. Wind caught my feathers and kept me aloft, and then instinct took over and I flapped my wings, taking me higher.

A laugh escaped my chest as we began to soar over The Strip, gazing down on the cars and casinos below. Lucifer had taken me on a flying tour of the city before, but he'd had to carry me then. Now I reveled in being able to fly by myself. The feeling was strange and yet so familiar, and like fighting, it came back to me easily. My body remembered, even if my mind struggled with it.

Lucifer flew alongside me, and somewhere over The Strip, it changed to a game of cat and mouse. One moment it was him chasing me, then I was chasing him. We laughed our way around loops of the tallest casinos, his darkness keeping us hidden from view.

Then Lucifer caught me, pulling me into his arms, holding me tight against his chest. My heart beat so rapidly, it seemed to pound throughout both our bodies. I caught my breath as I looked at him, drowning in his roguish green eyes—the eyes I'd loved as long as I could remember.

Slowly, so slowly years could have passed, Lucifer lowered his head. His mouth found mine, and heat rippled through me as he grazed his tongue across my lips, demanding to be let in. I sucked in a gasp as he gained entry and kissed me hard, his arms tightening around me, his black wings moving slowly to keep us midair.

When he raised his head, his smoldering gaze made my breath hitch with desire. He suddenly shot forward, carrying me through the air toward The Celestial at a speed no mortal could match. Wind tickled my heated skin as we flew through the night, and when we reached the penthouse, Lucifer reached out with tendrils of darkness and yanked open the sliding door to his bedroom.

We landed inside and he set me down on the floor. Before I could even protest, he gripped my black dress and yanked it off me. I'd purposefully chosen that one because it could come off easily, and I wore nothing underneath. The arrogant, satisfied grin on his lips told me he knew why too.

There was no hiding it. I craved him. Desperately. Last night had been like a delicious appetizer, but now I was ready for the main course.

His eyes raked over my naked body as I stood before him, and my nipples hardened in response. Then he stalked toward me, making me take a step back, and then another, until my back hit the wall. Right where he wanted me.

He took my chin and kissed me hard, holding me in place while he thoroughly seduced my mouth. Then his mouth danced across my skin, down my neck, teasing his way to my shoulders, and then my breasts. He spent some time there, licking and sucking, making me moan, before he continued his path downward. To my belly. To my hips. To the triangle between my legs.

He nudged my legs wider, his large hands gripping my thighs, before his mouth found my pussy and claimed it with a swift brush of his tongue. With a soft groan, I leaned back against the wall for support, my knees suddenly weak.

He looked up at me and met my eyes. "Admit it. This is where you want me. On my knees. Groveling at your feet. My tongue in your pussy."

"Yes," I cried out, as I dug my fingers into his thick dark hair and pulled his face back between my thighs.

He hoisted me up, putting my legs around his shoulders, giving him better access as he thoroughly devoured my pussy like a starving man. He fucked me with his tongue and sucked on my clit, and I was powerless to do anything but hang on and ride his face, my hips thrusting wildly. My climax came upon me like a tidal wave, and I yelled his name as the pleasure crested over me.

Then he stood up and dropped me down in one fluid motion, catching me in his arms, wrapping my legs around his hips. His cock entered me hard and fast, making me gasp at the sudden breach. He pressed me back against the wall, hands on either side of my head, and I clung to his shoulders. His hips pounded against me, slamming me back against the wall, his cock thrusting deep in a relentless pace. He fucked me like he wanted to become one with me, like he couldn't stop until he'd marked me inside and out. He needed this as much as I did, I realized—this connection, this confirmation that we were still mates, no matter what happened between us. I felt the mate bond thrumming between us, invisible and yet so powerful it couldn't be denied, and I threw my head back and gave myself up to Lucifer completely.

My pussy clenched around his cock as I came, and then he let out a guttural roar and slammed his cock deep into me. I felt his hot seed fill me, and he kissed me hard as we both shuddered with release. I held him tight, kissing him back, squeezing my thighs around his hips so he couldn't leave me just yet.

I rested my head back against the wall and sighed at him. "This doesn't mean I forgive you."

Lucifer carried me over to his bed and set me down on it. "You don't need to forgive me. But from now on you *will* sleep in my bed."

I bristled at his words. "I have my own room."

"The other room will still be yours to do with as you please. And then, every night, you'll return here to me. We both know you sleep better beside me, anyway. " He flipped me over onto my stomach, and then entered me again from behind, his hands rough on my ass and his cock already hard again. He bent over and said right into my ear, "You can hate me. You can fight me. You can punish me. But you will do it by my side. As my queen."

Any protest I might have made was lost as he claimed me over and over, all night long.

15

HANNAH

With a sigh, I plopped into my favorite chair in the library. It was my favorite place in the penthouse to relax, and after that training session, damn, I deserved a break. I'd fought Azazel and Callan together for the first time, and they'd kicked my ass. But we'd all known it wasn't actually a fair fight—at least not yet. There would come a day when I'd take them on and beat them, I was certain of it. Alas, that day was definitely not today.

I shifted and groaned, wishing my angelic healing would hurry up already. I'd landed hard on the roof, courtesy of Zel's enthusiasm, and if I'd been human I probably would have broken something. At the very least I would have sported a nice bruise, but because I was an angel, I only had some temporary discomfort while my body healed itself. One of the best perks of immortality for sure.

It had been a week since I'd returned to Las Vegas, and Zel and Callan now had to work really hard for their wins during our combat practice. My other training was going well too. Olivia helped me remember different aspects of angel and demon history and culture, while also getting me up to date on all the changes that had happened in the last forty years. Bastien taught me to regain control of my powers, and I annoyed everyone by reading their auras whenever I saw them. Lucifer's was especially intriguing to me, since the ring around his was as black as night, except for a few traces of light that shined through.

After that night with Lucifer, I turned the guest room into my office and personal space, and in my free time I began drawing up plans for Persephone's Garden. Every time I worked on it my excitement grew, and I couldn't wait to start ordering plants and really getting to work. My true self was starting to surface, and I felt more complete than I'd felt in several years—probably since the last time Jophiel had wiped my memory. I was Haniel mixed with Lenore, Persephone, Eve, and many more. A new Hannah, one I created myself.

I stood and walked around the room, trailing my fingers over the spines of the many books, but none called to me today. I came to a halt in front of the sword I'd grabbed from the wall and used against the gargoyles who'd invaded this space not long ago. Muscle memory had kicked in on that night, and I'd fought and defeated them like I was born to do it. I hadn't known then that I *was* born to do it

The sword seemed to call to me as I looked at it. I plucked it off the wall, enjoying the weight and craftsmanship, the perfect balance as I held it, so familiar from hundreds of years during which I'd clasped it in my hand. Morningstar. Lucifer's sword from when he was an angel.

As I balanced its weight and adopted a fighter's pose, something nudged at the edge of my thoughts, and I studied the sword, turning my hand so it gleamed and reflected the lights in the room. At a mental push, a mere urge, it pulsed with darkness, the only sword in existence infused with both light and dark power.

It responded to Lucifer's power. Only he could wield it. Lucifer...and me.

As I practiced with the sword, slicing it through the air, running through the familiar series of exercises and remembering what it felt like to fight with it, I lost track of time. Until Kassiel walked into the room.

My youngest son stopped short, staring at me with something like shock.

"Kassiel! It's so good to see you again." I lowered the blade and offered him a smile. I hadn't seen him since that first meeting, and I was eager to talk to him again, but he looked wary. Almost like he didn't want to see me. "Are you all right?"

"Yes, sorry. It's just strange seeing you in this body, holding the sword my mother wielded against angels." He raked a hand through his almost-black hair. "I only knew you as Lenore, and though Father told me about the curse and your reincarnation, I've never experienced it personally. I never met you as Haniel. Until now, anyway."

My heart broke a little at his words. I was essentially a stranger telling him I was his mother. He hadn't known me in over a century. How could I blame him for being hesitant? I'd lived the last forty years with no memories of having any children, so I didn't feel much like a mother either. I silently raged at the curse, and at Adam, and at Jophiel. They hadn't only kept me from Lucifer. They'd kept me from my sons too.

I wanted to reach out to Kassiel, but I stopped myself. He didn't seem ready for that yet. I sighed and set down Morningstar. "When I was Haniel, I wanted to see you, more than you can imagine, but my relationship with Lucifer had to be kept secret at that time. We made plans to tell you, but then Adam found me."

"I understand." He smiled, but it looked a bit forced.

I sat in one of the chairs and gestured for him to join me, hoping he would allow me a few moments with him to try to rebuild our relationship. "How are you? How have you been? I'm sorry that I missed so many years."

"It's not your fault." Kassiel slowly sat in the other chair, his movements graceful, every aspect of him reminding me so much of his father. "After Mother's—*your* death—I changed my mind about the war. I pleaded with Father for a truce with the angels, but he wasn't ready to listen yet. The war didn't end for many years after that, but I never stopped working toward it, even as I acted as a spy for Lucifer."

I let Kassiel keep talking, wanting to hear him, to just listen to his voice. My love for my son was so overwhelming it felt like it might burst out of my chest. How had I gone the last forty years without this feeling? And how did mothers live with this every day and not go insane? Or maybe we all were a little insane, but it didn't matter, because it was worth it. It was all worth it.

"Most recently I became a professor at Seraphim Academy on a mission for Lucifer, and with Olivia and the others, I helped stop a plot against demons," he said.

"Yes, Olivia told me all about it." I reached over and took Kassiel's hand, and to my relief he didn't pull away. "I'm so proud of you."

"What of you?" he asked, seeming a bit more comfortable now. "Tell me about this life. Lucifer gave me a quick rundown, but I want to hear it from you."

I bit out a sad laugh. "There's really not much to tell."

We talked for the next hour about our lives, catching up as if we were old friends, and I was delighted to hear that Kassiel shared my love of reading and history. In fact, he'd been the Angelic History professor at Seraphim Academy, which greatly amused both of us. I told him about my flower shop, and what Jophiel had done to me, and he told me about how he and Callan had hated each other for a long time. Of course, back then they'd had no idea they were basically cousins.

"What of your brothers?" I asked, hungry for more news of my sons. "Do you see them a lot?"

Kassiel shifted in his seat, looking uncomfortable again. "Not very often. Damien and I get together when we can, but he's in Faerie and outsiders are not welcome there. And Belial... I haven't spoken to him in years. Last I heard he's working as a bartender in New Orleans and laying low. Probably a good thing."

I frowned a little at that. I was beginning to realize my family was larger than I'd ever imagined as Hannah, but I sensed our family had grown distant and estranged, a side-effect of the curse, perhaps. But with the loss of my daughter so fresh in my mind, and the promise of one long, unbroken life ahead of me, I was desperate to reconnect with all of my sons and bring them together again.

———

After night fell, I decided to take a short swim in the infinity pool. It had been out there on the balcony all this time, tempting me with its cool waters, but for various reasons I hadn't taken a swim yet. On my shopping spree with Lucifer—which seemed like a lifetime ago—he'd picked out some skimpy little bikinis I would normally have been too shy to wear, but now I wore one confidently. Knowing who you truly were had a way of bolstering your self image.

Lucifer walked outside, carrying two drinks that looked fruity and fun, with little pink umbrellas in them. "I thought you could use a little refreshment."

I swam to the edge and took a drink from him. "Thanks."

"You deserve it. You've been working hard with the angels all week." A naughty grin crossed his lips. "And I've been working you hard after that."

I splashed him a little, rolling my eyes, even though his words made heat dance across my skin. All he did was chuckle and step back to avoid the water, and then he began slowly unbuttoning his shirt. As he revealed inch after inch of perfect skin and hard muscle, it was hard to concentrate on his next words.

"Tomorrow I plan to visit two of the Archdemons—Baal and Lilith—on a diplomatic mission to find out if the Lilim and vampires are working against me with the other demons."

I took a sip of my drink, tasting the alcohol and the pineapple. "Probably a good idea."

He unbuttoned his trousers next, but his gaze remained on me the entire time. "I'd like you to join me."

"I'm not sure how much use I'll be." After all, I was still learning my place in the demon world, and I wasn't sure it would help Lucifer's cause if he showed up with an angel on his arm.

"You might not be sure, but I am. I'm stronger with you by my side. I've always appreciated your advice and wisdom." His slacks fell to the ground, leaving him in tight black boxer briefs that did nothing to hide his impressive package. "We're a pair. Dark and light, wrong and right, day and night. For all eternity."

He dove into the infinity pool on the far side, where the water seemed to disappear over the side of The Celestial. Watching him was a luxury, with his waist narrowing from broad shoulders, and his taut stomach rippling with muscle. He plunged below the water and his form wavered beneath the surface as he swam in my direction.

He burst up in front of me, tossing his head back, his dark hair gleaming under the stars. Water ran in rivulets over his broad shoulders and down his hard chest, and I couldn't tear my gaze from his body. Everything about Lucifer called to me, making him impossible to resist.

"Well?" His rich voice sounded by my ear, and his wet skin brushed over mine.

I sucked in a breath as a rush of desire caught me by surprise. What had we been talking about? Oh, right. Going to see some Archdemons. "Yes, I will go with you."

"Good. I need you with me, Hannah." He moved closer and took hold of my hip. "And I want you. Now."

Desire shot through me, and the fire in Lucifer's eyes only strengthened it. He tilted my chin up, then his mouth came crashing down. I pressed against him, urgency thrumming a second heartbeat in my body, pushing unrelenting waves of desire through me. He drew a sharp inhale at the touch of my tongue against his lip and I pushed farther into his mouth, touching against the delicate skin there.

He wrapped his arms around me and crushed me to him, and the halter top of my bikini loosened before falling away. "Oops," he murmured against my mouth.

"Why, lord and master of Hell, what *do* you think you're doing?" I asked.

"Needing you... Wanting you..." He loosened the ties at either side of my bikini bottoms. "Having you."

His eyes darkened with lust as his hand slid over my ass to cup the left cheek, and he kneaded it slightly. I all but melted against him as I drew heavier breaths.

"Touch me, Hannah," he commanded, as he dropped his head to press his lips to my neck, soft open-mouthed kisses scorching me, searing his touch onto me, making me his.

I shivered and the water rippled around us as I slid my hand between our bodies. My bikini drifted farther away, but I didn't care. I touched Lucifer's abs, smoothing my way over the dips and ridges of the muscles there, and he inhaled a breath, far from unaffected by my touch. I paused, listening to the stuttered rhythm of his breathing, and he rumbled a growl of discontentment.

"Don't stop." He pushed his hips toward me, and the hard bulge in his boxer briefs jutted against my stomach. I arched my neck, giving better access for his kisses. His tongue flickered out in a lazy trail toward my collarbone.

I teased my fingers along his waistband, slipping them beneath it as he nibbled and nipped my skin. His hand slipped to my thigh, and I automatically widened my stance as my body begged for more. I groaned before I crashed my lips to his as I gripped his cock through the thin fabric.

He moaned and responded by pressing his hand between my legs, his fingers brushing my clit too fleetingly before he covered the area with his palm. He drew away and looked into my eyes. "Mine. It's always been mine."

I nodded, hoping my desperation for him didn't show on my face. I could barely hold still. I wanted to grind against him, and I pushed his boxer briefs down his thighs, freeing his glorious cock.

"Your pride's on display again," I said.

He chuckled as he looked down between us. "I better do something about that."

He grabbed my lips and lifted me against him, the water buoying me up so I could wrap my legs over his hips. I ground against him, bearing down just a touch. Fresh heat blazed through his eyes as he pressed himself against my entrance. Then he thrust upward, the movement so fast, I blew out a breath of surprise.

I ground down again, releasing a sigh as my body stretched around him. He groaned and pushed deep, filling me completely before setting a steady rhythm that rubbed me in all the right ways. The water lapping around us was strangely erotic, moving in time with our bodies as we joined together in this ancient. primal dance.

Lucifer leaned forward, supporting my ass with one hand as he gripped the edge of the pool behind me with the other. Something about his shift in position changed his angle and I groaned as heat pooled low in my belly.

My gasps became rapid pants, each more ragged than the last as I tried to brace against an onslaught of sensation building inside me until I couldn't fight it anymore. I clamped my thighs around him as I melted to nothing in his arms, feeling like I was the water from the pool, cascading down over the sides of the building. I rode my orgasm for as long as I could until the pulsing of my body brought Lucifer to climax too.

Lucifer dropped his head forward, his forehead resting against mine. "Do you forgive me yet?"

"No," I replied, though I didn't put much conviction in the word. I still wasn't sure if forgiveness was possible, but I'd stopped hating him, and my anger had faded. I understood more of why he'd killed me, and a part of me was secretly grateful. He'd restored me to my true self and broken the curse, giving us the possibility for true happiness for the first time in our ancient lives. I only wish it had happened differently. But that was true of so many things in my past.

"You will." Lucifer smirked as he ran his hands slowly up my arms. "You can kill me next if it will make you feel better."

I shoved him back with a laugh. "Don't tempt me, or I might take you up on that."

16

LUCIFER

I stepped out of the limo in front of Baal's mansion in upstate New York as the sun slipped behind it. The dark, gothic mansion was impressive in the waning light, the turrets reaching high toward the emerging stars, the wrought-iron gates both beguiling and unwelcoming. It was exactly what one might expect from a vampire king. The kind of place a soul could get lost in. I wouldn't have been at all surprised to find a graveyard around the back and a belfry of bats nearby.

I straightened my cuffs and glanced around, then reached out to help Hannah from the limo. She wore a long silver gown with the emerald necklace and earrings I'd gotten her on our first shopping spree, and it pleased me to see her finally wearing them. A sign she'd accepted her place as my queen.

She looked up at the mansion and bit her lip nervously, but I had complete faith in her. She'd always had diplomacy and astute business sense before in her many lifetimes as my queen. Those weren't qualities that would leave her just because she was still making the right connections in her memories.

A handsome male vampire in a suit opened the door for us and gestured us inside with a low bow. Another vampire in a suit brought in our bags from the limo, then whisked them off to our guest room. I had to give the older vampires credit for their hospitality, if nothing else.

Lilith stepped into the foyer to greet us, wearing a long gown the color of blood with a high slit up the thigh, her curves alluring because she couldn't wear them any other way. "Welcome! I'm so pleased you could join us. It's lovely to see you both."

She went to Hannah first, and kissed her on the cheeks. My mate smiled warmly and said, "Thank you for inviting us into your home. It's lovely."

Lilith laughed at that as she moved toward me. "It's not my home, but I appreciate the sentiment anyway."

"Lilith." I leaned forward to accept her cheek-kisses and touched her shoulder briefly. "I'm surprised to see you shacking up with Baal. You've never lived in one place for long."

"I'm only staying here because of Lena. She needed us after she and Ekariel were rescued from that horrid cult." Lilith shuddered a little, and I sensed the depths of pain in her voice. She'd spent years searching for her daughter, who went missing as a child, but once she found her, the girl was in bad shape after being in captivity so long. Baal had even resigned from his position as headmaster of Hellspawn Academy to help care for her.

"How is she doing now?" I took Hannah's hand in mine, reminding myself she was beside me, drawing some strength from her presence.

"Better." Lilith led us down a long hallway, this one only marginally less opulent than the grand entrance hall. "She no longer screams every night. Small victories."

"Glad to hear it." I sensed the mood needed to be lightened, and gave her a devilish grin. "And tell me, are you rekindling your old flame with Baal while you're here?"

Lilith's soft laughter echoed through the hall. "I do need to feed, naturally."

I raised an eyebrow. "And Gabriel?"

She lifted her chin with a secretive smile. "The Archangel does come to visit me from time to time."

"I knew it." I leaned over to Hannah and spoke in a low voice, as if sharing a secret. "Lilith and Gabriel had a secret affair years ago, resulting in Olivia. It seems to have started up again."

Hannah's eyes danced with amusement. "How scandalous. I wonder how many other secret relationships happened over the years between angels and demons."

"Oh, plenty." Lilith winked at Hannah. "Gabriel was certainly not my first angel, but we succubi do like to sample a wide variety of delights."

"If you're seeing Baal and Gabriel, that means you'll only need one or two more to be satisfied," I said. "Might I suggest Samael for one of the open positions?"

Lilith sighed. "Samael is angry with me for granting Asmodeus's wish to become mortal."

I lifted a shoulder in a casual shrug. "He'll get over it."

"He doesn't understand that it was difficult for me too. I don't want to see my son grow old and die." Lilith sashayed across a finely tiled floor as an impressive conservatory rose above us, the leaded glass windows dark at this time of day, with a mixture of floral and fruited scents hanging in the air. "But ultimately I want whatever makes Asmodeus happy, and I have to respect his decisions."

"For what it's worth, he does seem very happy with Brandy and her family," Hannah said.

"Ah, the things we do for our children," Lilith said with a sad smile.

We walked through a final doorway and out into an impressive garden. Winding paths led between mature bushes lit by tiny fairy lights, and candles hung in jars here and there. Night-blooming flowers filled the space with sweet scents, and tiny white blooms cascaded over a gazebo.

Hannah squeezed my hand tightly as she looked around. "It's magical."

Lilith only flashed a small smile of acknowledgment before she led us toward the gazebo, where a table and four chairs had been arranged, with candlelit wine already waiting for us. We all took seats around the table, and I poured us each a glass of wine.

"How are you, Hannah?" Lilith asked. "I see you've become an angel since we last met, but I won't hold that against you, I promise."

Hannah flushed. "Yes, it was a surprise, but I'm finding my way."

Lilith leaned forward and rested her hand over Hannah's. "I have no doubt you will. I'm sure you've discovered your son and my daughter are now an item. That makes us practically family."

"Yes, Kassiel and Olivia seem to complement each other well," Hannah said, but then she bit her lip. "I'm hoping to connect more with my sons. It's been so long since I last saw them, I feel like I don't know them at all anymore. And they don't know me either."

"I understand," Lilith said. "I've only recently reconnected with my daughters after years of being apart." She paused as if searching for the right words, her gaze far away as she looked out into the darkness beyond the gazebo. "It will take you some time, and it will be difficult, but it will also be worth it."

Before Hannah could continue the conversation, Baal emerged from the house, drawing our attention. He looked like a vampire from an old movie with long black hair, cold blue eyes, and sharp cheekbones.

"Welcome to my home," he said with a formal British accent, his gesture vast as he encompassed the house and gardens, his smile wide. He gave me a slight bow. "I'm pleased to have you here."

I nodded. "And we thank you for your hospitality, Baal."

As he sat down, he made another gesture with his hand and a man in a tuxedo brought out a cart laden with covered dishes, as if he'd been waiting behind a rhododendron all along. The aromas of well-cooked food overtook the delicate floral fragrances, and the waiter served a mixture of perfect vegetables and steak before quietly taking his leave.

When we were alone again with plates full of delectable food, I cleared my throat. "There's no point in pretending. As nice as all this pomp and ceremony is, I'm here to find out if you're involved with the other Archdemons in the conspiracy to overthrow me. I know you've long harbored thoughts of taking my place as the Demon King."

Baal let out a low chuckle. "Ah, Lucifer. I do appreciate how you've come straight to the point. Yes, in the past I planned to move against you, but not anymore. Your son helped rescue my daughter. I will not forget that." His gaze strayed back to Lilith, full of obvious love. "Besides, Lilith would never forgive me."

"And I would never move against my oldest and dearest friends," Lilith said, gazing between me and Hannah.

I glanced to Hannah and she nodded, confirming they were speaking the truth. I tried not to let my relief show. If I'd had to fight the vampires and the Lilim, on top of the other demons, I might actually lose the battle. Probably not, but why risk it?

"I appreciate your honesty and loyalty," I said. "What do you know of their insurrection?"

Lilith took a slow sip of her wine. "We know all the other Archdemons have turned against you. We believe Nemesis is leading them."

"Nemesis?" Hannah asked. "The Archdemon of the imps?"

"Yes, she's always been a jealous one," Lilith said. "Hungry for power. Did you know she's tried to seduce Lucifer many times over the years?"

"And always failed," I snapped. Nemesis had long been a thorn in my side, but I never thought she'd stoop so low as to actually plan a coup. "Why didn't you tell me this before?"

Lilith and Baal exchanged glances, before Lilith turned back to me, lowering her voice as she confessed, "They've threatened to hurt our children if we helped you. Even telling you this much is a big risk. But I can no longer remain silent."

"We refused to join them...but we can't help you either," Baal said.

I tapped my fingers against my wine glass as I glanced between the two of them. I understood their fears, but I also knew what was coming. "They're planning the release the Four Horsemen."

"No," Lilith said, her word more like a gasp.

"That is...unfortunate." Baal had always been a master of under-statement.

"I suspect you want Famine to show up about as much as I want

Death released," I said to Baal. I was driving the issue home, and we both knew it.

"You're right," he said. "I would prefer not to see either of our parents walk this world. But my hands are tied."

"What if..." Hannah spoke from beside me, her voice quiet, thoughtful.

"Go on." I knew that voice. It was a tone that had helped me out many times in the past.

"What if Baal pretended to join the other Archdemons?" She looked at me as she spoke. "Then he can feed information back to you."

"Like a spy." I rested my hand lightly over Hannah's, pleased with her for speaking up, before locking eyes with Baal. "They'll believe it, because you've always been outspoken about your desire to take my throne."

Baal chewed his food and sipped his wine, and we all did the same, giving him time to think over the idea. After a few moments, he set his glass down and nodded once. "I'll do it. But you will owe me a favor, Lucifer."

"I'm going to regret this, aren't I?" I chuckled, dark and low. I disliked owing favors to anyone, and much preferred when the power balance leaned in my direction. However, this favor would be worth it. "But you have a deal."

17

HANNAH

"Hannah, would you care to walk with me?" Lilith asked, as Lucifer and Baal continued the discussion of their plan. It had taken on a life of its own after Lucifer said the word *spy,* and I had a feeling they'd be working out the details for hours.

I rose to my feet. "I'd love that."

Lilith and I set off down the nearest winding path, tiny pieces of white gravel crunching beneath our feet. The garden was a huge oasis of plants and flowers, most of which I recognized at first sight, and I was curious to explore it some more. Besides, I felt much more at home out here among the foliage than anywhere else.

We wandered down various paths for a while before Lilith spoke. "I hope we can be friends again," she said as I stopped to admire a particularly pretty evening primrose. "Like we were in the old days."

She pretended to be distracted by the overhanging, feathery leaves of a weeping willow, but she'd never had a particular love for nature, that much I remembered. Well, nature that didn't involve naked humans, anyway.

I grazed my fingers over the delicate petals, trying to think of a polite reply before I looked at her. "I'm still sorting out my returned memories. You were Adam's first wife, weren't you?"

"I was, yes." She glanced down the path, deeper into the garden that seemingly had no end. "I was forced to marry Adam against my will, back when I was human. But I didn't love him, and I saw the darkness within his heart. I ran away, much like you did."

"You were once human?" I asked.

"Long ago, yes." She grimaced a little at the memory. "And much like you, I was also cursed. I was turned into a succubus for my crime of leaving Adam. The Elder Gods loved him. Probably because he was as awful as they were."

"Hence why they call your kind 'Lilim,'" I said.

"Yes, although please don't think I sired the entire line." She let out a delicate laugh. "They created many others after me. I was simply the first."

I stood from where I was by the flowerbed as I considered her words, which rang true. "I'm slowly remembering these things, but sorting through all of my memories has been difficult."

"In that case, there's something you should probably know about me before you remember it on your own and get the wrong idea," She sounded hesitant as she touched my arm to get my full attention. "I slept with Lucifer. Eons ago. After I met Adam, before Lucifer met you as Eve, when I had first become a succubus and I could barely control my newfound hunger. It meant nothing though. A simple dalliance to help ease my insatiable thirst. Once he met you, he had no interest in anyone else."

It meant nothing. Wasn't that what they all said? But Lilith was speaking the truth. Though I felt a quick pang of jealousy, I couldn't be upset about something that had happened so long ago, before Lucifer had even met me.

She continued before I could answer. "At first, I was jealous of you, and how you'd captured his eye so completely, but I soon came to view you as one of my closest friends. Besides, we both know Lucifer is not the type to share."

"No, definitely not." I cocked my head. "Your daughter told me about how challenging it was to feed a succubus's hunger."

Lilith's face broke into a big smile. Maybe she'd expected an angrier reaction than the one I gave her. "Isn't she lovely? I only recently reconnected with Olivia. I'm so proud of the woman she's become." She ran her finger lightly along a flower petal. "I had to give up Olivia when she was a child. It was for her own safety since she was the only angel-demon hybrid, and such a thing was forbidden back then. It was the hardest thing I've ever done."

"How did you go about reconnecting with her?" I asked.

She smirked and tossed her dark hair. "I made a nuisance of myself. I showed up in her life one day, and then I kept showing up. That's all you have to do."

"Annoy them until they love you back?" I asked with a laugh. "I wonder if that might work on Belial. I know he and Lucifer have had a falling out of some sort."

"It's best if you remember that story on your own, I think." Lilith drew me close to her, linking her arm through mine as she led me down another path. The light from the gazebo glowed gently at the end, and every so often a burst of male laughter drifted in our direction on the breeze. "But even though Belial and Lucifer are estranged, that doesn't mean they can't make things right. Nothing is too late while they're still both alive."

We emerged from the gardens back by the gazebo, but before we returned to our men, she stopped and looked me in the eye. "If you want your son in your life again, you should consider making a bold move."

A bold move... My breath caught in my throat. She was right. I had to find Belial, and make things right with him.

I had to go to New Orleans.

Lucifer shut the door of the guest room with a quiet click as I took in the space. A huge, wooden four-poster bed was hung with gauzy curtains, while a small fire crackled in a fireplace in the corner, with two small chairs flanking it. Every piece of furniture looked like it had been lovingly crafted, and I sensed they all had an impressive history. Pillows and throws were strewn artfully across the bed and chairs, and I wanted to lie down just to experience the comfort.

"You were brilliant tonight." Lucifer loosened his necktie, the noise of the fabric slicing through the room, his fingers swift as he made the masculine movement. "I knew you would have no trouble resuming your role as my queen."

"I'm happy I could help in some way." I sat in one of the chairs by the fireplace and fiddled with the soft throw hanging over the arm. "But there's something I want to talk to you about."

His brows drew low. "What is it?"

"I want us to visit Belial."

Lucifer shook his head. "It's not a good idea right now, with all that's happening with the Archdemons. Once things have calmed down, then we can see him."

"No." I stood, no longer hesitant, my voice firm as I took control of the situation. "I don't want to wait. What if Adam kills me, permanently this time? What if I never get to see my sons again?"

"Adam won't—" he started, but then he pressed his lips together as I narrowed my eyes into a glare.

"We can't know that for sure."

Lucifer moved to the great window overlooking the garden and rested his hands upon the sill as he gazed outside. His back was tense, his muscles tight and straining against his shirt. After some time, he sighed and turned back to me. "Very well. But it would be better if you went alone."

"What happened between you and Belial?" My memories from Eve and my other early lives were the hardest to access and the most faded due to time, unlike more recent lives like Lenore. I remembered Belial, but only in brief flashes and pangs of emotion. Love. Pride. Disappointment. Guilt. Sadness.

Lucifer scowled. "He rebelled against us, as all children do in the end."

Something had happened, something no one wanted to talk about, but it had clearly broken our family in two. I wasn't going to stand for that. "You should come with me."

"It's not a good idea. I won't stop you from going, but you'll have better luck speaking with Belial without me there. Just take Azazel with you. And Morningstar."

I grabbed my brush and began working it through my hair slowly as I considered his words. "Thank you."

He sat on the edge of the bed, folding his shirt sleeves up to reveal his masculine forearms. "For what?"

I set my brush down on the vanity and locked eyes with him. "For respecting my wishes. For treating me like an equal."

He inclined his head slightly. "I'm doing my best."

I stood and unzipped my dress, lowering it to my shoulders. "I know."

"Besides, you know what the best thing is about you traveling alone?" Lucifer's eyes took on a wicked gleam.

"What's that?" I let my dress fall the rest of the way to the floor, revealing a thin slip underneath and nothing else.

"Saying goodbye." He reached for me as I walked toward the bed. Without hesitation, I slipped my hand into his and he tugged, pulling me so I sprawled on top of him.

"Mmm..." He pressed his lips to my neck and pushed one of the thin straps of my slip from my shoulder. "I think this might need to be a very long goodbye indeed."

I relaxed completely under his touch as his mouth burned a trail of heat across my skin. I arched my neck, increasing his access.

"Just promise you'll come back to me," he said. "I won't lose you again." His words seared into me, sinking deep into my soul, before he flipped us, the movement so fast he was above me before I even registered the movement.

"Always." I reached up to touch his face, overcome with emotion. Deep down, he must be afraid I'd leave and never return. I wondered if he'd always had that fear, if every time he watched me be killed by Adam's hand he wondered if I would reborn again.

I curled my fingers into the hair at the back of his head and drew him toward me, lifting to meet his mouth, capturing his lips in a deep kiss. His tongue brushed against mine, and I was greedy for him, opening my mouth and arching my back, pressing my body to his in search of his touch.

He groaned as he explored my mouth, and my hand fisted tighter in his hair as he rocked against me, the bulge in his pants hitting just the right spot. Wave after wave of heat flooded me, and I dug my free hand into his ass as I ground against him, seeking a quick release even though the need to feel him inside me was almost overwhelming.

His hand slid up the side of my body, skimming the slippery fabric separating him from my skin. "I like this very much, but it's got to go."

I popped open a button on his shirt. "You're right. Our clothes arc in the way."

He lifted up and removed his shirt, then threw it across the room. His pants vanished too, leaving me with a naked devil looming over me. His eyes burned red as he looked at me through heavy lids, lust evident in his gaze, but also something else flickering in the fiery depths. Love.

He gripped the hem of my slip with a devious smile, but I caught his hand before he could continue.

"Don't rip it!" The man had destroyed way too many of my clothes already. "It's the only one I own."

He slammed my hand down on the bed, pinning me beneath him, his body looming over me as his lips seared my neck like a brand. "When we're back, I'll buy you an entire wardrobe of lingerie just so I can have the pleasure of destroying them every night."

His words sent a ripple of dark anticipation through me. As he pushed the slip up my thighs, the fabric skimmed my skin in a light caress, and a shiver ran through me. He moved down my body to kiss above my knee, then again in the middle of my thigh. Inching my slip upward, he kissed the new skin revealed, until he paused.

"Now, how loud should I make you call my name?" he murmured, as he smoothed his hands across my skin. "Loud enough that everyone in this house knows what I'm doing to you?"

I pressed my lips together as heat gathered in my cheeks. I'm sure the people in this house had heard worse with Lilith here.

"Yes." He coaxed my thighs apart. "Let's make you scream."

He kissed the inside of my thigh, sucking gently on the soft skin there before nuzzling forward. Higher. My hands were back in his hair, and he groaned softly as my fingertips pressed into his scalp. At first, all I was aware of was the warm air of his breath, but he quickly followed that with his equally warm tongue, and I squeezed his hair tighter as he ran it toward my core.

His fingers circled my clit, and I lifted my hips off the bed, trying to angle myself to nudge him closer to where I wanted his touch most. Then he lowered his head, and his tongue flicked out, grazing my clit. I tensed and tried to muffle an unexpected cry with my hand tight over my mouth. He sucked my clit into his mouth, and I gasped out meaningless sounds at the hint of teeth.

"Lucifer!" His name was a breath of air, and I pressed his head closer as he barely nipped at my clit then soothed it with his tongue as one of his fingers explored my entrance.

Then he switched his fingers and his mouth, his tongue dipping inside me as he rolled my clit with a laziness that kept me right on the edge of...something. I searched for it, chasing the elusive sensation of completion, but it was always just a second more away. He thrust his tongue inside me again, and I squeezed my thighs around him, but I still wanted more.

"Lucifer, I need you inside me." I pushed my straps from my shoulders, exposing my breasts as if to entice him farther up my body.

I thought he might ignore my words, but then he slowly began to move up my body, worshiping each bit of skin he passed with his mouth. He kissed each of my breasts, sucking on my nipples and flicking them with his tongue before he lay above me, his hard cock nudged between my thighs. Then he paused.

Impatiently, I used my newfound angelic strength to roll us both over on the bed, so I was on top of him. I stared down at my fated mate, my inevitability, and wrapped my hands around the base of his cock. "Now I get what I want."

He put his hands behind his head and grinned up at me. "I'm yours."

Slowly, I sank onto his cock, relishing every single inch of the stretch he gave me. My body tensed, then relaxed as the feel of him inside me ignited memories of all the times we'd done this before.

I began to move without thinking, rocking on top of Lucifer with his cock buried as deep as it would go. My clit ground against him, as his hands grabbed my hips and urged me on. Yes, this was exactly what I needed – to be in control. To take what I needed from him.

Switching my rhythm, I leaned forward and braced myself on the bed, arms on either side of his head, and kept rocking. This gave me room to pull up, letting him nearly all the way out of me, then falling back down and thrusting my body on his cock as hard as I could.

But it wasn't enough. I arched my back and rode him hard and fast, grinding down against him, while he held onto my hips and let me fuck myself on his cock. I demanded more and more and he gave it to me without hesitation.

He reached up and teased my nipples with his fingers, and I came apart, bucking wildly, yelling my pleasure as the climax shook through me. I had no doubt everyone in the house knew exactly what we were doing, and I didn't care.

As I sat there, panting through the last bit of it, Lucifer grasped my hips and rolled us over in one smooth motion, never letting his dick slip out of me. Connected. As we were meant to be.

Lucifer began to move his hips. "I am yours, Hannah. I will always be yours."

But his movements were too slow. "More," I begged.

"I want to savor it," he ground out.

"There will be many more times."

"And I will savor each one," he replied before claiming my mouth, plunging his tongue between my lips, and swallowing my gasps of pleasure as his body set a rhythm that I matched.

Lucifer moved in and out of me, drawing pleasure with every pass of his shaft. He thrust harder, never removing his gaze from mine. His muscles shifted and moved beneath my hands, and he knew my body so well, slowing and quickening, angling himself to press right where I needed him.

"Lucifer," I whispered. "I am yours."

Crying out, he pushed deep inside and stayed there as a second orgasm washed over me. I gasped out his name again as my muscles began to tighten, locking my body around him. This one came from deep within, half emotion and half release. I clutched my devil, pulling him close.

Nothing had felt this perfect in so long. I hadn't felt so whole in years. My heart knew him, knew he was the missing part of my soul. The missing piece that had always kept me awake at night. My other half.

He pressed his lips at the base of my throat and trailed over my neck, while his cock twitched inside, almost like he was ready for another round.

My body continued to pulse and spasm, and I laughed. "Enough."

"Never." His tone was joking, but his eyes were serious. "There will never be enough, Hannah. Not for me."

18

HANNAH

A car waited for us directly on the runway when Lucifer's private jet landed in New Orleans, and I descended the steps from the plane into the November sunshine and warmth. I paused and turned my face skyward, my angelic nature soaking up the bright light. Angels needed light to survive and to fuel our powers, while demons and Fallen needed darkness. Which was why Azazel emerged from the plane and ducked her head, donned her sunglasses, and grumbled under her breath.

The driver stared straight ahead as we slid into the cream leather seats, and I fished in my purse for the address of the bar where I hoped to find Belial. Kassiel had given it to me earlier, with a warning that Belial might not give me the warmest welcome.

I passed the paper over the driver's shoulder. "Drive straight here, please."

Zel cocked an eyebrow. "We should head to the hotel first."

"No." I bristled, annoyed at being questioned. "We go to the bar first."

Zel held up her hands in surrender, and I turned away from her and stared out of the window. I wasn't really upset with her, just anxious about this trip, especially now that we'd arrived. I tried to ignore my jangling nerves and focus on the New Orleans scenery—old buildings with tons of charm, colorful streetcars gliding down the road, people stopping to dance to music on the sidewalk. Any other day, this would have been incredible. But I was meeting my son, and fuck if it didn't feel like the first time.

I wiped my sweat-slicked palms over the side of my pants. It might have been easier if Zel had been more of a conversationalist, but when I shot a glance in her direction, she was looking out her own window, her mouth pressed into a tight line. Probably upset with me for overruling her, although that was something she'd have to get used to now. I was no longer clueless human Hannah, after all. I was her boss now.

"Have you been to New Orleans before?" I asked.

She dragged her gaze back to me and looked at me like I was an idiot. "Of course I have."

Okay, so we'd probably need to have a talk about her attitude at some point.

The limo eventually pulled over in front of a row of buildings. I hesitated, my hand on the door handle, like I was waiting for some sort of sign before I got out of the car.

"Take our bags to the hotel, please," I said to the driver. "We'll walk from here."

I got out of the car, and made sure to grab Morningstar and strap it to my back. Not that I expected to need it, but Lucifer had insisted I take it in case an Archdemon sent minions after me. I did feel more confident with it on, as I sucked in a deep breath and stared at the row of buildings on this narrow street. Many of the structures looked jammed together in a row, their second stories all displaying beautiful balconies with wrought-iron filigree designs, some with greenery cascading over the front. I spent a minute admiring the architecture, so different from anything in California or Nevada, but I had to admit to myself that I was only trying to delay.

"Why am I nervous?" I asked, with an awkward laugh. "He's my son."

She gave me a hard look. "Because he's Belial."

That didn't make me feel any better, but I continued forward.

The bar we were looking for was situated at the end of the street, in a two-story stone building with blue shutters on all the many tall windows. Big big red doors stood at the corner, and over them was a sign that read Outcast Bar, with a logo of two black wings that reminded me a lot of the painting in Lucifer's penthouse.

"I'll wait out here," Zel said. "Give you some time alone with him. He and I have...issues."

Great. I was on my own, then.

The bar appeared closed from the outside, but the door opened when I tried it. I stepped into the gloomy interior of the bar and looked around, giving my eyes time to adjust as I inhaled the smells of freshly waxed wood and spilled beer. It was early enough that the place was empty, with no bartender or staff in sight, giving me time to take in the rows of jewel-colored bottles against the enormous mirror and the clean glasses all hanging in their rows, ready for customers come this evening.

"Hello, Mother," a deep voice said. "It's been a long time."

I whipped my head around to see a muscular, broad-shouldered man walking out of a doorway, a wooden crate in his arms, the sleeves of his gray tee rolled up to show off his big, tattooed biceps. He had his father's chiseled jaw and nearly-black hair, and my— Eve's—dark brown eyes and olive skin. Like all our sons, he looked a lot like Lucifer, except Belial had turned the bad boy dial up to max. The kind of man you'd expect to ride a Harley and wouldn't want to be caught alone with in an alley. But he was still my son, and my chest tightened at the sight of him.

"How did you know who I am?" I walked forward slowly as he put the crate behind the bar and grabbed a rag, slinging it over his shoulder.

Belial leaned back against the mirrored bar wall and crossed his arms. "I've seen you in different bodies hundreds of times now. I always know."

He gestured for me to have a seat at the bar—a casual flick of his hand toward the stool in front of him. Shock made my movements sharp as I slid onto the barstool, adjusting slightly to accommodate the sword on my back. I hadn't expected to be recognized. I'd agonized all throughout the plane ride about how to introduce myself to him, and in the end, it didn't even matter.

"You don't seem surprised to see me," I said, as I rested my hands awkwardly on the bar.

He lifted a shoulder, his arms still crossed, showing off his ink. "You always come. I'm just surprised it took this long."

"There were some...complications." I couldn't tear my eyes off my son. So handsome, so strong, and so...distant. Closed off. Even though the longing to hold him in my arms was almost a physical ache, he clearly did not want a hug from me.

Silence stretched between us. I wasn't sure what to say and spent a minute glancing around the bar, noticing that it was well-kept but had an older feel to it. Like something that had been around for a while. "How long have you worked here?"

"I've owned this place for many years. You want a drink?"

"Sure. Anything is fine." I doubted I'd taste it right now anyway.

He grabbed a tumbler and poured scotch from the top shelf, then slid it in front of me. "The last time I saw you was when you were Lenore in the 1800s. I owned a different bar then. You visited me often with Kassiel when he was a kid." He smirked. "Always trying to bring the family together."

Not much had changed, then. I took a long swig of the generous measure of scotch. "Did it work?" I asked, even though I knew the answer.

He poured himself a shot of something clear and downed it, his face surly. "Nope."

This man was definitely one of my children with that attitude, although he probably got it more from Lucifer than me. They got all their bad habits from their father. Or so I told myself.

"What have you been doing all these years?" I asked, trying to get *something* out of him, even though it seemed like he had no interest in talking to me at all.

He spread his arms wide. "Pretty much what you see right now. I own a bar. I keep my head down. I stay out of the supernatural world."

I perked up a little at that bit of information. "Why's that?"

Belial let out a harsh laugh. "Because I'm the exiled prince."

I was about to open my mouth to ask what happened, when the red doors crashed open, the wood splintering at the hinges from the force. I barely had time to duck before a huge man barreled through on black, bat-like wings.

A gargoyle.

"Hannah!" Watch out!" Zel's voice rang across the bar as she followed after the gargoyle.

Shit. Gargoyles were damn hard to kill because their skin turned to stone when they fought. Light-infused blades were one of the only things that could injure them. Good thing I'd brought Morningstar. I whipped the sword off my back and it instantly ignited with blinding white light, as if reacting to the presence of the demons. My wings spread wide, blocking Belial, my protective instincts in overdrive.

But I needn't have worried. Belial jumped onto the bar and shot bright blue fire from his hands, hitting the gargoyles as they poured through the door. Their stone skin cracked, the sounds like thunder echoing around the room. My mouth fell open as I watched him as he wielded hellfire—the only person with that power other than his father.

I kicked myself out of my prideful staring and surged forward, my wings carrying me as I swung Morningstar and put all my recent training with Callan and Zel to good use. Morningstar glowed as it sliced through a gargoyle's shoulder, and around me the chink of Zel's weapons sounded as she fended others away. Hellfire blazed past and the air was filled with the guttural moans of injured and dying gargoyles.

As I swung around and stabbed the blade through a gargoyle's chest, another one grabbed my wings. He yanked hard, making me yell at the sudden, sharp pain, and shadowy tentacles surrounded the gargoyle, dragging him off me and throwing him against the mirrored wall, smashing it and sending liquor bottles flying. I assumed it was Belial or Azazel, but both of them were busy fighting across the room.

Then I realized the shadows came from me.

I stared down at the darkness swirling around me. Impossible. I was an angel, not a Fallen.

A woman with long black hair and black leathery wings stepped into the room, flanked by more of her kind. I recognized her as Bella aka Belphegor, Archdemon of the gargoyles.

"That's enough fighting, children," she purred with a soft French accent. "Time to take a nap."

She raised a hand and Zel closed her eyes and hit the floor, followed by Belial. I raised Morningstar to defend my son and my friend, but Belphegor's eyes landed on me, and I felt the pull of sleep dragging me down. I tried to fight it, rushing toward her, but my knees weakened. Two gargoyles grabbed my arms as heavy exhaustion settled over me, and I clenched my teeth as my eyes closed and I succumbed to the darkness.

19

LUCIFER

W hile Hannah took the private jet to see our son, I tried to distract myself with work at my desk in the library. I had a feeling Hannah would return disappointed, but I couldn't stop her from trying to reconnect with Belial. Even if I knew it would never work. Some things couldn't be repaired.

I eventually gave up on getting any work done and perused my library, gazing at the vast collection of books I'd gathered over my long years, along with some paintings and artifacts. One of my favorites was the painting of Eve being tempted by Lucifer, done as a commission for me by Michelangelo back during the Renaissance.

A few books had been piled up on one of the side tables by the armchair Hannah liked to sit in, and I picked them up and began to put them away. When I'd had this hotel built, I'd specifically requested this library be added to the penthouse, knowing how much my mate would love it once she found her way back to me. And she did. It thrilled me every time I found her in here, curled up under a blanket with a book. I'd built palaces for her once in an effort to impress her, but later realized all she truly ever wanted were gardens and libraries.

Samael stepped into the library, his dark brows drawn together. "How was your meeting with Baal and Lilith?"

His tone was sharper than normal, and I raised my eyebrows. "Did someone wake up with his wings in a bind again?" I sat at my desk and folded my hands upon it, feeling the old wood beneath my palms. "The meeting went well. They cannot outright help us because the other Archdemons have threatened their children, but Baal is going to act as a spy and provide us some information when he can. They've already given me the name of the Archdemon leading the rebellion—Nemesis."

Samael shook his head. "You should've taken me. Or Azazel."

I leveled a hard look at him in return. Samael wasn't actually angry because I hadn't taken him—or, indeed, Azazel—no matter the words he used to protest, but I waited for him to finish.

"You know Baal can't be trusted," he added. "How do we know he's not lying about all of this?"

I linked my fingers behind my head and sat back. "I think we both know the real person you're upset with isn't me, or even Baal. It's Lilith." His eyes blazed again, and I bit back a grin. Some days, Samael made baiting him so easy. It was barely even a game. "After all, she has been living there for a year now. I've never known her to stay with one man for so long."

Samael balled his hands into tight fists, his knuckles straining beneath his olive skin. "I don't care about that. The two of us were done centuries ago. But she turned Asmodeus mortal without even consulting me. My son will age and *die*. He's going to die, Lucifer. And there's nothing I can do to stop it."

The pain in his voice brought back my own grief at losing a child, though I tried hard to keep it buried deep down. I rose to my feet and crossed around the desk to his side, then set my hand upon his shoulder. "I am sorry about that, old friend. It might do you some good to sit down with Lilith and talk about it. She's just as upset as you are. Or better yet, visit with Asmodeus and his mate. Then perhaps you'll understand why he made his choice."

Samael huffed. "As if I have time for that with the impending apocalypse upon us."

"If it even happens," I said. "Has there been any sign of Adam, or any movement from the Archdemons?"

"Not yet, but our people are hunting for him. I've also sent Fallen soldiers to guard Pestilence's tomb."

"Good." Pestilence would have to be released first, before any of the others could be awakened. One of our safety precautions from when we sealed the Horsemen away. The destruction that even one of them could unleash upon the world was unfathomable—all four of them would mean the end of everything. It's why I let Hannah visit Belial, even though I knew it wouldn't end well. And why Samael shouldn't wait either. "You know, if things go poorly, you might regret not taking the time to connect with your family."

Samael scowled and crossed his arms. "I doubt Lilith would want to see me anyway."

I raised an eyebrow as I perched on the edge of my desk. "I wouldn't be so sure about that."

A knock sounded on the library door and I called for the person to enter. A beautiful Fallen named Einial walked inside and bowed low before us, her long blond hair curling at the ends over her shoulders. "My lord," she murmured.

"Ah, good," Samael said. "Lucifer, I believe you know Einial. I've chosen her for my new assistant."

I nodded. "A fine choice."

Einial was a few hundred years old and had been born a Fallen, unlike Samael and Azazel, who'd left Heaven with me long ago. She'd been one of Samael's spies for centuries, and was married to a sultry woman named Anig, an ancient vampire who didn't generally bother with the rest of demon politics.

She handed Samael a manila envelope. "The report you ordered on the comings and goings at Pestilence's location."

"Excellent." He opened the folder, while my phone dinged with an incoming message.

I glanced at the screen. Spam. Dammit—why was the king of the underworld still getting spam? But as I flicked to delete the message, I glanced at the time.

"Why hasn't Hannah checked in yet? She should have arrived

hours ago." Worry seeped into my chest, and I dialed her immediately. She didn't answer. I tried Azazel next. Nothing.

Samael grabbed his phone after I'd tried Azazel a second time. "I'll call the pilot."

Two minutes later, he set the phone down on the table and shook his head, his face creased with concern. "He hasn't seen them, and they haven't checked into the hotel either."

Something was wrong. The Archdemons must have gone after her. I knew it in my gut. But why now? Why not when she'd gone to visit Jophiel or Brandy?

Belial.

Of course.

I turned my gaze on Samael. "Fucking hell. They're after Belial. And Hannah led them right to him."

"I'll arrange transportation for us to head to New Orleans immediately," Samael said.

"Wait. Why do they want Belial?" Einial asked, her brow furrowed.

I grabbed my suit jacket, already on my way out the door. "Because he's the only one who can release Pestilence."

20

HANNAH

My head slammed against something, and a dull ache radiated through my skull. I tried to open my eyes, but they were slow to move, almost like they were stuck shut or pinned down. My throat ached, and I swallowed against the dryness of it, groaning a little as I did. I was in constant motion, my cheek scraping across a dusty, grit-covered surface as my body swayed. I moaned softly.

"Mother?"

At the sound of Belial's voice, I tried to open my eyes again, finally peering through two narrow slits into a dim, metal-walled room. Except, no. That wasn't right. The entire room was moving, and the low rumble of an engine vibrated through my body.

"Hot," I murmured. Shit, it was so dry and hot here. Like someone had left me baking in an oven. This was not New Orleans weather. Were we back in Nevada?

"Mm." Belial ground out his agreement.

Recollection came back to me. The bar. The gargoyles. Belphegor.

"Zel?" I could only manage one-word questions, and my voice was hoarse. I tried to look around, but my eyeballs ached. I couldn't see her.

"Not here."

Fuck. Had they taken her somewhere else? What if she was dead?

I grimaced against the fear and the aches in my body as I struggled to sit up. I couldn't do anything about Zel now. I had to focus on saving myself and my son. What I really needed was a drink, something to wet my throat. Hair slicked to my forehead, and tendrils of it were stuck with sweat to the back of my neck. The floor beneath me jostled again, and I groaned as my head bumped against the metal wall.

"We're traveling through the desert," Belial said. "Some sort of truck."

"Nevada?" I asked.

"Don't think so."

My arms were heavy, and I glanced down at the strange weight. A silver cuff hung around each wrist, like an old-fashioned manacle, only I wasn't chained to anything or otherwise bound. Each cuff was perfectly seamless except for a spot where chains could be added, with no obvious way to open it.

"Like our new accessories?" Belial asked, his tone laced with irritation.

"What are they?" They didn't look so bad. I shook one wrist experimentally.

Belial rolled his head against the corrugated inside of the moving truck. "They null our powers."

I paused. "No powers?"

"He shook his head. "And they're impossible to get off. I've tried."

"Fuck." There wasn't really another word for it, and my throat still hurt. But at least in this sitting position, some sort of breeze fanned across me. It was a warm one, but moving air was better than being suffocated in heat. I tried to reach for my wings, or any of my angelic powers, but it was like being human again. There was just nothing there.

I studied my son as he leaned back against the metal wall. Sweat creased his brow and his dark hair hung limp. A ragged tear ran up the side of his gray t-shirt. His eyes were exhausted but wary and alert. If he'd gotten injured, he'd already healed it.

It was my fault he was in this mess at all. For years he'd lived a quiet life running his bar, and I'd ruined all that.

"I'm sorry," I said. "For getting you caught up in this."

He gave me a wry smile. "I'm not mad at you. Though this kind of shit is precisely the reason I've stayed out of the supernatural world the last few centuries."

I nodded. There weren't any more words to express my regret.

We sat in silence for a while, the truck speed seeming to be steady, the road more or less smooth, the temperature constant. When things showed no sign of changing, I decided I might as well continue my plan of reconnecting with my son. We might not have much time left, after all.

"Tell me what happened with your father." I had a general idea, but those memories weren't making themselves super clear yet. I needed to know what I was up against before I could mend the rift between our family.

Belial lifted his eyebrows as if surprised by my words. "There's not much to tell."

I lifted my shoulders in a small shrug. "Then it won't take long to fill me in. It's not like we've got anything else to do but kill time back here."

He tilted his head back and stared off into space, his face hard. I thought he was going to ignore my request, when he finally said, "After you died as Persephone, Damien decided to stay in Faerie."

Damien. My middle son. Half-fae. Half-Fallen. Once I got out of this mess, I would find him next. "Why?"

Belial spread his hands. "What can I say? We blamed Father for your death. *All* your deaths. For the curse itself. But when you died that time, it hit us hard. As Persephone you lived a long time, and we had a..." He dropped his voice, looking away. "We had a real family for a while."

My chest tightened at his words. "I'm sorry. This has been so hard on you boys."

He shot me an exasperated look. "I'm thousands of years old. Hardly a boy."

I'll admit, it was strange calling this man my son, when he was centuries older than my current body. But at the same time, I had memories stretching back to when he was born. I vaguely remembered holding him in my arms as a baby. Damn, he'd been a fighter even then. Fighting sleep. Refusing to do anything we asked. Being way too smart and stubborn for his own good. I closed my eyes as memories of a brown-eyed, dark-haired toddler glaring up at me in defiance made me smile.

I turned that smile on Belial. "Ask any mother. You'll always be boys to me. *My* boys."

He shook his head, his mouth set in a tight line, but he knew better than to respond.

I gestured for him to keep talking. "What happened after Damien moved to Faerie?"

"The short version?" Belial asked, with a dark smirk. "I let my ego get too big and thought I could take Father down." He let out a harsh laugh. "I led an uprising against him to take the throne of Hell. As the oldest of the Nephilim, I had them on my side, along with some Fallen and demons too. But I failed, and I was cast out of Hell. I've been laying low on Earth ever since."

I nodded slowly as I listened. "Nephilim?"

"People like me. Half human. Half angel or Fallen."

"Right." I struggled through my memories of the time, but they were so vague. "Where was I during all this?"

"You hadn't been reborn yet."

That would explain why I had no memories of that battle. I did vaguely remember arguing with Lucifer in Hell over Belial's exile, but it had been years after the fact. I'd fought for Lucifer to pardon Belial, but he'd refused. He'd said too many lives had been lost in the uprising, and an example had to be made. He couldn't simply let our son try to overthrow him and claim the throne of Hell without some sort of punishment. Besides, if it had been anyone other than our son, the punishment would have been death. Exile was Lucifer being lenient. I'd argued that Belial had been punished enough, but

Lucifer wouldn't budge unless Belial made some sort of formal apology or reparations, which naturally Belial refused to do. And now here I was, centuries later, still trying to fix this mess.

Stupid, stubborn men. I loved them, but sometimes they were useless without a woman making sure shit actually got done.

There was something else too. Something I'd said in that argument with Lucifer about how Belial had lost something... No. Someone.

"You lost someone you loved in the uprising, didn't you?" I asked.

"Yes." He growled and turned his head away. "Tatra. One of Father's many casualties. Something I've never forgiven him for."

"I'm sorry." I felt for him, I truly did, and I knew how hard it would be to lose the person I loved. But I also understood Lucifer's position. Just like now, Lucifer had been forced to defend his throne. I'd been miserable about losing Belial, but I'd stood by Lucifer's punishment because our son had to be held accountable for his actions.

I blew out a soft sigh. "That was a very long time ago. Don't you think it's time to see if things could be worked out between you and your father?"

"No," he said flatly, and there was no room for argument in his tone.

I pressed my lips together to prevent myself from arguing further. I sensed if I wanted to bring my family back together, I needed to tread carefully to avoid scaring Belial off completely. Besides, we needed to get out of this situation first. I had no doubt Lucifer was already looking for us, but I wasn't going to sit around and wait for rescue. If there was a way for us to escape, we'd take it.

The truck turned and bounced a couple of times before the thin squeal of brakes being applied sliced through the air in the box-container we were in. Belial scooted in front of me to face the back door, his jeans scraping in the grit as he moved. I couldn't see his face, but I grasped his upper arm loosely as we sat in silence, the anticipation building as we waited.

After several long minutes, there was a grinding noise of bolts being released and the door burst open. I got a quick view of a dark sky hung with stars before two huge gargoyles with stone skin jumped into the container and grabbed Belial. My son shouted and fought as he was ripped from my hold. They dragged him outside and flung him unceremoniously to the ground, then grabbed me and did the same before I could even react.

We were in the middle of the desert, the moon lighting the vast, open space. Nothing but sand in every direction, other than our convoy of trucks. The land was eerie in its paleness, and a chill rippled over my skin. The sun had gone, and the air grew colder by the second now that we weren't insulated inside the moving truck. As an angel, the cold bothered me more than it had before. If I'd had my powers, I could have used light to warm myself, but the cuffs prevented that. At least Belial would be fine—as half Fallen, he would barely feel the cold, just like the other demons here.

I quickly scanned the area. There were at least thirty people around us, and most looked like fighters. I spotted Belphegor barking orders, and beside her was a gorgeous woman with flame-red hair. Nemesis. Archdemon of the imps...and the one behind the plot against Lucifer. According to Belial and Lilith, anyway.

Then Gadreel—Adam—emerged from another truck, and cold fear slid down my spine, mixed with molten rage. I watched him approach without shrinking back, hatred coiling tightly inside me like a snake waiting for its moment. I was going to kill that asshole for everything he'd done to me and my family over the years. I burned with the desire to take him down, but when I reached for my powers, I felt nothing.

Damn. I couldn't do anything with a swarm of armed gargoyles surrounding me and my son, keeping us in the dirt, forcing us to kneel. Adam had all of his strength and powers as a Fallen, and Belial and I were in magic-blocking cuffs. Plus, I still didn't know where Zel was.

"Hello, Eve," Adam said, as he towered over me. In this life as Gadreel he had sandy blond hair and blue eyes, with a handsome, boy-next-door face that concealed the monster within. "I'm so glad we're together again."

I glared up at him, even though I was terrified. For myself. For my son. "There's no 'together.' You kidnapped me. What do you want?"

Adam's grin grew wider. "For once it's not you I want, but your son. Although I'll gladly have you too."

I glanced at Belial, truly afraid now. What did they want with him?

Before I could ask, some of the gargoyles shackled my ankles with more of those cuffs, and then attached some silver chains to my ankles and my wrists. They did the same to Belial at my side, and then the chains were attached to the truck. I tried fighting against them, using my angelic strength, but the metal was magic and resisted all our efforts. Made by the fae, I remembered vaguely.

"What are you doing?" I asked the question without expectation of reply, but Adam met my gaze, his eyes amused.

He gestured at some of the soldiers, who were pitching tents behind him. "Setting up camp for the night. We have another long day ahead of us tomorrow."

I glanced behind us at the truck. I'd almost have been more comfortable sleeping in the box, locked in, away from the man who lived to kill me. If only I had Morningstar, but I hadn't seen any sign of it since the battle.

"Did you kill Zel?" I kept my words hard and emotionless, even though they felt like they were ripped out of my chest.

"No, of course not," Adam said, and the flicker of emotion in his voice surprised me. "Azazel and I were friends for a long time. We fought side by side, had each other's backs..." He straightened and grinned at me in the darkness. "She's decided to join us in our fight against Lucifer."

"What?" I shook my head. "She would never betray Lucifer. Or me."

"See for yourself." He grabbed my arm and yanked me to a standing position, so I could see over the front of the truck. On the other side of it stool Zel, her dark hair tied back, her daggers strapped to her side. She spoke with a green-haired man with pointed ears—a fae—who looked vaguely familiar, though I couldn't place him. When she saw me looking at her, she scowled and walked away.

Adam laughed as he threw me back in the dirt. "You don't know the depth of loyalty and camaraderie between us. Or her secret hatred of Lucifer. I knew she'd be easy to turn."

My heart pounded with the knowledge Zel was still alive, but I couldn't believe she would turn against us. She'd always been loyal. *Always.*

Belial turned around to scan the horizon. "Are we where I think we are?"

Adam looked pleased with Belial for noticing. "Yes, we'll arrive tomorrow. Lucifer's minions are already there, but it shouldn't be a problem." He left us in the sand and disappeared inside one of the larger tents. Belphegor joined him a few seconds later.

"Where are we?" I asked, turning to my son for answers.

Belial adjusted his position and rested his hands on his knees. "We're in the middle of Palestine. Near the Tower of Jericho." He gave me a level look. "Where Pestilence is sealed."

Fear spiked in my heart. Lucifer was right. Adam and the Archdemons were planning on releasing the Four Horsemen, even knowing it could set off the apocalypse. Maybe that's what they wanted. "Why do they need us here? Or rather, you?"

"They need my blood to open the tomb where Pestilence is currently sealed."

"Your blood?" My brow furrowed as I ran through my murky memories of Eve's past. "Lucifer said the Horsemen were sealed away by him, Archangel Michael, the fae king Oberon, and me."

"Yes, you—as Eve." Belial blew out a long breath as he tried to get comfortable on the hard ground. "Each Horsemen is hidden in a different realm, with Pestilence here on Earth, War in Heaven, Famine in Faerie, and Death in Hell. To unlock them, the Archdemons need someone who meets two criteria." He ticked them off on his fingers. "First, they have to be descended from one of the people who sealed the tomb. And second, they have to have been born in the realm the Horsemen was sealed in."

"Sounds complicated," I muttered.

"Complicated on purpose," Belial said. "You don't want any random person to be able to release the Four Horsemen."

"Good point."

"So to unlock Pestilence, they need a human born on Earth, with the blood of one of the original four." Belial spread his tattooed arms wide. "Since you're no longer Eve, that leaves me."

I ran through my memories—yes, Damien had been born in Faerie, and Kassiel in Hell, but Belial I'd had on Earth. I wasn't sure about how many children Michael and Oberon had, but they'd likely been born in Heaven or Faerie, not here.

And I'd led Adam and the Archdemons right to my son.

Fury and fear spiked up my throat, and my hands shook as I glared at the tent where Adam and Belphegor had disappeared inside. I had to stop them—from releasing Pestilence, and from using Belial's blood to do it.

Adam had hurt me far too many times. There was no way I'd let him hurt my son.

21

HANNAH

After an uncomfortable night where Adam did little more than throw a blanket over me—and only then so I didn't die prematurely in the cold night air—I'd woken up with stiff muscles and was already beginning to overheat in the unrelenting desert sun. Our captors gave us some granola bars and water, let us relieve ourselves, and then threw us back into the truck without ceremony. Belial tried to fight back against them, but Belphegor used her sleep powers to knock him out, and I decided to save my energy. Resolve burned low in my gut as they slammed the door shut, locking us inside.

The relentless forward motion of the truck and the low grumble of the engine, combined with the warmth of the day, almost rocked me gently to sleep. I spent the morning exhausted and dozing, curled up next to my son. Needless to say, this was not the reunion I'd been hoping for.

We awoke when they threw us some moist sandwiches, which we greedily chomped down. They were terrible, but we needed our strength.

"When we stop again, we need to try to escape," I said to Belial once the truck started moving again.

His laugh was harsh. "Sure. With no weapons and no powers. Against dozens of supernatural soldiers and two Archdemons."

"We have to do something." I sighed and leaned back, but couldn't get comfortable. "We can't let them awaken Pestilence."

Belial rubbed his chin, his dark stubble growing more pronounced while in captivity. "All right. If we find a moment when they're distracted, we'll take it."

"Maybe Zel will help us," I muttered. She couldn't have betrayed us. I refused to believe it.

"Azazel?" Belial barked out a laugh. "No way. She'd never lift a finger to help me."

Hours passed before the tone of the engine changed pitch and we rumbled to a stop. I drew away from Belial, instantly alert. Footsteps scuffed around the side of the truck and metal worked against metal again as the door at the back was unbolted. I watched for a chink of light appearing as it opened, but when it did I discovered it was already night, the vast black sky above us bright with stars.

Adam smirked as the soldiers dragged me from the back of the truck, but I looked beyond him, my chest squeezing at the sight of a strange, conical ruin, the stone rugged and crumbling. A wave of something like déjà vu came over me as I stared at the Tower of Jericho, and then I remembered it as it had once been—a beautiful structure of mixed stones with a massive staircase, envied for its height and for the advances it represented. Now it was mere ruins. Humans couldn't keep anything nice.

Nemesis approached from one of the other trucks, her ruby-red lips curved into a malevolent smile as she flipped flame-colored hair over her shoulder. As she came closer, I took in her curves and skin-tight clothing. She hadn't changed much over the years—wearing her allure like a favorite outfit. She'd always been jealous of me, I remembered. She hated me for becoming Lucifer's queen instead of her.

She and Belphegor conferred quietly, while I watched Zel, who stood in the background with her hands on her hips, staring off into the distance. I felt sick at the thought that she'd betrayed us, and wished I could read her aura to see the truth. Damn these cuffs.

A gargoyle guard nudged me forward, and I stumbled in surprise as our entire group began to move. As we approached the Tower, I saw people patrolling around it and on top of it. A dark shape flew overhead, blocking out the starlight, and I thought at first it was a raven, before realizing it was a black-winged Fallen. Did they not see us approaching?

Nemesis stood in the center of our group, her arms spread, and I realized she was using her powers of illusion to keep us hidden. Belphegor and some of her gargoyles led the charge, and I could only watch in horror as they approached the Fallen guarding the Tower.

With Nemesis's powers cloaking her, Belphegor walked up to Lucifer's guards, so close they should have been able to smell her, and waved her hand, putting them to sleep. She seemed to delight in their obliviousness, as they collapsed in the cold desert sand with a thump. I started to scream, to warn them, but a hand was clamped over my mouth. I struggled but couldn't do anything about the attack, and the cuffs at my wrists were a constant reminder of my powerlessness. I turned my head toward Zel, pleading at her with my eyes, but she ignored me and stared ahead, her lips pressed into a tight line. How could she stand there and do nothing?

The soldiers, who I assumed were all imps and gargoyles, rushed forward and began killing Lucifer's guards with ease as they slept. This wasn't a battle. This was murder.

Belial suddenly bucked his captors, spinning around and kicking them, while the main force was distracted with the Fallen. I began fighting off the two gargoyles holding me too, but just when I'd broken free, I heard Adam's horrible laugh. I turned and saw Belial face down in the dirt, with a gargoyle with stone skin kneeling on his back, and Adam's sword at his throat. I bowed my head in defeat and let the gargoyles grab me again.

Adam smirked at me, delighting in my misery as he always had. "You always were too soft."

I pictured killing him in varying horrible ways for all he'd done. But he was wrong—I was anything but soft. "Kindness and empathy don't make me soft. They give me the will to fight for what's right."

Adam rolled his eyes and sheathed his sword, then turned away as Belphegor approached. "Is everyone dead, Bella?"

"Yes. Philomelus has started the excavation now," she said. "It shouldn't be long."

Wait. I knew that name. I searched my memories and remembered the green-haired man I'd seen with Zel last night—that was Philomelus. A fae of the Autumn Court who I'd known during my time as Persephone. He'd had a twin brother, Plutus...who'd turned out to be the reincarnation of Adam. The two of them must still have a strong bond, if Philomelus was working with Adam now.

"Good." Adam lowered his head and kissed Belphegor, and the kiss soon turned into a full-blown make-out session, complete with roaming hands and way more tongue than anyone outside their relationship ever needed to see. "Let's go watch my brother work."

They held hands as they walked toward the crumbling tower, and many of the soldiers trailed behind them. Belial and I were made to sit by the trucks in the dirt. I asked for some water, and was completely ignored. I was freezing in the cold night air, but no one cared. All I could hear was a low rumbling sound by the tower.

Then the guard next to me suddenly dropped dead, his neck sliced open. Azazel spun and kicked and slashed with her light-infused dagger, taking out the other guards around us with ease. It happened so fast I barely had time to blink.

"Zel!" I exhaled in relief. "I knew you'd never betray us."

"Of course not. I had to trick that bastard so I could keep an eye on you." She tossed her dark hair as she sheathed her blade. "Can you believe Adam thought I'd join him just because we were friends when he was Gadreel?"

Belial got to his feet and eyed her warily. "Yet you just stood there and watched while they slaughtered your Fallen allies."

Zel's face flashed with anger. "My job is to protect Hannah. Have no doubt, their deaths will be avenged."

"Can you get these off?" I asked, holding out my cuffs. With them on, we couldn't use our wings, which made escape a lot trickier.

"I don't have the key. Adam's got it locked down tight." Zel searched the guards around us and held up some car keys. She tossed them to me. "Get in the truck and go. I'll protect you from the air."

"I'm not leaving you!" I ran for the nearest truck, the keys clutched tightly in my sweaty hands.

Zel's black wings spread behind her with a snap. "They'll come at us from the air. Someone has to hold them back."

She lifted off before I could argue, and Belial grabbed my arm and hauled me the final steps toward the truck. He'd grabbed a sword along the way. I should have thought of that. I got in on the driver's side, and tried the keys with trembling hands as Belial slid in beside me. The engine started up and I slammed my foot on the gas.

The truck peeled off, sending dirt flying in every direction as I headed for the road up ahead. Belial leaned out the window, looking back toward the tower, his stolen sword ready in his hand. I couldn't see Zel, but I assumed she flew over us with her daggers ready. My heart pounded in my chest as I maneuvered the huge steering wheel, knowing this was our one chance to escape, and it wasn't a very good one. There was nothing around us for miles except dirt and sand and stars. But we had to try.

The truck lurched onto the road, and I nearly let out a whoop of relief, until I glanced in the rearview mirror and saw it was filled with dark-winged figures gaining speed faster than should be possible, like something in a horror movie.

Belial saw it too, and he grabbed hold of the window and hauled himself up and out of it, then climbed onto the roof. My mouth fell open as I watched him, feeling a touch of pride even amid the danger. I so desperately wanted to go with him and protect him, but I had to keep us moving too.

The gargoyles reached us, and I heard the clang of swords striking above me, and the whoosh of air from powerful wings. A female gargoyle with blond hair tried to climb into the window next to me, and I slapped at her face, unable to do much else while driving. With her stone skin, it didn't do much, but then Zel yanked her off, slicing the gargoyle's throat with a glowing white dagger.

Suddenly the truck swerved and stopped, the tires squealing as they tried to keep going forward, but it was like something held us in place. I glanced out the side window and saw tentacles of darkness had grabbed the wheels, coming from Adam's hands. I kept my foot on the gas and yelled in frustration, as the gargoyles surrounded our truck.

Then Zel hit the window in front of me, cracking it instantly, and I screamed. She rolled off and fell to the ground, and I slammed my brakes. Where was my son? Was he all right?

Belphegor landed in front of my truck on bat-like taloned black wings. Adam set down beside her, holding Belial, who seemed to be passed out but otherwise unharmed. I took some small comfort in the fact that they wouldn't kill Belial, not yet anyway. They needed him.

Zel wasn't so lucky. As the gargoyles threw open the truck and hauled me out, they tossed me to the ground beside her. I couldn't tell if she was breathing or not, but she had a wound on her shoulder that was bleeding pretty badly.

"Nice try," Adam said, as he tossed my unconscious son down. "But there's no escape for any of you."

The last thing I saw was his horrid face before the world went black.

22

HANNAH

"The tomb isn't there."

Nemesis's voice roused me from sleep, and I cracked open my eyes. I was back in the dirt near the tomb, surrounded by more guards, with chains attached to my cuffs again. Night had fallen, and my skin prickled against the cold air. Belial sat beside me, already awake and alert, but wearing enough chains that he could barely move. Zel was still passed out beside him. Not dead, thankfully, but still bleeding, even with the rapid healing of an immortal.

I sat up a bit, noticing Nemesis standing a short distance away with Adam, Belphegor, and Philomelus. My one comfort was that they all looked pissed.

"What do you mean, it's not there?" Adam snapped, before they all stomped back in the direction of the tomb.

"Welcome back," Belial said to me in a low voice.

"I wonder what they mean," I whispered. "How could the tomb be gone?"

He shrugged, seemingly indifferent to our predicament. Or maybe he was just as exhausted and defeated as I was in this moment. Our escape attempt had failed, and we wouldn't get another shot. Things seemed pretty fucking bleak for us, except for the fact that they couldn't find Pestilence's tomb. That might buy us a few hours. It would have to be enough.

I tried to offer Belial some hope. "Lucifer will come."

He smirked. "Is that supposed to make me feel better?"

"We'll get through this. I promise." I leaned close to my son and, even though I knew he'd probably pull away, I put my arms around him. The words were spoken partly to reassure myself, and I expected him to make a snarky comment in response.

To my surprise, Belial let me hold him. He was huge, so much larger than I was that it felt like I was hugging a tree, but I breathed in deep, committing this moment to memory. If I died tonight, at least I'd have these few seconds where we'd reconnected.

Adam and the others returned, attracting my attention as they barked out orders to their soldiers. Belial and I were yanked to our feet, then dragged forward and shoved back down to the ground in front of the group.

Nemesis leaned down in front of me, so close I could feel her hot breath against my cheeks. "Where's the tomb?"

"I don't know what you're talking about."

Nemesis slapped me hard, making my ears ring, the impact so fast and shocking all I could do was take it. "I *said*, where is the tomb?"

Belial struggled against the men holding him and yelled, "Don't fucking touch her!"

Adam pulled Nemesis back. "Don't hurt my prize. Only I'm allowed to do that."

His *prize*? If he came any closer I would vomit all over his shoes.

As sharp pain blossomed across my face, I actually laughed. "I really have no idea. My memories are a jumbled mess."

"Maybe the son knows something," Belphegor said, stepping toward Belial with a knife in her hand.

"If you think that, you're bigger fools than I thought," my son said with a bitter laugh of his own. "Lucifer kicked me out of Hell centuries ago. I don't know anything."

"No, he doesn't," Adam confirmed. "But Eve does. I can get her to talk."

Adam looked at Belial for a moment, and then he slammed his fist into my son's stomach. I felt his grunt of pain in my own gut, and I clutched my chest as he bent over from it. Then Adam turned to me with pure evil in his eyes. "I won't kill him. You know that. But I'll make him hurt so bad he'll pray for death. Unless you tell me where the tomb is."

"I really don't know!" I yanked at my chains, desperate to get to my son. "I'm not lying. I don't remember anything, I swear it."

"Then you better remember fast." Adam grabbed Belphegor's knife and sliced it across Belial's upper arms. Two quick slashes that made him bleed, though his face betrayed nothing.

"No!" I yelled, as blood spilled across my son's tattoos.

"Don't tell them anything, Mother," Belial said through gritted teeth.

Adam sliced Belial's thighs next, through his dirty, ripped jeans, and hot tears fell from my eyes. I yelled at them to stop, struggling and fighting until my arms and legs ached, and Adam paused and looked at me.

"Stop," I cried. "I'll try to remember! Just let me think." I sifted through memories, images coming and going from my head as I pulled them forward and rejected them. I vaguely remembered being at the tower as Eve and spilling my blood onto the tomb, but that didn't explain what had happened to it after that.

"This is taking too long," Nemesis said. "Cut him again."

Adam slashed the dagger across Belial's back next, tearing into his already ripped shirt. Where his wings would be, if he could pull them out.

"Wait, stop!" Closing my eyes, I searched frantically, trying to sort anything that had to do with the tomb. "I'm trying!"

Belial cried out, his hoarse scream echoing off the ruins, and I jerked my eyes open to see blood pouring from his back.

"Wait!" I cried. "I've got something. Stop hurting him." My head began to hurt from the effort of forcing all the memories to comply. "Lucifer..."

"Lucifer *what?*" Belphegor asked.

The images flashed behind my eyes almost like I was watching an old, faded movie with some scenes missing. "He moved it. After Belial's uprising. He said he was doing it to be cautious." I slumped in relief, glad I'd been able to remember something so they'd stop hurting Belial.

But Nemesis surged forward, and her manicured nails lengthened, transforming into claws. She slashed at Belial's chest, and he gave another cry of pain. "Where?" she asked, her tone calm—as if she hadn't just spilled my son's blood into the desert sand.

"I don't know!" I cried. I closed my eyes again as I tried to cover the rapidity of my heartbeat, the franticness of my thoughts, and seem as calm as she did. I couldn't fall apart in front of them. Not if I wanted to protect Belial. And I needed to block out as many other senses as I could so I could concentrate.

I clutched my head, trying to remember. "I was human," I whispered. "On a ship. With Lucifer." I focused and concentrated as hard as I could, willing to do anything to keep them from hurting Belial. It was an older ship, with big masts and sails, the wood creaking as we sailed across stormy seas. Lucifer wore a billowy white shirt and trousers stuffed into large black boots. He turned and pointed across the waves.

Belial screamed again, his loudest yet. I couldn't open my eyes. I had to keep going. I sorted through the foggy memories. The ship docked, and the massive tomb was hauled off with ropes into a carriage. We continued through hard rain in the dead of night to a ring of stones in the grass.

"Stonehenge!" I opened my eyes. "It's at Stonehenge!"

Adam grinned and stepped close to touch my face, almost tenderly, but I jerked my head away. "I knew you would remember."

"Get ready to move immediately," Nemesis said to the nearest guard.

Oh fuck, what had I done? I'd led them right to Pestilence's location.

I turned to Belial, who watched me with inscrutable eyes, probably disappointed with me for revealing the location. I started to crawl toward him, horrified at the sight of his blood, wanting nothing more than to hold him tight. "I'm sorry," I said to him. "I had to do it."

But then Adam turned to Belial and offered him his hand. I paused, staring open-mouthed, as Belial took it and rose to his feet. Adam removed the cuffs around his wrists, and my son let out a relieved sigh, rubbing the skin there. Then a gargoyle handed Belial a small towel to wipe up the blood. His cuts were already healing, now that the cuffs were off, and I realized they weren't very deep.

"Thank you, Mother," Belial said, as he cleaned himself up quickly, then tossed the bloody rag to one of the nearby men.

"What..." I glanced between Belial and the others, who'd begun packing up and loading things into the trucks. Belial now moved freely between them, as if he was one of them.

"Prepare the jet," Belial ordered. "We're going to England."

"Belial, what's happening?" I asked, reaching for him. I didn't want to believe what I was seeing—my own son betraying me. "Belial!"

His eyes landed on me again, and they were hard. He looked at me like a stranger. No—an enemy.

"Knock her out."

"No!" I screamed as he walked away, my heart breaking even worse than when Lucifer had killed me.

Belphegor moved in front of me, and it all went dark.

23

LUCIFER

I stepped inside Belial's bar for the first time. I'd visited many times before, but I'd always watched from a distance, telling myself this would be when I finally stepped inside and spoke with my son. Now I feared it might be too late.

The place was a mess. Broken windows. Splintered chairs. Cracked tables. The mirrored wall behind the bar had been shattered, with smashed liquor bottles strewn about, making the room reek of alcohol. I picked up one of the menus scattered on the floor and stared at the Outcast Bar logo. Two tiny dots of blood marred the black wings stamped across the top. Was it Hannah's blood? Belial's? One of their attackers?

I dropped the menu and scanned the dark room, lit only by a bit of magic from my angelic friends. Clearly a fight had taken place here, but the victors had done a good job of cleaning up the evidence. If any had been defeated, their bodies had already been removed. Only these tiny drops of blood remained.

Good thing I had someone who could help with that. When we'd departed from Las Vegas, I'd brought Samael, along with Kassiel, Olivia, and her other men. Most of them were outside, combing the area for any clues, but Bastien was the one I turned to now. As the son of an Archangel, he had an extra power that I needed—the power to read objects and see the past through them.

Bastien stepped up to the bar and rested his hands upon the smooth wood, then closed his eyes. When he opened them, he turned toward me. "Gargoyles."

"I knew it," Samael muttered.

"What happened to Hannah?" I asked.

"Belphegor put her to sleep and she was taken away," Bastien said. "Along with Azazel."

I swore under my breath. This wasn't the first time Belphegor and her people had attacked Hannah. When I saw the Archdemon again, I was going to rip her apart, limb by limb. "And Belial?"

Bastien's dark brows furrowed. "He initially seemed to be knocked out by Belphegor—but once Hannah was asleep he stood up and brushed himself off. He walked out of the bar with Belphegor."

"No." The word slipped out of my mouth, even as the obviousness of it hit me like a punch in the gut. Belial was working with the Archdemons. Of course he was. He'd tried to overthrow me once before, and it hadn't worked, and now he was part of the plot to do it again. I should've known he would try again. What a fool I'd been to think perhaps we'd been ready to let the old grievances die, to hope that Hannah might finally be able to mend what had been so thoroughly broken.

"Any sign of where they went?" Samael asked. "Was Adam with them?"

"No," Bastien said. "To both your questions."

I found a half-empty bottle of bourbon and picked it up, downing the last of it, then tossed it against the wall, hard. As it smashed, the sound of glass breaking echoed through the bar. Hellfire danced across my fingers as I gazed across the room. I wanted to burn this entire place down. To make Belial feel a hint of the betrayal I felt now.

Samael rested a hand on my shoulder. "We'll find them. At least we can take comfort in the fact that Belial won't hurt Hannah."

Not physically, no. But emotionally? Belial could hurt her worse than anyone had done before. I knew, because he'd done it to me. I'd do anything to spare Hannah that kind of pain, especially when she'd suffered so much already.

From outside came the sound of a shout and a snarl, and then I caught sight of Callan's brawny frame throwing a large wolf through the already-broken window of the bar. The wolf hit the wall and crashed to the floor, and everyone around me drew weapons and charged out into the night.

Shifters. I should have known they'd be involved in this too. How unfortunate for them that they'd chosen a really bad moment to pick a fight with me.

I turned to darkness and flew through the open doors, then reformed outside in the midst of a battle. Giant bears and massive wolves fought in the dark street against my angelic allies, while Kassiel and Olivia took on a group of huge hawks in the sky above us. I unleashed the hellfire that had been simmering under my skin ever since learning of Belial's betrayal, and the air became filled with the smell of burnt fur and the guttural roars and whines of dying shifters.

Then a black wolf the size of a bus barreled into me, knocking me to the ground. Eyes that glowed like magma stared at me as two massive paws held me down, their burning claws digging into me, ripping my suit. The wolf's black lips curled into a too-human sneer, as he growled, "Submit, Lucifer."

"Fenrir," I said with a cold laugh. "I'm so honored you decided to leave your little hut in the middle of Montana to come visit me, though your manners could use some work. Then again, that's always been true."

The Archdemon of the shifters snapped at me with his giant fangs in response, but I blasted him with hellfire and he had to leap off me to avoid it. He landed on top of Belial's bar, so large he took up nearly all of the roof, and as he roared he sent burning magma toward me. I used darkness to smother it, and he launched into the air again. He was so big and fast I barely managed to dodge his massive claws. I flew up high, my wings spreading behind me, and spun to face him. He swatted at me with a massive black paw, and I maneuvered around it, then threw more hellfire at him. He blasted it with magma, and we continued the fight on the roof of Belial's bar and other nearby buildings, seeing who would make a mistake first.

Fenrir suddenly raised his head and let out a loud howl that rattled the windows of all the buildings on the street and set off a few car alarms. At his command, the shifters darted away on swift paws and wings, carrying their dead and injured with them.

"Leaving so soon?" I called out.

Fenrir leaped to the top of another building and snarled at me. "We'll meet again—once Pestilence walks the Earth."

He launched himself away from me, and I considered flying after him, but I let him escape. We'd have a reckoning later, I was sure of it. Right now I needed to focus on finding Hannah.

Even though it was the middle of the night, some humans must have seen the battle, because I heard screams and the sound of sirens. Fucking hell. The Archdemons clearly didn't give a shit about hiding our kind from humans anymore. No doubt they thought they would rule over humans like royalty once I was out of the picture. The fools. They ignored the fact that we were greatly outnumbered by humans, and if they banded together against us, it would not end well. For any of us.

I landed in the street, where the others had gathered, and winced a little. Fenrir's claws had carved two long slashes down my chest, and now they burned like I'd been touched by magma. Some of the others had been injured too, but the attack hadn't been a serious one, or Fenrir wouldn't have abandoned it so quickly.

At least he'd confirmed one thing—they were going after Pestilence.

"What was the point of that?" Olivia asked, staring off in the direction the shifters had fled.

"It was a distraction," Samael said, from where he emerged from the sidelines. "I just got a call from Einial. Shifters destroyed our private jet."

"They want to slow us down," I said. Belial and the others had to be on their way to Pestilence's tomb by now. He must have kidnapped Hannah because he suspected I'd moved the tomb, and she was the key to finding it. Hannah and I were the only two people in the world still alive who knew where it was. I'd used only humans for the transport to be extra cautious. Not even Azazel or Samael knew the new location. Since Belial took after me far too much, he must have suspected as much. I'd trained him too well, back when he'd been heir to the throne of Hell.

"I can find us other transportation, but it will take some time," Samael said. "Hotel Immortelle is nearby. We can get cleaned up there while I make the arrangements."

I nodded as I tore off my ruined jacket, even more angry seeing how Fenrir had ruined my Armani suit. Hotel Immortelle was owned by my company, Abaddon Inc. I hated this new delay, but there was really no other choice but to go there and plan our next move.

Marcus eyed the thick gashes across my chest. "You should let me heal that."

"No time," Kassiel said, as the sirens grew louder. "We need to get out of here immediately."

Everyone in the street looked to me for their next command. I had to make a decision—head to Palestine to the old location of the tomb and hope we could catch up to them—or head to England and try to stop them when they arrived at Stonehenge. *If* they went to Stonehenge.

I wrapped darkness around us to better conceal our group. "Head to the hotel, and prepare for a long flight. We're going to London."

24

HANNAH

I awoke to a low hum and the feeling of being in motion without even moving, along with the smell of recycled air. I kept my eyes closed rather than alert anyone to the fact I'd woken up while I tried to gather some knowledge about my position. I was on a plane, and when I moved my arms, they chinked softly like they'd done overnight in the desert, so the small silver chains appeared to be back.

I didn't hear anything else, so I slowly opened my eyes and looked around. I was in the cargo area of the plane, wedged between crates. I stretched out my neck, trying to remove a kink there from sleeping in such an awkward angle as I took in my surroundings. Two armed men stood by a nearby door that likely led to another part of the plane, but otherwise I was alone.

Belial walked through that doorway with a tray of food in his hands. He set it on one of the crates beside me and then perched on the edge of another one. "Hello, Mother. I'm glad to see you're up."

I stared at him as I tried to work out what to say. The pain of his betrayal was like nothing I'd felt before. Worse than when Jophiel had stolen my memories and my powers. Worse than when Lucifer had taken my life. At least they'd been acting with my best intentions at heart. I couldn't say the same for Belial.

"Where is Azazel?" I managed to ask. "Is she all right?"

"She's fine."

I watched him closely while I spoke the question I was scared to ask. "Are you really working with the other Archdemons? To overthrow Lucifer?"

"Working with them? No." A dark smile spread across his face, and for a second he looked far too much like his father. "They're working for *me*."

Anger warred with disappointment and guilt, and those emotions clogged my throat so I couldn't speak. How could my own son do this? Was it my fault?

No. Belial had made his own choices, as he'd always done. I might have failed him as a mother, but I couldn't take complete responsibility for my son having shed his conscience somewhere during his very long life.

He gestured to the food he'd set in front of me. "Eat."

"What, and let you poison me?" I pushed the tray away as if to underline my point, but fuck, it smelled good. I was absolutely starving. How long had I been out?

He frowned down at me, as if our positions were reversed and he was the parent disappointed with a willful child. "Of course not. You're not to be hurt in any of this."

I raised my eyebrows as I cast my mind back to when I'd believed I was human. I could still taste the fear from some of those moments, and it was worse now that I knew he was behind them all. "Oh? What about the imps throwing me off a roof?"

His face darkened, his eyebrows pulling down into a fierce glower. "They were not supposed to do that, and the ones involved were punished for it."

His words confirmed that he really was behind it all from the beginning. "And the gargoyles trying to kill me in Lucifer's library? Or the dragons attacking me in the Grand Canyon?"

He waved a dismissive hand. "They were merely trying to kidnap you, nothing more."

"And Adam?" I narrowed my eyes. "You're working with the man who has killed me over and over. How could you do that? Or is that a detail that you've conveniently forgotten?"

"Sometimes we must make allies with our enemies to achieve our greater goal." He sighed as he leaned back on the crate. "Trust me, I have no love for Adam, but he came to me as Gadreel years ago with a proposal to take Lucifer down. I agreed on one condition—that you would not be harmed."

I shook my head, still in disbelief, or maybe just not wanting to believe the horrible truth about my own son. I'd thought we were finally connecting. I'd believed our relationship could be salvaged. And it was all a setup.

"You tricked me," I said, with a lump in my throat. I would not cry. Not in front of him. "You pretended to be kidnapped. You faked our escape attempt. You made them torture you. All to get me to trust you."

"I'm sorry, Mother. It was the only way. I always suspected Lucifer had moved Pestilence's tomb to keep it safe from me."

"For exactly this reason," I muttered.

"Correct. He knows me well." Belial's tone suggested that I didn't, and I agreed with him on this one thing. I didn't know my son at all. "My sources told me that only you and Lucifer were involved in the transport, which meant I needed your help in finding it."

I thought back on everything that had happened the last few days. "How did you know I'd come visit you?"

"Oh, you're very predictable. I knew once you were reborn and had regained your memories you would find me and try to make peace with me. You always do. All I had to do was wait for you to be reborn, and for Gadreel to find you. It took longer than I expected, but as soon as he located you, we were ready to act."

"But why?" My voice cracked. "Why would you do all this?"

"You mean, why am I trying to take down Father again?" Belial asked. "The same reason I tried before. It's time for someone else to rule Hell."

I snorted. "And that person should be you."

"Ideally, yes, but that isn't as important as you might think." He crossed his tattooed arms. "Look at all the democracies around the world. They get new leaders every few years to prevent any one person from becoming too powerful and ruling like a tyrant. Lucifer's held the throne for thousands of years, and the demons are ready for a change."

"But Lucifer's been a good king all this time!"

"Has he?" Belial arched an eyebrow. "There are many who would disagree with that. Haven't you noticed he favors the Fallen and has tasked them with keeping the other demons in line? As if demons need to be babysat and corralled like unruly toddlers. Or what of his decision to expel everyone from Hell and force them to live on Earth?"

"He had to do it to save demons from extinction. The war had to be ended, and Hell had become unlivable."

"Many of the Archdemons believe otherwise. They wish to return there and begin to rebuild. To create a new world for all demons."

"And you think they'll let you rule it?" I asked, with a sharp laugh. "Have they failed to notice you're not a real demon either?"

He scowled at that, as if I'd insulted him. "I have no interest in going to Hell. I plan to rule those who remain on Earth—the Nephilim like me, and those demons and Fallen who prefer to stay here. The Archdemons can fight amongst themselves over how to rule Hell once they get there."

I could only stare at him in horror. "What happens to me in this grand plan of yours? And Lucifer?"

"You'll be safe, of course. Safer than with Lucifer, because of the deal I made with Adam. As for Father..." He shrugged, but his eyes were hard. "That depends a lot on him. I don't want to hurt him. I don't want him dead. But sometimes casualties happen in a revolution. If he won't step aside peacefully, he will have to be removed."

His callous words shook me to my core. Did he truly not care if his father lived or died? Or was this his pride speaking? Of course, he'd tried this once before. The only reason he wasn't on the throne of Hell now was because he'd failed. Back then, I'd thought Lucifer's punishment too harsh. Now I wasn't sure it had been strong enough.

I straightened up, as much as I could in my chains, and adopted a commanding tone. "Lucifer is my mate, and I am his queen. If you think I'll sit back and let you overthrow him—and possibly kill him— you are sorely mistaken."

"How can you stand beside him after everything he's done?" Belial slammed his fist on the crate beside him. "I've watched you die so many times. Over and over, for thousands of years. An endless cycle of finding you only to lose you all over again. And it's all his fault. You wouldn't be cursed if not for Lucifer."

"Belial, no." My heart ached for all he'd seen and all I'd been powerless to prevent. "You can't blame Lucifer for the curse, any more than you can blame me. It was all *Adam's* fault. He's the one who killed me all those times. *He* put us through all of this. It was his hand, not your father's. How could you possibly work with him?" I blew out a breath, feeling an urgent need to make Belial see the truth instead of this lie he'd concocted in his head. "You said the two of you made a deal, but just the other week he tried to kill me. Did he mention that to you?"

Belial's mouth twitched down, but he didn't reply.

"He also killed your sister." I hadn't planned on telling any of my sons about this loss, at least not yet, when it was still so fresh in my mind, but Belial had to know what type of man he was dealing with.

"Sister?" Belial asked.

I could barely get the words out, but I struggled to continue. "In my last life, when Adam killed me, I was pregnant. He took my unborn daughter from me. Your sister. I bet he left that fact out too when you made that deal."

Belial's jaw clenched. "I had no idea. I'm sorry."

"Besides, the curse is broken now anyway." I leaned back on the crate behind me, feeling hollow and exhausted after my last confession. "If I die, I die for good. If Adam kills me again, there's no coming back this time. Do you still trust him, knowing that?"

My son's eyes widened, just a touch, just enough to let me know this was a surprise to him. But then he recovered quickly and pushed the tray toward me again. "Eat your food. We're going to land in London in a few hours."

I turned away, unable to deal with my traitorous son any longer. After Jophiel had given me back my memories and I'd learned about the death of my daughter, connecting with my sons had become vitally important to me. Family was *everything*, I'd realized, and it had become my mission to bring us all together again. Maybe I'd been too optimistic to hope that I could turn us all into one big happy family so quickly, but now I realized there had never been a chance of that. Belial had gone too far into the darkness, turning his back on his family and everyone who loved him.

"Nobody is going to hurt you. You're under my protection now." Belial rose to his feet and hovered over me, waiting for me to look at him, but I didn't budge. "And once Lucifer is gone, you'll see it's for the best. For everyone."

25

LUCIFER

The large, gray stones loomed around me, only illuminated by the thin sliver of the moon. I patted one of them with the flat of my palm. They were holding up well, considering the level of interest the humans seemed to have in Stonehenge. Timepiece? Alien stone circle? Who the hell knew what other conspiracy theories they'd cooked up between them. I didn't care. The more, the better, as long as they didn't realize I'd hidden one of the Four Horsemen of the Apocalypse in the center of these stones. I was pretty sure *that* conspiracy theory hadn't surfaced.

Not that I'd created Stonehenge, of course. I'd simply needed another ancient place that was heavy with the magic of the Elder Gods, like the Tower of Jericho, to hide all traces of Pestilence's energy and power. When I'd chosen this as the new location for the tomb, hundreds of years ago, I'd had no idea it would turn into a bizarre tourist attraction. Humans really were odd little creatures.

But perhaps they sensed the god's latent power, deep under the surface. Perhaps they were drawn to it, and that's why they flocked to this place in droves. Over one million visitors a year, or so I was told. I nearly laughed at the thought of how angry that would make Pestilence, if he knew what was going on above him.

Focusing on my amusement was a good distraction from dwelling on my fear and anger. I'd received word that all my guards at the Tower of Jericho had been slaughtered, but that the attackers had vanished soon after that. The report had no word about Hannah, Belial, or Azazel—or much else for that matter. But Baal had come through and confirmed they were heading to England in search of the tomb, and that Hannah was still alive.

So here we were, waiting to ambush them. I couldn't decide if I was more angry at the thought of seeing Adam or Belial. All I cared about at this point was rescuing Hannah and stopping Pestilence's resurrection. Damn everything else.

I flew up to join the others who were circling overhead in the night sky. Samael and Kassiel kept the area shrouded in darkness, while Olivia used her angelic power of invisibility to hide us from onlookers. Callan and Marcus looked ready for battle, while Bastien scanned the area with his Ofanim senses, which would be able to see through any illusions Nemesis or other imps used. Having a group of angelic allies was certainly proving to be useful these days.

"They're coming," Bastien said, pointing toward the south. I followed his gaze but saw nothing there. "Nemesis is hiding their approach, but they're all there. Belphegor. Adam. Belial. A green-haired fae male. And about twenty or thirty imps and gargoyles, from the looks of it."

"Any sign of Hannah?" I asked. "Or Azazel?"

"No."

Damn.

"Get ready," Samael called out, and the others readied their weapons, including the other loyal Fallen who had answered my call to battle.

Bastien released a flash of light, and the demons in the air and on the ground were suddenly visible to all of us. I caught sight of Belphegor in the sky, surrounded by gargoyles, and I felt her try to use her Archdemon power of sleep on us. We'd prepared for this though, and Marcus used his healing powers to combat it, protecting our group. He flew after her, with Callan at his side wielding burning light against the gargoyles.

Nemesis suddenly turned into dozens of versions of herself, all of them wielding long, deadly black claws. Bastien shot the illusions with the light of truth, while Kassiel worked to take down the real Nemesis. My Fallen clashed with the gargoyles, and Olivia used her succubus seduction to distract and confuse the imps. Adam, Belial, and the green-haired fae were in the back of the group, and I surged toward them, while searching for any sign of Hannah and Azazel.

There! Far in the rear, away from the brawl, some soldiers were holding Hannah and Azazel captive. I turned away from Belial and Adam, losing them amidst the chaos, and shouted for Samael to follow me.

Before I could even get there, Hannah and Azazel bucked free and knocked their captors out, then started running across the grass toward me. Silver cuffs circled their wrists, like the ones they used in Penumbra Prison, no doubt blocking their powers.

"Hannah!" I swooped down and grabbed my mate into my arms. She let out a surprised cry, and then pressed her face against my neck.

"Lucifer! I knew you'd come!" She pulled back and looked at me. Her eyes were wide and glazed like she'd had a shock. "Belial! It's him!

"I know."

"He betrayed us," she continued, as if she hadn't heard me. "He's behind all this. We have to stop him!"

I met her eyes. Hearing Hannah's words had confirmed what I'd already suspected, and it only made the dark pit inside me grow larger. "I know."

Samael picked up Azazel, who looked pissed at being carried around like a child who hadn't gotten her wings yet. I worked at the cuffs nullifying Hannah's magic—Adam was certainly taking no chances this time. Or maybe I should blame Belial.

"Who has the key?" I asked.

Hannah's eyes hardened. "Adam, I think."

I'd figured as much. "We'll deal with them later."

We flew back toward the circle of stones and the battle, toward the sound of guttural cries and metal striking metal, toward flashes of light and bursts of darkness. Then there was a great rumbling below us, as the earth opened up in the center of the stones. The green-haired fae stood beside the new pit, and he used his earth magic to excavate the tomb from deep in the ground. Damn Autumn Court—why was one of them helping these traitorous demons?

The ancient black tomb looked as new as the day it had been sealed, with silver and gold symbols—words of power and warning in languages not spoken anymore—completely covering the outside. The tomb had been made long ago by the most powerful fae enchanters, who could imbue objects with the powers of others.

I set Hannah down with Samael and Azazel, out of harm's way, and rushed toward the tomb—but I was too late. Belial stood over it, and time seemed to stand still as he slashed his hand with a dagger and let the blood drop onto the tomb. The symbols began to glow, drawing everyone's eyes.

The lid of the tomb suddenly burst open, and with it came an enormous blast of power, knocking everyone back with as much force as if we'd been hit by an explosion. Some crashed into the large stones, while others tumbled out of the sky and landed on the grass. I managed to spread my wings and catch myself, but the extreme force still knocked me away from Hannah and the others.

No one moved as Pestilence emerged from his tomb for the first time in thousands of years. I could only watch on in horror, knowing it was too late to stop what was coming.

Pestilence didn't have a body, of course. We'd taken care of that long ago. The Elder Gods couldn't truly be killed, since they were primordial deities representing the basic building blocks of the universe. They could only be weakened and contained.

Pestilence oozed out of his tomb with a putrid odor—the smell of sickness that can't be cured, that rots away at your body until there's nothing left. He rose up like a spirit, a mass of sickly yellow energy that pulsed and buzzed, radiating pure evil and so much power it was oppressive. Now that he was released it would be nearly impossible to capture him again, though he needed a body to come to his full powers.

"I command you to submit," Belial said, his voice hard as he faced down the malignant essence. "Give me your strength so I may defeat my enemies."

The putrid specter laughed, a sound of pure malevolence. It crawled over my skin like a physical touch, oily and painful. "If you want my power, I require a sacrifice of the heart. Something you love. Or...someone."

"No," I yelled, and rushed forward, but half a dozen gargoyles leaped on me to stop me. I bucked them off, using darkness and hellfire. The battle had stopped as we'd watched the horror unfolding in front of us, but now everyone seemed to come out of their daze and the fighting started up again.

"Stop it, Belial!" Hannah yelled, running toward him, her hands still in cuffs, her blond hair flying back.

Belial grabbed her arm and drew her against him, raising a dagger to her neck, and my heart stopped. With a roar, I ignited everyone around me with blue hellfire, trying to get to my mate before my son could sacrifice her.

Belial looked into Hannah's eyes, and whatever he saw there made him pause. She reached for his face, and at her touch, he dropped the dagger and stepped back, his hands shaking. Unable to sacrifice the one person he still loved.

I slammed into him a second later, knocking us both back into one of the huge stones so hard it actually fell over. He fought me and threw me off him, just in time for us to see Adam standing before Pestilence.

"I command you to serve me," he shouted.

Hannah was only steps away, and I feared he would reach for her as his sacrifice—but then Adam grabbed Belphegor from beside him, and stabbed a glowing knife through her throat. She looked at him with wide, shocked eyes as her life spilled out of her neck, before she collapsed into the grass.

"No!" Belial yelled, and many of the gargoyles around us screamed and cried out.

Pestilence cackled. "A powerful sacrifice. Yes, you will make a fine vessel indeed."

The specter rushed toward Adam and entered his body through his eyes, ears, nose, and mouth. He filled Adam with his essence, making his hair turn white, his skin becoming a sickly yellow, while noxious, revolting power emanated from him. Even Adam's allies stepped back, their fear plain to see in their eyes. He'd been dangerous and evil before, but now he was something so much more. A god of vile torment and endless suffering, who turned glowing white eyes toward Hannah.

He reached to grab her and I moved as fast as I could, but Belial was closer. Our son put himself in front of her, blocking Adam's touch. Adam-turned-Pestilence grabbed him by the neck and breathed a cloud of horrible air at him, then threw him down. Belial hit the ground in front of his mother, his face turning green and his eyes glazing over, as his body twitched and curled up in pain.

"No!" I yelled, as I threw hellfire at Adam, trying to distract him from my mate and my son. Samael and Kassiel joined me, wrapping Adam in chains of darkness, while Callan shielded Hannah and Belial with a wall made of light. Behind us the gargoyles fled, their Archdemon defeated, and my allies took out the rest of the imps.

Adam hissed at us and slid away, like the slippery eel he'd always been. And they'd likened me to the serpent? They'd always had the wrong guy.

"Adam!" Nemesis cried out, as Olivia stabbed her with a glowing white dagger on the other side of the stone circle.

A spectral white horse appeared, and Adam grabbed Nemesis around her waist as he mounted it, his motions far faster and more practiced than I'd ever seen them. I ran forward, using my wings to propel me as fast as I could, but he rode away, the horse galloping quicker than any earthly beast could run.

"Help!" Hannah yelled.

I turned toward the sound of her frantic voice and saw her kneeling over Belial. Marcus dropped to his knees beside her and put a hand on our son's forehead. Belial wasn't dead, I saw with relief, just suffering from Pestilence's sickness. Glowing white light surrounded him as Marcus worked to heal him. *Could* he be healed? I wasn't sure.

Slowly the green tint to my eldest son's skin faded away, along with the glaze over his eyes. He still looked weak, but he blinked up at his mother, who was stroking his hair, his head in her lap.

Kassiel crouched down alongside them, his eyes narrowing as he focused on Belial. "How could you? Do you have any idea what you've done?"

Belial stared back at him defiantly, even in his weakened state. "You wouldn't understand. You've always been the favorite."

I pressed my lips together as I stared at my sons. It wasn't a question of favorites. I loved all my children, but this was the second time Belial had led a rebellion against me. How could I forgive him for that?

Belial must've felt better, because he threw Marcus off him, his eyebrows drawn, his expression angry. He launched into the air, flying away as fast as his black and white ombre wings would carry him. Kassiel spread his wings to follow, but I grabbed his arm.

"Let him go."

My youngest son turned to me and raised his eyebrows as he snapped his wings back, his obedience unquestioning. "We can't let him get away! Not after what he's done!"

"Adam is the bigger problem now. We've got to stop him." I turned to Olivia and her other mates. "I need your group to track him down."

Olivia nodded and Callan said, "We'll find him."

Kassiel turned to his mate. "I'm staying with my parents. Don't get close to this asshole. Just keep an eye on him from afar."

Olivia pressed a kiss to his forehead and whispered a few words, then she and her other mates launched into the air in the direction Adam had vanished.

"Come." I turned toward Kassiel, Samael, and Azazel as I spread my wings. "We're going home."

Hannah stared at the spot where Belial had been on the ground, her face pale and her eyes in shock. I lifted her up into my arms, fitting her body to mine, where it belonged. She needed some rest to recover from everything she'd been through at the hands of Adam and our son, and we still needed to get these damn cuffs off.

Then we would figure out how to stop the impending apocalypse.

26

HANNAH

When Lucifer had said we were going home, I'd expected a long trip back over the Atlantic, not this. My gaze traveled over the large stone manor house and the sprawling grounds, which sparked the feeling of familiarity inside me.

"Welcome to Blackwing Hall," Lucifer said, as he set us down in front of it.

I reluctantly let go of him, still shaken from everything that had happened. I desperately needed a shower and some new clothes—I'd been wearing these for days—and then maybe I could process what I'd just seen.

"This is where we lived when you were Lenore," Lucifer said, as he led me toward the entrance. "Do you remember?"

"I...I think so." The memories were so fleeting and I was so damn tired. Not just physically, but emotionally. I didn't want to think anymore.

"I grew up here," Kassiel said, as he walked beside us. "Here and in Hell. It was important to you that I spend time on Earth too, so I would empathize with humans since so many of your past lives were as one."

Yes, that sounded right. Standing here, in front of this house—

our home—felt so familiar. Memories floated through my mind of our family being together here. Once I'd had a chance to recover I'd like to explore them some more, but this wasn't the time.

A blond woman in a pantsuit walked out of the impressive, wooden front door at the top of the stone steps. "Everything is ready for you, my lord." She turned toward me and bowed her head. "My lady."

"Thank you, Einial," Lucifer said as he swept through the door while holding my hand.

I stumbled forward through the great entryway, and then Lucifer paused and held up my hand, looking at my wrist, which still had the silver cuff on it blocking my powers.

"We need to get these off," Lucifer said with a growl.

"Here," Kassiel said, stepping forward and holding out a small silver wand, about the size of his pinkie finger. "I got this off Adam during the fight. Before he turned into that *thing*."

"Good work, son." Lucifer took the object and touched it to my wrists. The cuffs instantly clicked open, and a rush of power and a sense of wholeness filled me. I took a deep breath and stood a little straighter, already feeling more like myself again.

He passed the key to Samael, who unlocked Azazel's cuffs, as he asked, "I'm assuming our suite is ready?"

Einial nodded. "Yes, Samael asked that I prepare the bedrooms and main living areas. Everything has been looked after very well over the years by the staff."

"Good." Lucifer rested a hand on my lower back, steadying me as he addressed the others. "We'll discuss everything after Hannah's had a chance to recover."

We left them in the main hall, and Lucifer led me down long corridors that I barely noticed, until we entered a suite, the one we'd occupied before, so many years ago. I glimpsed dark furnishings and a large four-poster bed, but couldn't really focus on anything at the moment.

Lucifer turned to me and took me into his arms. "I was so worried."

I clung to him tightly, so relieved to be with him again. He pressed his lips to mine, the kiss soft and sweet—reverent almost. I relaxed against his chest, savoring his presence. The scent of him was so familiar. It wove through so many of my memories over the years. Lucifer. My rock. My constant. My husband.

"Are you all right?" he asked, his gaze raking over me. "Did they hurt you?"

"I'm okay, but I could really use a shower and some fresh clothes."

"I'll have some brought to you." Lucifer pulled out his phone and sent out a text, probably to Samael or Einial. "Get as much rest as you need, and when you wake, we should have some news about Adam."

"He has Pestilence *inside* him now." I still couldn't believe what I'd witnessed. It seemed impossible, like something from a dream or a movie. I sank to the bed as some of the shock from the past few hours caught up to me. "He nearly killed Belial. The destruction he could unleash..."

I shivered as I imagined what Adam would do to me if he found me. He'd killed me so many times before, and all he had to do now was breathe on me. I covered my mouth briefly and shook my head as I imagined what he might do to any mortals he came across. There were no words to describe the horrors in my head.

I looked up at Lucifer. "How do we stop him?"

He rubbed the back of his neck, his brows furrowed. "It won't be easy. It took many angels, demons, and fae to take down the Four Horsemen when they were loose before, back when you were Eve. They're impossible to fully kill, which is why we destroyed their bodies and trapped their essence in magically-sealed tombs. We'll need to either capture them again, or send them to the Void realm, with the other Elder Gods."

I ran a hand through my dirty, matted hair with a sigh. "Then we'll need to act quickly before more of the Horsemen are freed."

"Yes, now that the Archdemons have released Pestilence, they'll go after War next. It's only a matter of time."

"War—he's buried in Heaven, isn't he?" I asked.

"He is, which should give us some time. Like Hell, Heaven has been sealed off, and very few can enter it."

I rubbed my wrists, which were still a bit sore from the cuffs. "How do we get in?"

Lucifer slid off his jacket and tossed it aside, looking somewhere between casual and disheveled. "There are keys, but only a few remain, and I highly doubt any of the Archdemons have one."

"Do *you* have one?"

He lifted an eyebrow. "No, I haven't had a key to Heaven in a very long time. But I'm sure we can find someone with one."

I pressed my palms to my eyes, knowing I needed to get up and shower, but the thought of moving was too exhausting to consider. Especially when my heart still ached so much.

"I can't believe Belial would go this far," I whispered.

"I can," Lucifer said, his voice sharp.

"I think there's some good left in him," I ventured, remembering when Belial dropped the knife, and the lost look in his eyes when he couldn't sacrifice me. "If I could just get through to him..."

"There's no use. He's too far gone." Lucifer's jaw clenched. "It's my fault, not yours. I haven't been the best father to our firstborn son. If I could change the past, I would. But there's no hope for a reconciliation with Belial at this point."

Jutting out my chin, I shook my head. "I refuse to believe that."

"Hannah, you've got to stop harking after the past." His features hardened as he spoke, his eyes becoming cold and unfamiliar. "It's done. He's broken. There's no fixing him."

I rose to my feet and glared at him. "Belial's our *son*, and we will *not* give up on him."

Lucifer's eyes burned as he stared back at me. "I already gave him a second chance once. I won't do it again. Not this time."

"We're his parents! It's our job to give him a second chance, and a third, and a fourth, until we finally bring him back to us!" I was so angry and frustrated that darkness I didn't know how to control lashed out at Lucifer, making him lurch back in surprise. It disappeared an instant later, so fast it made me wonder if I was seeing things.

"What was that?" Lucifer asked, his brow furrowing. "Did you just use darkness?"

"I don't know!" Rising to my feet, I shot him my most scathing glare. "All I know is that I won't be staying with you tonight."

I stalked out of the room before he could say anything further and before I needed to slow down and think about what I'd just done. My hands were trembling and I stumbled forward, nearly running into Einial, who was carrying some clothes and a towel with her.

She regained her balance quickly. "Oh! I was just bringing these to your suite."

"Thank you." I glanced back at the door I'd just slammed behind me. "But I'll be needing my own room now."

———

When I opened my eyes the next morning, Zel was on the foot of my bed playing on her phone.

"Morning," I said groggily, no longer surprised by anything she did.

"Come fight." She slipped her phone away, but I couldn't see where to in one of her usual skin-tight, leather outfits. It was more straps and criss-crosses than anything else. "I'm bored."

Somehow I doubted it was boredom that had brought her here. Like me, she'd been through an ordeal, and Azazel often got out her emotions by punching things.

"All right." The thought of fighting appealed to me more than I expected. Maybe I had some shit to work off too.

She leaped to her feet with a triumphant grin. "Hurry and get dressed. I'll meet you outside."

I was pleased to see that Einial had brought me more clothes, including some that were suitable for exercising in. Samael's new assistant seemed to be well on top of things.

Ten minutes later, we were on the back lawn. I eyed Zel as she went through some warm-up moves, looking beautiful and deadly. She stretched in the fine drizzle that seemed to keep the air at one hundred percent cold humidity. I glanced up at the gray clouds that seemed to be a permanent fixture in the sky. I'd never seen such a gloomy place. As I warmed up, the damp soon permeated my clothes, and I was glad I'd tied my hair back—it would have been a ball of frizz, otherwise.

It suddenly began raining and Zel stretched her arms to the sky and cackled. "Yes! Bring it on!"

It was official. She might have lost her damn mind. I hugged my arms around myself, already soaked and shivering. "You're enjoying this weather?"

"I love it. It's so nice to be back here instead of hot, dry Las Vegas." She threw me some side-eye. "You know, as Lenore, you loved this weather too."

That made sense, since I'd been a Fallen then. But angels tended to want to live in warm, sunny locations, and I was no exception. I shivered and rubbed my arms. If only Einial had prepared for this and gotten me a thicker jacket to wear. Hell, *any* jacket. She must have forgotten I wasn't a Fallen too.

"Come on." Zel jerked her head to a large expanse of lawn under the cover of some tall, sprawling trees. "The sooner you start moving, the sooner you'll warm up."

I huffed and headed over, knowing she was right. I couldn't just stand around waiting for the sun to appear. Right now, it didn't even feel like England got a turn with the sun—like the sun had rolled over in bed rather than bothering to rise.

We launched into our usual combat routine, as we'd done during our other training sessions, before we'd been kidnapped. Moving did warm me up, and it helped me burn off some of the stress of the past few days too. Things started to feel almost normal again.

As we sparred, my mind drifted to my time here as Lenore, when I'd trained with Zel just like this. Zel and that other woman with the red hair.

I dodged a quick jab and twisted away and spun back. "Being here brings back a lot of memories. I keep seeing another woman with you in them. A woman with red hair." I ducked Zel's swinging fist and moved to counter it. "What happened to her?"

Azazel froze, her hands lowering from their defensive position, and my blow hit her right in the face. Harder than I'd planned, because I never thought my punch would actually land.

She staggered back and spat, her bright red blood hitting the ground between us. "What the fuck, Hannah?"

"Sorry, I didn't mean to—"

"Why would you bring that up?" She rubbed her palm roughly over her jaw, muttering a sentence where I caught nothing but the last couple of words. "Stupid angel."

I watched her, realizing I'd hit a nerve. I didn't want to upset her further, but I also sensed this was something important, something I should know. Azazel was my best friend, I now understood. Not just in this lifetime, but in *all* of them, going back all the way to Eve. If there was some pain in her past, I wanted to be able to help her through it.

"Zel," I said, moving closer to my friend, my voice softening. "What happened?"

"Shut up." Her voice was cold and hard, and her face looked really pissed now. Her anger masked her pain, but it didn't conceal it completely. Not from me, anyway. "Her name was Veslea. She was my fated mate. Like Lucifer is to you."

"She was a shifter," I whispered. As soon as I heard the name, more came back to me. "A hawk. She worked for Lucifer during the Great War. No, that's not right. She worked for *me*." She was my scout. My spy. My messenger. The person I trusted most, other than Azazel.

"Yeah, thanks for the reminder. You don't have to regurgitate memories for me as they occur to you." Zel half turned away, and when she spoke again, her voice was smaller. "Veslea was killed by an angel not long after you—Lenore—died."

A wave of grief washed over me, and I gripped Zel's hand. "I'm so sorry."

She didn't shake me off, but nodded a little at my words.

"You thought Lenore was killed by an angel, too, didn't you?" I asked, fitting all the pieces together. This was why Zel hated angels so much. It made total sense now. It probably explained a lot of her attitude too, including why she'd been so rude to me at first. Imagine if you'd lost your mate, and your best friend kept dying on you, leaving you alone. How hard it must be to get close to anyone after that, fearing they might leave you next.

"Yeah, I didn't know it was Adam until Gadreel betrayed us." She snorted. "Not that Adam doing it makes it any better. That asshole."

Her voice sounded so bitter...and sad. Gadreel had been her friend for over a hundred years. She'd lost another person close to her.

I wrapped my arms around her, resting my head against hers, taking a moment to grieve with her. She stiffened, but then she lightly rested a hand on my back too, giving me the bare minimum of a hug in return. She'd held me like this not long ago, when I'd remembered who I was. Now it was my turn to offer her some silent comfort. I grieved for Veslea too, who'd always been loyal and exceptionally clever and so full of life. A perfect soul, gone too soon, lost to the horrors of war.

Azazel pulled away. "Come on. We have to get you in shape if we're going to face Adam and Belial again."

Her mention of my son made me apprehensive again. I had no idea what I'd do when I saw him again.

"What's the deal with you and Belial?" I asked, as we moved back into combat-ready stances.

She blew out a breath. "I killed his girlfriend during his last rebellion, when she was storming the palace in Hell. He hates me for that, and I hate him for being a traitor to his own kind."

Her words about my son made my hackles raise, and darkness lashed out of me again toward her. She rolled out of the way and yelled, "What the fuck was that?"

I spread my hands as the darkness vanished. "I...uh... I channeled some darkness last night. And back at the bar when we were attacked. Think you could help me figure it out?"

Zel's eyebrows arched, the movement rapid. "You did *what?*"

"Maybe I'm becoming a Fallen," I said with a laugh.

She scowled at me. "It doesn't work like that."

"How does it work?" I asked.

She narrowed her eyes at me, as if she thought I was messing with her. "The only people who became Fallen were the ones who left with Lucifer in the beginning. We settled in Hell, but we didn't do well in the land of darkness. Angels need light to survive, and there's not much of it there. So Lucifer summoned Nyx, the Elder Goddess of night, and begged her to help us. She turned all of us into demons, giving us many of their abilities—the ability to see in the dark, the immunity to the cold, and the power to use darkness instead of light. After that, all Fallen were sired from one of the originals, like me and Samael."

I nodded slowly, her words bringing back knowledge I'd lost. "And yet, the other demons don't believe you're really the same as them."

"It's bullshit. They were created by the Elder Gods, just like we were." She put her hands on her hips. "So there's no way you, an angel, could suddenly be using darkness powers now."

"But it keeps happening whenever I'm upset. Just like my angelic powers did, before I could control them."

Zel's brow furrowed. "Then we'd better work on getting these under control too."

I was sure the question in her mind was exactly the same as the one in mine. How the hell was I able to use both light and darkness?

27

LUCIFER

Olivia and her mates returned with news of Adam in the afternoon, and Samael summoned us all into the great hall of the manor so we could discuss our next move. We'd spread out around the banquet table, and I sat at the end with Hannah beside me, though she still wasn't talking to me after last night. She'd spent most of the day training with Azazel, and she looked a lot better than she had last night. Last night, when she'd somehow used darkness against me. I planned to ask her about that later, once we were alone. For now, we had more urgent matters to discuss.

"How bad is it?" I asked, already sure of the answer. Given the population increase the world over, Pestilence's arrival would be about a thousand times worse than the last time. So many innocent mortals... Well, perhaps not *innocent*, but certainly undeserving of the kind of destruction Adam currently wrought.

"It's bad," Callan said. He'd always been rather blunt.

Olivia's face was pale. "Adam vanished in London, but he left a trail of sickness along his path."

"Hundreds of mortals have fallen ill," Bastien added in his matter-of-fact voice.

"I couldn't keep up." Marcus bowed his head. "There were just too many who required healing."

"I'll notify Archangel Raphael to send Malakim to minimize the damage Adam's causing." My blood simmered as anger twisted through me. "The mortal world can't find out about this. It endangers us all."

Not to mention, if humans discovered the existence of Pestilence, it would create an immense global event, and anything that humans did in response would interfere with my own control over the situation. I pulled out my phone and shot off a quick text, the easiest way of communicating with Raphael, then began another one off to Gabriel, the leader of the Archangels. My fingers flew across the phone screen and the texts were sent off. In the old days, when we wished to confer with the angels, we had messengers. Modern technology was truly incredible.

"There was no sign of where Adam went?" Kassiel asked.

Olivia shook her head. "No, we lost him in the city."

"Wherever he emerges, death and disease will follow," Samael said. "We must stop him before it's too late."

I slipped my phone back into my pocket. "Even though we don't know where he is, we know where the Archdemons will go next. Heaven."

"To release War?" Azazel asked, leaning forward. "Are they that stupid?"

"Apparently," I said dryly. "The good news is that Heaven is sealed off, and only a few people have a key. Archangel Michael had one, which should have been passed to you, Callan, upon his death."

Callan's eyebrows darted up. "I didn't even know there was a way into Heaven anymore."

I drummed my fingers along the wooden table. "Yes, Heaven and Hell both have a few keys that allow entry, though they're extremely rare and hardly ever used. The last time I know of the key to Heaven being used was just before your birth, Callan. Michael and Jophiel wanted you born there." Truly, angelic pride put my own to shame.

"Also news to me." He rolled his eyes. "Great. I bet my mother has it."

"At the very least, she might know where it is," I ventured, though I didn't want to see Jophiel either—I still hadn't forgiven her for hiding Hannah from me.

"We'll have to pay my sister a visit," Hannah said, her voice firm. "She owes me, anyway."

I glanced at her face, noting how her mouth was set in a grim line at the thought of seeing her sister. Jophiel owed *both* of us for what she'd done.

Samael cleared his throat. "I also have some news about Belial. Our contacts at Penumbra Prison said he arrived there a few hours ago. He demanded to see Archangel Azrael, but we don't know the details of the conversation, or where Belial went after that."

Azrael had been the corrupt former leader of the Archangels, but he'd been sent to Penumbra Prison to rot after Kassiel and the others had taken him down. Since I'd helped them, Azrael would no doubt be willing to help my son move against me in any way he could.

"Belial must have gone there to get information on how to get to Heaven." I closed my fingers into a fist. Damn him. My own son, always a step ahead of me in plotting my downfall.

"Azrael tried to use the Staff of Eternity to open Heaven and Hell, but we destroyed it," Olivia said. "I doubt he would go through all that trouble if he'd had a key."

"Perhaps," I said. "But he might have told Belial where he might find one. Even more reason to visit Jophiel immediately."

"I'd like to visit the prison myself and see if I can learn anything more," Samael said.

I nodded. "Take Azazel with you."

"I'm ready," she said, rising to her feet. "No sense in wasting time."

Hannah stood too. "Let's make an early night of it. Tomorrow will be a long day."

Everyone filed out of the room to head to their own suites. Everyone except me and Hannah. She gave me an icy look as she prepared to part, but I said, "Wait."

She paused at that and turned around at the command in my voice.

I leaned back against the table and crossed my arms. "I watched you training with Azazel from one of the windows earlier. Were you going to tell me about your new powers?"

She set her hands on her hips. "First, don't take that tone with me. Second, I have no idea what's happening to me. Suddenly I can use darkness *and* light."

"Show me."

Her brow furrowed as she held out her hands and concentrated. I carefully schooled my features, deliberately keeping my expression blank so as not to reveal my shock as Hannah proceeded to produce both light and dark magic, one in each palm. Impossible. Even I couldn't do that.

"Are you using powers from your past lives?" I asked. "Do you have any of the other abilities you once had? Persephone's magic, for example?"

She shook her head and cut off the flow of magic. "No idea. I don't think so. Not that I know of, anyway."

I stroked my chin. "Very curious."

"I'm going to bed," she said, turning for the door again.

I moved in front of her to block her path. "No. Not without me."

She arched an eyebrow. "Excuse me?"

"I told you I was done with you sleeping somewhere other than by my side. I let it pass last night, because you clearly were exhausted and not thinking straight, but no more. I'll tie you to the bed if I have to, but your place is nowhere else than beside me."

Hannah's eyes flashed, but not in anger. Oh, she liked that idea, even if she wouldn't want to admit it. "I'll sleep where I want to sleep."

I scooped her up into my arms. Perhaps a little tying up was exactly what she needed. "It seems you require a reminder that you are my mate and my queen."

"Lucifer!" she cried, but she didn't fight me. She liked it when I exerted my dominance in bed, even if she wanted to be equal in all other areas of our relationship.

I carried her to our suite, my heart thudding as she stared up at me with defiant eyes. The bedroom door flew back as I kicked it open, revealing the four-poster bed in the center of the room.

I drew the blankets back and laid her on the bed, then used my own powers of darkness to shred her clothes, removing them without even touching her. She gasped at the sudden touch of my shadows as her skin was exposed, and her nipples hardened in the cool night air. I raked my eyes over her naked body possessively.

I commanded the shadows to become binding, twining around her wrists before anchoring to the posts at the headboard. Her eyes widened, but her cheeks were flushed with desire, and she didn't protest. She could have stopped this at any moment with her own magic, but she didn't. She wanted me to continue.

My cock strained against my trousers as my gaze roamed her body, bared before me. The shadows yanked her legs apart next, binding her ankles to the other posts, exposing her already wet pussy to me. Then I let the darkness run over her body like a caress, stroking her nipples, sliding against her clit, while I watched. She let out a breath and her pupils dilated as she moved her hips, and one of my shadow tentacles slid inside her pussy.

"I don't even need to touch you to make you come." I slowly fucked her with my magic, showing her who was in command, while she whimpered and writhed.

Hannah needed a lesson, a reminder that I was her king, and she belonged to me. I climbed up onto the bed and kneeled over her, yanking open my trousers and pulling out my cock. "Open your mouth."

Her lips formed a slight pout, and I rubbed the head of my cock against them, making them part for me. I slid my hard length into that perfect little mouth, smothering her cries as I made the tentacles thrust deeper into her, teasing her clit at the same time. She gasped around me as I rubbed against her tongue, and I groaned at the exquisite feel of having her soft lips around me again.

With her hands and wrists bound, all she could do was take everything I gave her, while she gazed up at me with wide eyes and moaned around me. Her mouth was so wet and hot, and I loved the way she tried to suck me deeper, even as she was being thoroughly ravaged by the shadows around us. I grabbed the edge of the head-board above her as I rocked in and out of her mouth, and her little whimpers got more frantic as my magic brought her to orgasm. I spilled my seed into her mouth and across her lips, making her drink it down, before I finally released her.

She watched me with a dazed look as I climbed off the bed and removed my clothes. My cock was already hard again. There were benefits to being the devil, after all.

I trailed my fingers over her smooth, flat stomach, over her ribs and to the curve of her breast. She tensed, not even breathing, as she waited to see what I'd do. She was powerless, but happy to be that way. No, she had plenty of power, and we both knew it. Hannah was in my bed, bound and spread for me because she wanted to be.

I drew closer to her, then bent over her beautiful body. "My queen."

I took one of her nipples between my lips, sliding my tongue over it as I sucked it deeper into my mouth. She moaned, the sound coming from deep within her, and she twisted as she tried to move her hands and legs. "I want to touch you."

"This isn't about what you want. This is all about me."

"Then take me," she begged.

I lifted myself over her body, lightly touching her nipples with my chest and she bit her lip at the contact, muffling a groan. My cock nudged against her entrance, and I surged forward, filling her completely. Proving she was mine. Again. Still. Always.

She arched her hips against me, taking me even deeper as she strained against her shadow bindings. I bowed my head and kissed her roughly as I thrust into her, my rhythm gaining in pace. Then I reared back, grabbing her hips and lifting them up to meet me as I kneeled between her thighs. She cried out over and over with each stroke of my cock, and I loved seeing her give herself up to me like this.

As her cries became more frantic, I rocked into her faster and harder, using my immortal strength and speed to fuck her like no one else could. As an angel, she could take it, and soon she tensed beneath me, her face contorting in a way that truly made me king. She writhed and screamed my name, and I thrust inside her one last time before the pulse of her body around my cock tipped me over the edge.

The shadow bindings around Hannah's wrists and ankles disappeared, and I gathered her up in my arms. She wrapped herself around me and I held her close, looking into her blue eyes, so full of truth and light. The perfect match to my darkness.

"I love you," I said, my chest suddenly tight. "And I need you. Now more than ever."

"Yes, you do," she replied with a slight smirk. Then she touched my face tenderly. "Whatever else happens between us, I will always fight by your side. Now and forever. I am your queen."

I gripped her tighter at the thought of what we up against in the days to come. For once, I wasn't sure we would be victorious—but at least we would face it together.

28

HANNAH

During the entire long plane ride from London to San Francisco, my thoughts had flitted between apprehension at seeing Jophiel again, fear at what Adam and Belial might be doing now, and exhilaration from the previous night with Lucifer. Even when I was angry, I couldn't resist him, and the way he clutched my hand in the limo now told me he didn't want me anywhere except right beside him. Lucky for him, I had no interest in being anywhere else.

We drew to a stop in front of the obnoxiously large white house my sister owned, and I took a deep breath as our driver opened the car door. Even as an angel I had to take a minute to stretch my back when I stepped out of the limo. After an eleven-hour flight and then the drive from the airport, I was ready for a strenuous yoga session. Yoga...or something else athletic. I eyed Lucifer's ass as I followed him up the steps. Callan was right at my heels, along with Olivia and her other mates.

Jophiel threw the door open and stared at us, her eyes wide, her mouth slightly agape before she seemed to recall herself. "This is quite the unexpected visit. I'm happy to see you..." Her eyes landed on Lucifer and her tone turned frosty. "Some of you."

"Can we come in?" I asked. "We have something urgent we need to discuss."

"Of course." She stepped back. "Come inside."

Lucifer and I stepped inside first, then moved out of the way so Callan and Olivia could follow us. Kassiel, Bastien, and Marcus remained outside, keeping an eye out in case the Archdemons arrived.

Jophiel put her hand on Callan's arm, looking up at her son with love. She touched his face gently. "I'm so pleased to see you. It's been too long."

He bowed his head slightly. "I wish we were here under better circumstances."

She turned to Olivia next and gave her a nod, but no other acknowledgment. I sensed this was the reason for the tension between Callan and his mother. Or at least one of the reasons.

Jophiel led the way to her living room and we all settled around the space, taking spots on the couch or sitting in the fancy armchairs, though Olivia remained standing long enough to pick up one of the tiny crystal angels on display.

"Please don't touch those," Jophiel said in a stern voice. Olivia quickly set it down and took a seat beside Callan, while Jophiel studied each of us in turn. "I can tell this isn't a social call. Why are you here?"

"The Archdemons have released Pestilence," Lucifer said flatly. No preamble, no sugar-coating. Just the facts. "He's possessed Adam's body."

Jophiel's face paled, and her fingers curled at the base of her throat. "No. The first Horseman? Why? How?"

"It's a long story, one we don't really have time for right now," I said, knowing Jophiel would feel the truth in my words. "But we all saw it with our own eyes. It's real."

Lucifer leaned forward, meeting Jophiel's stunned expression. "We both know that means War is next. We need Michael's key to Heaven so we can be ready to stop them."

"Michael's key?" Jophiel asked, still in shock from everything we'd just told her.

"Do you have it?" Callan asked.

"Yes. I was saving it for when you were ready." She turned her glare upon Lucifer again. "But I won't give it to the King of Hell, no matter the circumstances."

Callan rose to his feet, and his large form seemed to command the room. "That key is my birthright. I should be the one protecting it."

"No," Jophiel said, completely unaffected by Callan's display. "It's safer with me. You've clearly failed to stop Pestilence. What makes you think you can stop War too?"

"Jo, please," I said. Maybe a direct plea would help her see beyond her old prejudices against Lucifer. "You're in danger as long as you have the key. It's a target on your back. Adam or one of the Archdemons will find you eventually."

Her face registered the merest hint of surprise. "I'm shocked you care."

"Of course I do. You're my sister." I spread my hands. "I'm pissed at you. I'm not sure I'll ever be able to forgive what you did. But I still love you. I don't want you to die. And we really need your help."

"If War is freed, it will mean the end of peace," Lucifer said. "Not just for humans, but for all of us."

"Yes, I've heard stories of what happened last time from my parents." Jophiel pressed her lips together in a tight line as she considered. "Though I grew up hating demons, and you most of all, Lucifer, I supported Michael in ending the Great War. I have no wish to go to war again." Her eyes rested on Callan and then on Olivia, and her face softened. "Especially when my son has found happiness."

Olivia's eyes widened. I wondered if this was the first time Jophiel had ever hinted at accepting her as Callan's mate. I wanted to tell her not to take it personally. Jophiel saw everything in black and white, and Olivia's very existence was a shade of gray.

"Thank you," Callan said, reaching forward to squeeze his mother's hand.

She gave him a soft smile as she rose to her feet. "I'll go get the key, but I want to be part of the fight against Pestilence. If you go to Heaven, take me with you."

"Very well," Lucifer said, inclining his head slightly.

She walked from the room, and I blew out a small breath as my shoulders slumped in relief. As we waited, Lucifer sat back in his armchair and crossed his legs, like this was his place instead of his former enemy's. Callan's hands tightened around Olivia's, and she leaned against his shoulder.

I was watching them when something at the corner of my eye made me turn my head. "What was that?"

"What?" Callan asked, instantly alert.

I stared at the wall on the other side of the room. The one with the dresser against it. There had been movement there, like a ripple in the air. Everyone's gaze followed mine to where I'd seen...something. I stood and walked closer and felt a sense of wrongness, like when someone told a lie, except it was coming from that corner.

Using a move Bastien had taught me, I lifted my hand and light blazed from my palm as I directed it toward the wall. The illusion was ripped apart, revealing Adam and Nemesis standing in the corner of the room. No one had sensed them before—not even Jophiel. Nemesis was more powerful than I'd known.

Lucifer and the others immediately leaped to their feet, responding to the new threat. But before we could react, Adam raised his arms, the air turning thick and sludgy in front of him, and it spread farther into the room, coating everything with an oily film. It happened so fast, I didn't even have time to draw on my powers, and then the others were bending over and coughing behind me. Only I seemed to be spared.

Adam looked like something from a nightmare, his skin yellow and blistered, his white hair coming out of his scalp in clumps, leaving raw, bald patches that oozed a putrid looking liquid. When he turned his gaze on me, his glowing white eyes had taken on a glint of madness, almost like he was feverish, which he likely was. Perhaps the raw sickness he carried with him all the time held him in a state of suspended decay.

Nemesis tried to create more illusions, but I radiated the light of truth to stop her, then threw darkness at Adam, though it was mostly ineffective, partly because I still didn't really know how to control it. I backed up, trying to get to Lucifer, when the window beside me shattered and Belial flew inside—wielding Morningstar. Of course he'd taken it. I should have known. Even so, for a brief fleeting moment I thought he might have come to help, until I saw him go after Callan.

Jophiel ran into the room, her sword held high, as she defended her son with a roar. She traded blows with Belial, until Adam released a wave of the sickness directed solely at her. As it hit her, the color drained from her face, and she wobbled as the sickness stole her ethereal glow—whatever had lit her from within that I hadn't noticed until now. She swayed, moving in slow motion, as her gaze became panicked. She hit the floor and Nemesis was immediately beside her, plucking what looked like a large diamond from her body.

I screamed for Marcus, as the world around me turned to complete chaos. Kassiel and the others who'd been outside rushed in, throwing up their arms to combat the smell of sickness in the air. Bastien immediately took on Nemesis, using his Ofanim powers to combat her illusions, while Marcus began to heal Jophiel, and Kassiel tried to drag a sickly Olivia out of the room.

Lucifer recovered from Adam's attack first, and he rose to his feet and summoned a sword of shadow in one hand and a ball of hellfire in the other. I gathered darkness and light and stood beside him, preparing to take on Pestilence. If nothing else, we would die together.

We released our magic at him, and though he staggered back from the attack, it wasn't enough. Adam raised a hand and blasted us both with enough power to send us crashing back against the farthest wall.

"I'm a god now." Adam's horrid laughter filled the room. "Nobody can stop me. Not even the mighty Lucifer."

Nemesis grabbed Callan by his blond hair and yanked his head back. Belial moved forward and rested the blade of Morningstar to his neck, where a thin line of blood appeared. "Anybody moves," he said, "And pretty-boy dies."

"No!" Olivia and Jophiel cried at the same time, but Jo's voice was weak and insubstantial. Little more than exhaled air.

"Use the key," Nemesis ground out, her words directed at Callan as he tried to resist her hold. "Or we lay waste to all these people you love."

Callan glared at them as Nemesis pressed the gemstone into his hand. It glowed slightly as soon as he touched it, like it contained a touch of Heaven's light within. "I won't."

Adam grabbed Bastien and infected him with his sickness, making the angel's skin turn a sickly green. "I will keep going. You can watch everyone in the room grow sick and die, until you open the way to Heaven."

"Fine." Callan's teeth were clenched, and we all knew it was far from fine. "But I don't know how you expect me to do this. I've never seen this thing before, let alone used it."

"It will respond to your will." Even Adam's voice was changing, becoming more of a hiss and losing the rich tones it had held before. "The key will recognize you, son of Michael. It knows your bloodline."

Callan took a shaky breath and held the gem out before him. The room filled with an other-worldly light, and a shimmering hole appeared. It shone and sparkled, the colors pearlescent, and it was nearly impossible to tear my eyes off of it.

"You're coming with us." Adam grabbed my arm suddenly, yanking me to my feet. "You're mine. You've always been mine, Eve."

"No!" my sister suddenly yelled. "You will not hurt my family!"

Jophiel spread her beautiful copper wings and launched herself at Adam. She looked so deathly ill I wasn't sure how she even moved, but she managed to knock him back, releasing me from his grasp. In return, he flung his hand out, sending a concentrated stream of sickness just for her. The diseased air twisted around her, making her gasp. Jophiel dropped to the floor, hitting the carpet with a thump and not moving again.

Rage poured through me, giving me strength, and I channeled my light and dark energy, sending out pure waves of it woven together like an intricate braid, aimed straight at Adam. The blast drove him back, but the Elder God inside him fought me.

"Come on already," Nemesis yelled, halfway through the portal. Belial had already disappeared inside it, I saw with a huge wave of sadness and disappointment. "Leave her!"

She still had an iron grip on Callan and dragged him through the portal with her, and Adam cast me one last glare before he followed. The portal closed instantly behind them, leaving the rest of us with no way to follow or fight.

29

HANNAH

Marcus rushed everyone outside, away from the noxious fumes, and he carried my sister with him. We all stumbled out onto the front lawn, the others coughing and weak, barely able to walk. I grabbed onto Kassiel and helped him regain his footing, needing to be near my son, to make sure he was all right. Once we'd made it to safety, I wrapped my arms around him and gave him a tight hug, relieved he was okay.

I pulled away to see Marcus kneeling beside my sister. He looked up at me, his expression mournful, his eyes glazed.

"No," I whispered. "It can't be. She can't have—" I'd been so pissed at her, so damn angry, but now... She was gone. "Can't you resurrect her? You brought me back!" My words were desperate and thin, like even they held no hope at all. Why hadn't I been born a healer too? Who cared about truth, when the people you loved were dying around you?

Marcus's face crumbled. "I wish I could, but I'll barely have enough energy to heal everyone else as it is. I'm sorry."

Marcus's shoulders slumped, and I staggered backward into Lucifer's waiting arms. He held me close as I sobbed, my grief loud in the shocked silence that filled the air. Marcus moved to Olivia next, healing her from the poison Adam had spread. Everyone had been hit by it, but some had been worse off than others. Kassiel, to my relief, had barely inhaled any of it, and was only coughing a tiny bit. Olivia, on the other hand, had been inside from the beginning and could barely move, and Bastien was in pretty bad shape too.

When Marcus finished with the others and moved to Lucifer, my mate held up a hand. "I'm fine. Save your strength."

Marcus nodded, with shadows like purple bruises beneath his eyes. He'd worn himself out healing everyone. I'd been the only one untouched by Adam's disease—he wasn't ready to kill me yet. He always did like to make me suffer first.

If not for Jophiel's final act of bravery, Adam would have dragged me through the portal with them too. I could only imagine what torment he'd had planned for me in Heaven. I only wished we'd been able to stop them from taking Callan too.

"She sacrificed herself for me," I whispered. "She did horrible things, was so..." I stopped and searched for the right word. "*Misguided* at times, but she did bad things for the right reasons." I looked at Lucifer and begged him to understand, although I couldn't speak those words.

His hand curled around mine. "That I will agree with. She did everything she did out of love."

Another sob escaped me. "I never got to make peace with her for what she did, and now it's too late." I would have forgiven her eventually, just as I forgave Lucifer. It wasn't in my heart to hold grudges for too long—except when it came to Adam. That fucker was going to pay. Someday. Somehow.

Olivia sat on the grass against Kassiel, curled up in his lap, with Marcus and Bastien on either side, their hands resting against her. They were all upset, worried about Callan, and occasional tears slid down Olivia's cheeks. I was worried too—he was my nephew, and Jophiel's son, and I owed it to her to rescue him.

"They won't kill him," Lucifer said, stroking my back. "They need Callan to open War's tomb. Even afterward, I doubt they will. He's Michael's only living son. He was born in Heaven and they'll keep him alive in case they need his blood again."

Olivia looked at Lucifer hopefully. "Are you sure?"

He nodded. "Try not to worry. He's strong."

"Yeah, but Adam is too powerful," Marcus muttered. "How can we possibly defeat him?"

"Once War is released, it will be too late to stop the apocalypse," Bastien said. "And now they have the means to do it."

"The best we could do is get Pestilence out of his body and entomb his essence like they did last time," Kassiel said.

Lucifer pinched his brow. "We'd need to get the fae on our side for that. Unfortunately, the High King and I don't get along much these days."

Kassiel arched an eyebrow. "You made peace with the angels, surely we can convince the fae to work with us on this."

They continued discussing this but I tuned them out, staring at my sister's sickly pale skin. My stomach suddenly lurched and I turned away, hoping it would pass. It didn't, and I rushed away from the group, around the corner of the house. I pressed my hand to my mouth, my stomach roiling and trying to reject its contents, and I found a bush to duck behind.

I quickly hurled up all the food I'd had on the airplane. Tears gathered in my eyes as they always did when I was sick, and I wiped them away as my stomach moved again. I waited, gagging on nothing, but although my muscles moved, nothing else emerged. Sweat beaded on my forehead from the effort, and I leaned back against the wall behind me.

Shit. This really wasn't the time to develop a weak stomach.

"Are you all right?" Lucifer asked, concern written across his face.

"No," I said, wiping my mouth. "I just watched my sister be killed by the first Horseman of the apocalypse. I'm definitely not all right."

"I understand." He waited for me to join him, and I took his arm, leaning on him more than I wanted to as we walked back to the others. "The horrors of Pestilence's powers must have gotten to you. I've seen it happen before."

I nodded slowly and he dropped a kiss to the top of my head. I still felt a bit sick, and the shaky, fragile feeling hadn't left me, but I attempted to look stronger than I felt as we rejoined the rest of the group.

Lucifer stood at my side, his hand on my shoulder, as he surveyed the others. "It's time to go."

"Go?" Marcus asked. "Where? We can't get into Heaven."

"We can't stay here and wait for other demons to come and pick us off," Lucifer said, his voice commanding. "We'll head to Las Vegas, gather our allies, form a new plan, and then go after Pestilence."

Olivia sniffled and stood. "Let's go figure out how to rescue Callan."

Their group shuffled toward the limo, but I couldn't move from the spot where I stood. Not without Jophiel. "We can't just leave her here."

"I'll have someone come take care of her body," Lucifer said as he took my hand. "I'll handle everything. I swear it. Just come with me now."

I nodded and looked down at my sister as I wiped away fresh tears. My son had helped do this, while her son had tried to defend us, and now they were both lost to us. While there was still a chance of rescuing Callan, I was starting to think I'd never get my eldest son back. Maybe Lucifer was right, and there were no more chances for Belial.

Maybe Belial was lost to us forever.

I barely noticed as Lucifer herded me into the limo and we drove away. I barely noticed as we got back on the private jet and took off. I barely noticed when we landed in Las Vegas sometime later. I was numb. Going through the motions, but empty inside. Trying to find any small sliver of hope—and failing.

30

LUCIFER

I looked out of the penthouse window, seeing myself reflected in the glass, my whiskey in my hand. Behind me, Hannah paced back and forth, her arms crossed, her body language turned inward. Olivia and three of her mates reclined on the leather sofa, with Kassiel, Bastien, and Marcus sitting so close to her they should have been crowding her, but she seemed to need them all. Maybe she did —she was part succubus, after all.

I took a deep breath before turning to face the room. What a disaster today had become. I'd already summoned Samael and Azazel home, and they were on their way back from Penumbra Prison, where they'd learned absolutely nothing. I'd taken care of everything at Jophiel's house, sending her body off to the angels. I'd called Archangel Gabriel and asked him to meet me here to discuss our next steps. My head buzzed with my long list of things to do, but I was working through them and everyone in the room had a glass of wine, so at least there was that.

Hannah was the thing I worried about most though. She'd barely said a word since we'd left Jophiel's house. She'd been ill again on the airplane, but she'd refused to let Marcus heal her, saying she was fine. I'd tried to convince her to go to bed and get some rest, so she could mourn in private, but she'd said she wanted to be here when Gabriel arrived.

I checked my watch, wondering where he was. As if conjured by my thoughts of him, the Archangel appeared in front of me, and I steeled against a flinch, fighting not to react. The King of Hell was never taken by surprise. But fuck, I really hated when he did that.

"Where's my daughter?" the sandy-haired Archangel said by way of a greeting.

I understood. I'd be concerned only for Kassiel if I were in his position. I nodded over his shoulder, and he turned around, his arms already outstretched.

Olivia jumped to her feet as soon as saw him. "Father," she cried and ran to him.

He caught her and pressed her to him, and my heart gave a tug for the daughter I'd never experience this love with. I shoved that grief down, knowing I couldn't deal with it now.

Gabriel wrapped his arm around his daughter and led her to the black leather sofa before Kassiel explained in greater detail everything that had happened over the last few days, picking up all of the things I'd left out of my quick, urgent communication.

Gabriel sighed heavily when the tale was finished. "You've really gotten yourself into a mess this time, haven't you, Lucifer?"

"I refuse to take credit for this one." I poured Gabriel a stiff drink. It always amused me to see angels drinking. Humans thought they were so pure. Oh, if only they knew the truth.

Gabriel frowned as he took the drink. "The loss of Jophiel is a heavy blow to the angel community. She was not only one of our Archangels, but also the CEO of Aether Industries, our largest employer."

"Her son was taken by Adam," Hannah said in a quiet voice. "We need to honor her memory by rescuing him."

Gabriel's eyes landed on her. "Haniel. I thought you were lost to us. It's been so long since I saw you."

"I was lost, in a way," she replied. "But not anymore."

"She's right, we need to find Callan," Olivia said. "Do you have a key to Heaven?"

Gabriel swirled his drink around, the ice clinking against the sides. "Yes, Michael entrusted me with one when he sealed off Heaven."

I nodded, his words confirming my suspicions. I'd done the same thing when I'd closed Hell. Lilith had my backup key—she was the only Archdemon I trusted. Well, more than the rest, anyway. What was trust really, besides a short list of people less likely to stab me in the back on any given day? A list that grew shorter by the hour.

"Shouldn't we already be on our way there?" Kassiel asked. "Every moment we delay they get closer to War's tomb."

"We can't rush into this," I said. "Our failure at Jophiel's house showed us that much. We need to gather our allies and formulate a plan."

Gabriel nodded. "If they're traveling through the ruined, abandoned landscape of Heaven, it will take them some time."

I finished my whiskey and set it down on the bar. "Yes, they can't exactly hop on a plane over there. We'll take the jet to the equivalent location of the tomb here on Earth, and then use the key to open the portal. That way, we might even surprise them."

"What's the plan once we get there?" Hannah asked.

I steepled my fingers as I considered. "The priority is to stop them from releasing War. If they do manage to free him, we need to make sure he doesn't possess anyone. There's a small chance we might be able to re-seal him in the tomb, but not if he's taken a new vessel."

"Pestilence required a sacrifice," Bastien said. "Will War ask for the same?"

"I believe so, yes," I said.

"What about Pestilence?" Marcus asked. He still looked haunted after the healing he'd done earlier. I can only imagine how anathema Pestilence would be to a Malakim like himself, whose duty was to preserve life.

I spread my hands. "The best we can do for now is to distract him and possibly kill Adam's body. Once we stop the threat of War, we can contact the fae and work with them to trap Pestilence again."

"I need to make some calls." Gabriel finished off his drink and rose to his feet. "The tomb is in the equivalent of Mexico, just outside Cancun at Chichen Itza. I can teleport there myself, but I can't take everyone with me."

I nodded. "The rest of us will take the jet first thing in the morning."

"I'll organize some angels to help. This is a threat we must all stand against." Gabriel turned to Olivia. "I'll see you soon."

He disappeared in the blink of an eye. One second there, the next gone—his Archangel power. He'd always been my favorite Archangel, but damn, that was annoying.

The others all stood too. "We'll see you in the morning," Kassiel said, giving Hannah's arm a quick squeeze before he left.

After they retreated to their own guest suites in the hotel, I sent a message to Raphael to let him know what we had planned. We'd need the help of the strongest Malakim to combat Adam's plague powers. Frankly, we needed all the allies we could get at this point if we were going to stand against Pestilence.

"Go on to bed," I told Hannah. "I'll be right there after I send a few more messages."

She nodded and left the room, and I called Einial and went over some of the logistical aspects of our journey tomorrow. Once that was done, I considered contacting the fae, but there was no time. I couldn't exactly text them over in Faerie, after all. The fae were not exactly up to date on current technology.

As I walked across the living room, movement outside the window caught my eye. I was instantly alert, ready for another attack, when I spotted a female gargoyle hovering outside. She had black hair tied back in a bun, and she spread her leathery, taloned wings and set down on the balcony outside.

As I walked closer, I recognized her as Romana, Belphegor's eldest daughter. Great. Just what I needed right now was another headstrong child seeking revenge for the death of their parent. A death I had nothing to do with this time.

I threw open the sliding door. "What are you doing here?"

"Is it true?" she asked, with a slight French accent. "Is she dead?"

"I'm afraid so."

"Tell me."

I gestured for her to sit on one of the lounge chairs on the patio, as the night breeze teased at our hair and clothes. She perched on the edge of her seat, like she was a bundle of nerves that were ready to launch herself off the chair at any moment.

I sat across from her and quickly laid out what had happened, including Adam's betrayal and murder of Belphegor. The whole sordid tale. I wasn't sure how much Belphegor had involved her daughter in her plots against me, but Romana didn't seem surprised by much of what I told her—except for the end, when Pestilence emerged and Adam sacrificed Belphegor for the power.

Romana seethed, her hands gripping the side of the chair, her skin turning to stone. "I will kill him myself for what he's done."

I nearly laughed at the idea that she could succeed where I had failed. However, we needed allies if we were going to defeat this threat, and I was never one to pass up an opportunity. Even though the gargoyles had tried to kill Hannah while Belphegor led them, I sensed a chance to give them a new beginning.

"You are the new Archdemon of the gargoyles," I told her. "I need to know now—will you stand against me? Or against the people who betrayed your mother?"

She considered for a moment, and I saw the thoughtfulness in her brown eyes, before she bowed her head. "I stand with you, my lord."

I rose to my feet. "A wise choice. Tomorrow we fly to Mexico to stop Adam and the others from releasing War. You and your gargoyles would be very useful in that fight."

"We will join you. I will have revenge for my mother's death." She slowly dropped to her knees before me, her eyes lowered. "I pledge my loyalty to you, Lucifer. I will serve you as your Archdemon."

That was unexpected, but certainly welcome. I gestured for her to stand. "Rise, Romana. I thank you for your oath. We leave first thing in the morning."

"We will be ready." Her wings snapped out and she disappeared off the side of the balcony, into the night air.

I gazed out at the Las Vegas lights, trying to calm the turmoil in my head at the thought of what we would face tomorrow, but there was only one person who could soothe me. When I walked into my bedroom, Hannah was curled up in a ball under the covers in the middle of the bed. I undressed quickly and climbed under the blankets behind her, wrapping my arms around her.

"I never got to forgive her," she whispered.

"I'm sorry." There wasn't much else to say. No words would help her pain. I was all too familiar with loss, as were all immortals, and I knew it never got any easier.

"I was mad at her, but I didn't want her to die."

"She knew. She knew the moment you told her you loved her."

"Do you think so?"

I wanted to erase all uncertainty and guilt from her. Her immortal life would be a long time to bear that weight. Assuming we survived the next fight. "I'm sure of it. She loved you too. That's why she sacrificed herself to save you. That's why she did everything."

Hannah sighed. "I know. Her love was...overbearing. But it was true."

My arms tightened around her. "We're going to stop Adam, I swear it."

"How?" She let out a sad laugh. "Elder Gods can't be killed."

I didn't have the answer, but I had an idea. A possibility. The only thing as powerful as an Elder God...was another Elder God.

Could we get War to defeat Pestilence?

31

HANNAH

Cancun was warm and sunny, and all of the things the travel websites promised, yet still perfectly miserable. My sister was dead, my nephew taken, my son lost. Everything was wrong. As someone who was grieving, it was like a slap in the face that the day was so gorgeous. It should've been raining and bleak. Everything needed to be gray. Like I was.

But as we stepped off the jet and the sunshine beat down on my face, I at least felt a little stronger physically. As an angel, that warmth and sunlight helped, as did the ocean breeze blowing against my skin. I turned my head toward the bright sun, hoping it would burn through all the darkness inside me.

Lucifer rested his hand on the small of my back as he breathed in deeply. "We'll have to return someday. When things calm down."

I nodded, though we both knew it would be a miracle if we survived the day. Besides, all I cared about was defeating Adam. For thousands of years he had tortured and killed me. He'd tormented and tricked my family. He'd murdered my daughter and now my sister. I was ready to make him pay.

Our private jet had been packed with our allies, and they spilled out onto the tarmac now. Numerous black SUVs waited to drive us to the location of the tomb, and I hurried toward the first one. I didn't want to waste any more time. The few hours of rest we'd gotten were needed, but not at the expense of preventing Adam from releasing War.

"How long is the drive?" I asked, as I piled into a car with Einial and Lucifer.

"Two hours," Einial said. "Roughly."

"Others will be meeting us there," Lucifer said. "Assuming Gabriel and Raphael came through."

"They will," I said. Gabriel had only spoken truth last night. The question was whether his additional angels would be enough. Without some protection against Adam, I didn't see how we'd even be able to fight him, but we had to try. There was no other way. I'd never been content to just roll over before, and now that I had Lucifer back and the promise of forever with him, I wasn't about to roll over now. I reached for Lucifer's hand and entwined my fingers with his. No, I wasn't ready to give this up.

The car fell silent as we drove, and I assumed all of us were contemplating the coming fight. We left the airport and drove over a bridge, then headed through Cancun, which reminded me a lot of Southern California—big blue skies dotted with wispy clouds, palm trees on either side of the road, white buildings with signs in Spanish.

I spotted a glimpse of the ocean between the buildings, and I lowered my window to get a bit of the fresh sea air. We rolled to a stop outside a restaurant, and I was hit with the strong smell of seafood. Normally, I loved seafood, but today the thought of it turned my stomach. I gripped the edge of the leather seat and gritted my jaw against the sudden and strong wave of intense nausea.

A memory rose up from about forty years ago, when I'd been pregnant with my daughter, and a similar smell had sent me running to the bathroom. None of my other pregnancies had caused nausea, but I'd been ready to hurl for pretty much the whole time with my last one.

A particularly gnarly wave of nausea hit me when the wind brought more of the fish stink into the car. I quickly raised the window and clutched the seat with white-knuckled hands, fighting to keep my breakfast. I'd gotten sick yesterday, too, but I'd thought it was a reaction to Pestilence and everything we'd just been through. But what if it wasn't?

Fuck. Shit. Fuck. Could I be pregnant?

"Are you okay?" Lucifer asked, watching me with a worried twist to his mouth.

I nodded and grabbed a bottle of water. As I sipped it, my stomach settled a little, but the movement of the car from the back-seat made me feel sick again. I wanted to yell at my body to get it together. This was so not the time.

"Hungry?" Lucifer asked, then turned to Einial. "Do we have anything to eat?"

"Yes, of course." She opened up a backpack full of an assortment of savory and sweet snacks.

I nearly gagged but stopped myself in time as I shook my head. Then I spied a pack of plain crackers and snatched them before Einial closed it up again. "Thanks," I muttered. "Just feeling all this stress, I guess."

Lucifer squeezed my leg as I opened the crackers. I nibbled them slowly, trying hard not to think about the whole eating thing. Just auto-pilot chew, chew, chew, swallow. Holy crap. A baby would be an insane complication. Huge. At the worst possible time in my life. But I couldn't keep my hand from drifting towards my stomach. An insane complication, but also *ours*.

As we left the city and drove along a highway flanked by thick greenery, I pushed the nausea to the back of my mind. It was nearly gone now, and really might've just been lingering effects from Pestilence's power. A baby, no matter how incredible it would be, just wasn't an option during this fight. Just to be safe, I'd take a pregnancy test as soon as this was over though.

"Where is everyone?" I asked as we pulled up in front of the old ruins of the ancient city of Chichen Itza. I wasn't sure if I'd ever been here before, but it was obvious there should've been tourists everywhere. Yet nobody was waiting at the base of the long Mayan staircase or taking pictures of the ancient structures. "This place should be packed."

"I pulled some strings." Lucifer made his influence sound like child's play, but even now his reach still had the power to amaze me. "We have the site to ourselves today."

We parked the cars and got out, and I glanced around, taking it all in. There was a huge, flat, open area where the city had once stood, and thick greenery surrounded it on all sides, making this the perfect place to gather our allies and prepare for battle. The immense pyramid stood out in the distance, but there were other structures too, including an area with hundreds of stone columns lined up in rows. My love of history and mythology made me wish I could spend the day here like a tourist, learning everything about it.

"That used to be a market," Lucifer said, nodding toward the rows of pillars. "This city was truly spectacular long ago."

We approached the pyramid as everyone else got out of the cars and began to follow us. It was huge, with tens of thousands of limestone blocks, and the stones seemed to glow with an ethereal light as the sun sank in the horizon. I stared at the steep steps, and noticed serpent heads at the base. It was magnificent, and this close to it I felt a low thrum of power, like a subtle vibration in the air around me.

"You feel it, don't you?" Lucifer asked, watching me closely.

I nodded. "What is it? I felt the same thing at Stonehenge."

"This pyramid exists in multiple realms," Lucifer said. "As do many other old structures that humans consider wonders of the world. Like Stonehenge or the Tower of Jericho. The Great Pyramid of Giza. The World's Biggest Ball of Twine."

"Twine?" I asked.

He shrugged. "The imps."

Ah. That explained it.

He ran his fingers along one of the ancient stones. "In the old days, these locations acted as bridges between the realms, and they were ruled by angels, demons, or fae. Back when the humans worshipped us as gods."

The sun lowered behind the pyramid, bathing the world in a

rainbow of reds and oranges, while we walked back toward the large, flat area of grass. Others had begun to gather in large numbers. Olivia and her mates, of course. Samael and Azazel and other loyal Fallen. Our surprise allies the gargoyles, led by their new Archdemon, Romana. Plus a large contingent of angels, including a group of Malakim healers that Archangel Raphael had brought.

Archangel Gabriel stood among them. He was a handsome man with sand-colored hair and a welcoming face, the rare angel who looked more like a human than an immortal. We'd met multiple times back when I was Haniel, and I'd always liked him. I'd known Raphael a bit too, although more by reputation than anything—he was a huge flirt, with dozens of children, all from different women over the years. He was also ridiculously handsome and charming, with shiny dark locks, olive skin, and a captivating smile.

Everyone was busy preparing for battle, wielding weapons and wearing armor, while their leaders barked out orders. I felt completely underdressed, wearing something akin to my workout gear, and Lucifer had on one of his signature black suits. Armor wouldn't protect us from Pestilence's powers anyway. Better to be comfortable and able to move around with ease, I figured.

While Lucifer conferred with Einial, I gazed across our impressive force, made up of both angels and demons—people who I'd never expect to fight side-by-side. An impending apocalypse brought together strange allies indeed.

I walked over to Kassiel, my heart aching at the sight of him in his sleek, black battle gear. One son, going to fight another. We hugged each other tight, knowing this might be the end for one or both of us, and I prayed to whatever god might be listening to protect him.

"Do you think we can save him?" Kassiel asked, and I knew he was speaking of his brother.

"I don't know, but I won't stop trying." I took Kassiel's face in my hands and looked upon him, my heart overflowing with love, and then kissed him on the forehead. "I love you. Be safe out there."

"Love you too, Mom."

He had a few quiet words with Lucifer next, while Zel came

over and wrapped an arm around my shoulder. "Remember every-thing I taught you and you'll be fine," she said.

I hugged her close. "Don't die out there. I need you to watch my back."

She huffed as she hugged me back. "As if anything could stop me from doing that."

All around us people said what could be their final words to those they loved. Everyone here knew this was a battle many of us would not walk away from. If any of us did.

Lucifer turned toward Gabriel, "Are we ready?"

"Yes, we're all set." Gabriel pulled out his own key, a clear gem about the size of his palm and already glowing faintly. But then he paused and an expression that looked almost sad came over his face.

"What is it?" I asked.

Gabriel drew in a long breath as he stared at the gem. "I haven't been to Heaven in over thirty years. Some of the angels here have never even seen it."

Lucifer rested a hand on his shoulder. "I know exactly how you feel."

Gabriel shook himself out of his thoughts, then held the gem out in front of him. Bright light burst out of it, opening a huge, shim-mering portal to another world. My breath caught at the sight of it, and the idea that Heaven was on the other side.

Angels and demons alike began to stream into the portal, vanishing as soon as they stepped inside. I longed to follow them, and yet I was apprehensive about it too. What waited for us on the other side?

Lucifer turned to me and met my eyes, silently asking if I was ready. I nodded at him and took his hand. We stood together, ready to face whatever was on the other side of that portal.

Then we stepped through.

32

HANNAH

As soon as we were on the other side, my powers heightened, and the boost soothed my soul. Coming home—there was nothing else like it. Breathing deep, I closed my eyes and soaked in the warm light and influx of energy from simply being in this realm. It was truly Heaven. Pun intended.

Every angel that had been here before had a look on their faces like they'd come home at last, while the younger angels were completely awestruck at visiting Heaven for the first time. Meanwhile, the demons squinted and grumbled, their powers diminished in the land of light.

The sky was that deep coral color that I remembered being the closest Heaven ever got to night. Here, the sun met the horizon, but never went any lower. It sank and the light dimmed, but it never went out. I could only imagine what it would feel like during the middle of the day with the sun high in the sky.

Beside me, Lucifer's grip on my hand tightened as he looked up at the sky. Unlike other demons, he could also feed on light, a remnant of when he was an angel. I wondered when he had last been here.

"How does it feel being back?" I asked.

He dropped his eyes to me, his expression bittersweet. "Like being both home and homesick, all at the same time."

Somehow I knew what he meant, because even though this body had been born here, it wasn't truly home anymore, any more than Hell or Faerie was. Home was Earth.

No. Home was wherever Lucifer was.

Our fighters took to the sky, spreading wings of white, black, and every shade in between. We flew toward the pyramid, which was just a pile of crumbled ruins here in Heaven, unlike on Earth. A sad result of the war. There were so many things that were gone or destroyed in this realm, casualties of the horrible fighting between Heaven and Hell that had lasted for thousands of years. I was sure Hell looked much the same.

As we approached in the sky, I saw a large group standing in the ruins of the pyramid below, and a great gaping hole in the center of it. A tomb had been pulled out of it, and Callan stood beside it, flanked by Belial and Nemesis. Nemesis sliced Callan's hand, and his blood sprayed across the black tomb, making the symbols on it glow.

"No!" I yelled, knowing we were too late.

War erupted from the tomb with a huge roar, sending out a blast of energy that knocked everyone back, including those of us in the air. He rose up like a red cloud of fury, his spirit radiating anger and hatred, as he grew so huge he blocked the last sliver of sun that rested on the far-off horizon.

"Stick to the plan," Gabriel called out, as we all reeled from the shock of seeing him already freed.

The plan. Right. Distract Pestilence. Get War back in his tomb. We could do this. We had to. Or this would be the end for all of us.

Our forces slowly recovered and flew toward the pyramid ruins. Toward two of the Four Horsemen of the apocalypse. Our group was led by some of the Malakim healers, who created an aura of healing magic to block his powers. Pestilence flew in front of us on sickly gray wings, and below him was the green-haired fae Philomelus, along with a black wolf about the size of a truck. Fenrir, my memories supplied—Archdemon of shifters. There was also an assortment of imps and shifters around the ruins too, and they began to fight with our varied group of allies.

Chaos broke out as magic and weapons clashed, but then Adam released his magic, and it quickly burned through the healing wall the Malakim had put up, forcing us to retreat. There was no way we could get closer or stop War with Pestilence's magic blocking us, making us sick and weak.

Adam lifted his hand, a manic grin creasing his swollen and pus-filled face as he prepared to unleash a wave of sickness upon us that would probably end the battle. But then Callan stood up from beside the tomb, clutching his side as if in pain, and launched into the air.

"Callan!" Olivia screamed as he flew forward and knocked into Adam, knocking him back. But my nephew was too late. A rush of Pestilence's power vaulted toward us.

Then a wall of pure, strong light appeared out of nowhere, blocking Adam with a magical shield. Callan held up a hand as he flew in the air near Pestilence, keeping the monster's sickness contained.

Damn. He really was strong. Heightened by the light and power here in Heaven, Callan's shield held steady against every onslaught Adam sent our way, allowing us to press forward. Olivia and her mates, along with a small group of gargoyles, quickly surrounded Callan, protecting him so he could keep us shielded. I spotted Kassiel among them, and I was hit with a wave of pride and fear, but knew he was capable of defending himself. It was his brother I needed to worry about.

There were so many of us that our sheer number would've overwhelmed any other enemy in any battle, but Adam continued to sicken anyone who pressed through Callan's protective shield to attack. Adam slowed under the constant barrage of the attack, but wouldn't fall. Philomelus helped him by throwing huge stones and other parts of the ruins at our forces, but Samael and Azazel swooped down to stop him.

Lucifer and I battled our way through the chaos, his hellfire and darkness taking out anyone who dared stand against him. I used everything I'd learned over the past few weeks about light and darkness to fight alongside him, as we flew to the center of the ruins, where Belial stood with Nemesis.

Before Lucifer and I could reach our son, Fenrir suddenly leaped into the air and smacked us both with his clawed paws. I managed to twist and roll, flapping my silver wings rapidly, but Lucifer recovered faster. He shot hellfire at Fenrir, who fought it off with something like lava bursting out of his fanged mouth. I blasted Fenrir with blinding white light, making him stumble back and shake his head, while Lucifer chained him with darkness. Fenrir burst free of the shadow bonds with a great shake and a roar that shook the earth, and I wished more than anything that I had Morningstar.

Maybe I could improvise. I created two huge daggers made of shadow, a trick I remembered from my years as Lenore, and then wove light around them. While Fenrir tried to snap at Lucifer's wings, I launched myself onto his large back, settling into the thick fur. Then I stabbed each blade into his shoulders, making him scream and rear back. Just enough for Lucifer to hit him with a direct shot of hellfire.

Fenrir bucked me off him and I went flying, but Lucifer caught me in his arms. When I looked back, Fenrir had shrunk to a normal size wolf, and he stumbled into his group of shifters and disappeared amongst them. Turning tail and running away.

"Nice thinking," Lucifer said, nodding to my twin blades. "Now let's put War back where he belongs."

The path had cleared before us, and we flew as quickly as we could. War's enormous, rageful spirit hovered mid-air over his tomb, his burning red eyes watching Nemesis and Belial below.

"This Horseman is mine," Nemesis yelled, shoving my son back, her sharp black nails extended for battle.

"You can't handle that kind of power," Belial snapped. He held Morningstar in his hands and it glowed with bright white light. His wings were out, and they were beautiful—black at the top, then fading to gray, then white at the bottom.

"And you can't make the required sacrifice." Nemesis laughed, the sound cruel. "Or did you forget what happened at Stonehenge?"

War's horrid laughter filled the air. "Yes, fight little ones. Your anger and hatred only make me stronger. Fight to the death, and I will claim the victor as my prize."

The closer I got to War, the angrier I felt, but I was able to shake it off, my Ofanim senses allowing me to feel the emotion as a lie. I landed beside Belial, hoping to reason with my son. I didn't know if I'd get this opportunity again.

Before I could try anything, Belial slashed Nemesis with Morningstar and roared. As she hit the ground, the look in his eyes terrified me. My son had been inflicted with War's madness. There wasn't anything I could do. Not with him in this berserker state.

But I had to try.

I cast the light of truth on him, hoping to free him from War's grasp. "Belial, stop!"

"War is mine." He turned toward me, his eyes seeing me a little clearer, thanks to my magic. "It's the only way."

"Please don't do this!" I ran forward, making it halfway to him before Lucifer stopped me by grabbing me around the waist and hauling me back.

"Hannah, no!"

"Let me go! We can't let him become a monster!" I fought Lucifer off, desperate to get to my son, but his grip held tight. If Belial became War, we'd either have to kill him, lock him away...or watch as he destroyed everything we loved. "Belial!"

"I won't let that happen to him," Lucifer said in a voice so confident it made me stop struggling. "Do you trust me?"

"Yes," I said, without hesitation. Despite his harsh words before, he loved our son. He'd do whatever he could to protect him.

He glanced quickly at Belial, who was approaching War, then looked back at me. "I don't have time to explain, but I think I can stop this and save our son. Maybe take out Adam at the same time. But you're not going to like it."

"Do it," I said, even as my heart broke at his words. "Whatever it takes."

Lucifer nodded grimly. "Whatever it takes."

"I love you," I said, fearing it might be the last time I ever had a chance to say those words to him.

"I love you too." He pulled me close and pressed a hard, passionate kiss to my lips. "With all my heart."

A huge piece of stone suddenly came crashing down beside us. Philomelus approached us, no doubt trying to stop us from interfering with Belial and War. "Go," I said, pushing back from Lucifer. "I'll take care of this. Just save our son."

"I will." He gave me one last lingering look, before spreading his shadowy wings and launching toward War and Belial.

I held my breath and fought back the fear and worry for two of the men I loved most, before turning to defend them from another threat.

33

LUCIFER

I landed hard in front of Belial, blocking him from War. "Stop!"
"Get out of the way," Belial yelled.

He'd been arguing with War over the required sacrifice as I approached, still unable to take the life of one he loved. I saw it as a sign that there was still some small goodness left in my son's heart. If War got a hold of him, that tiny shred of light would be snuffed out forever. I couldn't let that happen—even if it meant sacrificing myself to save him. And if I got control of War, I might be able to defeat Pestilence at the same time. I had to try, anyway.

"Take me." My command boomed forcefully across Heaven, loud enough that War paused. "I'm far more powerful than my son in every way."

"Are you?" War asked, his voice cracking the air like thunder.

I stood taller, spreading darkness around me like a cloak. "Need I count the ways? I'm older and stronger. I have more magic. I'm the king of all demons. You'll never find a better vessel."

"You..." War's spectral form glared down at me with malice. "Son of Death. You were one of my captors."

Shit. I should have known he'd recognize me. But I could turn this around. "That's right. I defeated you before, but now I'm offering you a chance to take me as your vessel instead. There's no one stronger than me, and you know it. I fought against you in the Elder War, and I fought against angels in the Great War. Now I'll fight *with* you."

"You also ended the Great War," Belial growled, then looked over at War. "He's grown weak in his old age. He fights for peace now."

War fixed his vile gaze on my son again. "Hmm. I sense you are good at sowing conflict. You *are* enemies with your own father, after all."

"No!" I flew forward. I couldn't let him take my son. I'd seen what it had done to Adam. No matter what had happened in the past, I would never consider Belial my enemy. Not even after he'd betrayed me so many times. Not even after this. Here. Now. He was my son. And I would do whatever it took to save him—as I'd promised Hannah. Even if it meant sacrificing myself. "Belial is weak. He's stood against me numerous times, and I've always defeated him. He's the biggest disappointment of my life."

"Then sacrifice him," War said. "And you will have my power."

Despite my hard words, even I couldn't do that. "No. There must be another sacrifice you will accept."

"Yes. The angel woman." War stretched out a long finger toward Hannah, where she fought against the fae man. "Your mate."

I clenched my hands at my sides. "I will not take her life."

"Ah, but the sacrifice I require is one of the mind." War leaned close, surrounding me with his spectral energy. "She will live, but I will take her from you. Choose now, or I offer the boy the same deal. We both know he will take it."

I looked up at him, fearing what he meant, but knowing I was running out of time. This was probably the best deal I would get, even if my heart wrenched at the thought of losing Hannah in any way. All I could do was pray she would be able to save me from what I was about to do to myself. "Swear she will be unharmed, and I will agree."

"Father, no!" Belial yelled, rushing toward me with Morningstar.

"I swear it," War's voice boomed. "I accept you as my vessel."

At his words, War slammed into me with a rush of power, chaos, and hatred. I felt like my body was ripped apart only to sew itself back together, then torn apart all over again. Every pore oozed pain and torment. A needle for every day I'd ever lived stabbed into me— and I'd lived for so many years. The agony felt like it lasted for hours or days, maybe even weeks. My knees hit the ground, overwhelmed by the fight to remain myself amongst all this overwhelming rage. It had only been seconds, but the anger inside me had built for centuries. And now it was free.

Something inside me had been stripped. Something important, but what was it? The idea that an integral part of me had disappeared bothered me greatly. I couldn't quite put my finger on it. On that one thing I needed to remember. Was something missing?

No matter. I was Lucifer and War and a *god*. Purpose and power filled me as I gazed across the battlefield at the angels and demons still fighting each other. As they should be.

I spread my hands and laughed, using my magic to stir their emotions. I tweaked that part of their minds that allowed the puny creatures to give in to their base instincts. Their primal sides. Their rage.

They turned on each other and fought harder, not knowing or caring who fell before them. And they died, one after another, fueling my power. Making me whole.

Give them anger.

Give them War.

34

HANNAH

I blasted Philomelus with a combined hit of darkness and light, sending him flying back hundreds of feet. Azazel swooped down where he landed, her blades glowing, and I gave her a quick salute before turning back to help Lucifer.

But I was too late.

"No!" I screamed, as War surged into Lucifer, his angry essence surrounding him and sinking through every pore. Lucifer spread his arms as he accepted it, and understanding crashed over me as my heart shattered into a thousand tiny glass shards. He'd done it to save our son from such a fate—but now he'd cursed himself in the process, and the thought of losing him was unbearable. Maybe he could fight it. There was no one stronger than Lucifer. If anyone could control War, it was him.

Paths of angry red and orange light broke through Lucifer's skin, like it couldn't be contained. It burst out of his body like molten lava seeping through cracks in the ground, pulsing with iridescent fury. He spread his wings wide, and they glowed red instead of their usual inky darkness. Black feathers lit by rage.

Furious and overwhelming power pulsed from Lucifer, filling everyone on the field. As the energy hit all of those waging war against each other, they let out shrieks and cries filled with mindless anger, and began slashing and hacking at whoever was in front of them. Friend or foe, it mattered not. Rage had taken hold of them, and they fought with renewed vigor. If Pestilence weakened and sickened them, War did the opposite. He was a shot of caffeine straight to their anger centers.

And I was the only one who could stop it.

I launched into the air and flew in the lighted dusk to Lucifer, hovering in front of him. My mate was in there somewhere, no doubt fighting against the Elder God that had taken his body, and I had to reach him somehow. It was my only hope of ending this madness and turning him upon Adam.

"Lucifer, stop this!" I touched his arm and squeezed, willing our connection to help him focus past the influence of the god he'd welcomed into his body. "Listen to me! You have to fight it!"

He turned his head toward me with eyes that burned red like hot coal and gave me a scathing look. "Who are you?"

I blinked at him, confused. "It's me, Hannah. Your mate. You...you don't recognize me?"

Lucifer's impossibly handsome face was marred with hatred as he shoved me back. "I'd never mate with an *angel*."

I caught myself with my wings, even as his words shook me deep to my core. This was bad. What had War done to him? "I know you're in there." The words fell from my lips, a desperate attempt to have him acknowledge me. "Lucifer, you have to push through this!"

"Of course I'm in here. I once made the mistake of ending the war against the angels, but War has reminded me who I really am." He sneered at me as he spoke, while the battle raged around us. "It's time to take over Heaven and reopen Hell. Then we'll conquer Earth, and Faerie too." He surveyed the scene of chaos in front of him with satisfaction. "Soon every realm will kneel before me. Their king. Their *god*."

No, I refused to let him become this monster. I would make him remember somehow. I gripped his shoulders, forcing him to look at me. "Lucifer! You are not War! I know you can fight this. You know who I am. I'm Hannah. I'm *Eve*! You are my mate. And you love me." The wind whipped my last words away. "I know you do, even if War's made you forget."

Lucifer's furious red eyes burned brighter, and he grasped my wrist tightly but didn't strike me down. I stared back at him, searching his face for any hint of the man I loved.

"Mother!" Belial grabbed my arm and yanked me back. "There's nothing you can do. He doesn't remember you."

"No!" I cried. My soul felt like it was being torn in two as Belial dragged me away. I'd just gotten Lucifer back, just remembered everything about our past together, and now I'd lost him again. Even though we were no longer cursed, fate seemed to want to keep us apart, to make us suffer for the chance to be together.

But maybe there was hope. Lucifer let us go. He could've killed me easily while I'd pleaded with him, but he hadn't. More than that, the anger that affected everyone else had managed to spare me and Belial. No matter what Lucifer said, there was a part of him that wouldn't hurt me. That knew me, deep down, in the dark depths of his soul. Just like when Jophiel had made him forget Haniel, but he'd ended the war with the angels anyway. No matter what happened, I would always be with him.

As Belial pulled me to safety, I gazed out across the pyramid's ruins and watched the battle going on around us. Angels and demons, who were previously on the same side, now fighting each other because of Lucifer's magic. *War's* magic.

Too many people were injured or dead, and Lucifer wasn't going to stop here. War wouldn't ever let him stop, and even Lucifer wasn't strong enough to fight the Elder God's influence. Now Lucifer would go to Earth and restart the war against angels, and then he'd keep going until War conquered all. When he was finished, what would even be left?

I couldn't let that happen.

Lucifer had saved our son, but in doing so, he'd lost himself. It only made me love him even more, because it was exactly what I would have done. We'd been through countless lifetimes together, and my love for him—and his for me—was the one constant through all of them.

But now I had to stop him.

I turned to Belial, frantically coming up with a plan that probably wouldn't work, but was our only hope at stopping War. "Where's the key to Heaven?"

"I have it."

"Give it to me."

Belial scowled, but he took it out and rested the gem in my hand. It lit up immediately at my touch, reacting to my angelic nature. Only a few hours ago, this had been stolen from Jophiel's hands. Grief threatened to return, but I pushed it away. No time for that now.

"We need to get everyone out of here." I beat my wings hard against the air as I flew over the remaining living warriors, and then I remembered what Bastien had taught me. What he'd reminded me I could do. I gathered the light of truth in my palms, my powers so strong here in Heaven it felt like being hit by an electric bolt, and shot it over the field. As it hit everyone fighting, War's madness relaxed on them, just a little. Just enough to make them pause.

I landed in the middle of them and held out the gem, like I'd seen Gabriel do. The key reacted to my angelic blood as I thought of Earth, and a shimmering portal opened up. I concentrated and made it bigger, so multiple people could enter at once.

"Hurry!" I yelled, my voice booming across the field. "Go through the portal!"

The warriors seemed to snap out of a daze and began moving toward the portal, but I'd forgotten about Adam. With all the insanity going on, he had watched from atop his spectral white horse with a triumphant look on his face, loving the chaos and the death all around him. Now he focused on me and his eyes narrowed—and then he charged.

"I'll hold him back," Belial said, gathering hellfire in his hands. "Get everyone out of here."

I wasn't sure I could trust Belial, since he'd been on Adam's side only moments ago, but I couldn't stop to argue or question him.

All of the angels and demons still capable of moving headed to the portal, some of them crawling or helping others through, some flying on injured wings. Fenrir carried an unconscious or dead Nemesis on his back, but I didn't care at this point if they got away or not. All that mattered was getting everyone back to Earth so I could do what had to be done.

Belial flew around Adam so quickly he was a blur, attacking him with Morningstar, with hellfire, with darkness. Giving our forces enough time to escape. Whenever someone stopped and growled with War's rage again, I threw out more beams of light, focusing all my energy on making sure the truth won out. As I did, Gabriel opened a portal on the other side of the field, allowing even more people to escape.

An enormous spectral horse appeared in the distance, the color of dark red blood. It galloped toward us, passing by the angels and demons on the grass and approaching War. Lucifer mounted the massive beast and I knew we were out of time.

"Hurry!" I yelled. If they didn't get through soon, I'd have to leave some behind.

Belial suddenly hit the ground beside me, rolling in agony from Adam's sickness. The first Horsemen then rode across the field on his white horse and slipped into Gabriel's open portal, sickening anyone nearby along the way. The portal closed an instant later, and I swore under my breath.

Lucifer turned toward us and kicked his steed, his hatred and fury an oppressive cloud all around us. No doubt planning to do exactly what Adam had done.

We were out of time.

Across the field, Gabriel grabbed hold of someone with black wings—Azazel—and flew straight for my portal. A few others remained, stumbling to get through, and I feared they weren't going to make it. I had to give them a few more seconds somehow.

Before Lucifer's steed reached the portal, I blasted him with darkness and light, pouring everything I had into knocking the great love of my life backward. I wouldn't leave Gabriel or Azazel behind. I couldn't.

My son pushed himself up to his feet, his face twisting with resolve. Blue hellfire poured from his hands, packing enough punch to knock him back long enough for the remaining angels and demons to get through.

"Go!" I yelled as I shoved Belial toward the portal.

He shook his head. "Not without you!"

I had no time to waste arguing with my willful son. I was his mother, dammit. He should listen to me. As he turned to face Lucifer again while letting out a wracking cough, I wrapped darkness around him like a chain and tossed him through the portal.

Lucifer came closer, magnificent as he sat high on his steed, and I stood blocking the way. It was just me and him now. As it always had been.

"Get out of my way, angel," Lucifer commanded, his horse stomping its feet impatiently, turning the ground to lava with every step. But he still didn't attack me.

"I love you," I said, my voice choking with emotion and tears pricking my eyes. "I'll come back for you, I swear it. I will find a way to free you."

I rushed through the portal just as he charged me, then closed it right before War and his red horse came riding through. Leaving Lucifer alone in empty, war-torn Heaven.

35

HANNAH

I collapsed to the ground, my body spent, my soul broken. Fuck, that had been close. If I'd been a second slower, War would have made it to Earth. I could still smell brimstone from his horse on me, and my hands shook with both terror and the horrible realization over what I'd done.

I'd locked my mate in Heaven. I'd left him as a monster. I'd done it to save everyone in this realm and every other, and I knew if Lucifer was in his right mind he would have approved of my decision—but that didn't make it any easier. Lucifer was lost to me, and I wasn't sure how I would ever get him back.

I gazed across the field, my eyes adjusting to the darkness. No one was fighting any longer, no matter what side they'd been on before. Imps lay next to angels, shifters groaned beside gargoyles. Archangel Raphael had been smart enough to stay behind on Earth with some Malakim to heal us in the event of something like this, and they flew across the field now, tending to everyone who needed it. I spotted Marcus bending over Kassiel, healing his wounds, and breathed a sigh of relief to see my youngest son was all right. I also saw Azazel speaking with Samael, and Olivia hugging Callan while Bastien looked on. All of them wonderfully, miraculously alive.

Adam had vanished though, and there was no telling where he'd gone. Although I'd managed to cage War, we still had Pestilence to deal with. Somehow we'd have to stop him before he did irreparable damage to this world we all shared.

"What have you done?" Belial stared at the spot where the portal had disappeared. He let out another horrible round of coughing, clutching his chest, and then collapsed against me.

"Help!" I yelled, and Archangel Raphael himself hurried over to me. He surrounded Belial in bright white light, slowly removing all traces of Pestilence's disease from him. It was a miracle Belial had fought it off so long. When the healing was done, I thanked Raphael and he flashed me a wink and a flirty smile, before rushing off to the next emergency.

"Why?" Bastien muttered, as he stumbled to his feet again.

I rested my hand on Belial's tattooed arm, willing him to understand. "I had to trap Lucifer there. It was the only way to contain him. He's an Elder God now, so he won't die. He'll just get angrier and angrier. But this gives us time to figure out how to get War out of him and remind him who he really is."

Belial clenched his fists, his frustration pouring out of him, so thick I could almost see it. "This wasn't supposed to happen. I was going to take on War to stop Pestilence. That was my plan, once I realized I'd fucked up by letting Adam become Pestilence. Father ruined everything."

My poor, misguided, stupidly brave son. He was far too much like his father. Probably why they'd never gotten along.

"He did it to save you."

Belial's face screwed tight with anger. "*Why?* Why would he save me after everything I've done?"

"Because you're our son." I wrapped my arms around him and hugged him tight, unsure which one of us needed to be held more. "No matter what you do, we will always love you."

The muscles of his back tightened at my words and he pulled away, his face hard. "You shouldn't."

Then he stormed off, he steps stiff and angry. I stared after him, but let him go. At least I'd confirmed what I'd always suspected—

that he wasn't totally evil. There was hope for him yet. And Lucifer knew that too, or he wouldn't have sacrificed himself to save Belial.

Gabriel moved through the crowd to stand by my side. "Good thinking back there. You saved us all."

"I did what I had to do," I said with a sigh.

"I'm just glad the angry haze from War has passed. All I wanted to do was fight. I'd been about to declare open war against the demons again." He looked at me, his eyes full of pity. "I'm sorry you had to leave him there, but it was the right thing to do. We can't let War start the battle between angels and demons again. Not when we've worked so hard for peace."

"We won't." No matter what else happened, I wouldn't let that battle start again. I was an angel, yes, but my heart was with the demons. I belonged in both worlds—and I would give my life protecting the peace between them. "And somehow we'll stop Pestilence too."

Gabriel held out his hand. "I look forward to working with you and your people on that."

I stared at his hand, confused, and then shook it. It took me a few seconds to realize what he meant.

With Lucifer gone, I was in charge.

I straightened up and regarded the Fallen and demons spread across the field. Some who'd been loyal, and some who'd strayed. They were all my subjects, and I would bring them together again. I would protect them. Guide them. Lead them. It was what Lucifer would've wanted.

I would find a way to save Lucifer—even if I had to kill him. Until then, I had to be strong. For our people. For Lucifer. For our children. Including the one I suspected was growing inside me now.

I was the Demon Queen.

It was time to rule.

INFERNAL GOD

CLAIMED BY LUCIFER BOOK THREE

1

LUCIFER

Heaven had once been beautiful. Now it was as desolate as my soul.

For months I'd been trapped here among the empty ruins of this once great civilization, under the sun that never truly set. Though I'd been born here thousands of years ago, living in Hell for so long had changed me. I desperately longed for night, for even one minute of complete darkness, but such a thing was not to be found in the Land of Light.

All I knew was a burning rage that simmered below my skin, fueling me in place of food or water or sleep. I needed none of those things now that I was an Elder God. I'd become War, second Horseman of the Apocalypse, and my purpose was to sow chaos and discord—as soon as I escaped. I had to find a way back to the human world to find the woman who had imprisoned me here. *To kill her.*

As I gazed across the shimmering ocean before me, I patted the neck of Strife, my one companion in this wretched place. The smell of brimstone and the sound of hoofs against the stone had become as familiar to me as breathing during our time here. Like me, my trusted steed required no sustenance, and no matter how hard or fast he ran, he never grew winded or fatigued. He'd simply appeared after I'd become War, and though he couldn't speak, we had a connection I didn't understand yet couldn't question. I was a Horseman, and Strife was my horse. It was that simple.

I nudged Strife across the white, gleaming sand toward the flowing waves. He moved faster than any horse, as fast as the sports cars I used to drive when I lived among the humans. Together we'd raced across Heaven for so long I'd lost track of the days as we searched for a thin spot between worlds. We'd checked all the places in Heaven that I knew had once been portals to the other realms, where I might be able to use my power to break through to Earth. All but one.

The Bermuda Triangle. Also known, rather fittingly, as the Devil's Triangle. There was a reason humans tended to go missing there. I hoped to exploit it.

White-hot rage burned in my gut as I pictured the woman who had trapped me here, and I squeezed Strife with my calves and heels, urging him to go faster, ride harder. Anything to get us out of this place so we could begin enacting our revenge.

Her alluring face had consumed my thoughts since the moment she'd disappeared through that portal, leaving me imprisoned in Heaven with Strife. I couldn't stop thinking about what I would do with her once I found her. I would bend her to my will, force her to her knees, make her pay for what she'd done. I would utterly destroy her. And then I would destroy her world.

Soon, war would spread across Earth, and then into all the other realms. Angels, demons, humans, fae—none would be spared my wrath, and all would bow to me. As it always should've been. As was my right.

I was the King of Demons. I was a Horseman of the Apocalypse. I was a *god*.

I urged Strife into the waves, where his hooves skimmed across the surface of the water. He could run over sea or land, desert or snow, it didn't matter. I spread my wings as we rushed across the dark blue ocean, enjoying the feel of the salt water on my skin and feathers. I held on with my knees and spread my arms, relishing in the power coursing through me. War had strengthened me, given me divine and righteous purpose. Nobody could stand against me. Not anymore.

After hours riding across the waves, I sensed something up ahead, a change in the air, a tingling sensation across my skin. We grew closer with every stride, and I wiped saltwater from my face for the thousandth time as I focused on the small island with an unmistakable magical signature.

Long ago, the realms of Heaven, Hell, and Faerie had permanent gateways open to Earth, and ancient monuments had been erected at the sites of them. When these gateways were closed, many of the locations became old ruins, like Stonehenge, or Chichen Itza. Others were lost in time, like the Hanging Gardens of Babylon or the Lighthouse of Alexandria. This spot was one of the latter, an island that no longer existed on Earth, though it remained here in Heaven.

Using my knees, I urged Strife up onto the sand. Ancient stones of a once-great civilization loomed before me. This island had been abandoned long before Archangel Michael closed off Heaven permanently, and all that was left were a few crumbling pillars and stone walls covered in overgrown vines. Palm trees and lush green vegetation had taken over, but Strife had no problem finding a path through it until we found the center of the island. The large stones here formed a circle around a thin sliver of light, shining like a ray of pure sunshine, suspended in midair. Just a tiny tear in the veil between the worlds, but it was enough.

Strife pawed impatiently at the sandy dirt with his hoofs and blew fiery air out his nose. I felt it too. *Humanity*. Desperation and decay, with a strong tinge of passion and fear. The feel of their world beckoned me toward it. I'd found my way to Earth. Soon I would have my revenge, my glorious retribution.

I touched the sliver of light and pushed my power into it, drawing on the considerable reserves available to me as War. Old magic formed a barrier between the worlds, and I sliced through it, tearing the hole wider. Light burst through as I ripped the jagged portal open, until it was big enough to walk through.

Strife charged forward without hesitation and we passed

through the portal. His hoofs splashed against the water as we emerged on Earth in the middle of the ocean, the island reclaimed by the dark depths of the sea long ago. I drew in a deep breath of crisp salty air, as the sun sank below the horizon and the sky darkened. Finally, the glorious night.

The stars and moon appeared overhead as Strife galloped forward across the dark blue waters. Toward my kingdom in Las Vegas. Toward the woman.

It was time to get my revenge and retake my throne. Then my apocalypse could begin.

2

HANNAH

L as Vegas heat was intense in May, but as an angel, I reveled in it. The warmth from the bright sun overhead was one of my few comforts these days. If I was being honest, life had been a bitch since I'd trapped Lucifer in Heaven. With War possessing him, he was safest there. I knew that, but I hated every second he was gone, and until I could find a way to save him from himself, I didn't see that changing anytime soon.

Six fucking months and still no sign of a solution. It didn't help that for the first three of those I'd done little more than sleep and puke my guts up. Morning sickness, afternoon sickness, evening sickness, all the damn time sickness, and my body didn't care that Lucifer was gone and someone had to step up to rule.

That person was me, of course. Pregnant, exhausted, heart-broken me. I'd barely managed to keep things together, but somehow I did it.

I became the Demon Queen.

With a lot of help from my friends. All of them pitched in during my time of need, going above and beyond in their efforts, and I couldn't have done it without them. Azazel protected me and kept me from losing my sanity. Samael and his assistant Einial ran the business side of things and kept the other Archdemons happy. Olivia and her angelic mates became my intermediaries with the angels, while my youngest son Kassiel helped me research everything I could about the Four Horsemen. They were all family—but they couldn't fill the void that Lucifer had left.

I took a deep breath and inhaled the floral scent around me from the other project that had kept me busy over the last few months— Persephone's Garden. The Celestial Resort and Casino's newest relaxation zone was almost ready to be revealed to the public in all its glory. There was nothing else like it on the Vegas Strip, a lush expanse of green with bursts of color forming a tranquil oasis in the middle of the desert city. Nature doing her thing with a little help from me. I'd included all my favorite plants, from olive trees and weeping figs, to lilies, violets, and irises. My favorite spot was a stone bench surrounded by Persephone's signature flower, the narcissus, better known as the daffodil.

There was only one last thing to complete—the magnificent waterfall. I moved along the path toward it, letting the fine spray soothe my heated skin. Once it was finished, the waterfall would become a gateway, allowing guests to walk underneath it to access other parts of the garden. The only thing unfinished was the secret cave behind it, which would not be for hotel guests, but possibly the most important thing I'd ever built.

Pride filled my chest. Lucifer had given me this space and I'd found my happy place in creating this garden over the past few months. I'd filled it with life and beauty, and although I could only just now bear the scent of some of the flowers, it was *my* place. Somewhere I could be fully me, with no demands on my time or my energy, where I could be alone with my tumultuous thoughts.

Or nearly alone. Even now, my ever-present gargoyle guard had fanned out into whatever pattern they'd determined would best protect me in this space. They weren't intrusive, but they were always nearby, usually in their human forms so as not to scare the hotel guests. Should any threat arise, they'd instantly sprout wings and talons, their skin turning to stone as they protected my life, and that of the precious cargo I carried.

The irony of it all didn't escape me. It wasn't all that long ago that I'd killed gargoyle after gargoyle in the penthouse when they'd attacked me, and now they were my biggest line of defense. How things had changed.

"Hannah," Azazel's voice called out from across the garden. She was near the lilies, and she carried their scent as she approached.

I stroked my hand idly over my bump and turned to face my best friend. As I did, my daughter kicked against me, and I smiled at the reminder of her presence. But then my smile faded as I wished Lucifer could be here for this, to experience her first movements and the joy she brought. I was nearly at the end of the second trimester. He'd already missed so much. I'd never even had a chance to tell him I was pregnant, let alone with a daughter.

"The Archdemons have gathered for the meeting," Azazel said. Her thick hair was braided down her back and her dark skin gleamed under the setting sun, though she squinted against it even in her sunglasses. The hour was later than I'd realized, and soon it would be dark. That was when the demons came out in Las Vegas. My demons.

I nodded but winced a little as my baby kicked again, this time right in the ribs. She was a strong one already. Much like the daughter we'd lost once before. Sometimes I wondered if this was the same soul come back to me, giving me a second chance to be her mother. There was no way to know of course, but the idea brought me a tiny bit of peace.

This time I wouldn't lose her. This time, if Adam tried to hurt her, I'd rip his fucking throat out. And this time, he'd stay dead.

Zel noticed me wince, and her hands immediately moved to her waist, the hilts of her daggers against her palms. "Is everything okay?"

Theo, the captain of my gargoyle guard, appeared beside us as if summoned by Zel's concern. He was tall and muscular, with black hair and a slight French accent, and his hands were already turning to claws. "Did you sense a threat?"

I shook my head and flashed them both a quick smile. By now I was used to them being overprotective, even if it could be annoying sometimes. "No, it's nothing. I'm fine."

Theo gave a cursory look around the garden anyway. "Let me know if you need anything, my queen."

"I will, thank you."

He bowed stiffly, then retreated again. Theo was the younger brother of Romana, the new gargoyle Archdemon. Their mother, Belphegor, had conspired against Lucifer in a plot to overthrow him, but Romana and Theo had chosen a different path after her death. They'd sworn loyalty to Lucifer, and now served me in his absence. A good thing too, because the gargoyles had proven to be the only people immune to Pestilence's plague attacks as long as they were in their stone form. That was one of the reasons Azazel had chosen them for my security. A smart move, since Pestilence aka Adam came for me three months ago.

It was hard to tell how much of him was Adam anymore versus Pestilence. They seemed to have merged into one horrid entity hell-bent on destroying the world...and taking me as their prize. I supposed that meant there was still some of Adam left in there, which gave me hope for Lucifer too.

There was no way I was letting Adam take me, and I'd burn the whole world down before I let him hurt this baby. He'd already taken a daughter from me once, but never again. So when he came for me, as I knew he would, I was ready. My unusual mix of light and darkness powers had only grown stronger with my pregnancy, and my gargoyles and I managed to fight Adam off, weakening him enough that he had no chance but to turn tail and run. No one had seen him since.

Probably a good thing, since before his attack he'd been making people sick all over the country. With Archangel Raphael's help, I'd formed a task force comprised of angelic healers and gargoyle warriors, who worked to clean up the chaos Pestilence caused. It was only a matter of time before he emerged again, and when he did, we would be ready. I glanced back at the waterfall, peering past the water at the cave behind it. A cave with a tomb inside it strong enough to hold an Elder God.

Or so we hoped.

3

HANNAH

I walked, or perhaps slightly wobbled, into the meeting room with Zel at my side. I tried to appear cool, calm, and confident, hoping I looked like I knew what I was doing, even while my daughter continued to press against my ribs in the most uncomfortable way. Life didn't stop when you were pregnant, especially when you had a kingdom of demons to rule.

Samael was already there, along with the Archdemons Lilith, Baal, and Romana, to represent the Lilim, vampires, and gargoyles, respectively. I nodded to each of them as I took my seat at the head of the long table, but I couldn't ignore the fact that there should have been three more Archdemons present. The dragons were still staying away, remaining neutral after the death of their leader, Mammon. His son, Valefar, had not officially stepped up as Archdemon yet, and I suspected he was waiting to see what happened before he chose a side. The dragons' numbers were so low that I couldn't blame him for being cautious, even if I hoped he would join us.

The other two Archdemons, on the other hand, would not be welcome even if they came crawling back at this point. Nemesis, Archdemon of the imps, and Fenrir, Archdemon of the shifters, had gone too far in their attempts to overthrow Lucifer. They couldn't be forgiven for what they'd done. If it weren't for them, Pestilence and War wouldn't be released, and Lucifer would still be here. Of course, some of the blame also rested on my oldest son, Belial. He'd been the mastermind behind it all, at least at first, but I hadn't seen him since we'd trapped his father in Heaven. He appeared to have turned a corner at the end of that battle, as if he might have regretted acting against his father, but his continued absence troubled me. Now I wasn't sure where his loyalties lay.

Samael's dark eyes met mine in a silent question, asking if I was all right, asking if we could begin. He'd become indispensable to me in these last few months, a true friend I could depend on for anything, even though I knew he was hurting too. He wasn't one to show emotions, but Lucifer was his oldest friend, and he dearly missed him also. I gave him a slight inclination of my head, signaling I was ready.

Samael nodded to me and cleared his throat. "Now that our queen is here, we can begin. May I have everyone's attention?"

"You *always* have my attention," Lilith murmured as she gave him a little wink. As usual, she looked gorgeous with her dark curls and blood red lips, her green eyes accentuated by a low-cut dress of the same color. As the oldest succubus, she oozed sensuality even without trying, a perfect representative for the sin of lust.

Samael allowed his gaze to linger on her, but his eyes turned hard as they moved to her lover, the vampire Archdemon Baal. Samael and Lilith had been an item thousands of years ago, and so much history between them led to a lot of unresolved issues. Not least of which centered around their son, Asmodeus, and the fact Lilith had turned him mortal so he could be with my human friend, Brandy. I wasn't sure Samael would ever get over that, or accept that he would absolutely lose his son one day. Even so, it was impossible to ignore the way Samael and Lilith looked at each other, and as a succubus, Lilith needed more than one lover to keep her sated. I secretly hoped the two of them could work out their issues one day, but Samael was pretty damn hard-headed sometimes.

"Thank you for coming." I leveled my gaze at each of my

Archdemons, who inclined their heads slightly in return. Even though I'd been born as an angel in this life, they'd all accepted me as their queen over these last few months, and I appreciated their loyalty. With their acceptance, the other demons had fallen in line too, and no one had questioned my position so far. "Has anyone learned anything regarding the whereabouts of Pestilence?"

Romana growled a little at the mention of the man who killed her mother. Like her brother, she had black hair, stony gray eyes, and a slight French accent, and she wore a skintight bodysuit. "No, nothing. My gargoyles have been searching for him, but he must be laying low and recovering his strength after his attack on you."

Zel leaned back in her chair and crossed her arms. "Do you think he plans to free Famine and Death next?"

"It's unclear what he wants, other than Hannah," Lilith said with a slight shake of her head.

"I've recently learned that Fenrir and Nemesis still plan to release the other Horsemen," Baal said, as he ran a hand through his long black hair. His British accent made me think of Lucifer with a pang in my chest, though Baal's was much more formal, to go with his antiquated black suit. Baal had been spying on the imps and the shifters for us, pretending to be their ally in this conflict, even though it was risky. "Though their attempt to overthrow Lucifer was thwarted when he became War, they've regrouped and decided on their next steps."

"What is their plan now?" I raised an eyebrow. Of course they had a plan B. I wouldn't have expected anything less from Nemesis and Fenrir.

Baal turned his icy blue eyes on me. "They're going to Faerie to release Famine in the hopes of taking you down. They have an issue with you becoming our queen, as you can probably imagine."

"No surprise there," I muttered.

"They'll have an issue with anyone sitting on the throne who isn't one of them," Zel said with a snort.

"Yes, and if somehow they did succeed, they would turn on each other next," Baal said. "They have no loyalty to each other either."

"Do you know if Belial is working with them?" I asked, though I was almost afraid to hear the answer.

Baal shook his head. "No, I haven't heard them speak of him lately. I don't think he's involved with them anymore."

That was a relief. Perhaps there was still some hope for my son.

Samael steepled his fingers. "We've already been working with High King Oberon to protect Famine's tomb in Faerie. Should Fenrir or Nemesis arrive in that realm, we'll be notified immediately."

"We must be prepared to do battle against not one, but potentially three Horsemen," Romana said with a slight growl. "And if the fourth one is freed, we are all doomed."

The thought of fighting Lucifer made my heart clench, but of course she was right. I had no idea if there was anything left of my mate in there now that War had possessed him, though I refused to give up hope. I pressed my hands against the table and addressed the others. "We're doing everything in our power to prevent that outcome. We have a tomb prepared to hold Pestilence, should he return here. War is trapped in Heaven, and all the keys to that realm have been hidden."

"What if he escapes?" Lilith asked softly, with a touch of sadness.

I swallowed hard. "I'll try to save him, however I can. And if I can't...then I'll stop him. Do not worry. I'll do whatever has to be done."

Silence fell upon the table as we all looked at each other with grave expressions. None of us wanted to take down Lucifer, but we all knew it might have to be done to stop War. I'd been preparing myself for the horrible possibility for months now. Would I kill Lucifer if it was the only way to stop him? Yes. But I'd do everything in my power to find another way first.

The meeting closed out with more general demon issues, and when the Archdemons left, I breathed a sigh of relief and headed back to the penthouse to relax. As I entered, my first instinct was always to wonder what Lucifer would think of the changes I'd wrought in his absence. Nothing major, just a touch of my own style here and there. A few lush plants and more color, especially greens and blues, with comfortable pillows and throws draped across the furniture. It was a lot more soothing now, which both the baby and I desperately needed during these trying times.

I trailed my fingers over the fronds of a fern as I headed straight to the library. It had long been my favorite room, but now I glanced at the huge pile of books I'd been studying each night, and even my soul sighed. It was a mammoth task, but it was for Lucifer. For him, I'd do this every night for the rest of my life.

I opened my notebook and glanced at the latest I'd learned about the Elder Gods and the Four Horsemen. None of it seemed very hopeful. The Elder Gods couldn't be destroyed because they were ancient and primordial, representing basic components of the universe such as light and darkness, death and life. Just as one could never completely eliminate pestilence, war, famine, and death from the world, so too could those Elder Gods never be truly defeated. But they weren't all-powerful. For one thing, much like the fae, they couldn't lie. Of course, they were probably as tricky as fae too. Or even worse.

For another thing, outside of Void they required host bodies if they wanted to be corporeal. In addition, the Horsemen required a sacrifice from that host in exchange for giving them all the powers of a god, although I wasn't sure if that was true of all the Elder Gods. Pestilence required a sacrifice of the heart, which Adam had given when he'd killed his lover Belphegor. War needed a sacrifice of the mind, and it seemed he had taken Lucifer's memories of me as his payment. Famine supposedly asked for a sacrifice of the body, while Death needed a sacrifice of the soul—whatever that meant.

Not for the first time, regret and guilt squeezed my chest for trapping Lucifer in Heaven, but I'd had no other choice at the time. I couldn't let him come to Earth, not once I saw that War had taken over and turned my mate into someone else. Someone I didn't recognize...who didn't recognize me.

We were running out of options and out of time. At some point, we'd have to stop at least one of the Horsemen, if not all of them. We had the tomb in my garden, taken from Stonehenge and repurposed, but we weren't sure if it would truly hold an Elder God for long. It might contain Pestilence for some time, but what of the others? War was still out there, and Famine might be released soon. We might be able to defeat them—but if Death was released, I feared we would be completely screwed.

I flipped open one of the old tomes that described the Elder Gods during the ancient times when all the different realms were connected. In those days, Elder Gods often fought and defeated each other. They couldn't be totally destroyed, but they could be subdued and removed from their hosts, which gave me some small amount of hope, although it was mixed with a heavy dash of terror.

I was starting to think the only way to save Lucifer was for one of us to take control of another Elder God. Of course, that would require a sacrifice, and there was no guarantee whoever did it would be strong enough to not be consumed by the god in the process. Or that they wouldn't need saving, once they too became a monster.

No, there had to be another way to get through to Lucifer. I just needed to keep reading through all these books, and surely I would find something. I had to.

I was the only one who could save Lucifer from himself.

I sighed and got up, stretching my aching body, then headed back into the main part of the penthouse and to the kitchen to grab myself something to eat. I had a feeling it would be a long night, and I was starving again. As I opened the fridge and began scanning the shelves, something caught my attention, something tugging against my soul, and I turned around.

With a boom that seemed to shake the entire building, the huge windows overlooking The Strip burst in, raining glass all over the penthouse. Instinctively I threw up a wall of darkness woven with light to protect myself from the blast, and when I lowered it, my mouth fell open. Framed between jagged shards of hanging glass was my mate, the person I most wanted and most dreaded to see.

I scrambled back toward the other side of the room, my voice trapped in my throat, preventing me from screaming for my guards. This couldn't be happening. It was too soon. We hadn't worked out a plan yet.

Lucifer's black wings spread wide, and anger and hatred burst out of his skin with an ominous red light, the same color as his eyes. Eyes that fixed on me with such fury it made my hands tremble and my pulse spike.

Lucifer had arrived—and he looked like he wanted to murder me.

4

LUCIFER

I roared, making the walls shake as I landed inside the penthouse. My throne room, now defiled by the blond woman in front of me. How dare she lay claim to my seat of power and then turn it into a fucking garden. Everywhere I turned, there were more flowers, and the air smelled of nature. I could almost hear the plants growing. Another reason to end her. Slowly. Painfully. While she begged for mercy on her knees.

"What the fuck do you think you're doing here?" I asked, as I stalked across the room. The pull toward her was irresistible, and I devoured the sight of her full hips, heaving breasts, and lush lips. I sensed her fear, and it was intoxicating. Damn right she should fear me. All living things should. "You locked me in Heaven and now you claim my home as your own?"

Even with terror coursing through her veins, she stood straighter, defiantly staring back at me with those magnetic blue eyes, while her hand lingered protectively over her belly. "No, Lucifer. I live here—with you. This is *our* home. Don't you remember?"

"Liar!" I yelled.

Her eyes widened like she knew what I was about to do before I conjured a sword made of hellfire and shadows. It was darkness wreathed in red fury, and power coursed through me when I held it over her. But as I looked down at her face, that beautiful face that had haunted me for months, my sword never fell. My grip tightened around it, but I couldn't deliver the killing blow.

Something stopped me from ending her. And worst of all, she knew it.

Instead of screaming in fear and running away, she stepped closer, so close I could smell her. Flowers, vanilla, and something else, something primal and all feminine that made my cock harden.

"Lucifer, put the sword away," she said. "Remember who you are. Remember *me*."

"I know exactly who I am," I growled. "And you will die."

"No, I won't. You can't kill me." She put her hands on my shoulders, and the sword I held vanished like smoke. "You won't."

I wrapped my hand around her throat, but my fingers wouldn't tighten. Instead my grip became more of a caress, and she sighed and closed her eyes. As if she *liked* it. How could she possibly crave my touch? And the more important question—why did I crave hers even more?

"Who are you, woman?"

She reached up and stroked my face tenderly, as she looked at me with something I didn't understand. Her touch was a bolt of electricity that stormed through me, lighting me up in a way the anger and the hatred didn't. "I'm Hannah, your mate. Your queen. From the dawn of time, we've been bound together by fate. You sacrificed your memories of me when you became War, but I know, deep down, the man I love is still in there."

She was wrong. I was Lucifer and War and there was no room for love in my wrathful heart. Especially not for an angel. Yet her touch stirred something in me, and my hand slid from her neck down to her breasts, while I watched her lips part with a soft gasp. At the sound, my other hand grabbed her hip possessively and pulled her against me, before I realized what I was doing.

Then she was in my arms and my mouth was on hers, my lips rough and demanding, crushing hers as I stole her breath. My tongue stroked the warm, wet softness of her mouth as I deepened the kiss further, backing her against the wall, one arm wrapped around her, one hand resting on her hip. Everything about kissing this woman felt right, and I couldn't get enough of her. From the way she kissed me back and clung to my shoulders, she felt it too. How?

I didn't know. Didn't care. I had to have her. My cock demanded to be sheathed inside of her, and I would pound her hard until I had answers. I nudged her legs wide, sliding a hand between her thighs, finding her wet and ready. She gasped and arched against me, and I let out a low hum of satisfaction. Soon I'd make her scream my name.

I ripped her loose dress down the front, exposing her bra and panties, but then I saw the fullness of her belly and paused.

Fuck. The woman was *pregnant*.

My hand came to rest across her abdomen and I felt the life growing inside of her. It called out to me, filling me with an unmistakable truth.

Mine.

The woman carried a life. And not just any child, but one my blood recognized as its own.

Impossible.

I stumbled back, forcing my eyes up to her face. "How?"

She looked almost sad as she stared back at me. "It's yours, Lucifer. But you know that, don't you?"

"It can't be. I would never breed with a filthy angel!"

She sighed and reached for me again, but I drew away. I couldn't trust her. I didn't know her. She was nothing to me. Yet somehow she carried my child within her. What. The. Fuck.

"You can fight this," she said, stepping closer to me. "Fight it for me. For your daughter. For us."

Daughter? I didn't know what she was talking about, but something wasn't right about this. Conflicting thoughts and emotions warred for control in me, making me unable to tell what was true or not. She had tricked me somehow, confusing my thoughts, and I had to get away to make sense of it all.

My wings snapped out and I let the familiar anger and hatred fill me. Yes, that was better. That was real. That was *me*.

Without another glance, I launched myself out through the broken windows, the taste of her still on my lips. I couldn't kill the woman, not while she carried my child.

But I would return.

5

HANNAH

Damn, I almost got through to Lucifer.

I stared through the shattered windows where his red glowing wings had carried him into the night. He'd come here to kill me, I had no doubt about that, but he couldn't do it. Even though he didn't remember me, he'd felt the mate bond thrumming between us, pulling him toward me until it was impossible to resist. When he kissed me, I felt my Lucifer shining through, and I knew he wasn't all lost. He could still be saved—but I had to do it quickly before he started another war between angels and demons, or something worse, something I couldn't even fathom.

There was only one way—I'd have to use Famine to take War down.

The penthouse door burst open and Theo ran inside, followed by the other gargoyles in my guard. I hastily grabbed my ripped dress and tried to cover myself up, but my hands trembled and my heart pounded so loudly I could barely hear Theo's words.

"My queen, are you all right?" Theo had his sword out and he gripped my elbow protectively, ready to guard my body with his own while his gargoyles scoured the penthouse and took to the skies to search for the threat.

"I'm okay," I said, trying to pull myself together as I looked down at the glass all over the floor. Those poor windows had been replaced more times than I could count at this point. "I'm not injured. Just shaken, that's all."

"Who did this?" he asked.

I hesitated, but there was no hiding this from Theo or anyone else in my inner circle. "It was Lucifer."

Theo swore under his breath in French. "He escaped? Where did he go?"

"I don't know."

Azazel flew through the front window, a murderous look on her face. "I'm going to kill him," she muttered as she landed and her wings disappeared. She took one look at me in my ripped dress and narrowed her eyes. "What did he do?"

"Nothing. I'm fine." Lifting my still-shaking hand to my lips, I ignored the slight sting his rough kisses had produced. There was no denying how much his touch had turned me on, and that had a lot to do with why I was still trembling. I'd missed Lucifer so much over these last few months, and with these pregnancy hormones raging inside me, I'd been unable to stop my body from reacting to him. Even now, need pulsed between my thighs, begging for him to return and finish what we started.

Zel didn't look convinced. "The baby?"

I rubbed my bump and was rewarded with the familiar feeling of her rolling over. "She's fine too. He didn't hurt us. He never would."

Zel crossed her arms. "We don't know that for sure."

"We'll double our guards immediately," Theo said, his head bowed. "I apologize, my queen. This should never have happened. I'll investigate immediately why my gargoyles weren't here to defend you."

I waved his apology away. "As impressive as your guard is, I don't think any of them could have stopped Lucifer tonight. But I nearly got through to him, which means there is hope."

Zel's face softened. "Hannah, I know you think that, but—"

I held up a hand to stop her protest. "I *will* find a way to save him. Call a meeting immediately with all my advisors. We have a lot to discuss and only a short time to develop a plan."

———

L ess than an hour later, I sat in a rocking chair Zel had turned up with one day for the nursery, which had once been my bedroom in the penthouse, and then my office. She'd given no explanation, but the chair was plush and comfortable, and I'd loved sitting in it ever since. It had been a sweet gesture on her part, and it was the only thing in this room so far. I hadn't decorated the nursery yet —mainly because I kept stupidly hoping Lucifer would do it with me. Maybe such hope was foolish, but I couldn't allow myself to give up on it. If I did, I would truly sink into despair, and I'd had enough of that already in all my lifetimes.

Zel poked her head in the door. "They're here."

I joined everyone in the dining area of the penthouse, which had been cleared of glass already, and sat at the head of the table with the people who had been willing to drop everything to rush to my side. Samael and Einial, of course, plus Azazel and Theo, along with my youngest son Kassiel, his mate Olivia, and her other men, Callan, Bastien, and Marcus. They'd become my inner circle over these past few months. "Thank you for coming on such short notice."

"What happened here?" Kassiel asked, his green eyes filled with worry as he took in the broken windows. Pride and love filled my chest when I looked at my youngest son, with a touch of grief because he resembled his father so much. Our youngest son was truly the best of both of us—smart, loyal, and brave, and always fighting for peace.

There was no sugarcoating what happened, so I simply said, "Lucifer has broken out of Heaven."

Many around the table gasped or widened their eyes in shock, but Samael simply asked, "How?"

"I don't know."

"What did he want?" Olivia asked.

I let out a weary sigh. "I think he wanted to kill me, but he couldn't do it. Even though he didn't remember me, he knew me on some level. When he discovered I was carrying his child, he seemed...confused. Or conflicted. Then he left."

"Any idea where he might go next?" Callan asked. He was a fierce angelic warrior and the son of my sister, Jophiel, who had died while protecting me from Pestilence. Since then, Callan and I had grown closer, clinging to what family we had left.

Bastien, another angel and always the logical one in the group, stroked his chin. "Considering last time he tried to reignite the war between angels and demons, I suspect wherever he's going, it won't be good."

"Don't forget he can also turn people into frenzied warriors," Marcus added, reminding me of those final moments in Heaven and the chaos Lucifer had caused. As a Malakim healer, Marcus had been one of the angels responsible for dealing with the aftermath of that fight.

"All the more reason he needs to be stopped immediately," Zel said.

Kassiel turned to her. "Or saved."

Zel scowled. "We'll see."

I pinched my brow, fighting off exhaustion. "Lucifer is a threat, there's no denying that. Before we do anything else, we need to warn Archangel Gabriel that Lucifer is back on Earth."

Einial spoke up for the first time. "I'll get right on that."

"Thank you." I nodded to her before continuing. "I don't know if there is a way to save Lucifer or not, but we're going to try. I did come across something in my research that has given me hope. We might be able to use another Elder God to subdue War and free Lucifer. Which means we need to go to Faerie immediately."

"You want to free Famine?" Kassiel asked, his eyes filling with horror.

"I do, yes. Before Nemesis and Fenrir do it first."

"No way," Callan slammed his hands on the table. "This is way too dangerous. Especially for you in your current state."

"It's the only option we have right now," I said. Callan had lost both his parents, and I understood that he couldn't bear the thought of losing me or his future cousin either. My nephew tended to be overprotective of those he loved anyway, but even so, he couldn't stop me from doing what I had to do. No one could. "If we release Famine ourselves, we can control the situation."

"But one of us will have to make a sacrifice to host Famine," Olivia said in a quiet voice.

"I'll do it," Kassiel said, and everyone else at the table chimed in offering their bodies instead. Warmth filled my chest, along with a heavy dose of sadness. There was so much love at this table. So much bravery. I couldn't bear to lose any of them either.

Zel rose to her feet. "It has to be me. I'm the oldest and strongest, and unlike the others here, I have nothing to lose." Her dark eyes turned to me, glimmering with both pain and determination. "You know it's true."

I pressed my lips together, but then nodded. Azazel was a good choice, as much as I hated to admit it. She was one of the few who might be able to control the Elder God inside her, and unlike the others, she wasn't in a relationship. She'd lost her fated mate years ago, and as far as I could tell, she had never truly gotten over it. I wasn't sure she could.

But she was also my oldest and dearest friend, who had stood by my side for centuries, across hundreds of different lives. What if she became a monster like Lucifer? Would I have to stop her next?

The thought brought tears to my eyes, but I knew she was right too—it had to be her.

"It's decided then," I said. "Azazel will become Famine's host. Einial, please send a message to High King Oberon informing him we will need admittance to Faerie as soon as possible."

"I'm going with you," Kassiel said. "And we'll need to get Damien too."

My chest tightened at the thought of finally seeing my other son. I'd wanted to visit him in Faerie for months now, but it had never worked out with everything else going on. Now we needed him—Damien was one of the only people who could open Famine's tomb.

"Before you go, let me check on you," Marcus said, rising to his feet. "Are you sure you're not injured from Lucifer's attack?"

"I'm fine," I said, for what felt like the hundredth time. No one seemed to believe that Lucifer had never really been a threat to me. Or that I could take care of myself, even while pregnant.

"You should let him check you out, Mom," Kassiel said. "Or at least check the baby. We want to make sure you're both fit to travel to Faerie."

"Okay, okay." Yes, I was six months pregnant, but I was also an immortal being with Archangel blood and memories dating back thousands of years. I wasn't exactly fragile. But I knew their concern was only a sign of love, so I made myself let it go.

Marcus walked around the table to crouch beside me. I turned enough for him to put his hand on my bump, and a soft white glow emitted from his palms. "Your daughter is strong and powerful. Just like you."

"Thank you." I let out a slight sigh of relief. Not that I'd been worried, but after losing a daughter before, it was always a comfort to know this one was doing well.

"I should go with you too," Marcus said, as he stood up. "Just to be safe."

"No, I need you to stay here in case Pestilence returns," I said. "If he does, the people at this hotel will need your healing desperately. You'll remain, along with Olivia, Bastien, and Callan."

Callan jumped to his feet. "Fuck that. I'm coming with you. The others can stay, but you need at least one angel with you. That's my cousin in there, after all."

I pressed my lips together, but then reluctantly nodded. I should have known he would be eager to go with me as soon as I told them my plan. "All right, and we'll take some of the gargoyles too. Samael and Einial, I need you to keep things running here while I'm gone."

"Of course," Samael said. "We'll be prepared in case Adam or Lucifer should return."

For their sake, I prayed that didn't happen, or I might not have a kingdom left once I returned from Faerie.

6

LUCIFER

A thin sliver of moon hanging over California lit my way as I galloped toward Angel Peak, a small angel-only town where Archangel Gabriel currently resided. Like a fool, I'd once made peace with the angels, but War had shown me the error of my ways —and now it was time to start that ancient battle once again. It was eternal and endless, the conflict between light and dark, good and evil, day and night. It was not about the victor, but about the fight itself, and it must continue.

The angel woman, the one living among the demons and carrying my child, she wouldn't want war. Somehow I was certain of that. But what she wanted didn't matter. All that mattered was bringing the angels to their knees. Then the humans, and the fae after that.

Using my powers of darkness made concealing myself easy in the shadows of the night as Strife rocketed through towns, down highways, and over large swathes of land. It felt like no time at all before we stopped in the front yard of Gabriel's quaint little mountain home, situated near Seraphim Academy, where all the good little angel boys and girls went to school.

"Gabriel!" I thundered as Strife cantered around the house. "Show yourself!"

When I reached the back porch, I found him waiting for me. Gabriel was sipping a beer and seemed to be expecting me. With his sandy hair, faded jeans, and friendly face he looked like someone's favorite uncle, not the leader of all of angelkind.

"Hello, Lucifer," he said in a sad voice. A *weak* voice. "They told me you'd found a way out of Heaven. I wondered if you'd pay me a visit."

"We have unfinished business between the two of us." I jumped from Strife and he reared back with a loud squeal, then thundered away. He'd return when I needed him.

"You want a beer?" Gabriel asked, before holding one out to me.

I narrowed my eyes at him, wondering if this was some kind of trick. Did he think he could poison me? Or was his plan to make me drop my guard in the hopes of surprising me with an attack? Surely he knew that wouldn't work. "No, I don't want a fucking beer. I'm here to declare war against your people."

Gabriel let out a long sigh. "And here I thought we were friends."

"Friends?" I spat on the ground. "We've been enemies since the Elder Gods made us."

"That's not true and you know it. We were friends long ago in Heaven, before you turned your back on us and left for Hell. Sure, we had a few years where we didn't see eye to eye for a while and kept trying to kill each other, but then we became friends again after the war ended. Besides, our children are in love. That makes us family now."

"Children?" I bristled at that. "I have no children."

Gabriel whistled softly. "Damn, War's really done a number on your head, hasn't he? It's bad enough he made you forget Hannah, but to forget your own sons...that's truly evil."

Sons. Plural. How was that possible? How could I not remember any of that? Something wasn't right. Something big was missing from my past, and I needed it back. I raged inside, fighting at

War's hold as I searched for answers, but he was too strong. The anger overtook me again and all I knew was fury.

"Enough of your lies!" The sky had begun to turn purple near the horizon, a sign of the coming dawn. With War inside me, I had no fear of being overpowered by Gabriel, but I wanted to get this over with already. I forged my sword of hellfire and shadow and pointed it at the Archangel. "As King of Demons, I declare war against the angels. Prepare your people for battle."

Gabriel rose to his feet and his silvery wings spread out behind him. "I cannot do that, Lucifer. You know I would never willingly send my people to war against the demons again. Just like you would never go to war against us again if you were in your right mind. We both know what it cost us last time. We lost Heaven and Hell, and for what? Our pride?"

Fury coursed through me as I raised the sword. "If the angels won't fight willingly, then I'll make them. I'll destroy your towns. Your schools. Your homes. War will come to your people, and once I slaughter everyone they love, they'll have no choice but to fight back —or surrender like the cowards they are." Hatred for this angel who thought himself good and pure tightened my chest. In reality, he was spineless, unable to win a war he'd fought for a millennia. Now he tried to trick and taunt me with his words of deception and peace. Friends? How could I possibly be friends with one such as him? "But first, you will bow."

Walking forward, I released my War powers toward Gabriel, sending my rage into his own mind. Gabriel was strong, probably one of the strongest minds I'd ever encountered, but I'd controlled him before, and I could do it again. And after a few minutes of struggling, even the mighty Archangel Gabriel gave in.

Weak. Pathetic. Like all the angels were.

No, not all of them. The woman who'd locked me in Heaven wasn't weak. She'd fought back against me. And now that she carried my child inside her she would only be stronger.

I forced all thoughts of her from my mind as I fueled rage into Gabriel, until his eyes and wings glowed with red light. His face filled with hatred as he looked upon me, and I knew if I released him, he'd go for my throat.

"The angels will prepare for war," he said. "Where shall we begin the battle?"

"In Las Vegas." It was the seat of demon power here on Earth, and if we took out some humans at the same time, even better. The woman was also there, but I'd deal with her. Somehow.

The Great War was beginning again, and soon it would consume the entire world.

7

HANNAH

I woke early the next day, adrenaline already coursing through my blood. Lucifer had forced our hand with his escape, but I was ready to rescue him. I had a plan now. Would it work? I had no clue. But I didn't have any other ideas, and we had to try something. I couldn't let my husband remain a monster any longer...or let him destroy this world and every other one.

I fluttered about the penthouse as I got everything ready, ate a healthy breakfast, and then went to don some battle gear for whatever we might face. Except maternity stores didn't exactly make armor for pregnant angels, so I settled for comfortable clothes I could easily move in instead. If everything went well, there should be no need to fight, but it was best to be prepared for the worst in situations like these.

I headed out to Persephone's Garden with a thick circle of gargoyle warriors around me. The attack from Lucifer had shamed them, though I'd learned that Lucifer had used his War powers to cloud and confuse their minds. They'd never stood a chance against him anyway—better for everyone that they'd stayed away. Even so, Theo had been extra vigilant ever since, and I feared I'd never get a moment of privacy again.

When I arrived at my favorite bench, I was shocked to find someone else sitting on it—Belial. My eldest son wore a black t-shirt that showed off his muscles and tattoos, along with dark faded jeans and combat boots. If you didn't know better you might mistake him for his father, except Lucifer would never be caught dead in that outfit.

He stood when I approached, and my guard immediately surrounded him with swords and claws, some quickly shifting to their gargoyle forms. Belial looked unfazed by it all and didn't even bother to unsheath Morningstar, the sword strapped to his back that had once been his father's.

I rushed forward and belted out a command. "Stop! That's my son!"

"He's a traitor," Theo said, narrowing his eyes at Belial. "He's a *threat*."

"He's not a threat to me." I waved them off, and the gargoyles reluctantly lowered their weapons and backed away. I moved closer to my son and took him in. "What are you doing here? Where have you been?"

"You're looking good, Mother," Belial said, his eyes dropping briefly to my stomach. Then he looked at me again with a challenge in his gaze. "I heard you're going to Faerie. I'm coming too."

"How did you hear that?" I bristled, wondering if we had a spy in our midst. Belial clearly had been keeping tabs on me since he didn't seem surprised by my pregnancy, and he knew to be here at exactly the time of our departure. Someone was giving him information. Who was it—Samael? Einial? Definitely not Azazel, she hated him...

He gave a small shrug. "I have my ways."

Stubborn child. I bet it was Kassiel. They were brothers, after all.

I sighed and crossed my arms. "Why do you even want to come? How do we know we can trust you?"

Belial's jaw clenched. "It's because of me that Pestilence is freed, and I planned to make it right by becoming War and taking Adam down. Father ruined that, and now he needs saving too. If you're going to use Famine to fight him, I want to be there."

"What of Nemesis and Fenrir?"

"I'm not working with them anymore."

His words rang with truth, and I checked his aura and saw no other hidden lies or deceptions there. I nodded slowly, knowing the others wouldn't like it, but unable to deny how relieved I was to see my son again. He'd made a mistake—okay, a hell of a lot of mistakes. But he was still my son and I would always give him another chance.

I was about to tell him he could come with us, when Azazel rounded the corner with Callan and Kassiel. They were dressed for battle, and Zel let out a shout and rushed forward at the sight of Belial, daggers in hand. Callan growled and charged too, and this time Belial began reaching for Morningstar. Only Kassiel's quick movements blocked them before a fight broke out, his body moving to shield his brother from harm.

"What is *he* doing here?" Zel asked, her dark eyes flashing with anger.

I stood beside Kassiel in front of Belial. "He's coming with us."

Callan shook his head. "No way."

"I have to agree, my queen," Theo said. "My official position is also no."

"We should give him a chance," Kassiel said, his voice still calm and steady. Yes, it was definitely him who'd brought Belial here. They'd probably been talking for months, and though I was annoyed that Kassiel hadn't told me, I had to respect his loyalty to his brother.

"How can we trust him?" Callan asked.

"He spoke the truth when I questioned him." I cast a firm look at everyone standing before me, and channeled my authority as queen into my voice. "Belial's coming. That's my final decision."

Theo stiffly bowed, Callan scowled but nodded, and Zel regarded me with a stony expression, but in the end even she inclined her head. Belial just stood there with his arms crossed like he didn't give a damn about what was going on. A lie, of course. Though he might fool others with his uncaring facade, I knew his heart was in the right place and that he actually cared more than he would ever say.

As they all put their weapons away, Einial entered the garden with a woman with burnt orange streaks in her black hair, which was tied back to show off her pointed ears.

"This is Mirabella," Einial said. "One of our messengers to Faerie. She's half-Fallen, half-fae of the Autumn Court."

Mirabella dropped to a deep curtsy before me. "My queen, I'll be opening the portal to Faerie."

"Thank you," I told her. "Can you do it from here?"

She straightened up and nodded. "Time and space are different in that realm, so you don't need to go to a particular place before you cross over—all I have to do is focus on the destination, and the portal will take us there."

"Convenient," I said.

"I'll take you as close to High King Oberon's palace as I can. Are you ready, or do you need more time?"

I glanced at my companions briefly, but none of them had any protests. We were all here, and there was no reason to delay. "We're ready."

She nodded and removed a small gemstone from her pocket. It was similar to the one I'd used to open Heaven, but this one swirled with a rainbow of colors, all constantly shifting and changing in a pattern that was mesmerizing. She held it out before her and the colors shot out in a beam and formed a glowing portal, large enough for all of us to pass through. Einial stepped back, since she would be staying behind, while Theo and some of his soldiers went through first to ensure it was safe.

Once they'd determined there was no threat, I walked through the portal, discovering another world, one of nature and color and the heady perfume of flowers. A light spring rain fell upon us, and if I remembered correctly, that meant it was morning here also. Faerie was unique in that it went through every season over a twenty-four hour period, from blazing hot summer days to bitter cold winter nights.

We stood in the middle of a courtyard surrounded by white pillars wrapped in dark green ivy, and I looked up at the sky, so blue it almost sparkled like the ocean. To my surprise, Faerie felt like home, just like Heaven had. I breathed in the scents that drifted tantalizingly from the oversized blooms that grew up around us, and something woke inside me, unfurling and stretching, taking over.

Power.

I spread my fingers and tiny white flowers appeared before them, sprouting up from the dirt and grass at our feet, growing faster than was possible in nature. A strong breeze picked up, toying with the blades of grass, making the flowers dance, and I let out a bright laugh. As Persephone, I had been a princess of the Spring Court—and my powers had returned.

"What was that?" Callan asked.

"When Hannah was Persephone, she had the unique ability to make plants grow," Zel said, with a slight shake of her head. "You should have seen what she did to the palace in Hell."

"How are you getting these powers?" Belial asked. "First darkness, now this. You never had them in your other lives."

"I believe it's my Archangel gift, allowing me to tap into the powers from my past lives," I said, as I caused more plants to grow around us. Even when I'd believed I was human, I'd sought out plants and flowers, finding them soothing and restorative. I'd been unable to unlock this power until I felt Faerie's energy all around me, but it had been inside me all along—a reminder of my life as Persephone. My fae powers from the Spring Court were back too, allowing me to control air as well.

Kassiel nodded like he could follow my thoughts. "Yes, that makes sense. Jophiel's power made people forget. Your power is to remember."

My smile fell at the mention of my sister, but it did make a strange sort of sense. I'd recovered most of my memories from my previous lives, and now I was able to tap into those powers too. "Let's hope I can help Lucifer do the same."

Everyone had come through the portal now, with Mirabella stepping through last. The portal closed behind her and the gem in her hand dulled. "The High King lives in the castle at the top of that hill," she said, pointing ahead of us at a large mountain with a gleaming white fairy tale castle on top of it, with spires and arches and silver towers. "This is where messengers and other visitors wait to be granted entrance. Transport should arrive shortly."

"We could always just fly up there," Belial muttered.

"It's best to follow the High King's protocols," Mirabella said. "Those who cross him don't often survive."

"I met him once, and I have to agree," Kassiel added, his mouth twisting.

Zel rested her hands on her daggers. "Something's coming."

Shapes appeared on the horizon, and I shielded my eyes with my hand as I watched them approach. "What are they?"

"Griffins," Mirabella said. "From the High King's personal fleet. It's a great honor."

The beasts touched down in the courtyard, surprisingly light on their taloned feet and graceful for such large creatures. They had the bodies of lions and the wings and heads of eagles, and on their backs they had golden saddles with fae riders sitting in them. There was no mistaking the riders as anything other than fae, with their pointed ears, ethereal beauty, and unusually colored hair.

Most surprising of all—my son Damien rode at the front of them.

As he dismounted his griffin, I rushed toward him, unable to help myself. Of all my sons, Damien was the one who most resembled me—or at the least me when I had been Persephone. His eyes were the color of periwinkles and his hair was an indigo so dark it looked black until the light hit it and revealed the truth of his fae heritage. As a prince of the Spring Court, he wore a small crown of gold with jeweled flowers, along with a billowy black silk shirt and trousers, plain but obviously made by the finest tailors. He flashed me a charming smile as I approached, the one that had always made me forgive him no matter what he'd done—and he'd always been a very mischievous child.

"Damien!" I drew him close, my heart overflowing with love. It had been so many decades since I'd seen him last, in another life entirely. "Or should I call you Dionysus?"

He made a pained face and laughed. "No, I don't use that name any longer. Damien is fine."

I pulled back to really look at him, noticing a darkness in his gaze that had never been there before, though his smile never faltered. "I missed you so much."

"It's always too long between your lives. Though I heard Father put an end to the curse finally. Kassiel's told me a few things, but I'd love to hear about it from you."

I reached up to touch his glorious hair, so beautiful under the sun. "Yes, we have lots to catch up on."

"Indeed." He grinned and swatted my hand away from his hair. "Like how you're carrying my sister."

"It's weird, isn't it?" Kassiel asked, as he drew closer to us. "We've all lived for hundreds of years, yet now we're getting a baby sister."

"Not so weird to us," Belial said. "We went through it with you, after all."

"It's good to see you both again," Damien said, and the brothers all did those manly hugs that mostly consisted of back-patting and grunting. My heart melted at the sight of the three of them together for the first time in...well, probably centuries. Our family was finally reunited once again. The only person missing was Lucifer. I resolved once more to get him back, and to recreate this moment again with him at my side.

"Good to see *me*, you mean." Kassiel lifted his chin at Belial with a grin. "We're still not sure about this guy."

Damien arched an eyebrow. "What's he done now?"

"I'll tell you later," Kassiel said, while Belial scowled at them both.

"I look forward to the full report." Damien gestured toward the castle above us. "Right now the High King is waiting, and I suggest we make haste."

"Yes, we don't want to keep him waiting," I said. "Especially since I have a feeling we'll need his help."

"Then let's begin the next part of your journey." Damien stepped forward, placing his hand on my elbow. He led me toward the griffins, and the other fae riders stood and bowed their heads. We stopped in front of one that had been tethered to Damien's griffin and had no rider.

"I haven't seen griffins in so long." I reached out and allowed the griffin to nudge its head against my fingertips. Its warm breath fanned over my skin and its curved beak poked against my hand. Without warning, it dropped to its knees, turning its head inquisitively as it seemed to wait for my next move.

"She's accepted you," Damien said with a smile. "That's an invitation to climb on her back."

I ran my fingers through her luxurious white feathers as I settled onto soft, golden fur and a firm saddle. Like most magical beings of myth and legend, griffins were native to Faerie, and they served as transportation for the nobles of the different courts. "It's good to know I haven't lost my touch with magical beings after all these years."

Damien mounted the griffin beside me. "I never had any doubts."

My companions were seated behind the fae riders, and I was the only one honored with a griffin of my own. I hoped I remembered how to ride one.

Once everyone was settled on their griffins, our beasts leaped into the air and spread their wings, taking us toward the castle and one of the most dangerous men alive—the High King of the Fae.

8

HANNAH

We flew through the air toward Oberon's castle, and riding the griffin was entirely different from flying under the power of my own wings, with her sleek muscles flexing beneath my thighs and the steady beat of her wings sending currents of air to wash over me.

The castle loomed before us, sparkling in the sunlight as if the entire building was made of crystal. Perhaps it was. Turrets stretched high into the air, with colorful flags representing each of the different courts waving slowly against the blue sky. Even here there were trees and flowers everywhere, seamlessly woven into the architecture. The fae were deeply in tune with nature and the elements, one of the few things I missed about being one of them.

The griffins set down in the courtyard in front of the palace, where dozens of guards in elaborate silver armor and plumed helmets were stationed. A man in fine livery stood on the wide steps leading up to the massive door inlaid with gems and carved with ancient runes. He bowed low as I approached, with my guards and companions fanning out behind me, and my sons at my side.

"Your majesty, the High King is expecting you," he said. "Please follow me."

The man cast a slightly disparaging glance over my group as the door opened behind him, moving silently despite its size. He led us inside the palace, into a great entry filled with more guards and a few noble fae dressed in their finest clothes with hair in every shade of the rainbow. I looked closely, but didn't recognize any of them. Not really a surprise, since it had been many centuries since I'd been Persephone, and I'd spent much of my time in Hell during that life anyway.

As the man led us further into the castle, I took in my surroundings and felt like I'd gone back in time—or stepped into my previous life. Almost nothing had changed in hundreds of years in this castle, and I suspected that was true of all of Faerie. Technology didn't work in this realm, and the fae were resistant to change in general. It was one reason they preferred to stay neutral in conflicts and to live in isolation here in Faerie, with very few people coming or going from this realm.

An air of hushed calm hung in each of the spaces we moved through, until we stopped in a waiting room outside two large doors that I remembered led to the throne room. There were other fae here chatting with each other, all nobles judging by their clothes and the jewels decorating their bodies. Each one was dressed in elegant clothes that looked like something from the 1800s, and they gave us judgmental looks as we entered. My group was all dressed for combat, not courtly life, but there was nothing to be done about that now.

A tall, willowy woman stood by the window, and she wore a pastel pink gown of the finest silk. Her hair was the color of purple hydrangea and atop it was a crown similar to Damien's, but much more elaborate. She turned slowly, revealing herself in such a way that my breath froze in my chest.

"Mother?" I stepped forward to greet her, but her periwinkle blue eyes were cool and devoid of care as she leveled her gaze at me. Demeter was the Queen of the Spring Court and my mother when I'd been Persephone. It had been many centuries since I'd seen her, and my heart overflowed with joy at the thought of reconnecting with another member of my family.

She took me in slowly, her eyes scanning me head to toe while a tight frown crossed her lips. "You're not my daughter in this life."

I drew back as if she'd slapped me across the face. How could she be so callous and cruel? My children were no less mine because this wasn't the body that had birthed them, and she would always be my mother, no matter how long it had been.

"Mother, please." I hated explaining myself, and tried not to sound weak as I asked for the recognition of our relationship. "I know I've been gone for a long time, but I've regained my memories and my powers. I am truly your daughter once more. In mind and spirit, if not in body."

"I mourned my daughter's death. She is gone, and you...you are a stranger." She walked past my group, leaving the fragrance of lavender in her wake. Her words cut deep into me, and I stared after her as she joined another group of fae with her back to me.

Even Damien looked shocked and horrified by his grandmother's comments. "I'm sorry. I asked her to come with me to this meeting, but I didn't realize she would react that way upon seeing you."

"It's not your fault." I sighed, and tried now to show how much it bothered me. Demeter had always been a difficult mother, and some things never changed. After all, she'd made Lucifer agree to that ridiculous deal that had forced me to spend half my time in Hell and half my time here in Faerie, even though I'd been a grown adult who could make my own decisions about my life. To call her an overbearing parent was putting it lightly.

All thoughts of my mother vanished when the man who'd led us here held up a thin, silver fanfare trumpet, which he began to blow as soon the doors opened to admit us. I stepped inside the throne room first, walking down a long white carpet with my entourage behind me. In here there were even more guards in full armor, along with more nobles in long gowns or elegant suits who studied us with haughty looks.

The man we'd followed in bowed deeply from the waist. "Presenting Queen Hannah of the demons, along with her guests."

High King Oberon sat on a wide stage on a huge throne of tooled gold and silver designed by some of the finest craftsmen in

Faerie. Exquisite metal vines twisted together so that it looked like the king was sitting on a chair made of plants and flowers, yet he managed to lounge as if he was completely relaxed. Behind him were huge windows looking out at the sky, with a stunning view of much of Faerie below it.

The most powerful fae of all time focused his eyes on me, while my group bowed low to him. I nearly bowed too, and then remembered that I was his equal now. Above his pointed ears was a crown done in the same style as his throne, and he had long black hair and cold eyes, with an expression that somehow looked both bored and cruel all at once.

"It's been a long time," he said to me in his haughty voice. "I preferred you as Persephone, though I do enjoy the irony of you being an angel now. And Demon Queen, no less."

It took all my self-control not to roll my eyes. Was everyone in this realm stuck on the idea of me as Persephone? Yet while I might have changed, Oberon was still the same asshole as always.

Though I did notice one change from my previous life—there was no throne beside him anymore. I'd recently learned that my aunt, his wife, Titania, was dead, and most believed that Oberon was responsible. She was my mother's older sister and a powerful fae queen, but she'd been unable to produce children, and in Oberon's desperation to have a son and heir, he had many affairs. In retaliation, she cursed him to only have daughters. The rumor was that for many years he'd tried everything to break the curse, but when nothing worked, he'd killed Titania in a fit of rage. I believed it. The man was evil. Unfortunately, I had to play nice while in his realm.

I gritted my teeth behind my tight, closed-lipped smile. "Thank you for seeing us on such short notice. As you saw in my message, Lucifer has recently escaped the confines of Heaven."

"You mean War," Oberon corrected. "I suspect there is little left of Lucifer in there."

"We'll see about that." My fingernails bit into my palms as I forced myself to keep my cool. "He wants to start a war that will encompass all the realms, including Faerie. He must be stopped— and we believe the only way to do so is to use another Elder God."

A few shocked gasps went up around the throne room before it fell into deathly silence once more. Oberon straightened at my words and curved his hands over the arms of his throne. "You wish to release Famine."

"We do, yes."

He tilted his head as he considered. "Releasing one Horseman to stop another is a risky gamble. Still, Famine hates War, so you may have some success if you wish them to battle it out. But then what do you do with the winner? Or the loser, for that matter?" He stroked his chin. "There might be another way to save Lucifer."

"What is it?" I asked, unable to hide my eagerness. I'd searched all the books for any other solution, but hadn't come across anything viable, but perhaps Oberon had knowledge even more ancient than I could access.

"If someone is possessed by an Elder God, that person can wage the battle inside themselves—an internal fight to defeat the god and take their powers." He raised his eyebrows. "Only a few people would be strong enough to do such a thing, but Lucifer is one of them."

My heart sank. "Except he failed."

Belial turned to me. "He only failed because he lost all his memories of you, so he didn't want to fight War. He has no reason to wish for peace without you."

"He's right," Damien said. "You were always the one to calm Father, from the very beginning."

Kassiel nodded. "And it's because of you that he ended the war with the angels at all."

A tiny ray of hope fluttered in my chest again. "So if we could get his memories back, he might be able to fight War and defeat him. But he sacrificed those memories—how would we get them back?"

No one seemed to have an answer for that.

Oberon waved a lazy hand. "Perhaps it's impossible. You may have to trap the Horsemen again in tombs, as we did in the old times. Or you could always try to send them to Void."

Void—the realm where all the Elder Gods lived. It was

completely sealed off from anyone entering or escaping it, mainly to protect all the other realms from the powerful beings inside it.

"How would we do that?" I asked.

"Lucifer had a key to Void long ago," Oberon said. "Given to him by his father. Perhaps he still has it hidden away somewhere?"

"I don't remember anything about the location of a key." I turned to the others who'd come with me. "Do any of you?"

All of them murmured no or shook their heads. Damn. Another dead end. Even if I wanted to send Lucifer to Void, which I would only do as a last resort, the places he might have concealed a key were too numerous to count. It would take far longer to search for it than it would take Pestilence and War to destroy the realms between them.

I drew in a breath as the path ahead became clear. "Then we have no choice but to release Famine."

"Do you have someone willing to make the sacrifice?" Oberon asked.

Azazel stepped forward. "I'll do it."

"I also volunteer," Belial said.

"As do I," Damien chimed in.

Oberon drummed his fingers on the throne. "Perhaps one of you is strong enough to control Famine. Perhaps not. I'll be sending some of my own people with you to be certain it's handled correctly."

"I wouldn't expect anything less." In truth, I'd worried he might come with us. After all, he was one of the people who had trapped the Four Horsemen originally, and I thought he might want to be there when the one in his realm was released. I supposed Oberon didn't like getting his hands dirty anymore. He'd been different back when I was Eve. Not such an asshole. A real leader to his people.

The High King raised his chin. "I can't have a Horseman of the Apocalypse traipsing about my realm. We've kept Famine contained so long due to our strong ties with nature, but once that tomb is open, there's no telling what will happen to our realm."

"You know I will not allow Famine to harm Faerie," Damien said, with a small bow to his uncle. "If I must be the one to make the sacrifice, I would do it to protect our people."

"I know you would. That's the only reason I'm allowing this endeavor at all." Oberon's eyes hardened and his voice turned sharp. "And if all else fails—make sure to open a portal to Earth so Famine can destroy that world instead of ours."

Yep. Still an asshole.

9

LUCIFER

L as Vegas was sprawled out below me, all the lights, all the power, all the greed. I breathed it in, using it like fuel before turning my attention to The Celestial and my penthouse at the top. It wouldn't take me long to amass my demon warriors and lead them forth into battle. As soon as the angels arrived, we'd wreak havoc and destruction upon them, and on the unsuspecting mortals residing in the area. None would be spared my wrath.

My wings beat against the night as I soared over the city, concealed by darkness. Something about flying by the Stratosphere tickled my mind, like a memory I couldn't retrieve, but then War's presence crushed the feeling. He was always there, entwined with my own self, and soon I forgot anything except overwhelming rage.

I dropped down in front of The Celestial, sheathed my wings, and adjusted my suit. This time I planned to enter my kingdom properly, and I would announce myself to my people so they knew who they truly served. As for the woman? I planned to lock her away, keeping her caged like a songbird until she gave birth to my child. Then I would decide what to do with her.

But as I stepped inside my casino I noticed it was disturbingly empty, and heard shouts and screams up ahead by the bar. I walked quickly, passing human bodies on the ground around the blackjack tables and in front of the slot machines, each one an unnatural color and covered in putrid boils. A few were still alive, groaning and clutching their heads or chests, their features set in grim masks as they writhed on the carpet.

Pestilence. The name slithered through me, my whole body reacting to the slimy feel of it. Yes, he was here. Another Horseman. A brother of sorts, though not one welcome at my door. But why was he here? What did he seek? Did he plan to ally with me—or challenge me?

I found him at the Styx Bar, surrounded by gargoyles in stone form, who were managing to hold him off and resist his attacks, though I suspected that wouldn't last for long. They paused when they saw me, some of them opening their mouths in shock and fear, though some turned hopeful eyes upon me, as if I might save them from their fate. Save them I would, but only because they belonged to me. I wrapped my power around them, bending them to my will, taking away all their thoughts except those of combat and violence.

Pestilence turned toward me and snarled, his eyes glowing white and filled with madness. The body he'd claimed had not fared well under his control, and his skin was yellow and blistered, his hair white and thin, and his body reeked of decay and disease. Just being this close to him made me feel contaminated, though my powers protected me from much of his sickness.

"Why are you here?" I asked in a way that stiffened Pestilence's shoulders. "This is my domain."

"You know why." He cocked his head with a manic grin. "Or perhaps you don't. Have you forgotten our ancient feud as well?"

His words stirred something inside me, but once again it was just out of reach. The body he'd taken had belonged to Gadreel, a Fallen who had once served me, who turned out to be the reincarnation of Adam. I remembered all of that, though not why he'd betrayed me, nor why I carried such immense hatred for Adam.

I clenched my hands into fists and allowed my anger to seep out of me in a red glow. "What do you want? Answer me!"

His own putrid yellow power emanated from him too, clashing against my own. "I'm here for Eve."

"Eve?" I knew no one by that name.

He let out a sharp laugh. "You really don't remember. Good. That will make this much easier. Step aside and I'll get her out of your hair so you can continue with your plans of war. You can have this place. All I want is Eve."

My eyes narrowed as his words stirred up a fresh wave of wrath inside me, and my heart beat like Strife's hooves were thundering over my ribs. "You speak of the woman living in my penthouse."

Pestilence stepped forward with a challenge in his eyes. "She belongs to me, and I'm here to claim her."

"No." The worst burst out of me so vehemently it made the liquor bottles and the mirrors in the bar shake. It even made Pestilence step back, toward the gargoyle warriors under my control, who patiently waited to unleash their frenzy, though they snapped their teeth at him and tried to scratch him with their talons.

Pestilence lifted an eyebrow. "Are we back to this age-old fight then?"

I didn't know what he was saying, but I knew, deep in my bones, down in my very soul, that the woman—Hannah or Eve or whatever she was called—wasn't his. The life inside her wasn't his. They were *mine*. All mine.

"Get out of my hotel." I spat the words.

"It doesn't need to be like this," he said. "Not anymore. We're the same now. Two Horsemen of the Apocalypse, with the same goals of spreading chaos upon the land. We can forget the past—hell, you've already done that—and move forward as brothers. Once we release Famine and Death we'll be even stronger. We'll rule all the realms—even Void itself."

I stepped closer to him, forcing him back against the wall, my hands balled into fists. "I'm already the king here, and I'm not good at sharing. Get the fuck out of here before I destroy you."

He met my gaze, one corner of his lips lifting. "You can try, but you both know we can't be killed."

"Pestilence can't—but that body can."

I brought one of my fists up and landed it on his face, bursting one of the throbbing pustules there. The fluid inside it burned like acid as it ran over my skin, but I shook it off. I wasn't done. I summoned my sword and prepared to strike him down, but he slithered away like the slippery beast he was.

When I turned to face him, he stood on the other side of the bar wielding a bow and arrows. Each tip pulsed with yellow and black power, a combination of his Pestilence sickness and his Fallen darkness. He unleashed arrows faster than humanly possible, but I threw up a shield of darkness to stop him, then blasted him with blue hellfire laced with red rage. He launched over it with sickly gray wings that had lost a lot of feathers, and he was surprisingly spry for someone who looked so ill. I released my gargoyle guards and they leaped in front of him, blocking his path. He turned back to me and fired off more arrows, but he wasn't fast enough against me, a being created for one purpose: to fight.

I launched myself forward and sliced into him with my sword. He let out a horrifying screech, then managed to stab me with one of his arrows. Weakness and disease coursed through me, trying to slow me down, but I struggled against his powers, refusing to let him stop me. I couldn't let him get to that woman or my child. I'd burn this whole place down before I let that happen.

I lifted the sword and slashed at him, cutting into his shoulder and down his chest. He let out a horrifying screech as the hellfire stung him, and then he barreled through the gargoyles as he flew out of the casino. I rushed after him, my own wings giving me speed, but once I made it outside I saw him jump on his horse and ride away, slipping into the crowd of tourists and gamblers. Screams followed in his wake, but his horse was so fast, many had barely any time to react as he passed by them.

"Follow him," I commanded my gargoyles. They weren't as fast as his horse was, but since he was injured, they might have a chance of catching up. I could have gone after him, but I had more pressing business here, and I was satisfied that the fucker wouldn't return to challenge me anytime soon.

Besides, I had to check on the woman before I did anything else.

Though I felt only hatred and rage toward her, I needed to be sure my child was protected.

I flew up to the penthouse, but it was dark. There was no one inside.

The woman was gone.

10

HANNAH

Huge white columns soared into the air, gleaming under the soft moonlight at the temple where Famine's tomb was located. Our griffins circled over it, allowing us to take in the entire structure. It clearly hadn't been touched in many years, and nature had nearly swallowed it up entirely. All except for the massive statue of Oberon at the front of it. It had to be at least forty feet tall and depicted him seated on a throne decorated with gold and precious stones, while wearing a crown and holding a scepter in one hand. The entrance to the temple was underneath the throne, so you had to pass under Oberon's watchful eyes to enter.

There had once been a similar statue on Earth in Greece, depicting Oberon in his guise as Zeus. For many years he'd been worshiped on Earth under that name, but the statue had been destroyed long ago. Only its counterpart here in Faerie remained.

The day had passed from the awakening of spring, through the heat of midsummer, and now we were relaxing in a temperate fall that was rapidly cooling to winter. The light had changed, growing softer, falling in pale strips between the columns as our griffins sat down in front of the statue. I dismounted, taking in the untouched surroundings. I hadn't been here since I was Eve, when we first sealed Famine away. Belial had only been a child then. There was nothing else for miles except for this temple and the thick, dark forest surrounding it.

"Of course the entrance to the tomb would be under his feet," Belial muttered, as we took in the stone doors in front of us. They were covered in vines and other plants that had grown wild, but I flicked a hand and they released their hold on the stone and retreated back into the earth.

Damien cast his eyes up at the statue with distaste. "Yes. Oberon would trust no one else to guard a thing as dangerous as Famine."

I turned back to take in the large group of people who had come with me on this mission. My sons, all three of them eager and determined to save their father, despite any issues they had with him. My nephew Callan, hovering near me protectively, and Azazel, who stood with a grim set to her mouth. Theo was organizing his gargoyle guards into a formation around the tomb, while the fae warriors sent by High King Oberon stood impassively to the side, as if they could only be bothered to get involved should something go wrong. Our messenger Mirabella, who I'd learned had a father in the Autumn Court, stood apart from them, ready to open a portal for us back to Earth whenever we wished.

"We're all ready," Kassiel said. "The fae are opening the temple doors now."

I nodded, before turning to Zel. "Do you still want to do this?"

She scowled. "Want to? Not exactly. But it needs to be done, and I'm the best person for the job."

I took her face in my hands and stared into her dark eyes. "Promise me you'll fight Famine and will somehow remain yourself. I can't lose you too, Zel."

She put her hands over mine and gazed back at me with determination and love. "I promise. Long ago I swore to protect you and to fight by your side, and I'm not stopping now."

I nodded and stepped back, blinking away tears in my eyes. "I love you."

"Don't get all mushy on me, little angel," Zel said with a grin, her face softening. Then she brought me in for a tight squeeze and whispered, "I love you too, but don't you dare tell anyone."

The temple door opened with a loud rumble and a plume of dust, and Zel and I stepped back to watch. I couldn't see anything inside except darkness, but Callan and I could fix that with some angelic light.

"Let's move," I told my team, gesturing toward the entrance. So far there was no sign of Nemesis or Fenrir, but I didn't want to stick around and wait for them to show up either.

Theo went in first with some of his guards, along with Callan, who lit the way with a bright ball of hovering light. I went in next with Azazel, Damien, and Kassiel, using my own light to illuminate a dusty stone corridor with stale air, barely large enough for two of us to pass through side by side. More of my gargoyle guards trailed behind me, along with a few fae warriors at the back. The rest stayed outside, in case any threat should arise there.

The hallway became more of a tunnel, slanting down, down, down. No one had been inside this temple in thousands of years, and as we went deeper into the Earth, the space became more and more oppressive. I couldn't wait to get back outside.

Eventually the downward slope of the tunnel led us to another large door, this one covered in magical runes just like Pestilence's and War's tombs had been. The air here was especially stifling, and my stomach turned at the horrible power emanating from within the tomb. The baby kicked too, and I rested my hand over her, trying to silently reassure her.

"This is it," Callan said. "Famine's tomb."

Kassiel examined it closely. "It's built right into the temple itself."

Belial gestured at Damien to go forward. "You're up. Make us proud."

Damien grimaced, but stepped close to the door and pulled out a small knife. Only a few people could open Famine's tomb, including Oberon himself, or one of his daughters—and my son Damien. To do so, you had to be born in this realm, with the blood of one of the people who had sealed the tomb originally.

Damien looked over at me and I nodded, though inside I was

trembling. We had to do this, but that didn't mean I was ready for what was about to happen. Were we really going to release the third Horseman upon the world? Would this plan work, or were we only bring doom upon ourselves?

Damien drew the blade across his palm in a neat slice. I winced, but he didn't so much as flinch, and then he pressed his bloody hand against the tomb's door. The runes began to glow, casting all of us in an eerie green haze. Then the door flew open with a burst of power so strong it knocked all of us back. I slammed against the nearest wall, and only my newly-remembered air magic cushioned my blow and protected the baby.

"I'm free," a horrible, croaking voice sounded from inside the dark depths of the tomb, and then a cloud of sickly green seeped out of the tomb with the smell of decaying plants and rotten food. As we all recovered from the blast and got back on our feet, the green fog coalesced into the vague shape of a woman, though her features were blurred and kept shifting like smoke. "I am Famine...and I must feed. Who will make the sacrifice and gain my powers?"

"The third Horseman is a woman?" Callan asked beside me.

Zel rose to her feet and dusted herself off. "I will make the sacrifice."

As soon as the words had left her mouth, one of the fae guards moved behind her and stabbed a sword through her chest. I screamed as Zel was impaled, then saw through the fae guard's magical disguise—revealing a gorgeous woman with fiery red hair. Nemesis.

I blasted her back with a gust of air, while Callan jumped forward to catch Zel as she fell. Blood gushed from her chest, and I cursed myself for not allowing Marcus to come with us, and for not seeing through Nemesis's illusions sooner. I'd barely paid the fae guards who'd followed us inside any attention, and now Zel was dying. What could I do?

"Take her body and heal her," I yelled at Famine, as I desperately tried to cover Zel's wounds and stop the bleeding. Zel was barely conscious, her body shutting down as it tried to heal itself.

"No," the rasping, feminine voice boomed. "She is too weak. She would not survive."

Two gargoyle guards I recognized suddenly rushed into the area, and one of them yelled, "My queen, shifters attack outside the temple! We're surrounded!"

I swore under my breath, and turned to the others with me. "Defend the perimeter and get Zel to a healer! I can stop Nemesis myself." When my sons all looked like they would argue with me, I held up a hand and yelled, "Go!"

Callan carried Zel outside, and I prayed it wasn't the last time I would see her alive. Damien and Kassiel followed, along with some of the guards, though Theo and Belial stayed with me.

Famine's form began moving toward the exit too. "I hunger...who will feed me?"

"I will," Belial said, moving in front of Famine, shielding the rest of us with his body. My heart lurched into my throat at the thought of my son becoming a Horseman—but he was also probably the best option here, I was sad to admit.

Famine sneered at him, and then with one ghostly hand she knocked him aside. "I require a female host."

"Take me," Nemesis rose to her feet, with her imps—who had all been disguised as fae guards—behind her wielding weapons. "I'm the one you want."

Famine's green spectral form moved toward her, but there was no way in Heaven or Hell I was letting Nemesis get control of this Elder God. This was my one chance to rescue Lucifer from War, and I wasn't going to lose it. Nemesis had betrayed us time and time again, and now she'd stabbed Zel—I wasn't letting her win.

"No." I strode forward with both darkness and light emanating from me, my air powers whipping at my hair, while thorny vines grew up out of the ground at my feet. It was time to show that bitch what happened when you crossed the Demon Queen. "Famine is mine."

My thick vines wrapped around Nemesis, stabbing into her bare skin with the thorns, but she grew long, black talons and sliced through them, then managed to scamper away to the other side of the cave. Belial and Theo began fighting against the other imps, but the only one that mattered to me was Nemesis.

She split herself into dozens of copies, all of them slashing at me with swords and claws, but I cast out the light of truth around me and found the real Nemesis. I shot her with light and darkness, but she was so fast she seemed to almost blink away, and managed to dodge everything. No way was she escaping though. With a roar, I created a tornado of air laced with light and darkness, then unleashed it upon her. It caught Nemesis inside it, and then my vines reached up and tore her apart, limb from bloody limb. Though I'd never reveled in death, I watched on with grim satisfaction as Nemesis was destroyed.

Don't fuck with a pregnant woman protecting her family.

"My queen, are you all right?" Theo limped to my side, one hand wrapped around his waist.

Imp corpses were scattered over the ground, and Belial delivered the final blow to one of them with Morningstar. Then he turned to survey the pieces of Nemesis lying all over the ground in a pool of blood.

"Shit, Mother," Belial said. "I never realized you were so brutal."

"I did what I had to do." I looked around the cave and my breath caught. "Where is Famine?"

Belial sheathed his sword. "She must have escaped during the battle."

We rushed up the tunnel and emerged into a snowy battlefield. Shifters and imps fought against gargoyles and fae, and I was relieved to see that both Damien and Kassiel were all right. I scanned the area and found Famine's green spectral form floating above them all. She hovered over Mirabella for a few seconds, then turned around and reached for a large white wolf with ice coating its fur, who stood beside Fenrir.

Famine was looking for a new host. I couldn't let that happen. But Zel was gone, carried off by Callan to safety, and Famine wanted a female body.

There was only one person strong to contain her.

Me.

11

HANNAH

A path of dead, brown vegetation led directly to Famine. Plants withered and died, flowers lost their petals, leaves turned black. Shifters and gargoyles alike fell to their knees in her path, as if they'd lost all the strength to fight or even stand.

She was feeding.

Everything about it made my soul revolt. I was a goddess of spring and nature, and she was the opposite of everything I held dear. Yet I had to offer myself to her...there was no other choice.

Fenrir, in his giant wolf form, saw Famine coming for the ice wolf and jumped in front of her, baring his fangs. Whoever that wolf was, Fenrir didn't want her taken over by Famine. And here I'd thought Fenrir didn't care about anything or anyone except himself. But Famine couldn't be stopped, not by Fenrir, and she tossed him aside, then closed in on the white wolf.

I unfurled my silver wings and launched myself toward Famine, using my wind powers to give me a boost. "Famine!" I yelled.

The Elder God turned toward me, just as the ice wolf shifted back into a beautiful woman with white hair and pointed ears. She pulled out a gem and activated it, using a key to open a portal that she and Fenrir slipped inside. It closed before Famine could escape back to Earth. Like the coward he was, Fenrir had turned tail again —and left behind most of his shifters.

Famine let out a frustrated growl now that her host had vanished, but then her energy turned upon me. Being near her was like facing an energy drain—her very presence made me feel tired, hungry, and weak. Like I hadn't eaten or slept in days.

"I command you to submit," I said, repeating words I'd heard Belial use with Pestilence, but then I added my own twist. "Famine, I need your help."

"Is that so?" she asked with a sickening cackle.

"I need to defeat War. I'm told you are the only one who can stop him."

Her spectral form grew dark and angry. "Yes...War must suffer..."

Not exactly what I wanted, but I let it slide. "Serve me, and we'll take him down together."

"Mother, no!" Belial called out. He stood beside Kassiel and Damien, who also echoed his sentiments, but I ignored them. My sons had to know this was the only way now that Famine was freed.

"Are you willing to make the sacrifice?" Famine asked.

I hesitated. I was willing to do anything to save Lucifer...except endanger our unborn child. "That depends on what you ask of me. I am with child, and I won't let you do anything that would hurt her."

Famine's essence moved closer as she considered me. The entire glade around the temple fell silent as everyone watched our exchange. No one fought anymore—they were too weak thanks to Famine anyway.

"I was a mother once too," she said in a quieter voice. "Perhaps you know my son, Baal."

"I do, yes. He is an ally of mine." I vaguely remembered Baal saying that Famine was his parent, but I'd stupidly assumed he meant his father.

"There were other children too," Famine continued. "War murdered some of them. The others...perhaps they are still alive. Perhaps I will be able to find them."

"Then you understand that I would do anything to protect my child."

"Yes. I will not hurt this child. I swear it."

Relief loosened my chest around the breath I'd been holding. As an Elder God, she couldn't lie. "Then what sacrifice would you ask of me?"

"The sacrifice of your fertility. Your baby will remain safe and whole. She will be powerful and strong. I will ensure it. But this child will be your last. After she is born, your body will bring forth life no more."

I wrapped my arms around myself as her words sank in. The last. It was difficult to contemplate. I hadn't given thought to having more babies after this one, but the idea that it would be impossible made me feel hollow inside. I smoothed my hand over my bump, feeling the baby move inside, knowing once she was born I'd never experience this miracle again.

I swallowed hard as tears pricked my eyes, but then I turned and looked at my three smart, brave, handsome sons. Lucifer and I had been blessed with them and with this daughter growing inside me now. As long as this unborn child would be safe, I could accept never having another one after her.

"I accept this sacrifice."

"Very good." Famine moved toward me in a way that reminded me of a swarm of bees. "I'm looking forward to being a mother again."

Something in the way she spoke the words iced my blood. There was a finality in her tone, as though the child would be hers, and not mine. She thought she would take control of me, but I was going to fight. I remembered Oberon's words about how one could defeat and then become an Elder God, just as Famine's ghostly form surrounded me. Her power enveloped me and seeped into my skin, oozing into my pores, sliding into every hole until she'd slithered deep into my soul. Overwhelming hunger and desperate need made me nearly tear out my eyes, along with a melancholy so strong I could barely breathe. I was fueled by deep, intense longing, not just for food, but for power. For life.

Fighting against Famine's immense power was impossible. How had I ever thought I'd be able to defeat her? She stretched through my body, taking it over, claiming me as her host, and I couldn't stop her. No wonder Lucifer hadn't found his way without his memories. He'd never had a chance.

I gazed across the battlefield, at the dead grass and the weakened beings all kneeling before me. I could see their auras, their power, their essence, and I breathed it in, drawing upon their strength, claiming it as mine. It was my nature to feed, and none could stop me from draining every last living thing around me. Only then would I be strong enough to stop War.

My eyes fell upon the three men before me, the ones who called my name over and over. Damien sagged, his beautiful skin dimming as I sucked away his life force. Kassiel was on his hands and knees, his face pale. Belial, the oldest and strongest, fought back the hardest, but even he eventually fell under my might.

As he hit the ground, my senses came back to me and I recoiled. What was I doing? I couldn't allow Famine to leech power from those I loved. Those were my children she was draining, and behind them, my friends and my allies. I had to stop her from killing them all. I had to gain control somehow.

I forced myself to release the energy I'd stolen, allowing it to return to the people around me. Famine tried to exert control over me again, but this time, I knew what she was doing and I fought back. I could feel it now, a duality where I needed to hold on to myself, to make myself strong so that I didn't fade behind Famine. She would be the driving force if I let her, until we merged into one terrible, awful being that would drain the life out of every living thing in every realm, until there was nothing left.

Famine struggled harder, pouring more of her power over me, while attempting to reach out and steal life from everything around us. I countered her by sending out living energy into the surroundings with my Persephone powers, bringing the plants back to life around us, fighting her blight with my power of growth. That only made her more angry, but it also made me realize something—I was the direct counter of Famine. She made crops wither and die, and I made them grow and flourish.

I was Persephone, the goddess of spring and death. I was Eve, who had trapped the Four Horsemen originally. And I was Hannah, an angel of truth, and the motherfucking Demon Queen. Famine thought she could take over my body and raise my child as her own, but she had no idea how powerful I was. Especially because it wasn't just me. I had my daughter too, a little piece of Lucifer nestled in my body. My baby was strong, and together I knew we could subdue Famine and contain her.

My daughter kicked like she understood my need for us to fight together, and I drew on my love for Lucifer to center myself. I gazed upon my sons, all of them standing again and looking at me with such love it overwhelmed me. My family was my strength. Love gave me power.

This is my body, I told Famine. *And you will submit to me.*

Never, she cried, as she raged inside me. The overwhelming feeling of desperation, need, and hunger that could never be sated filled me, but I stared at my sons and pushed it down. I focused on life and love, using my memories of all my past lives to fuel me. I'd been reborn hundreds of times, my soul strengthening every time, and each life had given me a tiny bit more power. Enough power to defeat even an Elder God.

I forced Famine into a small space inside me, squeezing her tighter and tighter, draining her of strength and will until she faded away into nothing. The intense hunger and longing vanished, along with her presence. The only thing that remained was her power, coursing through my body like crackling electricity, now mine to control.

Famine was gone, and I remained.

No, that wasn't right.

I was Famine now.

An Elder God. A Horseman of the Apocalypse. A being powerful enough to stop War.

A black horse appeared out of the night and rode toward me, and I held out my hand to her nose. She breathed over me with warmth and recognition as she nudged against my fingers. I knew this horse, and it knew me. *Misery*, something inside me supplied. That was her name.

As I pondered this strange bond with this horse I'd just met, my sons rushed over to me. "What was that?" Belial's knuckles were white around the hilt of Morningstar, which was glowing with both white and black light.

"Are you okay?" Kassiel asked.

Damien peered at me. "Is Famine in there?"

"I *am* Famine." I stroked the horse's flank, then turned to face them with wonder. "But I'm also still me."

Belial arched an eyebrow. "You defeated her?"

Kassiel grinned. "Of course she did."

"How?" Damien asked.

"I used my love for my family to give me strength," I said, rubbing my bump as I smiled at my sons.

"That's corny as fuck," Belial said, rolling his eyes.

"Maybe, but it worked, didn't it?" I gave each of them a warm hug, so relieved to still be myself, but now with added hope. If I could defeat Famine, then surely Lucifer could defeat War too. He just needed me to guide him and help him remember who he was.

I glanced around the area, and most of the shifters and imps had either fled or been killed. Most of my people were still standing, except for Callan and Zel. They were on the ground under a dead tree, and I rushed over to them.

"How is she?" I asked.

Callan looked up at me with a pained expression. "She needs a healer right away."

While Damien called for Mirabella to open the portal to Earth, I kneeled beside my best friend and placed my hand on her cheek. She was weak, and I felt her life force in a way I never had before. A little voice told me it would be so easy to drain her of what was left— the lingering remnant of Famine's essence, perhaps. Something I would have to learn to live with and control.

But if I could take energy and life, could I give it too? I was able to do it with plants, why not people?

I rested my hands over the huge, bloody gash in Zel's stomach, which I'd avoided looking at because it was too horrifying to consider. While angelic healers like Marcus used their connection to the light to heal, I was different, and my power came from nature. Just like Famine did before, I drew upon the life force of the plants around us, making the grass turn brown again. The tree over us withered and died, its leaves falling upon us like rain. I gathered all of it inside me, and then I funneled it into Zel.

The magic kicked her own immortal healing into overdrive, and she gasped as her eyes popped open. Her stomach knit back together and color returned to her face, while she stared at me with shock.

"What...?" she asked.

"I'll explain everything later." I stroked her cheek with tears of relief in my eyes. "But if you could stop almost dying on me, that would be great."

She shrugged a little, though it made her wince. "I make no promises."

"My queen, the portal is ready," Mirabella said, from behind me.

"Thank you." I ordered everyone to go through it, while I did my best to repair the area. The spot where I'd healed Zel would never recover though, I feared. It would remain lifeless, a grim memorial to her neath death.

Callan carried her through the portal, and then there were only a few of us left. I glanced back at the tomb and the statue towering over it one last time, feeling a strange mix of affinity and hatred for the place, no doubt from this new part of me that had been trapped there for thousands of years.

Mirabella lightly touched my elbow. "Before you go, I wish to thank you for saving me and Eira from Famine."

I blinked at her. "Eira?"

"Fenrir's daughter, the ice wolf. She's half-fae from the Winter Court. Her mother died when she was a baby, so she was raised by Fenrir among shifters. She was a messenger for the demons like me, and a good friend, at least until Fenrir turned against Lucifer." Her voice trailed off with a hint of sadness. It was a good reminder that this civil war had torn apart our people, and Lucifer and I would have to do a lot of work to heal it, even once we stopped Fenrir. At least Nemesis was gone now.

"I do everything I can to protect my people," I said to Mirabella.

She bowed low, and I turned toward the portal. It was time to get back to Earth to face Lucifer.

To face War.

12

LUCIFER

After realizing the woman and my child were gone, I'd destroyed the penthouse in a rage. I barely remembered any of it, and only came out of my berserker frenzy when Samael and some angels rushed in to try to stop me. How foolish they were, thinking they could stand against me. A touch of my power turned them into mindless warriors craving blood, and now Samael served me once more. As for the angels that were with him, they were chained up in the basement of The Celestial. We'd use them as prisoners of war, or possibly bait, if needed.

I poured myself a drink and stood on the edge of the balcony, gazing down at the city I owned. A city that would soon know bloodshed and terror as the war between angels and demons began once more. Samael was currently rallying our forces, preparing them for battle. Soon the angels would be here too. My blood raced at the thought of the fighting that would soon break out across these brightly-lit streets. I craved the clash of weapons and the spray of blood, the cries of agony and of triumph.

I turned back to look at the destroyed furniture inside my penthouse. The black leather couches and the piano had been familiar to me, bringing back many memories, but other parts of my past were gaping black holes. Now they were in pieces, the leather ripped, the piano smashed. No matter. It was better this way. There wasn't a room in my home that didn't smell of the woman, and her presence invaded me with every breath I drew.

But she wasn't here now. Samael wouldn't tell me where she'd gone either. Somehow he managed to resist that one question, but I would get an answer soon. Those who wouldn't bend to my will would break.

I needed to find the woman and bring her here. Now that I'd kissed her, her absence created a hole in my chest, one I hadn't expected and didn't know how to fill.

As soon as I had that thought, War filled me with fury at the woman for making me feel that way. Now that I'd taken my rightful place as Demon King, I needed nothing and no one but myself. Especially not *her*.

Samael appeared in the entrance of the penthouse. "Lucifer."

"Your king," I corrected him. I gave him a hard look, and he inclined his head.

"My king. A large group of angels is approaching the city."

"Excellent." I downed the rest of my drink. "Are our soldiers ready?"

"Yes, but..." He hesitated, and I felt him fight against my control. "Are you sure this is the best course of action?"

"You dare to question me?" I slammed my empty glass onto the bar, and it shattered in my hand. "The war against the angels never should have ended. I made a mistake when I made peace with them, but the days of peace are over now. We won't stop until they surrender, or we destroy every single one of them."

Samael gave a quick shake of his head but pressed his lips into a line. "Of course, my king."

The bastard was stubborn, no doubt about it, and far too calm for my War powers to incite. But I had other tricks as Lucifer. I hadn't used my persuasive powers on Samael in a very long time, but I couldn't have him questioning me either.

"You followed me when we first left Heaven and made Hell our home. You will follow me again now." I laced power into my words and gave him a cocky smile. "We can't let the angels win after all these years, can we?"

"No, we can't," he murmured. His strength finally gave out against my own, and he bowed his head. "I will follow you anywhere, my king. Even into this war."

"There will be no war," the woman's voice said behind me.

I jerked my head toward the penthouse entrance, where the angel woman known as Hannah stood. Something about her was different, and it took me a moment to realize why—she emanated the power of an Elder God. How the fuck was that possible?

Three tall, dark-haired men fanned out behind her, and more confusion invaded my mind like there was something I needed to recall. I looked at them closely but they weren't familiar, even though they tugged at my brain like the woman did.

"It's already done," I told her. "War is coming to this city, and then to the rest of the world, and then to every other one. There's nothing you can do to stop it."

"I can stop *you*." She walked toward me, and as she got closer, that ancient, all-consuming power radiated from her. A power I recognized as being akin to my own.

"Famine?" I asked. No, that wasn't right. The angel woman wasn't Famine, yet Famine's power radiated from her, both calling to and repelling War. They were old enemies, and War wanted me to destroy her. *Kill, kill, kill,* he told me over and over. But I couldn't keep my gaze off the angel woman's lips, or the fullness of her breasts and hips, or the slight swell of her stomach where she carried my child. My daughter. I breathed in without thinking, taking a fresh wave of her scent deep inside me.

"I released Famine and became her host, just like you did with War," she said. "But then I took control and I defeated her, claiming her power as my own. You can do this too, Lucifer."

I stared at her, trying to comprehend how this could be possible. I felt the briefest spark of hope, before War trampled it down and raged within me.

Kill her, he ordered.

"Get away from me," I managed to say through gritted teeth, as I glared at the woman. On the inside I was being torn in two, divided by my need to both kill and protect her. "Stay...back..."

"No, I won't do that." She rested a hand on my chest. "War wants to convince you that everything is conflict and anger, but that's not true. Reach deep inside yourself and try to find peace."

I gripped her hand tightly, but couldn't let it go. "There is no peace inside me."

"That's War talking. The man I love has fought for peace for years. He ended the war with the angels. He fought by their side when they were threatened from within."

"I am not this man you speak of."

"You are. You just don't remember because War took your memories of me, and of our children." She turned back to the three men. "Our sons. Belial. Damien. Kassiel."

I cast another glance at them, all looking as if they were ready to attack me and defend their mother should I make a move against her. I was suddenly struck by the sense that they were also my blood, and saw some of my features in their faces reflected back at me. There was no denying the child inside her either. The woman spoke the truth.

"I will kill you all," War forced me to say, as he tried to exert his control again.

"No, you won't," she said. "You'd never hurt them. You might not remember them, but you know them. After all, you became War to save our oldest son, Belial."

I had no memory of what she spoke of, yet somehow I knew it was true. Inside me, War sent rage and hatred through my veins, trying to overwhelm me with bloodlust, but I fought him off. I had to know the truth of what had happened to me. But he was so strong, it seemed impossible to defeat him.

"Lucifer." The woman's voice called me back to her, and she reached up to stroke my face. "You know I'm your mate, deep down, even if you can't remember me. Embrace that feeling. You're not yourself right now. You sacrificed your memories for the good of all of us, but now you need to trust me. Believe in me and in our love. Believe in our family."

I started to shake my head, denying her words. She was nothing to me. Nothing. I was Lucifer, and War, and love did not exist in my world. "No!"

She cupped my cheek and kissed me, her mouth soft and gentle but unrelenting. I gathered her in my arms and returned the pressure, my tongue probing against her mouth. There was something about this woman. I couldn't get close enough.

She pulled back and took my face in her hands, staring into my eyes. "Fight War, Lucifer. You can defeat him. Let me help you."

"I can't. He's too strong."

"You are stronger."

Then she kissed me again, opening her mouth and touching my tongue with hers. Heat sizzled between us and I drew her closer, until we were almost one body. At the same time, I felt some of my anger and rage leeching away from me, along with my life force. Famine's magic stole energy and power, and she took that away from me as her mouth moved across mine.

My hands moved down to cup her stomach, to feel the life growing inside her that I'd helped create. A small little kick answered me in return, like my daughter was reaching out to me, calling for her dad. She needed me, and it gave me all the strength I needed to keep fighting.

War raged inside me, but he was growing weaker as Hannah leeched his rageful energy away. I clung to her, but War wouldn't let this battle end so easily. He suddenly unleashed a wave of frenzied anger, and gargoyles and Fallen rushed into the penthouse to attack my sons. They even came for my woman. My daughter.

"No!" I roared, as I pushed War back down and made the attackers stop. He would not hurt my family. I'd been willing to sacrifice myself, but not them. Never them.

You need me, War said. *I can make you great.*

I'm already great, asshole.

"Focus on peace and love," Hannah's voice said, coming to me through the swirling rage inside my mind that I desperately tried to fight off. "I know you can do this."

I pushed my mate away as my knees buckled, and I clutched my head. "I can't."

She reached for me again and took my hands, holding them in hers as she watched me, her gaze gentle. Pale light began to surround her, something I recognized as the light of truth. An Erelim angel trick. "Remember who you are. Yes, you are the Demon King, but you're also my mate. My husband. My destiny. You're the man who searched for me in every lifetime. Who waited patiently for me to be reborn every time. Who broke the curse and sacrificed himself to save the people he loves. Remember me. Remember *us*."

Her light surrounded me, and it all came back to me like being struck by a lightning bolt. I remembered it all. Eve and Hannah and every other life. Our sons. *Everything*.

I'd stopped the war against angels and fought for peace because of Hannah. Because of my family. Remembering them gave me the final push I needed to fight back against War, to ground him into dust.

He tried to escape my body, probably to find another host, but I latched onto him with my power and kept him inside me. Then I pummeled him with everything I had, until his essence exploded within my body in a flash of angry red hatred.

And then he was gone.

War's voice no longer echoed in my head, and his anger didn't tense my muscles or drive my thoughts any longer. Yet something from him was still inside me, a permanent part of me now.

I was Lucifer, but I was War too.

"Hannah." I captured my mate against me, as relief and love filled my chest. "I knew you would find a way to save me."

"I'm sorry it took so long."

"I'm sorry I tried to kill you."

She smiled up at me and shrugged. "You didn't put much effort into it."

"Is it done?" Belial asked, from behind us. "Are you free?"

I turned toward my sons, my heart swelling at the sight of all three of them together. My family—all here to save me. Including this new gift growing inside Hannah now. "Yes. I'm free."

13

HANNAH

I wrapped my arms around Lucifer and pressed my face against his chest, so relieved to have him back I could barely breathe. I no longer sensed War's presence, and instead felt only the man I'd loved for thousands of years.

He touched my cheek and I looked up at him. Love shone in his eyes, and no trace of War's red, angry glow lingered. Except now he *was* War, just as I was Famine. We'd been many things during my numerous past lives, but this was most unbelievable.

Lucifer turned toward our sons again with a smile. "You're all here. It's been so long."

"I couldn't have saved you without their help," I said, my heart bursting with pride and love. I'd wanted our entire family together again, and now I had my wish. It wasn't going to be the last time it happened either. I'd fought too hard to save Lucifer and bring this family together again, and I was going to keep it intact.

"Thank you," he told them.

"Father, it's been too long." Damien stepped forward and clasped Lucifer's hand as I drew away to allow them to embrace. I'd reunited with my sons, and now it was Lucifer's turn. Kassiel also moved to hug his father, and only Belial hung back, uncertainty in his eyes. But when Lucifer turned to our oldest son, it was with a hint of wry amusement playing at his lips and forgiveness in his gaze. Eventually, Belial stepped forward and shook Lucifer's hand. He said something low, something only meant for his father to hear, and Lucifer nodded.

Then Lucifer turned back to me and pulled me into his arms again. His hand crept lower between us until it rested against my swelling stomach, and his eyes looked at mine with awe. "Another child. I never imagined it might be possible."

I nodded and placed my hands over his. "A daughter, according to Marcus. She's strong too."

"I can tell. Strong like her mother." He looked so happy, but then he sighed. "I've missed so much of your pregnancy. I'm sorry."

"It's not your fault. I only had the first inkling that I might be pregnant when you became War, but I wasn't sure until after we left Heaven and I had Marcus examine me." I hesitated, debating whether to tell him about my sacrifice with Famine, but perhaps that was better saved for a private moment. Instead, I glanced around the penthouse, noting how it had been torn apart while I'd been gone. "What did you do to this place?"

He shrugged. "I destroyed it in a fit of rage when I came back and found you gone."

I sighed. "This poor penthouse. It's been through so much."

Lucifer nodded, his face thoughtful. "Yes, it has. Perhaps it's time to move on from it."

"My king," Samael said, behind us. I'd barely even noticed he was there during all of this.

Lucifer scowled and waved a hand, and Samael's shoulders slumped a little in relief. "There. Now you're no longer under War's —or my—control."

"That's what I wanted to talk to you about," Samael said. "The angels are coming to attack the city. They should be here any minute."

Lucifer swore under his breath. His wings, fully black again with only a slight red aura, unfurled as he turned to me. "It seems

I've started a war with the angels, and now I need to put an end to it."

"Of course you did," I said, with a slight shake of my head. "I'm coming with you."

Lucifer took my hand and pressed a kiss to it. "I wouldn't expect anything less, my queen." He turned back to Samael. "Please have all the demons stand down, and try to undo anything else I did when I was War. Kassiel, I locked Olivia and her other men up when I was War, and I apologize for that. Perhaps you and your brothers can free them now."

"We're on it," Kassiel said.

While the others took care of things back at The Celestial, Lucifer and I flew off the balcony and into the night. My silvery wings also had a barely noticeable green glow radiating from them, the only hint of my new status as an Elder God. Lucifer raised an eyebrow at them and I shrugged, and we held hands as we soared through the crisp night air. Reunited once again, and damn it felt good.

Just outside the city, we found about a hundred angel warriors flying toward Las Vegas over the desert, led by Gabriel. He wore gleaming silver armor and carried a spear, his expression menacing. Something angry lurked in there, something that would only be satisfied by the spilling of blood. Every single angel prepared to attack the second they saw us, but to my relief they waited for Gabriel's command.

"Is this your idea of a battle?" Gabriel called out to Lucifer. "Where are your demonic soldiers? Or is your ego really that large?"

"There will be no battle today," Lucifer said, and then he extended his power outward. "I release you."

The angry haze lifted from Gabriel's eyes and he blinked at us in confusion. "Lucifer? Hannah?"

"I'm sorry, my old friend." Lucifer rested his hand on Gabriel's shoulder. "I was not myself. I do not truly wish for a war with your people."

"Nor do I," Gabriel said, before he turned to face his soldiers.

"Stand down! Return to your homes. There will be no fight here today."

The angel warriors all seemed a bit confused, but sheathed their weapons and began flying away. Some looked relieved that they wouldn't spill demon blood today, while others looked disappointed. Soon, only Gabriel remained, the three of us hovering in the air as we faced each other.

Lucifer broke the silence. "You offered me a drink before, and I turned it down. Let me offer you one now."

"I accept," Gabriel said. "I'd love to know how you broke free of War's spell."

The three of us flew back to the penthouse together, our shoes crunching on broken glass and splintered wood as we set down inside our ruined home.

"I'm sorry for the mess," I told Gabriel with a sigh. "Lucifer had something of an anger management problem, but we've taken care of it."

"Where is War now?" Gabriel asked.

"He's gone," Lucifer said, as he poured two drinks from the one liquor bottle that had somehow survived his wrath, plus a glass of water for me.

Gabriel drew his brows together. "How can an Elder God be gone?"

"Famine is gone too," I said. "Although that's not exactly correct."

Lucifer gestured between us. "You're looking at what's left of Famine and War."

"How is that possible?"

I accepted the glass of water from Lucifer. "I released Famine, became her host, and then defeated her."

Gabriel's eyes widened. "I had no idea that could be done."

"Oberon told me it was possible, though he didn't seem to think it would work." I tilted my head as I considered. "I suspect for most people, it wouldn't. I was able to combat Famine because my essence is the opposite of hers. Just like Lucifer's is really the opposite of War's—once he remembered who he truly was." With Famine's added strength and magic, I'd been able to use my Erelim light of truth, boosting it to unheard-of levels in order to bring back Lucifer's memories. I'd never have been able to do that before becoming an Elder God myself—only Famine could weaken War enough for my other powers to succeed.

Gabriel took a sip of his drink with a grin. "Lucifer...a man of peace. Who would have guessed it, all those years ago?"

"Don't spread that rumor around," Lucifer said with a smirk. "I need to keep my villainous image, after all."

"I don't think that will be a problem." Gabriel finished his drink and set his glass down. "I'll leave you two to catch up, while I make sure there are no angels lingering behind with thoughts of taking out a demon or two." He clasped Lucifer on the shoulder. "It's good to have you back."

After he flew away, I turned to Lucifer, relieved to finally have him alone at last. We did have a lot of catching up to do—and many things to discuss.

14

HANNAH

L ucifer took my hands and drew me toward him. "Not a day passed that I didn't think of you, even when I was War. Your face haunted my every thought, though I didn't understand why."

"I thought about you every day also. I felt so guilty for locking you up—"

He placed a finger over my lips. "No. You did the right thing."

"I know I did, but I still hated it, and things were so hard without you..."

"Hannah." My name was a soothing caress, as visceral as any touch. He dropped a kiss to my hair and smoothed runaway strands from my face. "From what I've seen and heard, you did an amazing job while I was gone. You stepped up and became queen to our people, all while pregnant. I'm only sad I missed so much."

"You didn't mean to be gone." I laid my hand on his chest, feeling the reassuring beat of his heart under my palm. "You did what had to be done."

He rumbled a sound that could have been agreement or frustration, then smoothed his hand over my belly. "I'm here now though, and I'm not going anywhere. I'll be by your side every second of these last few months of your pregnancy, until you're begging me to leave you alone. Foot rubs? I'm your man. Strange cravings? Not a problem. Awkward pregnancy sex? Anytime you want."

I laughed a little at that, but then I remembered that this would be the last time we'd be going through all of this. I turned away, my eyes filling with tears, but Lucifer caught my chin.

"What is it?" he asked, his voice full of concern.

"To save you, I had to make a sacrifice too." I swallowed the lump of sadness in my throat.

Horror filled his eyes. "Is something wrong with the baby? Did... Did Famine...?"

I shook my head quickly before he believed the wrong thing. "No, Famine hasn't hurt her. She's just..." I stopped talking, but frown lines formed between Lucifer's brows, and I had to finish before he imagined any worse. "She's the last baby I can have."

He wrapped me in his strong arms, pressing me against his chest. "I'm so sorry, Hannah. I'm so sorry she's taken that from you."

"From us," I mumbled against his shoulder. I held him tight, feeling the sadness deep within my bones as my sacrifice really sank in. Lucifer clung to me too, no doubt feeling his own sorrow and grief.

He pulled back and wiped a tear from my eye. "I'm sorry. I had no idea you'd given up so much to save me."

"I won't lie, it hurts. I'm not sure I even want another child after this one, but to know it's impossible..."

"I understand, and I feel the same."

I tried to smile. "But we have four healthy children, right?"

He nodded, still watching my eyes. "That's an heir and more than enough spares. Of course, our heir tried to overthrow us multiple times, but we have time to work that out with him."

A short laugh escaped me at that. "It was so good to see them all together. We need to keep our family close from now on."

"I've been thinking the same thing. I made so many mistakes with our family before, but things are different now. The curse is broken, and we won't have those long years without you. Our daughter will never have to try to adjust to her mother in a new body, like our sons did."

"No, she won't," I said with relief. "And now that we're Elder Gods we can finally defeat Adam, so he won't ever be a threat to her."

"Adam..." He growled a little at the thought. "He came here as Pestilence while you were gone, but I fought him off. I believe I weakened him, but I'm sure he will be back."

"We'll be ready when he does. We already have a plan in place."

"Of course you do." Lucifer pressed a kiss to my forehead. "I'm constantly amazed at your strength. Every lifetime, you inspire me. But in this one, you've truly outdone yourself, my queen."

"Thank you. You're not so bad yourself, you know." I draped my arms around his neck. "Now, about that awkward pregnancy sex..."

A sexy, masculine sound of amusement rumbled deep in his throat. "Whatever my wife needs."

"Is there anywhere in this penthouse that isn't trashed?" I asked.

He picked me up like I weighed nothing, then carried me into the bedroom we'd once shared, where I'd slept alone for months. The bed remained untouched, still covered in black silk sheets, with my added teal pillows.

"Even in my frenzied state, I couldn't destroy this," Lucifer said, as he set me down on it. His voice was low and deep and sent a shiver of anticipation through me. "Although I'm starting to think maybe we need a new place to live..."

I grabbed his shirt and yanked it open, sending buttons flying. "Stop talking and fuck me already. It's been six months since I've seen you, and these pregnancy hormones have been killer."

He gave me a wicked grin as he removed his shirt, revealing the smooth, muscled chest I'd missed so much. "I used to wait lifetimes for you. Six months is nothing."

I grabbed a pillow and hit him with it. He took it from me and tossed it aside with a chuckle, then pinned me to the bed, taking care not to crush my stomach. His kiss devoured me, while his hands entwined with mine above my head. My body arched toward him, the need to have him fill me so strong I thought I might scream. All I could do was kiss him back harder and rock my hips against him, silently begging him for more.

He rose up, just enough to yank off my shirt and tear off my bra. Then he stared down at me, his fingers brushing over the swell of my body and cupping my breasts. "Incredible."

"There have been some changes while you were gone." I squirmed, midway between embarrassment and amusement.

He met my gaze with a hungry look in his eyes. "I love you like this, round with my child. I'm going to savor every second of it."

"Start now," I murmured, reaching for his pants.

"So impatient," he teased. He unfastened my pants and tugged them off, taking my panties too. I was still wearing the clothes I'd worn to fight Famine in and they were a bit dusty, but none of that mattered to him.

He admired me for a few seconds, then he sank between my legs and kissed the side of my knee, and my breath caught. I anticipated him kissing along the inside of my thigh, but as I held my breath, waiting, he moved away and started at the other knee.

"Like I said, I'm going to savor you."

I huffed but closed my eyes because Lucifer savoring me... I'd missed it.

His fingers gripped the outsides of my thighs as he parted them farther, and my breathing increased just from the anticipation. His tongue touched my skin, and I moved my hands until I pushed them through his thick, dark hair.

I tugged, trying to pull him closer. "Lucifer."

He made that rumble of amusement again, but then he took pity on me and covered my clit with his mouth. I let out a breathy moan at finally getting a sample of what I craved, as his tongue moved across my folds, tasting every inch of me like he couldn't get enough. He buried his face in my pussy, and I lost all thought as he sucked my clit harder. He feasted like a starving man, as if I was the best meal he'd ever had.

"Mmm." He hummed his satisfaction. "You missed me."

"So much." But my words were broken by harsh breaths as his mouth worked magic on me. My hands were back in his hair, tugging at the dark strands, and he responded to me, applying more pressure, licking and sucking harder and faster. Then looked at me, his eyes glowing red, before lowering his head again to flick his tongue over my clit in one possessive stroke. It was enough to send me spinning away from him as all of my muscles tightened and released. I hung in a moment of free fall, my breath held in my chest as I rode the feeling.

My body pulsed and I gasped for air as Lucifer rose up above me with a dark smile. Then he slowly dragged his trousers off, his large, perfect cock jutting forth with obvious need. I wasn't the only one dying for release here.

I sat up a little and took his cock into my mouth, just for a few seconds, unable to help myself. I needed to taste him too. He caught his breath, and I relished my small degree of control over this man who was used to controlling every other element of his life. Here, he was mine.

"Fuck, I missed you too," he said, as he gripped my head lovingly. But then his need overwhelmed him too and he let out a groan and jerked his cock out of my mouth.

He laid back on the bed and pulled me on top of him, making me straddle him. With fingers digging into my hips, he lifted me up while looking me in the eyes, his intense and glowing red. I wondered if mine were glowing too, but that was my last thought before I sank down, sliding him inside me.

It felt amazing, both of us joined together at last. I wasn't sure if it was because I was pregnant or because we were both gods now, but I felt him so much more than I ever had before, both physically and on a spiritual level. Our souls were entwined, just as our bodies were.

"You feel so good." Lucifer groaned, a deep sound that vibrated right through both of us. His hands were on my hips, before he ran them over my ribs and to my breasts, touching me everywhere, like he'd never felt me before. Then he thrust up hard, filling me so deeply it made me gasp. It was exactly what my body needed though, and now I wanted more.

At first Lucifer let me set my own rhythm as he fondled my breasts, watching them bounce over him, and I threw my head back and enjoyed the pleasure building within me. I rode him harder and faster, and I loved the feel of his cock sliding deeper into me with each thrust. But then his hands returned to my hips and he growled as he began to thrust up, matching me, holding me at the angle he wanted, fucking me harder and faster like he couldn't get enough.

He reached up to tangle his hand in my hair and pulled my face down to his, kissing me in a way that left no doubt that I belonged to him. His possessive fucking only fueled my own desire, and I let go and allowed him to take control of my body completely. I melted into him as we moved as one, each of his thrusts teasing more heat through me until I screamed his name and dug my nails into his skin, shouting my pleasure. As the orgasm rocked through me, power erupted out of me, and then Lucifer's breathing changed and he joined me with his own rush of energy. Glass shattered around us, but I barely noticed as he thrust a few last times, dragging out the moment where we'd never been more connected.

As my throbbing body returned to gentle flutters, I fell over his chest, rolling slightly to the side to allow for my cumbersome shape. Then I noticed the plants growing all over the room, which I must have created when he made me climax. Oops. Lucifer's orgasm had demolished more of the penthouse too, destroying what little had still been standing.

He followed my gaze and raised an eyebrow. "That's new."

"Was it just me, or was sex even more intense as an Elder God?"

"I'm not sure," he rumbled, as he reached down to slide a finger inside me. "I think we should do it again to be sure."

"Already?"

"Definitely." He grabbed me and set me on my knees, then mounted me from behind. His cock was already hard and pushing against my entrance, begging for entry. "After all, we have six months to make up for...and I have the stamina of a god."

After that, there were no more words as I pushed back against his cock, taking him in deep, while he reached forward and grabbed my hair to yank my head back. He took me hard and fast, like he would die if he didn't claim every inch of me—but we were gods now and nothing could harm me. I reveled in every second of it, until he had me screaming his name again and tightening around his cock, squeezing out his own climax while our power shook the entire floor of the penthouse.

"If we keep this up, we might need to move," I said, as my body trembled under the lingering effects of my last orgasm.

"I've been thinking the same thing." He wrapped me up in his arms and kissed me. "But right now all that matters is we're together —and nothing is going to tear us apart ever again."

15

LUCIFER

I glanced at the pile of books on the desk again. Hannah had left no stone unturned, no tome unopened. There were books open I doubted she could even understand, but I could imagine her taking her time turning the fragile pages looking for a familiar word or a diagram in a margin. How often had she spent late nights in this room searching for the way to rescue me from War's clutches?

I didn't need an answer. Instinct told me she'd made every night a late one during her search. Somehow she'd risen to Demon Queen during my absence as well, all while pregnant—and pretty ill too, from what I'd gathered.

I'd always known Hannah would rescue me. It was one of the reasons I'd taken such a risk in the first place. But seeing the evidence of all her hard work made me appreciate her efforts even more.

I breathed in the scent of my library—the ancient pages, the leather chairs, and now the slight floral scent from Hannah's plants. Though I'd destroyed much of the penthouse when I was War, I'd left enough of this space untouched for me to work at my desk for a few hours, trying to catch up on everything I'd missed in the last six months.

I'd missed a lot, it seemed. Time hadn't passed the same for me with War in my body. I hadn't thought about normal things or needed to eat or sleep. I'd had two focuses.

One, escape the confines of Heaven. Two, bring war and chaos to the world.

Hannah stepped into the library, absolutely glowing in a pale green floor-length dress that showed off her rounded belly. Pride and love filled me, and I immediately stood and crossed the library to her, taking her in my arms. I'd never truly felt lucky before. Certainly not like this.

"Hello, my love. How are you feeling this morning?" I asked, as I drew her against me.

"Strange. I don't need to sleep or eat anymore...but I still like to do both of those things." She shrugged. "How are you?"

"I'm brilliant. Never better." I pressed a kiss to her forehead. "Is it time for the meeting?"

"I believe it is."

"Come with me?" I lowered my voice and spoke against her ear. "We'll have time to nap later."

She rolled her eyes. "Of course I'm coming to the meeting. I can't let you loose with my Archdemons until I see that you know what you're doing."

"Oh, they're your Archdemons now?" I took her hand and led her out of the library, excited to be sharing my throne after so many lifetimes I'd spent without her. "I see how it is—I leave you alone for a few months and you take over completely."

"What's that saying? What's yours is mine, and what's mine is mine..."

"That does sound like marriage, yes."

As we held hands and grinned at each other like young lovers, we took the elevator down a level, to the command center. The demons working there bowed and some even clapped as we entered, and I gave them all a cocky grin and a little wave, though Hannah shook her head at me. It never hurt to remind them that I really did live up to all the stories about me.

We stepped into the conference room, where our allied

Archdemons were waiting for us, along with Samael. They all rose to their feet when we entered, and Lilith actually rushed forward and threw her arms around me. Then she hugged Hannah next.

"You did it," she said. "You actually managed to save him."

"She did," I confirmed, with a wry smile at my wife. "I owe my salvation to Hannah, though I would like to thank each and every one of you for your part in keeping the demon world running smoothly over the last few months. Romana, thank you for your loyalty and for your people's help in guarding Hannah. Baal, I truly appreciate the risks you've taken in spying on Nemesis and Fenrir for me. Lilith, Hannah's told me your counsel and support were invaluable to her, and I thank you for that."

"I think I speak for everyone when I say it was an honor to help however we could," Lilith said. "However, we're all relieved you've returned to us."

"As am I. I thank you all for your loyalty during this difficult period, though there is one more person I must thank—Samael." I turned to my oldest, dearest friend. "You've supported me through all these years, and when I was gone, you stood by Hannah's side in my absence."

"I did what anyone would do in such a position," he said, his voice deep yet humble.

"No, you always manage to go above and beyond, my friend." I rested a hand on his shoulder, and he stoically nodded, though I could see in his eyes that he was pleased.

"Is it true you're both really Elder Gods?" Romana asked. "What happened to War? And Famine?"

"Yes, it's true," Hannah said.

"You could say we defeated them...and then took their place," I added.

"They're truly gone then?" Baal asked.

Hannah's eyes grew sympathetic. "I'm sorry. If I could have done it without defeating your mother, I would have. If it makes you feel better, she seemed to still care for you, in her own way."

He held up a hand. "Do not apologize. It's actually a relief to know she's gone. I no longer have to live in fear of my mother awakening and destroying the world."

I knew exactly how he felt—except my father, Death, was still out there, locked away in his tomb, waiting to be set free. With Famine released, we were one step closer to his awakening, and that thought terrified me like nothing else.

"Nemesis is dead too," Hannah said. "I killed her in the battle in Faerie at Famine's tomb. Unfortunately, Fenrir got away."

"Do you think he'll go after Death next?" Romana asked.

"Possibly, if he's still stupid and stubborn enough to continue this battle," I said.

"He is," Baal confirmed.

"Even so, he can't get into Hell, where Death's tomb is located," Lilith said. "Lucifer made sure of that when he sealed that realm up all those years ago. Only he and I have the keys."

"A good point." I turned to Samael. "Let's make sure to get extra protection on Lilith."

"That's not necessary," Lilith said.

"No, he's right." Baal took her hand, and I noticed Samael narrowing his eyes. "We must protect that key at all costs."

"What of Pestilence?" Romana asked.

The very thought of him made me bristle. "When I was War I fought him and weakened him, but I have no doubt he'll be back."

"We already have a plan in place for Pestilence's return.' Hannah looked at me as she spoke, then turned to the table. "But I think we should have something else ready if it doesn't work."

"Somehow I doubt Adam has any interest in fighting off Pestilence's control, like you two did," Samael said.

"No, that won't work. We need another plan." Hannah turned to me. "Oberon said you once had a key to Void. Do you still have it?"

A chill ran down my spine. Whatever I'd expected her to say, it hadn't been that. "We're not using that."

"But you've been to Void before," Baal said.

"Yes, thousands of years ago, and I risked a lot by asking Nyx to make the Fallen into demons so they could survive in Hell. I'm lucky I made it back at all."

"How did you even get such a thing?" Romana asked.

"My father, Death, gave it to me. Before we became bitter enemies."

"It might work," Samael said, his voice thoughtful. "The key is the only thing that can send the Elder Gods to the Void."

I cast a hard look around the table at my allies. "Yes, but opening a portal to Void could also let other Elder Gods out. We don't need any more of them on our hands, now do we?"

They all murmured their agreement, and I considered the matter dropped, but I sensed they were all still wary. They wanted an easy solution, but when facing threats such as these, there wasn't one. It was always a matter of choosing the best option between multiple shitty situations, then praying you made the right decision.

I rose to my feet, forcing them to look up at my full height as I towered over them like the king I was. "Now that Hannah and I have the powers of War and Famine, Pestilence won't be able to stand against us. In the meantime, use all of our resources to hunt down Fenrir. I want him brought to justice immediately."

Hannah looked at me and nodded, before I sat beside her again —in my rightful place as Demon King.

Damn, it was good to be back.

16

HANNAH

As we stepped through the archway that led to Persephone's Garden, the first hint of nervousness took root in my chest. Lucifer had given me this space six months ago, back when it was nothing more than an empty lot and a dream. He'd known I would miss the flower shop and would need a connection to nature even in the middle of the Nevada desert. But then he was gone, and I'd had to design and implement the garden all by myself, trying to make it a place that the guests of The Celestial Resort & Casino would enjoy. Now I dearly wished for his approval.

It had been two days since Lucifer had become himself again and things were starting to feel normal once more. Azazel had fully recovered, thanks to my gift of energy, followed by Marcus's healing. Belial and Damien were staying in the hotel for now, though I doubted they would stay for long. The meeting with the Archdemons had gone well, and Lucifer and I were getting used to being Elder Gods. There were definitely some benefits to not needing any sleep.

Lucifer held my hand as he let me lead the way through the winding paths, under the dense trees and past the perfectly arranged plants toward the waterfall. "It's gorgeous."

"You like it?" I asked, turning a big smile on him. The sound of the waterfall soothed me instantly, and I inhaled the sweet fragrances of the flowers.

He nodded and raised my hand to his mouth, brushing his lips over my knuckles. "It's beautiful. Just as I knew it would be. As all your gardens have been."

"I was nervous doing it without your approval since this hotel is your baby," I said, as I walked to my bench. After I sat, I patted the smooth stone beside me. "This is my favorite spot."

"Might be my favorite spot, too." He grinned and sat as close to me as he could, pulling me into his arms. He dipped his head and kissed my neck, a promise of more to come. "You didn't need my approval. You had my complete faith when I gave you the project."

I arched my neck to grant him better access to my skin. "I know, but it would have been nice to be able to run decisions by you first..."

"I doubt I would have been much help. You know I'm not good with all this...nature. I leave that to you."

I rolled my eyes. It was true, Lucifer couldn't name any of the flowers near us if he'd tried. He was completely useless in that area. "We're hoping to open it to hotel guests next week."

"They're going to love it. It's really going to elevate the hotel's profile."

I practically beamed with pride at his comments, but then I noticed his frown as he stared at the waterfall. "What is it?"

"I can't believe I'm saying this, but I think we should move away from Las Vegas." He looked out over the garden like he could see the city itself through the foliage. "I love the very air here. It's saturated in sin, but I want to concentrate on you, and on our daughter."

I leaned against him, finding that spot on his chest that seemed to have been made just for me to snuggle against. "I've been thinking the same thing. We need a fresh start. The Celestial is great and all, but a casino is not the best place to raise a child."

"No it's not, and I'd like to move somewhere safer, and more easily defensible." He gave a rueful glance up at the building. "Those damn floor-to-ceiling windows."

I let out a laugh. "I know! We must have spent a small fortune repairing them over the last year or two."

"It's like no one knows how to use a door anymore," he muttered.

"Including you!"

"That doesn't count. I wasn't in my right mind then."

I stared at the waterfall as I voiced the secret dream I'd had over the last few months, one I'd been scared to even really consider since I didn't know if I'd be able to get Lucifer back. "While you were away, Asmodeus bought Brandy a house on the beach in southern California. I was thinking I'd like to live near her, since I miss her a lot, and she's pregnant too. We could raise our kids together." Then the hope faded as the reality of the situation hit me again. "But I also don't want to put her or her family in any danger. You and I are always going to be Lucifer and Hannah, Demon King and Queen, War and Famine. We're never going to have a quiet life."

"No, although at the moment that sounds lovely." He stared at the waterfall for a few moments, then turned back to me. "We should do it. We'll always have duties and responsibilities, and there will always be some danger, but we deserve happiness too. As for Brandy and her family, we'll make sure they are well-protected at all times."

Could we really make it work? I wasn't sure. While Lucifer had been gone, it felt like everything in the demon world was so precarious, like it could all easily crumble to dust if I wasn't there to hold it together. But maybe if we managed to stop Pestilence and Fenrir things would calm down for a while. We'd be able to step back from the demon world, delegate more to our Archdemons, and enjoy a small amount of peace. I could dream, anyway.

A soft whinnying sound caught my attention, and we turned to see our two spectral horses moving through the grass. My ever-present gargoyle guards drew their weapons, but I held out a hand to show them this wasn't a threat. War's horse was red and huge, both beautiful and terrifying at once, though he no longer left fiery hoof prints behind him. Mine was smaller and jet black, with a luxurious mane that blew gently in the breeze.

"Where did they come from?" I asked.

Lucifer took my hand as we rose to our feet and walked over to the horses. "I'm not sure, but they will vanish when not needed. Perhaps they live in the Void and can cross over somehow."

"That's so strange."

"The strangest thing for me was that Strife was the only one I could speak with the whole time I was locked in Heaven." He greeted his horse like a long-lost friend. "Not that he ever said much back, but I enjoyed his company nonetheless."

The red horse nuzzled against Lucifer's hand, and I reached out to touch mine more tentatively. Her coat was smooth and clean, and I ran my hand over it, wondering what it would be like to ride her. She had no saddle, but I had memories of riding horses in various past lives, though I was surely out of practice now. I was tempted to climb onto her back, but I was pregnant. Then again, I was also a Horseman now, and somehow I knew I wouldn't fall off this horse that I was bonded to on a spiritual level.

"My horse is named Misery, though I'm not sure how I know that," I said. "We've only met once so far, right after I became Famine. I'm not sure what I'm supposed to do with her. Did I need to feed her? Brush her? House her?"

"They're Elder Gods themselves, in a way," Lucifer said. "Or maybe they're part of our own essence. I don't really know. Either way, they don't need to eat or sleep, just like we don't, though they might enjoy a good brushing now and then."

"I guess we're bound to them for the rest of time," I said. "If we get a new place to live, we should make sure there's a space for them."

Lucifer patted his horse with a smile. "We should go for a ride sometime. The only thing I enjoyed while in Heaven was riding Strife—he's faster than even I can fly."

"Good idea. Out in the desert sometime maybe?"

Our conversation was interrupted by a scream outside the garden, over by one of the hotel's pools. Lucifer and I were instantly on alert, and my gargoyle guard surrounded us with weapons drawn and their bat-like wings already out. When we rushed toward the sound, we were met by Azazel, her weapons drawn.

"It's Pestilence," she said. "He's here."

17

HANNAH

A ripple of fear went through me, but I kept calm and nodded. I'd prepared for this, and I just had to make sure everything went according to plan. "Sound the alarm and have everyone get into position!"

"What's the plan?" Lucifer asked. We hadn't had time to go over it yet—we'd thought we would have a few weeks before Pestilence returned, at least.

"Just follow my lead." I didn't really have time to explain, not when Pestilence was on his sickly white horse, trotting around the large sparkling blue pool that had dozens of guests in or around it. Now they were either screaming and running, or falling to the ground sick—or worse. A few dead bodies already floated in the pool, and I swallowed hard at the sight of them. Pestilence laughed as he spread more sickness out in a putrid cloud and my hatred for him only increased, which I didn't think was possible.

My gargoyle guards rushed to form a barrier in front of Pestilence, their stone skin protecting them from his deadly plague, and that allowed a few more of the tourists to escape. What we didn't expect was that Pestilence wasn't alone this time—he'd brought a group of imps and shifter allies, and they all radiated disease like some sort of super-spreaders as they chased down other unsuspecting humans.

"He could infect the whole Strip if we don't stop him!" Lucifer said, as he summoned his War sword of hellfire and darkness and wielded it in front of him.

"I need to get Pestilence back into the garden," I said. "You take care of the others."

Without even stopping to question what I had planned, Lucifer altered his trajectory and headed toward the imps and shifters. I trusted him to take care of them, and I walked toward Pestilence slowly, hoping the others were already moving into position at the waterfall, or this plan would fail. The being that had once been Adam turned his attention toward me, a smile spreading over his sickly yellow face, one of the boils on his chin pulsing like it had a heartbeat.

"Eve, my love." His voice had changed, no longer the sound of my first husband's voice, but now tinged with something far more ancient. His eyes were all white, no pupils at all, and it was hard not to look away when he stared at me with them. "You've changed."

"I wanted to be like you." I took another step forward and let my Famine essence unfurl. My body glowed with a faint green light, and I would bet money that my eyes did too. "Your equal."

He cocked his head. "You released Famine?"

"Yes and I made the sacrifice." It was hard not to gag as I approached him. "Now we can be together. All we have to do is take out War."

He rubbed his hands together. "Yes, and then we can rule this world side by side as gods. That's all I ever wanted."

"I know." I forced a smile. "Come, let me show you my horse, Misery. She's in the garden waiting for me. We can talk more there."

Pestilence dismounted his own horse and sent it away with a gesture. The white beast rode away, turning incorporeal and running over the pool before vanishing. Then the rotting corpse-like Horseman walked alongside me, while my gargoyles hung back, though it clearly pained them to do so. I eyed Adam closely, wondering how he had become so far gone. Lucifer had changed too, with the red angry glow always bursting out of his skin, but he hadn't lost himself as much as Adam had—he must have been fighting War's influence even without his memories of me. I wondered what horrible thing I would have become had I failed to defeat Famine—probably some gaunt, haggard figure with sagging boobs and jagged fangs, always trying to find my next meal. I shuddered a little at the thought.

No one stopped us as we entered Persephone's Garden, and I led Pestilence toward the waterfall. Now that I'd let my Famine powers out, they begged to drain all the life from the plants in the garden, but I held myself back.

"What made you change your mind?" Adam asked.

"When Lucifer became War he was lost to me. He forgot who I was." I cast a glance over at Adam. "You would never do that."

"No. Never. Over hundreds of years, I always found you. Even when he didn't."

"I know. I became Famine because she has the power to stop War—and so I could be a Horseman like you." I gestured at Misery up ahead, who stood beside the waterfall. "Ah, there's my horse now."

As we approached the waterfall, my gargoyle guard moved in close, with Theo at the lead. Pestilence jerked his head around, just as Belial, Kassiel, and Damien emerged from the hidden cave below the water.

"What's this?" Adam asked.

"It's time for you to go back to sleep." I still had the powers I'd accessed in Faerie, and they were stronger here in the garden I'd created. At my thought, vines wound around Pestilence, binding his limbs, and his face contorted.

"You can't hold Pestilence!" As he spoke, he struggled, and the vines started to wither and die from his poison.

I drew on Famine, finding the vacuum always in the center of me, the one always hungry for power. I focused on Pestilence, drawing on him, taking his energy away. Making him weak.

He screamed as he realized what was happening. "What are you doing? You lied to me!"

"And it was all too easy... You'd think you would know by now that I will never be yours."

Out of the corner of my eye I saw Lucifer flying just outside the garden. He had the imps and shifters fighting each other with a touch of his War frenzy, while Belial and Azazel picked them off on the sidelines and protected the innocent humans. It was almost beautiful as Lucifer moved his hands like the world's most violent conductor. Then he finished his orchestral movement by destroying them with darkness and hellfire. Perfect takedown.

And my cue to finish what I'd started with Pestilence.

I directed the vines to pull Adam under the waterfall, using the walkthrough feature I'd installed. Theo hit a hidden button and the wall slid open to reveal Pestilence's tomb. I'd had it brought here from Stonehenge, banking on the fact Adam wouldn't be able to leave me alone and would return again. And where Adam went, Pestilence went too.

Damien was already inside, with the tomb open and ready. He'd told me it wouldn't work as well the second time around, since the runes weren't fresh—whatever that meant. I had to take the chance though. We had no other option.

Pestilence struggled and glared at me. "No! You will die!"

He sent out wave after wave of disease and horror, but my gargoyle guards were immune and they blocked me from it. Still, it took all of my power to drag him to the tomb, and even then I wasn't sure it would be enough.

With a roar, Adam suddenly broke free of his vines, then materialized a golden bow and arrow and began shooting me with them. One hit my arm and made me instantly feel sick, and I yanked it out and prayed whatever it was wouldn't harm the baby. I knocked him back with a blast of air, then used a weave of darkness and light to shield myself from more arrows.

Just when I thought Adam might actually break free, Lucifer rushed in and tackled him, knocking him backward.

"Get in that tomb, you bastard." Lucifer's face twisted with rage —fury created by all the times Adam had wronged us over the years. He shoved Adam hard, and they both fell into the tomb and began wrestling. Lucifer launched himself out a second later, his body covered in boils from Pestilence's magic, and then blasted Adam with bright blue hellfire. Belial joined in with his own hellfire from the other side of the cave, and I used a combination of vines and air to lift the lid of the tomb and use it to cover Adam.

The second it was closed, Damien spilled his fae blood on top of it, and the runes began to glow. The lid buckled and nearly came off as Pestilence struggled, and Belial rushed forward to add his own. I created a blade of darkness and sliced my own hand, then Lucifer did the same. Angel, demon, human, fae—all represented in our family line. As soon as all the blood mingled, the runes flashed bright, and the tomb sealed. Then it all went dark in the cave.

"Is it done?" Belial asked.

"Yes, but the seal won't last for thousands of years like the previous one did," Damien said. "And I think anyone powerful enough could open it, if they tried."

"But it will hold for now, right?" I asked.

Damien inspected the runes. "Yes, I believe it will hold for at least a decade or two, assuming no one tampers with it."

"That's enough time for us to find a better solution." Lucifer wrapped an arm around me. "An excellent plan, my love."

"Thank you, but it wouldn't have worked without everyone doing their part." My shoulders sagged in relief as I leaned against him. Adam was locked away, and couldn't harm me anymore—or my daughter. We might actually be able to have something akin to a normal life.

For a while, anyway.

18

HANNAH

T he next morning I sat in my garden on my bench, gathering my thoughts. We'd cleaned up everything from Pestilence's attack, and the angels had been able to heal most of the hotel guests. Unfortunately, many others were killed during the attack, and Lucifer had to use his persuasive powers to cover it up so it wasn't all over the news. We planned to offer compensation to each family that had lost someone, since it was our fault they'd been attacked at all. It definitely pushed me more in favor of moving out of the city to somewhere more remote, where we wouldn't put so many innocent lives in danger.

The good news was that our plan worked, and Pestilence was securely locked away beneath the waterfall. I felt his power emanating softly throughout the area, and I was certain the humans did too, because it seemed to draw them to The Celestial—and to the garden. His ancient power lured them in without harming them, just as it had done when he was under Stonehenge. A strange benefit of him being locked there, since it would only bring us more business. About time Adam did something that helped us after all these years.

My horse suddenly appeared and approached me. I held my

hand out to her and stroked over her face. The horse harrumphed softly, blowing warm air from her nostrils.

"Misery," I murmured, as I took in her black velvet coat, inky with a darkness I almost couldn't define. "One day we'll ride."

Lucifer had ridden his horse all over Heaven and much of Earth, too. Part of me longed to experience that freedom for myself, and I patted Misery again. The two of us were stuck with each other for the rest of eternity it seemed, so I'd better get used to her.

I tiled my head as I stared into her dark eyes. "I think we need a better name for you. Something not quite so dreary."

Misery whinnied softly at that, and I felt something like approval through our strange connection. I didn't get words from her, nothing like that, just a little hint of her thoughts and emotions.

"Blackie? Midnight? Ghost?"

She didn't like any of those. I was pondering some others, when a movement from the nearby olive trees drew my attention. I rose to my feet, but I wasn't worried. Security had been increased even more since Pestilence had been locked up in the garden, and I was well guarded today.

I smiled as Damien strode from the olive trees, something I'd planted because they reminded me of our home in Faerie. My handsome middle son was a perfect mix of fae and Fallen, and I desperately wanted to spend some time with him after all these years.

"Hello, Mother," he said as he approached with a sad smile.

I stood and held out my hands to him. "Is everything all right?"

"It's been nice being here with all of you, but I must return to Faerie to continue my work. I think I've done all I can here." His gaze drifted to the waterfall and the cave beyond.

"I understand, and I appreciate everything you've done. Before you go, can you sit for a while?" I dropped as gracefully as I could back on the stone bench and patted the space next to me. "It's been a long time since we've caught up properly, and I've only just found you again."

My chest tightened a little at the thought. Thanks to the curse, and then Jophiel hiding who I was for so long, I hadn't seen Damien in years. I'd managed to reconnect with my other sons a little, but it was always a bit awkward. They weren't the men I remembered, and I wasn't the mother they knew. But it was important for me to try, especially with a new addition to our family on the way. I didn't want to be a stranger to any of my sons ever again.

"Yes, I have some time." He sat beside me and gazed across the space. "This garden is lovely. It reminds me of our Spring Court residence."

I beamed at his compliment. "That's exactly what I was trying to emulate, using everything I remembered from my time there. Although when we went to Faerie to release Famine, I realized it would be impossible to truly copy such a place on Earth. This was the best I could do."

"Do you miss Faerie?"

"Sometimes, but it was so many lifetimes ago..." I shrugged. "I have a connection with all the realms, but my place is here on Earth at the moment."

"And mine is in Faerie. Though I hope to be able to visit you more often now. A baby sister is a good excuse, after all. Speaking, of how's my sister doing in there?" He nodded at my stomach and I automatically passed my hand over my bump, happy when my daughter kicked in response.

"She's great. Famine promised she'd come to no harm, and she hasn't."

"I can't wait to meet her. I'll make sure to come back after she's born. I just can't be away from Faerie too long."

"Lucifer told me about the work you're doing there," I said. Damien was pretending to be one of Oberon's most loyal princes, but in truth he was spying on the High King for Lucifer.

Damien nodded, his face serious. "Oberon has kept Faerie neutral for years, but I'm sure he is plotting something big, though I don't know what."

"Is it true he killed Titania?" I asked. Though I'd never been close to the Queen, she had been my aunt, after all.

He glanced around and lowered his voice. "No one can prove it, but everyone knows he did."

"How did my mother..." I paused and started again. "How did Demeter take her sister's death?"

"Not well, but as Queen of the Spring Court she can't openly do anything against Oberon. I'm pretty sure she would act against him if she could though. I've been trying to find others who might help overthrow him someday."

I lifted an eyebrow. "That sounds dangerous."

He shrugged. "Yes, but someone needs to protect the future of Faerie."

I squeezed his arm gently. "Just be careful, okay?"

He rolled his eyes and grinned at me. "I am, don't worry."

"I always worry. That's what mothers do." I reached up to touch his shiny blue-black hair, which was stunningly beautiful under the sun. "What of love? Any special men or women? If I remember correctly, you were quite the charmer as Dionysus. The stories about your parties were legendary. Why don't you use that name anymore?"

He coughed and jerked his head away. "That was the old me. I've changed a lot in the last few thousand years."

"What happened?" I asked, hearing the touch of sadness in his voice. Like most immortals who'd lived thousands of years, he'd gone by many names during his lifetime. Dionysus had been his fae name, and Damien his demon one. I was surprised he used the demon one now, despite living in Faerie.

"After you—Persephone—died..." He paused, as if finding the right words. "Things were different. Belial left Hell, then tried to overthrow Father. I tried to stay out of it, and at first, I threw myself into the parties, booze, and orgies, but later I realized it was just a way to numb myself to the pain of it all. Eventually, I chose a different path."

It pained me to see my most carefree and jovial son so heavy-hearted. While I'd been alive, his life had been a celebration of wine, sex, and merriment. He'd once been a great actor and patron of the theater too, but I supposed now he used those skills as a spy. "Belial told me you both blamed your father for my death."

"It was a difficult time for both of us. I'm not sure I ever told you this, but Belial and I were the ones who found you dead, after Plutus and Philomelus killed you."

That was unusual—normally the curse had me die in Lucifer's arms, but there were a few exceptions, and it probably pleased Death to bring misery upon my sons too.

Plutus had been Adam's incarnation while I'd been Persephone. He was an Autumn Court fae, along with his brother Philomelus, who'd gone along with everything horrible Plutus had done. Recently Philomelus had been helping Adam release Pestilence and War, but I bested him during the battle in Heaven, and Azazel got in the killing blow.

"If it makes you feel any better, Philomelus is dead. And Adam..." I gestured toward the waterfall. "But why did you blame your father?"

"You were killed on one of your trips to Faerie as part of Lucifer's deal with Demeter to spend half your time in Hell, and half there. You tried to get him to go with you, but Lucifer refused, saying he had to stay and rule the demons from the palace in Hell. He always hated going to Faerie, so you went alone—and because of that, you died."

As Damien fell quiet, I smoothed a hand over his back. "It wasn't Lucifer's fault. It was Adam, and the curse. But that's over now."

"You were safer in Hell," Damien muttered. "Father should have broken the deal with Demeter and kept you there. Or gone with you at least."

I sighed. "Yes, probably, but it's easy to look back at the past and think of all the things we could have done differently. Trust me, with hundreds of past lives and just as many gruesome deaths, I could chase those thoughts for hours. But at some point we have to accept the mistakes we made and try to move forward."

"I know, and I did. I didn't speak with Father for a long time, but eventually I stopped blaming him for what happened. I don't think Belial has ever forgiven him though." He patted my hand. "Maybe he'll come around now."

"Yeah, maybe." But I couldn't help but worry he might not.

"A new sister will help with that. Father and I reconnected a lot after Kassiel was born, mostly thanks to you. That's when I offered to work for him as a spy."

I smiled at the memories of my life as Lenore, one of my last few moments of happiness with my family before recent events. "Yes, I remember."

"Do you?" Damien cocked his head as he studied me.

"When Lucifer broke the curse, all my memories came back. I remember almost everything, though it comes and goes, as memories do."

"Everything? Like the time when I nearly fell into the fire pit?"

I arched an eyebrow. "You mean when Belial was supposed to be watching you?"

He laughed at that. "And all the times you caught me in bed with someone?"

I groaned and ducked my head. "Unfortunately, yes. Both men and women. Sometimes both at the same time. Things a mother should never have to see."

Damien only laughed harder, and I was happy to see some of my old mischievous, carefree son back again. We chatted a bit more about memories of the past, laughing and smiling as we reminisced together. He caught me up a bit more on his life in Faerie, and how he had won over Oberon after many years, and how his grand-mother continues to be a thorn in his side even though she obviously cares. I told him more about this life, and everything Jophiel had done to keep me safe from Adam, and how Lucifer broke the curse. But eventually the hour grew late, and it was time to say goodbye.

Damien glanced toward the setting sun. "I should go."

"Do you really have to?"

"Unfortunately yes, but I will be back soon. I promise." He pulled me into a last hug before he opened a portal to Faerie, and I breathed deep at the smell of home that emanated from it.

"You better."

I gave him another hug, and then held back tears as he disappeared inside the portal, though I was confident I would see him again soon.

Time had been tough on our family, but I was certain that things would be better going forward. I was going to make sure of it.

19

LUCIFER

I looked out over one of the crowded bar areas on the first floor of the Celestial. Tourists came here to drown their sorrows after losing too much money on the slots. Funny how humans continued their lives oblivious to all else going on around them, truly blinded to anything outside their own sphere of understanding. Clinking glasses, chatter and laughter formed the soundtrack to the evening and a sports event flickered on a television just barely in view, tucked around a corner. But none of that interested me.

I peered deeper into the shadows, and there he was. Belial. Alone on a stool and in the furthest reaches of the bar, almost as if he'd set a warded circle around himself to keep people away.

I started to stride over to him, but stopped a short distance away, unsure of my welcome. He looked up, amusement flashing briefly through his eyes as he witnessed my hesitation. I grinned and nodded brief acknowledgment. Yes, any sort of hesitation was uncharacteristic of me, but in this instance, it wasn't weakness. It was the closest I'd come to asking him for consent to join him, and he was too like me to not know that.

He glanced at the barstool next to him. Just a flicker. If I'd have blinked, I'd have missed the invitation, but I'd known not to blink. Belial wouldn't ask twice.

"Drink?" I asked. When had I last bought my son a drink? For that matter, had I ever bought one for him? Of course, I wouldn't actually buy one now either. I'd just wave, and a bartender would keep them coming.

My oldest son lifted his glass, the ice chinking softly inside. "Got one."

I waved anyway. This wasn't a conversation to have without the accompanying burn of good quality whiskey. "How are you doing?"

He answered my uninspired question with a dry, humorless chuckle. "Small talk, really?"

"We've got to start somewhere, don't we?" This was our first real conversation in centuries. I had no idea how to begin it, but I couldn't let things go on this way any longer.

"All right then." He raised an eyebrow, and for a second he looked so much like his mother when she'd been Eve. "I'm just dandy. How are you?"

His voice was dripping with sarcasm. This was never going to be an easy conversation, and I hadn't expected Belial to make it any easier. Still, he could help me out a little here. My whiskey arrived at that moment, and I took a long sip of liquid courage.

"I want to thank you for helping your mother in Faerie. She says she couldn't have done it without you."

Belial simply nodded and sipped his drink. I dragged a hand through my hair, trying to find the right words to connect with my son. This was much harder than I'd expected.

"I'm sorry." I blurted out the words in my head. They weren't the words I'd intended to say, and Belial stiffened, tension in all of his muscles. His head moved toward me almost as if he might look at me, but it was little more than a twitch he didn't complete in the end.

I laughed, the sound self-deprecating. "I realize those aren't words you're used to hearing from me."

He acknowledged me with a quick contraction of his lips, but he still didn't look in my direction as I studied his profile.

"I know I wasn't the best father to you. I was..." I paused, my mouth dry. I'd been about to say I'd been busy, but that wasn't right. "I was stupid."

Belial cut a glance toward me, and it was all the invitation I needed to keep speaking.

"When you were born, I'd just left Heaven to become king of Hell. You were only a baby when I begged Nyx to turn the Fallen into demons. Then a small child when we defeated the Elder Gods and locked away the Horsemen. Then a teenager when Adam killed your mother the first time as part of the curse. I spent your entire childhood struggling to prove myself as the Demon King and to keep the denizens of Hell in line. But I should have spent it with you." I sucked in a deep breath as I continued. I had to get this out, or I might never have the courage or the opportunity to speak like this again. "Especially after Eve was killed. I didn't know how to handle being a father or being a king without her—and I wasn't sure how the curse worked, or if she really would return. But I should have seen how all of those things were affecting you too. I should have been a better father. I tried to do better with your brothers, but I failed you, and I'm sorry."

He met my gaze properly, and I released a breath at the sudden connection. "Fuck. I've waited thousands of years to hear you say those words."

"I wish I hadn't waited so long to say them." I gave him a wry grin. "Maybe you wouldn't have tried to overthrow me. Twice."

One corner of his mouth curved, the half-smile bitter. "Not some of my finest moments, I'll admit."

"Do you really hate me so much you want me dead?" I asked in a low voice, almost afraid to hear the answer.

He looked down at his hands, wrapping around his drink. "No. I didn't want you dead. I have a lot of regrets. Like siding with Adam and releasing Pestilence. I tried to fix it by becoming War, but we all saw how that turned out."

I didn't speak. This all felt too fragile to disrupt.

"To answer your question, no, I don't hate you," he continued. "Maybe I did at various times in the past, but not anymore. But I don't regret trying to overthrow you either time. Each time I did it, you'd become out of touch with the people you ruled over, and I knew it was time for a change. No one should rule unchecked for thousands of years. That's the way to despotism. You might not have seen it, but both times the revolution was brewing behind your back even without me. I simply ignited the spark."

I considered his words, and some of the things the Archdemons had said over the last year. Many of them were unhappy that I ended the war with the angels and made us leave Hell, even though I did it to save the demon race. I had no regrets there. Still, perhaps I'd acted too harshly. Perhaps I should have consulted them more. I'd also discovered that many felt Fallen were not truly demons, and that I held my kind above all of the other demonic races. Perhaps I did, as I used them to watch over the other demons and keep them in line. Maybe Belial was right and it was time for a change, though I wasn't giving up my throne so easily.

I stroked my chin as I considered. "Your point is valid. I've started to see that some of that is true, and I'd love to talk with you more about this. Believe it or not, I do not want to become a dictator."

"Yeah, whatever." He shrugged and sipped his drink, back to acting like he didn't give a damn, but I knew better. Like me, he cared—maybe too much, even though he would never admit it. And like me, that was often his downfall. But I was admitting it now.

I raised my glass. "Of course, now that the curse is broken and your mother is ruling beside me, I have a feeling she'll keep me in line too."

Belial managed to chuckle at that. "No doubt. Not to mention a miniature version of her running around soon."

I groaned. "That's right. It's been so long, I forgot how difficult those early years can be sometimes. I actually think I blocked out the toddler years with all of you. Especially Damien's. What a little monster he was."

Belial actually laughed at that, and we both took a sip of our drinks, settling into a companionable silence. I was having a drink with my son, and all was right in the world.

Belial cleared his throat. "I'll leave Morningstar with you before I go."

I started to open my mouth to accept but I waved my hand instead. "Keep it for now. I want you to be safe, wherever you are."

Morningstar was my angelic sword, forged for me in Heaven back when I'd been an Archangel. When I'd left for Hell and become a Fallen, the sword had changed, allowing it to channel both darkness and light. Only those of my blood could use the sword now, along with Hannah, since she was my mate. It would always come back to me, but for now it felt right with Belial.

He shrugged. "It's not like I plan to use it. I'm heading back to New Orleans. Back to my bar. Back to staying out of this shit."

"I'm not sure that's possible for ones such as us, but I wish you well, and hope to see you again soon." I offered him my hand.

He took it firmly, and we shook hands, meeting each other's eyes. I looked upon my son as an equal, and he looked back at me with something other than hatred and anger.

It was a start.

20

HANNAH

I leaned against Lucifer as we sped along the highway in the limo. We were fresh off his plane and he'd practically whisked me into the car without letting me catch more than a glimpse of a clear blue sky. I hated that he wouldn't tell me where we were going, but he'd said he didn't want to ruin the surprise.

As I gazed out at the freeway we were driving down, my thoughts wandered to my sons, as it often did. I wondered what they were doing now. Belial had gone back to New Orleans to rebuild his bar and try to live a quiet life, Damien had returned to Faerie to spy on Oberon, and Kassiel had gone to upstate New York to teach a class at Hellspawn Academy, the university for demons where I supposed our daughter would go someday. Or would she go to Seraphim Academy, since she was part angel? Hmm.

Lucifer smoothed his hand over my shoulder. "Are you all right?"

I shrugged. "I just miss our sons. I only just found them again and now they're all gone."

Lucifer chuckled but he drew me tighter against him. "It's only been a month since we saw them. A blink of an eye in an immortal lifetime."

"I know." Some days I still felt so very human, even though that had all been a carefully constructed lie.

His hand drifted to my very round stomach. "Soon we'll have another child to look after for many years. We should try to enjoy our last few moments alone together while we can."

"Is that so?" I asked, my voice growing husky. One benefit of being an Elder God—we never ran out of stamina. A good thing too, since these damn pregnancy hormones made me horny all the time.

He pressed a kiss to my neck, as his hands slid back up to palm my breasts. "I like the way you think, my love."

"Do we have time?" I asked, glancing out the window. We were heading toward a freeway exit now.

"Yes, if we make it quick." He raised his head and met my gaze, his wicked green eyes alight with desire. "I have so much I want to show you today."

"I have so much I want to see. How proud are you feeling today, Lucifer?" I grinned at our old joke, but my words came out almost as a low purr.

"Around you, I can barely control my pride."

He pressed his mouth against mine, while I reached for the zipper on his pants, carefully cupping his hard bulge as I did. Sudden desperation for him spurred my movements. He'd said we should make it quick, after all. Lucifer got the hint and shoved my own pants off, but the stretchy maternity pants made it difficult to do anything with grace or speed.

"What do you desire, darling?" He moved his hand to the top of his pants, unfastened them the rest of the way. Then he freed his cock and palmed it, stroking the hard length.

"I want you, Lucifer."

His rhythm increased as he continued to touch himself. "How do you want me?"

"Here. Now." I was wet for him. So very wet. I watched his fingers moving over his skin, and I whimpered my need.

He gazed upon me with a perfect mix of lust and love. "You've always been my greatest temptation. Every face, every name, every time. Only you."

"Always you, Lucifer." I shoved panties off and moved to sit upon him, facing away, lowering myself onto him before either of us could say another word.

He inhaled sharply and his hands went to my hips, partly to steady me, but almost like he might impose a rhythm. I grabbed his hands and brought them to my breasts instead. He played his long fingers across them, stroking my nipples through the fabric before he started working at my buttons, releasing just enough of them that he could access my skin and dip down beneath my bra.

This wasn't calm and gentle. This was shoving clothes out of the way and grinding on Lucifer to find my pleasure. He swept my hair aside and nibbled my neck, then bit down harder, although not enough to draw pain. Just enough to say he could mark me if he wanted. That I was his. I arched to give him more skin, and he pushed his hips upward, thrusting hard.

I rolled against him, rubbing against the spot that made me cry out. He held on, his hands over my breasts and his mouth at the side of my neck as I lifted up and sank back down. Slow at first, then faster and faster, until the only sounds in the back of the limo were my heavy breaths and the slap of our skin connecting.

"Lucifer." His name left my mouth over and over, like a chant, and it grew faster as I began to lose control. He moved with me, catching hold of my urgency. Finally, my body tightened around him and I sucked in a ragged breath. He pulled me against him and strained upward one last time with his own release. Our orgasms rocked through us, but luckily we'd gotten better at controlling our new powers, and we managed not to destroy the limo we were sitting inside.

"Hannah," he murmured against my ear, before smoothing some of my hair back. He pressed a kiss to the back of my neck as our movements slowed, our lust sated. For now.

The limo stopped, and I glanced out the windows to see a glorious blue sea. I'd been so distracted by Lucifer I'd completely ignored the final part of our journey. Our driver got out of the car and waited patiently for us nearby, giving us time to get dressed. He'd probably heard far too much, even though the privacy screen had been in place. Oh well. We'd give him a big tip at the end of this.

Once dressed, I got out of the car slowly, letting the soft breeze soothe my too-warm cheeks, and inhaled the fresh sea air. "Where are we?"

"Southern California." Lucifer adjusted his suit as he stood beside me. "In fact, we're just a mile away from where Asmodeus and Brandy live now."

"Thank you, Lucifer." I threw my arms around him, and he hugged me close.

"I thought it was time to move forward with our discussion about finding a new home. I wanted you to see this one." He indicated a giant fence with a big gate.

I couldn't help my laugh. "I never in a million years thought I could own a fence as big as that one."

"You can, if you so desire."

The gate opened as if he'd willed it so, and a sweeping driveway lined by palm trees led to a large white house. The grounds of the estate stretched far and wide in every direction, with the sparkling blue ocean behind it.

I paused and looked around at the greens of the trees and the blue of the sea. "This is gorgeous."

"It gets better." Lucifer took my hand as we started along the driveway. The scent of the flowers hung heavy in the hot afternoon air, and I walked slowly to savor them. "You haven't even seen the house yet."

"Forget the house. I think I'd be happy to live outside." I laughed and swung our hands as we walked, freed from my worries by the hope of future happiness.

"Then let's explore the grounds first." Instead of leading me to the front door, we went around the side, where we discovered a large sparkling pool and spa, an outdoor kitchen with a seating area and a cabana, and lots and lots of land, all overlooking the ocean. "There's more than enough room for our horses to roam, and for you to create another garden here."

My mind was already swimming with ideas for what I could

design for the space. We continued on, past a guest house that looked bigger than the house I'd lived in with Brandy, and a walkway that led down to a private beach. I stood at the top of it, soaking in the sunshine. Even though I was so much more than an angel now, I still loved it. "It's perfect."

"You like it?" he asked.

I let loose a breath, "I love it."

Lucifer watched my face closely with a small smile. "Let's head inside."

We approached the two-story house, which had an incredible system of miniature waterways running around it between more palm trees. The house boasted wide glass windows and whole walls that seemed to simply fold out of the way to allow the exterior and interior to merge into one luxurious space. My heart beat wildly as I coveted all that I saw. I almost didn't need to see the inside. Lucifer knew me so well after all this time—if this was the house he'd selected to show me, there was no doubt it was the perfect one.

As we stepped through the entrance doorway, I squeezed Lucifer's hand in mine. A big open concept living area flowed into a chef's kitchen and out through a wall of glass doors with access to the vibrant green lawn and turquoise pool, with the ocean glinting in the sun behind it. A glorious staircase led upstairs, while a hallway led off to other rooms to the side. The house was empty of all furniture, but I could already imagine how I would decorate it— lots of black and white, plus sea greens and ocean blues, with a splash of earthy sand tones.

As Lucifer led me further inside, he said, "There's plenty of room for the boys to stay, it's close enough to hop back to Vegas quickly, and it's secluded enough to give us both privacy and safety."

"You don't need to give me a sales pitch," I said with a laugh. "I'm already sold."

Lucifer smirked. "You haven't seen the best part yet."

I lifted an eyebrow. "The bedrooms?"

He shook his head, mock disappointment on his face. "Really? No, love. The library."

I perked up at that. "It has a library?"

A wicked grin lifted his lips. "Of course it does."

We stepped inside, and my mouth fell open. Row after row of white bookshelves lined the big space, which had a view of the ocean behind a spot that looked like the perfect reading nook. It was even bigger than Lucifer's library in Vegas, and I could already imagine all the glorious hours it would take to organize our books in here. Plus, we'd need new ones to fill all these shelves. Naturally. In fact, I was pretty sure I'd need an entire wall to shelve all my favorite romance novels.

There were two guest bedrooms on the first floor, along with an office and a yoga studio we would turn into a sparring room. After we checked them out, we finally headed upstairs. The second floor opened up so you could see the living room below, before leading off into the other bedrooms. The primary bedroom was huge, with an attached room that would be perfect for when the baby was young. The bathroom was just as impressive, all newly remodeled with intriguing 3D tiles that looked like waves, that I just had to run my hand over. The other bedrooms upstairs were also a good size for our daughter to grow up in or for guests when they visited.

"I've seen enough," I said, as I leaned on the handrail on the landing overlooking the first floor. Everything about this home felt right. I could see us raising our daughter here, our horses would have plenty of space, and Brandy was close by. Plus the estate would be easier to defend and more secure than a penthouse in a big city. "Let's make an offer today. I want this house."

"It's yours." Lucifer wrapped his arms around me from behind. "I already bought it."

I spun around in his arms. "You did?"

"The second it came on the market, I made the previous owners an offer they couldn't refuse. I hope you'll forgive me for making the decision on my own, but I wanted to surprise you, and I acted quickly to make sure we didn't lose the property to someone else. It was too perfect to pass up."

"I love it, and I love you for knowing how much I would love it."

"Good." He bent to kiss me, then took my hand and led me into our future bedroom with a naughty smile playing across his lips. "I think we should celebrate our new home."

"Now?" I asked with a laugh. "We don't even have any furniture yet!"

"I don't need furniture to give you an orgasm." He took me further inside, to the bathroom, and gently set me on the counter. "Besides, if we're going to have sex in every room of this house, we'd better get started."

I shook my head with a rueful smile as he dragged off my pants again, but then his head was between my thighs and his tongue was on my pussy and all I could do was lean back and let him pleasure me. A deep feeling of rightness settled over me, as if destiny had finally led me to this moment after thousands of years of suffering, and now I would have my chance to relax and enjoy my happiness.

I just had to ignore the little voice inside me asking me if it could really last.

21

HANNAH

I wrapped my arms around my beach ball-sized belly and tried to breathe through the contraction tightening through it. It was a week before my due date, and we'd finally managed to move many of our things into our new house in California and bought enough furniture to make it livable. Now all we needed was to set up the nursery. I'd thought we would have another week or longer—all my sons had been born late, but this morning I'd started having contractions. I was sure they were false ones, but it motivated me to get the crib set up immediately—just in case.

"Screwdriver." I held my hand out toward Lucifer as I lifted the headboard of the crib.

"Darling, what exactly are you doing?" He managed to sound both curious and horrified at the same time.

I narrowed my eyes. "This nursery furniture isn't going to put itself together."

"There's an actual man in the room willing to do this for you."

I rolled my eyes. "Okay, actual man. But I think you might need to remember I'm a god now and can do pretty much anything. Even while pregnant."

He took the crib piece off me and set it down before tugging me into his arms and dropping a tender kiss on my lips. "Oh, believe me, I never forget that."

I pressed my palms against his chest. "No distractions. This crib needs to be built right away. We have no idea when this little lady is going to arrive. It could be today, for all we know."

His eyes widened as he glanced down at my belly. "We're not ready yet. Keep her in."

"I'll ask, but I have a feeling she has a mind of her own already." I handed him the screwdriver and sauntered over to the nursing chair. "Now screw like the wind."

He grinned. "Usually when you say that we're both naked."

I chuckled softly and was relieved to be able to sit down for a while. I closed my eyes and rocked myself back and forth on the chair Zel had given me as I rode out another contraction. Shit, they were getting closer, weren't they?

"Where'd Zel get to?" I asked. She'd moved into the guest house as soon as we'd mentioned the new place. No waiting to be invited, no waiting for permission, she just packed a bag to come along with us, then set herself up as head of security for the estate, running it all from the guest house and overseeing a small battalion of guards. I loved Zel, but she could definitely be...intense sometimes. It had only gotten worse after we asked her to be the baby's godmother. Still, if I was going to have this baby today, I wanted her nearby.

"I don't know, but I should order her to help me with this crib. She's a lot more handy than I am." Lucifer looked to the door like he might actually run down to the guesthouse and fetch her.

Despite Lucifer's complaints, he continued to get the crib set up, while I rested and gazed across the nursery. Over the last few days I'd decorated it like a secret garden, with little floral touches everywhere. The room made me happy and calm, and I hoped our daughter liked it too.

"Knock knock," Samael said, and I looked up at the unexpected voice at the doorway.

"So much for increased security," Lucifer grumbled. "Looks like Zel's letting in any old riff-raff these days."

I beckoned Samael in with a smile. "Perfect timing. You can help Lucifer look like he knows what he's doing with that crib."

Lucifer shook the screwdriver at me. "I beg your pardon, but I've finished the crib, thank you very much. Although now I need to mount this changing table to the wall. Can't have it tipping over in an earthquake."

I shook my head. "How humbling that even though we are gods we still have to worry about things like earthquakes."

"Have you come with an update?" Lucifer asked Samael, as he began attaching the mounting straps to the wall. Samael had been running things from Vegas ever since we moved out here, allowing us to step back from demon matters so we could focus on the new house and the baby.

"I have." Samael gave a small bow, but I noticed he didn't step forward to help Lucifer with his task. "The imps have been leaderless ever since Hannah killed Nemesis. They haven't chosen a new Archdemon yet and are fighting amongst themselves for control."

Lucifer grinned. "Why am I not surprised? At least that should keep them out of our hair for a while."

"Indeed."

"And the shifters?" I asked my question as I rode out another contraction in my rocking chair. This one was stronger, and I had to grip the armrests through it. "Have we found Fenrir?"

Samael cast an inquisitive look at me, as though he'd noticed I wasn't well, but was too polite to say anything. "No, I'm sorry to say he hasn't been seen. We believe he and the other shifters loyal to him are in hiding for the time being, no doubt plotting their next moves."

"I'm sure they're trying to figure out a way to release Death even now," Lucifer said.

"Would they really be that foolish?" I asked. "Surely they can see there's no way they can win at this point."

Lucifer leaned against the wall as he took a break from his work. "Fenrir is stubborn, and long ago an Erelim angel had all these prophecies about Ragnarok that he believed. He probably thinks releasing Death will set that off."

I thought back to everything I knew about Norse mythology. "Isn't he meant to die in Ragnarok though?"

Samael sniffed. "In the ancient days, every Erelim angel had their own prophecy about the apocalypse, and most of them contradicted each other. Some of these prophecies we've already stopped from coming true over the years. Like that 2012 Mayan Apocalypse."

Lucifer groaned. "Don't remind me. What a pain that was."

"What are you talking about?" I asked.

"A portal to Void was meant to open on the day the Mayan calendar ended in Tikal in Guatemala," Samael explained. "It could have released dozens of Elder Gods, but we managed to shut it down before anything happened."

"Just like we're going to stop the Four Horsemen's apocalypse before it happens too," Lucifer said.

Samael nodded. "Pestilence's tomb still holds, and Theo and his gargoyles are guarding it. They'll report any changes to me immediately."

I prayed Pestilence stayed locked up for a very long time. I wanted my baby to grow up without the threat of Adam casting a shadow over her childhood. He'd already done so much harm to our family—all I wanted was to not have to worry about him coming after us again.

Samael lapsed into silence, but something about the conversation felt unfinished. Lucifer glanced up like he felt it too.

"Is everything else okay?" I asked. Samael was Lucifer's greatest friend and ally, and we both owed him a lot. If he was unhappy with the current situation, we would fix it however we could.

"Yes." At first I thought Samael wasn't going to say anything further, then he cleared his throat and looked away. "I took your advice, Lucifer. On the way here, I stopped to see Asmodeus and his new family."

"Really?" I leaned forward, so excited by this unexpected turn of events I barely noticed the contraction. Okay, that was a lie, it hurt like hell.

Samael had been so upset by his son Asmodeus turning mortal

that he'd refused to have anything to do with him for the last few months. Lucifer and I had begged him to give his son a chance, to meet Brandy, to forgive Lilith for making their son mortal. All we wanted was for him to talk to his son, if nothing else. Especially now that Brandy was pregnant too.

"How did it go?" Lucifer asked, as he gave Samael his full attention. He knew all about reconnecting with estranged sons, and how challenging it could be.

"It went well. I've come to accept my son's decision, even though it pains me. I can see he is truly in love, and has found a family that makes him happy." He hesitated. "I'd had no idea my son wanted something like that. I thought he was happy as an incubus, but now I realize how miserable he'd been. I just never expected him to end up with a human."

"Brandy is his mate," I said, feeling defensive of my best friend. "And she's a good person. She took care of me when I had no idea who I was, and accepted me when I told her I was an angel dating Lucifer."

Samael inclined his head. "I have nothing but respect for the woman who managed to tame my son."

"And Lilith?" Lucifer asked. "Have you spoken with her?"

Samael scowled a little at that. "No. Not yet."

Lucifer rested a hand on his friend's shoulder. "If there's anything I've learned from all of this, it's that family is everything. They say time heals all wounds, but maybe this one could use a little help."

Samael's lips pressed into a tight line, but then he said, "Fine, I will make an effort to speak with Lilith, even if only to stop this infernal flirting she does in front of Baal."

"About damn time," Lucifer said.

Another contraction shook through me, and this one was followed by a feeling like I'd peed myself. I'd had enough babies to know that meant my water had broken.

"It's also time over here," I said, unable to deny it any longer. "Send for Marcus. The baby is coming."

Lucifer dropped the screwdriver. "Now?"
I nodded. "Now."

22

LUCIFER

Hannah grimaced more than smiled and she gripped the hand I'd offered her with all the strength of a god. Good thing I was one too, or she'd have broken me.

"That's it. Keep breathing." I'd intended to be soothing, but she shot me a glare and I closed my mouth, relegated to be the hand she was holding. Marcus waited at the foot of the bed, but I was under strict instructions to stay by her head and leave the business end to someone else, which suited me just fine.

It had been a long labor, and even though Hannah had borne three children before, she hadn't done it in this body, which made everything different. Equal parts anticipation and sadness floated through my mind as Marcus told her to push. Meeting a daughter for the first time would be a wondrous thing, especially after our last one had been taken from us too soon, but I was also keenly aware this would be the last time I ever experienced this. And while that burden was mostly Hannah's, she'd sacrificed herself for me and that responsibility weighed heavily.

But I couldn't afford to think of that now. Not while my mate needed me. Besides, the excitement outweighed the sadness. Today we would complete our family.

I tried to listen while Marcus coached Hannah through the birth process, but my attention was all on my mate, holding her hand through every breath she gasped. I knew the pain of this moment would fade, as it had with each of the boys, and we'd be left with a miracle.

My love for Hannah grew as I watched her amazing body bring forth the life we'd created together. Even this was a sacrifice of sorts —volunteering her body for our love. I'd lived thousands of years and seen many amazing things in that time, but this was the most incredible and unbelievable, the way life continued.

"One more push!" Marcus's voice was calm and soothing, and he was probably easing Hannah's pain as he guided our daughter into the world. Still, I saw her tense up and it made my protective side come out.

"Are you sure you've done this before?" I asked Marcus. I knew he was a great healer, Archangel Raphael's son even, but did he really know how to deliver a baby?

Marcus rolled his eyes and ignored me. I scowled and considered threatening him and everyone he loved if he didn't get this baby out immediately, but then Hannah's eyes met mine and I forced myself to be calm. Deep breaths. I swept Hannah's hair away from her forehead and let her grip my hand. I couldn't do anything else but be with her. In this role, being the Demon King was essentially useless.

Suddenly Hannah let out a guttural roar and a wave of power released from her. A heavy gust of air rushed through the room, sending medical supplies flying. Light and darkness burst out of Hannah all at once, and bright green plants suddenly grew up around us, before immediately withering and dying. Through it all, Hannah drained the life of everyone around us as she cried out, and though my powers as War protected me from the brunt of it, I saw Marcus stagger and grip the edge of the bed, his body weak.

"Hannah!" I cupped her chin, forcing her to look at me. "You must control your powers!"

She blinked at me and then the soul-sucking feeling of her

draining our life force died off. She drew in a deep breath as she regained control of herself. "Sorry!"

I pressed a kiss to her forehead as she relaxed a little and the room returned to normal. Marcus recovered quickly and got back to work, and soon a thin cry pierced the air as our daughter was brought into the world. Hannah's eyes widened as the baby girl was placed on her bare chest, allowing her to connect immediately with this beautiful, wrinkled, sticky creature that was our baby. I wedged myself onto a thin sliver of bed beside Hannah, wrapping an arm around her as I gazed upon both of them with love.

While Marcus healed Hannah up, she cradled our daughter, and I cradled her, stroking her hair. No words were needed as we shared a moment of quiet, calm love.

"Take the baby, Lucifer," she eventually murmured.

Suddenly I was accepting our daughter into my arms, and I held her against my chest and smiled down at her. She seemed to look at me with recognition, and a small pink arm waved from inside her blanket as I settled her in the crook of my arm.

"Perfect." The word came out as a whisper, and I barely saw Hannah's smile widen before I refocused all of my attention on the child in my arms. I stroked her cheek with the very tip of my finger, careful of the new, fragile skin. "Just beautiful."

Love surged through me, and my chest tightened. The sound that came from my mouth could have been the start of a laugh or a choked sob, and I didn't care if neither was the expected reaction from the Demon King on the birth of his only daughter.

I kissed the baby's little red face and reached for Hannah's hand. My amazing mate had done it again. I was truly the luckiest immortal in the world.

"What are you going to call her?" Marcus asked.

"Funny enough, we haven't discussed that." I perched on the first chair I found and gazed at my daughter's little face, her beautiful blue eyes, and I offered my finger for her to grasp. I glanced at Hannah, and she smiled as she moved her gaze from me to our daughter and back again.

"How about Aurora?" she asked softly. "After your mother."

My chest tightened as I looked into my daughter's eyes again, the color of the sky at dawn. "Yes, that's perfect."

"I'll let you come up with the middle name," Hannah said, as she leaned back and closed her eyes, no doubt exhausted from everything her body had just gone through.

I considered various names for some time. Since Hannah has chosen to honor a member of my family, I thought it only fitting we do the same for her. "How would you feel about Jophiel?"

Tears gleamed in Hannah's eyes as she smiled at me. "I think Jo would approve."

Marcus and his assistant—who I'd barely even noticed was here this whole time—finished cleaning up, and left us alone for some privacy, saying they would return to check on us shortly. I handed the baby back to Hannah, and she began attempting to breastfeed.

"She's powerful," I said quietly, as I watched them. "I can feel it, even here. The perfect blend of both of us."

"With a little bit of Elder God thrown in for good measure," Hannah said with a laugh.

"Do you think Famine changed her?" I asked.

"No, not at all. But my becoming Famine changed Aurora too, since we were still connected." Hannah sighed a little. "Famine said she wanted to be a mother again, and I sensed she would never hurt this baby. If anything, she made sure Aurora was protected during the transition. I had no love for Famine, but I appreciated that."

I smoothed a hand over my daughter's fuzzy head. No one like her had ever been brought into existence before. Half angel, half Fallen, with a touch of Elder God. I already knew she would be destined for greatness. Of course, we first had to get through the toddler years. Or worse, the teenage years. Somehow I had a feeling she wouldn't make them easy on us. She was a fighter, like her mother.

Our daughter had the power to destroy the world—or save it. I only hoped we were up to the challenge of being her parents.

23

HANNAH

The next few months passed in a sleepless, newborn haze, although Aurora didn't suffer from lack of attention. Our closest friends came to visit regularly, and Zel took her godmother duties far too seriously, proving the intensity we'd predicted from her was right on the money. She'd already tried to give Aurora two tiny knives like her own, and I'd had to explain that it would be a few years at least until my daughter would be ready for combat training.

Despite being an Elder God and not needing sleep, I was somehow exhausted most of the time, and it was a relief when Lucifer suggested I go out and finally take my horse for a ride. We'd made a small stable for the horses on one side of our estate along with a big grazing area, and even though the horses didn't really need any tending to, they seemed to enjoy having a space of their own.

I went out there now, breathing in the glorious fresh air, and found both horses together in the grass. Misery immediately came over to me and nuzzled me with her nose, and I smiled. I'd been so busy I hadn't made much time to get to know her, and I was excited to go for a ride and have a little me time, something that was rare as a new mother.

I climbed onto her back with ease, my body somehow knowing what to do even though I hadn't ridden a horse in centuries. I wove my fingers in her thick black mane, and then she took off with a triumphant leap, racing down the grass. Strife just shook his head and stayed behind as we galloped around the estate, and then we trotted down the rocky path to the beach. Once on the sand, Misery took off at top speed, and I threw my arms out and laughed as the sunshine filled me with life.

Riding across the beach gave me a lot of time to be alone with my thoughts without a baby demanding my attention. I wondered how my sons were doing, and hoped they would visit us soon, but I knew they were all busy with their own lives too. I thought about Samael running things from Vegas, and how nice it was to have some time to step back from all of that. I loved being the Demon Queen, but I also loved being Aurora's mother. My thoughts then turned to Lucifer, who seemed to enjoy being a father again too. The only thing that bothered me was that we hadn't been very intimate since Aurora was born. Hell, we'd barely had a moment alone together since then. I knew that was normal though—after all we'd been through this three times before—but thanks to Marcus and my Elder God healing my body had long been ready. It was more a matter of finding time and energy with a newborn. I just hoped that having a baby—a baby we both knew would be the last—wasn't going to change our relationship. Each experience seemed more important and immediate when we knew it was the last time we'd ever go through these moments, and I wanted to sear them all into my memories forever.

I wasn't sure how long I rode up and down the California coast, but eventually it was time to return to the stable. As I slid off Misery's back, I felt our connection strongly, this horse that was mine and yet also free. A part of her soul was bound to mine through some ancient magic I didn't understand, but I welcomed her calm, steady presence.

"I'll ride you again soon," I promised, as I patted her back. "And you still need a name. How about...Shadow?"

A soft neigh signaled to me that she liked that name, and it was settled. It seemed fitting somehow, since I was an angel that lived between light and darkness. Shadow wandered off to stand with Strife, the two of them content in their new home. Like this, they certainly didn't look like horses of the apocalypse. I wondered if Lucifer would rename his horse too. We were still Famine and War, but we kept those dark parts of ourselves in check using everything else we were. We'd figured out how to control our powers...and our cravings. Sometimes I did still get an urge to drain all the life out of every plant around me, but like someone battling an addiction, I worked through it and overcame it.

I checked the time—nap time. One of my favorite times of day, especially when I looked down at Aurora's sleeping form. Tiny eyelashes against delicate cheeks, a cherubic mouth, a face so peaceful and innocent it seemed unreal. Sometimes I watched her for hours, almost unable to breathe past the love constricting my chest. How could I have forgotten it felt like this?

I strolled into Aurora's nursery, preparing to get everything ready for her nap, nearly tripping over the millions of toys and baby products. I'd had three kids before Aurora, but I'd never had so much *stuff* before. Some of it did certainly make things easier though. I'd have killed for one of those automatic rockers when Belial was a baby—that boy had been the worst sleeper ever. Modern women had no idea how easy they had it compared to the olden days.

Inside the nursery I found the light already dimmed, the blackout curtains tightly closed, and a shirtless, muscular man standing near the crib. Lucifer turned toward me and held a finger to his lips, as he cradled our sleeping daughter against his chest. I smiled back, feeling a burst of love at the sight of them together like this. Lucifer and I had been through so much over the centuries, both together and apart, especially over these last few years—but it was all worth it for moments like these.

Also, Lucifer half-naked and holding our baby? Seriously hot.

My mouth practically watered at the sight. Then he bent over to put Aurora in her crib, giving me a view of his perfect ass, and I nearly fanned myself. Who would have thought that the devil could be such a good dad?

We stepped outside and closed the door, and Lucifer asked, "Did you have a nice ride?"

"It was great. I really needed some alone time. Thanks for watching Aurora."

"Of course. We had a lovely day, although it took a bit of rocking to get her to sleep. I forgot how hard all this newborn stuff is. You'd think after three other kids it would get easier somehow..."

"I know." I took his hand and tugged him toward our room. "In fact, I was just thinking maybe we should have some alone time too."

He arched an eyebrow. "Is that so?"

As soon as Lucifer entered the bedroom, I shoved him against the wall and plastered myself against him, my hands smoothing over his shoulders as I lifted myself on my tiptoes for a kiss. He only hesitated for a fraction of a second before his arms wrapped around my waist and he held me tight against him. He spun us around so I had my back against the wall, and his tongue slipped between my lips as he deepened our kiss.

"Hello there," he murmured against my lips as heat shot to my clit. "Is someone feeling a bit randy today?"

I ran my hands along his sculpted abs. "Like you didn't do this on purpose, walking around all half-naked like that."

He donned an innocent expression. "It's hot today."

"You're right, it is hot. I should take off my clothes too." I grabbed my shirt and pulled it over my head.

His eyes raked over my exposed skin. "Probably a good idea. In fact, we should both take a nice refreshing shower to cool off, don't you think?"

"It has been some time since I showered," I admitted with a laugh. Mom life didn't leave much room for showers at the moment.

"Time to get you cleaned up." He picked me up and carried me into the bathroom, then set me down while he turned on the shower.

It was big enough to house five people at least, with water spraying from multiple directions, plus the perfect little bench.

Our clothes were quickly shed, and then we stepped aside into the hot water, behind the steamed-up glass walls. As I stepped under the spray, I pressed my naked breasts against Lucifer's bare chest. He dropped his head, his mouth hot and urgent against my neck, his tongue against my collarbone, and I whimpered when pure need flooded me. I ground against him, relishing the hard length of his cock pushing against my skin as he rolled his hips. I could feel all of him against me, melting me, turning me molten under his touch.

As the water sprayed on us, Lucifer drew his fingertips across my breasts, and my nipples hardened instantly. His hair looked black while wet, and his gaze burned with darkness and the promise of pleasure to come. His mouth crashed against mine again, his hands in my wet hair, his body wrapping around mine. I could barely breathe. But really, who needed to breathe. I had Lucifer, who moved between kissing my mouth, my face, my shoulders and however much lower he could reach.

He groaned and lifted me, his hands supporting my ass as I wrapped my legs over his hips. His mouth trailed heat all over my skin, and I pushed my hands into his hair to hold him closer. His cock nudged against my slippery wet skin and he hissed out a breath.

"Lucifer." His name was little more than a strangled sound on my lips, and he responded straight away, pressing the tip of himself inside me before I even knew he was there. "More."

His mouth was a tight line of control as he eased more of his length into me. I stretched around him, and he groaned. "Fuck, I needed this," he growled as he began to rock into me. "I needed you."

"Then take me," I said, my legs tightening around him. "Take everything."

My back hit the cool tile, and Lucifer put his hands on either side of my head as his cock plunged deep inside me. He moved with the speed and strength of a god, fucking me so hard I was surprised the tile didn't crack, but then he paused, his breathing ragged, like he'd only just realized what he was doing.

"You won't break me," I said, and some of the tension in his muscles disappeared. "I'm a god too. I can handle it."

He pumped into me harder and faster, making me cry out in a mix of pleasure and pain. I was the only one who he could fuck like this, with complete abandon and all of his strength, and the knowledge he would never hurt me. He brought us both to the kind of orgasm you shouted through, the kind that made you forget your name or where you were, the kind that made your body ache in a good way for days.

But he wasn't done yet.

Abruptly, Lucifer held me closer and stepped out of the shower, dripping wet. He walked out onto the balcony, setting me down on the low edge of it, as the soft breeze tickled our water-coated skin. Then he dropped one hand between us, using his finger to stroke over my clit, even as his cock remained hard inside me. He leaned over me, his hips moving slowly, his finger lazy over me, his lips suddenly at my nipple, his tongue drawing it into a fresh peak. I briefly wondered if any of our staff was watching us, but then all thought was gone as his fingers pinched my clit and his teeth brushed against my breasts.

"Don't stop." I clutched his upper arms as I watched his shoulders flex and move like he was made of pure muscle. Lucifer was so hard and strong inside and around me still, even after that first incredible orgasm. He thrust into me faster, his movements so familiar yet still exciting, and I gasped as he took hold of my hips, raising me to adjust his angle. With the afternoon sun shining down on us and the ocean at my back, I threw back my head and lost myself in the moment.

My lips parted as I sucked in a breath and every muscle tensed inside me as pleasure rushed to my core. His eyes widened as my pussy gripped him tight, and then his seed spilled inside me for a second time. Together we hung in a moment of ultimate pleasure, as if our power had managed to stop time. For all I knew, maybe it did. It wouldn't be the strangest thing I'd seen.

"Hannah," he murmured between kisses, and though it was only my name, it said everything I needed to hear. It told me that he still loved me as much as he always had. It told me that even though we'd had a baby, our relationship with each other hadn't changed. It told me that our love was eternal.

Then the baby cried out, and we both sighed, pressing our foreheads together with a little laugh. Time to get back to work.

24

HANNAH

I scanned the gardens with a smile, watching our guests mingle under the pastel pink and yellow tents. Everyone was here, and my heart danced a happy beat seeing all the people I loved grab champagne and little pastries to celebrate Aurora's birth. Soft music played in the background, and the cool sea breeze kept the air from getting too hot, even under the bright afternoon sun. It was a perfect day for a party.

Before angels and demons moved to Earth, having a baby was so rare and special that it was common to have a big celebration so that others could come and pay their respects. Now that our two races lived on Earth, our fertility had increased and these parties were not as common. We decided to have one anyway, mainly as an excuse to get everyone together in one place, and because Lucifer seemed to want a party. I could take the guy out of Vegas but I couldn't take the Vegas out of the guy.

Lucifer wrapped his arm around me, appearing as I thought of him—as he often did. "What are you thinking about?"

I turned and kissed him, a fleeting brush across his lips. "Just how much you must miss your life in Vegas."

He glanced at the sleeping baby in my arms. "I don't miss it at all. This moment in time is so fleeting. I want to spend every second with my daughter while I can."

I knew exactly how he felt. Something like sorrow tightened my chest as I watched Aurora, her chubby hand a fist by her face as she slept. Each of these moments was my actual last. Last baby cries, last night wakings, last set of firsts—sitting up, crawling, walking, talking. Even so, I had no regrets at all. I'd saved our family, and knowing Aurora was our last child only made me appreciate every second with her even more.

And today was a day to celebrate her.

Lilith walked down the path toward us, dressed in a short sundress that was both sexy and cute, and I smiled as I saw her. Baal and Gabriel accompanied her, and it never ceased to amaze me that she'd managed to coax both an Archdemon and an Archangel into sharing her. I was glad she was back with them though, especially since she had a daughter with each one.

Then I nearly fell over with shock when Samael appeared and took her hand, then leaned close and gave her a quick kiss. A real kiss too, not just some polite cheek kiss. Were they together now too?

"Did you know?" I asked Lucifer, trying to keep my smile in place, even though my eyes were surely bulging out of their sockets at this unexpected surprise.

Lucifer donned a huge grin. "I guess Samael did a lot more than just talk to Lilith."

It was about time they'd gotten together. Lilith had been flirting hardcore with Samael for a while now, and it was obvious to everyone that Samael still had feelings for her, even though he'd done everything he could to resist her. Obviously he'd finally succumbed to her many charms, and gotten over whatever issues they'd had. Perhaps there was just no resisting a force of nature such as Lilith.

"Well, well," Lucifer said as the four of them arrived within conversation distance. His eyes danced with amusement and he wore a self-satisfied smirk. "Fancy seeing the four of you together."

"You all look great," I said, although that was probably no better a phrase to lead with. "It's really wonderful to see you all...getting along so well."

Lilith chuckled, deep and throaty. "Thank you. We're so happy to be here."

Baal rolled his eyes, while Gabriel just shrugged. Samael looked embarrassed by it all and said, "It's all very new, of course."

"Now you need one more to complete your set," Lucifer told Lilith. "What about that fae lord you used to be involved with?"

Lilith's eyes flared, a small smile capturing her lips. "Never say never."

Gabriel clasped his hand on Lucifer's shoulder. "Glad to see you're back to yourself again, old friend, and congratulations on the new baby."

"Thank you." Lucifer glanced over at Olivia, who stood with Callan, Marcus, Bastien, and Kassiel as they talked to Raphael and a few other angels. "You sure you don't want another one yourself?"

Gabriel let out a hearty laugh. "I think two are enough for me right now. Although I wouldn't mind a grandkid. Those seem like all the fun with none of the responsibility."

"Grandkids are wonderful," Baal said with a nod. Long ago he'd had numerous children with different women, forming an entire line stretching back thousands of years, known as The House of Baal. Of course, he also had a teenage daughter with Lilith named Lena, who was only now coming into her demon powers. It still remained to be seen whether she would be a vampire or a succubus — demons could only be one type, and it emerged when they were eighteen.

"Yes, they are," Samael said. He donned a rare smile, his eyes landing on Asmodeus and Brandy, who was holding their newborn son, born a month after my own. "I look forward to getting to know mine."

"May I hold her?" Lilith asked.

"Of course." I started to pass Aurora to Lilith, but then Zel popped up.

"Careful!" Zel said, making Lilith jump.

"I assure you, I know what I'm doing," Lilith drawled. "I've had many more children than you, my dear."

"Zel takes her godmotherly duties very seriously." I waved at Zel to back off. I often wondered if someone told Zel that godmother meant twenty-four-hour bodyguard. I loved Zel, but sometimes it was a bit much.

"Just looking out for my girl," Zel muttered, before slinking away with a scowl.

Samael came to stand at Lilith's elbow, and Lilith and her mates all gazed down at my sleeping baby. Baal stroked her head softly, and Gabriel touched her little hand. It struck me then that years ago, none of this could have happened—angels and demons celebrating the birth of one that shared both their blood.

"She's gorgeous," Lilith said, as she handed Aurora back to me. "Thank you for letting me hold her."

She headed off to speak with Romana, who stood with Theo and some other gargoyles. Her entourage followed behind her, and I could barely hold in a giggle at the sight of all of them, even stoic Samael, acting like puppies at her heel.

Lucifer wrapped an arm around me and drew me close. "Did you ever think we could pull this off?"

"Hmm?" I half turned to him, enjoying the faint scratch of his cheek against mine.

He waved in the general direction of our guests. "Angels and demons at a party together, honoring a child born of both races."

I shook my head with a smile. "I was just thinking the same thing."

When Lucifer had first found me as Hannah, this sort of thing had been impossible to even consider. Angels and demons had been at war, and we'd had to hide our relationship for fear of what would happen if anyone found out that the devil was in love with the daughter of an Archangel. Now such pairings were becoming more and more normal.

"It's all thanks to you," I said, pressing a kiss to his cheek. "You brought peace to our people. It was no wonder you were able to defeat War. You're the opposite of him in every way."

"Just as you're the opposite of Famine." He lifted a shoulder in a casual shrug. "But I only did it out of love for you and hope for a future where we could be together."

"Now we're living in that future." He and I would do everything in our power to keep this peace too, especially now that we had Aurora. Years ago, she would have been forbidden. An abomination. Some might have even called for her death. Now she would live in both the angel and demon worlds, like me, and I hoped she would be embraced by each side.

Suddenly the sky darkened as large wings covered the sun. Three dragons flew overhead, circling down to us, and everyone went on alert. Weapons were drawn, wings expanded, and claws came out. Lucifer and I were ready to unleash the Elder Gods inside us, if needed. But then the dragons set down calmly on the beach, shifted into their human forms, and began walking toward us with no obvious hostility. The man in front was tall and muscular with short black hair and a sharp jaw, and though I'd only seen him in his dragon form, I knew this was Valefar, their leader.

"We come to pledge the dragons' loyalty to the Demon King and Queen," Valefar said, as he dropped into a bow before us, his fist over his heart. The man and woman behind him did the same. "And to pay our respects to the little princess."

We'd long been hoping the dragons would finally join us again, but I'd never expected them to show up today like this. Lucifer had one hand on me, gripping me tight as I held Aurora protectively, and he glanced at me with one eyebrow raised. Silently asking me if Valefar spoke the truth. Though Valefar's words had all been honest, I checked his aura anyway, and saw no deception or malice there. I gave Lucifer a subtle nod in return, and he let me go and took a step closer to Valefar.

"Welcome, Archdemon Valefar," Lucifer said. "We're pleased you could join us, and we accept your loyalty oath."

Valefar rose up and gestured at his companions, who each offered a small, wrapped present. "We've brought gifts for your daughter."

"That's very kind of you," I said, as Lucifer took the gifts. "Please enjoy the party and make yourselves comfortable."

"Yes, later we can discuss how best to return the dragons to the fold," Lucifer said. "For now, grab some champagne."

"Thank you." Valefar and his companions gave us another bow, and then they headed for the bar. Romana walked over and began talking to him while the bartender poured him a drink, and it was clear the two of them knew each other already. Perhaps she'd convinced him to side with us.

That only left the imps and shifters unaccounted for, but the imps still had no Archdemon to lead them, and no one had seen Fenrir since he'd leaped through the portal out of Faerie. Even the other shifters we'd spoken to, some of whom still sided with Lucifer, had no clue what he was up to at the moment.

Suddenly a portal opened up on the other side of the garden, startling all the people at the party, who had just gone back to talking after the last surprising arrival. But now the fae were here, and they always liked to make an entrance.

Damien stepped through first, followed by my mother, who looked radiant in a pale yellow gown with real daisies growing out of it. Fae fashion could be a bit...extreme. Damien was much more subdued in a simple white silk shirt and black trousers, and he took his grandmother by the elbow and led her toward us. Lucifer tensed beside me at the sight of Demeter, though he stepped forward to give his son a hug.

"It's good to see you again, Damien." Then he shot a hard look at my mother. "Demeter."

"Lucifer." Her voice was frosty, and her gaze equally cool as it moved from my mate to me. "Hannah."

I ignored her as I hugged my son, then handed him the baby so he could meet her properly. Aurora's eyes popped open and she giggled and cooed at her brother, who laughed with her.

"You've already decided I'm your favorite brother, haven't you?" Damien asked, as she grabbed his finger. "Oh yes, she's a clever one."

I turned toward Demeter and offered her a smile. "Thanks for coming, Mother. Would you like to meet your granddaughter?"

My mother's face immediately changed, losing all hint of frostiness, lighting up as if from within, becoming truly beautiful the way only a fae could. She held her arms out to Damien, and as soon as she held Aurora against her, she touched the baby's face gently with a smile. Then she reached out a hand to me, and I took it. How could I not? She was my mother, the only one still alive from all my previous lives. I knew this hadn't been easy for her—to lose a daughter who was then replaced by a stranger, more than once. I looked at Aurora and couldn't even imagine.

My mother's fierce protectiveness of the daughter she'd loved reminded me of Jophiel and her desire to pause me as Hannah so she wouldn't lose me. Demeter clung to her grief over Persephone in the same way. Though I didn't agree with their actions, I knew they did them out of love, and I tried not to judge them too harshly. I'd lost my chance to reconcile with my sister, but maybe I still had a chance with my mother. Even if she was only here because of my daughter, it was a start.

After my mother had finally released Aurora, and Zel had stopped hanging around like some kind of armed hellhound, Lucifer and I sat with our children around the fire pit as it burned to embers and the sky darkened. Guests had drifted away or left the party entirely, and the only ones still left were family. Even Belial was with us. All of our children, gathered in one place, for the first time —but hopefully not the last.

Kassiel held Aurora and smiled down at her as he rocked her to sleep. She was perfectly content and happy there, but then he passed her to Damien and she began to cry immediately.

"Thought you were good with women, Damien." Kassiel smirked at his brother, and Damien briefly covered his sister's eyes to flip his younger brother off.

"Only ones that aren't my sister." Damien turned his attention to Aurora, and she soon giggled at the expressions he made, her gaze tracking every movement of his face. "Besides, we can't all be the perfect brother."

Kassiel shrugged as he leaned back and took a sip of his beer. "I'm just happy I'm not the baby in the family anymore."

"You're always going to be the baby brother, Kass," Belial said with a grin. "I still remember changing your diapers and rocking you to sleep."

Damien offered the baby to Belial. "Show us how it's done then, old man."

Belial snorted. "She seems happy where she is."

"Oh no, I insist."

Despite his boastful words, our eldest son looked uncomfortable as he awkwardly took the baby into his tattooed arms. I snuggled against Lucifer, content to watch my sons pass their sister between them, and curious to see what would happen next.

Belial's hard expression softened as he looked down at his sister. She stopped yawning and reached for his face, touching his lips, and clubbing his chin with her little closed fist. He grinned and caught her hand, and she moved her mouth like she had something to say. He said something softly to her that was only for her ears, and then she settled down and closed her eyes. Within a few seconds, she was asleep.

Belial leaned back in his chair and gave us a cocky grin. "See? Still got the touch."

"Maybe you just bored her to sleep," Damien said. "I heard it's a common problem with your women."

"What women?" Kassiel asked with a snort. "Hasn't Belial been celibate since the 1600s?"

Belial rolled his eyes. "Don't make me come over there and kick both your asses. I could do it without even waking her up, you know."

Lucifer chuckled softly. "As amusing as that would be to watch, there will be no fighting tonight. Don't upset your poor mother."

"I'm just glad you got her to sleep," I said, amused by their banter. It had been so long since we'd all hung out together like this, and I wasn't sure when it would happen again. I just wanted to sit here and soak up this moment for as long as I could. After all, none of us knew when another threat would emerge and put us all in danger again. It was inevitable, being who we were, and all we could do was try to enjoy the peace while it lasted.

25

HANNAH

Time passed, and still no threat had emerged. I was starting to think my idyllic life might actually be the new norm. How was that possible? I didn't know, but I wasn't going to question it, not after living hundreds of tormented lives where I was brutally torn apart from everyone I loved. Maybe the universe had finally decided I should get a reprieve.

I sipped my coffee as I looked at the two babies lying on a mat in front of me. There was only a month between them, but while Brandy's son Isaac was content to sit on his butt and survey the world from the cushions that propped him in place, Aurora already seemed desperate to move and get going, rolling to things that interested her and attempting to inch across our hardwood floors like a worm. Occasionally, she got close enough to Isaac to take one of his toys, and that was the most animated he became—his voice loud until Brandy soothed his little hurt feelings with a replacement block.

We had baby playdates like this every week, and it was fun seeing our kids grow up together. I just loved living so close to Brandy, since it reminded me of when we were roommates and would hang out all the time. It was also nice to be around someone who was human, who treated me as an equal and not a queen, who reminded me of what it was like to be mortal.

Brandy handed her son another block to gnaw on and gazed at him with adoration lighting her eyes. "Six months and all he wants to do is chew on things."

"That's what babies do," I said with a laugh. "I'm pretty sure Aurora is getting her first tooth. She's been so fussy lately."

Aurora reached into the air like she could see something besides dust motes in the sunlight filtering through the open windows. The smell of the Pacific drifted in off a gentle breeze, and palm trees rustled and rattled together in our gardens. I leaned back against a cushion and curled my legs under me, content with this new calm, normal existence.

"How's Lucifer doing, being so far away from his empire?" Brandy's lips formed a mischievous smile.

"He doesn't seem to mind. Besides, he can run pretty much everything from his office here, and Samael takes care of the rest." Brandy didn't need to know too much about demon business, no matter how much I loved my friend. Her life was much more simple, even though she was married to a former incubus. Besides, she was safer if she didn't know everything. "How's Asmodeus?"

"He's good, although he's super bored now that he doesn't have a job running Lucifer's strip clubs for all the Lilim. He's been joking he's going to open up a male version of Hooters called Peckers and fill it with incubus servers."

I nearly spit out my coffee as I laughed. "That would be hilarious."

"Yep. I think he might be serious too. He says succubi get all the attention, and he wants to provide more opportunities for incubi to get fed without hurting humans."

It was just like Asmodeus to still be watching over his fellow demons even though he was now mortal and removed from our world. "Then he should do it. I'm sure Lucifer would support it."

"Maybe. I told him he should just open some little cafes along the coast, but he said that wasn't sexy enough." She laughed and shook her head. "Once a sex demon, always a sex demon, I suppose."

I shrugged. "We can't change our true nature, even if we're made mortal."

Brandy was about to reply when her eyes widened. My head jerked back to Aurora, who wasn't on the floor beside Isaac anymore, but in the air, making unsteady progress as she chased a seed that had blown in on the breeze. Two wings had emerged from her back, one pure black and trailing darkness from it, the other as white as fresh snow and glowing brightly. They fluttered uncertainly, barely keeping her airborne as she made her way clumsily toward the window that held her fascination.

I launched myself to my feet, my breath stuck in my chest, my mug clattering to the floor and spilling coffee everywhere. "Aurora! No!"

I caught her in my arms before she fell out of the air and held her close to my chest, my heart pounding fast. Brandy jumped up and closed the open window, and I gave her a grateful nod. Aurora immediately started crying, unhappy that I'd stopped her from doing what she wanted, and oblivious to the danger of it all. Fucking hell. How was she flying already?

Lucifer rushed into the room, a sword already forming in his hand, darkness swirling to create the blade. "What's wrong? Is there an attack?"

"We're fine." I glanced down at the baby in my arms who giggled up at me as she moved her wings. "I think."

"Shit." His eyes raked over her and he ran a hand through his hair, blowing out a breath. "Wings? Already?"

"Is that not normal?" Brandy asked, glancing between us.

"No, not at all," I said. "Angels don't get wings 'til they're twenty-one."

"Oh shit," she said.

"Indeed." Lucifer took Aurora from me and held her up, examining her. She quieted down now that her dad held her. "I've never heard of anyone developing wings this young. Sometimes angels do get them early, either at seven or fourteen, but that is extremely rare."

"She's only seven months!" I said, my voice rising with my panic. "How can she have wings already?"

"They're beautiful, though." Lucifer lifted a couple of the black and white feathers and stroked them with care, and Aurora giggled.

A montage of all the ways Aurora could now hurt herself flickered through my mind, and I sank onto the sofa with a groan. Everything needed to remain closed from now on. And locked away. Nothing was safe from her now. "All the childproofing we've done... What use is it now?"

Lucifer lightly tapped Aurora's back between the feathers, and her wings vanished. "We always knew our baby would be special."

"Yes, but I never expected this! Not for many years, anyway."

Brandy handed Isaac another toy. "I don't envy you my friend. Aurora's definitely special, but I can tell she's going to be trouble," she said with a laugh.

Lucifer grinned. "Yes, she is. The best kind of trouble."

I glared at him, worried he wasn't taking this seriously. All our sons had wings, of course, but they'd gotten them at twenty-one. Back then, I'd thought that had been a challenge. Oh past Hannah, how little you knew.

"Let me take her out flying with me," Lucifer said. He'd been asking if he could do it for some time, but I'd been too worried to say yes before. "She'll be perfectly safe in my arms the entire time. She clearly wants to experience the feeling of it, and I can give her a taste of it and show her the proper way to use her wings."

I sighed and rubbed the bridge of my nose. "Fine. Just don't go too far."

26

LUCIFER

I looked down at Aurora, wrapped snuggly in the fabric Hannah had helped me wind around my body. I was pretty sure Hannah had wrapped us extra tight—more to prevent Aurora from taking off on her own than to ensure I didn't drop her into the ocean. As we flew, I imagined what my enemies would say, seeing the devil with a baby strapped to his chest, but the thought only made me laugh.

Real men wore babies.

Aurora giggled as sea spray coated our faces with a fine mist of salt water, and her little wings moved uselessly against her wrap. Oh, she was trouble, all right. And she wasn't even one yet. How were we going to handle her?

"One more loop around?" I looked down at her, and she shrieked her excitement again as I banked left and swooped a wide arc over the waves. I cupped the top of her head under my palm as water splashed higher than I'd anticipated. I'd never experienced protectiveness quite like this, even with my sons. It was different this time, maybe because she was a girl, or maybe because I knew she would be my last child.

"We need to head back, little one," I said, and she pouted on cue. That face got me every time, and I dipped lower, almost trailing her through the ocean. She shrieked and laughed again, and I chuckled as I smoothed a hand over her wet hair.

"Your Mom's going to kill me for bringing you back drenched in salt water." But I looked at Aurora's face and couldn't find any regret in me. This time together was too precious.

I landed on our carefully manicured lawn, not far from the pool with the tiny Roman-style tiles that Hannah seemed to like. Then, as if thinking about her had summoned her, she burst through the door from the house, running toward me at top speed with a panicked expression on her face.

"Lucifer! There you are!"

Shit. We'd been gone too long, and now I was going to get an earful. I held up my hands in surrender. "We were perfectly safe the entire time, I promise."

"It's not that." Hannah pushed her windswept hair back roughly from her face. "Samael just called. Lilith is missing!"

My heart seemed to stop. "What? Three mates and they can't keep it straight where she is?"

Hannah shook her head. "She was traveling without any of them. All of her guards were found dead. Ripped apart by shifters."

I swore under my breath in languages not spoken on Earth any longer. "Fenrir must have taken her because he knows she has one of the only keys to Hell."

Hannah's eyes widened. "That means they're going after Death. Oh no—Kassiel!"

She sprinted toward the house, and I followed right at her heels. Once inside the kitchen, she grabbed her phone and dialed Kassiel. If Fenrir was trying to release Death, he would need Kassiel—the only person I knew of who could open the tomb, since they'd have to be both born in Hell and carrying the blood of one of the people who had sealed Death away—me, Eve, Michael, and Oberon.

While the phone rang, I unwrapped Aurora. She immediately cried and reached for her mom, and I passed her over to Hannah and took the phone to speak to our son. Luckily, Kassiel answered on the first ring.

"Hey Mom."

"It's me actually."

"Dad?" He always sounded suspicious when I called him.

"Lilith is missing, and Fenrir might be coming for you next. You need to go into hiding. Take Olivia and her other mates with you for protection and leave immediately." There was no point in sugar-coating or small talk. We didn't have time for any of that.

"I understand." Kassiel's tone was serious. "We'll leave right away."

"Get a burner phone in case they're tracking us somehow and check in when you're safe."

"I will."

"Tell him I love him." Hannah touched my arm, her eyebrows draw together.

"I heard," Kassiel said. "I love her too. And you, Dad. Look after my sister, okay?"

My chest swelled with a potent mix of love and fear. "I will. You look after yourself too. Love you, son."

We said goodbye and I turned to Hannah, whose eyes reflected all the same worries I had. It pained me that I couldn't be there physically to protect Kassiel. Maybe I should have had him come here. Or maybe that's what Fenrir expected. Maybe it was better if Kassiel was hiding somewhere that I had no knowledge of. Maybe it was better if he was far from Aurora if shit went down. Maybe not. Fuck. I hated having to make decisions like these.

"Is Kassiel safe?" Hannah cradled Aurora closer, pressing our daughter's head to her shoulder.

"He's as safe as he can be." Then I blew out a sigh. "I need to call Samael."

"I spoke to him just before you returned. He's already sent people to search for Lilith. He's very worried, of course."

I nodded, but knew it wouldn't be enough. Fenrir was too damn crafty, even without Nemesis at his side. "We have to prepare for the worst. If Death is freed..."

Hannah shuddered. "We can't let that happen."

"But if it does, we have no way to stop him once he's released." I closed my eyes as I faced the inevitable. "We have to get the key to Void."

"I thought you might say that." Hannah nodded slowly. "Where is it?"

"In Hell. I hid it in the lowest reaches of our palace before I sealed the realm off. I figured it would be safest there."

Hannah considered this. "The palace is in the equivalent of Egypt. That's a long journey."

"I know. I'll take the private jet and come back as soon as I can."

"No way. I'm coming with you. I don't want to be apart from you for that long. Not after losing you for six months."

"What about Aurora?" I glanced at our baby, at her hands as they grabbed at locks of Hannah's blond hair, at her wings fluttering in excitement. She still wasn't very good at putting them away yet. "That's a long time for us to be away from her."

Hannah shrugged. "She can come with us. Consider it our first family vacation. Besides, despite what Zel thinks, she's safest with us."

I rubbed my chin as I considered it. Hell should be completely empty, but if Fenrir was there waiting for us, we'd probably be able to stop him. After all, we were the Demon King and Queen. Who better to protect our baby in Hell? Whereas if we left her here with Zel, and Fenrir came here looking for us—or for Kassiel—Aurora might be in even more danger. Besides, Hannah and I were a team. After being separated for so long, both in this life and every other, we didn't want to be apart again.

"Very well, we'll go together," I said.

Hannah picked up her phone again. "I'll call Einial and have her make the arrangements."

I took the baby from her as she made the call. The private jet was only a short drive away, but then it would be a long flight to Egypt. Our daughter's first trip.

I hoped it proved to be an uneventful one.

27

HANNAH

Our palace in Hell was located in the equivalent of the Valley of the Kings. After our private jet landed at Cairo Airport, we checked into our hotel room, and then flew out of the city on our wings under the cover of night. Considering it was her first time away from home, Aurora was doing amazingly well. She slept for some of the flight, and we managed to keep her entertained the rest of the time. Mostly she was just curious about everything she saw. Even now she gazed around from her position on Lucifer's chest, her blue eyes wide as we swooped through the air, hidden from view by the shadows we'd gathered around ourselves.

Once we were out of Cairo, we found an empty patch of desert to cross over into Hell without anyone watching us. We landed gently on the sandy ground, and I glanced around, noting we'd managed to find somewhere actually deserted. "Here?"

"Yes, this should work." Lucifer had a protective arm across Aurora and he pulled the wrap up to shield her head against the sand that thickened the air. Somewhere along the way she'd fallen asleep, lulled into slumber by the sound of Lucifer's heartbeat and the feel of him gliding through the air.

I stood back as Lucifer produced a gem that seemed to swim

with shadows. It emitted a black glow that was almost like the absence of light. A black hole, sucking all light into it.

"The key to Hell." Lucifer lifted it to eye-level, twisting it like he was examining the multi-faceted sides. Then he held it out in front of him and the dark glow spread out and formed an inky black portal before us.

A shiver ran through me as I wondered what I would see on the other side. Last time I'd been in Hell, it had been a battle-ground, and I'd been fighting for the other side. I also remembered it during our golden years, when I was Persephone and he was Hades and we filled our palace with love and life. I was anxious to see what Hell was like now, after it had been abandoned for so long.

Lucifer entwined his fingers with mine, and together we stepped through the portal into the land of darkness.

People thought Hell was all fire and brimstone, but that was angel propaganda. Hell was an endless night full of twinkling stars and brisk air, with night-blooming flowers that faintly glowed with light and animals that could see in the dark. It was still all of those things as we entered it, but it was also a barren, gray landscape, where instead of the ground being covered with golden sand, flakes of ash drifted into piles and dunes. That was new—there had never been ash, at least not until the angels burned everything down. It pained me knowing I had once been a part of that, before I'd remem-bered who I really was.

"We're home again." As I spoke, the words settled into my brain with the ring of truth. Just like Heaven and Faerie, this was also my home. Maybe even more so than those places. I'd lived in Hell during so many of my past lives, sometimes for centuries, sometimes for only a few days, but this was my first time visiting as Hannah. Even so, my soul recognized this place as home.

"My domain." Lucifer spread his arms wide as he gazed across the barren landscape. "I've returned."

"You know, since we're bringing Aurora to Hell, we should also take her to Heaven sometime. She needs to connect with her angel heritage as much as her demon one."

He grimaced as a faint shudder worked through him. "You know, I think I've spent far too much time there already recently."

"It'll be different this time. You'll have your family with you."

"We'll discuss this some other time," he conceded, and then let out a low whistle. His horse, Strife, appeared in the distance and rode toward us at top speed, with Shadow just a step behind. We mounted them when they got close, and they took off toward the south, leading us to our first destination.

As we galloped beside the Nile river, my heart sank at the sight of all the destroyed, abandoned buildings, and the complete lack of life anywhere around us. Hell had once been beautiful and prosperous, and it hurt to see it so forlorn. I completely understood why Lucifer had moved all the demons to Earth, since it was the only way to save our people, but it was depressing to see the aftermath of that decision. I stole a glance at Lucifer's face, and judging by his pained expression, he felt the same way.

Soon the great pyramids of Giza appeared in the distance under the soft moonlight, like beacons pulling us toward them. They existed in this realm just as they did on Earth, but with one big difference—in Hell, Death was entombed beneath the Great Sphinx, which was originally built as a monument to him. The entire Giza plateau was once a gateway between the worlds, and the barrier was still weaker here between Earth and Hell, especially with Death's power emanating from the Sphinx. It was no wonder that Giza was thought to be a very haunted place on Earth. The humans might not know why they were both drawn to and revolted by the place, why they went inside only against their better judgment yet couldn't seem to stop themselves—but we did. Death's essence reached across all of the realms, calling to anyone who dared come close to his tomb. It was the one thing no mortal escaped, the last great fear. Even us immortals would succumb to it eventually.

We took some time riding around the pyramids and the Sphinx, checking to make sure Death hadn't been released, but everything was quiet. There was no sign Fenrir or anyone else had been here in decades. I breathed a sigh of relief, until I heard whispered voices on the wind, saying my oldest name.

"Eve...the cursed queen...the lady of many deaths...free me and find peace..."

I shuddered as I tried to block out the horrible words that chilled me to the bone. I was all too familiar with death, and had no interest in experiencing it again. I turned to Lucifer, and his jaw was clenched, his mouth set in a tight line, and I knew he heard something too. What horrible things was Death whispering to him?

"Let's get out of here," I suggested.

Lucifer wrapped Aurora up even tighter, as if he could shield her from the dark presence all around us. "With all haste."

We rode off into the night as fast as our horses would take us, leaving the deathly whispers behind. The other Elder Gods hadn't been able to reach out of their tombs like that, but then again, Death was the most powerful of them all.

———

W e reached our old palace some time later, and the sight of it made my soul weep. The huge columns framing the front were usually alive with climbing plants and flowers that glowed with soft blue light, but now they hung in dead swathes, like tattered drapes from some long-forgotten bygone age. More ash littered the ground, and entire sections of the palace had crumbled to dust.

I flicked my fingers to try to inspire some life in the plants and was rewarded when some veins of green appeared. The plants rustled as they moved, stretching toward me to draw more power, and soon they began to grow again. Tiny little glowing flowers appeared once more, struggling to come back to life. Other than those small movements, the entire place remained desolate and sad, like the soul of the place had died without us here to tend to it.

I sighed and took Lucifer's hand, squeezing it tightly. "I miss this place. I miss what it was."

"I do too." He touched one of the columns as we walked by, his fingers trailing over the smooth black stone. Aurora stirred a little from where she was strapped to his chest and blinked at the glowing flowers with sleepy-eyed interest. "Perhaps we can rebuild once we've got everything else under control."

I turned to him with raised brows. "You would open Hell once more?"

"Someday, yes." He gazed up at a statue of him that was now in pieces. "I've been thinking a lot about this ever since speaking with Belial. Closing Hell and moving all the demons to Earth is one of the reasons the Archdemons revolted against me. Perhaps I shouldn't have been so hasty to close it off completely. At the time, I thought it would be best, just like Michael thought it best to close off Heaven and move the angels to Earth. Both realms were destroyed by our long war, and both races were dying out. We needed to move to Earth to have any chance of survival. But what if that was the wrong decision? I see now that it caused strife for many of our people."

I leaned my head against his shoulder, and stroked Aurora's head where it rested against his chest. "You did what you thought was best for our people at the time, and I know you'll do the best you can going forward, no matter how hard those decisions are to make. Maybe that means starting to rebuild Hell so the demons can return —eventually."

He wrapped an arm around me. "As long as I have you by my side to help me make these decisions going forward."

I shoved him playfully. "Well, obviously."

Aurora began to cry and struggle against Lucifer's chest. After being strapped to him for so long she was probably desperate for some free time, and probably hungry too.

"I'll take her and give her a snack," I said. "You can get the key to Void while we wait outside."

"Probably for the best." Lucifer began unwrapping the baby. "It looks quite dusty inside. I'll be back in a few minutes."

I pulled a blanket out of the diaper bag and set it down, then put Aurora on top of it and began feeding her one of those fruit and veggie pouches that were so convenient. Another thing I wished I'd had in the old days. She devoured it immediately, and I gave her some water, then searched around in the bag for something else to feed her.

Suddenly a growl ripped through the air behind me. I leaped to my feet in front of Aurora, my wings flaring out, with light in one hand and darkness in the other. A three-headed hellhound the size of a horse stood before us, its black fur radiating darkness and its eyes glowing red. Drool dripped from the long, sharp fangs on each of the heads, and sharp claws pawed at the ground as if it might charge us.

"Cerberus, no!" Lucifer cried out, from where he'd appeared in the entrance to the palace.

The hellhound paused, and then launched itself at Lucifer, wagging its tail. Three long tongues came out and covered Lucifer, who held up his hands to defend himself. Aurora giggled and squealed and I made my magic vanish, my shoulders relaxing. Cerberus had been our pet and guardian while in Hell, and it seemed he was still protecting the palace after all these years.

"Down!" Lucifer said, and Cerberus sat and looked up at his master, tail still dancing. Now that the hellhound realized there was no threat to the palace, his demeanor had changed entirely.

"Did you know he was here?" I asked.

Lucifer rubbed Cerberus's many heads. "Yes, he and all of the other hellhounds stayed here when the demons left for Earth. We couldn't exactly bring them along, after all."

"No, I suppose not." I held out a hand and approached him slowly. "Cerberus, it's me. Eve. Persephone. Lenore."

Cerberus tilted his heads, seemingly curious as he examined me. One of his noses sniffed my hand, then he bounced forward, three tongues ready to lick me. I gave him a hug, rubbing the thick fur along his neck.

"It's good to see you too," I said. "Want to meet our newest member of the family?"

Cerberus peered at Aurora next with three big doggy grins, and she giggled and reached for him with both arms. He laid a long lick up her cheek, and she laughed even harder.

"I feel so bad that he's been here all this time." I smoothed a hand along the hellhound's back. "Think he'd like to come home with us?"

Lucifer raised an eyebrow. "A three-headed dog in California?"

"He'd be the perfect guardian and playmate for Aurora." Three pairs of eyes on my child who seemed determined to fly before she could walk sounded perfect at the moment. If we tasked Cerberus with keeping her safe, he would do everything he could to protect her. "As long as he stays at the estate, it should be fine."

"I can't argue with that." Lucifer patted Cerberus on the back. "Do you want to come back with us, old boy? We could use your help defending a new palace."

Cerberus let out a bark and wagged his tail harder, and I guessed that meant yes.

"It's settled then," Lucifer said.

I began packing up all of Aurora's things, eager to leave this forlorn place. "Did you get the key to Void?"

"Yes, I did." Lucifer held up a small velvet drawstring bag, then tucked it into a pocket. "Let's go home."

I glanced back at the palace that had once been our home. Perhaps one day it would be again. But for the moment, our place was on Earth.

28

HANNAH

Cerberus nudged Aurora across the floor, butt-scooting her along with one of his noses, and her peals of laughter rang out around the nursery. Even Zel smiled at the close bond that had developed between them.

Lucifer wrapped an arm around my waist, drawing me closer. He nuzzled a kiss to my neck. "Think anyone would notice if we took an hour for ourselves?"

I lifted an eyebrow as I grinned. "A whole hour? What a luxury that would be."

He laughed and kissed my neck again, but then his phone rang, and he cursed under his breath. "It's Samael."

I nodded, my smile dropping immediately. It had been a week since we'd gotten back from Hell, and there had been no news about Lilith's whereabouts. "You'd better get it then."

Lucifer huffed out a sigh as he answered. "Hello, Samael. Everything all right?" He paused and his eyes landed on me. "Yes, she's here."

I turned to Zel, worry already nagging at my gut. "Could you watch Aurora while we take this?"

"Of course," Zel said.

Lucifer and I headed out of the nursery and into our bedroom, shutting the door behind us. I sat on the edge of the bed as Lucifer tapped his phone and said, "Okay, we're ready."

"We have an emergency here in Vegas," Samael's deep voice said from the phone's speaker. "Pestilence has been freed and we're under attack."

"What?" I asked, jumping to my feet again.

"How?" Lucifer asked.

"Our cameras show it was Theo who released him," Samael said.

Theo? I gripped Lucifer's forearm. No, that made no sense. Theo had been my guard for months. I trusted him with my life. He'd helped me become Famine, and he'd been there when we sealed Pestilence inside. Why would he free Pestilence now?

"Are you sure it was him?" I asked, my voice trembling a little.

"We're sure." Samael spoke on a sigh, the words almost an apology. "We need your help. Pestilence is attacking The Celestial as we speak. Our people managed to evacuate it as best we could, but I fear he's going to spread his plague to everyone in Las Vegas within a few hours."

"We'll be there in an hour," Lucifer said, before hanging up. It wasn't even a question of whether we would go or not. We were the only ones who could stop Pestilence—especially if the gargoyles had turned on us. And with the tomb no longer an option, our only hope was to use the Void key to send Pestilence to that realm.

I glanced around the room, wondering if I should pack anything or change my clothes, and instead opted for just throwing on my sneakers and a bra. Would anyone care if the Queen of Hell showed up to fight Pestilence in yoga pants? Probably not. Assuming anyone was even alive by the time we got there.

I rushed back into the nursery, where Aurora was riding on Cerberus's back while Zel fed the hellhound a biscuit. My chest tightened as the reality of the situation sunk in, and I accepted that I would have to leave Aurora behind. It was too dangerous for her to go with us this time. She would be safer here. I knew that, but it was still hard to leave her.

"We have to go to Vegas," I said, as I grabbed Aurora and pulled her against my chest. "Pestilence is free."

"Oh fuck." Zel rose to her feet. "Do you need me to go?"

"No, I need you to stay here and watch Aurora." I felt a slight pang of guilt that one of the greatest warriors of all time was relegated to babysitter duty, but there was no one else I would trust more with my daughter.

Zel nodded. "That I can do. Cerberus and I will keep her safe."

"Thank you." I hugged Aurora to my chest, kissing her face a hundred times. "Mommy will be back soon, I promise. I love you so much."

Lucifer came into the nursery and took Aurora from me, then said his own goodbyes while I wrung my hands nervously. We'd never left her behind before. Not even for date night. Not while Fenrir was still out there. Now we were going into certain danger, and there was no other option but to leave her here.

I took Aurora again and gave her more kisses and hugs, then reluctantly handed her to Zel. I opened my mouth to tell Zel about bedtime and what to feed her and everything else I could think of, but Zel held up a hand to stop me.

"I got this. Go save the world."

I hugged her close, then walked out of the room with Lucifer. We got in our Lamborghini, and Lucifer drove out of the estate so fast the world became almost a blur around us. The private jet waited at a nearby airstrip, and Lucifer was already on the phone telling them to get it ready to go.

When he hung up, we settled into uneasy silence. Finally I said, "I can't believe Theo did this."

"Another traitor," Lucifer said with disgust. "Maybe he thinks he's continuing his mother's plans after her death."

"That would mean he's been waiting all this time for the right moment to act." I swallowed hard, feeling the sting of his betrayal deep inside.

Lucifer shook his head. "I didn't know him as well as you did, so I can't say for sure. But we always knew there could be gargoyles who believed so earnestly in Belphegor's mission that her death wouldn't stop their actions. Theo might be one of them."

"And Romana?"

"I think she is loyal." Lucifer sighed, his hands gripping the steering wheel so tight his knuckles were white. "I guess we'll find out soon enough."

I nodded and stared out the window as we zoomed down the highway. "I hate that we have to leave Aurora."

"She'll be all right," Lucifer said, his voice gentle. "Zel will be there, along with Cerberus. Neither of them will let anything happen to her."

"I know. And our estate's well-guarded and has plenty of security measures in place... I still hate it."

"Me too." He rested a hand on my thigh. "We'll take care of this problem and be back in no time."

I prayed he was right. I'd gotten so used to our perfect, happy, almost-normal life, but deep down I'd known it could never last. A threat would always emerge that we would have to face, and every time we would be forced to leave Aurora behind, knowing we might not come back. It had been the same during all of my lives. No wonder all of our sons had issues. We'd done the best we could with them, but we'd always had other duties too, duties that were so important we couldn't pass them off to other people. It was hard being a parent when you had to save the world all the time. I hadn't really understood that until now, and I feared we would repeat the same mistakes with Aurora. But what else could we do?

Stopping Pestilence would help, for a start. Adam had been a threat during all of my kids' lives, and if he were finally out of the picture, we could relax a little. It was time to take the fucker down.

29

LUCIFER

I tightened my thighs to spur Strife on as we left the airport and headed into downtown Las Vegas. We'd known something was wrong before the jet even touched down, as the sun glinted off the buildings bold enough to stretch their glassy tips farthest into the sky. This city was an oasis of life in the middle of the Nevada desert, but even from a distance, we could tell that Vegas was sick. Plumes of black smoke rose from various spots along The Strip, and I feared what we would find when we returned to The Celestial.

As we drew closer to my resort, the extent of the damage became clearer. Windows had been blown out, bodies were strewn across the pavement and covered in boils, and even the plants had withered and died from the sickness in the air. Our horses brought us to Hannah's garden that had once thrived with life, but now everything here was dead, the flowers black, the leaves spotted and brown. Up ahead, the waterfall recycled murky yellow water, and behind it was a huge hole where Pestilence's tomb had been hidden away. The tomb itself was gone. Or destroyed. I wasn't sure. But where was Pestilence?

Hannah surveyed the damage in the garden she'd created, her fingers flickering idly over various plants, coaxing life back into them, although the movement didn't seem to be deliberate on her part. She looked absolutely horrified by it all, her face paler than normal, her eyes wet with unshed tears, especially when her gaze landed on the tourists that had died. Entire families, destroyed by Pestilence's plague. Intense rage filled me at the sight. These people had come to my hotel for a family vacation or a fun weekend getaway and now they were dead. It was my responsibility to keep them safe and happy while at my resort, and I'd failed. Now all I could do was avenge their deaths...which I would do with relish.

Sirens sounded from the street, and the sound of human misery and suffering thickened the air. I kept the War side of me locked away most of the time, but now I let it surface. The fury made me stronger, as long as I could control it.

"I'm going to rip Adam's fucking head off," I growled.

Hannah shot me a look full of menace. "Not if I do it first."

"We need to find Samael. Let's check the war room."

Hannah nodded, and our wings unfurled at the same time, mine black and shadowy, hers silver and bright. We launched into the air and flew up to the penthouse, which had sat empty for months, but had been destroyed anyway. Pestilence had even peed all over my leather couch. That fucking prick. Hannah just let out a long sigh as she surveyed the damage.

We marched down the stairs rather than take the elevator, uncertain of the electrics and stability of the infrastructure. I'd never seen my command room so busy. Demons scurried between desks and spoke into headsets while typing furiously on their computers. Lights flashed on monitors and maps, showing the activity of my demons across the city and wider areas. Occasionally, alarms went off, attracting more frenetic activity at various desks.

Samael watched over everything, his arms folded tightly across his chest, his face expressionless but his jaw tight. He turned toward us as we approached, and something that looked like relief flickered across his features before he clamped down on it and returned to being expressionless. He nodded a greeting, and I motioned toward the meeting room. We'd be able to watch from within the glass walls without being overheard.

"What's happening?" Hannah spoke first—as soon as the door closed.

"Where is Pestilence?" I asked.

"You're too late," Samael said. "He's gone."

"Gone?" Hannah asked. "Where did he go?"

"No one knows. He rode off on his horse into the desert."

"And Theo?" I asked. Another fucker who needed to die.

"Also gone. He left as soon as Pestilence was freed, and took many of the gargoyles with him."

Dammit. We were too late. Pestilence had gone, leaving destruction and sickness in his wake. My vengeance would have to wait another day.

"Where's Einial?" Hannah asked. Normally she was at Samael's side, helping him run things.

Samael's face fell. "Dead. Killed by Theo when she tried to stop him from opening Pestilence's tomb."

Hannah covered her mouth with her hand, her eyes wide. "Oh no. I'm so sorry."

"Pestilence will pay for what he's done," I growled. "What about the humans?"

"We've put word out about a terrorist attack," Samael said. "Chemical weapons. It's something the humans will believe and rally behind."

"Good thinking." It wasn't like any of them would believe that demon factions were currently releasing the Four Horsemen of the Apocalypse, or that Pestilence had destroyed much of the Las Vegas Strip. "What can we do?"

"We've got everything in hand here, but you can speak to the press perhaps. Or try to find Pestilence, though I'm not sure how you'll locate him."

I agreed, but Pestilence's disappearance grated against me. "It's surprising he left so quickly. He must have known that Hannah and I would come for him. Wouldn't he want to face us? To try to take Hannah, if nothing else?"

"Maybe that's why he left," Samael said. "He knew he couldn't face both of you together."

Hannah tapped her lips. "Maybe... Or maybe he's going to meet Fenrir somewhere for the real attack."

Her words sparked a horrible idea inside my head. "What if this was all a diversion?"

Hannah's eyes widened. "What do you mean?"

"It's possible." Samael stroked his chin. "There's certainly enough damage control here to keep us all busy for a while."

"And it got us both away from home." Hannah gripped my arm tightly, her voice rising with her panic. "We need to get back to Aurora."

I nodded, heart pounding, gut twisting with fear. "Samael, you've got this covered. We need to return home."

"Go," Samael said. "I'll keep you updated on any new developments."

I nodded and clasped Samael's shoulder briefly before Hannah and I left the room at a near run. I tried to keep my panic in check, but instinct told me something wasn't right, and that things were about to get a lot worse.

Then again, things getting worse was a given until we found Pestilence.

———

Hannah whipped across the grass on Shadow, always a couple of hoofbeats ahead of me like she was being chased by hellhounds rather than simply returning home. I felt that same urgency and urged Strife on too.

"Are you all right?" I shouted my words into the wind racing past, hoping Hannah heard me.

"No." It was one word tossed over her shoulder. "I have a really bad feeling."

"Me too."

She remained silent the rest of the ride, but there was a tension in her posture as she sat on Shadow's back, and her face could have called forth thunder.

We arrived at our estate, but Hannah didn't even wait for

Shadow to slow before she leapt off her back and took off toward our house. That's when I realized how quiet and empty it was on our estate. Something was wrong. Worse than Vegas.

Death lingered here.

"Hannah—wait!"

But she sped up, my call spurring her on rather than holding her back. She pushed the front door open and screamed.

I was with her within moments. Two of our guards lay dead on the hardwood floor, their bodies lying there peacefully, as if they'd gone to sleep and never woken up. There was no sign of a struggle. An unnatural quiet blanketed the house, and the air was too still.

"Aurora! Zel! Cerberus!" Hannah ran from room to room, her voice going shrill as she screamed the names over and over. I searched too, my heart in my throat, my fear so strong I couldn't say anything at all. We checked everywhere. The bedrooms. The office. The kitchen. The pool.

The nursery.

The house was empty aside from dozens of dead guards. There was not one single living person on the estate, as far as I could tell, though nothing else had been touched.

Hannah was in a complete panic, her eyes wild. "Where is Aurora?"

I shook my head and drew her into my arms, partly to keep myself from falling apart. "I don't know."

"Or Zel? Or Cerberus?"

I had no answer to that either. As I'd searched the house, I'd been terrified that I might find one—or all—of them dead, just like the guards. It was a small relief—very small—that they weren't here. They could still be alive. Taken by whoever had done this.

Oh, who was I kidding? I knew who'd done this. Of course I did. The presence was unmistakable, even after thousands of years apart. I smelled it lingering in the air, heard the ghostly whispers on the breeze, and felt the eerie chill trailing down my spine.

Death.

My father.

Somehow he was free—and he'd taken my daughter.

30

HANNAH

Everything inside me screamed and sobbed. It was a miracle I wasn't doing both of those on the outside too, but I was using every ounce of control I had to keep it together. Falling apart wouldn't save Aurora, and I had to act quickly. I had to do everything I could to find her, even if all I wanted to do was break into a million pieces.

Lucifer threw his arms out to the side and let out a guttural roar that made the windows of the house shake. His eyes were red, and fury radiated off of him in menacing waves. The part of him that was War was emerging. I considered stopping it and trying to calm him down, but then said fuck it. If there was ever a time to be Famine and War, it was now.

"We'll get her back," I told him, as my own desperation brought out my endless hunger and thirst. This time, it was an all-consuming yearning to save her. A mirror across from me showed that my eyes were glowing green too, and I embraced the power. To save my daughter I would become a force to be reckoned with. I would tear apart the entire world if I had to, if that's what it took to find her.

Yes. I could do this. I'd rescued Lucifer from War, for fuck's sake. I could find my daughter, a three-headed dog, and my demon bodyguard. It wasn't like they'd be easy to hide, and it must have been Fenrir who'd taken them. This didn't look like a shifter attack, but who else could it have been?

A noise stirred behind us, like the sound of people moving and the rustle of fabric. Lucifer and I shared a "what now?" look, before we turned to face whatever this was from our spot in the middle of the living room. But what I saw made my stomach drop.

The dead guards around us rose to their feet, their completely black eyes staring at us. As they stepped forward, their movements were jerky, unnatural, and they raised their weapons in threat. From the corner of my eye I saw more coming down the staircase, and others in the garden and by the pool heading toward us. They said nothing, but their intent was clear, and Lucifer and I summoned our magic to defend ourselves.

The undead guards threw themselves at us with abandon, slashing their weapons and shooting their guns, even though there was no chance they could win against us. A cocktail of terror and grief mixed inside me as we fought them off with blasts of light and darkness. But every time we knocked them down, they got back up again.

All right then. I'd seen enough zombie movies in my time as a human, and I knew there was one surefire way to stop the undead. I created twin swords of twisting light and darkness for myself and for Lucifer, which easily sliced off the heads of our former guards. I felt sick to my stomach as I took them down, these men and women who had once worked to protect us, but were now being used against us. I knew they were already dead, but I hated it anyway. I remembered all of their names. Every single one of them. And they'd died because of us.

One of the guards suddenly stopped before us and croaked out with a rasping voice, "Death awaits you in Hell."

"What did you just say?" I asked, as a chill ran through me.

"If you want your daughter back, come find him," the undead continued.

Lucifer sprang forward and sliced his sword through the guard's neck. The head tumbled to the floor and rolled across the hardwood, scattering small droplets of blood everywhere.

That was the last of them. I vanished our swords, my hands shaking as the horrible truth of the guard's words sank into me. I turned to Lucifer and met his angry gaze, my eyes wide. "Death took Aurora?"

"Yes, it must be him." Lucifer spoke through gritted teeth. "He's been freed somehow."

Another horrible realization hit me, and my panic spiked again. "Kassiel!"

Lucifer reached into his inside jacket pocket and withdrew his phone. "Call him."

I took the phone with shaking hands. If Death had been released, Kassiel had to have been there. They needed his blood—and he wouldn't have gone willingly. So how much blood had they spilled? Was he still alive?

The screen blurred and I could barely read the list of contacts. Lucifer took the phone back and tapped it a couple of times before handing it to me. As it rang, I drew a shaky breath, and when Kassiel answered, I blew it all back out in a hurry.

"Kassiel?"

"Mom?"

The sound of his voice filled me with relief. "Are you okay? Where are you?"

"I'm fine. We're still in hiding. Why, Mom? What's happened?"

"He's okay," I said to Lucifer, and my husband closed his eyes, his jaw visibly relaxing. I hit a button so Lucifer could hear too as I asked Kassiel, "Are you safe where you are? Are the others with you?"

"Yes, they're all here. What's going on?"

"They've released Death," Lucifer said. "And he took your sister."

"What?" Kassiel yelled from the other side of the phone. "Where?"

"To Hell." Lucifer tensed again, his hands curling into fists, his knuckles going white. "Death wants us to find him there."

"Then I'm coming with you," Kassiel said. "We all are."

I tensed at the thought of putting another of my children in danger, but we would need his help. We would need everyone's help to face what we were up against. "We'll let you know when we have a plan. Stay safe."

We told Kassiel we loved him and then hung up. As soon as I did, Lucifer spun away from me, a cry of rage tearing from him as he conjured a shadow blade from nowhere and smashed it against the fireplace. Then the dining table. And the sofa.

He raised the weapon again and I yelled, "Stop! Destroying our house won't get her back!"

Lucifer looked at me, his gaze a burning mix of fury and grief. In his eyes, I saw the same desperate pain resonating within me, and knew he would burn the entire world down if that's what it would take to get Aurora back. I'd let him do it too. I'd throw on the gasoline and strike the matches. With Lucifer at my side, I'd become the villain, the terrifying goddess of hunger and misery, the bringer of the apocalypse. All to save our child.

"We'll find her." I held out my hands to Lucifer, and his blade disappeared before he walked over to me. He slid his fingers into mine, and we stared back at each other with resolve. A new strength straightened my spine as power rippled along my skin, moving back and forth between me and Lucifer. Ancient power. Godly power. "We're Lucifer and Hannah. Demon King and Queen. War and Famine. No one can stop us, not when we're together."

Lucifer nodded slowly, his rage shifting to determination, his hands squeezing mine. "We've fought together for all of time, and we won't let anyone take what's ours. I'll make the calls and rally the troops. If Death wants us to meet him in Hell, we're bringing an army with us."

Our horses appeared just outside the open sliding glass doors, their eyes glowing like ours were as they angrily stomped their hooves and shook their heads. They were ready for battle too.

We were Horsemen, and it was time for the apocalypse to begin. *Our* apocalypse.

31

HANNAH

We were back in Egypt, but this time Aurora wasn't giggling happily from her usual position on Lucifer's chest, and my heart ached at the loss of her. The Great Sphinx loomed over us under a moonless night that cloaked us in darkness, and just as well, because Lucifer and I had gathered all of our allies here at the Giza Pyramids.

We had an army.

With Lucifer at my side, we made the rounds to make sure everyone was ready and knew what to do before we opened the portal to Hell. Once on the other side, everything would happen fast, and it would all be chaos. As we walked across ancient sand-beaten stones, I shivered, but not from the cold. Death truly did linger around this crumbling monument, even here on Earth.

Samael hovered nearby, staring at his phone like he was still considering the logistics and organization of the mission—always one step ahead and completely reliable under every circumstance. It made me sad seeing him without his assistant Einial, which only increased my resolve to avenge her death. She'd been good to me while Lucifer was in Heaven, and it was a damn shame she'd been another of Pestilence's casualties.

"Everything is ready," Samael said, when he finally noticed us approaching. "We only await your command."

There was a touch of sadness in his eyes I hadn't seen before. I stepped forward and gave him a hug, realizing he was also worried for a loved one. "I'm sure Lilith is with them."

"I hope you're right." Samael blew out a breath. "She went with them willingly, so perhaps they haven't harmed her. Baal got the full story from their daughter, Lena. Fenrir kidnapped them both, and Lilith agreed to use the key to open the portal to Hell only after Lena was released and her safety assured."

"I can't fault her for doing that to save her daughter," I said with a sigh. Not when I stood here with an entire army to rescue Aurora. Mothers moved mountains. We always would.

Baal and Gabriel stood a short distance away among a few other vampires and angels, all donning their weapons and armor. Baal wore black and red armor with spikes, befitting a vampire lord, while Gabriel wore gleaming golden armor perfect for an Archangel. Together, they looked particularly formidable as they prepared to go into battle to rescue the woman they loved. As Gabriel raised his spear, I'd never seen the Archangel look so foreboding, and I had a sudden flash of what he'd be like if he'd become Fallen instead of Lucifer.

After a few more words with Samael, we moved to speak with Romana, who stood in gargoyle form, her bat-like wings folded behind her. She barked commands to the gargoyle soldiers in front of her, and then turned toward us with blazing eyes. She wore Theo's betrayal like a shroud, like it had personally stained her, and now she had the ferocity of a woman with a lot to prove.

She bowed toward us. "My king and queen, I wish to apologize for my brother's actions."

"There is nothing to apologize for," Lucifer said.

"We know you weren't involved in his betrayal," I added.

Romana shook her head, her mouth twisted in an angry scowl. "No, but I should have seen it coming. Theo was always Belphegor's most loyal child, and I think he believed he should have become

Archdemon instead of me, even though I am older than him by many centuries, and..."

"And what?" I asked, sensing there was more to this story.

Romana glanced about, and when she spoke again, she'd lowered her voice. "Theo is not entirely demon. He is half angel. Archangel, to be precise."

Lucifer arched an eyebrow. "Who is his father?"

"Michael," Romana said, her voice barely above a whisper.

My mouth fell open. That would make him Callan's half-brother. Lucifer tensed beside me too at the name.

Romana continued speaking in a low voice, as if telling us a secret. "He and Belphegor had a short fling about two hundred years ago, long before there was peace between the angels and demons. Theo was raised in Hell by our mother, who kept his parentage a secret. According to her, Michael refused to acknowledge Theo as his son. It's one of the reasons Mother hated angels so much, and why Theo hates them still."

"Michael's son, born in Hell..." Lucifer said, then closed his eyes and nodded. "That must be how they opened Death's tomb."

Of course. They hadn't needed Kassiel at all because they had Theo all along, carrying the blood of one of the people who had sealed away Death originally. Damn. If only we'd known the truth about him sooner.

It was too late to worry about what we might have done differently. I touched Romana's arm lightly. "Thank you for coming today, Romana. I know it's hard to be divided in your loyalties."

She stood up straight, her leathery wings twitching. "There is no division. My brother will be brought to justice for what he's done. As will the rest of them."

Lucifer began to speak, but he was interrupted by a colorful portal opening up in the sand. My mother stepped through it wearing elaborate, shining armor with flowers engraved on the breastplate and along the arms and legs. Her helmet was designed to look like an armored crown, and she carried a staff in her hand. Damien left the portal right behind her in his own similar armor, and with him were about a dozen other soldiers from the Spring Court. My people, once.

I rushed over to them and gave my son a big hug, then turned to my mother. She embraced me too, to my surprise.

"Daughter," she said, as she stroked my back. "I understand your pain all too well."

"We came as soon as we heard," Damien said. "We're here to help get Aurora back."

Demeter pulled back from me and regained her composure immediately. "The Spring Court will not sit idly by while one of our own is attacked. And unlike Oberon, we will not ignore a threat that will spread to all of the realms if not stopped now."

"I'm so glad you're here," I said, glancing between the two of them. "Both of you."

"Yes, thank you." Lucifer moved up behind me and nodded at my mother. "We gladly welcome the help of the Spring Court in this battle."

Demeter offered him a smile that was more winter than spring... But it was a start.

Damien waved at Kassiel and Belial, who were standing with Olivia, Marcus, Callan, and Bastien. We headed toward them, leaving Demeter behind with her soldiers, and Olivia threw her arms around me.

"I'm so sorry about Aurora," she said, as she squeezed me close.

Callan pulled me in for a big bear hug next. "I'll do whatever I can to get my cousin back. We're family, after all."

"Yes, we are," I said, wondering when I should tell him about Theo. Maybe when this was all over, if any of us were still alive. Instead, I turned to give my thanks to Marcus and Bastien.

Kassiel wrapped an arm around me, and we moved over to speak with Damien and Belial. I gazed at my three sons, noting how different they were. Damien in his fae court armor, his blue-black hair flowing in the wind. Kassiel in a suit much like his father's, and sharing the same green eyes. Belial in ripped-up jeans, motorcycle boots, with Morningstar strapped to his back. I loved them all so much, and though I worried about each of them getting hurt in the upcoming battle, I accepted that they were grown men too. If they wanted to fight for their family, who was I to stop them?

"Don't do anything stupid and get yourselves killed, or I'll kick your asses," Belial said to his brothers.

"That doesn't even make sense," Kassiel replied with a shake of his head.

Damien gave his brothers a mischievous smirk. "He's just worried we're going to steal all the glory in the battle."

Belial crossed his arms. "Hardly."

"Just be careful out there," I couldn't help but add. I was still their mother, after all. "I love you all so much."

Kassiel rested a hand on my shoulder, his demeanor going serious. "Don't worry. We'll get Aurora back."

"Yes, we will," Lucifer said, gazing at his sons with unabashed pride. "On that note, I have tasks for the three of you I can't trust with anyone else. Kassiel and Damien, I need you to find Azazel, Lilith and Cerberus. Free them and get them to safety."

"It will be done," Damien said.

Lucifer looked at Belial for a few seconds before he spoke, his words heavy. "Belial, I need you to rescue your sister. Your mother and I will be busy fighting Death and Pestilence. We need you to keep Aurora safe."

"I swear it on my life." Belial pressed a fist to his heart. "On my very soul."

They stared at each other and I sensed that the enormity of Lucifer's trust in Belial had lifted a great weight between them.

Then it was time to begin. We hugged our sons again, and moved to stand in the center of the Giza plateau between the pyramids. Lucifer wore black and silver armor along with a spiked crown covered in rubies, and his entire body glowed with a slight red tint. Beside him, I wore the gold and silver armor I'd once donned as an angel, except I now wore a matching crown to Lucifer's, although mine had emeralds for the gemstones.

All of the people assembled before us quieted down, waiting for the Demon King and Queen to speak. I gazed out across the soldiers we'd gathered, an impressive mix of angel, demon, and fae, all willing to fight and die to rescue the people we loved and save the world from the impending apocalypse that Pestilence and Death would bring.

I waited for Lucifer to begin, but he gestured for me to take the lead. I cleared my throat and raised my voice, infusing it with power so it would boom out into the night. "Death has been released. He's free and he's waiting for us in Hell, and he's taken my daughter and my friends. We must stop both him and Pestilence to prevent the apocalypse they will bring to all the realms. They have powerful allies, but we have an army too. One built of love and respect, not of fear and anger. Because of that, we will succeed. I have no doubt."

A roar rippled through the crowd, growing louder as the soldiers gathered before us fed from each other's enthusiasm. Famine reached for their power until I almost glowed from it, though I made sure to send it back to them. They would need all their strength for this upcoming battle.

"We have a plan." At the sound of Lucifer's voice, everyone fell immediately silent. "We must stop this threat today, before Pestilence and Death spread their evil to the other worlds. I will open a portal to Void, and Hannah and I will force Pestilence and Death through it, while the rest of you keep their forces busy. Once they're through, we must close the portal to Void immediately, to make sure no other Elder Gods enter our world." He looked at me with love and devotion. "Failure is not an option, but we won't fail. They may have two Horsemen, but so do we. Let's show them what our apocalypse looks like."

With that, Lucifer held out the key to Hell and a huge black, shadowy portal opened up. Big enough for many soldiers to enter at once. I spread my silver wings, and Lucifer spread his shadowy ones beside me, and together we flew into Hell to save our daughter—and defeat two Gods.

32

LUCIFER

My army poured through the portal into Hell, with Hannah and myself in the lead. The air on this side was colder, the sky was darker, and the scent of death was everywhere.

Death lounged on a throne under the head of the Great Sphinx. My fucking throne, which he must have had brought over from the palace just to spite me. He wore Fenrir's body, and I wondered what the Archdemon had sacrificed in order to gain Death's power. His eyes shone an eerie purple, and his body had already begun changing, becoming almost...skeletal.

What a fool. There was too much power for Fenrir to even stand a chance against Death. He couldn't contain it, never mind control it. Not that he wanted to. All Fenrir wanted was to destroy me and take my place as king, and it seemed his interests aligned with my father's.

I held up a hand to halt my forces behind me as I took in what we were facing. Pestilence—Adam—stood to the right of my father, and on the other side of him was Theo. War's fury bubbled up inside me as I thought of all the things I wanted to do to them, but then my gaze landed on the cages just behind them. They were all made of jagged bone that looked like it had sprung up out of the ground and then been bent and twisted to Death's will. Inside each cage was someone I cared about deeply. Lilith. Azazel. Cerberus.

Aurora.

She made her way around her cage, her black and white wings fluttering to keep her airborne as she bumped her head against the bones with each jerky ascent. My rage became a volcano inside me about to explode at the sight, and Hannah's hand tightened around mine, letting me know she'd seen it too.

I forced myself to look away, to study the horde my father had amassed all around us under the shadow of the pyramids. Shifters, imp, gargoyles, and others who had decided to defy their Archdemon to fight me. Their forces surrounded ours, but we could take them. Fuck, I could probably take them single-handedly with my rage at seeing Aurora in a cage. I was barely in control of myself, and Hannah gripped me tighter like she knew that. Fury burned through me, and I took a deep breath as Hannah and I landed in front of my father.

Death's laugh boomed from Fenrir's mouth, and it sounded wet, like something inside him was broken. "So good of you to join me, Lucifer."

"Father." I looked straight at him as I greeted him, giving him the honor of our relationship without making myself submissive to him. I wouldn't bow and scrape to Death, but I could remind him we were family once.

"And Eve, in a new body." Death tilted his head as he studied her.

"Thanatos," she said in a low, menacing voice. I was impressed she remembered his name from all those years ago.

His haunting eyes landed on me again. "I see you finally broke the curse. Certainly took you long enough."

My hands clenched into fists at my side at the reminder of what he'd done to us all those centuries ago. How he'd managed to haunt us even while locked in a tomb for thousands of years.

"Not all of us are so eager to bring death upon those we love," I said through gritted teeth.

"You always were weak." Death raised himself from my throne

like he still hadn't gotten used to controlling a body and all of the articulated joints yet. He rolled rather than walked toward us, his limbs strangely fluid. "No matter. I've taken over as the rightful King of Hell, a role that's been vacant since you saw fit to abandon this realm."

"I am still the King of Hell."

He laughed again. "Don't waste your breath. Your people need someone strong to lead them, someone who will rebuild Hell and make it a true land of the dead. Once that is done, I'll spread my kingdom to Earth, then to Heaven and Faerie." He indicated the angels and the fae in my army. "How nice of you to bring representatives."

"We're not going to let you do that," Hannah said.

"Why would you stop me?" His eyes narrowed as he studied us closer. "Even if you could, which we all know is impossible, you are War and Famine. Your purpose is to serve me, the leader of the Horsemen, as we take over all the worlds and remake them in our image." He indicated everyone around us, and gestured wider still, like he could encompass all of the realms. "Come, let us rule together. The Four Horsemen of the Apocalypse, as prophesied, as it should be." He stretched his mouth into a grin. A grimace. A leer. "We can put the past behind us."

"Hannah and I will never work with you," I replied. It wasn't like I was being presumptuous, speaking for my mate. Not when our baby was trapped in a fucking cage made of bones.

"Give me my daughter back." Hannah spoke in a voice like steel. It was a cold, hard demand, but Death laughed again.

"I can't do that." He stole a quick look over his shoulder and flicked Aurora a small wave, just a little movement of his fingers. "I have big plans for my granddaughter."

"What plans?" I asked.

"I'm going to raise her as my own. My little prodigy. A perfect blend of light and dark with the added essence of an Elder God. She will learn from me and rule by my side. She'll be the child you weren't, the child you could never be. And one day, when she's older, she'll be the perfect host."

"You fucking bastard." As if I didn't already have enough reason to stuff him into the Void. No way was he raising my daughter to be his next body. "You won't harm a hair on her body, and you won't rule anything, because we're stopping you today."

"You can't stop Death. I'm inevitable."

"We'll see about that." I gave my army the signal they'd been waiting for, and they let out a triumphant roar and began to march forward. I turned to Belial, who'd landed just behind me, and handed him the key to Hell. "If anything happens, get our family out of here."

He nodded and flew off toward the cages, with his brothers beside him. It was the only thing I could do to make sure they were safe should Hannah and I fail. Of course, if we failed, nowhere would be safe. Not from Death.

Hannah and I shared a look, one of love and devotion and fierce determination, and I pulled her close and kissed her hard, in case it was the last time. She clung to me tightly like she would never let me go, and then we stepped back.

She sighed as she glanced toward the throne. "Time to save the world again."

"I'll take my father. You deal with Pestilence."

"Gladly," she said. "I love you."

"I love you too. Always."

I released my wings and let my fury free, feeling it race through my body, dragging heat and electricity with it. I crackled with rage, and the part of me that was War gave me strength. It reminded me that even before I was War I was made for battle, forged from death and light to be the fiercest of Heaven's warriors, then remade into the Prince of Darkness, the Father of Lies, the King of Demons.

If anyone could defeat Death, it was me.

33

HANNAH

As Lucifer and I flew toward Death, the monster lifted his arms and a wave of power rolled out of him. It didn't do anything to the two of us, nor to our soldiers, but instead settled over the land with a murky purple light. Mere seconds later, skeletal hands burst out of the ground as corpses came back to life. Dust gathered and reformed into undead soldiers, both angels and demons who had perished over thousands of years during the Great War. Others were more recent corpses, their skin hanging off or in various stages of decay, their wings ragged, their light long extinguished. They charged toward our army, along with the others Death and Pestilence had gathered to fight for them.

Zel rattled the bones of her cage uselessly, her face a mask of rage as Pestilence spread sickness over the shifters rushing forward. Boils broke out over their skin and they became graying, dying shadows of themselves. They raced in among our army, becoming walking contagions. Theo leaped up on his leather wings and flew into battle with them, his stone skin protecting him from Pestilence's plague.

The roaring cries of war filled the air as angels, demons, fae, and undead collided, but I only had eyes for one man. Adam. He'd killed me repeatedly, time after time ripping me away from Lucifer and my children. He'd killed my last daughter before she'd even had a chance to live. Now he threatened my other daughter's life, and I wasn't letting him get away with it this time.

He was mine.

As battle raged behind me, I ignored the clash of swords and claws and the blasts of magic. I had only one duty—to stop Pestilence, while Lucifer stopped Death. It came down to the two of us. No one else could do this, and we couldn't fail. We wouldn't. I was too fucking mad. Not just because they'd taken my daughter, but because of everything Adam and Death had done to me for thousands of years, going back to my very first life as Eve. They'd tormented me enough, and I was done. So fucking done.

Adam's face was a nightmare of yellow skin and puss-filled boils, his grin a gash in his face. I landed in front of him and formed my sword of darkness entwined with light.

"So nice of you to return to me, Eve," he said, as he drew his golden bow and arrows. "I'd like you to know I've given up on convincing you to rule by my side."

I snorted. "That's a relief."

"Is it? Because now the only other option is for you to die." He shot a plague-tipped arrow at me, but I used a blast of wind to shoot it wide. He hadn't really intended on hitting me with it though. He was just taunting me. "I'll take the most pleasure from your death this time, I think. Maybe I'll even fuck your corpse when it's done. One last time, just you and me, like the old days."

I leveled my sword at him, trying not to gag at his words. "You disgust me—and it's you who is going to die today. A final death this time. One there is no coming back from."

"How can I die, when I have Death on my side?" He held out his hand, sickness flickering over his skin as he unleashed it upon me. I used a mix of air and light to block it and send it away from me, while darting to the side. He rapid-fired a dozen more arrows so fast I barely had a chance to deflect them, and then I went after him with my sword. His sickness leeched across my skin, making me feel tired and weak, but I fought it with everything I had.

At that moment, Lucifer opened the portal to Void with a tearing sound I'd never heard, like it had destroyed something in the fabric of the universe, like the realm itself was fighting this intrusion. The portal was a kaleidoscope of endlessly swirling glints of light moving dizzyingly against deep black, as hazes of gray mist drifted across it.

The portal was open—which meant I had to get Pestilence in it. As much as I hated to admit it, killing him was near impossible.

Or was it?

We all stood transfixed for a moment, staring at the portal, before springing back into action. Out of the corner of my eye I saw Lucifer fight against Death, trying to maneuver him toward the portal. I barely had time to notice though, as Pestilence dodged my every blow, not even breaking a sweat as I danced him across the plateau toward the portal. As we grew closer to it, he suddenly sprang at me, his face an abomination of evil as he gripped my shoulders and yanked me forward.

"I had thought death for you, Eve." Again, he used my first name, the one guaranteed to remind me of all we'd started as. The one he seemed to cling to as proof of his birthright. "But now I think you should be in the Void. Lost forever to your family."

Panic flared through me as he shoved me away from him and I fell toward the portal, but before I could save myself, Kassiel blocked me with his body. He helped me stand and said, "Go get him, Mom."

Then he flew off toward the cages, where Damien and Belial were already there trying to free our family. Aurora cried in her cage, and when I turned toward her, she waved her arms at me, her terrified eyes fixed on mine across the distance between us. She needed me, and it broke my heart to see her in such pain, but at least her brothers were there. They would keep her safe, I had no doubt. My heart burst with a mixture of anger, grief, pride, and love, making me even more determined to finally remove Adam from our lives.

I poured my emotions into my magic and made thorny vines grow up from the ground all around Adam, trusting my soldiers to keep Death's army from me while I focused. My plants wound around Adam's legs to hold him in place, and around his hands to trap his bow, then around the rest of his body until I could barely see him beneath the writhing green. But I didn't intend to suffocate him. Oh, no. For every painful death he'd given me he deserved so much more than mere deprivation of air. I squeezed my vines tight enough that a few bones cracked and the thorns dug deep into his flesh, and he cried out in pain.

But Pestilence was too strong, and he was already working to break free of my vines, tearing them off his body and making them wither and die with his sickness. That's when I called on my Famine powers to steal energy and power from him, dragging it out of his body and into me. I grew stronger, while he grew weaker. He tried to fight me with everything he had, but I was too much for him. I kept pulling and pulling, my hunger demanding more and more of Pestilence's essence, until I ripped the Elder God out of Adam entirely.

Adam staggered, his knees hitting the ground, his body weakened and battered by hosting Pestilence for so long. The Elder God hovered above me, a yellow spectral essence, a tainted cloud of putrid sickness. He spread his plagued fingers across the battlefield, searching for his next host, but I wasn't going to let that happen. I wrapped a swirling mass of air infused with light and darkness around him, then forced him into the portal. Pestilence screamed, a shrill, horrifying sound that made everyone on the battlefield feel queasy, as the portal to Void sucked him inside, like it too was greedy to lock him away.

Pestilence was gone—leaving only Adam behind. I was his judge, jury, and executioner, and I'd tried him and found him wanting. Today, I was his reaper.

My entire world narrowed to just me and Adam. I stepped closer to him, clearing his body of the remaining vines that still clung to him, leaving grazes and cuts where their thorns had started to burrow. His body was covered in Pestilence's boils, his hair almost gone, his skin still a sickly color, though his Fallen powers tried their best to heal him. For a second I saw Gadreel, who I'd thought had been my friend, but who had tricked me for numerous lives. A bitter reminder of all that Adam had done.

He deserved to suffer for his sins.

"Eve... My Eve." His voice was weak, pleading, and it fueled the hate inside me. "I knew you'd come back to me. Heal me and we can be together finally."

"No." He didn't deserve any more words, and nothing I said would ever get through to him. He'd been a possessive, abusive husband when I was Eve, and after I'd left him, he'd only gotten worse. He'd never been able to let me go, his obsession carrying across multiple lives—thanks to Death's curse—for thousands of years. I had nothing in my heart for him but loathing for everything he'd stolen from me. I was literally a different person because of him. A different person again and again, always losing everything I held dear, then having to search for it over and over, knowing I would only lose it again.

I didn't plan to lose anything I loved ever again.

His face changed when he realized I wasn't going to help him. "Whore," he yelled, followed by a dozen other obscenities, along with, "I'll kill you!"

"No, Adam. It's time for your final death."

I plunged my dark-and-light sword into his chest, slicing him open with a hard slash of my blade. His eyes widened at me, and he spat blood from his lips as he tried to fight back, but he wasn't strong enough to do anything to stop me. I felt his life force flicker, and it would have been so easy to steal his life and end his suffering, to feed my eternal hunger... But I did not.

Instead, I hit him with all of my rage and suffering, with all of the love I felt for my family, and the grief from when he'd taken me from them over and over. Light and darkness, air and vine, truth and hunger—all of my powers mixed together to rip him apart, atom by atom. His face became a mask of pain as he was torn asunder, his screams echoing across the battlefield, and then he was no more. My power devoured him, wiping him from existence entirely.

Adam was gone, and only I remained.

Our eternal battle was finally over.

34

LUCIFER

E ven though I'd become War, my father still managed to overpower me. We wrestled like I was a child trying to move a man as I attempted to force him toward the Void portal. I was starting to think Death would be impossible to defeat. No one won their final war against him, though many had tried. How had I ever believed I might be the one exception?

I glimpsed Aurora behind him, now in Belial's arms but still reaching out toward us, her cries for her parents almost lost to the sound of battle. I couldn't let my father take my daughter away and raise her. No good came of having Death as a father figure. If anyone knew that, it was me.

"Oh, Lucifer," Death said. "You could have ruled all the worlds. I expected so much from you, my son. Instead you had to fall in love with that mortal woman. She made you weak."

Why was everyone always trying to convince me that loving Hannah made me weaker? "No. Loving her has only made me stronger."

"You're wrong." Death shook his head at me, then gestured at Aurora and Belial. Undead immediately surrounded them, trying to tear my daughter from her brother's arms, but Damien blasted them all back with a burst of air. Zel, Lilith, and Cerberus, now freed by Kassiel, all leaped into the attack too, easily slicing down the skeletal attackers.

"You see," I said, turning back to my father. "Love wins."

But I'd been so distracted by the attack on my family that I hadn't noticed Death lunging toward me, and he managed to rip the Void key right out of my hand. Then he let out a guttural roar as he clenched it within his palm. Rays of light of every color shot out of it, before he closed his fist and shattered it into a million pieces. The portal to Void immediately closed behind him.

Fuck.

"Careless, Lucifer," Death chided. He wrapped his free hand around my neck and pinned me against him from behind. "Weak. Powerless. Useless. What a disappointment you are. Are you even my son? Or did that angel lie to me?"

"I guess I'm a mama's boy," I growled, as I grabbed his arm and flipped him over me. His back hit the ground hard, but then he slithered away, too fast for a mortal eye to see. But he wasn't getting away. I didn't know how I would stop him, but this had to end here. Maybe we could put him back in his tomb, which had to be behind him somewhere. There was a solution, I just had to find it.

I shot brilliant blue and red hellfire at him, but he always managed to escape it. I kept firing, pushing him back and back, toward the battle behind him. Then I released all my War powers and grabbed hold of every one of his undead soldiers, turning them against each other. Against him.

They swarmed his body, a writhing mass of bones and dead flesh, and I felt a deep sense of satisfaction at the sight. But then an ear-shattering roar burst out of Death and he shifted and grew, becoming a giant black wolf with glowing purple eyes and talons that turned the ground black around them. Fenrir's wolf form, now with an apocalyptic twist. Shit, maybe this really was Ragnarok.

Wolf-Death launched himself at me, and only the swift beat of my wings got me out of the way in time, though he did manage to rake a claw down my side. His mere touch leeched life out of me, and a deathly chill spread through my body. I sucked in air as I tried not to let Death overtake me. I was too strong to be so easily defeated—but how long could I last against this apocalyptic Death wolf?

Fingers curled around mine, and I looked into Hannah's face, smears of blood covering her cheeks, her hair coated with a fresh layer of fine gray ash. She'd managed to defeat Pestilence and Adam, and now she was by my side again, ready to face our other eternal enemy.

"Let's finish this." She sent a little life-giving energy into me, allowing me to fight off the last of Death's touch. "I can rip Death out of Fenrir. I just don't know what we'll do with him after that."

"I'll get him back in the tomb." Time for plan B. Or Q. Or whatever the fuck we were on at this point.

Hannah held her hands out, her body emitting a green glow as she sucked at Death's essence. He let out a skin-crawling howl that echoed throughout the battlefield, making everyone cover their ears. Then he charged her with his wolf body the size of a dump truck. I blasted him with hellfire so strong it knocked him back and set his fur on fire, but he stood up and shook it off, snapping at me with his massive fangs. Then a giant paw tried to rip me apart with its claws, but I flew around him and kept firing at him, distracting him while Hannah leeched away his life force. He grew weaker and weaker, the purple in his eyes dimming, his movements slowing down.

"I've nearly got him," Hannah ground out.

Purple essence seeped out slowly, unwillingly, from Fenrir's mouth, nose, and ears. I rushed to the base of the Sphinx, looking for Death's tomb—but it wasn't there.

Death suddenly released Fenrir's body, launching out of him, forming what looked like a spectral Grim Reaper in the air as it hovered over us. Fenrir shook out his wolf body, but then the two began to merge again—Death trying to return to its host. I shot all of my power into Death, holding him back with everything I had, but knew it wouldn't last. We had to kill Fenrir to sever the bond.

I quickly sought out my sons, even as I struggled to hold Death back. Belial was closest, and oddly enough, the one I trusted most with this task. I met his eyes and pointed at Fenrir, and he nodded as understanding settled over him.

Belial handed Aurora to Damien, unsheathed Morningstar in one quick movement, and plunged my old sword into Fenrir's throat. He acted quickly, bringing Morningstar down fast and sure, no lack of certainty and no hesitation. Fenrir couldn't even struggle, not as the light-infused blade cut him down, and he hit the ground hard. As he died, his body returned to his human state, looking small and broken on the ashen ground.

Fenrir was dead, but Death still remained. An Elder God with no tomb to lock him inside, and no Void portal to send him through. But he needed a body.

Death yanked himself free of my hold, and his essence began to float forward toward the person he'd already chosen as his new host. Death was the absence of indecision—and I knew his choice even before he got there.

Aurora.

"No!" I began to run toward my children. "Not her!"

Damien tried to rush away, carrying Aurora in his arms, but Death's skeletal army surrounded them from every side, with Theo at the head of them. Kassiel began to fight them off, and Olivia and her other mates joined him, but Death was too fast and too powerful.

Belial flew in front of Death's essence, shielding his siblings with his wings, his beautiful ombre feathers spread wide. He thrust Morningstar into the air, right into the middle of Death's essence, and the mist swirled around the blade, almost like a caress, spiraling to Belial's hand and arm like it was tasting him.

"Take me," Belial said. "Not the girl. She's only a child, and still weak. You'll be too easy to defeat in her body. But I'm also your grandchild, and I'm almost as ancient as you are. With our power combined, we'll be unstoppable."

"Belial!" Hannah screamed. "Don't do this!"

I grabbed her hand and held her back. "No. He can do this. I have faith in him."

She looked at me like I was insane, but there was only one

person here strong enough to contain Death. Hannah and I couldn't do it—we were already Elder Gods. It had to be Belial.

"But what if we lose him?" she whispered.

I squeezed her hand. "We won't."

"Why do you want this power?" Death asked Belial.

Our oldest son straightened up, his eyes blazing with fury. "To defeat my father once and for all and take my rightful place as Demon King."

His words were like a blow to my chest. After all we'd been through, did my son truly mean that? Had he done all of this just so he could have a chance to grab an Elder God's power? Had I really been so wrong about him?

Death cackled. "I like you, grandson. Perhaps my pedigree merely skipped a generation. Yes, you will make a fine host, at least until the girl is older. But I require a sacrifice."

Belial closed his eyes briefly, and then he looked at his mother, his gaze lingering on her as his face remained stoic. Then he turned his eyes upon me, and I saw the truth there, as if I'd had a touch of Hannah's power. Belial didn't want Death's power. He was only doing this to save his sister. He was doing this for *us*.

He looked at Aurora next, still in Damien's arms, and his jaw clenched. "Anything," he told Death.

"I require the sacrifice of your soul," Death rasped.

"Belial, no!" Hannah yelled, rushing forward to try to stop this somehow, but I wrapped my arms around her, wishing there was some other way to defeat Death and save my son. If Hannah and I could defeat the Elder Gods inside us, I had to believe Belial could do the same. Somehow.

Belial cast one last glance at us, as if saying goodbye, before he nodded at his grandfather. "Done."

Then I could only stare in horror as my son became Death, the destroyer of worlds.

35

HANNAH

As the last of the purple essence disappeared into my son, my tortured cry rang loud and harsh over the landscape and then echoed back, like the whole of Hell shared my grief. Behind us, the battle was still going on, but none of that mattered. All I cared about was that I was about to lose my son to Death.

I gripped Lucifer's hand, dragging him along with me as I crossed the distance between us and Belial, my wings bursting from my back when my legs didn't move fast enough. Damn it all. An Elder God couldn't have another one of my men. Death wouldn't take my son.

"Belial!" His name ripped from my throat. "Belial, you have to fight!"

Belial was kneeling in the dirt, shuddering with the aftermath of becoming Death, but then his head snapped up and his glowing eyes met mine. A horrible cackle escaped from his mouth, as purple magic slithered up and down his body, making his veins and bones glow from the inside out in a most horrifying way.

Theo landed in front of me, trying to block me from getting to my son, but Lucifer grabbed the gargoyle by the throat. He reached out with a tendril of darkness and picked up Morningstar, which had fallen when Belial had become Death, and yanked it into his hand. Without hesitation, Lucifer used the glowing sword to slice Theo's head off. When it was done, Lucifer tossed the gargoyle's body aside like it was a doll, then handed Morningstar to Kassiel and wiped his hands.

I couldn't even take satisfaction in the traitor's death, because all I could see was Belial, spreading his purple-tinged wings as he gazed across the battlefield at his undead army. When Belial had been a kid, he'd had horrible nightmares, and I would stroke his head and tell him everything was okay until he fell asleep again—but this was one monster I couldn't rid him of. If my sheer will had been enough, he would have returned to me immediately.

"Fight, Belial!" I called out. "Remember who you truly are!"

"Who I am?" He let out another horrible cackle. "I am Death. Belial is no more. He was weak, and now he is gone."

Lucifer clenched his fists. "No, he's not. You are Belial. Our first child. Our strongest son. I know you can fight this. Don't let him win."

Belial suddenly launched himself at Lucifer, wrapping his hands around my mate's neck. Lucifer's eyes went wide as Death sucked the life out of him, making him go pale. "I am Death, and you will die!"

Instead of fighting him, Lucifer wrapped his arms around his son in a hug. "If you need to kill me, then so be it. If I could give my life to save you, I'd do it. I'd gladly sacrifice anything for you."

Death roared and released Lucifer, retreating away from us. He shook his head like he was confused, and I knew it was Belial trying to fight him off. All he needed was a little help from his family.

I gestured for my other sons to come close as I moved toward Death. Just like with War, I had to trust that Belial wouldn't hurt me. With Lucifer at my side, Kassiel moved to stand on the left, and Damien on the right. Aurora launched herself away from Damien and flew over to me, and I caught her in my arms, kissing her on the face, so relieved to have her back again. My entire family, reunited once again—and now we had to save one of our own.

"Belial, we love you," I said to him as he glared at us. "Focus on that. Focus on your family."

"Don't let past hurt dictate your actions, brother," Damien said.

"Please come back," Kassiel added. "We're all here waiting for you."

"Love is a lie," Belial said. "Love makes you weak. Love is *nothing*."

"That's Death talking," Lucifer said. "Not you."

"What would you know of love?" Belial asked, glaring at his father. "You neglected me as a child. You cast me out of Hell. You pretended I didn't exist for centuries. Now you speak to me of *love*? Where was your fucking love then?"

"I'm sorry." Lucifer's voice caught a little. "I've made many mistakes. I let my pride keep me from doing what was right. But I've always loved you, and I've always been proud of you, even if I was terrible at showing it. I promise I will do better going forward."

Belial responded by raising his arms, and his undead army charged toward us, plowing over our other soldiers to get to us. He was losing this battle against Death, and we had to do something. Something more. At first, I thought perhaps I could drain him of power, like I'd done to Adam and Fenrir, but then we'd be stuck with Death with no host and nowhere to put him. We had to get Belial to defeat Death instead.

I thought back to when Lucifer and I had defeated our Elder Gods, and how we'd called upon our opposite natures to fight back. With Famine, I'd used growth. With War, Lucifer had used peace. Which meant with Death, Belial had to use life. But how? He didn't possess that gift.

No, but I did.

Lucifer glanced at the oncoming horde of undead, but our soldiers were holding them off, for now anyway. Demeter and her fae warriors used air magic and elegant swords to keep them at bay. Gabriel and the other angels shot light and flew on shining wings over the battlefield. Baal, Lilith, and Samael led the demons and Fallen forward, and among them I saw Zel slicing into shifters and gargoyles, and Cerberus tearing skeletons apart limb by limb. They were all giving us time, time enough to save our son.

I propped Aurora up on my hip, and then reached for the other's hands. They got the idea, and my family all linked hands as we circled around Death. He glared at us with purple eyes, but Belial held him back from attacking, as I'd known he would.

"What are you doing?" Death asked with a cold laugh. "You cannot stop me."

I released my Famine powers, but instead of taking energy, I gave it. I channeled life from my family and funneled it into Death, making him scream. Lucifer also released War's powers, but he reversed them, sending feelings of love and peace into our son instead of anger and hatred.

"Death will not take my son from me," I called out, as I felt Death fighting back, trying to quell my life-giving power. "I am a goddess of life, and my children carry that gift too. You cursed me to die again and again, but being reborn over and over only made me stronger. Now I give that power to Belial."

It was working. Death was weakening his hold on Belial. I saw my son's eyes shining through again. But I wasn't sure it would be enough, even with all of us sending life and love into him. Death was just too damn strong, like a black hole that sucked everything into it.

Then Aurora suddenly flew out of my grasp toward Belial, and I let out a little cry as I reached for her. It was too late though, and she landed in his arms, grabbing onto him. Belial lowered his head to her, his movements almost robotic as he caught his baby sister in his hands. I held my breath as I waited to see what would happen next. I was terrified, but I had faith too. Faith that Belial wouldn't hurt his sister. Faith that love would prevail.

"Yes, you will be an excellent host one day," Death said, and my hope faltered.

But then Aurora reached up to touch Belial's face, and they stared into each other's eyes and something passed between them. Power. Life. *Love.*

"Be be be," Aurora said, her voice clear even among the battlefield. Was she trying to say his name? He blinked at her, as if he wondered the same thing. She looked at him with pure baby adoration, her eyes shining with love for grumpy older brother, and that was enough to push him over the edge.

Belial threw his head back with a roar, and an inner war waged inside him, one we could do nothing more to fight. It seemed to last for an eternity, but then Belial prevailed, and all the purple glow around him vanished back inside his body. He staggered, and I rushed forward to take Aurora from him, while Lucifer caught him in his arms.

Belial coughed. "He's... He's gone."

"Yes, my father is gone," Lucifer said. "But Death remains. You are an Elder God now."

"How do you feel?" Kassiel asked.

"Fucking great," Belial said sarcastically, as he pulled away from Lucifer and stood on his own.

"How is this possible?" Damien asked.

I gave a little shrug as I smiled at my sons. "Love is stronger than death."

Lucifer nodded. "Yes, love persists, even after someone is gone. It's the reason we grieve someone, or smile at the memory of them. It was the one thing Death hated more than anything else, and the reason he cursed me and Hannah all those years ago. Love is the only thing he could never kill."

"That's lovely, but would you mind stopping your undead horde before they kill my grandmother?" Damien asked, tilting his head toward the battle behind us.

"Oh. Right." Belial lifted his hands in silent command and the undead all fell, their bones collapsing to the ground or becoming dust once again.

Once they were gone, the battle was over. The remaining shifters, imps, and other traitors surrendered, and we could all breathe a little sigh of relief at last.

I drew Aurora into my arms and wrapped her tightly to my chest, dropping kisses into her wisps of blond hair. "Good girl," I whispered. "Did you see what you did? You saved your brother." I hugged her to me again and her fingers batted my cheek. I turned my head to kiss her little hands as Lucifer gathered us both against him, wrapping us in his arms and his wings.

He released a sigh and bent to kiss Aurora's head. "You're both incredible."

Aurora giggled and reached for his feathers. He let her touch them for a few moments before he took her from me, and his wings folded away. I went straight to Belial next.

"Are you all right?" I asked, wrapping my arms around him and giving him a long, tight squeeze. I'd almost lost him today.

"I'm fine," he said, slowly pulling out of my pincer hold. "Thanks to you."

He said that, but I was his mother, and I knew it was a lie. Something about him was different. Colder. Emptier.

But of course he was different. He was a god now.

Lucifer walked over next and clasped Belial on the shoulder, while still holding Aurora. "I knew you could do it."

"Did you?" Belial asked, genuinely surprised.

He nodded. "I never had any doubt you would find your way back to us."

"Be be be," Aurora said, and Belial gave her something that was almost a smile as he held out a hand to her.

"But you sacrificed your soul," Kassiel said. "What does that mean?"

Damien tapped his lips. "Father sacrificed his memories, but those were returned. Could Belial's soul be restored too?"

I shook my head. "I don't know. I hope so."

Lucifer put an arm around my waist. "We're all here. Together again. If there's a way to save Belial's soul, we'll find it."

Belial rolled his eyes. "I'm fine. Really."

He did seem all right, so it was hard to tell what exactly losing his soul had done to him. I prayed it was nothing, and that he would be able to move forward with his life—now with a bit more power. Either way, I knew I'd be back in the library looking for answers as soon as we returned home. That was what I did, after all.

A pale horse suddenly galloped over to us and bowed its head to

Belial, who looked surprised by this turn of events. He was a Horsemen now, like Lucifer and I were. But there were only three of us on Earth now, and perhaps that meant the threat of the apocalypse was over. After all, all the prophecies said there had to be four.

As Hell quieted down around us, I leaned against Lucifer as we gazed across the battlefield at the aftermath of our apocalyptic war. A war we'd somehow won, despite all odds. Marcus and some other angels were healing the injured. Romana and Azazel had rounded up the remaining enemy soldiers and subdued them, while Cerberus growled and kept the prisoners in line. I spotted Demeter among the fae, adjusting her armored crown. Everyone I loved had come to fight this battle with us, and we'd prevailed.

A huge wave of relief washed over me as I turned toward Lucifer, who was still holding Aurora. I wrapped my arms around the both of them, holding them close. We were free. Free of Death's curse. Free of Adam's threat. Free to have a normal life. Well, as normal as life could be when it consisted of angels, demons, fae, babies who could fly, and three-headed hellhounds. Not to mention a couple Horsemen of the Apocalypse.

"We did it," Lucifer said, before pressing a kiss to my lips. "We won."

I nodded, tears of happiness filling my eyes. "Let's go home and celebrate."

36

LUCIFER

Hannah and I entered the conference room in The Celestial, which we'd decided would still be our base of operations for our empire, even though we made our home in southern California now. Las Vegas was the main hub for demons on Earth and that wouldn't change. After all, with the internet and a private jet we could rule from anywhere. Damn, I loved this century.

My queen and I took our places at both heads of the table and I let my gaze slowly fall on each of the people in front of me. It had been three weeks since we'd stopped Death and Pestilence, and I'd called a meeting of Archdemons, both new and old. I had some changes to make to prepare for the future of our people, to usher them into a new era.

Lilith sat to my left, fully recovered after her kidnapping and looking as lovely as ever. On my right was Baal, wearing a suit that looked like it has been made during Victorian times. Next to him was Romana, across from Samael, both of them looking stoic. Then down by Hannah was Valefar, representing the dragons for the first time, and Bastet, the leader of the feline shifters, and the newest Archdemon in our ranks. She'd been quick to pledge her loyalty to me after Fenrir's death, swearing her people would root out the corruption and bring the other shifter clans in line. Since the insurrection had mostly involved wolves and bears, I was willing to let her try. Besides, she'd hated Fenrir for thousands of years, and was thrilled to take his place—and that was enough to keep her loyal. For now, anyway.

The final seat at the table stood empty. No Archdemon had been chosen for the imps yet, and from what I'd heard, their ranks were in chaos. One of the many things on today's agenda.

"Thank you for joining us today," I said. "We have much to discuss."

"Yes, big changes are coming," Hannah said, as she took her seat with a smile.

The Archdemons bristled and glanced between each other. "Are the rumors true?" Romana asked. "Are you stepping down?"

A hearty laugh erupted from me. "No, of course not. Why would anyone think that?"

The demons settled down at those words. Immortals didn't like change. They tended to be stuck in their ways, even if those ways were outdated and it was obvious that a new way would be better for them. Of course, change was necessary for the survival of our people. I'd been doing a lot of thinking over the last few weeks, and realized that was where I'd failed as a ruler before. I'd been either too hesitant to change, or I'd embraced it too hastily. But now I had Hannah ruling with me to help find the right balance.

I slowly sat in my executive chair like it was a throne, my back straight, letting my hands languish on the armrests. "The first business on the agenda is a promotion. Samael, please rise."

"Yes, my lord?" He reluctantly stood up, towering over the rest of the table.

"Samael, Hannah and I are pleased to announce that you are now officially an Archdemon, representing the Fallen."

"I... I don't understand," he said. "The Fallen don't have an Archdemon."

"They do now," Hannah said with a big smile for her friend.

I nodded. Until now I'd acted as both Demon King and leader of the Fallen, but it was time to delegate more. Plus, Samael deserved a promotion for everything he did for us. "It's something I should have done centuries ago."

"Agreed," Lilith said, giving Samael a sultry smile. "You've basically had the job all these years anyway, Sam. It's high time you were recognized for it."

"Thank you," Samael said, bowing his head, and the other Archdemons offered their congratulations. "I will do everything in my power to serve the Fallen as their leader."

"I know you will," I said. "And I hope this will address another issue—the belief among some that Fallen are not true demons, or that I favor them over other demon races. That is false. We are all creatures of the night and children of Hell, and Hannah and I will rule over all demons equally and impartially."

This was something Mammon had brought up as a reason why he was trying to overthrow me, and after speaking with some of the other Archdemons privately over the last few weeks, I'd discovered it was a larger problem than I'd realized. I hoped that by making Samael the Archdemon of the Fallen it would solidify him as their leader and representative, and allow me to treat all the demonic races as equal subjects. After all, I wasn't really Fallen, not anymore, and neither was my queen.

I steepled my fingers on the table as we moved on to the next order of business. "As for the imps, we will give them one more week, and if an Archdemon is not named, we will choose one for them. Does anyone have a person they would like to nominate?"

"That won't be necessary," a lilting voice said from the doorway. Audible gasps went up around the room as our unexpected guest strode into the room. I hadn't seen the man in hundreds of years, and though he could change his appearance at will, I recognized that cocky swagger immediately—Loki.

Today he wore wavy black hair, cheekbones that could cut glass, and mischievous green eyes, with his trademark crooked smile. An ancient imp, he was the cousin of Nemesis, and also the father of Fenrir, who had taken after his wolf mother in his powers. Was Loki here to swear his loyalty—or here for revenge?

I rose to my feet, preparing myself in case he launched an attack. "Welcome, Loki. It's been a long time."

"Where have you been all these years?" Bastet asked, with a toss of her dark brown hair. The way she said it made me think they had once been an item.

"Oh, you know. Here and there." Loki waved a hand with a mysterious smile. "I've been hanging out, doing my own thing, but it seems I'm needed now. I'm here as the new Archdemon of the imps, and ready to swear my loyalty to good ol' Lucifer and his lovely queen." He winked at Hannah as he said that, and I barely held back a growl.

Instead, I raised an eyebrow at Hannah, silently asking her if he was speaking the truth. She studied him closely, no doubt reading his aura, and then nodded to me.

"Oh good, I see I have your approval." Loki swept into an elaborate bow before us. "I am your humble servant, my king and queen. I pledge my loyalty to you, and swear to serve as your Archdemon to my best capabilities."

I didn't like this, not one bit. Loki was the most famous trickster of all time, and damn crafty too. If he'd emerged after centuries there had to be a reason, one we might not know for many years—and I didn't believe for one second it was because the imps needed him. But what was that saying—keep your friends close, and your enemies closer?

I flashed him one of my own charming smiles. "We're so pleased to have you with us. Please, take a seat."

Everyone's eyes were on Loki as he draped himself across the chair. "With pleasure."

Hannah cast a warm smile around the table and drew everyone's gaze back to her when she spoke. "Now that the Archdemon issue is settled, we can move on to the next thing on our agenda. Hell."

"What about it?" Baal asked.

I sat back in my chair. "We're going to start rebuilding it."

That got everyone's attention.

"Do you plan for us to return there?" Valefar asked. It was another thing his father, Mammon, had wanted. After speaking with the other Archdemons, it seemed many of my subjects also wanted that—while many others had absolutely no desire to leave Earth.

"Eventually, yes," Hannah said. "Once we've rebuilt some of Hell and determined it is habitable again, we'll open passage to any demon who wants to return there. We know many have made their homes on Earth and will not want to leave, but there are others who long to return to our old realm."

"We'd like to set up a team with representatives from all seven demon races to lead this project," I said. "Please choose five of your people whom you think would be best for this task and report back by the end of the month."

Baal gave me a respectful nod. "This will go a long way into reuniting our people."

"Will it?" Lilith asked. "Or will it set up another divide of Earth versus Hell demons?"

"We'll try to prevent that from happening by allowing demons to pass freely between the two realms," Hannah said.

Valefar stroked his chin. "My people would approve of that. Hell is much safer for my dragons than Earth, but with our numbers so few, we also need to be in this realm to reproduce and rebuild our race."

Bastet leaned toward me and asked, "But will you be ruling the demons on Earth or the ones in Hell?"

"Both." I leveled a gaze at anyone who might try to challenge me, then gave them another disarming smile. "Although I won't be able to do it without my Archdemons. I'll need all of you more than ever. I see a bright future for our people—but it will take all of us working together to usher the demons into the next era."

Loki gave me a slow clap and then grinned at the others. "Well, I don't know about the rest of you, but I'm sold. Sign me up, Old Scratch."

I tried not to grit my teeth at that old nickname and instead kept my smile on my face. "Excellent. Now, if there are matters that any of you would like to discuss, the floor is open."

Bastet began speaking about her plans to deal with the various shifter packs, and the others chimed in with some ideas or questions.

As the meeting went on, I found my eyes drifting back to Hannah, watching her command the room with ease. She'd changed so much, it was hard to believe she'd once been the innocent woman who'd come to my door asking me for a favor. My Eve. My Persephone. My Hannah.

Her eyes met mine, and she gave me a smile that was just for me, filled with love and respect. She was my equal. My mate. My wife.

My queen.

37

HANNAH

I stretched and rolled over in bed, not really wanting to be awake but being awake all the same. Not that I needed sleep, of course. I just liked it. It made me feel a little less...godlike.

"Good morning." Lucifer's voice was warm and full of promise, and as his hand skimmed my hip, I suddenly didn't mind being awake at all. He kissed my neck, his soft hair brushing my cheek, before I'd even opened my eyes. I had a feeling he'd been up for hours. Unlike me, Lucifer couldn't be bothered to sleep.

"Morning," I murmured back, luxuriating in his touch and warm mouth as he nibbled his way along my jaw.

The house was so quiet. Peaceful.

My eyes flew open. "Aurora."

Lucifer's hand was against my cheek, his eyes looking into mine. "She's still asleep. Just be here with me." He resumed his gentle nibbling as his hand swept my hip again, then rested over my ribs so his thumb pressed softly against the underside of my breast.

I wanted to offer him encouragement, but couldn't tear my thoughts away from a sudden mental onslaught of party plans, caterers, guests, and a one-year-old birthday girl. There would be time for Lucifer later. I'd make sure of it.

"As much I'd like to continue this, I have shit to do," I said with a sigh.

Lucifer laughed at my eloquent words. "What shit?"

"Party shit," I clarified. "Aurora only turns one once, and people are coming here expecting a party, not to join us in our bedroom for the world's most powerful orgy."

His eyes flickered with interest. "An orgy? How very old school. You know I'm down for it."

"Maybe some other time." I laughed and pressed my palm to his chest as I lifted away from his body. "I call the shower first."

I paused for a fraction of a second, knowing what I'd hear next.

"Let's conserve water," Lucifer drawled, as he stood in all his naked glory.

I grinned. Fine, maybe the party shit could wait a little bit longer.

———

I looked out over our friends and family the same way I had after the final battle with Pestilence and Death, but this time the air around me rang with laughter rather than the aftermaths of battle. Today everyone we loved was gathered to celebrate Aurora's first birthday, and I couldn't be happier. Tents had been set up around our garden once again with outdoor couches and tables, and a huge buffet stood at one side, along with an open bar, naturally. Lucifer wouldn't have it any other way.

I glanced around for my daughter, and spotted her with Demeter. Of course. Demeter had perhaps the greatest patience for holding Aurora's hand while she tottered along, trying so hard to walk. Round and round the garden, her chunky little thighs carrying her forward, while her wings tried to lift her up.

Balloons waved here and there in the air, and Aurora reached for them, flying up, up, up, then sending them bouncing away with her clumsy attempts to capture them. Demeter caught her and smiled, kissing her cheeks, doting her with grandmotherly love.

Demeter was still a bit frosty with me and Lucifer, but she had nothing but warmth for Aurora.

Behind her, Lilith sat with Brandy and Asmodeus, holding little Isaac as he bounced on her lap. She looked positively smitten with her own grandchild, while Samael, Baal, and Gabriel chatted beside her. Olivia, Lilith's daughter with Gabriel, came to sat with her, taking the baby from her arms with a smile. Callan, Marcus, and Bastien dropped onto a table nearby, and I smiled at this huge family Brandy had somehow gotten herself involved with. I bet she'd had no idea what she was getting into when she fell for Asmodeus, but judging by her smile and the love her son was getting, she didn't mind one bit.

They were my family too, of course. Olivia was tied to my son and my nephew, making us all connected. I wouldn't have it any other way.

"Nice party," Zel said, draping an arm over my shoulder. "Am I allowed to give Aurora her daggers yet?"

I sighed and laughed, all at once. "Not for another few years."

"Damn. I was so looking forward to beginning her training."

I leaned against my best friend. "She's still too young, but in a few years you can teach her everything you know. I can't imagine a better mentor for her."

Zel grumbled. "Fine, I guess I can wait a little longer. At least until she's walking properly."

"Thank you." I studied her face, searching for signs of sadness. "But is this enough for you? Are you happy here with us?"

Zel shrugged. "I'm content. I have purpose. I'm with people I love. That's enough for me."

I nodded slowly, but hoped one day Zel would be able to find love again, even though her mate had died. Was it possible to have a second fated mate? I wasn't sure, but at this point I'd settle for Zel meeting a nice woman who made her smile.

I searched the party for my sons, and spotted Damien and Kassiel sitting together at the far edge of the tents while drinking beers. Relaxing together, trading quips, and rubbing Cerberus's many heads as he tried to steal the cheese off their plates. But where was Belial?

I spotted him standing by himself, gazing out at the ocean. He had his hands shoved in the pockets of his jeans, and the wind whipped at his dark hair. My heart clenched at the sight of him, worried something was wrong, but then Lucifer joined him there and the two of them spoke softly to each other. Whatever they said was lost on the wind before it reached my ears, but I was just happy they were speaking again.

Belial still seemed different, but he swore that he was fine, and I wasn't sure what—if anything—I could do for him at this point. Like me and Lucifer, he had to learn how to deal with being an Elder God, with Death being a permanent part of him now, and everything that entailed. It wasn't easy, but Lucifer and I were there for him if he had any problems. As for the matter of his missing soul...well, I still wasn't sure what that meant, but I would find out. When Lucifer and I put our minds to something, nothing could stop us.

As I continued to watch the party guests, Lucifer moved behind me, resting his hands on my hips and pressing a kiss to my neck. "What are you thinking about?"

"Fate," I said. "Life. Love."

He nuzzled my neck. "Sex?"

A short laugh escaped me. "Is that all you think about?"

Lucifer's hand had already drifted to my ass. "When you wear skimpy little dresses like that, yes.'"

"Later," I said, a promise I intended to keep. "After the guests have gone."

"I'm holding you to that."

———

True to his word, Lucifer found me out on the balcony later that night. The party was finished, Aurora was in bed, and I was staring at the ocean, much like Belial had done earlier.

"Still thinking about love?" Lucifer asked, as he moved toward me. He was shirtless now, wearing only black slacks that fit his body perfectly.

"With you? Always."

"You did make me a promise." His hands skimmed along my sides, as he raised up the dress I was wearing to expose my thighs. "I had an idea... Something we haven't done in many years."

My eyebrows darted up at that. "What would that be?"

He yanked the dress off me, while at the same time his shadow magic ripped off everything I'd been wearing underneath. Then he dropped his own trousers, freeing his impressive cock.

He took my hand as his black wings stretched out behind him. "Come with me, love."

My own silver wings extended, and together we flew up into the night, both of us completely naked, though Lucifer's shadow magic kept us hidden from anyone who happened to look up. Once we were hovering above our estate, I took it all in, enjoying the view of our home. Our palace on Earth.

But that wasn't why Lucifer had brought me up here. He drew me toward him, his wings spread wide behind him, and then his mouth crashed down on mine while his hands found my thighs again. His kiss was rough and demanding, as were his fingers as he moved across my skin. My desire immediately spiked as I realized what he had in mind.

I brought my hands to Lucifer's shoulders and his muscles flexed and moved beneath my touch as he continued to trail kisses over me. Wet, open-mouthed kisses down my neck. A hint of teeth. The flick of his tongue over my collarbone, and the soft caress of his fingers over my breasts, spiraling my nipple until it hardened and I arched against him.

"I see I have your attention now," he said with a smirk.

"Mmhmm." I threaded my fingers into his hair as his lips closed over my nipple before he sucked it into his mouth. Then he moved his ministrations to my other breast and his cock rested hard and heavy against my thigh. I grinned as he drew back and forth across my skin a little. "I see I'm not the only one at attention."

"If only you knew how you've tormented me over the centuries.

Able to make my body respond with just a glance, or the sound of your breathing, your fragrance lingering in a room after you've left..."

"I know exactly what you mean." I tugged on his hair, wanting his mouth back on mine, while my wings flapped slowly behind us to help keep us aloft. The wind blew lightly against us, the night air cold against my skin, but I knew Lucifer's touch would keep me warm.

He obliged me, his lips widening into a grin before they captured mine and his tongue slipped into my mouth, slow and smooth and seeking something, but in no hurry. Taking his time because we suddenly had plenty of it. No emergencies, no one to fight, no one in danger.

I kissed him back, reveling in our freedom, and I worked my hand beneath his body and mine, tracing the valleys between his muscles, then down to stroke his cock, which hardened even more as he drew a sharp breath.

"Tease."

"You wouldn't have me any other way." I laughed and pressed a kiss to his throat.

"I'd have you every other way, Hannah." He gripped my legs and spread them around his hips, while his black wings beat behind him. "All the ways. And I'll have you now."

I wrapped my arms around his neck and ground against him. "Promises, promises."

While we hovered in the air, he rolled his hips forward, and the head of his cock probed between my folds. I tightened my legs around him as he filled me completely, making me cry out with the perfection of it. I dropped my head back as I savored the feel of him inside me. The closest two people could get. Two mates, joined together as one, our souls intertwined as much as our bodies were. We were the king and queen of night, and we consummated our love amongst the stars.

Lucifer's hands were on my hips as he began thrusting into me, using his wings to propel him forward with more momentum. He started out slow and easy, hard and deep, but then I used my own wings to push back against him, making our pace speed up. He grunted and suddenly flew up higher, impaling me on his cock as we became one with the night, reaching for the moon, and I held onto his shoulders and let him take me for a ride.

We shot through the air, moving faster than should have been possible, our bodies joined together. Fucking in the air was like nothing else I'd ever experienced, a true give and take, and every thrust was met with a flutter of wings to keep us aloft. Lucifer's feathers brushed against me, their delicate touch the perfect contrast to his demanding movements. His fingers were almost bruising against me as he moved my body against him, hitting just the right spot every time.

We had sex as only gods could, pumping stronger and faster than any mortal could take, our pleasure heightened by the power coursing through us and the way our wings kissed the air as they moved. I reached up to stroke his feathers, and he let out a loud groan.

"Fuck, Hannah. Come for me." His breaths came faster as he pummeled me. "I want to feel you squeeze my cock as you lose control."

"When I'm ready." I wanted to drag this out as long as possible, but I couldn't stop the pleasure building inside me. He was too good. He was touching all the right places, and soon all I could do was gasp and moan as he took me harder and faster. His hands rested on my ass, kneading me there, demanding I follow his orders.

"I said, come for me," he growled, as his cock plunged deep.

I arched back against him, my wings flaring out as the orgasm flooded me with heat and power. Lucifer groaned too as I tightened up around his cock, my legs still squeezing around his hips, unwilling to let him go until he'd fully released himself inside me. He pushed upward one last time as we clung to one another, our wings barely keeping us afloat as overwhelming pleasure made us lose control of ourselves.

"I love you," he said, burying his face in my neck. "Across every lifetime. For all eternity."

"I love you too. Always."

We pulled apart so we could do a few lazy laps over our home, but our hands stayed intertwined the entire time. As I gazed over at my mate, his eyes bright under the twinkling stars and soft moonlight, all I felt was love and peace. Against all odds, Lucifer and I had found each other across hundreds of lifetimes, and managed to defeat the curse that kept separating us. We overcame Death, and finally took down Pestilence. We no longer had to live in fear of what Adam might do to us, or to our children. We were free.

Most importantly, we'd brought our family back together—and we'd resolved to never let it be torn apart again, no matter what threats we might face in the future. Whatever happened, we were ready for the next chapter of our story.

It was time to live.

DEATH LORD

CLAIMED BY LUCIFER BOOK FOUR

1

BELIAL

I n New Orleans, very little separated the living from the dead. Tombs sat above ground in the dozens of cemeteries across the city, where visitors left daily offerings to appease the restless spirits. Songs of the dead echoed through the French Quarter, telling the story of the city's violent, tragic past. Tourists flocked to ghost tours and combed abandoned buildings, hoping to get a glimpse of the supernatural.

If only they knew how close Death truly was.

From the rooftops, I watched my prey move through the alleys below, blending into the darkness almost perfectly. The only thing that gave him away were the scuffs of his shoes along the pavement, and the occasional flicker of his shadow over a lighter patch of alley.

I followed along the edge of the building above him without making a sound, my form cloaked in darkness. He carried on, unaware that he was being stalked by something far worse than him. Death was already in the air—I could taste it on my tongue like a familiar, intoxicating drink. It grew stronger by the minute, and I knew I'd only have so much time before I'd have to act. Because *he* would act soon.

My stomach clenched, empty and wanting. Unnatural hunger

burned inside me, a pounding need that had to be fulfilled. I had to feed soon...or else.

The man stopped in a patch of light and I got my first good look at him. He was on the shorter side for a modern-day male, with tawny hair that looked messy and a long nose that defined his face. He glanced around as if checking to make sure he was still alone, but he never thought to look up, still oblivious to the danger above him. He had no idea that Death stalked the streets of New Orleans alongside him, searching for the next doomed soul to consume.

He slid into an alley with intermittent, flickering lights, where a shape slumped against the wall. The shape stirred and croaked out words too quiet for me to hear. A dirty hand came up, peeking out of blankets, asking for a handout. The man I'd been following sneered and towered over the helpless human, and I knew it was time.

I jumped across the rooftop to the next building, landing softly. The tang of magic filled the air as the man changed into a large bobcat, revealing his true nature as a shifter—a type of demon representing the sin of wrath. He snarled and the human screamed, trying to get away as the bobcat readied to pounce, fangs bared.

I dropped down from the roof in a swirl of darkness, my cloak fluttering behind me, my hood concealing my face. I landed directly between the shifter and the human, just as the bobcat lunged. I knocked him back with a blast of darkness, and he hit the wall on the other side of the alley with a sickening crack. But that wasn't enough to kill a shifter. He recovered fast, back leg lifted in a limp, and his eyes widened at the sight of me—and then he ran.

Of course he did.

Disgust curled my lip. This was the third person he'd attacked in as many days, but this time I was here to stop him before he left another body behind.

I summoned Ghost, my horse, who appeared out of the shadows, bowing his pale head as he approached. I mounted him easily and we took off after the bobcat, racing down the dark alleys across cobblestones and cement, a mix of new and old. A rush of adrenaline flowed through my veins at the chase, and the promise of what was to come—because there was no escaping Death.

In his panic, the shifter ran into a dead end, and I cornered him against a wall. As I leaped off of Ghost's back, the shifter returned to his human form in a swirl of magic. I gestured for Ghost to vanish again as I stalked toward my prey.

"No..." he muttered, his eyes wide as he looked up at me. "It's you..."

"I see my reputation precedes me," I said in a low voice.

"Please, spare me," he gasped out.

"Like you were going to spare that man back there?" My hand snaked out of my cloak to grab hold of the shifter's throat and I lifted him up in the air. "I think not."

At my touch, life began draining from the shifter into me. He choked, scrabbling uselessly at my arm as I tightened my grip. His power flowed into me, sating that deep, aching hunger that plagued me constantly. I closed my eyes and breathed in deeply, relishing the brief moment of peace.

Something cold and painful plunged into my back, and I jerked my head to look over my shoulder. An ice spear protruded from my cloak. *What the fuck?*

I dropped the bobcat shifter, who collapsed onto the ground in a heap, too weak to do anything for the moment. Whoever had interrupted my feeding was going to pay for it.

I reached around and grasped the spear, gritting my teeth as I pulled it out of my shoulder and shattered it in my hand. When I looked in the direction of where the spear must have come from, I spotted a woman standing about twenty feet away. My breath caught as we locked gazes, not only because she was gorgeous, but because her pale blue eyes burned with a deep, fiery hatred that contradicted her icy powers. Pure white hair flowed down her back, and she wore all black leather that looked like it was made for combat. She lifted her hands up and magic hummed in the air as her ice hit me like a brick wall. I brushed it aside with a flick of power, and she bared her teeth, her fingers lengthening into claws.

Great, another shifter. These two must be working together, which meant they both had to die. Fine with me. My appetite was insatiable and I could feed all night long, especially if it meant getting other murderers off my streets.

As she threw another blast of ice at me, the bobcat shifter took the moment to dart away. Damn it. I'd have to hunt him down again after I drained this one of life.

"You're going to regret that," I said as I enveloped the shifter in thick, inky darkness. She struggled as it wrapped her limbs tight to her body until she could hardly breathe. She let out a gasp, her bright eyes flaring as she looked at me defiantly. She didn't seem scared.

You will be, I thought with satisfaction as I stalked forward, tightening my darkness around her in slight increments. She'd already ruined my hunt, so I didn't mind making her suffer just a little bit before I drained her of life. She struggled harder, seeming intent on getting away from me. She bared her canines as I drew closer, trying to bite my hand as it lifted toward her.

"Don't worry, it will all be over soon," I said as I wrapped my hand around her throat. Our eyes locked and I was struck again by her beauty, even as my fingers tightened on her soft, delicate skin. A shame to kill one so lovely, but if she was working with the bobcat shifter then she deserved this fate.

I began to drain her of life...but nothing happened.

Something was different. It took me a few heartbeats to realize I didn't feel the overwhelming need to feed anymore. For once, I wasn't absolutely starving for life.

Instead, I felt a different type of hunger. Like lust, but stronger. I wanted to devour her, but in a completely different way than usual. My thumb brushed against her pulse, which was beating rapidly, and my gaze fell to her lips. I had a sudden desire to pull her closer and claim her mouth with a rough kiss. Or to throw her over my shoulder and carry her back to my bar, where I'd spread her legs and feast on her pussy.

My hunger for death had been replaced—by a hunger for *her.*

2

EIRA

B elial tossed me to the ground as if I'd scalded his hand and he couldn't let go of me fast enough. I landed hard on the dirty cement and clutched my neck, drawing a deep breath into my aching, burning lungs. He could have killed me easily, just like his other victims—so why had he stopped? And what was that weird sensation I'd felt when he'd touched me? Something that felt...*right*. Even with his hand around my neck, choking the life out of me. Which made zero fucking sense.

I looked up at the man the press called the Grim Reaper of New Orleans as I tried to catch my breath. Belial's tall, muscular frame towered above me, and his presence bled into the space outside of the physical bounds of his body, taking up more room than he had any right to. He wore a black cloak with a hood that completely hid his face, though I'd caught a glimpse of his hard eyes and chiseled jaw when he'd stared at my mouth like he'd been about to kiss me. Another thing that made no sense.

"Who are you?" he asked in a low, dangerous voice.

Anger flared inside me at the sound. He was the reason shifters had been going missing all around the city. He was also my father's killer. I had to stop him at all costs.

"I am vengeance." As soon as the words left my mouth I launched myself upwards, shifting mid-lunge into a huge white wolf, my claws and fangs crystallizing into lethal ice.

But he dodged my attack easily, moving so quickly I almost missed it. I twisted and tried to attack again, but he simply maneuvered away in the blink of an eye once more. No matter how much I attacked, he didn't fight back, but simply stared at me. I couldn't see his expression, but I got the impression he was studying me, or perhaps sizing me up. Like a specimen laid out under a microscope, bright lights trained on me and a giant eye watching my every move.

I shifted back into my human form and threw multiple shards of ice at him in quick succession. He didn't dodge this time, but simply raised a hand up. Blue flame lit in his hand, melting the ice, and I froze at the sight—*hellfire*. Only Belial and his father Lucifer possessed such a deadly power, and if it hit me, this would all be over.

Was that how he'd killed my father?

My anger flared once more, burning deep in my stomach, and I let out a yell as I rushed Belial. I formed an ice sword in each hand and swung them around, preparing to attack. He formed a sword made of darkness and easily parried my attacks, as if my years of combat training was nothing against him. Damn it! What would it take to kill this asshole?

I raised my swords to strike again, but a rush of dark power rolled out of Belial in a wave. My jaw fell open as something burst through the cement at my feet—a bony white hand. A choked scream escaped me as more hands reached up all around me, grabbing for my boots and anything else they could use for leverage. I could only gape in horror as freaking *skeletons* started crawling out of the ground, moving closer with jerky movements like something out of a nightmare.

Belial only looked on as bony fingers reached for me. I chopped and dodged, but the skeletons were relentless and their undead hands wrapped around my upper arms, holding me firmly in place. I gritted my teeth, unsure how I was going to get out of this alive, as I conjured shards of ice, but they did little against the skeletons surrounding me.

Belial stalked forward as I struggled against the skeletons, but there was no escaping them. He drew close enough for me to get another glance at his annoyingly handsome face under that dark hood. My chest clenched, and not entirely from fear.

Don't get distracted, I chided myself. *He's the son of Lucifer, of course he'd be devastatingly sexy. He's also going to fucking kill you.*

I lashed out with my ice magic, trying to make one last-ditch effort to get away. Finally, some of the control the skeletons had shifted slightly, and I shoved at that with all my might, my heart thundering in my chest. I scrabbled with the tiny bit of freedom I'd won, throwing everything I had against it. If I was going to die tonight, I was going to fight against Belial as much as I could.

But it wasn't enough.

Belial grabbed my arms with impossible strength and speed, snapping a pair of silver cuffs on my wrists.

"What are you doing?" I cried, as I looked down at them, trying to jerk my hands away. The instant they were on, I felt hollow—like my magic had been stripped away completely. I tried to call my wolf, or summon my ice magic, but it was like a cage surrounded me, preventing me from accessing my powers.

With a sinking sensation, I realized I recognized these silver cuffs. I'd seen them on prisoners of the fae during my time in Faerie, and they blocked all magical powers, basically turning the person wearing them into a regular human. I'd never experienced them before, and after feeling my magic blocked from me like this, I never wanted to feel it again. But why was he doing this instead of simply killing me, like he'd almost done to that other shifter?

The skeletons disappeared, fading to dust all around us. Belial didn't need them anymore, since there was nothing I could do to get out of the cuffs. I could *run* though. I glanced around, looking for the best escape route.

"Don't even think about running," Belial said, with that low, hard voice, as tendrils of darkness snaked around me, trapping my arms at my sides.

"Let me go, asshole!" I shouted, trying to summon my anger again, along with my courage. "Or at least have the balls to kill me already!"

Belial's eyebrow arched at that, and then a tendril of darkness snaked its way up my neck and sealed itself across my lips. I screamed against it, struggling harder, but it held tight. There was nothing I could do but glare at Belial, trying to relay exactly how I felt about him through my eyes.

"I'm not going to kill you," he said. "At least, not yet."

"Why not?" I asked, but it came out a garble of repressed, furious sounds.

"You're coming with me."

He scooped me up into his strong arms as my muffled protests got louder and more frantic. I struggled with everything I had, but between the cuffs and his shadow bindings, there was nothing I could do. Besides, he was way too powerful, much more so than I'd expected.

He cradled me in his arms like he was rescuing me, as his huge wings snapped out behind him. They were impossibly beautiful—his feathers inky black at the top, then fading to gray, then turning to white along the bottom tips. I'd be impressed, if I wasn't being kidnapped.

With a sweep of his wings, we lifted into the air. My eyes nearly bulged out of their sockets as we flew higher, while shadows swirled around us, blending us into the night. If I had access to my hands, I would cling to him for dear life. As the twinkling lights of New Orleans zipped beneath us, I prayed he wouldn't drop me. Then again, maybe I'd be better off if he did. A quick death, rather than whatever he had in mind for me.

Where the hell was Belial taking me—and why?

3

EIRA

Belial's feet finally touched down on the roof of a building in the French Quarter, and I let out a long breath, my muscles relaxing slightly. Was flying across the city amazing? Yes. Was it terrifying? Also yes.

I still had no idea where the Grim Reaper of New Orleans was taking me either. Was he going to torture me? As part fae and part demon, I healed faster than any human, although that wouldn't be true with these damn silver cuffs on. I struggled again for good measure as Belial walked toward a door on the roof, but he didn't even seem to notice my efforts.

He threw the door open and stomped inside, narrowly smacking my head against the door frame. I snapped, "Watch it," but the stupid shadow muzzle on my mouth turned it into gibberish. This asshole was getting an earful when he finally took it off me.

The stairwell inside was nearly pitch black, but my demon eyes let me see well enough in it. Not that there was much to see as we went down three flights to another door. Belial threw this one open too, and I craned my neck to look around. We were in a basement with no windows, filled with bottles and barrels of alcohol, cleaning supplies, crates of snack food, some bar stools, napkins, and table cloths, and a refrigerator. Had he taken me to his bar? I'd been watching it for a few days before I'd made my move against him, trying to learn his habits and his schedule. That was how I'd known he would go out tonight...to hunt.

I'd given up struggling at this point, and I didn't even try to yank at the darkness as Belial finally set me down. It was obviously futile. He had me in the magic-draining silver cuffs, and his own magic was airtight. I was sure he could hold me like this for as long as he needed. All I could do was glare up at him and hope he combusted on the spot from the hatred searing in my veins.

He dropped me in a heap in the corner of the room on the dirty floor, and I let loose another stream of swear words he couldn't understand. I fell silent when the clink of metal against metal met my ears. My fears were confirmed a moment later when Belial pulled chains out from a cabinet and started toward me with them. I scrambled back, my bound feet trying to catch footing and failing, and then my back hit a wall. I was well and truly trapped here with this psychopath who seemed impossible to kill.

Belial let the chains drag along the floor as he cornered me at the wall. He released the darkness cocooning my wrists, but only to snap a chain to the silver cuffs. I watched helplessly as he attached the other end to a hook on the wall. I didn't bother tugging on it. The chain was thick enough that I'd almost call it overkill.

He quickly searched me all over, presumably for other weapons, his hands roaming across my body over my combat leathers. I froze as he touched me, and even though there wasn't anything sexual about it, my breath hitched anyway at how near he was. He found no weapons, but did confiscate my phone, the bastard. Then he reached into a cabinet and pulled out another set of silver cuffs.

"No!" I cried out through my muffle. I strained against the length of the chain, trying to get away from him, but there was nowhere to run and no way to escape. He captured one foot and held it tight so I couldn't kick him as he attached the cuff around my ankle, and then quickly slapped the other one on before I could try to kick him again. He added another chain to those cuffs, and attached it to the same wall hook. Why did he need a wall hook?

Did he keep many prisoners down here? Fuck, what kind of sick bastard was he?

Belial stepped back to admire his handiwork. I glared at him, hating him with every fiber of my being. He waved his hand and the pressure sealing my mouth shut vanished. Finally.

"Let me go, you fucking psychopath!" I snapped instantly.

He arched a dark eyebrow. "Now why would I do that when I just got you here?"

A tremor of fear ran down my spine but I refused to let it show on my face. "What are you going to do to me?"

"I haven't decided yet." He leaned against a stack of crates, crossing his arms, and observed me. His dark gaze wandered over me in a long, lazy roll, and then came back up to my eyes. He smirked as if he'd just seen something incredibly funny. "Tell me who you are... or better yet, what you are."

I debated not telling him a single thing. But then, what was the point in hiding it? He already had me chained up, and he could probably torture the information out of me if he needed to. "My name is Eira, and I'm the daughter of Fenrir."

Understanding flickered across his face, so slight that I would have missed it if I wasn't watching so closely for his reaction. "Is that why you're here to kill me?" He sounded almost amused. "Revenge for your father's death?"

"That's not the only reason," I growled.

I hadn't been at the battle in Hell where my father had been killed, but my older brothers were there and they'd told me everything. Sure, my father had fought a war against Lucifer, but it was Lucifer's eldest son who'd dealt the killing blow. My father had made many mistakes, but I'd loved him anyway, and I couldn't forgive Belial for his death. Even so, I hadn't planned to go after him until shifters started going missing or turning up dead all around New Orleans, and when my brothers came to investigate, they disappeared too. The media had called the "vigilante" the Grim Reaper of New Orleans, mentioning how he only killed criminals, rapists, and others the police never caught, but I knew what he truly was—a murderer who had to be stopped.

"Where are my brothers?" I asked. "Have you killed them?"

"I have no idea what you're talking about," Belial said.

"Liar! You've been killing off shifters in this city, and even more have gone missing. Did you bring them down here before killing them? Is that what you're going to do to me?"

He snorted. "You're the first I've chained up down here in many years."

"Wow, I'm honored," I said, my voice dripping with sarcasm. "How about you free me and we finish what we started in that alley"

"Are you so quick to go to your death?" He smirked, looking haughty and amused and way too fucking handsome for his own good. "We both know you can't kill me. After all, I am Death."

"What are you talking about?" I asked, shock running over me like a bucket of ice water.

Belial just shook his head. "You want to kill me because of Fenrir's death when you don't even know the whole story."

"No, I want to kill you because you're a murderer and you have to be stopped. The trail of bodies you've left across the city is proof. Just like the shifter you were about to murder tonight."

Belial let out a sarcastic laugh. "Is that what you think? I was only attacking that shifter because he was going to kill that homeless man. He's killed many over the last few days, and I'd finally tracked him down and was about to stop him—when you attacked me."

"I didn't see any homeless guy." I'd watched Belial from the shadows as he'd jumped down and grabbed the shifter by the throat, completely unprovoked. "Just you and the shifter."

"I don't give a fuck if you don't believe me," he said, as he tore off his cloak and tossed it aside, giving me a better view of his large, muscular body. "But over the last few months, crime has been increasing in New Orleans, and most of it has come from shifters. I'm only protecting my city, taking out the criminals that can't be stopped by the police. Can you imagine a human police officer going up against a shifter? It would be carnage."

"Why didn't you kill me, then?"

Belial's mood shifted in an instant. He'd been resonating a low-level threatening aura this whole time, setting my teeth on edge and making my hair stand on end, but it suddenly intensified. He didn't so much as move, but something shifted in the air. "That's a good question."

Before I could say anything else, he rushed forward and grabbed my throat.

4

BELIAL

I'd thought that it was just a fluke, but when I wrapped my hand around Eira's throat again, there wasn't so much as a flicker of hunger.

Ever since I'd become Death, I'd been completely insatiable. It had changed me as a person, and I didn't like who I was becoming. My need to steal life was all-consuming, and on some nights I could hardly control it, like trying to contain a hurricane with my bare hands most days. All I could do was direct it toward the evil in the city, taking out the other murderers to hopefully spare other lives. If I had to kill, I would protect the city I loved at the same time.

But the moment I touched Eira, it all changed. The raging and howling in my head for the death of every living thing around me quieted, as if I'd snuffed it out like a candle. I tightened my grip around her throat and tried to drain the life from her. I sucked and sucked, but I couldn't draw a single drop of life from her.

I leaned closer, letting go of her throat and drew in a deep, long breath. She smelled like shifter and fae, a rare hybrid for sure, but nothing that would explain my unusual reaction to her. Beyond the lack of hunger, there was an incredible pull I felt toward her, and nothing I could do to slow it down or halt it. I *wanted* her. Badly.

"Why?" I murmured, only half-aware of what I was saying, as I breathed in her wonderful scent. "Why are you special?"

Eira didn't answer. She was holding perfectly still, possibly with fear, or maybe just as caught up in this as I was. I opened my mouth to ask her something else, but then she drew in a deep breath and slammed her head into me as hard as she could. She jerked her limbs against me all at once, trying to push me away, or topple me over so she could escape, but it didn't do any good. She had no idea who she was up against.

I gripped her chin and shoved her head against the wall so she couldn't move. I smiled, amused that she was still fighting me. Somehow she thought that she could actually kill Death.

"You think you can get away so easily?" I asked, enjoying the feel of her so close to me. I wasn't sure why I'd brought her here, I'd just known I couldn't let her go—not until I learned more.

"I was hoping you'd be distracted," Eira growled.

"Keep trying," I said, as I caressed her chin with my fingers, pressing my body against hers. I couldn't stop myself. I needed to be closer. "Who knows, maybe someday you'll manage to beat me."

"Or you could just let me go," she asked, her voice disgusted. But I noticed she didn't try to fight me again, and she leaned into me too, like she couldn't help herself. She inhaled sharply and her eyes dropped to my mouth, and I spotted desire flickering across her face. She wanted me too, despite her fear and her hatred. What the fuck was happening to us?

And it only got worse with proximity. I could hardly hold myself from back from nosing along her exposed neck, from tasting the sharp beat of her heart and her soft, smooth skin. I wanted to *bite* her, to consume whatever part of her was so alluring just to make it *stop*. Or maybe the only solution was to taste her somewhere else, like between her thighs, before I plunged my cock into her. I grew hard just thinking about how much I needed that. Needed *her*.

"What do you want from me?" Eira asked breathlessly, breaking the spell. I blinked, realizing that I'd nearly pressed my mouth to her neck, and I pulled back slightly so I could look her in the eye.

I didn't have a good answer for her. There was no reason for me to keep her, except that I couldn't let her go. For one thing, she wanted to kill me, and I didn't want to have to pull ice spears out of my back all the time. But that wasn't why I'd really brought her here. I had to find out why she was different, why I couldn't drain her life, and why she soothed the raging hunger inside me for death...and awakened another kind of hunger. Then, once I figured out what the hell this thing was between us, I could stop it. The last thing I needed was a distraction.

If I was smart, I'd pull back and leave her to stew for a bit, and maybe that would cool her awful temper so she could talk to me in a calmer state. But when I looked at her, the overwhelming urge to kiss her washed over me. Lust, I could understand, but this was deeper. I wanted to *devour* her. How long had it been since I'd felt that particular urge?

Eira's pupils dilated like she felt it as well, and she licked her lips. My eyes fell to the movement, and I swallowed, my mouth suddenly, inexplicably dry. She wanted this, too, that much was clear in her eyes, and for a moment, I felt like we were both on the same page. Everything else faded into the background, and all that mattered was the need to seal my lips to hers. Would they taste as sweet as they looked?

No. I couldn't. I was Death, and there was no way I could get involved with anyone. I could kill with just a touch now, and it didn't matter that this particular urge didn't apply to Eira. She was from a different world, and I didn't need to drag her into mine in such an intimate way.

I stepped back and tried to regain control over myself. The want had a keen edge that wasn't going away, and I had to battle against it in an entirely different way from the usual hunger for death. It was dangerous, and I shouldn't tempt whatever it was.

But I couldn't let Eira go either.

She was glaring at me again, her beautiful face filled with hatred. No matter what strange desire drew us together, she still blamed me entirely for her father's death, and that wasn't going to be something that we could get past with a kiss or even a good fuck. But I needed to know why and how she affected me this way, and I had to keep her close long enough for that. I had no doubts that if I left her tied up in my bar's basement, she'd find a way to get out, but there were other options. It was just a matter of convincing her to go for them.

"I've noticed shifters going missing, too," I said finally. "It's not because of me though. Yes, I'm going after the ones who are dangerous and are killing humans, because they need to be stopped. But the others? I have no idea what's happening to them, and I'd like to find out. Maybe it's tied to the increase in violent crime over the last few months." I leaned back against the fridge, keeping my distance from her as much as I could. "Why don't we work together to find out why the shifters are going missing?"

"You want to work...together?" she asked, like I'd just said the most ridiculous thing she'd ever heard in her life.

"Yes. That is, if you can stop trying to kill me for a while."

Eira tilted her head back and shot daggers at me with her cold eyes. "I'm not sure if I can resist the urge."

"I assure you, it's completely futile. I *cannot* die, and it doesn't matter how many ice spears you throw at my back. It does hurt though, and kind of puts a damper on the idea of us working together." I shrugged casually. "The other option is that I can just leave you chained up down here, and go do it myself. I can't have you interfering with my work. Either you stay out of my way, under lock and key, or you work with me. Which one is it going to be?"

"That's really not an option," Eira said, twisting her sexy little mouth up into a scowl.

"At least I'm giving you the choice," I said. "Anyone less generous might have taken offense to you repeatedly attacking me."

"Fine," Eira spat. "I'll work with you, and I'll do my very best to try and not kill you."

She still had that defiant tilt to her head, like she expected me to revoke the offer because of her attitude. *If this was any other circumstance, I'd tease back,* I thought. She was just my type, gorgeous and smart and feisty as a hellcat, but I had no time for any sort of feelings. Right now, all there was, was the mission.

I stepped forward and unhooked the chains from her wrists and ankles. I crouched down in front of her and carefully undid the cuffs on her feet so that she could walk properly. I half expected her to try and kick me and escape, but apparently somehow I'd convinced her that fighting and running wasn't the best idea.

She might just be biding her time to find another escape route, but I hoped I'd be able to show her that I was willing to help her out. There was clearly more going on than what she was telling me. She had seemed very emotional about the shifters going missing, which made sense if she was looking for her brothers, whoever they were. Hopefully that desire to find them overruled her other desire to kill me, at least for a little while.

As I was pulling away from her leg, my fingers slid against the exposed skin of her ankle. Something crackled in the air between us. I wanted to lean in and lick her skin, but I steeled myself and let her go. But I stood up slowly, still caught in her spell. Touching her was intoxicating, and I couldn't get enough.

Eira was looking at me, eyes wide, cheeks flushed. I slid my hand along her neck, and she let out a long breath as her body trembled slightly. Her eyelids fluttered shut like she was going to give in, and she swayed toward me. I let out a harsh gasp, fighting desperately for control, as my mouth drew closer to hers with every second.

I drew back sharply. I couldn't do this. She hated me, and I had no business trying to seduce her. We'd just agreed to not kill each other, for fuck's sake.

No, I'd have to simply suffer through it. I turned away and started up the stairs without waiting to see if she would follow me.

5

EIRA

I looked down at my wrists once more to make sure they were actually freed from the wall. Had Belial really let me go? The silver cuffs still blocked me from using my powers, so it wasn't true freedom, but it was something. I looked around for a weapon to use against him, but all I saw were bottles of alcohol and an old mop. I grabbed the closest bottle of wine I could find and scrambled to follow Belial up the stairs.

I couldn't believe the turn of events over the last few minutes. I'd gone from thinking I was going to die, to agreeing to work with my father's murderer, who was supposedly trying to help the city, even though I'd watched him attempt to kill a shifter in cold blood.

And then there was that weird, crazy desire I felt whenever he was near, which I was desperately trying not to think about. Every time he touched me it was like fireworks were being set off all throughout my body, and intense need filled my core, demanding I touch him back. Or worse, kiss him. No way was I ever doing that, so my body needed to calm the fuck down already.

"Are you ever going to take these cuffs off?" I asked, holding my hands up. The silver caught the dull light and winked. It was excruciating to be cut off from my magic and so powerless. I wondered if this was what it felt like to be human. No wonder they needed so much protection.

"I will when you can be trusted to not stab me in the back with a spear of ice."

"Wow, you're really hung up on that, aren't you?" I sighed. "So, basically...never. How am I supposed to help you if I'm cuffed? I can't use any of my magic or shift at all. I could fall down these stairs and die because I can't catch myself."

He snorted. "I have faith in your ability to walk up a flight of stairs. Although I could carry you, if you're so worried."

The thought of Belial taking me in his strong arms again sent a shiver of lust and fear through me. "Keep your hands off me," I snapped.

Except my traitorous body secretly wanted him to touch me all over, for some dumb reason. Back in the basement, I'd been so sure that Belial had been about to kiss me, and the weirdest thing was that I'd been about to *let* him. My body wanted me to get close to him, telling me I could lean into him, close my eyes, and trust he would protect me, which made no sense at all. Why would my survival instincts be misfiring so hard when it came to Belial? I had never had them fail me like this before. In fact, I'd always prided myself on being able to trust my instincts and be right about a person. But now? Belial was just pulling up a bunch of question marks along with this strange desire that pulled us together like magnets.

I kept having to remind myself that he was the enemy, and that turning my back to him would be like laying myself out in front of a target and begging to be hit. I'd only agreed to help him because I wanted to figure out what had happened to those shifters he'd claimed he hadn't killed, including my brothers. If I stuck with him for a bit, I was sure I'd be able to uncover the truth of what was going on.

I'd also use the time to try and figure out how to kill him. He'd said he was Death, but I wasn't entirely convinced, or even really sure what that meant. Even if he was Death, there had to be a way to kill him. I'd start looking for his weaknesses and how to exploit them in my favor. No one was infallible, and I'd figure out what made Lucifer's son tick—and then use that to end him.

Belial led us through another door and into the bar he owned. I'd only seen it from the outside, where it sat on the corner of a street in the French Quarter, with blue shutters on tall windows and big red doors at the entrance, along with a sign that said Outcast Bar with two black wings on it. Inside, the bar was a mix of new and old, like it had been around for decades but was also managing to keep up with the modern era. Without my shifter senses my nose felt clogged up, but I could still smell alcohol and food in the air, something like burgers and fries maybe.

Along the back wall was a huge mirror with many different bottles of alcohol, and behind the bar was a beautiful woman with Asian features and long black hair, who was polishing some glasses. She wore a black corset that was half leather and half lace and showed off all her assets.

"I just closed up for the night," she said, hardly glancing up as Belial sat down at the bar.

I followed him a bit more slowly, glancing around and noticing that the place was mostly empty, with only a few stragglers hanging around. Of course, he wouldn't want to bring me to his bar when it was open. It would be too easy for me to slip away in a full crowd of people, magic-dampening cuffs or not.

"Surely you can spare the owner of this establishment a drink?" Belial asked.

"For you, sure. But what about your guest?" The woman shot me a brief glance, like I was barely worth her time.

"She needs one, too," he said. "She tried to kill me."

I gaped at him. Who would go around telling people that?

The bartender gave me a second, more appraising glance, and then shook her head and let out a laugh. "Okay, yeah, she deserves a drink."

"Actually, I'll take care of the drinks," Belial said. "Your shift is done. Go home, Yumi."

Yumi hesitated, looking at me again. This time, I saw a small flicker of worry in her gaze, and wondered if the two of them were an item. The thought annoyed me more than it should. "Are you sure?"

"We're just going to have a drink and talk." Belial's eyes slowly slid to mine. "Isn't that right?"

I held up my cuffs and muttered, "Not much else I can do."

Yumi just shrugged and set down the glasses. "Fine, but let me know if there's any trouble and I'll come right back." She shot me a look of warning and then tossed down her towel. She obviously felt protective of Belial in some way, and the wolf inside me wanted to snap my teeth at her for some odd reason. Luckily she stalked away before I could act on the irrational urge. I had zero reason to feel jealous of her. Nope, none at all.

"What do you want to drink?" Belial asked, shaking me out of my thoughts. Was he really going to pour me a drink like we hadn't been at each other's throats less than an hour ago? What game was he playing? Was he going to poison me? I didn't trust him at all. He had no reason to trust me either, or share a drink with me in his bar like we were old friends catching up after several years apart.

"I'll take whatever you're having," I said, unable to focus enough to actually choose a drink. Belial stepped behind the bar, rolling up his black sleeves and revealing dark tattoos all along his forearms. I watched his chiseled face as he poured us two drinks, just some whiskey on the rocks. I couldn't figure him out at all. What was his deal? Did he really want us to work together?

Was he as disturbed by the disappearances as much as I was, or was he the ultimate villain behind everything? It annoyed me beyond measure that I couldn't trust my instincts on this, and all I could do was watch him closely and try to stay alive.

Once he'd poured us both some whiskey, he leaned against the bar and rested his heavy gaze on me again. "Tell me what you know about the missing shifters."

"I thought you knew everything that happened in your city." I carefully picked up my glass and eyed it, wondering if it was safe.

His broad shoulders moved in a lazy shrug. "I know a lot, but I'm not a shifter. Maybe you know something I don't."

I took a sip of my drink as a test, before telling him anything. I didn't immediately fall to the ground, frothing at the mouth, so there was that at least. I set it down carefully on a coaster, still eyeing it like I was waiting for it to grow legs and walk away. But when the smart burn of the whiskey slid down my throat and I didn't keel over, I decided he truly wasn't going to kill me. At least not now.

I rested my elbows on the bar and met Belial's steady gaze. "Over the last year, at least thirty shifters have gone missing, and all different kinds too. Some just vanished without a trace, but a few of them were last seen in or near New Orleans."

"I had no idea it was that many." He took a long swig of whiskey and then set his own glass down next to mine.

"We've been trying to keep this hidden for as long as we could, but then we learned that some imps have gone missing around here too."

Belial rubbed the stubble on his chin. "I have noticed an increase in imps attacking humans too over the last few months."

"And no doubt you decided to deal with them with your own vigilante justice," I said dryly.

He gave me an evil grin. "I do what I must to protect my city."

"Uh huh." I shook my head, glaring down at my drink. A drop of condensation traced its way down the side of it and landed on the coaster.

"Archdemon Bastet wanted to investigate. She's the current leader of the shifters, now that my father is dead," I added, just in case Belial was completely out of touch with the world. "She called a meeting between shifters and imps, and Archdemon Loki, who leads the imps, decided that my brothers should be the ones to go to New Orleans to investigate."

Belial leaned forward a bit. "Is there any particular reason he suggested them for the job?"

"Loki thought that if they took care of this problem, it might help the image of the wolf shifters. We're trying to get back into good graces with Bastet and the other shifters after Fenrir's uprising against Lucifer. You know, the one you were involved in?"

"Oh, right, that," Belial said, sounding amused.

I gritted my teeth. How could he be so flippant about the thing that had caused my father's death and the total disgrace of the wolf shifter demons?

"Why would Loki help you?" he asked a moment later, before I could snap something at him. "He's a notorious trickster who cares for no one but himself. It could be a trick."

"It's not a trick," I said through my clenched jaw. "Loki is my grandfather. He's just looking out for us after you killed our father. His *son*."

Belial leaned back but didn't look convinced. Yes, Loki was known for tricking people, even those who thought they were close to him. But he wouldn't do it to family. "Go on," Belial said, motioning for me to continue.

"Skoll and Hati came to New Orleans to investigate two weeks ago. They told me they'd found something, but when I tried to reach out to them a couple of days later, there was no answer. They'd disappeared off the face of the earth, and no one has seen or heard from them since."

My fingers tightened around the whiskey glass, as I remembered the utter terror I'd felt when I couldn't reach them anymore. I'd packed up and flown down here as soon as I could, taking on the investigation myself. But when I'd gotten here, all I'd found was a cold trail, and rumors of the Grim Reaper of New Orleans that was enacting vigilante vengeance around the city. The Grim Reaper...who turned out to be Belial—my father's murderer.

I took another sip of whiskey and made my voice calm again as I looked up at Belial. "When I came to investigate, the only person I found killing shifters was you. No trace of my brothers, or any other leads. Their trail simply went cold."

Belial refilled his whiskey glass as he considered my words. "I have no idea what happened to your brothers, but I have noticed something odd in the city recently. I've noticed the shifters here have been attacking humans more often than ever before, and when I try to stop them, they're often filled with an almost mindless, animal rage, like they can't control their wrath."

"That's odd," I said, frowning. Shifters always had a problem with rage, of course. We were the demons of wrath, although we could feed on any strong passionate emotion. Anger was just the easiest one to find and provoke.

"The people in New Orleans also seem more violent and angry lately," Belial said. "There's been a major uptick in violent crimes committed every day. The news channels are all telling people to be home before dark just to be safe." He let out a frustrated breath. "I'm doing the best that I can to protect the city, but I can't be everywhere at once. It's getting out of hand, and I'd just like to find the source."

You and me both, I thought, looking him over. He seemed genuinely upset, but he could be a very good actor. I still didn't trust him.

"Do you have any leads at all?" he asked. "You mentioned that your brothers said they found something that could possibly help."

"They never got to share the information with me," I said, shaking my head. "I'm staying at Hotel Immortelle like my brothers were, but I didn't find any information there on what happened to them. It's like they just vanished."

"Hmm." Belial downed the rest of his whiskey in one gulp and then considered me again. "I suggest we get some rest and then start searching. I'm sure you're exhausted after stalking me all night and trying to kill me."

"Does this mean I'll be going back to that wonderful dungeon you have in the basement?" I glared at him. "Are you going to chain me up again?"

"Not if you control yourself." Belial turned a lazy grin on me. "Unless you're into that sort of thing?"

The sultry purr in his voice sent an unwanted rush of desire through me. "With you? No way in hell."

He chuckled low in his throat, like he knew I was lying, as he gathered our glasses and put them in the sink. "Fine, no chains, but you'll stay with me tonight so I can keep an eye on you."

"Lucky me," I muttered. I could already tell this was going to be a long night.

6

EIRA

Belial led me back out the way we'd come and up the stairs again, to a heavy metal door protected by an electronic lock. I watched as Belial unlocked it with a code and then ushered me inside, to what I assumed must be his living room. It was the epitome of masculinity, with exposed brick walls, dark wood framing, and a leather couch that looked both impressive and comfortable. A huge TV sat on one end, while shelves crammed full of books, both new and old, lined the opposite wall. Big windows looked out over the French Quarter, along with a balcony draped in thick, dark curtains. I spotted an open kitchen with dark granite counters and stainless steel appliances, along with a dark metal dining table, and a hallway leading off to more doors, presumably bedrooms. It was all exactly what I'd expect from someone like Belial, except for one thing: the art all along the walls. Dozens of paintings that looked like they came from all different eras, as if he'd stolen each one from a different part of an art museum. I didn't know enough about art to know the artists or even the eras, but I had to admit that the man kept surprising me.

Belial stalked across the room to the hallway, where he grabbed a blanket and a pillow from a cabinet. "You can sleep on the couch."

He shoved both of them at me and I eyed him warily. "You actually expect me to sleep here?"

"Sleep or don't, that's your problem." He loomed over me, his eyes dark and deadly. "Just don't even think about running."

"Or what? You'll chase me down and chain me up again?" I rolled my eyes.

"If you try to run, my horse will stop you."

"Horse?" I asked, looking around. It had to be a metaphor of some sort. "What horse?"

"That one." Belial gestured behind me.

I turned and immediately jumped, because a huge pale gray horse had somehow appeared behind me without making a sound. It was bigger than any horse I'd seen in my life, and had glowing purple eyes. I'd seen a lot of stuff in my time, but I could still be shocked.

"Where the hell did that come from?" I asked, gaping at the horse. Despite it's very equine face, I had the feeling that it was looking at me with disdain, like I was a fly on its back that it could flick away with a single swish of its tail. It probably could. Those purple eyes gave me the creeps.

"Horseman of the Apocalypse, remember?" Belial asked. "It comes with the job."

So maybe he really was Death after all. Shit. No wonder I couldn't kill him. I swallowed hard, as the horse tossed its head in a very haughty manner, and then disappeared again.

"Where did it go?" I asked.

"I don't know," Belial said, shrugging.

"You don't know where your horse goes?" I asked, incredulous.

"Ghost and I respect each other's' privacy," Belial said, like it was the most obvious thing in the world.

Okay then. Maybe Belial was just plain off his rocker. And here I was, stuck with him all night. That did not bode well for me, but at least I'd accepted he wasn't going to kill me just yet. He wouldn't have brought me a pillow and blanket otherwise. I'd much rather be back in my hotel room, but at least I wasn't chained up to a wall in a basement either. At least here I might be able to snoop around and find out more about Belial, including how to defeat him.

"There's not much in the kitchen, but feel free to eat or drink anything you find."

"Let me guess, you're one of those guys who can't cook and orders in every night."

He shot me a hard look. "I'm an excellent cook. But now that I'm an Elder God, I don't need to eat anymore."

My mouth dropped open at that and I fumbled for a good response. "How does someone become an Elder God?"

"It's a long story," he muttered. "Get some rest."

I glanced down at my leather combat gear. "Could I at least go back to my hotel room to grab some clothes?"

"No."

"Fine, I'll just have to sleep in my underwear," I muttered, and started fluffing up the pillow.

"Hang on," he said, his eyes narrowing. He spun on his heel and disappeared down the hallway, then returned a minute later and tossed something at me. "Wear this."

I caught it on reflex, snatching the bundle of fabric out of the air. A black t-shirt, like the one Belial wore.

"Thanks?" I said, making it more of a question than anything else. Belial's eyes flashed again, and he sauntered closer. I held my ground, tilting my chin up. I wasn't going to let him intimidate me, no matter how much taller and stronger he was than me. He didn't stop, getting close enough that if either of us leaned forward just a bit, our chests would brush. He was close enough to kiss.

His mouth opened and closed like he was about to say something, his eyes flashing with annoyance, but then he reached up, touching my hair. He threaded the white strands through his fingers and I sucked in a breath, trying to figure out what he was doing. The action seemed almost involuntary, like he couldn't help himself. For a moment, I was so caught up in it that I couldn't do anything other than sway in and wonder where the hell my night had taken such a weird turn. Then I blinked. *The enemy,* I reminded myself for what seemed like the thousandth time.

"Don't touch me," I said, and then shoved him back as hard as I could.

He was so solid and ridiculously overpowered that even with all of my strength, he hardly swayed. But he stepped back all the same. "Bathroom's down the hall. Get some rest."

What an asshole, I thought, glaring at his retreating form. Once he was gone, I looked around the living room once again. Really, what was I doing? I was staying in this murderer's house like it was no big deal. Unfortunately, he might be my only viable lead, and he might give me clues that could lead me to my brothers. Hopefully I could uncover a way to kill him while I was at it, and finally avenge my father.

Besides, I was trapped here, between the silver cuffs on my wrists and that freaky horse that could show up at any moment out of nowhere to chase me down. Was Belial really Death? That would have been good to know before I'd tried to kill him, but my brothers hadn't mentioned it, and I hadn't heard it from anyone else either. Maybe Lucifer and his people were keeping it on the down low. Not that many people talked about Belial much in the demon world anyway. He'd been an outcast ever since he'd been exiled from Hell hundreds—thousands?—of years ago. All I knew was that he'd been friends with my father...and then he'd killed him.

I looked down at the shirt I was clutching, realizing that I'd clawed the material so much I was distorting the fabric. I smoothed it out, and then lifted it to my nose. I could smell Belial on it, and I was beyond pissed to report that he smelled *amazing*. I debated tossing it aside, but if I was actually going to get some rest, I'd be better off not trying to sleep in my combat gear. With a sigh, and a glance down the hallway to make sure Belial was gone, I began removing my clothes and folding them up. Then I yanked Belial's shirt over my head, inhaling sharply. Unwanted desire rushed through me, making my thighs clench, and I couldn't decide if I wanted to snuggle the shirt even more or tear it off myself. It was surprisingly soft, and large enough to hit me at the top of my thighs.

After a quick trip to the bathroom, I fluffed the pillow once more, and then collapsed onto the couch. I wanted to stay awake and snoop around, or make sure that he wasn't going to murder me, but I was exhausted enough that I couldn't think about doing anything other than lying down.

The moment I closed my eyes, I was sucked directly into sleep. I couldn't have fought it if I'd tried.

––––––––

I stood in the forest, in the familiar Montana wilds where my pack called home. I looked around, frowning. This wasn't where I'd fallen asleep, was it?

I took a step toward the stream flowing near my feet, where my brothers and I had often splashed as children. When had the direction of the water changed?

The rest of the forest was as dark as night, but I could see the sun in the sky up above. Something was clearly wrong, but I couldn't put my finger on it. I frowned, looking back down at the water. Had it always been that dark? I could have sworn I'd watched fish swim in the clear water many times before.

"Eira..."

I looked around, trying to see who was calling my name, but the forest around me was deserted. I turned back to the stream, trying to figure out what was happening and why everything felt so...off.

The voice spoke again, a low, raspy whisper that sounded like something directly from a horror movie. It was clearly female, but not immediately recognizable. "Eira..."

"Who's there?" I turned away from the creek, following the general direction of the sound, but no one was there. I couldn't see or smell anyone, but the sound of my name being eerily whispered drifted back to me again.

I spun around as the sound suddenly changed directions, my claws out and ready for a fight, but I was still alone. The eerie weather was really doing a number on me. I dropped my hands, shaking my head and letting out a small huff of laughter at my own paranoia.

A hand closed around my shoulder and I jumped half a foot into the air. A scream escaped my throat, but the sound got choked off when I looked down at the long nails dripping with blood digging into my shoulder.

I wrenched my shoulder away and spun to face the owner, my heart pounding out of my chest. She was dressed in all black, with snakes instead of hair, and a glowing red aura surrounded her. Her face remained indistinguishable, like no matter how hard I looked at her I couldn't quite get her features to stick in my mind.

"Eira," she whispered once again and it sounded like a death rattle from this close up. I shuddered and narrowly resisted the urge to brush my shoulder off. I still felt the ghost of her hand on my shoulder. "You have much anger in you."

"No shit," I muttered, although I was feeling a lot more fear than anger at the moment.

"We can help you channel it," another raspy voice said, as a second woman stepped beside the first one. She looked identical to the other woman, except with a green aura around her. "We know you seek vengeance. We can help you find it."

"How?" I looked between the two of them, wondering who they were, and how they possibly thought they could help me.

"Come to us," the first woman hissed, holding her hand out in a beckoning motion.

"We have what you need," the other one said.

She pointed to something behind me, and when I turned around, the world whooshed and I had the distinct feeling of falling forward. I gasped, trying to get my footing, but it didn't seem to matter. The next moment everything coalesced into something solid once again, and I came to a stumbling halt. I gritted my teeth, closing my eyes and trying to stop my head from spinning.

When I opened my eyes again, I drew in a sharp breath. If I knew the clearing by the stream like the back of my hand, this was the exact opposite. I'd never been here before, and I'd certainly remember it. A huge roller coaster stretched above my head, the metal twisting and turning, but it only took a glance for me to realize it was abandoned.

Vines grew on the skeletal structure, the metal was rusted in many places, and the entire concrete base was covered in graffiti art, layered over like people had been coming here for years to mark their spot.

I started walking toward an old arcade, with broken machines and more graffiti. No one was around and torn flags rustled in the wind, while abandoned carnival prizes lay abandoned and faded. The entire place gave me the creeps, and I wondered what had happened here. Where was everyone?

Somehow I was dead center in an abandoned theme park. I'd never seen it before, but it was distinctive enough that I figured I could find it again once I got out of this... whatever this was. I looked back at the roller coaster, trying to seal it in my mind. Remember this, I told myself.

I continued walking until I stumbled upon a large body of water. It faded into the hazy distance, and I couldn't tell whether it was a large pond or an actual lake. I squinted out at the horizon, and then looked at the half-dead grass under my feet at the bank.

Something was moving in the water. I peered down, trying to get a closer look at it, and then the surface erupted. I jumped back with a scream, stumbling on the uneven ground. From the roiling surface, the two women rose like some sort of eldritch creatures coming to suck the life out of me. I let out another scream and took a few more stumbling steps back.

The women reached for me, their limbs moving weirdly, as if they were puppets on strings that were being jerked in an inhuman way. "Come to us," the one with the red aura hissed as she lunged forward, as if she planned to attack me.

I turned around to run, trying to get away, but I couldn't move, my feet suddenly rooted to the ground. I opened my mouth to scream again, but it was sealed shut.

The women moved closer, hands outstretched as if they were trying to pull me toward them through sheer force of will. "Find us," the second hissed, curling her fingers over and over, like she was trying to grip onto me but couldn't quite make it.

I looked around wildly, trying to figure out how to get out of this.

There was nothing that could help me and no way to escape. I was glued to the spot, and their fingers would reach me at any moment.

Then a new clarity suddenly hit me. This was where I had to come. The women were right. I needed to find them. They would help me.

I belonged with them.

7

BELIAL

My door burst open. I sat straight up in bed, instantly on high alert. Who would break into my house at night—
Oh, right.

Eira came running into my room, dressed in nothing but the shirt I'd loaned her. I hardly had time to think about her being in my room before my eyes dropped to her legs. The shirt barely covered the tops of her thighs, and I found my cock hardening at the sight.

I'd already been awake when she'd busted through my door, since I didn't need to sleep anymore. I did still try to rest, more out of habit than anything, but one of the perks of being an Elder God was that I didn't need food, sleep, or water anymore. No, instead I had an insatiable thirst to steal souls, although it had been much weaker ever since meeting her, like her mere presence nearby calmed the urge. I'd been tempted to stare at her while she slept, trying to figure out what made her different, but I'd forced myself to stay in my room instead.

Eira's eyes dropped to my naked chest, her mouth opening slowly. At first, she seemed as caught up in the lust as I was, but then she shook her head violently and then looked back up at my face. Still, words seemed to fail her.

"Have you come to try to kill me again?" I asked, stretching my arms behind my head in a way that I knew would draw her attention. "Or are you in my bedroom for something else?"

Her eyes widened at my words, and her nostrils flared a little as her eyes traced the tattoos on my arms and the muscles in my chest, before going lower, to where the sheet had pooled around my hips. I always slept in the nude. Who knew it would be useful to put a mouthy shifter in her place?

"No way in hell," Eira finally spat.

"I can take you to Hell if you'd prefer, though I assure you my bed is more comfortable."

Eira huffed out an annoyed breath. "Could you shut up for two seconds? I had a...dream."

"What kind of dream?" I asked, arching an eyebrow.

"Not that kind." She rubbed her hands over her arms as if they were cold. "There were these two women..." She paused and then shook her head. "I don't know if *women* is a good descriptor. They had these long claws and hair made out of snakes. They told me to find them."

A chill ran down my spine at her description. I had a feeling I knew who she'd been dreaming about, though I hoped I was wrong. I slid out of bed, my thoughts moving quickly as I planned what to do next, but then Eira gasped and turned around. *Oh, right. Naked.*

"Can you at least give me a warning next time?" she growled. "And put some damn clothes on!"

"You're in my bedroom," I reminded her. "What, did you like what you saw a little too much?"

"In your dreams," Eira snapped.

I pulled on some loose sweatpants so Eira could focus, because I was sure she wouldn't be able to if I stayed naked. No matter how much fun it was to tease her, I needed to figure out if this dream that had freaked her out so much was actually anything to be worried about.

"I might know who you saw," I said. "The Furies. Did you happen to see a third one?"

Eira shook her head, frowning. "No, just the two."

"That's odd. They always come in a group of three. Never less." I grabbed a t-shirt and pulled it on. "Are you sure that's what you saw? Could it have been something else? Describe them to me again."

Eira looked annoyed, her hands going to her hips. "Yes, that's what I saw. They had snakes for hair, nails dripping with blood, and auras of color around them—one green and one red. I couldn't see their faces."

"That's how they looked in the old days when they walked the Earth." I ran a hand along my jaw, as I took in this new complication. "They're Elder Gods, and should be trapped in Void like most of the others. They have the ability to send images and dreams to people, even across great distances, but they shouldn't be able to do that unless they were somehow here in this realm."

"The Furies?" Eira asked.

"Yes, goddesses of anger, jealousy, and vengeance. They caused a lot of havoc in ancient times, before they were sealed away with the rest of the Elder Gods. But no one's heard anything about them in centuries, as far as I know."

"Well, that's what I saw." She bit her lip, her eyes distant. "I feel this odd compulsion to go to them, like I can't help myself, even now. I'm fighting it, but it's like someone's attached a string in my stomach and is pulling on it."

Shit. This was really not good. My parents and I were supposed to be the only Elder Gods on Earth right now, but if the Furies were somehow getting into people's heads, they had to be close "I wonder if they got the other shifters that way."

"You think they're the ones who are getting the shifters? I guess that would make sense." She tapped her finger on her lips as she thought, and I found myself looking at them again, wondering what they tasted like.

"Where were you in the dream?" I asked, trying to tear my own thoughts away from her allure.

"There was this old roller coaster that looked like it hadn't been used in years. It was in a theme park, and the whole thing was abandoned. There was a big pond or lake at the edge of it, and the Furies rose out of that."

I nodded slowly. "Sounds like Jazzland. It was an amusement park on the edge of New Orleans that was abandoned after it was destroyed by Hurricane Katrina."

"Sounds creepy," Eira said, shuddering.

"Very. It's rumored to be haunted, but then again, what isn't haunted in New Orleans?"

Eira shrugged at that and followed me from my bedroom to the living room. She didn't seem to be interested in going back to sleep, so I headed for the kitchen and started the coffee maker. Through the windows, the horizon was starting to lighten, and the sun would be coming up soon.

Eira sat at the island counter while the coffee began brewing. I stood over the sink and stared out the window at the city as it woke up, though it would still be hours before it really got moving. I'd never even considered that another Elder God might be loose, let alone *two*. Fucking hell.

My guest didn't speak either, her eyes staring off into space as though she was reliving the horrors of the dream. A fierce protective urge settled over me at the thought of the Furies targeting her, and I found myself pulling out some old cereal from my cupboard and pouring it into a bowl for her. I didn't have much food in my place anymore, but she needed to eat something. I added some milk, which I kept for my coffee, and then slid it in front of her.

"What's this?" she asked, blinking at it.

"Breakfast." I poured her a cup of coffee next. "How do you like your coffee? Black like your heart?"

She scowled at me, but at least the vacant look in her eyes was gone. "With lots of sugar and milk, actually."

"Ah, you're one of those types who likes coffee that doesn't taste like coffee."

"Exactly," she said, as she poured a ridiculous amount of stuff into her mug. "Why would the Furies be luring shifters to them?"

"I don't know, but it can't be good. The Furies are incredibly dangerous." I took a swig of coffee before continuing. "Like all Elder

Gods, they embody primordial elements of the universe and can't be completely destroyed. They were originally good, seeking to take out the evil of the world, but they got bloodthirsty and decided that *all* humans needed to be punished."

Eira snorted as she stirred her cereal. "Sounds a lot like what you're doing."

I leaned forward on the counter, my eyes narrowing at her. "I only kill those who have hurt others. People who need to be stopped, who the police can't or won't deal with."

Eira shrugged. "You're still a murderer. No matter how you try to justify it."

"You were going to murder me too, where you not?"

"That's different," she said. "I was stopping you from killing someone else."

"Exactly the same thing I was doing," I muttered, but I knew she wouldn't listen. She was too damn stubborn and had already created this narrative in her head where I was the bad guy. Okay, fine, I'd killed her father, but he'd needed to be stopped before he destroyed the whole freaking world.

"Go get dressed," I said curtly as I set my mug in the sink. "We're going to Jazzland to figure out why you're dreaming about it."

"We're going now?" Eira asked as she slid off the stool. I carefully didn't look at her exposed legs. I didn't need to tempt myself any more than I already was. It was clear that we weren't going to be anything more than reluctant allies, but that didn't seem to matter to my dick.

"Why wait?" I asked with a shrug.

"Fine with me," she said, rubbing at her stomach with a frown. "The need to go there is getting stronger every minute."

"Even more reason to go sooner than later. You can have the first shower."

She headed for the bathroom, and I watched the door long after she had disappeared behind it. The sound of the shower turned on and desire raged inside of me, as unquenchable as my thirst for death. I wanted to follow her into the bathroom, to see what would happen if I climbed in with her and began soaping that smooth skin or slid my fingers between those lush thighs.

Instead, I stomped back into my room and slammed the door, then grabbed my cock in my pants and jerked it hard, trying to relieve the pressure there. I pictured Eira soaping herself, running her hands along her body, as my hand slid along my cock, faster and faster. Then I imagined myself bending her over and fucking her from behind as the water sprayed onto us, while she cried my name and begged for more. The thought had me coming hard into my hand, but when I was done, I only wanted more. Only she could truly sate me.

Fuck. This non-stop pull toward Eira was becoming a real problem. Even worse, I had a feeling I knew what it was. I'd been trying to deny it ever since we met, but the urge to mate was only growing stronger by the minute. Soon I feared it would become overwhelming, and we'd be unable to stop what was coming next.

I knew this, because I'd lived through it once before—and this time it felt even stronger. Was it possible to have a second fated mate?

And how could I have one at all, when I had no soul?

8

EIRA

The urge to find the Furies, if that's truly who they were, grew with every moment that passed. By the time I followed Belial outside to his garage, the incessant pull was almost painful, like I was being dragged forward by my ankles, and only sheer willpower stopped me from dropping everything and taking off in a run. Well, maybe sheer willpower plus the other strange attraction I was feeling toward Belial. My pull toward him was equally strong, and at times it felt like I was going to be torn apart between the two conflicting forces.

He swung the keys around his finger as he circled a black Ducati motorcycle in the middle of his garage. He climbed on the bike with ease, and I hated how my eyes followed him, devouring his every movement. Seeing him naked earlier had set something off in me like a ticking time bomb of lust, and now I couldn't stop drooling over the asshole, even though I definitely was not going to fuck him. Even if he was the hottest guy I'd ever seen.

"Get on," he said, once he was seated on the bike.

"You have wings and a spectral horse, yet you ride a motorcycle?" I asked, mostly to hide my apprehension at climbing onto the bike behind him. There was not much room there, which meant I would be pressed along that big, hard body for the entire journey. I wanted it and dreaded it all at once.

"You can turn into a wolf, but you don't run around the city like that, do you?" Belial shot back. "I've been alive for thousands of years on Earth because I know how to blend in with humans."

"Walking around in a hooded cape at night is not exactly 'blending in,'" I said.

He snorted at that, but eyed me closely. "How old are you, anyway?"

"I just turned forty," I said, standing a little taller. Among immortal demons, age was measured in centuries, not decades, but I wasn't ashamed of my youth.

Belial let out a sharp laugh. "You're not even a century old. Practically still a child."

"You didn't think I was a child when you almost kissed me last night, old man," I snapped.

"And you definitely didn't think I was an old man when you ogled my naked body this morning. Now hurry up and get on the bike already."

I huffed and climbed onto the bike behind him. He wore a t-shirt that clung to his muscular chest—which, yes, I'd seen in great detail this morning—and showed off the tattoos that ran all along his arms. I tried not to touch him, but then the bike lurched forward and I found myself clinging to Belial to stay on it as we zoomed out of the garage and onto the street. The second my hands wrapped around those strong arms I felt that annoying spark between us, which only made me want to press my entire body against his. And that spot of his neck in my face was just begging for me to lean forward and set my mouth there.

I closed my eyes and breathed in deeply, trying to get myself under control as we drove out of the French Quarter and onto the highway. Between Belial and the Furies, I was losing my damn mind. Luckily, the ride was shorter than I thought it would be, and before I knew it, Belial was killing the engine on his bike. We were just off the side of a deserted road with dense plants on either side of us, and he gestured for me to hop off, then hid the bike in some shrubbery.

"Is this the place?" I asked, as my gut tried to tug me forward. *Keep going, almost there,* it seemed to whisper deep inside me.

Belial nodded. "We'll walk the rest of the way. Stay alert in case we're attacked."

"You know what would help with that?" I asked as we started moving through the trees and bushes. "If you took these cuffs off me so I could shift or use magic."

Belial kept charging through the foliage without looking back. "Not going to happen."

"I'm not going to run, if that's what you're worried about. I'm here to find out what happened to my brothers and the other shifters. I need answers."

"I'm less worried about you running and more about you trying to kill me again."

I rolled my eyes. "You're really hung up on that, aren't you? Especially for a guy who supposedly can't be killed."

"It's more of an annoyance than a real problem," Belial growled. "Thanks to you, that shifter got away last night. He'll probably be out there tonight trying to kill someone else. Which means I'll have to be out there too to make sure he doesn't. And if he does kill some innocent person? That's on you."

"Once again, the only person I saw trying to commit murder was you." I picked at the silver cuffs on my wrists, wishing I could get them off. "But if you're so worried, I'll help you watch over your city tonight. As long as you remove the cuffs, that is."

"Nope."

I shrugged. "Well, I had to try."

"Shut up and stay close," he said, as we came to the edge of the bushes.

In front of us was a faded, rusty sign that said, "Six Flags New Orleans" and below it, "Closed For Storm," except the first O was missing. We continued forward and climbed over a fence, while the Louisiana heat washed over me. With my shifter and Winter fae blood, I always preferred a cool, dark night over a sunny day, but if we did run into a group of demons, they'd be weaker at this time. Most imps and shifters would usually be sleeping now. That could give us an advantage.

Up ahead, rusted roller coasters loomed over the entire abandoned amusement park, which was somehow creepier in real life than it had been in my dream. We passed empty buildings that once sold food and tourist gifts, but were now covered in graffiti, their windows broken, their doors hanging off the hinges. You could almost hear the echoes of children playing and laughing along the cracked cement, a reminder that a place like this should never be so empty and lifeless. No wonder people thought it was haunted.

I lifted my nose to the air, hoping to catch the scent of another living being in this park with my shifter senses, but then I remembered the damn cuffs that blocked my magic. Damn Belial. I would get these cuffs off somehow.

The rest of the park was just as desolate, although nature had crept in and was slowly taking over the area. Debris littered the area, weeds and plants had grown up over everything, and I jumped at the sight of an actual alligator sitting beside the remains of a carousel. I nudged Belial but he just shrugged like he saw alligators all the time, but *he* still had his powers. I was basically a defenseless human right now.

Join us, a voice whispered in my ear. I whipped around, looking to see if anyone was there, but saw no one but Belial. "Did you hear that?"

"Hear what?" Belial asked, giving me an odd look.

I opened my mouth to tell him, but before I could, a rustling sound in the bushes caught our attention. Someone was out there, moving toward us. No—a lot of someones, and they were coming from every direction, forming a circle around us. My hands formed into fists, and I wished again that I had my magic or at least a weapon of some sort. Belial just stood beside me, taking it all in, his face hard and his eyes completely fearless.

Even without my wolf senses I could tell most of these people were shifters from the way they moved, although I guessed a few of them were imps too. They drew closer, surrounding us completely, cutting off every escape route. There was no chance to turn and head back to the entrance, and short of Belial breaking out his wings and flying us out, we were trapped.

"I'm pretty sure we just walked into an ambush," I muttered.

Before either of us could discuss what we were going to do to get the hell out of here, two giant wolves prowled forward. One was black with red eyes, while the other was white with blue eyes, but otherwise they were identical. As they stepped through the brush, their claws burned it and turned it to ash.

My heart leaped at the sight of my brothers, completely unharmed, and I rushed forward. "Skoll! Hati!"

Belial grabbed my arm and held me back with his supernatural strength. I glared at him and jerked at my arm, but he didn't let me go.

"They're my brothers, you big dumb oaf!" I turned back to them. "I'm so glad to see you guys. You have no idea how worried I've been. Why haven't you returned my calls or anything?"

Neither one of them answered, and both of my brothers stared at me like they had no idea who I was. When I stepped toward them again, they growled low in their throats.

Belial shoved me behind him, protecting me with his body. Which was totally unnecessary, because my older brothers would never hurt me. Would they?

"What are you doing here?" I asked them, stepping out from behind Belial.

"We're working with the Furies now," Skoll said, his wolf voice like a low growl. His red eyes blazed with inner fire as he stared us down like he was about to lunge.

Hati's claws scraped at the ground, turning the grass to ash. "You should join us too."

I frowned at my brothers, wondering why they were acting this way. Sure, they were both assholes, but this was different. This was wrong.

"Where are the Furies?" Belial asked.

"You..." Skoll said with a snarl. "We've been waiting for a chance to get you alone."

"Thanks for bringing him to us, Eira," Hati added. "Now we will tear him apart."

I held up a hand. "Yeah, I already tried that and it didn't go so well. The bastard's basically unkillable. But that's not why I'm here, anyway."

Hati crept closer, teeth bared. "Maybe you just weren't up to the task."

"Now it's our turn," Skoll said at his side. "Time to die."

Shadows gathered around Belial as he faced them down. "Try it, and we'll see who ends up dead."

I stepped in front of Belial this time, my pulse racing. I couldn't let my brothers attack—they had no idea how dangerous Belial was, and they'd probably both end up dead. But how would I stop them? They looked like they were about to tear through me to get to Belial.

"Now, now, let's not fight with our guests," a woman's voice said from behind us.

Hati and Skoll stopped immediately at the sound, lowering their heads in submission, though they continued to glare at us with obvious hatred. I gaped at the sight of them, then turned toward the voice.

Two hooded figures made their way through the ranks of shifters and imps, who parted around them without having to be told. I didn't have to see the women's faces to know that these were the Furies. My hackles went up and a chill ran across my skin as both of them stopped in front of us and threw their hoods back. They looked completely different from the women from my dream—the hair snakes and bloody claws were gone, for one thing—but they still radiated the same power.

"Welcome," one of the women said. She was tall and thin, with short black hair, tanned skin, and features that were more stern than pretty. "We knew you would come."

"You sent me the dream, didn't you?" I asked.

"Yes, and we're so pleased you brought Death with you," the other woman replied. Unlike her sister—who she looked nothing like—she was one of the most beautiful women I'd ever seen, with long, shiny chestnut hair and legs that seemed to go on for miles, along with a slitted dress to show them off. "We've been wondering when he would visit us."

"I see you've found yourselves some new bodies to possess," Belial drawled. "Which ones are you?"

"I am Anger, though you may call me Alecto," the black-haired one said, somehow making it sound like a threat. She gestured toward her sister. "And this is Jealousy, who some call Megaera."

"How did you get to Earth?" Belial asked.

"A portal opened in Void, and we felt Death calling," Megaera said.

Belial crossed his arms. "I didn't call you."

"Not you. The previous Death." Alecto's eyes narrowed, as if this was a sore spot. "We came through, but the portal closed too quickly for our third sister to make it. Now we must bring her to Earth, so we can continue our goal of punishing wicked humans."

"We served the previous Death," Megaera said, batting her eyelashes at Belial. "We would be willing to work with you too. We can give you *whatever* you need."

Jealousy rose up in me at the way she looked at Belial, and then I realized that was what she wanted. I suspected they both inspired and fed on the emotions they embodied.

To my relief, Belial didn't seem to care one bit about her offer, because he let out a sharp laugh. "How about you serve me by going back to Void? You don't belong on Earth, and there's only room for one Elder God in this city."

Alecto's eyes suddenly glowed red as she looked at him with pure fury. Apparently Belial's ability to piss off anything with a heartbeat extended to the Furies too. "If you won't work with us, then stay out of our way." The 'or else' was implied.

"Why are you gathering shifters and imps here?" I asked, as Belial stared them down.

Megaera turned her gaze on me and smiled in a way that felt almost predatory. "Those who are attuned to wrath and jealousy are simply drawn to us. You've felt it yourself, haven't you?"

"Let them go," Belial said in a low, dangerous voice. "These people are not yours to control."

Megaera laughed. "What if they don't want to leave?"

My brothers moved beside the two women, brushing up against them in a protective and almost loving way. They snarled at us, making it clear they would defend the Furies if we tried to attack them. The other people all around us seemed to step forward too, reminding us we were surrounded and outnumbered. Belial squared his shoulders and gathered more shadows around him, obviously ready to fight. But if we attacked, a lot of lives would be lost, and I wasn't sure who would come out the victor.

I touched Belial's arm to get his attention. "We should go."

He jerked his gaze to the spot where I was touching him, and then his eyes lifted to meet mine. His brow furrowed, like he was torn on what to do, but then he nodded. He shot the Furies a sharp look. "This isn't over."

I sighed and released him, relieved that he wasn't going to attack. We started to leave, but then a shiver ran down my spine.

Stay, a voice said in my head. *Join us.*

Both Furies stared at me intently, along with my brothers. I shook my head and looked away, trying to ignore the voices filling my head.

You have so much wrath in your heart. Don't you want vengeance?

Only we can give you what you want.

Shut up, I shot back, covering my ears even though I knew it wouldn't help. Belial gave me a questioning look.

Our sister is the Elder God of vengeance.

She can help you defeat Belial.

All you have to do is help us bring her to Earth...

I stopped dead in my tracks as their voices filled my head and took hold of me. Vengeance. Yes. I wanted that with such a deep pull that I actually felt myself take a couple of steps toward them. I would finally get closure for my father's death and extract my revenge on Belial. Rage surged inside me at the thought of him, along with jealousy of his powers. Why should he be alive, when my father wasn't? He had to die to pay for his sins. All it would take was—

"Eira, what is it?" Belial asked, gripping my arms tight.

His voice and his touch shook me out of the Furies' trance. I gaped at him as my head cleared and the rage and jealousy died down. Shit, that had been intense. Still, I couldn't deny that their offer wasn't tempting...

"Nothing," I said, taking a deep breath to steady myself. I jerked my eyes away from the Furies and focused on Belial instead. "Let's get out of here."

9

EIRA

I walked into Belial's bar in a daze, and it wasn't until we were seated at the counter that I realized we hadn't gone back to his apartment. I glanced around, surprised Belial wasn't worried about people seeing me in cuffs, but the place was empty except for us.

"Don't worry, it's not open yet," Belial said, like he could read my mind. "I thought you could use a drink, along with some food."

I nodded, still shaken by what we'd uncovered at the amusement park. While it was a relief to know my brothers and all those other missing shifters were alive, it was just as disturbing to see they'd fallen under the Furies' spell and become completely different people. If I'd stayed, would I have ended up like them too?

Belial poured me a beer, and then disappeared into another room behind the bar. I stared at my drink, going over everything that had happened, searching for more clues or a reason as to why the Furies were doing this. Eventually, Belial came back with a burger and fries, and set it down in front of me. The smell of hot feed made me perk up a little.

"Where did you get this?" I asked.

"The cooks are already here," Belial replied. "It's not poisoned, I promise. You look like you're about two minutes away from passing out. Eat."

He wasn't wrong. I ducked my head and dug into the surprisingly delicious food, while he watched me like he was studying me again.

"You really don't eat at all?" I asked.

He plucked a fry off my plate and tossed it in his mouth. "I can eat. I just don't need to."

I pulled my plate away from him. "Hey, get your own damn fries."

He smirked and reached for another one. "You're in my bar, so I think technically they're my fries."

I slapped at his hand. "Nope, you gave them to me. Mine now."

The smirk turned into an amused grin. "Would it make you feel better if I got my own food?"

"Much."

"Fine." He stomped into the back again, leaving me alone for a few minutes. Unfortunately, that left me alone again with my thoughts.

I didn't trust the Furies at all. Why were they luring shifters there? Did it have something to do with bringing their missing third sister to Earth? I shuddered as I remembered how it had felt to be under their compulsion, with their words rattling around my head. I needed to get my brothers away from them before they ended up hurt...or worse.

But a tiny voice inside me was curious about their offer too. I still wanted vengeance for my father, but I'd found no way to defeat Belial so far. If the Furies were telling the truth, they could help me defeat him. Which I still wanted. Right?

I wasn't so sure anymore. The last twenty-four hours had thrown everything in my world upside down. I'd come to New Orleans with the image of a clear-cut killer in my head, and I was ready to make him pay. But Belial had turned out to be different than I'd expected, and now I didn't know what to think. Yes, he was a total dick, and if he didn't take these cuffs off my wrist soon I was going to scream, but I didn't believe he was a cold-blooded murderer anymore. He seemed to really care about protecting New Orleans and finding out what was happening with the missing people, plus he'd protected me at the amusement park. Not to mention, there was that intense pull I felt toward him, though I was trying to ignore that as much as I possibly could.

Belial returned with his own burger and fries, but he remained standing behind the bar as he ate them. Did he want to keep some distance between us? Or was he standing over me to remind me he was the boss here?

I sighed as I finished off the last of my fries. "What are we going to do about the Furies?"

"We?" Belial asked, arching an eyebrow. "Are we on the same side now?"

"No, but we have a common enemy."

"Glad to know you feel that way. I was worried you might go over to their side, like the other shifters did."

"I almost did, until you shook me out of it," I admitted. "The Furies were inside my head, trying to convince me to join them. But more than that, there was this compulsion that I couldn't resist, like a voice inside me telling me to do whatever they said. By the time you stopped me, I was about two steps away from joining their little cult."

Belial stroked the dark stubble on his chin. "That must be how they got the other demons to fall under their sway. Shifters feed on wrath, while imps feed on envy, which Alecto and Megaera can create and control. If they used that in conjunction with their ability to get into people's heads, it's possible they could compel the demons to join them. But since you're part fae, perhaps you're more able to resist them."

"Maybe," I said, though I wasn't sure how good I'd been at resisting them. I had been closer to giving up and letting them have me than I'd like to admit, and I wasn't sure if I'd be able to stop them if they tried again. "They've turned my brothers into loyal guard dogs. How can we break their control?"

"I'm still figuring that out." He took a long sip of his beer as he considered. "Although sending them back to Void would do it."

"What exactly is this Void place?" I asked.

"An alternate realm where the Elder Gods are trapped. That's all anyone really knows. It's been sealed off for thousands of years."

"If it's sealed off, how are the Furies going to bring their sister over?"

"I wish I knew. They don't have a key to Void, or they would have done it already, but there are always other ways to open portals. It just depends on how much they know, and how far they're willing to go."

"But there must be a way to defeat them," I said. *And you*, I mentally added.

"They're Elder Gods, like me, so they can't be killed," he said. "We could kill the bodies they're possessing, but just like you can't remove all anger or jealousy from the world, we can't destroy them either. We need to either contain them in a specially crafted tomb made by the fae, or use a Void key to open a portal to send them back."

"And we don't have either one of those," I said with a groan.

"Nope."

Getting a tomb made by the fae would take too long, I suspected. If they agreed to help us at all. You never knew with the fae. "How do we get a Void key then?"

Belial smirked again, his eyes flashing with dark humor. "Why, so you can use it on me next?"

I hid my smile with my drink. "Well, now that you've given me the idea..."

He shook his head, but didn't seem especially worried. "My father had one, and together we were able to send Pestilence back to Void, but apparently we unknowingly let two Furies in at the same time. But the Void key was destroyed, and I'm not sure where to get another."

I tapped my fingers on the bar as I pondered our next move. "I could ask Loki. If there's anyone who knows how to find some rare artifact, it's probably him."

"Loki?" Belial practically spat the name. "Could we really trust anything the trickster tells us?"

"Do you have any better ideas?" I tilted my head, staring him down. "Ask your parents, maybe?"

He grimaced at that. "No way. Besides, they're in Hell right now, and I don't have a key to go *there* either."

"Sounds like Loki is our best option then." I extended my hand. "Give me back my phone and I'll text him now."

Belial scowled at me, but he reached in his pocket and got out my phone, then slid it along the bar. I grabbed it and immediately saw a message from my friend Mirabella asking me if I was okay. She was half-fae and half-demon like me, and together we'd worked as messengers between the two sides, going back and forth between Earth and Faerie. I'd given up the job once my father started his rebellion against Lucifer, but I'd remained friends with Mirabella through it all. I shot her off a quick reply, saying I was fine and I'd catch up with her soon, then sent another message to Loki, asking if I could talk to him, noting that it was urgent. Hopefully he would respond quickly. Loki was the kind of guy who called on you when he felt like it, not the other way around.

"I sent him a message," I said, and then quickly stashed the phone in my pocket before Belial could try to take it away. "Hopefully he responds soon. He'll likely want to meet in person."

Belial rested his hands on the bar on either side of me, towering over me. "If you're going to see him, I'm coming with you."

"Only if you play nice. He won't help us if you're rude."

"I'm always nice."

"We both know that's not true." I held up my cuffs. "If you were, you'd take these off and let me go back to my hotel."

"No, I think it's best I keep an eye on you." He cocked his head. "But I suppose we could get your things from the hotel."

"So you plan to keep me a prisoner for a while?" I asked, holding up my hands. The silver cuffs winked in the light, and his eyes fell to them.

"For now, yes. Show me you can be trusted, and maybe that will change."

"How exactly am I supposed to do that?" I asked, blowing out a breath in frustration.

He caught my wrists in his hands. "Stop fighting me and we'll find out."

At his touch, electricity seemed to zip along my skin, and my heart skipped a beat. His thumbs slowly rubbed my skin along the edge of the cuffs as he stared into my eyes, and within them I saw a hunger there that made my breath catch.

"I'm not fighting you," I said, my voice little more than a whisper. I bit my lip, and his gaze flickered to the motion, and then came back up to my eyes. The need in his eyes grew stronger, and he pulled me forward by the wrists, making me lean against the bar.

One of his hands came up to slide into my hair, turning my head slightly. His nose brushed along my neck as he breathed me in, and all I could do was melt into his touch, craving more. His breath moved across my skin lightly, traveling up my neck and to my chin and then to my mouth, where I eagerly waited for him to kiss me. Or throw me down on this bar and spread my legs for him.

Then a door banged open, and the spell was broken.

I jumped back, yanking away from Belial as I turned to face the sound. Yumi, the bartender from last night, stood in the doorway, her eyes moving between us. She looked at me suspiciously for a few moments and then headed toward the bar, shaking her head. Belial busied himself with tidying up our empty drinks, his face calm and collected, like we hadn't just been about to kiss...or more.

"Can you handle the bar tonight?" he asked Yumi. "I have something I need to handle."

"Of course." Yumi shot me another long glance, but nodded at Belial. "Be safe."

"It's not me you need to worry about," he said with a grunt as he stepped out from behind the bar.

"Are you so sure about that?" Yumi asked, crossing her arms as she stared at me.

What was her deal? Did she have a thing for Belial? Jealousy surged inside me at the thought, but I pushed it away. I felt her gaze burning holes in my back until we exited the bar.

10

EIRA

This time we took one of Belial's cars, a black Aston Martin, and headed into the Garden District along oak-shaded streets. Belial's hands were tight on the steering wheel the whole time, and a muscle in his jaw ticked in an almost rhythmic way. I wasn't sure what his problem was, and told myself I didn't care either.

His bad mood only got worse when we pulled up to the grand historic mansion with white columns and wrought-iron balconies. Hotel Immortelle had once been a wealthy family's home in the 1800s, but now it was a luxury hotel catering to demons and other supernaturals who visited the city. It was far more elegant than anywhere my brothers and I would have stayed on our own, but since we'd been visiting the city on official demon business, Loki had insisted we stay there. I couldn't deny the place was gorgeous though, and it was refreshing to stay at a hotel where they understood the special needs of demons. They even had lush, private grounds out back where shifters could roam freely in their animal forms.

A valet took the car and Belial scowled at the man, then looked up at the hotel like he was waiting for it to explode. "Get your things quickly."

"What's your problem?" I asked, as we stepped through the big black doors and into the lobby, which was just as luxurious as the rest of the hotel with an abundance of mirrors and gold gilding. A man by the front desk offered us aperitifs with or without blood (for the vampires, naturally), but we waved him away as we headed for the elevator.

"I've always hated this place."

"Any particular reason?"

"My father owns it," he said grudgingly. "We have some...issues. We've mostly worked them out, but I'd prefer to not hang around the place any more than I have to."

I should have known Lucifer owned the place. As ruler of the demons, he seemed to have his hand in just about everything. It was one reason my father had rebelled against him—too much power in the hands of one immortal ruler was dangerous. Of course, my father had failed and had paid the ultimate price for his crimes.

"Hard to imagine anyone having issues with you, with your glowing personality," I said as we entered the elevator, my voice dripping with sarcasm. "Especially Lucifer, since you tried to overthrow him with my father." I stabbed at the button for the third floor, while smooth jazz music played around us. "You know, before you killed him."

He shook his head. "You have no idea what happened with your father."

When the elevator door opened, I led the way down the hall toward my room, while Belial followed right at my heels. "So tell me what happened. From your point of view."

I swiped my key and the door clicked open. Inside, the room was large enough that we didn't feel cramped in it even with a huge four-posted bed and old-fashioned French furniture. My luggage was open in the corner with a few clothes spilling out of it. I tried not to feel self conscious as I slung a bra in alongside a shirt.

Belial sat in a wingback chair opposite the bed, and flipped on the Tiffany lamp beside him, causing the colored glass to shoot light across his handsome face. "Your father and I were...allies, if not exactly friends. We both wanted to see change come for the demons, and believed that a new ruler would be the best thing for everyone. So we decided to take down Lucifer, once and for all."

"Why?" I asked from the bathroom as I gathered up my toiletries. "He's your father."

"Lucifer had gone unchecked for too long. He was out of touch with what most demons wanted, and wouldn't listen to anyone who disagreed with him. He made rash decisions without consulting anyone, like ending the war with the angels and closing off Hell forever. But he's so damn powerful, no one dared oppose him openly."

"My father said similar things," I said. He'd always tried to keep me out of his rebellion against Lucifer, partly for my safety and partly to keep me more neutral since I worked as a messenger with the fae, but I'd heard him ranting about our ruler for my whole life. I'd never met Lucifer, but I'd been raised to hate him.

"The last person who had tried to oppose Lucifer...was me." Belial gave me a sardonic smirk as he continued. "That was what got me kicked out of Hell all those years ago. For my rebellion, he condemned me to live on Earth."

"The exiled prince," I said with a nod as I finished packing. Everyone in the demon world knew the story of Lucifer's eldest son trying to claim the throne, and being punished for it. It was no wonder Belial had some serious daddy issues. But with a father like Lucifer, who wouldn't?

"Yes, they love to call me that," Belial said, rolling his eyes. "But this time when I decided to overthrow my father, I wanted things to be different. Fenrir and I made a plan, and we got the help of some of the other Archdemons who felt the same way we did about Lucifer. Together we planned to awaken the Four Horsemen of the Apocalypse to defeat Lucifer, since he was too strong for any of us to take down on our own." His face darkened as he stared out the window, his eyes lost in the memory. "But once Pestilence was freed, I realized we'd made a huge mistake."

By now I'd finished packing, and I sat on the edge of the bed, eager to hear his story and finally have some answers. "Why did you change your mind?"

"Pestilence was too damn powerful and he wanted nothing more than to annihilate the entire world. That wasn't what I'd signed up for. Earth has been my home for centuries, and I didn't want it destroyed. I just wanted Lucifer overthrown."

"I mean, they are called the Four Horsemen of the *Apocalypse* for a reason," I said. "What did you think would happen?"

He scowled in response. "I was a fool. I'd been a child when the Four Horsemen were first defeated and entombed, but I'd forgotten how bad things had gotten then. Once Pestilence was freed and began spreading plague across the world, I knew I had to stop him. We freed War and I tried to use him to take down Pestilence, since the best way to defeat an Elder God is with another Elder God. But War needed a body to possess, as all Elder Gods do, and Lucifer sacrificed himself to save me from being possessed." His scowl only deepened at the memory, and he ran a hand through his hair. "My mother then became Famine to take *him* down."

I nodded slowly. "I was there when your mother freed Famine. My father needed me to open the portal to Faerie, where Famine was entombed, and I saw the horrible aftermath once she was set lose. Famine actually tried to possess my body." I shuddered a little at the memory of the Elder God draining my life away from me. "Your mother saved me when she let Famine possess her. Fenrir and I escaped before I saw what happened next though."

"She's impressive, isn't she? She's the reincarnation of Eve and has been many things in her past lives, but I think she's topped them all in her current life." He grinned at the mention of his mother, obviously fond of her. "She found a way to defeat the Elder God when it was inside her—basically resisting the possession while retaining all of the powers of Famine. She managed to save Lucifer, who defeated War and took possession of his own body again too."

"What happened next?" I asked. "How did Death get free?"

Belial's grin fell and darkness clouded his face again. "After all that happened, I couldn't stand against my father anymore. Yes, he'd fallen short as a leader many times, but he was still my father. He'd sacrificed himself to save me. He wasn't perfect, but he and I talked some things out, and he seemed open to changing how he ruled. But Fenrir didn't want to stop."

My muscles tensed, knowing what was coming. I had to know what happened, but I didn't want to hear it either.

"By then, most of our other allies had been killed, but Fenrir teamed up with Pestilence, thinking they would overthrow Lucifer together and then he would crown himself the new king of demons. They released Death, who possessed Fenrir's body, and they kidnapped my baby sister, Aurora, and took her to Hell." His hands clenched the sides of the chair at the memory. "My parents led an army into Hell to rescue her, and this time, I fought alongside them to rescue my sister and stop the Horsemen from destroying the world."

"And my father?" I asked, my voice barely above a whisper.

"By the time we fought, there was very little of him left inside his body. Death was completely in control, and I doubted Fenrir even wanted to fight him off. The only way to stop him was to kill him."

I swallowed, my throat dry, as I learned about this for the first time. My father had said it was too dangerous for me to come with him to Hell to release Death, and most of the shifters who had gone with him had either died or refused to talk about it. I'd learned about my father's death from my brothers, who had been there at the battle in Hell, but they hadn't told me all of this. They'd painted Belial as the villain, and made me crave vengeance for the death of our father, but now I knew the truth was a lot more complicated than I could have imagined. I'd loved my father, but he'd been no saint, and I'd seen him lose more and more of himself in his quest to become the king of demons near the end. Maybe I should have tried harder to stop him too.

Belial's eyes met mine. "I want you to know I took no joy in ending your father's life, and I did it quickly with the slash of my sword. He did not suffer."

I nodded and closed my eyes, letting his words soak in. A hollow, aching emptiness crept over me, replacing the anger that had burned within me little by little. I'd come to New Orleans for vengeance, but what I'd really needed were answers, and Belial had given those to me. Even if I didn't like them.

Belial's hand suddenly clasped mine, and my eyes snapped open. I took a shaky breath in, as I realized Belial wasn't the villain I'd painted him as. He'd made mistakes, just as my father had done, but he'd tried to make things right in the end...even if it had resulted in my father's death.

I wiped at my eyes as I asked, "But how did you become Death?"

He jerked his hand away from mine, his face going hard. "Once Fenrir was done, Death needed a new host, and we had no way to lock him up or send him to Void. He went after my sister, planning to possess her body, but she was just a baby." His voice shook a little, showing how much he cared for his sister. For *all* his family. "I told Death to take me instead, but after he possessed me, I was able to overcome the Elder God with the help of my family. I defeated him and became Death myself, instead of just a host body. And now I have to live with that for the rest of my life."

I sat on the bed, silent. My head was spinning with everything Belial had said. Grief settled over my shoulders like a shroud, but the burning need for vengeance was gone. My father had brought his death upon himself, and I had to accept that. I would always love him and miss him, but I could admit that he'd gone too far too.

"I didn't know," I said. "No one ever told me the whole story."

Belial stood up and crossed to the window, peering out at the darkening night sky. "It's not exactly a fun tale."

"No, but I should have known. He was my father and I loved him...but that doesn't mean he didn't make mistakes."

"We all did, and look where it got us." Belial turned back to me. "I never wanted to kill Fenrir, but I don't regret it either. I would do it again if I had to. Though we were once allies, we made our own choices and stood on opposite sides of the battle in the end." He moved to stand in front of me, towering over me with that strong, tall frame. "Now you must decide whether you want to stand against me too."

I stared up at him, my heart pounding wildly in my chest. A kaleidoscope of emotions flickered inside me, and I had no idea how to feel anymore. I'd once thought Belial was my enemy, but now he was my ally too. Would he become my enemy again when this was all over? And what about the overwhelming desire I felt for him whenever he was near?

But most of all, I worried that if I let go of the anger that consumed me, all that would be left was that aching emptiness—a loneliness and restlessness I had no way to fill.

"I haven't decided yet," I told Belial.

I stood and went to walk around Belial to grab my luggage, but he wrapped his hand around my upper arm to stop me. The point of contact flared icy-hot, and I stilled. When I tilted my head to look up at Belial, his lips were parted, as if on a word. That pull to lean in, to close the distance between us, struck me like a brick to the back of the skull. I swayed, and Belial's hand around my arm flexed and tightened minutely. It wasn't tight enough to hurt, and I could easily break out of it if I wanted, but I didn't want to.

"Eira," he whispered, and the sound of my name on his lips sent heat straight between my thighs. He said my name like it pained him, like he was desperate for something only I could help him with. "I don't want to be your enemy."

I didn't know how to answer that, especially when his other hand caressed my cheek, his thumb brushing against my lips, while he looked at me with so much need it actually burned. I was suddenly hyper-aware of the bed behind us, realizing Belial could easily throw me down on it. Did I want that? *Yes*, my mind whispered. *Take me. Take everything.*

I opened my mouth, not sure what exactly was going to come out of it, but before I could get a single word out, my phone chimed and the moment was broken. I shook myself free of Belial's hold, struggling to take a deep breath. *That was too close.*

I put some distance between us as I pulled my phone out of my pocket. A message had arrived from Loki. *I'm waiting at the bar for you.*

"Loki's downstairs waiting for me."

"That's convenient," Belial said, raising his eyebrows. "I didn't realize he was in town."

"Me either." I picked up my luggage, but Belial plucked it from my hands like it weighed nothing. If he was affected by what had just happened between us, I would never be able to tell. His face was completely impassive as he opened the door for me. Gone was the look of hunger in his eyes, and I found myself missing it.

I shook my head to clear it from those sorts of thoughts. I didn't have time to be thinking about Belial throwing me down on a bed and having his way with me, not when there were bigger problems to deal with, like stopping the Furies. It was time to focus on that, and I'd deal with the strange attraction between me and Belial later.

11

BELIAL

I grimaced as soon as I spotted Loki. It had been quite a few centuries since I'd seen him last, and even though his appearance had changed, he somehow hadn't changed at all. As an imp, he was a master of illusion and deception, and he was known as the world's greatest trickster for a reason. Somehow I doubted he'd become any more civilized since becoming an Archdemon either.

In his current form he had shiny black hair, perfect cheekbones, and a mischievous smile that never met his eyes. He lounged in a corner booth of the bar in an expensive suit, looking like he owned the place, but his eyes were watching everything, his clever brain always calculating.

Eira rushed toward Loki with an excited hop in her step, but I didn't bother hiding my dislike of the imp as we approached, letting the scowl show on my face.

In return, Loki looked at me like he'd come across a dead fish in his house. "I'd say it's a pleasure," he said smoothly, "but I'd be lying."

"We both know that's what you're good at," I quipped back.

Loki's smile turned downright devious as we stared each other down. We had our reasons to hate each other. Back when I'd first tried to overthrow my father, Loki had been my friend and ally, and together we'd planned the coup against Lucifer. But right when I'd needed Loki the most, he'd betrayed me. At the very last minute he'd switched sides, warning Lucifer of the attack, including the team sneaking into the castle from the back. The team that had contained my first mate, Soria, who'd died that night before I could save her. All so Loki could save his own tail. Cowardly bastard.

But Loki had reason to hate me too. After all, I'd killed his son, Fenrir.

Eira stepped between us, breaking the rising tension before it could escalate into a fight, or something worse. "Thanks for meeting with us so quickly."

Loki's gaze snapped toward Eira and he rose to his feet to embrace her. "Eira, darling. Always lovely to see you."

For a split second, I watched his face soften. Even if he didn't like me, hopefully his love for Eira would be enough to compensate. From that look alone, I knew that it wasn't likely that he would trick his own granddaughter.

"Sit and have a drink with me," Loki said, gesturing at the table. Eira slid into the booth across from him, and I grudgingly scooted in beside her.

"What are you doing here?" I asked, trying to keep the hostility out of my voice. I'd expected that he'd call her, not show up out of the blue at my father's hotel.

"When I didn't hear from Eira after I sent her on this mission, I came to New Orleans to make sure she was okay," he said, tilting his chin up at me like he was daring me to question it.

"Is that right?" I asked, meeting his gaze head on. I didn't believe him for a second. If he was in the city, why hadn't he contacted her sooner, or reached out first? If there was one thing Loki was good at it was lying, and he would do it more often than telling the truth.

But Eira didn't seem bothered by his answer and shot me an exasperated look. "Be nice," she muttered.

"Let me get you some drinks," Loki said, breaking my stare first. It didn't feel like a win. "You both look like you need some."

"Good idea," Eira said.

Loki flagged down the server and we ordered our drinks, before he spoke again. "What have you found out so far?"

"I found my brothers. They're alive, along with the other shifters and imps that went missing, but they're not exactly safe." She bit her lip and glanced at me, like she wasn't sure if she should keep going.

"What do you mean?" Loki asked.

"Two of the Furies are here," I said. "Alecto and Megaera. They're trying to bring Tisiphone over from Void next."

Loki's eyes widened slightly. "The Furies? That's...unexpected."

"They're gathering together shifters and imps like cultists, putting them under some sort of spell, using anger and envy to control them," Eira said, rubbing her hands over her arms as if she was cold. I had the sudden urge to wrap my arms around her, to protect her from whatever was bothering her, whether it was a chill in the bar or the memories in her head.

"I see," Loki said, frowning as he tapped his fingers slowly on the side of his drink. "Anger and envy. Yes, of course."

"They need to be stopped," I said. "You know what kind of damage they can cause."

"Yes, I remember," Loki said, giving me a hard look.

"We need to send the Furies back to Void, but we don't have a key," Eira said. "That's why I contacted you."

"Of course," Loki said, leaning back with an amused grin. "And lucky you did, because I doubt anyone else could help you with this problem."

"Do you have one?" Eira asked, sitting up straighter.

"No, but I did once. I hid it in Faerie to keep it safe." He tilted his head. "I can't get to it, but perhaps you can."

"How?" I asked.

Loki shot me another amused glance. "Eira has a key to Faerie. Didn't you know?"

I gritted my teeth. It took pretty much all of my willpower to not punch that smug look off of his thin, foxy face. "No, she failed to mention it."

Eira shrugged. "I used to be a messenger between Earth and Faerie, and I still have a key. There was no reason to mention it before since it was here at the hotel."

"But surely an Archdemon such as yourself can get to Faerie too," I said, giving Loki a pointed look. "There must be another reason you need us to get the key."

"Well, there is one tiny little complication," he admitted.

"Here we go," I muttered.

Loki ignored my comment as he continued. "I left it in a cave with a basilisk for safekeeping. The beast can see through illusion magic, which is why I can't get it myself. Of course that also means that no fae can get to it either, especially since it can kill with a single glance. A perfect hiding spot, don't you think?"

I narrowed my eyes at him. "If it can see through your illusion magic, how did you get it there in the first place?"

"I had help." Loki smiled mysteriously at me. I expected him to elaborate, but in his typical, slippery manner, he didn't say more.

Eira cleared her throat. "Okay, so it's in a cave with a basilisk that you can't get past because it sees through your illusion magic and can kill with a look. What makes you think we can get past it?"

"Because you have the God of Death sitting here with you. It shouldn't be an issue for him."

"And what do you want in return?" I asked, because obviously Loki wanted something. He wouldn't help us unless it benefited him in some way.

His smile turned predatory. "I'll tell you where the cave is, as long as you give me the key once you're done with it."

Eira opened her mouth, but I put a hand on her arm to stop her. There was no way I was getting Loki a key to Void. I said one simple word: "No."

"It's mine anyway," Loki said, waving his hand idly. "I'm simply letting you borrow it for a while."

"Yeah, after we go on a deadly mission to retrieve it for you." I snorted. "How do I know you won't turn around and use it on me the moment we hand it over?"

"Are you worried I'll send you to Void for killing my son?" Loki asked, voice carefully neutral.

Eira looked between us, her jaw clenched. She still didn't know how to feel about me, even after learning the whole story, and I wasn't sure she'd defend me from Loki if he tried.

"It wasn't personal," I gritted out.

"You of all people should know that death is always personal," Loki said, and his voice took on a sharper tone.

Touché, I thought. I met his gaze and stared him down again. This time the tension rose even higher, crackling through the air like lightning, and Eira's presence beside us wasn't enough to stop it.

She blew out a breath. "If you two are done having a dick measuring contest, we still have things to resolve."

Loki sat back, folding his hands on the table. "I give my word not to use the Void key against you if you give it to me. But I can't speak for Eira, of course. If she wants to use it, I won't stop her." He seemed wickedly delighted by the idea of Eira using the key against me.

"Fine," I ground out. "I agree to give you the key once we're done with it. If it survives the encounter, of course."

Loki frowned, as if he hadn't expected that, and his eye twitched. But I'd learned long ago it was always wise to go above and beyond when bargaining with the trickster.

"Very well," Loki said. "I give you my word."

"Your word's not good enough," I growled. "We tried that once, or don't you remember? I want blood."

Loki rolled his eyes. "You're always so dramatic."

He pulled out a small knife from his suit and cut his hand, before he passed it to me. I slashed my skin in the same spot, and we clasped hands and met eyes.

"I swear on my blood," I said, and Loki repeated the words. Power surged between us as we nodded, our bargain struck.

"Excellent," Loki said, as he released my hand and used a napkin to wipe the blood off himself.

"Where exactly do we go in Faerie?" Eira asked.

"I'll draw you a map."

"Good," I said. "Then Eira can open up the portal, and I'll go through alone and get the key."

Eira's gaze snapped to me. "No fucking way. I'm going too."

"It's not safe for you." My chest tightened at the thought of Eira facing down a basilisk. Unlike me, she wouldn't be immune to its killing gaze, and I was worried about her going up against it. I hated the idea of her being in danger. Why was I so worried about her? Wasn't she about two decisions away from stabbing me in the back? But there was something that connected us. *Are you my mate?*

Eira snorted. "When was the last time you were in Faerie? You need me to navigate the place. You'll never get to this cave without me."

"She has a point," Loki said.

I shot him a glare, and then downed my forgotten drink. Faerie was notoriously difficult to navigate, and I'd never been a fan of the place. Plus, other than that brief trip with my mother to free Famine, I hadn't been there in years. "Fine. But you'll do what I say when we fight the basilisk."

"Deal. *If* you take these damn cuffs off of me first." She shook her wrist in front of me, the silver of the cuffs catching the light.

Oh right, the cuffs. There was a good chance that the moment I took them off she'd be right back to flinging ice spears into my back again, but we needed her magic in Faerie. Could I trust her? I wasn't sure, even though something in my gut told me to give her a chance.

"Fine," I snapped. "But as part of that deal, you agree to stop trying to kill me."

"Oh, please do keep trying to kill him," Loki said, his eyes sparkling with mirth.

"I haven't tried to kill you since that first time," Eira said, raising her eyes to the ceiling in exasperation.

"Only because you haven't had the chance to try again," I said.

"I agree to stop trying to kill you. Happy? Or do we need to seal our deal in blood too?"

"I don't think that's necessary."

Loki chuckled as he watched the two of us argue. "If that's settled, I'll make you a map."

He grabbed a napkin and unfolded it, then waved his hand over it. The napkin turned to an elaborately drawn paper map that looked like it was a few hundred years old, featuring a big red X over a cave. I looked it over, but had no idea what most of the landmarks were, or where to even begin. Eira, on the other hand, gave it a quick glance and nodded, proving that I did need her after all.

"We'll let you know when we're done with the key," I told Loki, as I slid out of the booth, eager to be done with this meeting. "If we survive."

Loki stood too and his green eyes glowed slightly. "You'd better be sure Eira does, or I *will* destroy you," he said in a low, dangerous voice. "I don't care if you're an Elder God. I'll find a way."

Interesting. It seemed the self-serving imp actually cared for his granddaughter. Not enough to come with us, of course, but enough to throw idle threats my way.

Eira rose to her feet and tucked the map into her luggage. "I'll be fine. I can take care of myself, you know."

"I know you can, darling." Loki gave her a warm smile. "After all, you were trained by the best. Me."

I rolled my eyes so hard it almost hurt, then grabbed Eira's arm and practically dragged her out of there. She called out a 'thanks' to Loki as we headed outside, and then she glared at me, no doubt annoyed by my rudeness. Like I gave a fuck. I wasn't spending one more second in that trickster's presence if I could help it.

"See, I told you he wasn't so bad," Eira said, while I flagged down the valet.

"You call that 'not bad?'" I asked with a snort.

"For Loki, yeah. Trust me, he can be so much worse."

"I'm familiar," I said dryly. "We go way back."

"Right. I forget you're an old man sometimes. Must be the tattoos."

The valet brought my car around in record time, making me wonder if he knew who I was. Probably. Many people said I looked like a rougher, more muscular version of my father. I didn't see it though. I preferred to think I took after Eve in most ways. Except for my pride—that was all Lucifer.

I put Eira's luggage in the trunk and opened the door for her, before getting in myself. Night had fallen across the city, and this would normally be when my intense hunger to steal souls from the living rose up and became unbearable. Yet ever since meeting Eira it had lain dormant, or been replaced by hunger for her. The relief was palpable, but I wondered how long it would last.

"We should wait until the morning to go to Faerie," Eira said, while I drove. "It'll be a bit of a journey through Faerie to get to the cave."

I nodded. "You'll stay at the bar or my apartment tonight. I have some things to do."

"Like roaming the streets as a vigilante?"

"Maybe." That shifter from last night was still out there, though I was less excited about killing him now that I knew he was being controlled by the Furies. That had to be why more and more people were being attacked throughout the city—the Furies were inciting anger and jealousy, first in shifters and imps, and then in other people too. Stopping them would end a lot of the violence in New Orleans.

"I'm coming with you," she said.

"No." I wanted to test what happened if I put some distance between us. Would my hunger for death return? "I need to be alone tonight. And I think you do too. You learned a lot today about your father and you need time to process it all." I looked over at her, but she was staring out the window, her pretty little chin jutted forward stubbornly. "Grieve tonight, fight tomorrow."

She drew in a long breath and met my eyes, then nodded. "Grieve tonight. Fight tomorrow."

12

EIRA

Belial abandoned me in his bar, and though I was tempted to go after him, his words about needing to be alone had struck a chord in me. I decided to give him some space, partly because I needed it too. When I was around him my emotions were too raw and my head spun with conflicting thoughts. He'd killed my father—he'd admitted as much, and even said he'd had no regrets about it. I tried to be mad about that, to hold onto the simmering anger inside me, but it sounded like my father had lost himself to Death by that point. By defeating him, Belial had helped stop the fourth Horseman from going all apocalyptic on the world. I would always miss my father and wish he were still alive now, but I also had to accept that he had gone too far and needed to be stopped. I only wished my brothers had been more honest about what had happened.

Of course, Belial could be lying, but somehow I knew in my gut he wasn't. His story matched up with bits and pieces I'd seen and heard myself, and had filled in a lot of holes in my knowledge about what had happened. As much as I hated trusting him, something inside me told me he was telling the truth.

But where did we go from here?

"What'll it be?" Yumi asked, bringing me out of my thoughts.

When Belial had left me in the bar, he'd told Yumi I could order any food and drinks on the house. Then he'd warned me not to leave the building, if I wanted to get my cuffs off. Proving he was still an asshole.

"Rum and coke, please." I stared down at the menu in front of me. "And the Cajun pizza."

"Good choice," Yumi said.

She put in my order and then went to make my drink, while I watched her. She moved with the grace of a supernatural, and I wondered what exactly she was and how she'd come to work here for Belial.

"Do you have any idea where Belial went?" I asked, as she slid the drink toward me.

"It's better not to ask," Yumi said with a wry grin.

"Does he do this a lot?"

She nodded as she ran a cloth over the bar. "He slips out every night, usually between serving up drinks at the bar. He's gone about an hour or two, and when he comes back he usually looks...different."

I leaned forward. "Different how?"

She cocked her head as she considered. "I don't know. Better. More refreshed. Like he's just woken from a really good nap.

"Somehow I doubt that's what he's doing," I muttered. "Does he ever come back injured or anything?"

Her eyes narrowed. "Trying to find a weakness? Trust me, he doesn't have one."

"No, just curious." I took a long sip of my drink as I eyed her up. "Are the two of you an item or something?"

She let out a sharp laugh. "Me and Belial? No way. For one thing, he's my boss." Her eyes flashed with amusement. "For another thing, you're more my type than he is."

I couldn't help but feel a wave of relief. "Sorry. You just seem really protective of him."

She lifted one shoulder in a casual shrug. "I guess because he's protective of me too. He's like a big brother. Not just to me, but to all Nephilim."

Nephilim was the term used for anyone who was half human, and half angel or Fallen. Like Belial had been, before he'd become Death. "How so?"

Yumi leaned on the counter. "Many years ago, when Heaven and Hell were still at war, Belial set up a network here on Earth to help and support the Nephilim. Back then, our kind were all outcasts thanks to our half-human blood, but there were more and more being born every year. Belial took in everyone, whether they were part angel or Fallen, saying that Nephilim were neutral and not on either side of that pointless war. He gave them food, clothes, shelter, jobs, and whatever else he could." She refilled my drink, which I hadn't realized had gone empty. "Nowadays things have changed, of course. Angels and demons have called a truce, and over the last few years they've started to become more accepting of Nephilim. But Belial still runs the network and makes sure anyone in need gets help. He just does a lot of it on the internet now. We have a Facebook group and everything."

"I had no idea," I said, staring into my drink. Every single thing I learned about Belial changed my perception of him a little bit, making me doubt that he truly was the villain of my story.

Yumi disappeared into the back room, and then returned with my Cajun pizza, which smelled divine. The bar was starting to pick up as it grew later, and she wandered off to take some more orders while I ate, but then she returned, like she wanted to talk to me some more. At least she wasn't openly hostile anymore.

"How did you meet Belial?" I asked, before devouring another slice of pizza.

"For most of my life, I thought I was human and had no idea the supernatural world existed. When my wings sprouted, I panicked. My parents did too." She picked up a peanut from a little jar and popped it in her mouth. "Turns out my mom had a one night stand with a Fallen angel back in the day, and I was a result of that. It tore my family apart and I ran away, feeling like I was losing my mind and terrified of the changes happening in my body. Belial heard about me somehow and tracked me down in Oklahoma. He took me in, explained the entire supernatural world to me, and helped me learn to control my powers. He even got me enrolled in Hellspawn Academy and found my biological dad, who had no idea I even existed." Her eyes took on a faraway look as she tossed a few more peanuts in her mouth. "But I never really fit in at Hellspawn Academy, being a half-blood and all. So when I graduated, I came back to New Orleans and asked Belial for a job. Now this is my home."

"I'm sorry you went through all that," I said. "I know what it's like not to fit in anywhere either. I'm half fae and half demon."

She nodded. "It's hard, isn't it? Always straddling the line between two worlds, and never fully belonging in either. But I found my place here, and with the other Nephilim I have a new family." She gave me another wry grin. "Maybe Belial will help you find your place too."

"If he ever comes back," I muttered, which got an amused chuckle out of her.

"Oh, he will. I have a feeling he won't want you out of sight for long."

She moved away to help other customers, and I finished off my pizza while the bar grew more and more crowded. When I was finished I gave a little wave to Yumi, and then headed up the stairs to Belial's apartment. He'd given me my own access code and I punched it in now, then slipped inside and flipped on the lights. For a few seconds I simply stared at the space, taking it all in without his distracting presence at my side. Without Belial's energy dominating the room, it seemed a lot less imposing.

I decided to do a little snooping, telling myself he must have known I would do it. Who wouldn't? I checked out every single room, hoping to find some dirty secrets tucked away somewhere, but his place was surprisingly well organized, with very little clutter. I'd met immortals before who had a whole collection of stuff stored away in rooms and warehouses. People who liked stuff and were able to keep it forever? They took hoarding to a new level. But not Belial.

Belial still had a few interesting artifacts, but to my surprise, they were kept to the minimum—a few pieces of ancient Greek pottery, a small box of old jewelry from different eras, an old voodoo doll in the corner of his office, and a few other small things here and there. I wondered what the stories behind each of them were, but didn't find anything too shocking. He also had a vast array of first edition books from all sorts of important people. I flipped through a few, but mostly kept my hands off them, just in case they crumbled apart in my fingers. He had kept most of them in excellent condition, but there was only so much a book could take after existing for hundreds of years. I'd heard that Lucifer had one of the most impressive libraries in the world, and Belial seemed to have a miniature version here. It made me think he was more like his father than he cared to admit.

The most disturbing thing about the apartment was how little food there was in the kitchen. The man really didn't need to eat. Although I did find a bag of fancy chocolates, which I plucked from the shelf and ate as I wandered around the apartment some more. He'd told me to eat whatever I wanted, after all.

When I was done with my search I got ready for bed, grateful to have my own clothes and all my toiletries again. Then I found myself staring down at Belial's bed, at the dark gray sheets where he'd been sleeping naked last night. No, not sleeping. He didn't need to sleep either. So why should he get the bed while I was forced to sleep on his uncomfortable couch? Would he even be back tonight? I had no idea. It seemed a damn shame to let the bed go to waste, especially when it looked so comfortable. I'd doze off a little, and then move back to the couch before he got home.

The sheets caressed my skin like silk, and the pillow was the perfect blend of hard and soft. Plus it all smelled like Belial, even without my wolf senses (damn these cuffs), which made me only sink into the bed even more. No one would know, I told myself, as I drifted off to sleep.

I woke to the sound of Belial's deep voice. "What are you doing in my bed?"

Damn. Busted.

In that moment I had a choice—scrabble up and act embarrassed, or just fucking own it. So I did the latter. "It's more comfortable than the couch," I said with a yawn and a shrug. "No one else was using it."

Belial's eyes tracked my every movement with obvious hunger. "If you want in my bed so badly, I'd be happy to invite you."

The sultry tone of his voice left nothing to the imagination, and heat flooded me at the naughty images it conjured. I found my eyes wandering over him too. He wasn't wearing his hooded cloak, and the black t-shirt showed off all his muscles and tattoos. I'd already had a glimpse of what was underneath those clothes too and my mouth watered at the thought of another peek.

I dragged my eyes away. "Not if you're in it with me."

He took a step forward. "We both know that's not true."

Before he climbed in with me, I hopped out of his of bed. I wore only a little silk nightgown that left little to the imagination, and I put some distance between us quickly before we both got any ideas in our heads. Maybe a change of subject would help. "Where have you been?"

"I went hunting, but couldn't find that shifter from last night. It's possible the Furies are having them be more cautious or staying out of the city now that they know we're on to them."

"So no killing spree last night for the Grim Reaper of New Orleans? You must be disappointed."

He gave me a villainous smile. "No, the Grim Reaper was alive and well last night, protecting the city as best he could."

"Did you kill anyone?" I asked, a shiver running down my spine.

His eyes darkened and his voice turned hard. "I found a woman stabbed nearly to death, and a man about to rape her. I quickly dealt with him and then flew her to the hospital. I believe she made it. He did not. I feel no guilt about that."

I bit my lip and looked away, unable to chastise him for what he'd done. I'd have done the same thing if I'd been there.

"That took all night?" The words slipped out, and I wondered if I was starting to lose my mind. When had I turned into his nagging woman? And why did I care what he did with his time?

"I had to...test a theory." His eyes swept over me again with a frown. "I also went grocery shopping."

"Oh yeah, I noticed your kitchen was totally empty."

His lips turned up in amusement. "I don't need much, but you do. But I wasn't sure what you liked, so I got all sorts of things. Next time you can make me a list."

A pang hit my chest. "You did that for me?"

He shrugged. "You need to eat. And starting today you're no longer my prisoner, but my guest."

Excitement hummed through me at his words, and I gazed down at my silver cuffs. I couldn't wait to get them off, or to go back to Faerie, which I hadn't visited in over a year.

"Come on. I'll make you something to eat." He turned and walked out of the bedroom, and I watched his fine ass as he went.

I couldn't help myself.

13

EIRA

I quickly took a shower and got dressed, donning my combat leathers because you could never be too careful in Faerie. Besides, most of my other clothes would stick out there. The fae were definitely not jeans and t-shirts kind of people.

I was drawn back to the kitchen by the smell of food cooking. Belial was making a feast of eggs, bacon, and pancakes, and it was all for me. Unbelievable. Why couldn't he just let me keep hating him? No, he had to go and be nice to me, all while being so freaking hot it was hard to take my eyes off him. Asshole.

"Breakfast will be ready in a few minutes," he said.

I nodded and glanced at the map sitting on the bar counter. Loki had made it yesterday with his illusion magic, and I wondered how long it would hold. You'd never know by looking at it that it had once been a simple bar napkin. It even felt like old parchment paper when I picked it up to examine it again. The basilisk cave was located in Summer Court territory, which I wasn't thrilled about, but if we were lucky I could get us there without encountering many fae. As a messenger, I'd been all over the place in Faerie, and I knew all the landmarks Loki had mapped out for me. It should be pretty easy to get to, or so I hoped.

Belial served me up a plate of food, and I had to admit he was a good cook. He saved only a single piece of bacon for himself, explaining that it was one of the few things he missed the taste of. I couldn't blame him. I devoured my food quickly, eager to get moving, while he took a fast shower and got dressed.

When he returned, he held a small silver wand in his hand. "Let's get this over with."

He made a motion for me to give him my hands, and when he touched the little wand to my silver cuffs, they snapped open immediately. My power rushed back in, and it was almost overwhelming as it poured back into me all at once. I breathed in deep and let it settle until I felt complete again, and fully *me* once more. But just to be sure, I formed a ball of ice in one hand and turned my fingers to claws on the other. I was *back*.

I looked up at Belial with a smile on my lips, but he was watching me closely with narrowed eyes, like he expected me to whip out another ice sword and stab him. I didn't, of course. No, if I was going to try that again, I'd wait until he was caught off guard. But I was starting to doubt my plan to kill him a little more every day.

"Much better," I said, as I banished my claws and ice, then rubbed my wrists where the cuffs had been. My body instantly healed any bruising or soreness there, now that my magic was back, but I still let out a soft sigh, so relieved to have them gone.

"Ready to go?" Belial asked, and I nodded.

Together we threw some food, water, extra clothes, and some other necessities into a heavy outdoor backpack, which Belial strapped to his back. Then I dug around in a secret compartment of my luggage and removed a necklace there, with a round polished gemstone with a rainbow of colors moving inside of it. The key to Faerie. Even though I hadn't used it in over a year, I always kept it close to me. It was one of the few things I had left from my mother.

"Stand back," I said, as I clutched the gem and called upon my fae power to open the portal, picturing the location in my mind of where I wanted to go. A beam of colorful light burst out of the stone and expanded into a glowing, swirling portal, just large enough for us to pass through one at a time. I stared at the myriad of colors swirling in front of me, before turning to Belial. "Let's go."

"Ladies first."

"Don't worry, I didn't open the portal into a death trap," I muttered. But just so he knew it was safe, I stepped through first.

Belial's living room faded away as soon as I got to the other side of the portal, which took me to the edge of the Summer Court territory, to a forest I knew would be safe to enter without being noticed. I inhaled the sharp scent of the trees here, which were bursting with purple flowers that gave off a vibrant fragrance. All the colors seemed brighter here too, from the grass at our feet to the bright blue sky above us. It was a cool morning with a hint of chill in the air with the promise of a warmer afternoon. Of course, the seasons were different here in Faerie—all four of them played out across the space of a single day. Judging by the current temperature, I guessed we had arrived at the early spring portion of the day, with summer a few hours ahead of us, when it would get much hotter before settling into autumn before returning to winter in the evening.

It's been too long, I thought, as I looked around while Belial stepped through the portal. I was excited to be back in Faerie, even if it wasn't the Winter Court where I came from. I'd been to the Summer Court plenty of times while playing messenger, but I longed for the snowy, frost-ridden lands that held the key to my powers. Plus I had my own reasons for avoiding the Summer Court as much as possible.

Meanwhile, Belial squinted in the bright light as if it was hurting his eyes. I grinned at how out of place he looked here, even though I was sure he must have been to Faerie many times before during his long life.

I glanced down at Loki's map to check my bearings. "We're going to try to avoid encountering any fae," I said, before setting off through the trees.

"Works for me," Belial said, as he kept pace with me. "How long has it been since you were last here?"

"A little over a year."

"Do you miss it?"

"Sometimes. Being a messenger to Faerie gave me a purpose, at least. A chance to prove my mixed heritage was useful in some way."

"Did you grow up here?" he asked.

I was surprised by all his questions. Was he really interested in hearing all this? "No, my mother was killed by a rival in the Summer Court when I was a baby, and I don't remember her at all. I grew up mostly with Fenrir and my brothers on Earth, but I visited my Winter Court family members a lot as a child. But I've never really been accepted as either a shifter or a fae, but always as something in between."

"I get that," Belial said. "I was the first Nephilim, the product of Lucifer falling for the human woman Eve. It was quite scandalous at the time."

"I bet. Half-breeds are still not totally accepted among any supernaturals, but it made me a good messenger between the fae and demons. Well, at least until my father decided to go and start a civil war among the demons to try and overthrow Lucifer. That ended my messenger days."

"Would you ever go back to being a messenger?"

"I don't know," I said honestly. "It's what I'm good at and it's probably the best job for me, since I don't really fit in with either world."

"I understand where you're coming from," Belial said. "I was cast out from Hell a long time ago and sent to live on Earth long before most other angels or demons came here. I've done my best to make it my home though, and to help others like me."

I slanted a glance at him. "Yes, Yumi told me about your network of Nephilim, and about how you helped her out. And helped many others, it sounds like."

"I do what I can," Belial said with a shrug. "I know how hard it is to be alone and confused and unsure where your place is in the world, so I created a network for people like me, who can help each other out so none of us is every truly alone."

"Very noble," I said, almost grudgingly. "Yumi speaks very highly of you."

"She had a difficult time, but I tried to help her out as best I could. She's one of the younger Nephilim around. Now that angels and demons live on Earth, there are more half-humans than ever, and I want them all to not have to struggle like I did."

Something warm erupted in my chest as he spoke about Yumi and the others like a proud papa. He really did understand what it was like being an outcast, and I had the sudden feeling that we understood each other more than we originally thought.

Then it hit me—I *liked* him. Not because of his deadly good looks, or because of whatever desire tied us together. We had more in common than I wanted to admit, and I'd discovered he wasn't a total villain, but someone trying to make the world a better place however he could. Plus he kept trying to help me out too, even though I'd tried to kill him. Shit. Was I developing *feelings* for him? This wasn't supposed to happen at all. We were enemies, and I'd come to New Orleans to kill him. I'd only agreed to team up with him temporarily to find the missing shifters while also looking for a weakness in him. But it wasn't as simple as that anymore.

We lapsed into a comfortable silence for a while, simply walking through the forest, and Belial's shadows concealed us anytime we got too close to other fae. I checked the map frequently to make sure we were on course, and made slight alterations to make sure that we'd be staying out of the way of any large towns. As we traveled, the weather warmed up very quickly, and it was brutally hot by midday.

I'd nearly forgotten how intense the Summer Court's day could be. It would start cooling off soon though as it switched to fall and then winter, although it would stay warm enough for us to sleep outside at least. That was one good thing the Summer Court had going for it. The only thing, I thought darkly as I wiped my brow against the seemingly endless streams of sweat dripping down my forehead. Demons were not meant for the heat, and neither were Winter Court fae, which meant I suffered doubly for it. For some time I shifted into wolf form and ran while Belial flew overhead, which helped for a while, but we had to be careful that no one saw us like that. That was the same reason we didn't ride Ghost, even though it would have been faster and easier—the fae might have been able to sense his otherworldly presence in this realm. There would be too many questions if we were caught by the fae here, and we didn't have time for that.

It turned cooler as the sun set and the winter night set in. Eventually Belial and I stopped to camp for the night in a clearing that looked like it had been used by other travelers, judging by the remains of a campfire. Luckily Belial and I wouldn't need one of those tonight, as neither of us was bothered by the cold.

I gratefully sat down on a fallen log once we were settled and stretched my aching legs. It had been quite some time since I'd covered so much ground in one day and I was unused to it. I was looking forward to getting some sleep, although we'd have to take turns keeping watch to make sure no one came upon us while we were asleep.

Belial rummaged around in his backpack and then passed me a little brown bag. "Here. You need to eat something."

I raised my eyebrows as I caught it and checked inside, finding a sandwich and a bag of chips that he must have packed for me. Fuck, why was he so nice to me? I wished he would stop. Okay, not really, because I was pretty hungry, and I appreciated him thinking of me, but he really was making it hard to dislike him. "Thank you. Are you going to eat anything?"

"No, I'll be fine. I also don't need sleep, so you can rest as much as you want. I'll keep watch the whole night."

"Must be nice," I said. "What's it like being an Elder God?"

Belial watched me for a few moments, his eyes inscrutable in the low light. "I wouldn't wish it on anyone," he finally said, in a brutally honest tone.

I hadn't expected an answer like that from him, especially since he'd flaunted to me so many times that he couldn't be killed. "Why not? You're so powerful. Like seriously overpowered. You've said it so many times, that you're unkillable. Isn't that the best thing?"

"I suppose."

"I'm sensing a 'but.'"

"But the cost of such power..." he trailed off and shook his head.

"What cost?" I asked, holding my breath.

"It doesn't matter." He looked down at his hands, his voice hollow and his face stark. "Try to get some sleep."

I huffed at his dismissal. Why had he piqued my interest like that just to back down at the last second? He was being worse than Loki, but I had the feeling that he wouldn't take kindly to that comparison. "You can tell me, you know."

"Maybe another time."

"Stubborn ass," I muttered.

Belial just chuckled softly as I shifted into wolf form and settled on the ground in a softer patch of dirt. It was easier to sleep outside as a wolf, although I still moved around uncomfortably for a bit. It had been a while since I'd slept out under the stars like this.

I closed my eyes, but cracked them back open when Belial scuffed the ground standing up. He looked down at me with dark eyes as he draped his cloak over the ground and patted for me to lie on it. I hesitated only a second, before scooting over onto the thick fabric, but turned around so he couldn't see my face as the confusion inside me surged. The cloak smelled like him, and it was especially strong with my wolf nose. I tried to resist the urge to inhale for several moments, but then I gave up and breathed it in. I smelled traces of alcohol, leather, blood, and metal, but mostly the unmistakable scent of *him*. Something I knew I'd always be able to find now, and would never forget. I wanted to push the cloak away from me, to remind him that we were enemies and he had no business offering up his clothes like we were friends...or more. But I couldn't do it. Instead I just snuggled a bit closer, finally growing comfortable, while hating that I liked this so much, even as I fell asleep with his smell in my head.

14

BELIAL

W e got to the cave the next morning and hid in some bushes while we scoped out the situation. The cave appeared to be larger than I expected, and I got the feeling it extended far into the mountain behind it. Beside me, Eira stared intently at the entrance, eyes narrowed as if she was listening very hard for something. With her shifter senses, she could probably hear things I couldn't.

She glanced over at me. "I don't hear much. It might be asleep."

"I don't think that matters," I said. "It will probably wake up."

"I know that," Eira snapped. She seemed very irritated this morning, but I couldn't figure out why. When she'd woken up, she'd been in a bad mood, and I wished she would just tell me why instead of giving me the silent treatment.

We hadn't talked on the rest of the journey to the cave, except to discuss the plan. I would distract the basilisk since I was more likely to survive going toe to toe with it than Eira. Meanwhile, Eira would sneak into the cave and get the key. Then we'd get the fuck out of there as fast as we could, because basilisks were damn near impossible to kill, and I wasn't looking to try today.

I held out the scrap of cloth I'd crafted into a makeshift blindfold. Eira eyed it, curling her lips. "Are you sure I have to wear that?" she asked. "This would be a lot easier if I could see."

"You don't need to see. You can use your other senses to navigate the cave, and this is the best way to avoid accidentally looking at the basilisk on the way."

We'd already agreed on this plan, so she was stalling putting it on. I knew how much she hated the idea, but it was the only way I was letting her participate. I didn't care what she said—if she met the basilisk's eyes, even accidentally, she'd be dead. No fucking way was I letting that happen. For some reason I couldn't explain, her safety suddenly mattered more to me than anything else.

"Fine," Eira said with a heavy sigh. She shifted into her wolf form, and I crouched down. Her white shoulders tensed as I slipped the fabric over her eyes and tied it as tightly as I could without hurting her. My fingers brushed the thick fur at the nape of her neck, and I had to physically resist the urge to dig my fingers in and pet her. The strong, inexplicable pull dragged me toward her once again, and the never-ending hunger for death was sated whenever she was around, fading into nothing. It was only temporary though, as I'd discovered the other night when I'd gone out in the city on my own and put some distance between us. Still, she was the only thing I had found that could take it away. I closed my eyes and basked in the feeling for just a moment before I forced myself to pull away.

"Can you see?" I asked.

She moved her white head around, ears twitching forward to track my voice. She shook her head in a very humanoid movement. I watched her test her paws, stepping around a bush and then circling back around to face me dead center, while a pit formed in my stomach. Worry. Something I hadn't felt in such a long time. I wanted to protect her from everything, but she had insisted that she be part of it. I understood why—she didn't trust me at all. In her mind, if I went in the cave, there was a good chance that I wouldn't be coming back out to help her. I wasn't sure how to convince her otherwise.

She started to turn toward the cave, but I called after her. "Eira, wait."

She stopped dead in her tracks, her ears perking up. I reached forward, and she flinched slightly as I threaded my hand in the fur on top of her head and rubbed her lightly. Eira bared her teeth at me and let a low growl, but she didn't move away. Instead, she lightly pushed her head against my hand, as if she couldn't help herself. She'd never admit it to me, but I could tell she liked my touch.

After a moment, she snapped at my fingers with her teeth and yanked herself away. She disappeared into the plants we were currently hiding behind. I looked on with a heavy heart as I watched her fluffy white tail disappear into the distance.

Now it was time to work my magic. I couldn't focus for too long on Eira because I had to make sure I could lure out the basilisk so she could sneak in and get the key. I closed my eyes and cracked my knuckles. I sent feelers out, not surprised to find lots and lots of death in the area. To my deathly senses, it was like a beacon around the cave, lighting it up like the Vegas Strip at night.

I raised my hands and let the power of Death run through me. Most of the time I tried to keep this part of me locked away, sealed up to protect the living around me, and to keep the hunger contained as long as I could. Now I let it rush through me, such unfathomable power that it made me tremble, and I knew my eyes would be glowing purple, as they did when I tapped into the power of Death. I was an Elder God, one of the fundamental elements of the universe, unkillable and all-powerful, and for a moment I reveled in it. This much power was incredible, though it definitely didn't make up for the overwhelming hunger for stealing life I felt all the time. Until Eira, anyway.

The dead reacted to me like I'd rung a dinner bell, and started waking up slowly. It was sluggish for some of them, the ones who had been here for a long time, but many of the bodies were more recent. I was fairly sure they'd all tried to enter the cave before meeting their fate. Whether they knew what was inside or not, none of them had made it very far.

The newer bodies dragged themselves out of the ground, their movements jerky and unnatural. The older ones had been ground to pieces by time and dirt, but they reformed from the dust as skeletons, their bones creaking as they moved. Soon my army of the dead stood before me, with over two dozen of them. I nodded once, pleased with my handiwork. It should be enough to draw the attention of the basilisk.

"Go make some noise," I ordered.

The dead fae soldiers turned as one, walking over to the mouth of the cave. They rattled and chattered like a storm of the damned, and I focused on commanding them to be as loud as possible. For a few minutes, they raged on with no sign of anything from the cave. Then there was a loud roar, and a dark shape filled the entrance.

The basilisk was one of the more terrifying creatures I'd encountered before, and that was saying something. The back end of it was a giant serpent, the tail twisting far into the cave, but in front it looked like a rooster, with a giant pointy beak and sharp talons on its two feet, along with some feathered wings that didn't look big enough to actually lift the creature. I suspected it wasn't very good at actually flying, but that didn't matter when it had ten other ways to kill you.

The basilisk knocked the undead soldiers aside like they were nothing more than toys. They fell back to dust and the basilisk let out a huge roar, swiveling its huge head around to look for the source of the magic. I tossed a ball of blue hellfire in its direction, and just like that, I had the complete attention of one of the most deadly creatures on the planet solely on me. It's eyes locked on me, but nothing happened. At least Loki had been right about the death gaze not affecting me.

I volleyed a few more hellfire balls at the basilisk, which only seemed to piss it off. It crept out after me as I drew back from the cave, yelling and waving my arms above my head, trying to keep its attention solely on me as I used shadow magic and hellfire against it. It didn't seem phased by either, and started acting like it was going to head back into the cave.

Damn, what did it take to injure this thing? I'd have to step up my game if I wanted to get it out of the cave so Eira could sneak inside. I needed to make myself such a delectable target that it wouldn't be able to resist. It was just parrying my blows, looking generally annoyed, but not threatened enough to leave it's home to come after me.

I unfurled my wings and took flight to swoop above the basilisk, hitting it with hellfire from a new angle. It watched me, interest piqued as I flew above, and then it blew a long, hot blast of fire. I gritted my teeth and dodged, swooping off to the side so the fire shot straight into the sky.

Well, fuck. There could be dozens of nearby fae who had seen that fire, and I was betting they'd be here soon to try and figure out what was going on at the cave with the basilisk. We needed to get in, get the key, and get out as quickly as possible, so no one would learn why we were here.

I grimaced and dove down again, swooping in a bit closer, narrowly dodging a claw that went after me before trying again. It was dangerous to do this when the thing could move so fast. If I wasn't careful, it could swipe me out of the air, or grab me and swallow me whole. I wasn't about to test the full limits of my immortality.

To my surprise, the basilisk whirled around and sent its long serpent's tail careening at me at a breakneck pace. I cursed and shot upward as quickly as I could, trying to escape it before it knocked me right out of the sky. I shot back tendrils of black smoke, trying to pin the thing in place, but it tore through them like they were nothing more than tissue paper. I cursed and dropped the magic, going back to flinging balls of hellfire at it as I gradually drew it farther away from its cave. It was very reluctant to leave, not taking more than a couple of steps forward at a time, until I finally gave up and started getting in close enough for the basilisk to actually catch me.

It was stupid, but we were running out of time. I needed to be able to get Eira in that cave before it noticed her. She would only wait, blindfolded and in her wolf form, for so long. The longer we took, the more likely the basilisk would smell or hear her, and I didn't want her to try and fight it.

I landed on the ground some distance away, staring at the beast as I planned my next move. Hellfire should have torn it to shreds, but its skin must have been made of some pretty tough stuff. I wished I'd brought Lucifer's sword, Morningstar, with me, but even that might not have done anything to the basilisk. I was meant to fight demons and angels, as was the sword, not ancient creatures of legend.

I roused my undead army, or what was left of them, and had them charge forward to fight the basilisk again. If I could get close enough to the beast to touch it, I might be able to drain some of its life. I watched as the basilisk lashed out at my army with enormous claws, each the size of my entire arm. I definitely didn't want to find out how much they hurt.

I finally called my horse, Ghost, not knowing what else to do. He appeared at my side, looking less than pleased, and tossed his pale head. The basilisk let out a shriek, as if it had finally found a worthy opponent, and took a few steps forward. The horse simply blinked once at me with its glowing purple eyes, and then turned and pawed at the ground.

The basilisk slid out farther, its tail finally leaving an opening large enough for a white wolf to slip in. I looked around, trying to see if I could catch sight of Eira, but she'd done an excellent job of camouflaging herself and I had no idea where she was. I could only hope she'd be ready to go when the time was right.

I lit my hands with hellfire as Ghost continued staring the basilisk down, as if to say *bring it on*. My horse whickered once, and then we both charged at the beast. I ducked to one side, and the horse darted to the other, and the basilisk slid the rest of the way out of the cave in its attempt to come after us both.

Now! I thought at Eira, even though she couldn't hear me. Then I saw the flash of white fur as she darted into the cave, and I let out a sigh of relief. Of course, she also had to get out of the cave too, which meant my job here was just beginning.

I hopped on the back of Ghost, forming a sword made of shadow and hellfire, and charged the basilisk once more.

15

EIRA

The heat was almost oppressive in the cave. I had to open my mouth to pant to avoid overheating instantly, but at least it was a dry heat, not the moist, gross heat that was usually in dark, enclosed spaces like this.

I swiveled my ears around in lieu of my eyes, and flared my nostrils to catch the scents around me as I crept forward silently. The air smelled of death and sulfur, so strong it almost made me gag, and almost making me wish I'd done this as a human instead. Moving through the cave like this was difficult, but I managed to keep going, sticking close to the walls so I didn't lose my way.

As I continued forward, I caught scent of a huge pile of bones right in the middle of my path. I skirted it carefully, my flank brushing along the cave wall. I shuddered to think about what might be on that wall that was now on me, but I'd have to worry about getting clean later.

Outside, I heard the distant sounds of battle and hoped Belial was all right, especially when a particularly loud roar echoed through the cave. I had to move quickly to get the Void key to avoid either of us getting hurt. Wait. When had I started caring so much about that bastard? Dammit, I'd told myself this morning that I would avoid him as much as possible, get the job done, and then never see him again. But now all I could think about was making sure he, the unkillable Death, was okay, when I should really be more worried about myself.

I kept creeping through the dark, hot cavern, though my heart was in my throat the whole time. I just wanted this to be over already, so we could stop the Furies and save the shifters and imps they'd brainwashed, including my brothers. Why couldn't Loki have hidden the key somewhere a little more accessible? He'd told me it was way in the back within the largest cavern, under a loose rock. I wasn't looking forward to trying to find it blindfolded.

Finally, the quality of sound changed, and the air seemed to be a little less oppressive, and I realized I must have reached the large cavern. Loki had said it would be on the right side, and that I would find it about halfway back. Which really wasn't all that much help.

Please be here, I thought as I stuck close to the wall and kept going.

A sudden noise behind me made me freeze. I swiveled my head around, trying to catch the source of the sound. The smell of sulfur intensified instantly, and every hair on my body rose straight up. I still didn't know exactly what it was, but it was bad and my instincts were screaming at me to run. I had barely enough time to throw up an ice shield around myself as something hissed through the air.

Fire impacted against my ice shield and sizzled. I balked at the sudden rush of heat, almost too much to take. Who the fuck was throwing fireballs at me?

My shield crumbled as a horrible screech echoed through the chamber, and then something started stomping toward me. It sounded very similar to the thing outside that Belial was fighting, but from the sound of its movements, it was a lot smaller.

A baby basilisk!

Fuck, this was bad. I wanted to run with every fiber of my being, but I couldn't leave until I had the Void key. It had to be here somewhere. I scrambled at the wall with my paws in a desperate frenzy, trying to find the loose rock Loki had told me about, while also trying to keep an ear or two on the basilisk as it drew closer. The thing was moving slowly, like it wasn't sure it should attack me again, or perhaps it was waiting for its parent to come help finish me off. Either way, I created another ice shield around me, making it as big as I could and praying it would hold. Then I felt something shift. A loose rock.

I pushed it aside, but there were lots of rocks below it, and I couldn't tell if I'd found the Void key or not. I didn't have time trying to test every single rock either, not when the basilisk kept approaching. With quick movements, I nudged the blindfold aside with one paw and looked down at the space I'd opened up.

There, amidst the rubble and the dull stones of the cave, was a gemstone that looked very similar to my key to Faerie. It was small, round, and polished, but instead of being filled with a myriad of colors, it was a deep black with stars and mist in it.

I quickly grabbed it in my mouth, making sure to only look down at the ground in front of me. I spotted the shadow of the baby basilisk creeping closer behind me, like something out of a nightmare, and I quickly slipped my blindfold back down to protect my eyes.

Then I backed up, trying to find a way out of the cave without using my eyes, while also somehow getting past the baby basilisk that wanted to eat me for breakfast. The thing suddenly charged me, and I let loose a stream of icy shards at it, which made it pause long enough for me to put a little more distance between us. It unleashed more fire on me and began melting my ice shield, which wasn't meant to withstand this kind of power. Fighting this thing would be useless. I had to run for it.

I released a huge blast of ice toward what I thought was its face, trying to knock the thing back. It didn't work, but the creature let out a terrible screech, that sounded almost like a chicken's squawk. My back bumped into a wall, and I spun around to book it out of there, racing on my wolf's legs, but heard the damn basilisk coming after me.

I stumbled and fell over a rock in my path as I tried desperately to outrun the baby basilisk, but it was gaining fast on me. I held my breath as I rounded the pile of bones that meant that I was almost to the cave entrance, and I started running as fast as my four legs would allow. Finally, the basilisk, which had been gaining on me to the point of almost catching up, fell behind.

A slight flicker of hope broke through my terror me as the light from the outside of the cave filtered in through the tightly woven fabric of my blindfold. *Almost there... almost...* I burst into the light and started sprinting toward the cover of the trees nearby, briefly noting the smells of death, sulfur, horse, and Belial nearby. If I could just make it past the main part of the clearing and into the forest, I'd be safe. I hoped.

I'm going to make it, I thought, just before something huge and heavy plowed into me. A giant serpent's tail. It tossed me into the air several feet, and I let out a surprised cry and clenched down hard on the Void key as I went flying and landed awkwardly on my left side. Ow. That was definitely no baby basilisk. Somehow I'd gotten the attention of the mom. Or dad? I had no idea, and didn't really care, as pain lanced through me.

I scrambled up, trying to find my bearings, but then I was dragged down once again. Something sharp pricked at my thigh, and then set it on fire. I screamed at the feel of hot venom pulsing through my veins and heard Belial shouting as well. Some instinct made me shift back into human form, and the change in my size let me slip out of the basilisk's grasp, though I could do little more than scramble away on my hands and feet while unbearable pain spread through my body. The Void key had fallen from my mouth some-where along the way, and I reached around until I found it, clasping it tight in my hand. The blindfold slipped off of my face and I shut my eyes tight, not willing to risk meeting the gaze of either basilisk.

Pure adrenaline shot me forward, and I stumbled the rest of the way to the edge of the forest, fighting through the agony. The baby basilisk was hot on my heels, so close that I could hear its clawed feet hitting the ground and feel the reverberation run up my own legs. I screamed again as I launched myself forward, and then turned around and blasted the baby basilisk with as much ice as I could call at once.

It was too much. The venom was already taking root in my

system and making me weak, and then using so much power finally did me in. I collapsed and waited for the end.

But it didn't come.

Belial let out a roar that sounded less human than anything I'd heard from him yet, and then he landed next to me only seconds later. I heard the sizzle of him flinging hellfire, in such large amounts that I was surprised the forest around us wasn't already ablaze.

"I got the key," I muttered, unable to move. "Take it and go."

"Hold onto it. We're getting out of here."

He swooped me up into his strong arms, and I let out a sigh as I sank against him, finding comfort in his nearness. His large wings flapped, and then I felt the dizzying sensation of being lifted into the air at a speed so fast it took my breath away. I clutched the Void key tightly with one hand and gripped Belial's shirt with the other, deliriously trying to hold on as tightly as I could while he flew us away from the basilisks. Finally, I opened my eyes to watch the forest whizzing by beneath us and instantly regretted it as nausea made me gag.

After some time, which might have been minutes and might have been days, Belial slowed and started descending. We landed on the ground, and when I tried to put weight on my leg again, I let out a cry. The venom was acting fast, and I had no idea how long I'd be able to hang on. Belial watched me, his eyes dark and furious, but before he could say anything, his purple-eyed horse appeared out of nowhere.

"Ghost can run a lot faster than I can fly," Belial explained as he helped me onto the back of the horse, who tossed his head in annoyance.

"Where are we going?" I asked, my voice more like a frog's croak. I slumped forward on the horse's neck, unable to summon the strength to hold myself up.

"To get you help." Belial climbed on behind me, wrapping his arms around me, pulling me back against his hard chest in an almost protective manner. "I won't let you die."

"That's ironic, considering you're Death," I said with a delirious laugh, before everything went black.

16

EIRA

I opened my eyes to vibrant purple flowers creeping along a trellis above me, with a crystal clear blue sky behind it. The colors were so intense that I had to close my eyes again to stop them from tearing up. The sound of birds chirping and a bubbling stream met my ears. Everything smelled like flowers and a perfect breeze teased along my skin. It was so peaceful and idyllic, I wondered if this was a dream.

"You're awake."

My eyes flew open and I turned to face the sound of a melodious deep voice. A gorgeous fae male moved toward me, wearing a crown of ivy above his pointed ears. He wore a breezy white shirt that showed off his muscular chest, above black trousers that looked like silk. His hair appeared black at first, until the sunlight glinted off it, and I saw it was actually dark, luxurious blue. I blinked at him a few times, trying to figure out who he was. Something about him was familiar, but the shape of his face wasn't quite fully fae—it was a little too rugged and masculine. He must have been half fae, like me. The other half? I had no idea.

"Shit, I better not be at the Summer Court," I muttered before I could stop myself.

He laughed, and the sound was beautiful too. "No, this is the Spring Court, darling." He gave me a flirtatious wink. "Don't worry, you're perfectly safe here. I'll make sure of that."

Everything about him was charming, and it might have been endearing, if I hadn't woken up in this strange place and couldn't remember how I'd gotten here. "The Spring Court?" I asked, frowning as his words finally made sense.

His gaze swept across my body, though more in a concerned way this time. "How are you feeling?"

"Um. I don't really know." I tried to move, but everything felt sluggish. I also noticed I wasn't wearing my combat leathers anymore, but a breezy green dress covered in tiny purple flowers. "Nothing hurts, at least, but what happened to my clothes?"

"They were destroyed by the basilisk's venom. To save your life, Belial and I had to tear them off you."

My cheeks flashed with heat, knowing I'd been naked in front of the men, and that one or both of them had put me in this dress. "And then you dressed me."

"Don't worry, we were careful to preserve your modesty the entire time. Although you must know you are very beautiful, even when you're on the verge of death."

His hand reached toward my face, as if to brush away a piece of hair in my eyes, but before he could make contact, Belial stepped into my line of vision and knocked the fae's hand away. "Don't fucking touch her, Damien."

Damien just laughed and stepped back. "Wow, you really are possessive over her."

Belial shoved Damien away, and leaned over me himself. He ran his hands over my arms and tilted my head side to side, looking me over with a frown. Finally, he moved down to my leg, and I remembered. Ah, yes, the basilisks. What a fun time that had been. I grimaced at the memory, and wondered how I survived.

"I'm fine," I said, shrugging away Belial's hands from my body. I was a little groggy, but there was no pain. "Can you help me sit up?"

Belial helped me sit up, while my head spun a bit and then settled into normalcy. I looked down at my leg, but couldn't see a single trace of the wound that I'd sustained from the basilisk. It felt a lot better, with not even a twinge of pain as I moved it. When I clenched my hand reflexively, I realized that somehow I'd managed to keep hold of the Void key. I stared at it for a few moments, and then glanced up to find both Damien and Belial watching me.

"What happened?" I asked. "How did we get here?"

"I raced as fast as I could to the only place in Faerie that I knew could help you," Belial said. "Damien has a healing gift, especially good for poisons...and alcohol. It was particularly useful when he was in his Dionysus days as the god of wine."

"And orgies," Damien chimed in with a wicked grin.

Oh shit. I'd heard tales of the Spring Court palace. Which meant that the person standing in front of me had to be the Spring Court prince. I should have known immediately from the name and the crown on his head, but my brain was still catching up to all of this.

"You're safe here," Damien added as he noted my uncomfortable look. "No one will dare harm my brother's lady."

"Brother?" I asked, looking between the two men. That must be why Damien looked so familiar. He was Lucifer's son too.

Damien flashed me another flirty smile. "Yes, I'm Belial's younger, better looking, and far more charming brother."

Belial growled at that, and Damien shot me a look as if to say, *he's proving my point, isn't he?*

I hid a smile behind my hand. I liked Damien immediately. "Thank you for saving me."

"Thank Belial," Damien said with a knowing look in his eyes. "He somehow kept you alive on the journey here, which should have been impossible."

I frowned at Belial and opened my mouth to ask him what he'd done, but he shook his head.

"Now that you're better, we should get you back to Earth," he said.

"Please, stay the night," Damien said. "Or at least for dinner. Let Eira regain some of her strength. Demeter should be back by then too."

"Just one more reason to leave now," Belial grumbled. "She doesn't like me."

"No one does," Damien said, but he laughed right after, and Belial only rolled his eyes a little bit instead of threatening to kill him on the spot, so I figured it was a joke.

My brain was still a bit groggy, but even I realized they were talking about the Spring Queen—Damien's grandmother. I'd never met her, but I'd heard she could be...prickly. I didn't really feel up to being sociable at the moment though, especially with royalty. "I feel fine. I'd like to head back to Earth sooner than later."

Damien nodded. "Very well, if the lady insists. I can open a portal for you whenever you're ready."

"We're ready," Belial said, his voice leaving no room for argument. I got the sense he didn't want to be here a second longer than needed either.

"Of course." Damien clasped him on the shoulder, his face softening. "But I mean it, brother. You and your woman are always welcome here, even when you don't need anything. It would be nice to see you more than once every few decades."

"I'm not his woman," I said quickly.

Damien laughed. "That's not true and you know it."

Belial scowled. "Fine, I'll try to visit more often, but first we need to take care of a problem back in New Orleans."

"Whatever it is, I'm sure you'll be able to solve it," Damien said. "I'll open a portal back to your place now."

He stepped back so Belial could help me get to my feet. I let him lift me, and then pushed him away. I'd already been weak enough around him, and I needed to make sure he didn't think I needed to rely on him completely. I regretted it instantly when I swayed on my feet, but eventually I regained my balance. My supernatural healing was taking over now that the poison had left my body, and every second that passed made me feel a little stronger.

"You shouldn't be walking yet," Belial said, and before I could protest, he picked me up like I was a bride and he was about to carry me over the threshold.

"I can walk," I snapped. "Put me down." I didn't want Belial's brother to think I was some helpless woman who needed to be carted around like an invalid, but Belial just ignored me. Stubborn ass!

"See? So possessive." Damien chuckled as he reached into his pocket. He pulled out his own Faerie key and held it out, opening the swirling, colorful portal before us.

Belial started toward the portal but then paused and turned back to Damien. "You know, you can come and visit me as well. I'm only a portal away."

"I would, but every time I return to Earth, my visit somehow turns into a wine-filled orgy." Damien winked at me as he said it.

"Keep your dick in your pants and you'll be fine," Belial said, rolling his eyes. "Although I do have a great wine collection at my bar."

Damien grinned again. "All right, you've convinced me. I'll try to come visit you more too."

Belial nodded and carried me forward toward the portal. I'd given up resisting at this point, my body too weak to fight him off properly, even if this was humiliating. And kind of nice, at the same time, though I would never admit that out loud.

"Thank you again," he said to Damien, and then we stepped through the portal.

We arrived outside, in the alley behind Belial's building, and compared to Faerie, everything here seemed suddenly a lot dimmer. Belial immediately started toward the door, with me still clutched in his hands.

"Are you seriously going to carry me all the way up to your place?" I said, straining to get away from him. "Put me down."

"No, you need to save your strength."

"Maybe we should have stayed for dinner then," I said, slapping at his chest ineffectively when trying to wriggle out of his grasp didn't work. "Then I could have regained it."

Belial only grunted, and didn't give me an answer as he carried me up the stairs to his apartment. He entered the key code and kicked the door open, then stomped inside. He carried me all the way into his bedroom and deposited me onto his bed.

I sat up on the edge of it and glared at him. "You're fucking ridiculous. I'm not some damsel in distress."

"You're a damsel," Belial countered. "And you were in distress."

Fury washed up inside of me, and I threw an ice blast at him. I knew it wouldn't do anything more than annoy him, and he knocked it aside easily.

"Still trying to kill me even after I saved your life?" he asked, arching an eyebrow. "You know by now that won't work."

"No, but this will." I stood up and held the Void key to his neck. "I can use this on you."

Belial took a step closer, until we were basically on top of each other, as he stared into my eyes with a challenge. "You won't."

"What's stopping me?" I asked, suddenly breathless.

"This."

Belial's hands slid into my hair, and then his mouth crashed down on mine. Shock washed through me as he kissed me hard, followed by a rush of desire and a sense of *rightness*. I dropped the Void key almost instantly, my hands needing to touch him instead, to wrap around his neck and pull him even closer. His kiss seemed to melt the ice around my heart, and I couldn't get enough of it. I demanded more of his lips, his tongue, his taste. He groaned in response and devoured me with the same primal need, and something within me shifted. Like I'd had this aching, empty feeling inside me all along, but now someone had taken a cup and poured in Belial, filling me up for the first time ever.

We belong together, I realized, and then wondered what the fuck would have brought that thought on. Then it struck me, and I pulled back with a gasp, looking at Belial's face for any indication of whether he felt it too. His eyes flashed with possessive need, like he was ready to pull me back into his arms again, and my soul sang for him to do it. It was clear he'd been struck by the same madness.

Surely, it couldn't be—a mate bond? No. It wasn't possible. I wouldn't accept it. But it felt so damn *right*.

How could Death, the killer of my father, be my fated mate?

17

EIRA

Belial reached for me again and lust ran through me, answering his call, and I wanted nothing more than for him to rip off my clothes and claim me completely. But somehow I managed to back away, stepping out of range, still trembling with the revelation of what we were to each other.

"No," I said, shaking my head. "You can't be my fated mate."

"I am," Belial said, gazing at me with absolute certainty. "I didn't believe it at first either, but it explains the pull between us. Now the kiss has confirmed it."

"I don't believe it." I covered my face with my hands, trying to block him out, even though he was now a part of me I couldn't ignore. The kiss had activated the mate bond fully, and I knew, deep down, things would never go back to the way they were before. Fuck.

"It's how I was able to keep you alive," Belial said. "I shared some of my power with you and it brought you back from the dead."

I dropped my hands and gaped at him. "No. That's impossible."

"It's the truth. The sooner you accept that we're mates, the easier it will be on both of us."

I sank back down on the bed, feeling suddenly weak again. "How is this even possible? This has to be a mistake."

Belial watched me for a moment, and then opened up his closet and shoved his clothes aside, revealing a huge safe in the back. I'd seen it during my time snooping around the apartment, but obviously couldn't open it. He entered a code and the door swung open, and then he removed a huge, sheathed sword from inside. Okay, that was not what I'd expected to be in there.

"Take this," he said, holding it out to me hilt-first.

I stared up at him, trying to figure out why he was giving this to me, but his eyes were impassive. I gingerly wrapped my hand around the hilt. "Why?"

"This is Morningstar, an ancient sword forged specifically for Lucifer, and him alone. It burns anyone else who touches it."

"It's not burning me."

"Only Lucifer, his fated mate, and their children can hold it..." Belial paused, arching his eyebrows at me. "And their mates."

I quickly thrust the sword back at him. "And if I refuse?"

His mouth curved up in a smirk. "We both know you won't."

"I could reject you, you know. It's been done before."

"Impossible." Belial's eyes flashed with dark fire. "Now that I've confirmed you're my mate, I'm not letting you go."

A shiver ran through me at his possessive words, and I hated how much I liked them. I crossed my arms. "I don't want this."

"I wasn't looking for this either, but there's no way we can deny it." He set the sword down and took a step closer to me, like he couldn't fight the pull between us any longer. "Besides, I need you."

I clenched my hands into fists at the vulnerable note in his voice. *Don't get taken in by it,* I told myself sternly. "What are you talking about?"

He breathed in sharply, then sat on the bed beside me. "To become Death, I had to sacrifice my soul. I've been hollow ever since, like I'm missing a part of myself." He paused and his face tightened, almost as if he was in pain. "And then there's the hunger."

"Hunger?" I asked.

"The hunger for death. I have to steal life to sate it, or I'll lose control." He slanted a dark look at me. "That would be very dangerous for everyone."

My throat tightened. "Is that why you go hunting every night?"

He nodded. "If I have to kill, I can at least try to protect my city at the same time. But when I met you, everything changed. The hunger fades away when you're near. Every time we touch, I feel complete again."

"What does that mean?" I asked.

His hand cupped my cheek. "It means you're my mate. I've lived for thousands of years and even though I had another mate once before, I've never felt anything like this. I assumed I would never find love again, especially once I gave up my soul. But then I met you."

"Belial..." I swallowed hard, as I found myself leaning into his touch. "None of this makes any sense."

"You're my other half. There's no denying it."

This time when he pulled me into his arms and kissed me, I gave in. I pressed myself against him, letting his words echo through my head. I could *feel* the truth of them, and the mate bond was impossible to deny, no matter how much I wanted to fight it. All we could do was let it sweep us away.

The kiss between us grew more intense, and I trembled as Belial ran his hands over my body, tracing my curves through my thin Spring Court dress. When he captured my breast in his palm and gave a light squeeze, I gasped against his lips. My fingers tangled in his dark hair, needing to touch him, to keep his mouth on me for as long as I could. Kissing him was like being ravished, and I couldn't get enough.

His broke the kiss to my dismay, but then he trailed his lips down my neck, and I sighed and arched to give him better access. His mouth sent heat through me with every kiss, while his thumbs traced my nipples, making them hard as pebbles. Then his hands skimmed down my body, to my hips, and then to my thighs, where he fisted the fabric of my dress and pulled it higher. And higher. Giving him access to the soft skin of my thighs, and everything between them.

"Are you wet for me, my mate?" he asked, his voice low in my ear. "Let's find out."

His large fingers slipped between my thighs, and I realized the men hadn't bothered to put underwear on me when they'd dressed me. Typical. I couldn't complain though, not when Belial traced a finger over the folds of my pussy with a satisfied smirk.

"Mmm, very wet indeed."

His finger suddenly plunged inside me, making me gasp. My hands tightened around his tattooed arms, not to stop him, but to stop myself from falling over. I was still a bit tired from what had happened, but more than that, I was overwhelmed by what he was making me feel. Then he pulled his finger out and slid it into his mouth, tasting me, while his eyes locked on mine. Inside them I saw that hunger he spoke of, though I could see that he craved me and not death. The intensity of his desire made me weak in the knees, and I knew I wouldn't be able to resist him. Nor did I really want to anymore.

"You taste even better than I imagined," he said. "But I need more."

He fell to his knees in front of me and pressed his nose into the gap between my thighs, shoving the dress up even higher. I gasped as his face nuzzled against me and I gripped his shoulders, anxiously awaiting whatever he would do next. Anticipation mixed with desire and set my body alight. I could hardly hear anything over the sound of my beating heart.

Finally, he dipped his mouth between my thighs and found my clit. I let out a moan as he explored my pussy, taking his sweet time, like he wanted to devour every inch of me. My head fell back as he teased me with his tongue, licking and sucking, but never quite giving me enough to set me over the edge. His hands gripped my hips, holding me in place, and each tightening of his fingers against my skin sent little shocks of pleasure though me. Every muscle in my body was clenched tight, waiting for more.

Belial yanked my hips to the edge of the bed and began devouring me like I was is favorite meal. I dug my hands into his still-clothed shoulders, my claws shredding the material of his shirt like it was nothing. Belial didn't do anything but growl and double down, almost as if he was egging me into an orgasm, pushing me closer and closer to the edge of it. I leaned my head back, waves of pleasure running through me, as it built and built. Finally it was too much and I came with a shout, my legs trembling, my hands hanging onto Belial's shoulders like I might be lost if I let go.

"You taste divine," he said, licking his lips, and my already weak legs threatened to give out completely at that. He rose to his feet and began pulling off his shirt, drawing my eyes to his chest. I sucked in a breath as his skin was revealed before me, every perfect inch of his muscled body. He reached for his jeans next.

"Belial..." I said, making him pause. He probably thought I was going to push him away or end this now. Instead I looked up at him with everything I wanted clear in my eyes and said, "Don't stop."

"I don't intend to." With a carnal grin, he slid his jeans down, along with whatever was underneath. I'd had a glimpse of his impressive cock before, but hadn't allowed myself to really look at it. Now I gave myself permission to stare, and I drank in the sight of it —long, thick, and hard, and all for me.

Then he gripped the light fabric of my dress in his fists again, and lifted the entire thing above my head. I wore nothing underneath and his gaze roamed over me, taking me in while the hunger in his eyes only grew more intense.

"I've lived for thousands of years, but you're the most beautiful thing I've ever seen," he said, and my heart skipped a beat at the words. Then his voice dipped lower. "And now I shall claim you as mine."

He pushed me down on the bed, his hands almost rough, though I knew he would never truly hurt me. With desperate need, he yanked my legs apart and settled between them, like he couldn't wait even a second longer. Then his eyes met mine as his cock thrust into me, hard and fast. I let out a soft cry as he filled me completely and wrapped my legs around him, bringing him closer to me and pulling him in deeper.

Something clicked into place as he bottomed out, as if I'd been missing this my entire life, and now I was finally whole. I met his gaze as he began moving inside me, shocked at the feeling of how right it felt.

He's my mate.

I finally accepted it, unable to deny the bond between us any longer. Somehow fate had brought us together, and I knew it was never letting us go after this. Our lives were bound together forever from this moment onward. The thought of that still scared me, but it was hard to worry about it when Belial's cock was pounding into me, sending unimaginable pleasure through my entire body.

I wrapped my arms around him, trying to bring him closer, to pull him deeper. I wanted to feel him at the very core of me, deep in my soul. Belial let out a low growl, as if he felt the same need, and he yanked up my hips, trying to fill me even more. The friction against my clit at this angle, along with the slide of his cock in and out of me, had me whimpering. I was hardly off of my first orgasm, and he was already hurtling me toward a second.

"You're mine," he growled, but then he suddenly rolled us over, so I was on top, straddling him. "But I'm yours too."

"Mine..." I whispered, gazing down at him, feeling his cock pulsing inside me. The word felt strange on my lips. How had Belial gone from being an enemy to being *mine*?

"Show me," he ordered. "Ride me. Fuck me. *Claim* me."

I drew in a breath and pressed my hands to his chest, then began moving up and down on him. Slowly at first. It was easier to let him claim me. To be his. But I wanted him to me mine too. Desperately. And maybe he needed to see that.

With each rock of my hips, my pace increased, as did the pleasure. He dug his fingers into my hips and thrust upward to meet me, and soon I was riding him fast and hard, chasing my own pleasure, needing to feel that cock deeper and deeper inside me. I threw my head back and let go, and then my vision whited out and I clenched around him, spinning into another orgasm, this one even more intense than the first.

I cried his name as I rode him through my orgasm, and he groaned and thrust up harder in response as his own climax swept over him. I didn't want it to end though, so I kept going, until we were both so spent that he wrapped his arms around me and dragged me down against his chest, his cock still throbbing inside me.

Aftershocks of pleasure went through me as the mate bond sealed. It was done. I was bonded to Belial, and we would be mates forever now. Before I might have resisted it, but now I closed my eyes and gave in to the feeling. I wanted it, more than I'd ever wanted anything in my life.

I didn't know what would happen between us, or how we could ever truly be together, but for the first time in my life I finally felt like I belonged.

18

EIRA

I opened my eyes to a dark room and immediately knew I was alone. Belial's scent lingered in the air, but I didn't hear his movements anywhere in the apartment. The sleek, modern alarm clock on his bedside table told me it was 2 AM. I hadn't even remembered falling asleep, but then again, Belial had thoroughly worn me out last night, and I'd already been pretty tired from the whole nearly-dying thing. Good thing I healed fast.

I glanced over at Belial's side of the bed, even though I knew he wouldn't be there. Where had he gone? Down to his bar? Or on another one of his nightly hunts? He'd told me he had to kill to keep the hunger for death under control, but he'd also said that being around me calmed that need. Yet now he was gone again, and I didn't know what to think. Maybe killing was now a compulsion for him, an addiction he couldn't get over, no matter what he said. Why else would he leave me so soon after we'd just sealed our mate bond?

"What have I done?" I whispered, as regret and shame washed over me. I'd come to New Orleans to kill Belial, not sleep with him. *Definitely* not to become his mate. This was all wrong. But even now I couldn't stop wanting him. I pressed the palms of my hands into my eyes, as if I could forget every earth-shattering orgasm I'd had at his hands, and lips, and cock...

Stop it! I told myself. I sucked in a breath and tried to pull myself together. I needed to get out of this place so I could think without all of the reminders of Belial—and his absence—around me.

I ignored my discarded Spring Court dress on the floor and went for my luggage in the living room, where I pulled out a gray t-shirt and jeans. I'd go out and get some fresh air to clear my head, before coming back here, and Belial would probably never even know I was gone. And if he did know, why did I care? I wasn't his prisoner anymore. I could go where I wanted. If he had a problem with that, too fucking bad.

I left quickly, making my way down the stairs to the door into Belial's garage. His sleek Ducati motorcycle was parked beside his Aston Martin, and I debated which one I was going to borrow. I got on the bike and started it up, planning to ride around the city for a while with no real destination in mind. As I revved the motor, I considered going to Loki, but I wasn't ready to give him the Void key yet, and I had a feeling he wouldn't be amused by the news that I'd become Belial's mate. The two of them seemed to have some bad blood between them.

As I rode out of the garage, something strange bubbled up inside me, yanking me in one direction. It had been a few days since I'd last felt it—the call of the Furies.

I tried to ignore it, gritting my teeth and driving faster. I wasn't going to be under anyone's control. Not Belial's, and not the Furies' either. But the more I tried to deny the pull, the stronger it got, and somehow I looked up and found myself staring at the rusted, faded sign outside Jazzland. I didn't even remember the journey, like my body had taken over even while my mind fought back.

I got off the bike, wondering why they'd brought me here now. The abandoned amusement park was even more eerie at night, just like when I'd dreamed about it, and my skin crawled even as the tug in my gut made me take steps forward.

But as soon as I climbed over the fence and entered the desolate place, I got the feeling I was alone. I breathed in sharply, able to use my wolf senses now that I no longer wore the cuffs, but didn't smell any shifters or imps around me. The few lingering scents were a few days old, as if they'd cleared out of the place just after Belial and I had found them. But where had they gone? And why was I still drawn to this place?

The sound of quiet steps on the sidewalk made me freeze. Something flickered in the corner of my eye, and I jerked my head toward it. I raised my fists, ready to call on my ice magic to defend myself, but relaxed a tiny bit as I smelled my brother's familiar scent.

Skoll was in wolf form as he approached, his black fur blending into the night, but his burning red eyes gave away his position. Another sound on the other side of me caught my attention, along with a second familiar scent. I spun around as my other brother, Hati, crept toward me, his white fur bristling.

I glanced between both of them nervously as they approached, while tension hung between us. I'd never been afraid of them before in my life, but now I wasn't sure if they were truly themselves anymore.

When they made no move to attack me, I asked, "Where did the Furies go?"

"They prepare to bring Tisiphone to Earth tonight, at the Blood Moon," Skoll said.

That must be the name of the Fury of vengeance. "How?"

"Sacrifice," Hati growled.

That didn't sound good. "What kind of sacrifice?"

Hati bared his fangs in a dark, dangerous smile. "You'll see."

"Join us," Skoll said, as they prowled around me in a circle. "Together we can stop Belial. With the Furies, even he won't be able to stand against our might and power."

"Belial isn't the enemy," I said. "The Furies are."

"He's in her head," Hati growled.

Skoll's red eyes narrowed. "Eira, have you forgotten that he killed our father? Along with many other shifters?"

"I haven't forgotten, but you never told me the whole story. Like how Dad became Death, the fourth Horseman, and lost himself completely."

"Does it matter?" Skoll asked, his ears twitching. "None of that changes that Belial was the one to end his life."

"He needs to be stopped before he kills more of our people," Hati added.

I bit my lip, torn between my brothers and my mate. I understood how my brothers felt, because I'd shared the same feelings only days ago, when rage and a need for vengeance had consumed me. Besides, Belial could be out there right now, killing at this very moment, and I wasn't sure I would be able to ever stop him.

But I couldn't kill Belial either. He was my mate, no matter how much I'd tried to deny it, and we were bound together for the rest of our immortal days. I wasn't ready to admit that to my brothers just yet though. I could only imagine the way their rage would turn upon me if they knew.

I had to be careful here. My brothers were still being controlled by the Furies, and picking Belial over them could lead to my death. Besides, if I could convince them I was their ally, they might give me information, which I could use to stop the Furies tonight.

"You're right," I said. "He has to be stopped. I will join you."

"To join us, you must betray him," Skoll said, cocking his wolf head. "Can you do this?"

"Yes," I lied. "It won't be a problem."

Hati gave a sly, cold smile. "Good. Welcome back to the pack."

"Bring Belial to the Ursuline Convent at midnight," Skoll said. "We will deal with him then."

I nodded, feeling a lump in my throat. "We'll be there."

"And vengeance will finally be ours," Hati said.

They slipped away into the shadows and I drew in a deep breath, relieved to be alone again, even if this place gave me the creeps. I ducked my head and rubbed my arms against the chill in them, which had nothing to do with the weather, as I set off for the bike again.

A movement in the sky caught my attention and I looked up, not sure what to expect this time. Belial swooped down on his beautiful black and white ombre wings, his long cape flowing behind him. As he drew close, the cold look on his face could have killed on the spot. He truly looked like Death at that moment—and he was coming right for me.

But I wasn't afraid. I stood my ground, waiting for him to land, refusing to run away. I knew he would never hurt me.

"What are you doing here?" he growled, the second his feet touched the ground. "Why did you leave?"

"I could ask you the same thing," I said, glaring back at him. "I woke up and you were gone."

He raised his eyes to the sky. "I had something to deal with in the bar. I was coming right back."

"Well, how should I know that?" I asked. "I just needed to get away for a while, but then I found myself here."

His eyes narrowed and then he let out a low whistle and his horse appeared. Belial's hands wrapped around my waist, and then he lifted me up like I weighed nothing and deposited me on Ghost's back. He climbed on behind me, wrapping his arms around me tightly, like he worried I might run away at any second.

"You're coming back with me," he said, as the horse took off running.

19

EIRA

As Ghost raced forward alongside the highway, I struggled against Belial, pushing his hand off of my waist. Fury ignited inside me. He had no say over where I went or what I did.

"I'll jump off of your damn horse," I threatened. "You can't keep me like a pet."

"You're not my pet, you're my mate," Belial said, wrapping his arm around me once more. This time, he pinned my arms flat against my sides, and it was impossible to break free. "I'm not letting you go," he continued, his voice right in my ear. I could feel his lips brushing the delicate shell of my ear, and involuntary shivers went through me. "I lost my mate once before, and it's never happening again."

I could hear real pain in his voice, and I softened. He'd never spoken about this before, and though I was a little jealous he'd had a mate before me, I was also intrigued. "What happened?"

"She was a gargoyle named Soria and we were together for a century in Hell. But during my rebellion against my father, Loki betrayed us and she was killed."

"No wonder you hate him so much," I muttered.

"Indeed." His voice turned grim. "I lost the battle, I lost my lover, and I lost my family when I was exiled." The pain in his voice increased, and for the first time he sounded almost vulnerable. "I never thought I would ever find a mate again... Until now."

He tightened his hold against me more, but it felt reassuring rather than painful this time. I relaxed slightly against him. "Look, I don't know how or why we have this bond between us, but I'm not resisting it any longer. I wasn't running away. I just needed some space to think. Especially because I thought you had run away—or gone out hunting again."

"It seems we both overreacted a tiny bit," he admitted with a low chuckle. "The mate bond does tend to make one a little...crazy sometimes."

"So it seems."

"The feeling is stronger this time too." He nuzzled his lips against my neck. "I can't think of anything else but you."

"I know what you mean." My breath caught as his mouth brushed my skin and his hands tightened on my hips. Behind me, his cock pressed into my ass, hot and hard, and I couldn't help but squirm back into it. I wanted him inside me again, with a startling intensity.

"I think it's because I'm part fae," I gasped out as Belial's hand moved to cup my breast. "Our mating bonds are more intense than for demons and angels. The bond is almost all-consuming, especially at first. Or so I've heard."

"Yes, all-consuming..." He pinched my nipple while his teeth nipped at my neck. "I want to consume you right now."

I rocked back, trying to meet his cock, to get any kind of relief, and Belial let out a low growl. Ghost made an annoyed whine in response as his feet pounded against the pavement, while Belial's shadow magic concealed us from the few cars that drove along the highway at this hour.

Unable to stop myself, I reached back and slid my hand between our bodies, touching Belial through the fabric of his pants. He let out a harsh breath and rolled his hips into my body, then slid his free hand along the front of my jeans, dipping between my legs. He was talented with his fingers, even through the thick fabric, and he had me panting and moaning almost instantly.

I rubbed him through his pants, unable to get the leverage to properly take him in hand. Good thing the ride back to Belial's place was short. Ghost dropped us off with a disgusted snort, before disappearing into thin air.

Belial pushed me against the wall the moment we were inside of the building. I ran my hands over his chest, sliding my fingers under his shirt so I could feel the smooth, hard ridges of his abs.

"Should we go upstairs?" I asked.

"Do you want to wait that long?"

That was a fair point. I plunged my hand inside his pants and gripped his length. He let out a groan and thrust into my hand shallowly. I watched in wonder as his face opened, the last of the anger and hurt fading. It was replaced with pleasure, and when he looked at me, there was nothing but hunger in his eyes. He drew me closer and kissed me hard, the mate bond wrapping around us like a warm blanket, while he tugged open the front of my jeans. He slid them down without hesitation, taking my panties with them, just low enough for him to slide a finger into my wet pussy.

"Turn around," he commanded, and I did it without a second thought.

He moved behind me, pressing me against the wall, bringing his lips to the exposed skin of my neck. I heard him shove down his own pants and then felt his cock rubbing along my ass until it found the gap between my thighs.

I spread my legs wider and arched my back to give him better access. "Yes," I hissed as he slid his cock inside of me, my eyes fluttering shut.

Belial began slamming into me, hands on my hips to pull me back as he pleased. I put my hands flat on the wall, bracing myself against the impact. His pace was unrelenting, his body so strong it felt like he might tear me apart, but I welcomed it. I wanted it all.

It didn't matter how many times we did this, each time was just as good as the first one. There was something about the mate bond that made sex ten times better. I couldn't describe it, but it was like I was just now finding some hidden part of me that no one else had been able to touch.

I moaned as his cock hit me in just the right way, and then clamped my jaw shut, wondering if there was anyone around who could hear us. We were in the middle of the stairwell, where anyone could walk out and see us.

"Don't you dare be quiet," Belial growled. "I want to hear every noise you make for me. *Because* of me."

I squeezed my eyes shut as he found my clit with his fingers and began stroking it, while pounding into me again and again. Pretty soon I didn't have a choice but to let out little cries and moans as he claimed me with his cock. I wondered if people from the bar could hear me. *Do I even care?* I thought as my eyes rolled back in my head. *Not one bit.*

Then he suddenly pulled out and turned me around, plastering me up against the wall once more. "I want to see you when you come."

"Only if you come with me," I said, my voice breathless.

He growled at that as he wrapped my legs around his hips. I gasped as he entered me again, then reached forward and slid my hand around the back of his head, clutching at the nape of his neck. We stared into each other's eyes, turning this quick, desperate fuck into something so intimate it made my heart ache.

Overwhelming pleasure rocked through me like a lightning bolt and I screamed Belial's name, my pussy clenching around his cock. He continued slamming into me through my orgasm, but then he threw his head back and roared as his own release took hold of him. Then his mouth found mine again and we devoured each other, unable to get enough, even when he was still inside me.

Reluctantly, he let me go, and we yanked up our pants. Then he lifted me in his arms and carried me up the stairs. This time, I didn't resist. Fuck, I wasn't sure if I could even make it up the stairs right now, after what he'd just done to me.

Once we returned to his living room, Belial set me down on the couch. "I'll make you something to eat."

"How did you know I was hungry?" I asked.

He grinned as he headed into the kitchen. "You're part shifter. As far as I can tell, they're always hungry."

I couldn't argue with that. I relaxed into the couch, trying to remember what I'd been doing before I'd been pinned against Belial's wall. Right, the Furies. "My brothers were there when I went to Jazzland again, but otherwise the place was empty."

"Did they say anything?" Belial asked, as he pulled out some bread and cheese.

"They're going to bring the third Fury into the world tonight, during the Blood Moon." I stood and went to stand beside him, setting my hand on his back as he worked, the mate bond demanding I touch him.

"How do they think they're going to do that?" he asked as he put the bread and cheese in the skillet, making a grilled cheese sandwich for me.

"They said something about a sacrifice, which can only be a bad thing. They told me to be at the Ursuline Convent tonight at midnight so I could join them."

Belial frowned at that as he grabbed a spatula. "The Ursuline Convent is one of the oldest structures in New Orleans. The nuns there used to care for the dying during the yellow fever outbreak and for wounded soldiers during the Civil War. It's seen a lot of death over the years. It's also where the famous Casket Girls lived."

"Casket Girls?" I asked, my eyebrows shooting up. "That sounds morbid."

"Not as morbid as you'd think," he said. "They were French women sent to be brides to men in New Orleans. They lived on the third floor of the convent, but a lot of people believed they'd brought evil in with them. Some also believed they were vampires."

"Well, with a name like that, I can see why," I muttered.

"They weren't vampires, of course, but even now, the Ursuline Convent is considered one of the most haunted places in the city because of all of the death that happened there."

"Do you believe in ghosts?" I asked, cocking my head at him. I'd never seen one, but maybe he had, since he was a lot older than me.

Belial shook his head. "I've seen a lot of strange shit in my life, but never a real ghost. Some creatures like to pretend, but they always end up being something else." He finished frying up the sandwich and put it on a plate for me. "Still, with its dark history, it's one of the places where the barrier between worlds is a little thinner, which is probably why they've chosen that spot. The Blood Moon will also make their magic more potent tonight."

"Makes sense," I said, before taking a bite of the sandwich, which was as simple as it was delicious. I had to admit, I was enjoying being with a man who liked to keep me well-fed.

"Midnight, you said?" Belial asked, leaning back against the counter as he watched me eat.

"That's what they told me." I finished off the rest of the sandwich in record time.

"Then we'll be there tonight to stop whatever this sacrifice is, and we'll use our Void key to send the Furies back where they came from."

"Do you think that will be enough to free my brothers and the others the Furies have enthralled?"

"It should be. Once they're safely sealed back in Void, they won't have any power here anymore."

I nodded, but knew it wouldn't be easy. To stop the sacrifice and use the Void key, we'd have to go up against both my brothers and the Furies, along with all the other shifters and imps that followed them. Doing this would mean turning against my family completely, even though I was trying to help them. But in their eyes, I would be siding with Belial over them.

Choosing my mate over my family—could I really do it?

20

BELIAL

W ith the Blood Moon bright overhead, I carried Eira across New Orleans, keeping us wrapped in shadows so none would see us—although I suspected the Furies could sense my power as I approached. I sensed them too, like the presence of another Elder God or two was calling to me. With soft steps, I landed on the roof of the Ursuline Convent's main building, and pieces of it crumbled beneath me despite my caution. The white French colonial buildings below us were old, possibly the oldest structures left in New Orleans, and they formed a courtyard around a garden that looked almost like a maze.

I set Eira down and she nodded at me. She was dressed in all black, her white hair tied up in a bun, and my heart twisted at the sight of her. I'd do everything in my power to make sure she was safe tonight, but she was a warrior too—I would do her a disservice if I didn't allow her to fight.

With shadows concealing us, we walked to the edge of the roof to peer down into the courtyard below. Dozens of shifters, imps, and even humans were gathered there, all facing the steps of the Convent, where the two Furies stood. They had their hands up and their eyes closed, and I heard a low, rhythmic chanting coming from their direction. On either side of them, acting as their guardians, were Eira's brothers, both in their wolf forms, one dark, and one light.

The crowd was all staring forward, completely entranced as the Furies continued chanting, and many of them appeared hostile. Their faces were twisted, their hands clenched into fists, their feet stomping almost comically.

"The Furies are spreading anger and jealousy," Eira whispered. She closed her eyes and shuddered slightly. "I can feel it."

"Will it be a problem?"

She breathed out slowly and met my eyes. "No. I can fight it."

I stared down at the people below, who seemed to grow more agitated by the second. "They're whipping these people into a frenzy. Soon things will get violent."

"We have to stop them," Eira said.

Before we could act, the Furies' chanting became louder, drowning out everything else, and then a wave of red and green magic passed over the assembled group. Without warning, the shifters and imps turned on the humans and began attacking them, ripping them apart like they were nothing more than animals, killing them with claws and talons and fangs within seconds.

Eira gasped at the horror of it all and clutched my arm. "This is the sacrifice."

"Yes." I'd seen countless battles during my life, but this was a bloodbath, and it happened so quickly it seemed impossible to stop. "And with every death, the Furies channel the power into creating a portal to Void."

As we watched, deathly power rippled back into the space between the two Furies, where the air shimmered like a heat mirage. Space and time were literally ripping open, and the veil between worlds was growing thinner with every human's death.

Eira took a step forward, nearly launching herself off the roof. "We have to do something before the portal is open!"

"It's too late," I said. "It's already open."

Eira looked over at me, her jaw clenched, her eyes burning with determination. "I have a plan. Can you distract the shifters and the imps so we can get down there?"

"Of course." I reached out with my Death magic, knowing it would alert the Furies, but we were past any subtlety now. I latched onto the dead humans in the courtyard and sent life back into them, or some semblance of it, anyway. It was always easier to raise the fresh dead, and they responded to my call immediately.

The shifters and imps began looking around in confusion as their recent kills started twitching, standing up, or crawling toward them. My undead shambled forward in a mass, going after the imps and shifters with their jerky, nightmarish movements, and then they began fighting against the very people who had just killed them.

"That should keep them busy for a while." I pulled Morningstar from the sheath I'd slung over my back and handed it to Eira. "Take this when you go. And be careful."

"I will." She stared down at the sword in awe as it lit up with black and white light, showing it was deadly to both angels and demons. Her own ice magic coated the blade too, as she tested the weight of it. "Thank you."

I grabbed her and kissed her soundly, trying to communicate everything I couldn't put into words with that kiss. Now that I'd found Eira and accepted who she was to me, I had a hard time letting her go, but we had a job to do here. No one else would be able to stop the Furies tonight except us.

"Don't die on me," I told her.

"I won't," she said with a mischievous grin. "After all, I have Death on my side."

I wrapped my arms around her and lifted off the roof, then dropped us down right in front of the Furies. Behind us was the throng of shifters and imps fighting their recent kills, but they didn't pay us any notice. Eira launched herself toward Alecto and Megaera, and I unleashed my own power against them, sending a flaming ball of hellfire at their dark, hooded forms. It crashed against them and they were buffeted backward, their chanting cut off immediately. The portal spasmed and began to grow thin, like mist that was being carried away by the night.

The Furies each unleashed an earsplitting scream of anger as they dragged themselves up and turned their full attention to me. Eira's brothers descended from the steps, their huge wolf forms almost as dangerous as the Furies. I prepared myself to fight them all, drawing upon my reserves of power. There might be a lot of them, but I was Death. I could not be defeated.

"Wait!" Eira's voice rang out across the din, cutting through it all. "Stop!"

Was this her plan? I readied my next hellfire shot, ready to protect her with everything I had, while I waited to see what she did next. Her brothers and the Furies paused though, almost as if they'd been expecting something like this.

"You don't need to kill any more people as a sacrifice," Eira said, holding her hands up in a placating gesture. "I have a Void key, and I'll use it to bring the third Fury to Earth."

What? I glanced her way, wondering if this was a trick. She wouldn't really give them the Void key, would she?

The Furies cocked their heads with dark smiles. "We knew you would see things our way," Alecto said.

"The only thing I ask for is the power of vengeance from the third Fury to send Belial into Void," Eira continued in a cool, even tone, without looking at me once.

The world seemed to disappear under my feet, dragging me down with it. Or at least that's how it felt, hearing Eira's words. Shock rippled through me at her betrayal, and I could only stare at her, wondering if I'd had it all wrong.

The two wolves seemed to grin at her words, their eyes burning with hatred as they fixated on me. Had they gotten to her when she'd met with them?

Or had she been plotting this all along and I'd been too infatuated by her to notice?

"Vengeance will be yours," Megaera said, gesturing for Eira to step forward. "Give us the Void key."

"Release the others first," Eira said, glancing back at the mad horde fighting behind us.

Alecto sighed as if this was a true hardship. "Very well."

Another wave of power erupted from them, and the shifters and imps behind us suddenly stumbled and collapsed. I reached out with a tiny bit of my power and found they were alive, just completely drained of energy. Their demon healing would kick in soon and they'd be fine, albeit somewhat traumatized. I couldn't say the same for the humans they'd killed though.

As Eira stepped toward the Furies, I called out, "Don't do this, Eira."

Her eyes finally locked onto mine, and all I saw in them was rage. "Stay away from me."

I staggered back under the weight of her hatred. She'd really turned against me. She must have been pretending to care about me all this time, gaining my trust so she could look for a way to defeat me, all the while plotting to betray me. Now she finally had her chance.

This can't be happening, I thought. *Turn around, look at me. Give me a sign that what we had was real.*

She didn't.

Her brothers dodged in front of me, blocking me from getting to her, as she clutched the Void key in her hand. I'd given up the fight at this point anyway. Why bother, when my own mate wanted me dead? Did any of this even matter, without her?

Another thought struck me, one that had festered inside of me ever since I'd become Death. Did I even deserve to live? Perhaps I belonged in Void with the other Elder Gods. The world would certainly be safer without me in it. Especially if I didn't have Eira at my side, calming my hunger.

Maybe this was the end of Death.

21

EIRA

I held out the Void key and the portal burst open with a horrible
ripping sound, like the world itself was being torn apart around
me. A chaotic swirl of glittering lights and hazy mist formed against
a black background that seemed as empty and vast as space. My eyes
could barely comprehend the strange sights and the feeling of
unknowable power in front of me, and I quickly turned my gaze
away, fearing what would happen if I stared at the portal to Void too
long.

Instead, I finally allowed myself to look back at Belial. I'd been
avoiding it, afraid that everything would show on my face the
moment I did. I didn't want the Furies to doubt me for a second, but
now they weren't focused on me at all, but at the portal in front
of me.

Belial stared at me, his face completely dead, with only defeat
and heartbreak in his eyes. My heart wrenched in my chest, but
before I could consider it further, there was an inhuman shriek,
almost deafening in my ear.

I turned just in time to see a deathly yellow spirit full of rage
pouring through the portal. The fury and need for vengeance hit me
like a storm, and I doubled over. I coughed, as if it was something I

needed to get out of my body physically, and then I heard one of the Furies speak.

"Sister, take Eira's body. She is your vessel!"

I'd known this was coming when I made my deal with the Furies, but panic still spiked inside me as the spirit surged toward me. As the Fury drew near, I was hit with the absolute need for revenge, the certainty that defeating Belial and having my vengeance was the most important thing in the world. All I had to do was let this Fury take over my body, and together we would be unstoppable.

"No!" Belial yelled.

A roar of bright blue hellfire went past my ear and slammed into the Fury of vengeance, who shrieked and fell back. It was just enough to break me of her spell and I shook my head, trying to clear it of her influence.

The other two Furies turned on Belial, and I watched as they changed. Alecto had possessed the body of a shifter, and now she changed into a giant alligator before my eyes. She let out a wild scream that faded into a roar, while Megaera grew the black talons of an imp, thanks to the body she possessed.

The huge, lumbering alligator lunged at Belial, who started aiming half of his hellfire balls at her. Meanwhile, Megaera slashed at him with her claws and then exploded into ten versions of herself with illusion magic, all circling around and diving at him. When my brothers joined in the fray, their wolves out for blood, I feared Belial wouldn't be able to withstand it all. He might not be able to die, but the Furies were slowly inching him toward the portal, making him lose ground to avoid getting caught by claws or a heavy sweep from the Fury's alligator tail. I had to do something to save him.

While Belial shot hellfire at the Furies, his undead army came up behind him, and they tackled my brothers. The wolves snapped and tore at the zombie-like human corpses, but there were too many of them. With a flick of his deathly power, Belial knocked both of the wolves out, my brothers collapsing into the grass. I hoped they were only knocked out anyway, and not dead.

Now it was only the three Furies fighting against Death. Four immortals, locked in a power struggle that would only end when some of them were shoved into Void.

Finally, I saw my opportunity. I unsheathed Morningstar and raced toward Megaera, the green-eyed Fury of jealousy who was using the imp's magic to confuse Belial. She took a few stumbling steps back as Belial hit her with hellfire square in the chest, and she didn't hear me coming up behind her. I was able to grab hold of her loose robe and pull her back onto Morningstar. She let out a wail, scrabbling at me and the sword, but I encased her in ice, her body impaled on the sword. I knew it wouldn't hold her for long though, but I was already in motion. With shifter strength, I shoved her toward the portal, and heaved Morningstar out of her back as she fell into Void.

The other Furies screamed in response, and the alligator roared, "You dare betray us like this?"

She ambled toward me with unnatural speed, her jaws wide, her fangs glistening under the moonlight, and I knew she would chomp down on me within seconds. But then Belial lunged at her with a growl, picking her up with his impossible strength. He lifted the alligator over his head and swung her around like he was a wrestler, before tossing her into the portal. Yes! Two Furies down, one to go. But we had to make it quick, before the Furies came through again.

I turned toward Belial, hoping he would see in my eyes that this had been my plan all along and that I hadn't betrayed him—but before I could so much as say his name, something rammed into me from the side. I fell down the stairs, landing badly on an unconscious bear shifter, while Morningstar fell out of my hand.

The third Fury, still a cloud of noxious, yellow gas that radiated rage, hovered over me like a malevolent cloud. "My sisters told me about you," the rattling, wheezing voice said. "They said you wanted vengeance, and I will give it to you. All you have to do is let me in, and we can have our retribution together."

Her power surged into me, filling me with rage, hatred, and a need for revenge, but this time I fought back against it. I reached for the mate bond with Belial and focused on that. "No," I forced out through clenched teeth. "I'm done with vengeance. It won't change the past, and I have to move forward."

The Fury hissed above me, and her incorporeal body reached for me. "You will be mine," she snapped, as she surged toward me.

I blasted her with ice as I scrambled back, but it did little against her ghostly form. She surrounded me suddenly, and I coughed, blinking and trying to fight as my vision turned completely yellow. I was being smothered, like she had wrapped herself around me like some demented snake, and I fought against it with everything I had. I closed my eyes and imagined ice coming out of every pore of my body, adrenaline sending my power shooting through me like lightning, and the next moment I was free.

The Fury screamed, blown apart by my ice. I quickly shifted into wolf form and ran, heading back toward the portal. We had to get her inside it somehow. I stopped just in front of the portal and returned to human form, while the Fury coalesced into a spirit again a few feet away from me. She dove to attack me, but something long and black wrapped around her, pulling her back.

Belial stood behind her, and chains made of darkness suddenly burst out of him and wrapped around the Fury. He pummeled her with his magic as the shadow chains wrapped around her, trapping her inside.

"You!" she screamed, struggling to get free. I added my own ice around her, reinforcing Belial's magic, but it was obvious it couldn't hold her for long. The Fury was too strong.

Belial met my eyes, and a sudden calm came over his face, as though he'd made a decision. He rushed toward the Void portal, dragging the shrieking Fury with him. She broke free enough to latch onto him, the two of them struggling against each other, as he leaped toward the portal.

"Belial!" I screamed as he fell into the portal along with the Fury, and I desperately reached out to him. He extended a hand, as if he wanted to caress my face one last time, but I grabbed tightly onto it. For a moment, I thought I was going to be pulled in to the portal as well, and screamed with a new kind of rage.

Belial's hand started slipping through mine and I gripped on tighter, reaching into the portal to try and find his wrist with my other hand. Piercing needles pulled at my skin, as though the portal was trying to tear me apart atom by atom, but I refused to let go. I grabbed hold of Belial and dragged him toward me, until finally, my own hands reappeared.

Belial pushed himself out of the portal with a growl, and together we stumbled back a few feet. Belial turned to me, running his hands over my body as if to check and make sure I was okay, and then looked back at the chaotic, maddening swirl of colors and darkness.

"Do you still have the Void key?" he asked.

I nodded, grabbing it from the pocket I'd somehow managed to stash it inside. "Right here."

"Close the portal, quickly."

I nodded and held the key out, focusing on shutting the portal down. Opening it hadn't been any different from using a Faerie key, but closing it proved to be harder. The portal was like a door in the wind, fighting against my every attempt to shut it, and I could hear the echo of the Furies' voices on the other side. Belial reached over and rested his hand upon mine, adding his strength, and together we wrestled the portal closed.

All at once, it was silent. The overwhelming urge to join the Furies went away like it had never existed at all. The shifters and imps, who had been passed out throughout the courtyard, all seemed to wake up at once and looked around themselves in horror. There was some confusion and shouting, but screams of rage turned to whimpers of fear and panic as most of them started running away, as if they were terrified. Belial released his undead at the same time, and they collapsed in a heap, then turned to dust and floated away on the breeze.

I rushed toward Belial and threw myself into his arms before he could say anything. He embraced me tightly, burying his face in my hair and breathing me in, like he couldn't believe we were really still together.

"I thought you were going to send me to Void too," Belial said, his arms tightening around me.

"Don't be an idiot," I said, pulling back and punching him in the arm lightly. "I was only doing it to trick them."

"I figured that out eventually, but you could have warned me. That was reckless."

"*You're* one to talk," I added, punching him again for good measure. A little harder this time. "You were going to sacrifice yourself to save me."

"I couldn't let that Fury possess you. I know all too well there are costs to being an Elder God, and I wouldn't wish the same fate on you."

"But I almost lost you."

"It would have been worth it anyway, knowing you were safe." He took my face in his hands and gazed into my eyes. "I would do anything for you, Eira. There's no point in life without you. I love you."

My heart swelled as I looked at him. "I love you too."

"Does that mean you're done trying to kill me?" he asked, arching an eyebrow.

"Yes, I'm done with that. I've realized vengeance isn't the answer." I cocked my head to the side with a wry grin. "But don't piss me off or I might change my mind again."

"Noted, my mate," he said with a short laugh, before sweeping me into his arms and kissing me hard.

A low growl made us break apart and turn around. "Mate?" Skoll asked, his voice disgusted.

My brothers, still in wolf form, both watched us with fury in their eyes, but it was a pissed off look I recognized. They were no longer under the Furies' control, but they'd also just seen me kissing the man who had killed our father.

"Yes, Belial is my mate," I said, taking his hand and facing my brothers. "I know you might find that hard to accept, but there's no denying it."

Skoll and Hati exchanged a glance, and then Hati said, "We will talk about this later."

The two of them dashed off down the courtyard and disappeared the same way the other shifters and imps had gone. I had a feeling family dinners would be uncomfortable for a while, but at least they weren't controlled by the Furies anymore. They might never accept Belial as my mate, but I'd do my best to convince them he wasn't our enemy. I didn't want to choose my mate over my family, but there was no denying this bond between us anymore.

We would be mates for the rest of our lives—and mine felt like it was just beginning.

22

BELIAL

"——And then I pulled his dumb ass out of the portal," Eira said, tossing the rest of her drink back.

The chatter of the bar surrounded us, cocooning us in as we sat at the counter. We'd returned here after leaving the Ursuline Convent, and we'd both agreed we could use a good drink after everything we'd just gone through.

Yumi blinked a few times, looking between us with her mouth agape. "So you saved him? Wow. And here I thought the almighty Lord of Death could get himself out of any situation."

I scowled at them both and finished off my drink too. "I could have handled it."

"Yeah, sure." Eira rolled her eyes, before finishing off the story with how she'd closed the portal, trapping the Furies in Void.

"That's one crazy tale," Yumi said, as she poured us another drink. "I'm just glad that New Orleans is safe again."

"You and me both," I said.

Yumi's eyes suddenly widened at something behind me, and I turned, readying to defend my bar if there was a threat. When I saw who had her spooked, I released my magic with a sigh. Loki was a threat, but not in that way.

Tonight his black hair was slicked back and he wore a tuxedo with an emerald green bow tie and matching emerald cuff links, as if he'd just arrived from some fancy charity ball. He flashed us a dazzling, impish smile. "Hello, friends. I see you've survived the night. How fortuitous."

"No thanks to you." I narrowed my eyes at him. "We could have used your help tonight."

He waved his hand dismissively. "I had other pressing matters to attend to, and it seems you've protected the city just fine on your own. Though I'm surprised you're still here, Belial. I thought Eira would have sent you back to Void by now."

Eira reached over and grabbed my hand. "We've worked out our issues."

"I see that," Loki said, his eyes dropping to our hands and then flicking back up to her face. "What do your brothers have to say about that?"

"I don't think they're thrilled, but they'll just have to get over it. Just like the two of you will need to learn to be civil with each other."

"Not possible," I muttered.

Loki's face shifted to amusement. "Oh, Belial. I'm sure we can work something out for the sake of our darling Eira, can't we?"

I glanced at Eira, who looked at me with her bright blue eyes so full of hope it was impossible to say no. "Fine. I'll try."

Loki chuckled at that and then turned back to Eira. "Now that your mission to find your brothers and the missing shifters and imps has been successful, what do you plan to do next?"

"I'd like to go back to being a messenger between the fae and the demons," she said. "I miss visiting Faerie and I want to embrace both parts of who I am."

"That's an excellent idea, and I'm sure I can make that happen. I can always use a trusted messenger." His smirk turned on me. "Especially one who can call on some pretty deadly backup when needed. But first, I do believe we had a deal, and it's time for you to pay up."

I glared at his outstretched hand, knowing exactly what he was asking for. "We should have destroyed the damn thing."

"I'm surprised you didn't," Loki said.

"Eira wouldn't let me," I grumbled.

"I swore I wouldn't use it on you," Loki pointed out.

"Yes, but that's the only thing you promised. There are plenty of other things you could do with the key, like trying to send Lucifer to Void and so you can take over Hell as the Demon King."

"Now what would give you that idea?" Loki asked, his face the picture of innocence. "I would never do such a thing. Lucifer and I are old friends."

"Yeah, but so are we, and I wouldn't trust you not to shove a knife in my back."

"He won't do any of that," Eira said, though she didn't sound entirely convinced. She reached into her pocket and pulled out the glittering black stone, before handing it to Loki. "Here."

"I do appreciate you retrieving this for me." Loki's grin widened as his fingers clasped around the Void key. Then the key vanished, disappearing in a swirl of Loki's illusion magic. "I'll contact you soon about your new position."

Then I blinked, and he was gone. No one else in the bar seemed to notice, which made me wonder if he'd concealed himself from all the other patrons the entire time.

"He is a bit dramatic," Eira admitted.

"You act like he's harmless, but I know better." I tossed the rest of my drink back, and Yumi immediately refilled it. I nodded my thanks to her. "He's going to cause more chaos. That's what he does."

"He's not bad," Eira said. "He even helped us, in his own way."

I wasn't convinced. In fact, the only reason I hadn't challenged Loki was because I did believe he had a soft spot for Eira, and that he would never do anything to hurt her. But if that ever changed? He would face my wrath.

"I'll tell Lucifer to keep an eye on him. Now that he has that Void key, he will surely be plotting to use it."

"Speaking of Lucifer..." Eira started, sounding almost nervous. "When do I get to meet the rest of your family?"

"You want to meet them?" I asked, pausing with my drink halfway to my mouth.

"Of course. I already met one of your brothers, but I know you have more siblings, and I'd like to thank your mom again for saving me."

"And Lucifer?" I asked.

She hesitated. "As long as he can forgive me for my father's sins."

"He's forgiven me, by some miracle. I have a feeling he won't blame you for what Fenrir did either."

"Then yes, I'd like to meet him too." She brushed her finger along my jaw. "I'm all in now. Assuming you want me to stay in New Orleans, of course."

"What kind of question is that?" I asked. Wasn't it obvious I was never letting her go?

Before she could answer, I stood up and grabbed her around the waist, then tossed her over my shoulder. She let out a noise of protest, but didn't fight me as I carted her out of the bar, while Yumi rolled her eyes at the two of us.

I carried Eira all the way upstairs to my apartment, and once we were inside, I set her down gently on my bed and knelt in front of her.

"This is your home now," I said, reaching up and cupping her face in my hands. "Or we can get a bigger one if you want. Wherever you want to be, I'll follow. Whenever you're around, the hunger is gone. With you by my side, I won't ever have to feed on the souls of others again. I thought I was soulless, but the truth is, *you're* my soul."

"You're my home, too," she whispered. "I never felt like I had one until I met you."

"I love you so much," I said, sliding my hands down her shoulders. She was so beautiful, and I'd spend the rest of my life showing her just how much she meant to me.

"I love you too," she whispered. She drew me closer, and I

leaned into her, pressing myself against her to feel the solidness of her body. I'd already almost lost her, and I wasn't going to let it happen again. She moaned against my mouth as I pulled her hips closer to the edge, rising up so I was level with her. I ground my hard length against her stomach, and she pulled away with a gasp.

"Fuck me," she demanded.

"Gladly," I growled.

We both rid ourselves of our clothes so quickly a human might have blinked and missed it. The need for each other swelled again, as it often did thanks to this mate bond, but this time it was different. We'd almost lost each other tonight, but somehow we'd fought our own inner demons and won the battle, both against the Furies and against our pasts. Together we were ready to move on to whatever came next.

Eira's eyes burned with need as she crawled up the bed and spread her legs invitingly. Her pussy was already gleaming, inviting me in as well. I reached down and dipped my fingers inside, the warm heat of her surrounding me. When I pulled my fingers out, I reached them up to taste her. I closed my eyes, savoring her unique, wonderful flavor. I'd been hungry for so long, but she was the one thing that truly sated me.

"Enough," Eira said, pulling me down. "Fuck me properly."

"As you wish," I said, and flipped her over. She got on all fours, arching her back and pushing her ass back toward me. I grabbed hold of her hips and stilled her, need pounding through me. I rubbed my cock along her pussy, teasing her a bit more until she made a noise of protest, and then slammed inside.

She let out a yelp, grabbing onto the sheets below as she clenched around me, drawing me in deeper. I closed my eyes, savoring the feeling. This felt more like coming home than anything else I'd ever had. Eira was made for me.

I began thrusting, pounding into her so hard I thought it would hurt her. But she just arched her back and begged for more, always goading me into going deeper, faster, to try and consume as much of her as I could. I could never get enough of her, and I wanted *more*. I leaned over her, not slowing my pace at all, and nosed at her neck.

She smelled intoxicating, and I licked and bit at her skin until she turned her head and offered me her lips. She reached up with one hand and pulled me closer, somehow sliding me deeper inside of her.

"Yes," she moaned as she drove herself back on my dick once more. I bit the shell of her ear.

"Mine," I murmured as I pistoned my hips into her. She let out a little noise with each thrust, raising in intensity. She was already trembling around me, moments away from coming. I loved how responsive her body was. I looked forward to spending all my nights trying to draw every noise out of her.

There's time enough for that, I thought as she clenched around me, her voice going hoarse as she started coming. I pulled back to watch her entire body lose control, pleasure overtaking me as well. I held on longer, wanting to push her to the limits of however much pleasure she could take.

She shuddered, tightening around me, drawing me closer and closer to that edge. Finally, with a growl, I let it consume me. My movements slowed, and my vision went white with the force of my climax. I drove myself in one last time and emptied myself into her. She gasped, body still quaking with the aftereffects of her own orgasm.

When we collapsed onto the bed together, I pulled Eira to me immediately. She turned in my arms and nestled up against me, putting her head on my chest. We were both panting hard, and I knew that this was just the beginning. I wanted to fuck her into oblivion until the sun rose, but for now, I was content to just hold her.

She hummed happily as she draped her arm over my hip and pulled me even closer to her. When I smiled down at her, she looked back up at me, eyes glinting happily in the dim light of my bedroom. She really was my home, my fated mate, my everything. *Mine.*

23

EIRA

I looked up at the imposing black doors of Lucifer's palace in Hell, and then back at Belial, swallowing hard. It was a week after the battle with the Furies, and Belial had wanted to take me to meet his father as soon as possible. But nothing would have prepared me for this.

Lucifer's palace was in Hell in the equivalent of Earth's Egypt and looked like something that had been built around the same time as the pyramids, with huge columns covered in ivy and flowers that glowed in the night. A few sections of the palace were under construction, adding a startlingly modern contradiction to the ancient structure.

I'd never been to Hell before, since I'd been born in Faerie and raised on Earth. Most younger demons never had, not since Lucifer had ended the war with the angels, and he and Archangel Michael closed off Heaven and Hell and moved all the angels and demons to Earth. At the time, the two realms had been completely decimated and unable to support life, but now each side was slowly working to rebuild their homes. Starting with this palace.

Hell was completely different from how I'd pictured it too. Hell was the realm of eternal night, just like Heaven was the land of never ending day. An endless black sky stretched overhead, sparkling with countless stars and the thin sliver of the moon. There was no fire and brimstone, and instead it was quite chilly, not that the temperature bothered me, of course.

Belial glanced over at me, his jaw clenched so hard it looked painful. "I haven't been here since I tried to overthrow my father. It's...strange being back."

"You'll be fine," I said, taking his hand. "The past is in the past, remember?"

"Yes, but the past is long when you're immortal." He looked down at our intertwined hands with a scowl, but let me lead him to the entrance of the palace.

Before we could reach the huge doors, they suddenly flew open, and a toddler with wings—one black, one white—rode out on a three-headed dog. She laughed as she held the dog's collar like reigns and directed him forward. Then the girl caught sight of Belial and let out an ungodly shriek.

"Bel Bel!" She flung herself off of the dog and flew right into Belial's arms, her little wings flapping against the cool night air.

Belial laughed and caught her, spinning her around like this was completely normal. I'd never seen such joy on his face before, and she looked back at him with the same adoration. He was like a completely different person, and I knew this must be his sister, Aurora. The one he'd sacrificed his soul to save. The love they shared was unmistakable.

The three-headed dog nudged my hand, sniffing at me, and I tried not to panic. As I held very still, trying to see what he would think of me, his tail started wagging, and six eyes looked up at me, imploring. I tentatively reached out to pat his head. He wagged harder, and began bouncing circles around me. I let out a startled laugh, looking back over at Belial. This definitely hadn't been the welcome wagon I'd expected, but it was much better than anything I'd had in mind.

Belial grinned and set the girl down. "Eira, this is my sister Aurora, and the family dog Cerberus."

"It's nice to meet you both," I said.

"Aurora?" another voice called from inside. A beautiful woman with long blond hair and the face of an angel—literally—emerged from the palace, then relaxed when she saw Aurora was with us. "There you are. I see you've found your brother."

"Bel Bel!" Aurora said with a grin.

"I'm so glad you're here," Hannah said, as she embraced her son. I'd seen her once before while in Faerie, when she sacrificed herself and became the 3rd Horseman, Famine. She was just as impressive now, wearing a silver crown and a shimmering blue dress. Flowers grew at her feet, as if her very presence inspired them to rise up, and she glowed faintly as she moved. She had once been Eve, and then Persephone, and dozens of other lives throughout all of time, but now she was in the body of an angel for her final life. Her long love affair with Lucifer across countless centuries was both tragic and romantic, from what Belial had told me of it.

"You must be Eira," she said, smiling warmly at me. "It's lovely to meet you properly. Please come inside."

She beckoned us inside before we could have a chance to say no, and practically shoved Belial through the doors when he hesitated. I hid a smile as I followed them inside.

"We've spent the last few months restoring the palace here, and it's finally coming together now," Hannah said, as she led us through a grand hall with giant columns circled by vines and impossibly tall ceilings. Windows and high doorways cut through the roof and the higher portions of the walls, allowing winged demons to move in and out of the hall freely without stopping to land. Flowers that glowed with a soft blue light grew from every corner, and a large fountain in the middle of the hall was full of luminous fish.

"It's...much more alive than I thought it would be," I said.

"My mother has what you'd call a green thumb," Belial said. "A remnant of her time as Persephone."

I nodded, putting it all together in my head. Persephone had been a fae of the Spring Court, and was Damien's mother. Would Belial's flirty half-fae brother be here tonight?

As we continued walking, Aurora babbled excitedly at Belial in toddler speak, but I could only make out a few of her words. He seemed to understand though, or at least pretended he did, and seeing him interact with Aurora made my heart melt a little more. She was the reason he'd become Death, when he'd sacrificed himself to save her. I'd been so very wrong about him at first, but now it was so obvious to me how bright his heart was.

Hannah continued telling us about different renovations to the palace as she led us further inside, and each room was more impressive than the last, even the ones under construction. Finally she took us into a dinning room that was a lot less grand than some of the other rooms we'd been in, and I realized it was a more private space, reserved for just her family.

Damien was there, and he flashed us a charming smile when he saw us, but my eyes quickly looked past him to the other two men he stood with. My breath caught at the sight of Lucifer, who shared many of the same features as Belial but had a more refined air to him. While Belial was all tattoos and t-shirts, Lucifer wore an exquisitely made black suit and every inch of him, from his dark stubble to the silver crown on his head, was the picture of perfection. He was the kind of man who turned heads when he entered a room without even trying, and when he turned his eyes on me, my heart nearly stopped.

But then Lucifer smiled, and I could breathe again, because I saw only warmth in his eyes. He wasn't going to smite me down right here for being a part of my father's rebellion. I knew he could do it too, since he not only had all of his original powers, but also those of the 2nd Horseman, War.

Lucifer turned toward Belial with open arms. "Belial. So good to see you again."

Belial's eyes narrowed, as if expecting a trick, but he put Aurora down and reluctantly embraced his father. He took a deep breath in, and his shoulders relaxed a tiny bit, before he stepped back. "It's good to be back."

Lucifer smiled and patted him on the back, before looking over at me. "And this must be your mate."

"This is Eira," Belial said, motioning for me to come forward.

"An honor, my king." I dipped my head in deference to Lucifer, and then wondered if I should bow instead.

To my surprise, Lucifer took my hand and kissed the back of it. "Anyone who has tamed my son is most welcome here," he said, his eyes twinkling.

"I'm not sure he can ever be truly tamed," I said with a smile.

"You've come closer than anyone else though," the other man said with a grin.

I'd temporarily forgotten his presence in the wake of Lucifer's attention, but now I turned toward him. This man looked almost identical to Lucifer, and was so obviously his son that I could only stare at him in amazement. He looked like Belial too, and even a bit like Aurora and Damien. The family resemblance between all of the siblings was strong, and tied them all back to their father.

"I'm Kassiel, Belial's youngest brother," he said with a grin. "Damien has told me all about you."

"Don't worry, only good things," Damien said, winking at me. "I'm just glad you two finally came to your senses."

"I suspect she had to bash him over the head with a rock to get that to happen," Kassiel said with a laugh.

"No, but I did impale him with an ice spear one time," I told them.

"Ooh, I like this one," Lucifer said, as he clasped Belial on the shoulder.

Belial rolled his eyes, but he didn't move away either, and I had a feeling things between him and his father would be repaired a tiny bit more tonight. They had a long and difficult history spanning centuries, but I was confident that things were going to change going forward. *After all, he has me now.*

Hannah announced that dinner was ready, and we all sat down at a long table, where an assortment of glasses and fancy dishes lay arranged in front of us. Belial pulled my chair out for me, and I smiled at him as I took my seat.

As soon as we were all settled, the wine glasses all filled, as if by magic. I picked up my glass with a grin. "I'm liking this place more and more."

"Blame Damien for that trick," Belial said with a snort as he grabbed his own glass. "God of wine and all."

"I don't see you complaining," Damien said.

Lucifer stood, raising his own glass. "I would like to propose a toast." Everyone quieted down and he continued, smiling at all of his family members seated around him, from ancient Belial to baby Aurora. "If there is one thing I have learned in all my many years, it's that family is everything. I'm so happy to have all of you here tonight, including the newest member of our family, Eira." He motioned toward me with a mischievous grin. "I truly hope you can keep Belial in line, because I'd really hate to have to exile him again."

Everyone around the table laughed, while Belial shook his head. "My rebellious days are over." He took my hand in his own and gazed into my eyes. "I've found my place now."

Hannah practically beamed at these words, looking over at Belial with pride, before turning back to the others. "Now that Kassiel and Belial have both found their mates, it's time for Damien to find his mate too, don't you think?"

Damien waved her away. "You know I have no interest in settling down."

"He'll surely run out of eligible men and women soon," Kassiel said with a laugh. "If he hasn't found his mate yet, he must not have one."

Damien smiled devilishly over his wine. "Or maybe one man or woman will never be enough for me."

"Love is not the kind of thing you can predict or control," Hannah said to her son with amusement in her eyes. "Someday it might surprise you."

Lucifer reached over and took Hannah's hand. "It certainly continues to surprise me, even after all these years."

"Hey, if it can happen for me, it can happen for anyone," Belial said.

"And sometimes with the person you least expect," I replied, gazing back at him with the full force of my love.

"To family!" Lucifer said, and everyone raised their glasses and toasted.

I kept my eyes on Belial as we clinked our glasses together and drank, and I saw my love reflected back at me.

After years of feeling as though I never belonged anywhere, I'd found my place too—right here beside Death.

ABOUT THE AUTHOR

Elizabeth Briggs is a New York Times and Top 5 Amazon bestselling author of paranormal and fantasy romance featuring twisty plots, plenty of spice, and a guaranteed happy ending. She's a Stage IV cancer warrior who has worked with teens in foster care and volunteered with animal rescue organizations. She lives in Los Angeles with her husband, their daughter, and a pack of fluffy dogs.

Visit Elizabeth's website: www.elizabethbriggs.com

Join Elizabeth's Facebook group for fun book chat and early sneak peeks!